LEGACY OF THE BRIGHTWASH

KRYSTLE MATAR

First published by Imburleigh Book Company 2021

Cover illustration and design by Brad Bergman

Edited by Trinica Sampson

Maps by Soraya Corcoran

AUTHOR'S NOTE

Dear Reader,

Thank you for joining me here in the Dominion. Tashué's story depicts scenes containing and/or discussing instances of miscarriage, addiction, drug and alcohol use and/or abuse, prisoner abuse, police brutality, racism, and torture.

I tried to depict what it's like to try to love in a world that's terribly bleak, and that meant portraying that bleakness. It also meant portraying love, found family, hope, passion, courage in the face of overwhelming odds.

It's a rough world out there, and it's a rough world in here. Here's to trying to muddle through it all and finding love in the darkness.

Take care of yourself. Even if that means skipping this book.

Love,

K

For Tashué
For 18 years

ACKNOWLEDGMENTS

I used to think writing was a solitary endeavour. I've never been so happy to be wrong.

Thank you to my husband, who never gets tired of my babbling while I try to figure out these people who live in my head. You've been letting me talk at you for nearly ten years now, and without you, this book wouldn't exist.

To the late, great David Gemmell, whose books started me on this crazy adventure of being a "serious" writer (whatever that means).

To Anthony Ryan, who also put David Gemmell's name in the acknowledgements of his debut novel, convincing me to read a fantasy book again for the first time in ten years. Reading that book felt like coming home. Reading that book led me here.

To Ashley, my very first fan. The Brickwall made it, girl. We both love you a million!

To the amazing writing community on Twitter, who taught me so much about drafting and revising simply by talking about their process on such a public platform.

To Nick specifically, who included me in my first #FF, which brought me into the fold and allowed me to discover my people. Thanks, Nick!

To Mihir and the folks at FBC for the opportunity to work with Soraya—that map made the world so much more real for me, and really lit a fire under my butt to get this book finished!

To the self-published community, who took all the fear out of the prospect of doing this book myself. To the amazing book bloggers that keep us all going.

To Clayton, Luke, Angela, Dave, Justine, for trusting me and letting me participate in Dark Ends, even though I hadn't published anything yet, and for never once asking if I belonged. That book means so much to me, my little debut.

To Angela, I can't even begin to list the ways that you've been so helpful. This book is my baby, but you are the godmother. From your beta feedback to your moral support to your publishing experience, and everything in between. Thank you so much. I couldn't have done it without you. I'm blessed to have you.

To Justine and Brad for being amazing, and bringing my vision to life for the cover. For being supportive and enthusiastic and delightful. You guys rock!

To Isabel, for asking questions that I hadn't even considered, which made the world building and the characters so much deeper.

To Ronkwahrhakónha. What can I say that I haven't already? Thank you for sharing so much of yourself. Thank you for your insight, your wisdom, and your passion.

To Trinica, thank you so much for your enthusiasm! It was such a gift to me (and certain characters) to receive such glowing feedback from you, and your polishing was so helpful.

And to you, dear reader. Thank you for trusting me to take you on an adventure.

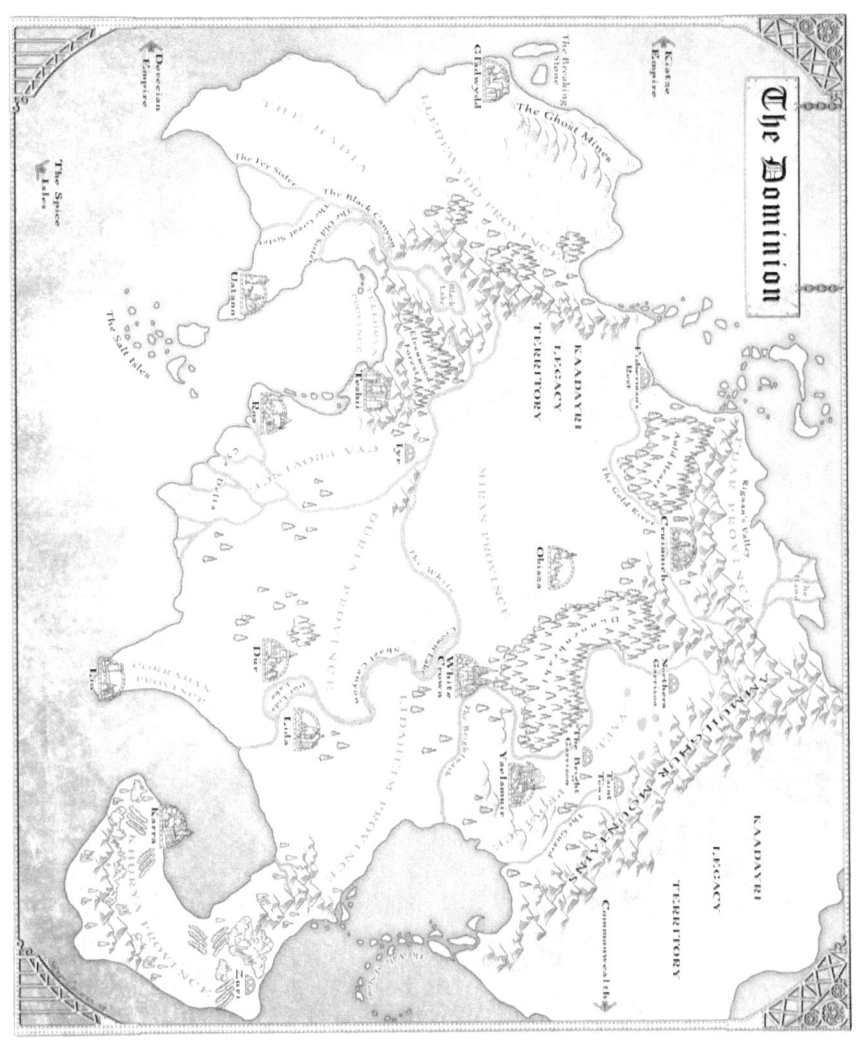

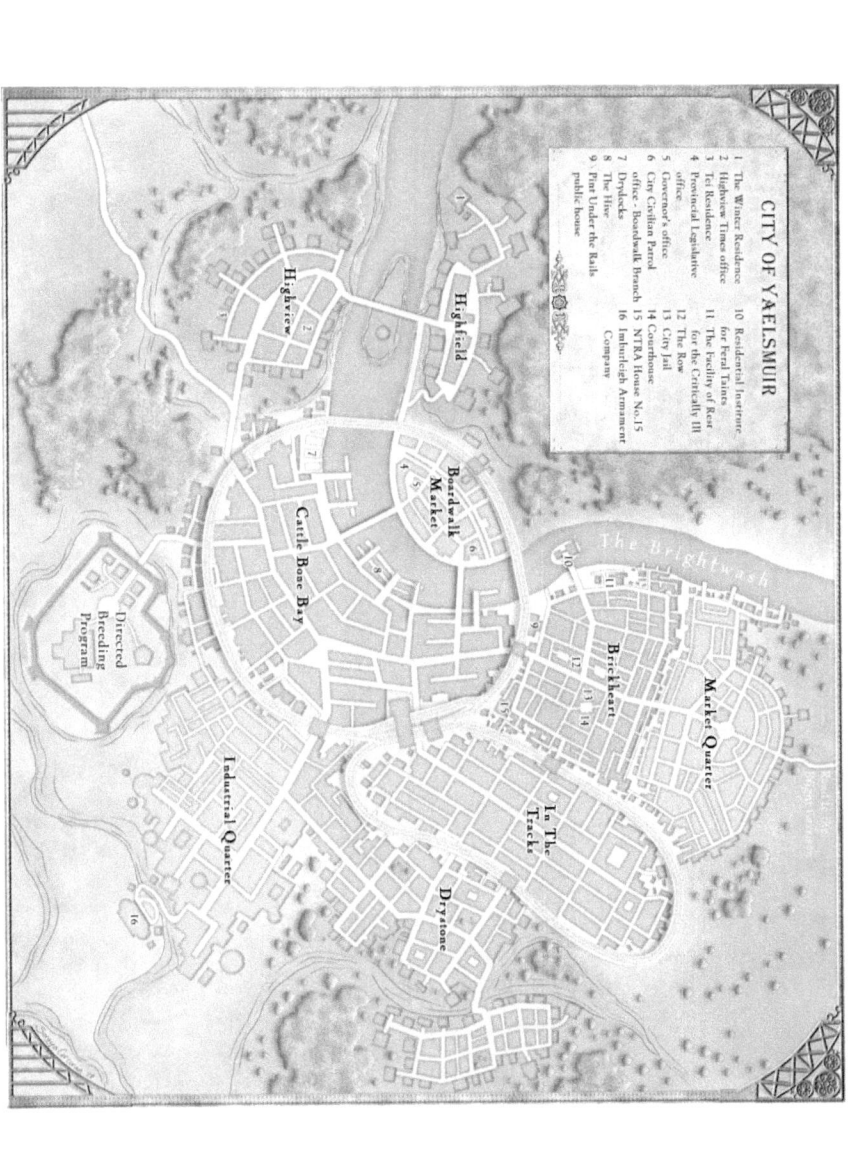

CITY OF YAELSMUIR

1   The Winter Residence
2   Highview Times office
3   Tel Residence
4   Provincial Legislature
5   Governor's office
6   City Civilian Patrol
    office - Boardwalk Branch
7   Drydocks
8   The Hive
9   Flat Under the Rails
    public house

10   Residential Institute
     for Feral Taints
11   The Facility of Rest
     for the Critically Ill
12   The Row
13   City Jail
14   Courthouse
15   NTBA House No.15
16   Imhrilcith Armament
     Company

Highview

Highfield

Boardwalk
Market

Castle Base Bay

Directed
Breeding
Program

The Brightwash

Brickheart

Market Quarter

In The
Tracks

Industrial Quarter

Drystone

1

TASHUÉ

DAY 1

I t had already been a long, exhausting day when the girl's body washed up on the bank of the Brightwash.

Tashué Blackwood trudged up the street, feeling the weariness in every part of his body. His station house had always been short-handed, but since one of their Regulation Officers died, everyone was working to the very limit of their strength. Some days he scarcely knew what time it was, what month it was, hours and weeks blending together into a trek through the city, knocking on doors, asking questions, filing endless stacks of paperwork at the station house.

Pint Under the Rail was a natural rest stop for him and the other Regulation Officers of Station House 15. As he headed toward the rickety little pub, tucked up against the elevated tram line that shuffled workers around the city, he heard the angry squeal of an infant.

He walked faster.

One of the Regulation Officers he worked with—the newest of them, Beckett Collstone—was in front of the *Pint Under* already, standing beside his wife. They had a pram between them, and his wife rocked it, trying to calm the angry little hurricane inside, but the babe wailed louder.

"Collstone, you finally brought your baby," Tashué said, stopping in front of the pram. "She doesn't look too pleased."

"No, sir, I guess not. Minna wanted to meet me for breakfast this morning, since I've been so busy, but little miss seems unimpressed with us for bringing her out in the cold."

"I don't want to be a bother, Beckett," Minna said. Her cheeks were flushed, but her eyes were distant and tired. Tashué knew that look, that new-parent panic. "If she's only going to scream, I don't want to disturb everyone."

"Nonsense, Miss Collstone," Tashué said. "Sometimes they just get overly tired and can't settle. Can I try?"

"Oh, please, Mr. Blackwood."

Tashué swept the baby up in his arms. She fit so nicely against his shoulder, even though her whole body was rigid with fury. "There now, sweet girl. Let's go warm up inside, see if that improves your mood."

He headed up the stairs with the infant at his shoulder, patting her back. Sweet North Star, how long had it been since his son was this small? He missed the simplicity of it sometimes. Some people hated the sound of a baby crying, especially when they had strong lungs and all the rage of Beckett's girl, but there was something easy about it. Babies cried, and you did your best to comfort them. Eventually, you found the thing that helped them, and they stopped. Sure, you were so tired that you couldn't think and you began to wonder if you would ever sleep again. But Tashué had learnt in the cavalry how to sleep standing up or sitting in the saddle, just for a moment. Just long enough that he wouldn't keel over from the exhaustion. And when they were babies, you didn't have to worry about the decisions they made. All you had to do was feed them and cuddle them and wait for their fury to exhaust itself.

"Beckett, you brought the baby!"

Tashué looked down the bar, where Kazrani leaned over her breakfast. She slid off her stool to meet Tashué, reaching up and sliding a tender hand across the back of the baby's head.

"Heavens, she's got a set of lungs, hey? What are you so mad about, missus?" The baby knotted a little fist in one of Kazrani's black braids, catching one of the silk ribbons. She grimaced as she teased the baby's hand open. "Did you finally settle on a name for her?"

"We named her Lenora, after Beckett's mother," Minna said.

"I told her she didn't have to," Beckett said, shaking his head. "My mother always had a temper. Now the baby's taken after the name, I think."

"Let me try, sometimes they just need a bounce," Kazrani said, reaching.

Tashué batted her hands away. "Back off, Lieutenant. I haven't held a baby in ages."

"Whose fault is that, then?" Kazrani muttered, but she retreated to her stool. "You're perfectly capable of making a few, if you would settle on a woman to make them with."

"Ha. I've done enough damage to the world with my offspring, thank you. The world doesn't need any more Blackwoods."

"There's only the two of you," Kazrani scoffed.

Tashué shrugged. "That's plenty and you know it."

"Another whisky morning, is it, Mr. Blackwood?" Pallwyth, the bartender, asked.

"Yes please, Mr. Pallwyth. Angry babies aside, it's been a long morning."

Pallwyth poured a generous measure of the cheapest whisky he had as Tashué rubbed Lenora's back, adopting the bounce and sway that always calmed Jason. Little by little, he could feel her start to relax. The warmth of his body and the heat in the room worked its magic, and she slumped against him. She was still crying, but it was half-hearted and unconvincing. It was the first time in so long that he'd been able to solve such a simple problem.

He shifted little Lenora's weight so that she sat in the crook of his arm. Her face was still red from all the yelling, but her features settled into something peaceful as she sank down into sleep. Her hat, displaced by the way he shifted her, revealed her wispy dark hair, which was starting to develop little curls. Minna stepped closer, untying the baby's hat with swift fingers and taking it off.

"You're a miracle worker," she breathed.

Tashué settled on his stool, scooping up the whisky. "You just have to be more stubborn than they are. Outlast them." He threw it back in one swallow. The copper whisky was the very worst money could buy—blended whisky made from the rejected batches from various distilleries in the city. It probably wouldn't kill you, but it burned like acid all the way down. "I'll hold her a while, if the two of you would like to eat with your hands free."

"Thank you, sir," Beckett said, settling beside Tashué. "Are your services available at night, too, or do we have to bring her down to the pub every time?"

Tashué sighed. "Would that I had time to come cuddle your baby for you at night. I still haven't assessed all of the cases I got from Maccus."

"You should eat something too, Mr. More Stubborn Than Babies," Kazrani said. She had already finished her bowl of the stew Pallwyth made—usually plenty of onions and potatoes and whatever scraps of meat were available—and took a bite out of a thick slab of dark bread. "You can't survive on whisky, coffee, and sweets alone."

Tashué shrugged, but only gently, nestling baby Lenora tighter to his body. "My hands are busy."

"Give him a mug of it, Mr. Pallwyth. That way he can pretend it's whisky and knock it back."

Pallwyth grinned. "Good idea, Lieutenant." He stepped to the wood stove he kept behind the bar with him. Now that the oppressive heat of the summer faded into autumn, Pallwyth stoked the fire in the stove to keep the dining room warm, and the kettle of stew took up residence on top of it. Pallwyth ladled a measure of stew into a tin mug and delivered it to Tashué.

The door swung open, letting in the noise of the street. It seemed louder than usual, more urgent. Another of their Officers, Duskan Hillbraun, stepped in, his eyes sweeping the inside of the pub. He scowled at Tashué.

"Who gave the ass a baby?"

Minna bristled, but Beckett lay a hand on her back as he leaned around her to look at Duskan. "You're especially sour this morning.

I take it things didn't go well with the Derccian woman from the songhouse?"

"I didn't like her that much anyway," Duskan muttered, settling on the other side of Kazrani and nodding at Pallwyth. "Is that your baby, Collstone?"

"Lenora," Beckett said. "Cute, isn't she? Looks just like her mother."

Duskan grunted. "If you say so."

"Don't mind him, Miss Collstone," Kazrani said, leaning around Tashué to look down the bar at Minna. "He's sour with everyone."

The sounds of the commotion outside permeated through the closed door. It sent a wave of agitation through Tashué, making him want to stand, but the weight of baby Lenora kept him in his seat. "What's going on outside?"

"Outside?" Duskan asked. "Fuck, what would I care? Something down by the riverbank."

How could the man wear the tin badge of the National Tainted Registration Authority and not be drawn to the chaos? How could he not want to help?

Tashué bit back a curse, drinking the cup of stew as quickly as he could. It was hot and salty, almost washing away the burn of whisky still on his tongue. He stood carefully, passing Lenora off to her mother. He needed to know.

He pushed the door open, and the sound amplified in front of him. It hit him like a wall of anxiety, rippling up from the crowd at the end of the street, where the cobbles gave way to the bank of the Brightwash. The street used to lead to a bridge that spanned the water, but it had been abandoned when sturdier bridges were built for the tram. The support pilings were still driven into the rocky bank, but the rest of the bridge was gone, materials salvaged for other things. The crowd pressed in close to the pilings, jostling against each other, collecting like a blood clot in an open wound. Their chattering filled his ears like the rattling of the tram, loud and trying to drown out coherent thought, but he kept walking, drawn to chaos as if he was bound to it with a rope. He was only distantly aware of Kazrani following him. She always followed him, no matter what. Beckett had followed her, and Duskan was dragged along in their wake by some fear of being left behind.

A woman lay stretched out on the ground, her own smaller crowd gathered around her. People fanned her face and called to her, trying to rouse her. Tashué made his way down the sloping streets. The cobbles ended a few yards from the water's edge, giving way to shale that crunched and shifted beneath his boots. He pushed his way into the crowd, until the mass of jostling bodies ended abruptly.

The girl had washed up on the bank among the detritus and trash that was carried through the city. Tiny and grey-fleshed, her body was made smaller and more heart-wrenching by her terrible mutilations. Her arms and legs had been cut away at shoulder and hip. Most of the wounds had healed, long keloid scars left in place where the flesh had been stitched back together, but one of the arm wounds was gaping and vile. Infection had eaten away at skin and tissue, so deep and raw that Tashué saw bone. Death and the river had cleansed her body of the usual redness and swelling and pus that came from such a terrible infection, but flies buzzed around the dead meat and the smell of rot wafted on the breeze. Her hair had been cut close to the scalp, leaving only black fuzz as it tried to grow back.

Her face punched Tashué the hardest, despite all the gruesomeness of the state of her. There was a familiarity to her features—the black hair, brown eyes warm despite their blank emptiness. Was it his imagination, that made him see his own son? Or was it the Rift, just upriver, looming over his shoulder like the whole edifice was watching him? The Residential Institute for Feral Tainted and Non-Compliants. Could the girl be from that place? It seemed a foolish thought—she was too young to have quickened yet. Without a woken Talent, there was no need for her to register, thus no reason for her to be processed to the Rift. Tashué's son *was* in there, locked away for refusing to register. But Jason wasn't a child anymore, and this girl would never grow up.

"Get people back." The words came almost unbidden from

Tashué's chest, but uttering them dragged him back to himself and out of the trance that the little dead girl had laid on him. "Get all these people back. And send for the Patrollers."

Kazrani nodded and turned on her heel, Beckett following her example. Duskan stood firmly in place, staring. He hadn't served in the military, unlike most Regulation Officers. Had he seen many dead bodies in his life? The world was a hard place, Yaelsmuir a hard city. But not everyone had death in their immediate orbit with such a simple, ugly truth. A child, no less.

"Mr. Hillbraun."

His name snapped Duskan out of his stupor and his wide eyes found Tashué's face.

"Get the people back before they touch anything."

"Not my job, is it?" Duskan sneered, the cloak of anger falling over him. "I'm a Regulation Officer and she's no tainted. Too young."

Tashué shook his head. "Doesn't matter. Someone has to take control until the Patrollers get here with a surgeon. They'll have questions."

"What difference does it make? Surgeon won't help her none."

Tashué gritted his teeth against the wave of frustration. "Surgeon's job is to declare her dead."

"Anyone with eyes can declare her dead!"

"Mr. Hillbraun," Tashué snapped, "get the crowd back!"

Duskan stepped away from Tashué, turning to the crowd, but he was still frozen, staring while Kazrani and Beckett herded the people away. It seemed so quiet without the crowd pressing down on the back of Tashué's neck, the babbling of the river almost drowning them out once they were further away.

"Make way! Make way for the Patrol!" A thin, reedy voice asked for passage through the crowd, lacking the authority to move all those bodies.

Kazrani added her voice to the din and Tashué glanced over his shoulder to see the crowd part. A boy pushed through, long and lanky and dressed in the uniform of the City Civilian Patrol, the black linen crisp and starched. Acne and facial hair vied for territory along his jaw. The boy froze at the sight of the child, going near as grey as she was. The surgeon burst through the milling bodies next, round and sweating and breathing hard.

"Aw, hell," the surgeon muttered, moving across the bank with faltering steps. "Hell." He made a slow circuit around the body, oblivious to the water lapping at his shoes.

The Patroller's attention was riveted to the child's body. He gagged, then snapped his teeth shut and swallowed hard. Tashué looked at him, at his wide eyes and grey face. He was so terribly young.

"What's your name, son?"

The Patroller looked at Tashué, his eyes uncomprehending at first. "What?"

"Your name."

"Jonhan, sir. Or, City Civilian Patroller Jonhan Kiplar, that is."

"You need more Patrollers here, Kiplar."

The boy nodded, his bowler sliding down over his eyes. "There's more coming. I was the closest. But there's more coming."

"You should start talking to people," Tashué said. "You need to find out what people know."

"Yes, you're right, sir. I know. It's just—I've never handled a murder before. I wouldn't know where to start."

Tashué nodded toward the crowd. "Start with the man closest you, ask if he knows anything."

"Yes, sir." Kiplar headed back across the bank, fumbling for his pencil and pad in his breast pocket.

Turning back to the child, Tashué saw that the surgeon had finally eased himself closer. Tashué looked down at the girl's face again, the familiarity of her making him ache. The little girl didn't have the hair to hide her ears. Some rational part of Tashué recognized how ridiculous it was that, of all the obscenities that had befallen the girl, he was fixated on her hair.

A hand gripped Tashué by the arm, pulling at his attention so abruptly that it almost startled him. He dragged his eyes away from the girl, finding Kazrani standing beside him, looking at him intently. Had she said something?

"What?"

"I said, Patrollers are here. We should leave them to it."

Tashué almost turned to follow her. One of the Patrollers stepped back toward the cobbles, waving his arms at the crowd to shoo them off.

"Time to leave! Off to your business now, the lot of you. Off now. Time to go!"

Kiplar staggered across the open space, pad and pencil still in his hand. "Sir, this man here suggested I talk to the crowd and see if anyone knows anything, sir."

The older Patroller turned to Tashué, giving him a hard stare. "Are you in service of the city, Mister . . .?"

"Blackwood. I'm a Regulation Officer."

"Ah, well. Thank you, sir, for your service, but unless this child is tainted, you have no authority here."

Kiplar shifted, looking down at his notebook. "So, we aren't to question the crowd, sir?"

"This child washed down the river, Kipper."

Kiplar grimaced at the nickname, but didn't say anything.

"Doubtful any of the crowd knows anything at all," the Patroller went on. "We shan't be wasting our time with questions that've no answers. Thank you for your advice, Mr. Blackwood, but we have the girl now."

"There's more to know than simply who she is." Something frantic built in Tashué's chest, something wild and raw. It had been a long time since he'd looked down on the body of a child so horribly mutilated. Not since he was a soldier had he seen such violence perpetrated on a child and he couldn't bring himself to walk away. Not with the knowledge that she would be discarded and forgotten, as if she were another pile of trash from the river. And with the memory of Lenora's weight in his arms, no less. He took a slow, deep breath, fighting through the rising tide of agitation. "Did anyone touch anything when they found the body? How long ago was it found? Did anyone pass here regularly enough to be able to help identify when it might have washed up?"

Kazrani edged closer still, tugging at Tashué's arm. "Captain, we should go. This isn't our job."

Tashué pulled his arm away from Kazrani's grasp. "I'm staying."

The Patroller glared hard at Tashué, his neck turning deep red. Before he could say anything, someone in the crowd stepped forward. A woman, a great shock of grey hair piled atop her head.

"I was here earlier, sir. It was seven, maybe eight in the morning. There was no child here then."

Tashué met the Patroller's stare. "There, see? There *is* information." He turned to the crowd. "Who else passed this way?"

Kazrani sighed. "Tashué…"

A great barrel of a man with a scraggly black beard stepped forward. "I did, sir, 'bout a half hour ago!"

"Take notes, Patroller Kiplar," Tashué said. "You never know what might help."

"That's quite alright, Kipper, there's no need," the Patroller grunted. His words sounded calm, but a glance across him showed his frustration, the way he had puffed out his chest like a game cock, the way he had both his fists clenched. "Mr. Blackwood is going now and he'll leave the investigation to the investigators."

"But, sir, my son found the girl!" Another woman had moved forward through the crowd. "He saw the body by the bank before anyone else. I sent him on home ahead of me, but I can have him back here if you wish to speak to him."

"That's quite alright, ma'am, I've no need to make matters worse by involving other children in this ugliness. You go home to your son, now. The Patrol is here and we shall handle things."

Anger burned in Tashué's chest. He reached for his cigarillo case, going through the motions of lighting one to help hold back the frustration. "The Civilian Patrol has a puzzling way of investigating things if it's their policy not to ask questions."

"That's quite enough Mr. Blackwood!"

Tashué swung to the woman. "Ma'am, would you escort Patroller Kiplar to your home so that he might have a word with your son?"

"Yes, of course," the woman said. "Anything for the wee one."

Kiplar and the woman slipped away as Bowman fumed.

"Mr. Blackwood!" the Patroller snapped.

"Yes, sir, I see your cock swinging in the breeze," Tashué said. He clamped his cigarillo between his lips to free his hands, retrieving his charcoal pencil from another pocket. "I'm sorry for threatening your manliness and all that." Unwinding a section of twine to reveal the end of the charcoal, he opened his penknife to sharpen the pencil to a good tip. "But the City Civilian Patrol is named not because they patrol civilians, but because they are a patrol *made* of civilians. Seems pedantic, I know, but it's an important difference." Satisfied with the tip, he folded up the penknife and replaced it in his pocket, retrieving his notepad. "Since you're a civilian, and I am a Regulation Officer, I do technically have authority over you."

"I'm not tainted, sir!" the Patroller snapped.

Tashué shook his head. "You aren't listening. I never implied that. No matter the circumstances, any person serving as a Regulation Officer holds implicit jurisdiction over any civilian. Even though neither you nor the child are registered, I can help to direct your investigation. And I'm telling you, sir, that you're to question this crowd for any information they might have so that you, *sir*, have a chance of discovering who mutilated and murdered a child. Am I clear, Civilian Patroller?"

The Patroller shifted his weight from one foot to the other, a bit of his bluster fading away. He seemed frozen in place, his eyes flicking around the crowd as if he were trying to decide exactly how intimidated he was.

"I said," Tashué snapped, using his best military voice, "am I clear, Civilian Patroller?"

"Tashué." Kazrani stood at his elbow and Tashué could feel the energy of her, a twisting, roiling knot of frustration. He couldn't bear to look her in the eye and see that look she had when she thought he was wrong. "We should go. Leave it to the Patrollers. We've our own work to do, don't we? We all have too many files to manage and we don't have time to stand around here. It isn't our job."

Tashué snarled, swinging on her. "Go then, Kaz! You have better things to do, fine. Go!"

"He's fucking losing it," Duskan laughed.

Tashué didn't look at Duskan because if he did, he would smash the man's face to pieces. He kept eye contact with Kazrani instead, his anger a shield against the sadness and the disappointment in her face. "Go ahead. Leave. You have more important things to do than find out who mutilated a child and left her body in the river."

"Don't look at me like that, Tashué Blackwood," Kazrani hissed, his anger only serving to wake some of hers. "I didn't kill her."

"Don't you want to know who did?"

"What does it matter who did it? She won't be any less dead if we know how she got there. You're the one that just said you don't have any extra time!"

Tashué shook his head, biting back the angry retort. He took a pull from his cigarillo instead, turning away from Kazrani. He took a deep breath as he listened to her walk away, studying the girl instead. When he was sure he understood the shape of the girl's face, he set the first sweeping lines to the paper with the charcoal pencil. The sketch came together quickly on his page, only a rough drawing to help him remember the details, like the round cheeks that weren't pudgy enough for a child so young and the long lines of her neck suggesting she would be tall if she had been given the chance to grow. The heart-shaped mouth, the broad, flat nose that reminded him of Keoh.

At the sound of running footsteps, Tashué looked over his shoulder. Kiplar was returning, bless him, his overly large coat flapping around him as he ran, one hand clutching his bowler to his head. He skidded to a stop at Tashué's side, his chest heaving.

"I spoke to the boy. He hadn't much to say, sir."

Tashué sighed, shaking his head at the fresh wave of frustration. "Children are notoriously hard to question. Have one of your comrades help you search the bank."

"The bank, sir?"

"The riverbank." Tashué nodded upriver. The thought came again, intrusive and obsessive, like ice flowing through his body.

Could she be from the Rift? The rational parts of his mind told him it didn't make sense, and yet, he couldn't escape the fear of that place, the loathing for it.

"Yes, sir." Kiplar hadn't moved away, looking at Tashué with wide eyes. "It's only that… well, sir, there is a rather lot of debris along the bank. How am I to know what pertains to the girl, sir?"

Tashué sighed, tearing his eyes from the Rift and looking down at the bank again. Kiplar was right, of course. There was so much trash, how could anyone tell what might help? "Just look to see if there are any other bodies, Kiplar. We should know what exactly we're dealing with."

"Yes, sir."

The youth darted away, gathering one of his colleagues to ease along the bank, heading upriver. The loose stone was slippery underfoot as they neared the water's edge and their movements were slow. They locked arms with each other, and Tashué was pleased to see them moving with their eyes fixed on the ground, the toes of their boots nudging whatever they passed before they moved on.

At the sound of cursing, Tashué turned back to the child. Bowman and the surgeon were wrestling the girl onto a stretcher that the surgeon had brought with him. Tashué saw something as they lifted her, a flash of faded black on grey and white mottled skin.

"Wait," Tashué breathed. He stepped closer and retrieved his pad. "Hold her there."

"What now?" the Patroller snapped. He looked precarious, leaning over the child's body, hands tucked beneath her side as he tried to find purchase to lift her.

"There's something there, on the back of her neck." Tashué dropped to one knee. The rocks were damp from the river. He reached out, gently lifting the child's shaved head. Her skin was cold, her skull heavy and limp, the stubble of her hair prickly and rough. There was a tattoo across the back of her neck, a scrawl of numbers in a combination Tashué didn't recognize. He scribbled them down, 1693-0237-4494.

"What's that, then?" The Patroller shifted, peering down at the tattoo. He shifted his grip to free a hand and reached out, running his thick fingers across the tattoo as if to check if it was real. "Who tattoos a child?"

"I don't know." Tashué flipped his notebook closed again. "I've never seen anything like it."

Bowman cursed as the child slipped from his grasp, her body falling hard among the stones. Tashué winced, but he reminded himself that she was beyond such simple things as pain and discomfort. Bowman took a step back, plucking a kerchief from his pocket and wiping his hands. Tashué slid his hands under the child's back, lifting her carefully. The sickly sweet rot smell of death wafted over Tashué, but such smells had long since lost their hold on him. She was terribly light even though she was all dead weight, her torso swollen with the onset of decay. He set her gently on the canvas of the stretcher, pausing to brush some dirt from her cheek.

"Where does the Patrol take bodies?"

"There's a crematorium down in the Bay that handles cases like this," the Patroller said, and the bluster had fallen away. Maybe a dead and mutilated child did affect him after all. "There'll be a notice in all the papers that we've found a child and if no one claims her in two days, she'll be incinerated. City doesn't waste space in the graveyards for bodies no one claims."

2

TASHUÉ

DAY 1

The crematorium employed a photographer, and under Tashué's direction, the man took two photographs: one of the girl's face, another of the tattoo on the back of her neck. He conceded her to the crematorium, the memory of her rotted wound etched so vividly in his mind that he was sure he'd go to his grave bearing the image.

Two days to be claimed, that's what the Patroller said—they'd wait two days before giving her body to the fire.

Tashué tried not to think too hard about that for now. Kazrani was right, after all. He had plenty of his own cases to manage as a Regulation Officer and he didn't have any more time to chase answers about the girl, not today.

He walked under the elevated tram line, leaving the Bay. His home in the Row wasn't far from the tracks, and he went there first. He needed more cigarillos, after spending most of his day in the company of a dead child. He hadn't smoked this much in a long time, but the tobacco helped to cleanse his mouth of the cloying taste of death.

Children played in the street outside his building, a thick knot of them, fighting and scrabbling over a ball made of rags. A familiar strawberry-blond head stood in the centre of the chaos, swamped by some of the bigger children but very much in control. He stopped for a moment, down the street of his own building, watching her a while. She was in another fight with the neighbour boy that had just moved in, the boy twice her size and looming over her, but she was resolute.

Such a simple thing, to watch children play, to watch the crowd shift and the argument fade and then the children scatter to resume their game. It almost let him forget about the dead child on the bank, the photographs in his pocket. Almost.

Taking a deep breath, he headed toward his building. Stella Whiterock sat on her front steps—of course she did. She often sat there in the afternoons, watching her daughter Ceridwen play until it was time for her to go to her night shift. The cool autumn breeze had Stella's hair again, lifting strands from the braids she kept when she was going to work. That hair, that copper coloured hair, with its corkscrew curls, could never really be tamed, no matter how hard she tried to contain it.

She smiled when she looked up at him, and that smile made it hard to breathe. "Good afternoon, Mr. Blackwood."

Tashué stopped by her front steps, leaning on the banister. *Don't have time*, he tried to tell himself, but he was rooted there now, locked in place by her presence. "Afternoon, Miss Whiterock. Your Ceridwen is becoming quite the rabblerouser these days."

Stella nodded, her eyes finding Ceridwen. "She has a way with her friends."

"A way with the whole crowd, I think."

The door to the building opened behind Stella, and she pushed herself to her feet. Tashué was suddenly aware of how close they were, her face inches away from his, almost as tall as him since she stood two steps above him. He took a step back, away from her, but it was too late. He'd already felt her breath on his face, smelled the scent of her hair. His mind betrayed him and he imagined what her hair must feel like, silky and messy and curly all at once.

She followed him as he stepped back—what was she doing? The closer she came, the harder it was not to touch her. Closer, closer, until she was down at the bottom with him. His hands itched with the desire to reach out to her. The warmth of her was delicious, even through their clothes.

The family that she had been making room for passed down the stairs in a great flurry of movement—both parents herded half a dozen children out of the building and up the street, some children peeling away to steal a quick word with their friends. But once the stairs were clear again, Stella didn't sit back down. She rested her whole body against the banister and stayed close, her head tilting back to look up at him.

She took the breath from him, looking at him like that.

He reached into his pocket for his timepiece, just so he could have something else to hold, something else to look at. He flicked the cover open, watching the second hand tick around its little circle at the bottom of the face.

"Do you have another busy day?" Stella asked. She was looking at his timepiece, too, which somehow only made her closer to him. The breeze had her hair again and it drifted up into his face.

"All of my days are busy," Tashué said. He snapped the timepiece closed again, replacing it in its pocket. This was the part when he said he needed to go because he should check in on at least one of his cases today, but he couldn't find the words. Not with her standing right there against him.

"You have a Saeati watch," she said, nodding to the pocket where the timepiece sat. "Those are very expensive."

"My father bought it for me, when Mr. Saeati was still in the Bay. They weren't so expensive back then."

Stella looked up, meeting his eye again. "Did your father come from the Bay?"

"No, he was born and raised here in Brickheart," Tashué said. He found his cigarillo case next, but it was empty. Stifling a sigh, he snapped it shut. "So was I, right here in the Row."

Stella smiled at that, turning her face away from him and finding Ceridwen. "I'll bet you caused all kinds of trouble, when you were a boy. Streets like this are ripe with mischief."

"You sound like you know a thing or two about mischief yourself, Miss Whiterock."

She smiled and blushed at the same time, her hand sliding through her stray hairs in an attempt to smooth them back down.

Don't lean closer to her.

He regretted it, saying the thing about mischief. Now he was thinking about her again, about the mischief he'd like to make with her, about how she stood so close to him, how it might be her way of telling him that she wouldn't mind it if he reached out to her and kissed her like he wanted to.

He took a step back, putting a little more distance between them. If he didn't step away, he *would* kiss her. He might have, too, a few weeks ago, back before her Regulation Officer died, back before her file had been assigned to him. He might have kissed her and pushed his face into her hair and tasted every inch of her body—but now he was her Regulation Officer and it wasn't possible anymore. He'd known plenty of Officers who took advantage of their position, who traded leniency for skin. He wouldn't. He wouldn't put Stella—anyone—in that position of wondering whether saying no to him would put her in danger. Of saying yes just to keep herself safe.

She didn't even know that he was her Regulation Officer now. Her file was technically his, but he hadn't opened it yet. Hadn't looked. It wasn't how he'd hoped to come to know Stella Whiterock.

"I should go," he forced himself to say. "I hope you have a nice evening, Miss Whiterock."

"Thank you, Mr. Blackwood. The same to you."

The second set of elevated tram rails cut through the city mercilessly, buildings razed in the mad rush to get them up. The quarter now contained inside the tracks had once been part of Drystone, Brickheart or the Market Quarter, but the razed buildings and the large tracks had redefined the area. Anything bordered by the loop that curved through the city was simply known as *In the Tracks*.

Glaen Forsooth lived In the Tracks. His job was to keep the brights lit through the night, the lamps themselves a project of mixed success. In wealthier quarters, they gave the long streets and stately manors an air of sophistication, an elegant glow. In quarters like Brickheart and In the Tracks, they only seemed to throw deeper shadows on the flaws and cracks and holes. Worse was when the tall wrought-iron posts were damaged, leaving them bent at odd angles like drunkards staggering home after too many pints. Criminals and mischief makers—those whom the brights were originally intended to discourage—had learnt where the gaps were, which alleys had the deepest shadows, which bright-keepers could be bribed not to work for a few hours.

Forsooth lived in one of the large tenement buildings built in response to one of the city's many housing crises. The population of Yaelsmuir had grown more steadily than any other city, with all the industries that burst to life in the area. For years, builders tried to make the most profit from what land they held by building massive residential blocks. Only the rooms against the exterior walls were fortunate enough to have windows—the rest lived in eternal darkness and stifling heat. Such horrific tenement buildings were fading away since the Queen had declared that everyone had the right to at least one window. Forsooth lived in one of the remodelled block tenements, where interior walls had been torn down and rebuilt to try to get at least one window per apartment.

Tashué smoked another cigarillo as he made the climb up, ignoring the clutter beneath his feet—leaves blown in the open window, dropped and forgotten pieces of paper, cloth, or food, carcasses of rat and roach and fly. Some days, there were people in the stairwells, searching for shelter in a city that didn't have room for them.

He knocked on Glaen Forsooth's door. Footsteps whispered behind other doors, creaking floorboards and door frames as other tenants leaned against their peepholes. When there was no sound from Forsooth's apartment, he knocked again, louder. Forsooth came, cursing under his breath. The door stuck in the frame, then swung on its leather hinges. His face fell when he saw Tashué.

"There was no appointment scheduled today," Forsooth said, but the little act of defiance was ruined by the way he stared down at his feet.

"Let me in so we can speak privately, Mr. Forsooth. Not here in the hallway where your neighbours can hear."

"Mr. Blackwood, I've thin walls and a broken window. I can hear the whore to my left with her clients, and the family to my right fighting all day. I am certain that they can both hear my business no matter where I'm standing."

"Nevertheless . . ."

Forsooth sighed and shuffled out of the way. He lived in a single room with one window, although the one window was nearly inaccessible, sitting at the end of a long, narrow hallway stretching from the foot of the bed to the north wall. Forsooth could walk to the window easily, but Tashué, taller and broader, would have a tight squeeze.

Forsooth stirred the coals in his wood stove, adding some smaller logs. "Do you take tea?"

"Thank you, no."

"I don't know why I still offer you tea. You never take tea."

Tashué sighed. "I didn't realize tea meant so much to you."

Forsooth shook his head, his shoulders going tense. "Tinmen never take tea because tinmen don't have souls. People who don't take tea in another man's home can only be men without souls. Yes, tea means very much to me. I've only the one window, and I use it to throw my shit down into the alley since there are no water closets above the third floor. The glass in the window is broken, probably from the tram line making it rattle all the time. The landlord won't fix it. Says I broke it, so it's my responsibility. I save my spare copper crowns, but of course there aren't many because the Authority pays a pittance. On windy days when my neighbours throw their shit, it blows in the cracks of the window. I asked the landlord if I can put shutters on at least. To keep the shit out. But the law says shutters aren't allowed anymore. Did you know that? I didn't. Apparently, shutters don't let in enough light, so the law says it has to be glass." He huffed. "At least I can still make tea. Tea is the cornerstone of civilization, Mr. Blackwood, and I could never trust a man who doesn't take it."

Tashué took a deep breath and held it for a moment, biting back the anger rising in his chest. Forsooth had long been one of Tashué's easiest cases, quiet and cooperative. Until recently, when he'd been seen with another tainted—Gianna Tarbrook, a healer from Drystone. Part of Tashué understood Forsooth's anger and frustration. After all, did he not just stand in front of Stella White-rock and feel his whole body ache for her? But he stepped away, because it was the right thing to do. And the National Tainted Registration Authority claimed the right to manage whom their charges could associate with. Non-compliance with the fraterniza-tion law was not taken lightly.

"You know why I'm here, Mr. Forsooth."

Forsooth shook his head, a pendulous movement filled with grief.

"You have been seen fraternizing with another tainted for the second time. If it happens again, I'll have to process you. You have to stop seeing this woman, or it will cost you your freedom."

Forsooth laughed, a wheezing cackle that shook his shoulders. "My freedom? Do you live in a tenement building, Mr. Blackwood? Do you have any idea the humiliation and the degradation that a human being withstands in a place like this? Gianna gives me a reason to breathe. She is like the sun rising after a long and terrible night. But the night was more than only a few hours; the sun set for me years ago."

Tashué took another slow, deep breath, letting it out bit by bit. "You should write poetry."

"Excuse me?"

"You're an eloquent man, Mr. Forsooth. You should write poetry and sell it to those pennycovers. They'd devour your poems, I'm sure, what with all the pain and darkness. It would be a better use of your time than fraternizing with another tainted. Might even get you enough crowns to fix your window."

"Are you mocking me?"

Tashué shook his head. "No, sir, I'm being serious. I don't live in a tenement building, but I do know people who have been processed. This tenement has more freedom than you'll ever see in the Rift. I think you've convinced yourself that this is the worst your life can be, but I promise you, you can still sink further. And if your freedom, such that it is, isn't enough to convince you to stop, consider this—if I process you for fraternization, then I'll also contact Gianna Tarbrook's Regulation Officer. She'll be processed, too. If you love her, you'll not subject her to that. This is the final warning."

"Why can I not see her?" Forsooth breathed. "What's the harm?"

What's the harm indeed? Tashué sighed, feeling the weight of his badge pulling down at the front of his jacket. What was the harm? Sedition. Rebellion. And if he didn't stop, the Rift.

The elevated tram hurtled past the building as they stood there, filling the silence with its clatter. The vibration rattled Forsooth's broken window. Tashué watched the tram pass, his stomach twisting at the sour feeling that it always brought with it, as if he could feel the misery of the tainted that powered it. His own Talent, still knotted deep in his chest and never quickened, allowed him to feel other people use their abilities. He hated the sensation that he got from the trams especially.

"It's not for me to say why laws should be followed," he said, once the tram was well past. "My job is to enforce them, not question them. Things could always be worse. There was a time when this room had no window at all, and nine other men would be in here with you."

"Forgive me if I don't dance with the joy of my circumstance. Perhaps if there were ten of us, we could afford a new pane."

3

TASHUÉ

DAY 1

The Residential Institute for Feral Tainted and Non-Compliants—the Rift—stood on an island in the Brightwash, its massive stone walls constantly enshrouded in spray from the river. An iron fence had been built around the old stone structure, an extra layer to keep its residents contained. It stood like a monolith to the nation's past, when the continent was divided into countries and city states, and war raged more often than not.

Tashué smoked as he stood on the bridge, hoping to banish the pressure in his chest, but it was no use. The grounds were stark and empty, the stone denying a foothold to any vegetation. When he glanced down river, he could see the pilings jutting up from the bank from here. That girl, so small and tortured, hadn't left his thoughts. The photographs still sat in his pocket, tucked into his notepad. Such a little thing, a photograph. And yet it was heavier than any other burden he'd ever taken on before.

With the cigarillo spent, he couldn't use it to stall anymore—he marched himself forward, trying to brace himself against the headache that clamped down on the base of his skull. The tainted in the Rift were kept contained not only by stone walls, iron fences, and the rushing river, but by a thick fog of protection that blocked the inmates and their visitors from using their Talent. Though Tashué's own Talent was so minimal he didn't need to register, he still felt the vice-like will blocking him from it. He wondered, as he had more than once, if the inmates got used to the sensation, if exposure to the vice took the pain away, or if they lived with the headache every moment of every day.

The attendant was a small man, walking with a shuffling limp that made every step look painful. What he may have lacked in physical intimidation, he made up with the guards that flanked him, the pair of them armed with utilitarian Imburleigh pistols and heavy truncheons.

"Good evening, Mr. Flinn," Tashué said, waiting at the gate.

"You're late today, Mr. Blackwood," Flinn said. He settled his spectacles on the edge of his nose as he looked at Tashué expectantly. "Haven't much visiting time left."

"I have an hour still."

Flinn shrugged at him. Tashué reached for his tin badge, passing it through the gate. Flinn was the keeper of the paperwork. He scratched Tashué's name and badge number down with deliberate care. He passed the badge back and checked his watch, marking down the time beside Tashué's information. Only when those notes were made did Flinn nod at the guards. Tashué had to duck to fit through the small door. He pinned his badge back into place on the front of his jacket as he followed Flinn into the building, a guard hanging back to close and lock the gate, the other stomping along just ahead of Flinn.

An attendant waited in a room behind a metal grate, where Tashué turned over most of the contents of his pockets. He handed over his Imburleigh pistol—a heavier piece than the guards carried—the big cavalry knife that he'd had since he served in the Dominion military, his timepiece, his cigarillo case, his pack of matches, the handful of coins he kept.

The visiting rooms were arranged next to a long hallway that stretched along the outer wall. There was a door on each side of the room, both of them locking to keep the visitor and the inmate trapped inside. Each room was cut in half by a table and strong metal grate, keeping inmates and visitors on their respective sides. Without access to Talent, no one could run brights, and the rooms were lit with oil lamps, which gave off juddering, dim light and too much heat. At least with autumn fading into winter, the rooms weren't so oppressively hot anymore.

Tashué sat at the table and waited. An ever-present hum filtered through the massive halls, an indistinct roar of so many bodies living in one place and the babbling of the river as it crested around the island. Tashué had come to appreciate all the noise. It used to be daunting, but he had learnt that the constant barrage of sound lay like a cloak over the visiting rooms, making it hard for the guards waiting outside to hear what was going on once they shut the door.

Tashué looked up as the guard stomped in. Setting eyes on his son never ceased to hurt, the frustration and regret and disappointment and fear of the last three years tearing through him every time. Jason sat across from Tashué, looking small and weary on his side of the grate. Jason hadn't inherited his father's height and breadth. He looked more like his mother—short and slim, with warm gold skin and hair as black as pitch, and tawny coloured eyes that were somewhere in between his own startling amber hue and Keoh's warm brown. But seeing the girl made Tashué realize that he had forgotten what Keoh looked like. When he pictured her, he saw Jason. But Jason's face was a blend of the two of them, Tashué and Keoh both. The girl made him remember Keoh's face scrubbed of the features that Tashué had contributed to their son. He remembered now how full and heart-shaped Keoh's mouth was, and her ears, overly large for her face. He remembered Keoh compulsively smoothing her hair over her ears, and Tashué, in his youth and ignorance, teasing her about them because he liked making her blush.

There were no new bruises on Jason this time. His eye was less swollen and the blood that had turned the sclera into a mottle of white and red was starting to fade. The other bruise, the one that came from a hit to the jaw that probably knocked a few teeth loose, had almost faded completely.

They sat in silence, staring at each other through the grate until the guard retreated out of the room.

"You look like shit, as usual," Tashué muttered.

Jason rolled his eyes at him, leaning his chair back to balance on the two rear legs. "Sorry. I didn't have time to dress up for you."

"Your eye is getting better, at least."

Jason's hand moved up to the side of his face, but he stopped short before touching it. He clenched his fists and Tashué saw the bruises on his knuckles. Were those new? He couldn't remember.

"Remind me what happened to it?" Tashué pressed.

"I fell."

"And broke your fall with your eye?"

Jason scowled. "You can save your interrogations for your cases."

Tashué bit back the frustration. He shuffled through his pockets instead, pulling out his various offerings: one silver crown, a handful of plump figs and a slice of dense bread made with grains and nuts, wrapped in muslin cloth to keep it clean. The grate was easily pulled up from the table, just enough to squeeze the items through. A few snacks seemed like such a small contribution to Jason's life, but Tashué had to do something. Jason was Tashué's flesh, his bone, his blood, but he was locked up like an animal, and there was nothing Tashué could do about that. He watched Jason diminish, every lost pound and every bruise gained chipping a piece of Tashué away. One day, he would know how to fix it, how to get Jason out. Until then, fruit and bread would have to suffice.

Jason leaned forward again, the front legs of his chair thumping back down on the floor as he reached for the silver first, stashing it away into a pocket in the rags that passed for clothing here.

"Did you get any more letters from your mother?" Tashué asked.

Jason unwrapped the muslin from the heavy bread, breaking off a few pieces and chewing them before answering. "This morning, just the one."

"What does she write about?"

"Nothing. It's babbling on paper. I don't ever recall her

babbling. In fact, when I try to remember her, I only remember her being quiet. Standing back, away from everything, as if she was afraid I'd break her."

"I think she was afraid she would break you. No one ever taught her to control her Talent."

Jason scowled at the answer, and Tashué could feel the familiar shape of the conversation and the way it was going to flow. It always went this way—a few questions, a bit of small talk, and it all somehow built up into a fight.

"How is she?" Tashué asked, trying to head off the fight. Maybe if he changed the subject often enough, he could spend a whole hour with his son without either of them getting angrier than they already were. "Your mother. Other than babbling, I mean."

Jason sighed, taking a fig next. He twisted off the hard bit that was left of the stem, pushing it back under the bent grate. "She's going to be retired soon. She said she had three miscarriages in a row, but now she's pregnant again. She says she hopes this one will survive, but she isn't sure it has a chance. Whatever happens to the babe, they'll retire her."

"That's good news."

"Is it?"

"It must be. Maybe she'll be released."

Jason leaned close to the grate, eyes wide and intense. "Will she? What happens to the Talented when they're retired from the Breeding Program? Do they get reassigned? Do *you* monitor any women who have been retired?"

The thought, and what Jason was implying, gave Tashué pause. "No, I don't have any, but that doesn't mean anything. Most of my cases are low strength. A woman strong enough to make it into a Breeding Program would get a much bigger assignment than anything we would keep in Brickheart."

"Are you sure?"

"Why, Jason? What have you heard?"

Jason shrugged, twisting the top off another fig. "Nothing specifically." He popped the fig into his mouth and Tashué could hear him crunching on the seeds. He'd never got used to that feeling, but

Jason loved figs. "I've been wondering. I was tempted to hope I would see her again, but hope seems such a stupid thing in this world."

The words cut through Tashué. His one job as a father was to protect his son from the hard world around them, but he had failed. He had so miserably failed. Fighting was almost better than this, because at least when they were fighting, rage and frustration filled all the hollow places in him and left no room for the shame.

"I'll find out," he croaked. "I'll find out what happens to them."

Jason nodded. Tashué tried to remember how old Jason was when last he saw his mother. He wondered if Jason even remembered what she looked like. If Tashué didn't have a firm memory of her anymore how could Jason remember someone he had last seen when he was a child?

Tashué's eyes were drawn down to the dark lines across Jason's collarbone, stark against his pale skin. Jason noticed him staring and his hand went to the tattoo, pushing aside the ragged collar of his shirt. *Blackwood J 1.1.658753.* The first number named his crime—1 was code for feral, refusal to register. The second marked the province he belonged to—1 again, for Yael, the first province to have the Authority at all. The third was his identity as a prisoner in the Rift. Tashué had wondered more than once if that meant that the Authority had really processed over six hundred thousand people into the Rift or other buildings like it. Jason seemed to think the numbers were random. Tashué hoped he was right.

"Do they tattoo you all in the same place?" Tashué asked, nodding to the mark.

Jason nodded, popping the last fig into his mouth. "Everyone."

"You don't see anyone with tattoos anywhere else?"

Another shrug. "Of course, but they had them before they got here. Or they get them after."

"But the Authority gives you all the same style tattoo? In the same place?"

"Yes," Jason huffed. "Why? Why do you care about tattoos all of a sudden?"

Tashué reached for his notebook, but muttered a curse when he realized he'd handed it over to the attendant. "I found a child, on the bank of the river. She had a tattoo on the back of her neck, three sets of four-digit numbers."

"Why don't you ask her where she got it?"

"Don't be a shit," Tashué muttered. "You think I wouldn't have tried that if I could? When I found her, she was dead."

The smirk died fast and Jason leaned forward, pushing the muslin back through the gap and smoothing the grate back into place. "I didn't realize dead children were part of your job."

"They aren't. But I can't do nothing."

"You always did have a soft spot for little kids. Fuck, that was so frustrating. All the other kids liked you so damned much and they were always asking to come visit because they wanted to see you. It made me so mad because I could never seem to get along with you, but there you were, a second father to half the fucking neighbourhood."

Tashué sighed, folding the muslin and tucking it back into his pocket. How could he explain that the reason he was so infuriated by Jason's choices was because he loved his son so damned much? He watched Jason stubbornly throw himself into his mistakes. Every time, Tashué desperately wanted to pull his son back onto a safer course. But every time he pulled, Jason bucked and fought like a stubborn horse.

"Do any inmates ever get pregnant?" Tashué asked instead.

Jason shrugged. "Of course they do. You know what people do when they're all locked up together. Helps pass the time."

"What happens to the children?"

Jason glanced back over his shoulder, still for a moment. It was easy to tell what he was thinking—how close were the guards? How much did they hear? "I don't know. Don't see any of them in here. There's all kinds of rumours."

"What kind of rumours?"

"Why?" Jason asked, swinging back to Tashué, leaning in close. "Do you think she came from here?"

"I don't know. She was just downriver and I thought… What kind of rumours, Jason?"

Jason shook his head, leaning back again. "I'm sure the Authority takes them. We're all tainted in here, after all. A bunch of bad meat. If people are making babies, they'll be tainted too, so the Authority must want them. Right?"

"What else have you heard, though?"

Jason opened his mouth to answer, but the guard came stomping into the room. Jason shot to his feet like he was caught at something he wasn't supposed to be doing, wiping the crumbs off his hands. The guard ignored the crumbs and the sweet smell of figs, patting Jason's pocket quickly and finding the silver crown. With it in her pocket, she marched Jason back out again.

"Fucking hell," Tashué muttered, pushing himself to his feet.

Flinn escorted him back out. Tashué lit a cigarillo as soon as he had them back, cloaking himself in sweet-smelling tobacco smoke. Was it the rumours that inspired the fear in Jason, or merely the defiant act of spreading them?

Wind whipped off the river, tugging at Tashué's clothes. Flinn's keys unlocked the gate and Tashué stepped through, released from the headache.

"Have a good night, Mr. Blackwood."

Tashué stopped. He turned to the little man, looking past the crooked spectacles to look Flinn in the eye. "My son is imprisoned in the Rift, Mr. Flinn. I come here three or four times a week to see him and most of the time he has fresh bruises. No new ones this time, thank the North Star. As long as my son is in this place, I don't have 'good' nights."

4

STELLA

DAY 1

Stella Whiterock was registered as tainted. She worked at the Facility of Rest for the Critically Ill, which sat on the bank of the Brightwash like a towering, ugly toad, all grey stone and hard lines. There weren't enough windows in the building, so brights lined the halls, casting ghoulish shadows night and day.

Stella hated the brights. She hated the whole building, all six floors of it. The uppermost floors were miserably hot, the basement and the ground floor bitterly cold. There seemed to be quite a bit of disagreement as to how the patients were to be distributed through the building. Sometimes the patients assigned to her were peppered thinly across multiple floors, sending her up and down the stairs endlessly, or they were packed more 'efficiently' on each floor, sometimes so tightly that there was only room to step between every second cot, sending her wading through bodies and the filth that the dying created.

Tonight, Stella had a dozen patients scattered across the fourth and fifth floors, sending her wandering through the halls and stairwells like a wraith. The Facility of Rest was not a healing place, but rather a hospice where people could go to die without their pain. Not everyone could afford the attentions of a proper registered healer, nor even could every ailment be solved completely by Talent. For those people—at least those that could pull together four copper crowns a day—there were whisperers who could offer their patients the solace of removing them from their pain. It was an easy thing to disconnect people's minds from their own pain, leaving them oblivious and distant. But whisperers were no healers, and though the pain was gone, the symptoms continued.

And so it was that Stella found herself on her hands and knees, washing another pile of vomit from the floorboards. There were attendants to mop up the various messes, but of course there were never enough of them.

Dumping the rags into the wash bucket, she stood slowly, her knees crackling their protest. The water and the rags and the filth all slopped around together as she lifted the bucket. Stella headed out of the big room, stepping carefully so she didn't slosh any of her foul water on her feet. Stella moved to the end of the hall where there was a wash basin and a water closet. She dumped the contents of the bucket into the basin, the acrid smell burning the inside of her nostrils. The water pump was stiff and creaky, and she felt the strain in her shoulders, her arms, her back. Her legs might have been well toned by all her numerous trips up and down the stairs, but pumping water wasn't one of her usual chores.

"Miss Whiterock?" came a familiar voice.

Stella looked up to see Daphne, the orderly who seemed to be in charge of the entire fifth floor, a mighty job even when the beds were under half full. She was a short woman, with a round face predisposed to friendliness, but mostly she looked weary and worn.

"Forgive me, Miss Whiterock." Daphne dragged her bucket to the sink and dumped in a similar soup of rags, dirty water, and sour smell. "Was there a mess?"

"Mr. Thorpe was sick again. You seemed busy so I thought I'd clean it myself."

"Thank you, Miss Whiterock." Daphne moved swiftly between Stella and the pump, taking over. "The girl in the east wing was stricken with a terrible bloody flux. She didn't last long, poor thing, but at least she was able to go quietly."

Stella leaned over the basin, rinsing her hands in the flow of bitterly cold water. The water from the Brightwash seemed to remember the ice it had melted from, up in the mountains. The cold dragged Stella back to herself, an ache forming in her fingers that anchored her in her own flesh.

"I'm sorry, Daphne. I really should be getting back."

"Of course, Miss Whiterock. I'll be around to your side in a few moments, I promise. If there is any other trouble, please come find me."

"It's fine. There's no rush."

Stella returned to the boy in her care, the one that was most frustrating of all her cases. He probably hadn't long left in him, his whole body carrying poisonous blood with every beat of his heart. His parents had taken him to a meat-monger instead of a proper healer when first he fell ill. After discovering the boy had cut himself on the toe and the wound had gone bad, the meat-monger cut off the rotting appendage. When it became clear that the infection hadn't been brought under control, they cut off the whole foot. Finally, they'd taken the boy's leg just above the knee in a last effort to save him, but it was all too late. The terrible infection burned through his entire body by then, eating him from the inside. The boy's parents had spent all of their money on the meat-monger and they couldn't afford the calibre of healer it would take to save his life.

Returning to the child's bedside, Stella lowered herself onto the edge of the cot and took the boy's hand. His skin was hot and clammy, the fever raging as his body battled vainly against the infection. But he lay peacefully, his other hand pinned beneath his cheek. With his mouth hanging slack, Stella could see the gaps where his baby premolars had fallen out, making Stella wonder how old he was. Surely no more than ten. No older than Ceridwen, who slept even now in a safe place, up on the top floor.

It was an easy thing to slip her consciousness into the boy's body, to hear his heart racing but weakening, fading beneath the strain. It wouldn't be much harder to slide her Talent a little further, to drag the infection out of his body and boost the strength of his organs and see the boy on his way—one legged, perhaps, but alive! Even though her registration papers said that she was only capable of small feats, her Talent burned in the centre of her and so too her desire to use it. The infection, though fatal, would be an easy thing for her to help him conquer. The body knew what to do, and Stella had more than enough strength in her Talent to lend him some, more than enough skill to see him safely returned to his parents.

It was a shame that he had lost so much when the solution was so simple. Any decent healer could have dealt with the infection when it was first discovered, and their attention would have been less expensive than three amputations from the meat-monger. But the very thought of going to a healer—someone tainted—was terrifying to some people, even though it was often the simplest and best solution.

She sent her Talent into him, just a bit. It flooded his body with fresh energy, lending strength to organs that were about to fail and pushing her own will against the invading infection. He would still have to battle the infection himself, but perhaps now he had the strength to survive it.

And even as she lent him that strength, a flash of fear passed through her mind. Such risks she took, when she healed people. The Facility of Rest wasn't a place for healing. People came here to die, and if she sent too many home, someone would notice.

And yet, she couldn't quite bring herself to feel bad about saving him. The boy deserved to live. Her skills allowed that to happen. What world was it if she let him die only because she was afraid for her own life? Living longer was not a good enough gift, not when an innocent child was in front of her and she had to choose.

"Rest, sweet boy," Stella whispered. "Rest a while longer."

5

TASHUÉ

DAY 2

The Directed Breeding Program of Yaelsmuir housed their breeders in a massive garrison standing alone on a hill to the south of the city. As he stood by the walls, Tashué looked back to see the whole city stretching out before him: Cattle Bone Bay, Highfield on the other side of the Brightwash, Highview looking north at it, the two tram lines slicing through it all with the elevated track.

It was easier to look out at the city than it was to look at the towering stone walls. He wasn't sure what he'd find in there, but the whole place left him feeling as small as he felt when he stood on the bridge and looked up at the Rift. Smaller, even. The walls of the Breeding Program were angular and aggressive, more menacing than the Rift. The double gates were shut tight, but the turret closest to the road held a great column of offices. Tashué wondered how much paperwork was contained in that turret, how many boxes of files were collecting dust. The Authority generated so damned much paper. Which floor was Keoh's file tucked away on? What happened to the files of the women 'retired'? Did they get shifted to a station house somewhere, or were they all still there?

Tashué cursed as he flicked the cigarillo to the road, crushing the ember with the toe of his boot. He turned away from the city, looking up at the turret instead. He took a deep breath and stepped in. The place smelled of stone and dust and paper and spent gas from the lamps. Like the Rift, the tiny windows did not let in sufficient light. The brights really were a fantastic innovation, something Tashué had come to realize with all the places he frequented that couldn't use them.

He didn't get far before he found a table that barred his path. A pair of guards were rolling knuckle-bone dice, a pile of half copper crowns as their wagers. An attendant sat among a pile of paperwork at the massive desk that stretched behind them. The guards glanced up as he rounded the corner, one half-rising from his seat.

"Sir? Are you here to apply for a visitation?"

"Yes."

The attendant's head popped up and she waved Tashué over. Tashué had to skirt past the guard's table to reach her, and the dice stopped clattering. The attendant shuffled through the papers on her desk, found the appropriate paper, and refilled her pen with ink.

"Your name?"

"Tashué Blackwood."

"Occupation?"

"I'm a Regulation Officer here in Yaelsmuir."

"May I see your badge?"

Tashué pulled the badge off his jacket, laying it on the desk between them. She pulled it closer, copying down the badge number.

"Who would you like to visit?"

"Keoh Gian Ly."

"What is your relation to this breeder?"

"She is the mother of my son."

"Were you ever married to this breeder?"

"No."

"Is there any family relation between you and this breeder?"

"I fucking well hope not," Tashué grunted. "What the hell is that supposed to mean? Is she my cousin as well?"

The attendant forced a smile, gesturing down at the paper. "I've a list of questions to ask and I need an answer for each one."

Tashué sighed. That, at least, he understood. "No, I am not otherwise related to the mother of my son."

"Is there an official reason for the requested visit?"

"If I say yes, are my chances of getting through the gates better?"

"If the answer is yes, you have to prove the official reason with supporting paperwork. Do you have supporting paperwork?"

"No," Tashué admitted.

"What is the reason for the requested visit?"

"Nostalgia?"

The attendant glanced up at Tashué, waiting for a better answer, before looking down and scratching something on the paper. "Your request will be submitted and you will be informed when a decision is reached."

"How long might I wait for such a decision?"

"The usual waiting period is four to eight weeks."

"Four to eight weeks?" Tashué breathed. "I'm sorry, I thought it would be a somewhat shorter time frame?"

"There are a lot of applicants, Mr. Blackwood, and these things take time. I'm sorry. Four to eight weeks. But it could be longer."

"Is there any way I can expedite this process?"

"Not unless you have an official reason to visit."

Frustration bubbled in him again, but he took a deep breath and swallowed it down. He knew the intricate system of the Authority well enough to know how they cloaked themselves in paperwork and regulations. Employees were given the rules to follow, rigid lines that they were meant to fit in, and copious amounts of paperwork to ensure that every decision could be traced.

"Fine," Tashué said, standing, picking up his badge and returning it to its place. "Is that all, then?"

"If you'll leave your address, sir, I can have any correspondence sent to your place of residence. Otherwise I'll have it sent to your station house."

"I'm at 52 Firth Street, unit 15," Tashué said. "I would prefer any correspondence to be delivered there."

"Yes, sir." She sighed after taking down the address, glancing up. "There's only so much that I can do."

"I know," Tashué said, running his hands over his face. "We're all just trying to do our jobs, aren't we?"

"We are indeed," the attendant said, pushing back her chair and standing again. "We're nothing but a great web of people, only doing their jobs."

The first floor of the station house was gloomy despite its high ceilings, its small windows barred. Heavy desks were bolted to the floor, iron rings on them used to lock any hostile tainted in place.

Just like the Rift, the station house used someone with Talent to block other tainted from their abilities. Tashué felt the familiar headache clamp down on his skull. He'd never get used to the invasion of another mind into his own.

He leaned on the desk that guarded the stairs, rapping his knuckles against the wood. The sound echoed through the hall even above the din. The young desk clerk sprang up from under the desk, long and lanky and not yet in charge of all his limbs.

"Yes, sir?"

Tashué raised an eyebrow at him. "Have you taken to napping under the desk, Lian? Are we really working you so hard?"

"No, sir, I dropped my pen, and I kicked it under here somewhere, sir. There's so many cracks and crannies, I can't seem to figure where it went, sir."

"I didn't realize pens were so crafty."

"No, sir, it's not the pen, just my feet." Lian looked down at the floor as if he meant to dive under his desk again.

"Lian."

Lian darted back up straight. "Yes, sir?"

"As much as I'd like to listen to your adventures, Commander Khosran wanted to see me this morning."

"Oh, yes, sir, my apologies, sir."

Lian fumbled for the ring of keys at his belt, struggling to get them off their chain. He fought with the heavy lock next. All his movements were too fast and uncoordinated, and he dropped the keys but managed to catch them before they hit the floor.

"Easy now, Lian," Tashué said. "Don't drop those keys. I hear there's cracks and crannies and whatnot for them to hide in."

Lian stopped, giving Tashué a shy smile. "Yes, sir. Sorry, sir."

The lock thunked as it opened, the door swinging slowly on old metal hinges. As Tashué stepped past the reach of the suppression, he sighed at the release of pressure in his skull. Since the tainted were only kept on the first floor and in the cells in the basement, there was no need to cast the suppression to the second floor.

The room upstairs was no less crowded than the floor below. There were desks and small table lamps scattered everywhere, but the main desk stretched across the far wall. Gaslights stood on brass sconces between each window, the glass covers polished and clean. Three stations were spread along the desk, with three elegantly wrought typewriters and a typist at each.

Tashué resisted the urge to fall in line to file his notes. Better to see Khosran and get it over with, whatever 'it' was. The door to the Commander's office was open and Khosran shot to his feet when he noticed Tashué.

"Mr. Blackwood! Please, come in. Have a seat!"

Tashué took a deep breath, heading into the office and pushing the door closed behind him. Khosran leaned across the large desk to shake Tashué's hand, which only served to make Tashué feel worse. Why all the enthusiasm?

"Sit down, Mr. Blackwood. No need to look so scared!"

"Yes, sir." Tashué sank into the chair, but it felt awkward, the chair a little too small and a little too close to Khosran's desk, the length of him too constrained to be comfortable. "What is this about?"

"Yes, right to business. My promotion has been approved. I'm to be shuffled off to some internal position where I'll be in charge of even more paperwork. I'm quite excited, really, to be working over at House One. It's quite the monument, isn't it? To the success of the Registration Authority."

Tashué fought down the urge to curse. The success of the Registration Authority had put Keoh in the Breeding Program and Jason in the Rift. *The success of the Authority pays your damned salary,* he reminded himself, *the success of the Authority gave you that badge.* And there it was again, the mantra his mother had drilled so securely into his mind, *follow the law and you'll stay safe.*

"Yes sir," he said finally. "Congratulations on your promotion, sir."

"Thank you. Of course that left the question of who would command this station house. I was asked if anyone here would suit for the job, and I suggested you."

"Me? Why?" Tashué blurted. He hadn't led anyone in years, not since he'd retired from the cavalry. He thought that part of his life was over. *Wanted* that part of his life to be over.

Khosran laughed. "Why? Because you have experience leading people. The Jitabvi, no less! If there is a more unruly group than Jitabvi hotbloods, I haven't yet seen it. I know we don't always see the same side of things, Mr. Blackwood, but I think we're different men serving the same purpose. I think this house will do well to have you in command. And the Chief Administrator agrees." Khosran shuffled through his desk, pulling out an envelope with Tashué's name on it, leaning across the desk to hand it over. "That's your formal invitation to the Imburleigh event, where you'll receive your brass badge. They've asked for military dress for anyone who served, and I believe you may bring one guest."

Tashué took the envelope, the paper heavy in his hand, his name on the front in deep black ink. Imburleigh's seal was embossed in one corner, the ridges standing high above the rest of the paper. "Why is Imburleigh Armament Company involved with Authority promotions?"

"It's an event they are running in support of Governor Winter's campaign, I understand. Something to do with the Provincial Police Force he wants to start. I expect he'll be taking some leadership from the Authority in order to train his police force, so it's something to consider if you want to work with the new force."

"Governor Winter has to be re-elected before he can start work on his police force," Tashué muttered.

"Yes, of course, but it's not exactly a gamble, is it?" Khosran asked. "Eirdis Redbone is lovely, but she hasn't got Winter money and Elsworth strategy backing her, has she?"

Tashué shrugged. He'd never thought much of politicians in Yaelsmuir. The first time he had ever taken an interest in voting at all was when General Wolfe ran for Mayor. "Are there any more Officers coming here, then? We were short handed before Maccus died and we're all at or above our maximum case levels."

"I made sure to remind Mr. Elsworth. He's assured us that he hasn't forgotten our request for more Officers." Khosran sat back, pulling out his timepiece. "I won't keep you any longer, if you need to file notes. But don't leave just yet. Mr. Elsworth is coming shortly and I believe he wants to speak to you as well."

Tashué froze, half-out of his chair. "The Chief Administrator wants to talk to me? Why?"

Khosran laughed, shaking his head. "Have you always been so scared of your authority figures wanting to see you? I doubt Mr. Elsworth bites."

Tashué scowled before he could stop himself, fighting the uneasy feeling back down. "It's probably leftover from serving in the military. The Generals only came looking for the Captains when they were looking to hand out floggings or bad assignments."

Another laugh, but the sound grated on Tashué's nerves. A lot of soldiers died on those bad assignments. "I don't think Mr. Elsworth is going to flog you."

"Here's hoping."

Tashué let himself out of the office, falling into line with the other Officers waiting for their turn with the typists. There were plenty of tainted in the Dominion workforce, keeping foundry fires lit, driving the trams that ran on two separate loops, lighting the brights, smelting, forging, weaving, healing. Their abilities built things with more strength and more precision than could the average human mind and hand. The Authority supervised most of the tainted in the Dominion, and there never seemed to be quite enough Regulation Officers to manage them all.

The line shifted again, and again, and Tashué found himself sitting at the desk. "One file for notes please, Celia. Forsooth, Glaen. And I'll need another to look at, the last of Maccus's files. Whiterock, Stella."

Celia nodded as she scribbled down the names, sending a runner to fetch the files. It didn't sit right with him, this part of his job. Glaen's words echoed in his head. *Gianna gives me reason to breathe. Why can I not see her?*

The runner disappeared into the back room where all the files were kept, piles and piles of paperwork, hundreds of lives reduced to black ink on off-white pulp. The runner returned with both files. Celia handed the Whiterock file across the desk and Tashué felt his heart skip a beat as he took it. It was nothing but paper and yet…

Celia's hands moved with practised efficiency, threading the page of notes for Forsooth's file into her machine. Her fingers hovered over the keys as she waited.

Tashué took a deep breath, meeting her eye. "Fraternization reported. Final warning issued."

The heavy clack of the keys struck his raw nerves and he bit back a curse. *What harm indeed?*

"Is that everything, Mr. Blackwood?"

Tashué nodded. Celia pulled the paper out of the typewriter, laying it in front of Tashué on the desk. She handed over her fountain pen and Tashué lay his signature next to the words she'd typed. It was a short page of entries and signatures. Glaen had been a good case, staying out of trouble, keeping up with the demands of his job. Until he met Gianna Tarbrook. And now both of their futures were in peril.

Celia replaced the sheet into Glaen's file and there was no more reason to stall. He had to open Stella Whiterock's file and read the history of her whole life, even though he didn't want to.

Tashué realized that Celia was talking to him and he looked up. "Pardon?"

"You'll be keeping the file?"

"Yes. Thank you."

Celia nodded. Smiled. She was kind enough not to comment on

his discomfort. He walked to an empty desk, sitting with the file in front of him. When Stella's file needed a new Regulation Officer, he'd taken it without hesitation. *This way I can protect her,* he'd told himself.

And that, of course, made him ask, *protect her from what?*

Footsteps echoed up the stairs, and he looked up from Stella's unopened file. General Nathaniel Wolfe, the Mayor of Yaelsmuir, appeared first. His long military career was also highlighted by his service on the Queen's voting council, which helped give the Provinces more control over their own governance. Tashué had voted for him already, and would do it again when his election came due in two years. It was the first time Tashué had ever had the pleasure of voting for a politician that genuinely seemed to care about the people of the city.

Behind him was the Governor's wife, Illea Winter. She entered the room as if she owned it, and she very well may have. There was no telling where the considerable wealth of her family was placed, which buildings had been built by her forebears, which institutions were funded by her patronage. That the Governor himself, Myron Winter, was absent was hardly surprising. The pair seldom appeared at the same place.

Rainer Elsworth, the Chief Administrator of the National Taint Registration Authority, walked behind her with his back ramrod straight, his smile mostly hidden beneath the long moustache that sat swept his top lip. He was everything Tashué hated about politicians—and in his control were the laws the governed every tainted in the Dominion.

Khosran stepped out of his office at their arrival, wearing his best smile. "Good morning, gentlemen, Miss Winter. I trust you made it through Brickheart without incident?"

The room fell silent, Officers and typists frozen in place. Station houses didn't usually host the government of Yaelsmuir.

"Of course, Commander," General Wolfe said. "Brickheart is hardly the most dangerous place I've been in my life."

"Speak for yourself, General!" Elsworth laughed. "Not all of us have enjoyed such an interesting life as you have." He reached out for a handshake as Khosran approached them, patting the smaller man on the shoulder. "Good to see you, Commander Khosran. And where is our Mr. Blackwood?"

General Wolfe's eyes scanned the floor, his face cracking into a warm smile when he found Tashué. Tashué shot to his feet, his arm going up to salute before he could stop himself.

"No need for that, Captain," Wolfe said, stepping closer. "I've told you before—I don't expect my friends to salute me."

"Yes, General."

General Wolfe chuckled, extended a hand. Tashué reached across the desk, accepting his handshake. "It's good to see you again, Captain. It's been entirely too long. Relax. You aren't in any trouble."

"Oh really? Then what brought the Mayor, the Governor's wife and the Chief Administrator of the Authority looking for me?"

"Consider it a special assignment, Captain."

"That isn't comforting in the least," Tashué grunted. "The Black Ridge was a 'special assignment'."

Wolfe reached out and patted Tashué on the shoulder. He understood, at least. "This won't be anything like the Black Ridge. Commander Khosran, is there somewhere more private we can talk to our Captain Blackwood?"

"Yes, of course, Mr. Mayor." Khosran stepped through the silent crowd, smiling at the people around him. "This way, into my office."

Tashué took a deep breath, gathering up Stella's file and step-ping around the desk. It took some shuffling to fit the five of them in enough to close the door. Tashué found himself pressed so close to Illea Winter's body he could feel the warmth of her. Tashué clutched the file close to his chest, looking at the faces around him one by one.

"You have an impressive history, Mr. Blackwood," Elsworth began, breaking the silence. "You served in the military for ten years, is that right?"

"I did," Tashué said. "Enlisted at thirteen."

"So young," Illea Winter said. "Admirable, Mr. Blackwood."

Tashué shrugged. "Seemed better than waiting for the draft to scoop me up. I wanted to choose my assignment rather than be placed somewhere boring."

"What made you choose the cavalry?" Illea asked.

"I didn't like the idea of marching everywhere."

"I see you've always been pragmatic, Mr. Blackwood," Khosran chuckled. "Our Mr. Blackwood has been a dedicated Officer at this very station house longer than I've been here. Nearly twenty years I believe—is that about right, Mr. Blackwood?"

"I'm sure it says in my file. What is this about, General?"

A flush crept up Elsworth's face. Illea covered her mouth with one hand, but that wasn't enough to hide her smile. Something had shifted in the room in response to his deference to General Wolfe over Chief Administrator Elsworth and it made him uncomfortable, being at the centre of that much tension. General Wolfe cleared his throat.

"This project would be under Mr. Elsworth's control, Captain. I'll let him take the reins."

"I'm sure you know there is an election forthcoming," Elsworth said, "with our Governor Winter for re-election. Do you follow election news?"

Tashué shifted, taking a deep breath. Back to politics, then. "Not especially."

"Our Governor's desire is to create a Provincial Police Force in the style of the National Tainted Registration Authority. As such, we had thought it a good time for us to remind the people of the success of the Authority overall."

"What does that have to do with me?"

"Are you always so surly, Mr. Blackwood?" Illea asked.

Tashué looked down at her, trying not to notice how close she was standing, how she was leaning toward him. "I try to be."

Illea laughed, and Tashué was struck by the sound. Everything she did was so effortlessly beautiful, so warm and intoxicating.

Khosran forced a laugh, too. To a different effect in the room. "Our Mr. Blackwood has a rather grim sense of humour, I'm afraid."

Illea calmed Khosran with a beaming smile. "It's fine, Mr. Khosran. The man's file speaks for itself. His sense of humour is a bonus."

"What is my file and my sense of humour needed for?"

"You are to be the face of the National Tainted Registration Authority," Elsworth cut in. "You will accompany us—the Governor, the Mayor and myself—on our various campaigning functions."

"What does that mean?"

Illea put her hand on his arm, giving an affectionate squeeze. "It means that we will dress you in our finery and feed you our best food. Whenever Mr. Elsworth wants people to notice you, he will talk about how excellent your history is and everyone will agree that the National Taint Registration Authority is a resounding success."

"Why do you need me for that?" Tashué pressed. He was getting tired of asking and not getting a real answer. "Plenty of other Officers have a military background. I'm sure plenty of them have better files than I do, with more experience in politics."

"But Mr. Blackwood, not many Officers can say they have a White Shield, can they?" Khosran asked.

Tashué took a deep breath, turning to Wolfe. "This is about the Ridge?"

"Of course it is, Captain," Wolfe said, but his voice was softer than everyone else's. He knew the weight of the Ridge. "The White Shield is no small achievement."

"Mr. Blackwood, honestly, you can relax," Illea said. "Yes, you are an exemplary Officer, and a Captain with a fascinating military history. But honestly? We chose you because you're tall and handsome. We'll have you fitted for some proper suits from Bellmore himself, and you'll look absolutely dashing. All of these things are excellent qualities in public figures."

"That sounds terribly uncomfortable."

"I promise, the food really is quite good," Wolfe said. "And the wine, Captain, is excellent. As is the gin and the brandy and the whisky."

"Oh, well, if there's going to be good whisky."

6

STELLA

DAY 4

The boy's fever turned even hotter through the second night. Stella sat with him, her Talent drifting through his body. She didn't interfere with the fever, for the heat of it did important work, killing away the vileness in his blood. But she guarded his organs, protecting the ever-vulnerable brain from getting too hot. By the time the sun began to lighten the horizon, the boy's body had begun to sweat, the first sign that the fever was breaking and the infection was conquered.

Stella roused Ceridwen from the cot bed on the sixth floor. The girl was nothing but a tangle of strawberry-blond curls sticking out from her blankets. Stella sat Ceridwen on the edge of the cot for a moment to fix her hair into plaits that would sit on the back of her neck.

"How did you sleep, Pigeon?" Stella asked as they headed back down the stairs.

"Fine. It was cold last night. Winter's almost here, I think."

"Almost," Stella agreed. "Might come early this year."

Outside, the crisp autumn air seemed to invigorate Ceridwen and soon she was skipping ahead, making up a song as she went.

She knew by now the limit of Stella's comfort, pushing to the very edge of it before she stopped and waited for Stella to catch up.

"What's for lunch today, Mam?"

"We'll make the pies? We made the pork and potatoes yesterday, remember?"

She nodded, skipped ahead, then stopped. Bitterly cold wind scythed through them as they made their way home, wet with the promise of rain. The clouds opened above them, fulfilling their promise when Stella and Ceridwen were within view of the Row— blocks of buildings that had all been constructed on the same blueprint, a courtyard in the middle of each block. Each building had been painted a different colour, as bright and merry as spring flowers. It had been many a year since the paint had been laid on the stone, and it was faded now, wind and weather and time slowly buffeting the cheerfulness away, as it always did.

The rain became a vicious torrent within a few moments. Stella caught Ceridwen's hand and they ran the rest of the way, heads ducked against the bitter cold rain, Ceridwen laughing and shrieking as they ran. Ceridwen darted up the stairs ahead of Stella, unlocking their front door.

"Get a fire going, Pigeon."

They peeled off their coats, and Stella dragged the coat tree closer to the stove. She used a cloth to squeeze the dampness from her hair as she watched Ceridwen lay the fire, small pieces of wood nestled among shredded paper and bark. Best not to help, to let her learn to do these things herself. She was perfectly capable, after all.

Turning away, Stella rolled a ball of dough onto the table, from the bowl where it had been waiting to be used. She punched the great mass down, forcing out some of the air before folding it over itself a few times. Ceridwen's fire was crackling and hot by the time Stella cut the dough into smaller balls. Ceridwen crouched in front of the stove, watching the flames dance.

"Close the oven door, Ceridwen. The fire's hot enough—you're just wasting wood now."

"Yes, Mam."

The door squeaked on its iron hinges, and Ceridwen struggled to get the latch in place. Stella bit her lip and watched Ceridwen fight against the stiff iron. Better to let her struggle and become stronger.

A knock on the front door froze Stella for a moment. She wasn't expecting anyone. It wasn't her Regulation Officer—the knock was strong and firm. Mr. Maccus was a slight man, with sloping shoulders and long, elegant hands that seemed more intended to play piano or hold a paintbrush. He didn't knock with so much force. But of course it couldn't be him. Mr. Maccus was dead.

Ceridwen had no such hesitation, shooting to her feet and skipping over to the door.

"Ceridwen, wait," Stella breathed.

It was too late. Ceridwen was opening the door. Stella pushed herself to her feet, fear rising like bile in her throat. She started around the table, but the chairs were in the way and she couldn't move fast enough. Had she been *found*? Even as her limbs went heavy and leaden with fear, she fought against those thoughts. She was being foolish. Death, when it came, wouldn't knock.

But when she saw Tashué Blackwood standing on the other side of the door, the relief was so total that her knees went weak. His bedroom window faced hers. She saw him on hot summer nights, sitting in his open window with a cigarillo, stripped to the waist to catch the cool breeze on his skin. She saw him often on the street in front of their buildings, rushing off to some task, or trudging back home. He liked fruit and sweet things like Ceridwen did. He shared whatever he brought home with Ceridwen when they encountered each other in the streets, but he had never come knocking before. There was so much about him that she was tempted to like, a gentleness to him despite all his scars and calluses, but he wore a tin badge on his jacket, shined and polished and displayed for all to see. Stella knew better than to trust any man or woman who worked for the National Tainted Registration Authority.

"Mr. Blackwood!" Ceridwen cried and she launched herself at the big man. "I didn't know you were coming to visit. Oh—you're soaking wet!"

"Yes, little warrior," he chuckled, rustling her hair. "It's raining outside. A lot." He was, indeed, dripping wet, a puddle forming around his feet. He'd tried to shake out his hair, which left it standing on all ends. He was considerably more dishevelled than Stella had ever seen him, and he smiled. But his eyes looked... sad? He seemed uncomfortable, shifting from one foot to the other. Was there a bit of a blush creeping up to his face? "Your mam wouldn't be expecting me. I'm sorry, Miss Whiterock, I'm here on... Authority business."

"Authority business?" Ceridwen echoed. "Did you know Mr. Maccus?"

"I did, little warrior. He was my colleague."

"What's a colleague? Is it like a friend?"

"It means we worked together." He looked up at Stella, trying to smile, but it was a weak effort. "May I come in, Miss White-rock? I have a few questions to ask, to make good all the paperwork."

"Are you to be my Regulation Officer now, Mr. Blackwood?" Stella asked, and her heart beat a little faster at the thought. He always made her heart beat faster, and the possibility of him coming into her home on a regular basis...

"Yes," he said softly, peeling off his coat. It was soaked through, clinging to the jacket of his suit. "I'm afraid I am."

She bit the inside of her lip. "Out of the way, Ceridwen. Let Mr. Blackwood in."

He stepped in only tentatively, just enough for Ceridwen to close the door behind him. He seemed frozen by something, held in place by the threshold. Was it the rain, still dripping from his coat, which he held over one arm? Stella stepped closer, drawn to him like she always was. She took his coat, draping it across the back of a chair to spread it in front of the fire, but of course it was too long and the hem trailed on the floor. She moved the chair around to the other side of the stove, out of the kitchen so no one would get flour on it or step on the hem.

"Would you like to help us make lunch?" Ceridwen asked, skipping back to the table. "It's fun to make hand pies."

"I'm afraid I'm not a very good baker, little warrior," Tashué said, the tension releasing from him only slowly. "Isn't it early for making lunch?"

"We make lunch when we get home so Mam can rest after. She works all night. I get to sleep but Mam has to help those people at the Facility. Are you sure you don't want to help? I can show you how to fold the dough so none of the juices leak out."

Ceridwen settled in her chair again and Tashué came to stand in front of the table. He didn't seem to know what to do with his hands, shuffling through his pockets as if he was looking for something and then giving up on his search. His arms were soaked, as was his collar and his shoulder and his back. Stella's heart fluttered in her chest as she looked up at him. How long had it been since she'd had someone in this apartment with her, other than Ceridwen? Life was so lonely in Yaelsmuir, so far from anyone she knew. She had spent so much time running from her past that she never seemed to have a chance to live anymore, and now here was this man who made her heart beat so fast that she finally felt alive again.

"Here, Mr. Blackwood," Stella said, passing him the same cloth she'd used on her own hair. "You might be more comfortable if you dried yourself off. Would you like to take off your jacket as well?"

"Ah, no. I'm alright," he breathed. He took the cloth, though, wiping his face, mopping water from the stubble that was growing on his cheeks, from his thick auburn hair. He gave a sheepish grin as he pushed his fingers through his hair, trying to smooth it back down. Those amber eyes of his held her in place, the intensity of the man like a lodestone that always pulled on Stella. He handed the cloth back, clearing his throat. "Thank you."

"Mam, I need some dough," Ceridwen said. "The oven is ready!"

Stella looked down at the table to avoid looking at him and spread a handful of flour before reaching for a ball of dough. Her fingers went to work and it helped her slow her heartbeat. She stretched the dough into a wider circle, sliding it across to Ceridwen.

"You should still help," Ceridwen said. "Even if you don't think you're good at it. The best way to learn something is to not be good at it first."

"That's very wise, little warrior," Tashué said. He stepped a little closer, leaning over to watch Ceridwen work. "What are you making?"

"They're like pies, but Mam uses bread dough. They do it up in Cruinnich, she said, because sometimes it's hard to come by suet or lard or butter. She said it's something her mam used to make and it makes her feel like she's at home."

"How long have you lived in Yaelsmuir, Miss Whiterock?"

Stella glanced up at Tashué. She wondered how innocent that question was. Was he making small talk, or was he checking to see if she knew what her own paperwork said?

"We've been here four years now," Stella said, reaching for another ball and stretching it. "We lived in Obisza before that, but I missed the water. We were only there a year or two."

"You've moved cities a lot. Do you remember Obisza, little warrior?"

"I only remember our neighbour, Miss Zee. She used to make vodka with bison grass in it, and she paid me a half copper crown to go pick grass with her. She was very nice. Mam still has a bottle of bison grass vodka. She doesn't like it very much, but it was a gift from Miss Zee, and it's nice to remember our friends, especially if we won't see them again on this side of the Keeper's Gate."

"You've been a hard worker for a long time," Tashué said.

"I like having my own crowns to spend. That way I can buy sweets that Mam can't afford. The Facility doesn't pay very well, but if I work too, then we can have more sweets."

"You do the laundry for people in this building, is that right?"

"Yes, sir."

"Anything else?"

"No, that's it for now. Mam says I have to learn to read and write and do my maths. That way I can learn to be a baker one day if I want instead of only doing the laundry. I don't mind doing the laundry, but sometimes the lye soap hurts my hands. But if I'm a baker, I can have all the sweets I want. And I can make other people happy, too."

"Bakers do good work," Tashué agreed with a nod. "I've never mastered the skill, so I wouldn't be able to have cherry pie without bakers. Or sweet buns. Or honey cakes."

"Or cookies! Mam makes good cookies. I bet Mam would be a good baker if the Authority would let her, but the Authority said she has to work at the Facility."

"She does good work at the Facility, too," Tashué said and his voice had gone soft and gentle. "It's a good thing she does, helping the people there."

Ceridwen's production had slowed considerably, her attention going to chatting instead of folding. All of the dough was stretched now and there was nothing left for Stella's hands to do. She stepped around the table, opening the small oven that sat above the fire box. She slid the first pie in. The heat from the stove chased away the deep chill that lived in her bones these days. She imagined the warmth of Tashué Blackwood's body for a brief moment. Surely it would chase the chill away even better than the stove did. How long had it been since she felt the embrace of a man, strong arms around her body, the scrap of stubble on her skin? She stepped away from the stove, trying to push those thoughts from her mind. But Tashué had moved and as she took a step back, their bodies collided, her shoulder pressing into his jacket where it was still the most wet. He caught her when she staggered, his hands firm and strong, warm through her sleeves.

Stella stepped away from him quickly, though the confines of the kitchen meant there wasn't much space to get far.

"I'm sorry, Miss Whiterock," Tashué said softly.

Stella felt her cheeks flush and she bit her tongue against the rising heat. "No need to be sorry, Mr. Blackwood. It's a tight space."

The smell of roasted bread filled the small apartment and Stella moved back to the wood stove again, easing the door open. The thin dough had cooked fast, the dome rising with steam and turning golden brown. Ceridwen had gotten a little further ahead and Stella pulled one off the table, crimping the edge closed where Ceridwen had missed a spot. She switched them, pulling the first out and adding the second.

"You're very good at that," Tashué said.

"I always liked baking. Mother expected us to help in the kitchen. Said it kept young people out of trouble if they stayed busy."

"Us?"

Stella hesitated only a moment, cursing herself. Her paperwork didn't say anything about siblings. "Me, and then Ceridwen, back when she was a babe. Before I left Cruinnich."

"I don't remember Cruinnich," Ceridwen announced. "I was too little when we left."

"Why don't you go get yourself some breakfast from the bakery, Ceridwen? Mr. Blackwood and I will finish making lunch."

"Yes, Mam!" Ceridwen was away in an instant, wiping her hands on the front of her skirt. "Will you still be here when I get back, Mr. Blackwood?"

"I'm not sure, little warrior. We'll see, I suppose."

Ceridwen hesitated. Stella could see the way her body vibrated in that way it did when she had more to say but wasn't sure if she should. She wanted to ask to stay, to visit. She nodded finally and turned, grabbing her coat again before heading out the door. The stillness and the quiet usually left in her wake was interrupted by Tashué's presence, by his breathing, heavy but even, by the scent of cigarillo smoke and wet wool from his suit.

"I'm sorry to ask about such sensitive details, Miss Whiterock, but your file says you are widowed and gives no other information. Was your husband also..." He hesitated again as if he'd gotten his mouth onto a flavour he didn't like. "Tainted?"

"No." Stella glanced up at him. Why had he hesitated? "He was a stevedore."

"How did he die?" Slowly, slowly, he asked those words. Worried he would break something between them, perhaps, by pulling would-be memories of her husband into the room with them.

Stella opened the oven box again, taking out the cooked pie. The bread was a little darker than she usually liked. She busied herself with the next pie, sliding it in place and clamping the door shut again. If only her husband was dead. "A rope snapped as they were offloading some cargo. The load hit him in the head. His father assured me that he died swiftly, as if that would offer some comfort."

"I didn't realize that Cruinnich had a port."

"Not Cruinnich. We lived in Fisherman's Rest at the time."

"Your paperwork says you came from Cruinnich."

"I was born there. I followed Náin to Fisherman's Rest, but when he died, I went back to Cruinnich again."

"Why did you leave after going back?"

Stella sighed, looking up at him again. "Everyone in Cruinnich knew that I was widowed. I could see people watching me as I passed. I couldn't bear it, all that pity."

He couldn't hold her gaze, looking down at his feet while his hands shuffled in his pockets. Whatever he was looking for—his cigarillos, perhaps—he seemed to change his mind and clenched his fists instead. "Is Whiterock your family name, then?"

"Yes."

Tashué nodded, his gaze drifting away from Stella, making it look like his mind had gone wandering off. "Has Ceridwen shown any signs of Talent?"

It was a strange word for a tinman to use. Talent was a word used among people who had it, to give themselves a little more dignity. Whereas 'tainted' was used by everyone else, a word used to crush them down and make them less human.

Stella shook her head. "No—and I'm sure she won't have any Talent at all if she hasn't shown anything yet."

Tashué nodded. Stella opened the oven again, pulling out the bread, but there were none left that were prepared. She smiled at Tashué, nodding at the bowl of filling. The potatoes and shredded pork smelled of onion and garlic and paprika.

"You should help me. It will keep those restless hands of yours busy."

"I... I wouldn't know what to do."

"You're a bright man, Mr. Blackwood. I'm sure you can follow directions."

He flushed, but grinned. "I'll try my best."

"Take off your jacket, then. Flour will stick to all that wet wool."

The flush deepened the way it had when she said the word 'mischief' a few days ago. Still, he shrugged out of his jacket, draping it over the back of the same chair that held his coat. Stella felt her eyes drawn away from his face and to his chest—to the leather holster that kept a revolver nestled against his body, an Imburleigh judging by the crest on the butt, branded right into the wood. The hilt of a knife stuck out as well. It was strange to be so starkly reminded that there were pieces of this man that she wasn't yet familiar with. Dark pieces, pieces rooted in violence.

Stella took a deep breath, sliding a pair of flattened dough circles over the floured surface of the table. Tashué rolled up his sleeves, revealing the military tattoo on his forearm—one of those missing pieces, perhaps. Stella had seen tattoos like that before, enough that she could decipher the symbolism. The horseshoe showed that he was cavalry, the sabre that he was an officer, the arrow that he lead Jitabvi warriors. His battalion—Maddox's Mad 8th—was scrawled in the horseshoe, and the silver officers bars stacked to one side showed he'd ended his career as a Captain. Did he have any other tattoos on his body? He had the amber eyes that identified many Kaadayri—which Kaadayri nation did his parents come from? Not all of them used tattoos, but the majority did. Perhaps he among the many that the Kaadayri considered 'lost'— men and women who hadn't been taught the customs of their ancestors, a casualty of the Dominion's effort to suppress the various Kaadayri cultures to make room for the endless industrial sprawl that the Authority was driving.

"Just put a few spoonfuls in the middle," Stella said. "Not too much or they'll burst open."

Tashué scooped some filling into the dough. Stella guided him in folding one side over, and crimping it closed. The hesitancy in his movement was a surprising thing to see. He was usually so confident.

"You and Ceridwen live here alone?"

Stella glanced over at him. "That's rather forward of you, Mr. Blackwood."

He cleared his throat. "It's for the paperwork, Miss Whiterock.

The Authority needs to be informed if you take up residence with anyone else."

"Ah yes, of course. The Authority needs to know if the tainted are mingling with normal people. No, there's no one else living here. Only me and Ceridwen."

She turned away from him, grabbing the pies they'd folded and sliding them both into the oven at the same time. When she turned back to the table, Tashué had dragged the last two pieces of dough closer and had spooned a measure of filling into his. Stella stood back a moment, watching him move, watching his body pull at the lines of his suit. His shirt didn't fit properly, the shoulders too narrow, the seams sitting too high. The waistcoat fit well enough, though, accenting his broad chest and his waist. The holster added bulk to his chest, the line of leather sitting naturally against the curve of his back—perhaps the only thing he wore that was tailored just for him. He filled the second piece of dough and his movements were more confident, more precise. There was a scar on his elbow, a curving pale line against the rich rusty hues of his skin. Stella had seen plenty of wounds and scars in her life and she could almost see the wound in her mind's eye—it would have been ugly, a large chunk of flesh cut and hanging loose, but not completely sliced off. She could see the little dots where the stitches had held the flap back in place long enough for the flesh to heal, whether by someone's Talent or by time and patience. Stella wondered if he had full range of movement, or if the skin had healed too tight.

He glanced over his shoulder before folding the dough over. She took up her place at his side again, using the spoon to push the filling back in as he pressed the dough down too hard and some of the pork tried to escape the sides. She thought she could feel his breath on the back of her neck, or maybe that was just her hair shifting and a little too much imagination. His fingers crimped the dough well this time, without guidance. It was funny to her, how all of her life seemed to blend together. Sealing dough to keep the filling in. Sealing flesh to keep the blood in.

Like Ceridwen always did, Tashué had somehow managed to get flour all the way up his forearms, and some on his waistcoat too.

"We'll make a baker out of you yet, Mr. Blackwood," she said, smiling. "It just takes patience and repetition."

"I've never been known for my patience," he grunted. He stepped back from the table and clapped his hands together, sending up a cloud of flour. Stella handed him a cloth and he cleaned his hands and arms as best he could, but white smudges remained. He shrugged it off, pulling his sleeves back down. "May I look around? Just for due diligence."

"Are you implying that I would lie to you, Mr. Blackwood?" Stella asked.

A spasm of pain crossed his face and he took a deep breath. "No, not at all, Miss Whiterock. It's just the procedure I'm meant to follow, for the paperwork. I don't mean to intrude."

Anger and bitterness rose in Stella's chest and she revelled in it. Usually she was too tired to feel much at all, but the frustration reminded her all of all the things she used to be. Her old self might have pointed out that submitting to the Authority meant a lifetime of intrusion, a lifetime of people she didn't know stepping into her home whenever they wanted with the capability to destroy her life with nothing but their word. But she wasn't that woman anymore. Instead, she smiled carefully, looking Tashué Blackwood in the eye and enjoying the way the heat of him seemed to smoulder in the centre of her, trying to catch on old, dead coals snuffed out by years of running and hiding and pretending. Different, this heat. Something angry and sharp, which she hadn't felt in a long time.

"It's alright, Mr. Blackwood. I understand it's your job. Was there anything in particular you were looking for? Maybe I can help you find it."

"Nothing specific, no. It's just good to see everything in its place."

Stella turned from him again, opening the oven to pull out the pies. Once they were set on the table, she led him to Ceridwen's room first. He cast those amber eyes around the space as if searching for something. It was a small room, narrow but long, the bed nestled against one wall with a tiny side table and a trunk at the foot. The window looked at Tashué's apartment, too, no doubt into the same size room as they stood in now, but Stella had never seen him at that window.

"She keeps a tidy room." Was there a hint of wistfulness in his voice?

"She doesn't use it much. She comes with me when I work my shifts. And she doesn't keep many belongings."

"She mentioned buying sweets with her wages. Is that all she buys?"

"I encourage her to save some of her wages, but otherwise she mostly buys her sweets. Or bread. Or cheese. Or extra butter. Mostly sweets, though. She has a sweet tooth, that girl."

Tashué chuckled. "Yes, we have a lot in common, she and I."

"You are rather popular here."

She thought she saw it again, the flush, the redness, creeping up his neck. He cleared his throat and straightened his back, motioning back toward the door. She stepped out of the way and he followed. It felt strange to allow him access to her own bedroom, where the bed was still mussed and her uniform for the Facility sat draped over the foot board, her housecoat hanging from the open door of the wardrobe. If Ceridwen's room was neat and tidy and neglected, Stella's room was overused, bearing the clutter of too much purpose and not enough time. He was gentleman enough not to say anything, though his eyes searched everything. Was he looking for proof of another person, perhaps? Clues of a life that Stella hadn't admitted to?

Tashué nodded and stepped back again, shifting his weight. "Thank you, Miss Whiterock. I know how uncomfortable this whole process can be."

"I'm sure the Authority appreciates your diligence, Mr. Blackwood."

He had that look again, that pain across his face. He stepped back, heading to the kitchen as if he wanted to put distance between himself and the word 'Authority.' Stella followed him, opening the wood box and adding another log. With an iron poker, she pushed it down into the bed of coals so it would burn slow and steady.

"There was something else I hoped to ask you about, Miss

Whiterock. If you had a moment. Is Ceridwen likely to be gone much longer?"

"She can stand in that bakery for an hour, trying to decide what she'll have. Why?"

He lifted his jacket from the chair to shuffle through his pockets, leaving smears of flour in the wool. "This wouldn't be something for her to listen to."

"Excuse me?"

The flush spread across his face in earnest this time and she smiled, her annoyance melting away again. What was it about him that he could pull her through emotions so swiftly, without once trying to? Nothing about him felt manipulative or forceful, presumptive or pushy.

"I didn't mean anything like that," he said. He pulled a small sketch pad, dog-eared and worn, out of his pocket. The way he took a deep breath in sucked all the fun out of the moment. "I was investigating a death. A body washed up on the riverbank and I noticed that the Facility wasn't far upriver from where the child was found. Would you take a look perhaps at what I have and tell me if you recognize anything?"

"A child? What makes you think she was from the Facility?"

"She had severe wounds. Her arms and legs had been removed, but one of the wounds hadn't healed. I suspect her death was caused by the infection. I wondered if someone had sought help for her at the Facility, so that she might die peacefully."

Stella shook her head. "We aren't in the habit of discarding our bodies in the Brightwash, Mr. Blackwood. Those that are trusted to us are either cremated or buried in the graveyard. People who can't afford our services donate their bodies to the colleges for the students who train there to study."

"I didn't mean to imply that the Facility was responsible. I meant—is it possible that someone had tried to have her treated but was turned away?"

"I suppose it's possible. But that sort of news spreads. Injuries that severe would be gossiped about endlessly, and I haven't heard rumour of a child without limbs being turned away."

"What fees are charged for the Facility?"

"Four coppers a day. Sometimes we can tell how long the patients will hang on. Mostly we charge them daily."

"And if they last longer than they can afford?"

"According to the policy, we're to turn them out into the streets," Stella admitted. "Typically we're able to keep them on without the administration noticing. And the fees are waived if the patient consents to have their body donated after death."

"Is it common for people to sign themselves over for experimentation?"

"It is," Stella admitted. "Most who come to us hardly have two coppers to rub together, never mind four."

Tashué nodded, looking down at his notepad as if to gather his thoughts. He flipped it open, taking the photographs that had been tucked between the pages and laying them face down on the table before Stella could see what they had captured. He turned the notepad to her, showing the lovingly rendered drawing of a child's face.

"This is her, the girl I found. I tried to imagine how she must have looked with some life in her eyes."

The weight of his grief struck Stella in the chest, making it hard to breathe. The skill involved in the sketch was incredible, the sweep of her jaw, the gleam in her eye.

"Did you see her anywhere around the Facility?" Tashué asked.

"No, I'm sorry. If I saw a child without arms and legs, I'm sure I would have remembered. I'm not so jaded that a thing like that would pass me by."

Tashué took a slow breath, reaching out and taking the notepad. He flipped a single page, then handed it back. "What about any other children—any at all—with a tattoo like this on the back of their neck?"

Breathe! Stella took the notepad again, cocking her head at the numbers scrawled across the page. "Who tattoos a child?"

"I have no idea. I've never seen anything like it. I take it you haven't, either?"

Stella licked her lips, but her mouth had gone so dry that there was no moisture to spare. "No, I haven't."

She handed the notebook back just to get it out of her hands, but some impulse made her reach for the photographs. Tashué opened his mouth as if to say something, reaching toward her hand to stop her, but it was too late, she had them up and saw the face of the child again. She wished she hadn't. Where Tashué's sketch was as much a show of art and skill as it was a likeness of a child, the photograph was a testament to death. An amazing technology, perhaps, but cold and distant. The girl's eyes were not-quite closed and entirely too blank. The photographer had captured the top of her shoulders where her arms should have been, and the abrupt end of flesh was startling.

"You found her?" Stella breathed, handing the photographs back. She wiped her hands on the front of her skirt, as if it could somehow remove the ache from her chest. The girl looked so small, so young.

"Well—I was there, when she was found. A few days ago."

"I didn't realize it was part of your job to investigate murders."

"It's not, generally, unless the victim is one of my cases. Or the killer is, I suppose." He tucked the photographs away, closing his notepad around them to hold them in place with the sketches he'd made. "I can't help but try. No one else seems to care." He sighed slowly, reaching for his jacket. It must have been terribly damp, but he pushed his arms into it anyway.

"You might try the charities near the Facility. There are a few run by the Sisters of the Star's Mercy, down on the riverbank. We take as many cases as we can, but I'm afraid there isn't room enough for all the wretched souls in the city. The Sisters take more than we do."

He nodded, pushing his arms into his coat next. He seemed terribly sad; perhaps the little girl sitting in his pocket was a weight on his shoulders. It was hard to imagine how this man who sketched the face of a dead child 'with life in her eyes' had come to wear that vicious tin badge. "Thank you for your time, Miss Whiterock." Tashué headed for the door, but paused again and turned back to

Stella. He stood for a moment, fiddling with his notepad as if he meant to say something else. "I'm sorry, Miss Whiterock. Honestly, I don't mean to intrude."

"You keep saying you don't mean to intrude," Stella said, the words escaping before she could stop them. It made her heart beat faster, speaking to him like that, made her hands tremble—and yet she gloried in it. This feeling, this heat in her belly and the twist of anger and hate, this was how she used to be, before everything changed so much. She took a deep breath, lifting her chin. "Then let's stand on equal footing, shall we? Were you ever married?"

He cocked his head to one side, surprised perhaps at her impertinence, but then part of his mouth started curving upward. "Very well—you're absolutely right. Let's stand on equal footing." He found his cigarillo case, flicking it open. "Do you smoke?"

Stella reached for a cigarillo, running it under her nose and taking a deep breath of the sweetness of the leaves. "Thank you. You didn't answer my question, though."

He paused long enough to light a match for both of them, shaking out the flame once both of their cigarillos were lit. "No, I never married."

"Very well. You said you were born in Brickheart, didn't you? Tell me about your parents, then."

"My mother was a registered healer and my father was a stone-smith with the directed work program."

"How is it that two people with such powerful Talents could make a son that isn't Talented?" Stella asked, although she knew the answer already. She could feel it in him, whenever he was near. Perhaps it was why he reminded her of a furnace, that heat inside of him that should have been a massive Talent yet remained locked away.

"I have a little Talent, I think. I've never quickened, so I've never needed to register."

"You said they *were*," Stella said softly. "She *was* a healer, he *was* a stonesmith."

He knew what she was asking, using his cigarillo to stall a bit and maybe hide the emotion. It wasn't a very good cloak, that cigarillo smoke. It didn't hide the tightness around his eyes or the way his smile faded. "My father died when I was a boy. My mother passed when I was away, stationed on the Black Ridge with the Derccian army."

"How did they die?"

Another few drags of his cigarillo, trying to compose himself. "Those aren't stories I usually tell." His voice was so soft that she barely heard him, his mouth set in a hard line.

"Nor is the story about how my husband died, and yet I gave it to you freely. I gave it because you are my new Regulation Officer, and you said we could stand on equal footing."

He fidgeted like a child in trouble, smoothing his coat and his sleeves and reaching into his pocket and out again, smoking all the while. When it was clear that she wouldn't let him wait her out, he took a deep breath.

"My father died of a stroke. My mother did her best to take care of him, but she couldn't ever fix his brain. She tried, but it was too complex, the damage too deep." He ran his hand over his face. "And my mother was killed by the husband of one of her patients. She tried to save a woman. Her colleagues insisted that she tried her very best, which of course I believe—she always did everything she could. The woman died anyway. The husband followed my mother out of the hospital one night after her shift, and killed her. No one did anything. One witness told me that he knew she had Talent, so he assumed she would save herself. But she wouldn't do that. For her, following the law was everything. She wouldn't even use her Talent to save her own life, because it would have been unlawful." He took another deep breath, his hands going into his pocket again and withdrawing his cigarillo case. He opened it, then flicked it closed. "Are we on more equal footing now, Miss Whiterock? Do you feel I've given you as much as you gave me?"

Stella's gut twisted with a wave of guilt, for he had in fact given her more than she had given him—her stories were lies, her dead husband fabricated, and his truth was so raw and emotional that she felt she had stolen something from him. She wished for a moment she could give it back to him, this thing that she had taken, that she could fold his emotions back into his chest so he could feel that they had never been exposed at all. Instead, she offered him a smile. She reached across the small gap between them, catching his fingers for just a moment.

"Thank you," she said. It felt weak, but she couldn't think of anything better. "May I ask what happened to the man that killed her? Was he arrested?"

"Arrested? No. He shot himself not long after. It took him some time to die, I was told, a few days or something. He was brought to the same hospital where my mother worked, and her colleagues did their best to save him, but like my father, his brain was too damaged and there was nothing they could do. At least, that's what they told me. The healers at that hospital were close, though. It does me no credit, but I like to think they let him die." He started fidgeting again, reaching for his timepiece and flicking it open. "I should go, Miss Whiterock."

"Of course."

Stella folded her hands in front of her, taking a half step back to help her resist the urge to reach out to him again. He lingered, meeting her eyes again. She wondered what he was looking for, whether he was tempted to say something more.

"Ah—I have… Thank you for your time." He turned away, heading for the door—it was so close to him, with his long legs it would only take him a few steps to reach it. Something like panic rose in Stella's throat.

"Mr. Blackwood!"

He froze, looking back at her.

Stella bit her lip, squeezing her hands together. "I hope you come again sometime soon. We could have a cup of coffee perhaps, and I could teach you to bake something else."

His smile was so large and warm that it made her feel flushed. "That sounds delightful. Another time, then."

"Soon, I hope."

He nodded, turning away again. He left so slowly, like he was dragging himself against a powerful tide. When he was gone, there was such a silence left in the room, a stillness that made her ache.

She closed her eyes, finding the knot of loneliness in her gut, and tried to cut it away with the same deft Talent that allowed her to separate her patients from their pain. But as it detached, it left a hole of emptiness and that was worse. Better to be lonely and feel the sharp edges of it, she thought, than to be empty and filled with nothing.

7

TASHUÉ

DAY 4

At least the rain had stopped by the time Tashué stepped out of Stella's building. Puddles sat between the cobbles and the cold, damp air chased away the warmth that had almost dried his clothes. The wind blew the clouds away, upriver, and Tashué's damp coat did little to protect him from the vicious chill.

It was a short walk to the tram station, at least. Tashué had no choice but to use it, even if he hated it. It would have taken him half the day to make the trip to Boardwalk Market by foot or by carriage. Stepping onto the last car with gritted teeth, Tashué stood next to the door. He held onto a leather strap hanging from the ceiling to steady himself against the lurch and rattle, feeling the weight of misery wafting through the whole ghastly contraption. He had never seen the inside of the front car, nor did he know any Officer who supervised a tram operator, but his experience assured him that the shifts were onerous and exhausting.

A woman with reddish hair piled atop her head caught his eye. For a moment he dared hope it was Stella, on her way across town. But of course it wasn't. Why would she have followed him onto a tram to the Boardwalk Market? He wondered at the impression he'd made, standing in the centre of her home and asking such personal, private questions. He would have liked such discussions to come freely, borne of trust, of friendship.

Tashué took a moment to orient himself on what felt like the *wrong* side of the river as he stepped down from the tram. He never would have set foot in the tailor's shop if Illea Winter had not sent him there. The sign out front bore only the name A. M. Bellmore and the window was draped in lace curtains of the purest white. If it weren't for the address on the card Illea had given him, Tashué might have walked right past the building.

He took a deep breath before stepping inside, forcing the emotions back down. Never mind his frustration over his situation with Stella—that was bad enough on its own—but her questions had rent open old wounds that refused to heal. He hadn't told her that the man that killed his mother called her a *filthy Kaadayri whore* while beating her to death. His mother had spent her whole life trying to fit seamlessly into the fabric of the Dominion. She had never learnt what it meant to be Pashibé because her mother had never taught her their culture in order to keep her safe, and still she died violently in the street.

With those old angers dragged back to the surface, it was hard to push them all back into the crevices of his soul, but he had to. He had been angry for a long time after his mother died, angry at the city that didn't protect her, at the man who called the kindest, gentlest woman he'd ever known a *filthy Kaadayri whore* while pummelling her to death, at the country that denied her and him their culture by making Kaadayri so afraid to live in their own skin that they didn't teach their children their own heritage. But anger hadn't helped him then, and it wouldn't help him now.

Now, he had to be measured for a suit because he was going to sit at a table with the Queen of the Dominion. A Queen who stood in White Crown and declared that all people deserve the right to live free and safe in their own country, a Queen who fought against poverty with every law and project that she sent to the Council. So maybe, maybe, it was safe to hope things were changing.

Inside, a long desk across the width of the building blocked access to the back. Wardrobes stood behind the desk, the wood dark and gleaming with oil.

"Can I help you?" asked the little man who stood behind the counter. A pair of spectacles perched on the end of his long nose.

Another deep breath. *It's not time for anger anymore.* "I've been sent by Illea Winter. I'm to attend a formal dinner at the Winter house. With the Queen."

"Mr. Blackwood!"

Tashué had only met her yesterday, but he would know Illea Winter's voice anywhere. Her silk dress was the same olive hue of her skin, giving her the illusion of wearing nothing when she stepped into his peripheral vision from the back room. When she smiled at him, the force of it struck him in the chest.

"Come through, Mr. Blackwood," she said, turning and heading back. "We have an exciting day ahead of us."

Bellmore plucked a thick book off the counter with Tashué's name written on the cover in ornamental calligraphy. "Follow me, sir."

Behind the wall of wardrobes, a larger room held a bank of mirrors and a long clothing rack. Plush seating and hardwood furniture clustered in the available corners.

"You were exactly right about his colouring, Miss Winter." Bellmore followed Tashué through. "The autumnal tones will suit him nicely."

"Autumnal tones?"

"Don't you worry yourself, Mr. Blackwood." Illea lay a hand on his arm and guided him to stand in front of the mirrors. She stood pressed against his arm, smiling at their reflection. "You're covered in flour! Don't tell me you're also taking up a career as a baker. I'm afraid you won't have much spare time once the election gets going."

Tashué wiped at the flour on his waistcoat again, though none of his previous efforts had helped him much. "No, my career as a Regulation Officer keeps me busy enough." Standing so close to Stella had only made everything worse, made the questions he was forced to ask more mortifying. And yet that moment where they stood shoulder to shoulder, so close he could hear how she held her breath when she was concentrating, was perhaps one of the best moments of his recent life. What was it about her that was so bewitching?

"Excellent," Illea said. "You may as well take off all your clothes now, since they're dirty and wet. You must have gotten caught in the storm? No matter, all of it off—Mr. Bellmore needs to take your measurements."

Bellmore took a long, slow breath. "You don't need to take off all your clothes, Mr. Blackwood. Only your overcoat and your jacket."

Illea grinned. "And your waistcoat."

"That's not necessary, sir."

"Of course it is. We can't get a proper appreciation of his colouring with all that harsh black. Down to your shirt if you please, Mr. Blackwood."

"Whatever you are comfortable with, sir."

Tashué let out a slow breath as he started his usual fight with his buttons, his right hand clumsy and half-numb. At least undoing them with one hand was possible. "I can't imagine there are many men who are able to tell Illea Winter 'no' when she asks them to take off their clothes."

"You are an astute man, sir."

"Do you like wine, Mr. Blackwood?" Illea asked. "I always like to have a nip at Mr. Bellmore's. Makes the whole process so much more entertaining."

Tashué slid his arms out of both garments and the boy came forward to receive them. "Thank you, but no." He checked his time-piece, trying to remember the long list of things he'd hoped to accomplish. Stella wasn't the only file he needed to check in with, but Illea and Elsworth had made it quite clear that his presence was expected at Bellmore's today, no matter how busy he was. "I have a lot to accomplish still today. I was hoping to make more room in my schedule to make time for all of this... campaigning."

"How very industrious of you, Mr. Blackwood. Rainer will be most pleased with your dedication."

Though the words sounded complimentary, there was something in Illea's tone that slid across Tashué's nerves, ugly and tense. He glanced at her as she settled on a large wingback chair, trying to read how suddenly the mood had shifted, but Illea only smiled at him. Bellmore's assistant delivered a glass of brandy to her, then gathered up the book and stepped closer to Tashué, handing Bellmore a rolled measuring tape.

Tashué unbuckled the leather holster around his chest, shrugging out of it. As always, he felt strange without the weight of his Imburleigh pistol and his old cavalry knife. He draped the holster across the back of a chair, stripping out of his waistcoat next.

"You've rather long arms, even for your height," Bellmore said, stepping forward with his measuring tape, unrolling it with a flick of his wrist. "I imagine it's difficult to find shirts that fit."

Tashué shrugged. "I haven't fit in a shirt since I was sixteen."

"A decent tailor would be able to help you, sir."

"Hard to afford a tailor on a tinman's salary."

Bellmore nodded. "Fair point, sir." He pulled his spectacles down his nose so that he could look over the silver rims as he kicked a small stool over to Tashué. "If you'll open your collar, sir."

Illea smiled. "Why stop at the collar when you could just take off your shirt?"

Tashué took a deep breath, looking at her again. Maybe the shift he'd felt earlier was his bleak mood rather than hers—maybe simply the mention of Elsworth set him on edge. What did that say about him? Shit. He wore his badge for the Authority—but the very mention of the man in charge of it set his teeth on edge? He couldn't even identify what exactly he disliked so acutely. Illea, on the other hand, drew Tashué in. She held his gaze as he fought with the buttons of his collar. Both relaxed and poised as she sat in her chair, she sipped her brandy and didn't let Tashué look away. Bellmore looped the measuring tape around his neck with a deft flick of his wrist, and the moment was broken.

"Do you have a preference as to lapel and button?" Bellmore asked.

Tashué cleared his throat. "No, sir, not particularly."

Illea laughed. "He was asking me, Mr. Blackwood. He'd already guessed that you wouldn't have a preference."

"Of course. Mr. Bellmore is also very astute."

"Thank you, sir."

"I would like a double-breasted, vaguely military style. As well as heavy-handed tapering around the waist to keep it looking slim."

Bellmore looked at Tashué over the rims of his spectacles, a long, appraising look. "That will accentuate his already broad shoulders, Miss Winter. I would recommend less tailoring around the waist to keep his proportions balanced."

Illea snorted. "Why would I want that? He has a delightfully brutish chest. We should celebrate that, not hide it. I chose him for his impressive girth. I don't want him 'balanced'."

Blush crept like fire up Tashué's neck, to his face, making his skin feel too tight. "My impressive—"

"Of course, Miss Winter," Bellmore interrupted.

Bellmore's assistant had turned away but Tashué could still see him in the mirror, the way he bit his lip and tried not to laugh.

"Are you taking notes, Mr. Noor?"

"Yes, sir," the young man gasped. He cleared his throat. "No balance. Impressive girth."

"Thank you, Mr. Noor," Illea said brightly.

"At your service, Miss Winter."

"I like this one, Alric. You should keep him."

Bellmore took a deep breath, turning and peering over the rim of his spectacles at his assistant. "He's unprofessional. Giggling. Like a child."

Illea shook her head, sinking into one of the chairs. "What's the fun in being professional all the time?"

"Some of my clients might not appreciate it."

"Well, I appreciate it, and I was under the impression that I'm the most valuable of your clients."

"Of course, Miss Winter. Arms to your sides, sir."

Tashué lifted both arms for Bellmore to measure them. Even as his base instincts were drawn to Illea, when he closed his eyes, he saw Stella. He reminded himself that it was inappropriate to be with

Stella given his position; he held her life in his hand. He had no right to put himself in a position to ask or take anything from her. When he opened his eyes, Illea was still watching him and he realized it wasn't mischief he saw in her face, it was hunger.

"Thank you, Mr. Blackwood, that's all I need from you." Bellmore stepped away, pushing his spectacles up his nose so that he could look at Noor's notes. "I'll need you back tomorrow for a fitting and then the suit will be ready for pick up the day after."

"So fast?"

"Mr. Bellmore has a veritable army of seamstresses to keep up with the demand of his label," Illea said. She gave a dramatic sigh, her whole body heaving with the motion. "But Alric, I'm disappointed. Are you sure you don't need him to take off his trousers?"

Noor snorted, nearly folding in half in an effort to keep the laughter in. Bellmore huffed at him, snatching his book from the youth's hands.

The buttons of his waistcoat were always challenging, an old wound making his fingertips half numb and clumsy. But loose button holes, large buttons, and practised movements made it possible. His holster was easier, the buckle big enough for easy handling. He turned to Illea, meeting her eyes again. Maybe he was half-mad over Stella because it had been so long since he'd had time to pursue anything like a relationship. Maybe he wasn't hungry *for* Stella specifically, he was just craving the warmth of another person's body. And here was Illea Winter, chasing after him—maybe letting her use him for whatever she had in mind was just the distraction he needed.

"I promise I'll take off my trousers for you at the fitting."

Her eyes widened and she sat up a little straighter. The way her chest heaved with the deep breath she took sent a thrill of pleasure through his body. She offered him her hand again and this time, he leaned down to kiss the back of her knuckles. He watched gooseflesh rise up her arm.

"It was a pleasure to see you again, Miss Winter."

"Mr. Blackwood, I think I underestimated you."

"I hope so."

8

ILLEA
DAY 4

Nathaniel Wolfe's estate sat atop the highest hill in Highfield. The road curved up the contour of the hill to Wolfe's front door, and then meandered back down to the edge of the cliff to the Winter estate, at the end of the road. Like most of the estates on Highfield, the Wolfe residence backed onto the massive Dunnenbrahl forest, the great sprawling woodland from which the Winter family made its early fortune.

Illea's carriage rattled along the cobbled streets, slowing as the horses made their way up the hill. Arriving at the Wolfe manor always set her into a battle against her own emotions, past losses laying like shackles on her soul. Some things wouldn't let go of her. Some things she couldn't let go of.

The brandy was still warm in her veins as she rolled up the hill, the excitement of Tashué Blackwood's lips still burning on the back of her hand. He was an intriguing man, better than she dared hope. His emotions were easily manipulated, but he was able to rally against them unexpectedly, rising to the occasion when he looked like he was going to be swamped by them.

The carriage rattled to a stop in front of Nathaniel's front steps and Illea's servant opened the door for her. She stepped down carefully, hitching up her gown so she wouldn't trip on the hem. Her arrival would set off a flurry of movement in the Wolfe home—her father made sure she'd learnt each person's role in a household. *How are you to judge how your staff is doing their jobs if you don't know what their jobs are?* It was calming for her to picture the ripple of movement that her arrival was setting off. Arriving at the Wolfe manor didn't need to feel so deeply personal. Her gut didn't need to twist and she didn't need to feel like she was betraying a dead man by flirting with Blackwood—or any other man for that matter.

The massive front door—made of slabs of Winter oak—swung open for her and she swept in, a trail of servants in her wake. She went straight to Wolfe's solarium where Nathaniel liked to host the smaller gatherings once the worst of the summer heat had passed.

He sat already in the solarium when she arrived, overlooking his sprawling grounds. He stood when she swept into the room, smiling beneath his thick salt-and-pepper beard. The beard almost hid the deep lines of his face, but not quite, and the recent appearance of so much white and grey made him look older, but somehow also gentler. Illea wondered, not for the first time, if his beard and his close haircut and his utilitarian suits were deliberately chosen to make him look approachable while reminding everyone of his military career, or if the appearance came naturally to him. Her father would have insisted that Nathaniel consider his appearance carefully, and they had been close.

He leaned over and planted a kiss on Illea's cheek and she leaned up, finding a patch to kiss above the line of his beard. "Nice of you to join us, Miss Winter."

Illea smiled, meeting the gaze of Nathaniel's other guest, Mallory Imburleigh. Mallory stood and they exchanged a flurry of kisses. Another wealthy family in Yaelsmuir, the Imburleigh family had built their fortune on guns. The Imburleigh Armament Company made the highest quality guns in the Dominion, possibly in the world. Mallory was only a few years older than Illea, with all the poise that was expected of the wealthy families of Yaelsmuir. None of them could claim any royal lineage, and so they needed to present their very best face to the Dominion. Illea wondered if families who built their wealth and power in other cities spent so much time measuring themselves against the royal family of White Crown, or if Yaelsmuir's proximity to the Dominion's capitol was what made them so obsessed with how they compared.

"How are you, Mallory?" Illea asked, smiling. "How was your journey back?"

"Muddy," Mallory sighed, stepping back to her seat and sinking down. "Those stagecoaches really are dreadful. Our rail line can't possibly come soon enough!"

"You spoilt the news for me, General Imburleigh," Nathaniel muttered. "What are you drinking, Illea? This is something to celebrate."

"A celebration?" All thoughts of men and ghosts and royal families disappeared from her mind like mist before the rising sun. "Will we have it, then? The rail line?"

Nathaniel smiled, gesturing to one of the chairs. Her favourite spot in the solarium, the chair that caught the most breeze and the least sun and looked out over Nathaniel's sprawling gardens, which backed onto the massive Dunnenbrahl forest. She could just see Amias's gravestone from where she sat, right at the edge of the forest. "Have a seat, Illea. Have a drink."

Illea stifled a sigh, sinking into her chair. "News like this calls for something stronger than wine."

"I've the Gladwydd whisky, the one that you think is sweet. I just had a fresh crate shipped in for the banquet."

"That sounds lovely, thank you."

Illea stared out the back windows as she waited, her mind racing. The proposal for building a rail line from Yaelsmuir to Obisza had been on the docket of the Queen's Council for what felt like ages.

"The stagecoach is truly an instrument of torture," Mallory said. "I can't believe no one tried to build an inter-city rail line sooner."

"It won't be as easy in the Dominion as it was for the cities of the Commonwealth," Nathaniel said as the glasses of whisky were distributed. "Their population is much denser than ours, and their cities are closer together. Each stretch of rail is much shorter."

"We have it, then?" Illea pressed, leaning forward in her chair and catching Nathaniel's gaze. "I want to hear you say it."

"Illea, you don't know anything," Nathaniel said, his voice pitching low in the way it always did when he wanted to sound paternal. "The Queen will want to tell you herself when she arrives and you can't let on that you've heard. My work on the Council is supposed to be strictly confidential."

Illea snorted. "You can't honestly tell me that the Queen's cousin doesn't tell the entirety of White Crown what the Council has decided the moment you all step out of those chambers."

"That may be so, but I am not the Queen's cousin. They're always looking for some excuse to dismiss me. If they're able to get rid of me, they'll throw the rest of the provincial representatives out one by one."

"Yes, yes yes," Illea muttered, waving a hand. "I know what the stakes are. I *know*. You are doing the invaluable work of the people. I won't say a word to the Queen, and neither will Mallory. Now tell me, please. I want to hear you say it."

"The Council voted on the rail line, and it's been affirmed. The Crowne and the Council will hear proposals by contractors for the Yaelsmuir-Obisza line starting next month. She'll announce it as soon as she gets back to White Crown, but that doesn't give you very much time to prepare at all."

"No, of course it doesn't," Mallory scoffed. "Why would they want to give the provinces a fair shot? Then we might actually catch the contract ourselves. Will anyone in Obisza bid for it, do you think?"

Nathaniel shook his head. "No, they haven't the capital to get started, unfortunately. The Council will structure the bids to delay payments, forcing the contractors to carry the costs for the first few miles. That way they can squeeze out any of the small players. That's why I wanted to tell the pair of you. If you two are able to put together a solid proposal, you have a decent chance of getting it."

Illea looked out across the garden again. Wolfe's garden blended seamlessly with the border of the forest, a small army of gardeners and botanists making the transition look both seamless and natural without ever looking wild. Her eyes drifted across the landscape as her mind raced. There would be a great deal of money to be made on a contract with the Crown for building the long stretch of track. Even if Illea missed the building contract, which was unlikely but possible, she owned every lumber yard between White Crown and Cruinnich.

Movement caught Illea's eye in the tree line. A pair of hunting dogs came running from the forest, the scraggly wirehair pointers that Nathaniel kept. They sprung through the grass, then turned around and looked back toward the forest. More movement and a man emerged, Ishmael Saeati. Even in the chilly air, he was stripped to his shirt-sleeves, which were rolled up to the elbows to show off some of his tattoos. Another three dogs came bursting out of the forest behind him, their brown and tan fur tangled with twigs and leaves and their faces deliriously happy. Ishmael lifted an arm and threw the big stick he carried, sending it spinning. The whole pack of dogs went bounding after it, tongues hanging out of their mouths and floppy ears bouncing as they ran. The dogs tussled over the stick, a seething knot of energy and fur. When Ishmael whistled, the little fast one was first to return. Ishmael's hand went into his pocket and produced some scrap of food and tossed it to her. She bounced off her back legs to catch it, then followed as he walked on.

Peace and pain warred for space in Illea's heart. The pack of hunting dogs had been Amias Wolfe's most precious possession; he had trained and bred them with near-obsessive attention. She couldn't remember a single moment when Amias didn't have one of his dogs with him. It was good to see the staff at the Wolfe house taking such good care of the breeding lines. Amias would have been so proud. But it was just one more reminder of everything that life was supposed to be. Did she like Ishmael Saeati so much because he reminded her of Amias? Or did she look for qualities of Amias Wolfe in every man she liked? Ishmael was always so restless, not unlike Amias, energy overflowing in him. It was probably what drove him out into the Dunnenbrahl in such miserable weather.

"I think we've lost Illea's attention," Mallory sighed. "He's very distracting, your watchmaker."

"That's why I keep him around," Nathaniel said. "He distracts people so that I can make better deals."

Illea shook her head, but kept an eye on Ishmael. Distracts people indeed—Mallory didn't know the half of it. "If the track from Yaelsmuir is six hundred miles, like the road, it will take nearly two million railroad ties to complete. Two million pieces of wood that are eight feet long and at least seven inches thick, nine inches high. That's a massive span of solid wood. I don't have enough lumber to meet that need, not on hand, so I'll have to organize some cuts. And of course treat the wood with creosote. And we add ten to twenty percent raw material to make room for mistakes, breakage, unforeseen circumstances... which brings us to nearly two and a half *million* ties. I would say there's a good chance I'll make money from this project, even if I don't get the contract with my workers." She sipped at the whiskey, enjoying the sweet burn. "How many pounds of iron goes into a mile of track, Mallory? Or would you indeed sell the Crowne steel instead?"

"I can't say that I know the exact number," Mallory admitted. "I'll have to ask someone. And it would be the choice of the contractor as to which material is best."

"You should know the exact number," Illea countered, leaning back into her chair. "You should always know what projects are coming and how you can meet the demand. And *you* should decide what you want people to use. You should ensure that those decisions are being made based on what benefits *you*."

An awkward moment of silence stretched in the solarium. Illea let her attention wander back to Ishmael. She tried to tell herself that it wasn't Mallory's fault that she didn't know her numbers. The Imburleigh family had a board of investors that had a say in how the factories were run. One of the investors owned the mines, and the Imburleigh factory had its own tainted-powered foundries, which processed most of the iron she used in her guns. Illea's father had taught her to do business the opposite way—own the supply, create the demand. Middle men were a liability, devouring capital and subject to errors in judgement.

Ishmael broke into a run, the dogs dropping the stick to give chase. His stride was long and easy, eating up the yards of garden seemingly without effort. His face and hands were still tanned from wherever he had been—somewhere sunnier than Yaelsmuir obviously—but his forearms were still somewhat pale. The biggest of the dogs kept trying to nip his heels, making a game of it. Ishmael took the whole pack of dogs back to their keeper, having thoroughly exercised them in the forest. It was hard to imagine him sitting still at a desk, tinkering with gears and springs or whatever went into pocket watches. But that was how his father had pulled the Saeati family out of Cattle Bone Bay and ostensibly, he still knew how it was done.

"Would the track follow the road, then?" Mallory asked, pulling Illea from her thoughts again. "If you had the contract?"

Illea shook her head, taking a sip of the whisky. "The track will replace the road. Anyone who wants to travel from Obisza to Yaelsmuir can travel by horseback over rough country, or they can take the train."

Mallory turned, leaning closer to Illea. "Who owns the rail line, after it's built?"

"The Crowne would want to, but since it's on Yael and Miran provincial lands, I'll push for legislation that helps to spread the profits," Nathaniel said. "If I can manage that, the Crowne will expect us to absorb some of the cost of maintenance as well, but I think I can get a fair deal."

"We'd have more opportunity to make money if we could own the trains themselves," Illea said. "The engines and the cars. Then we could run as many trips back and forth as we see fit."

"How many people in Obisza and Yaelsmuir could afford to purchase an entire *train*, Illea?" Mallory said.

"Not many," Illea admitted. "The Winter family. The Wolfe family. The Imburleigh family. We could pool resources, the three of us."

"It will be a massive undertaking to convince the investors to purchase a *train*."

"It's not about the engine, it's about how many cars it can pull, and what they're pulling. With the new factory you're building in Obisza, goods will need to be shipped back and forth between the two cities. Raw material and finished product alike. No matter who owns those trains, your investors will like the idea of using them to increase the shipping capacity. No more river barges and wagon trains. If you own the train and its cars, you can ship the goods you'll have to pay to ship anyway—and you can add a few passenger cars."

Mallory shook her head. "That all sounds very good, but how many people are really going to travel from Obisza to Yaelsmuir? What reason would they have for such a journey?"

"Whatever reason you give them."

"What reason shall we give them, then?"

Illea smiled and shrugged. "We have some time to think about that, don't we?"

Ishmael laughed at something the dog handler said, but they parted ways and Ishmael came into the solarium, carrying with him the scents of the outside. He smelled of sweat, of rich forest moss and cold autumn humidity. His hair was defying the hair oil he tried to use to keep it fashionably smooth and was starting to bend into the waves that would start to fall down in front of his face if he didn't keep pushing it back. His hands were dirty with bark from the stick, his shoes leaving muddy tracks across Nathaniel's floor.

"Good afternoon, Miss Winter. General Imburleigh."

"Good afternoon, Mr. Saeati," Mallory said, but her smile was stiff and uncomfortable.

Ishmael stepped around Illea, pausing to kiss her on the cheek on his way to the sideboard where all the alcohol was lined in crystal decanters. "You're into the Gladwydd whisky, Illea. What are you celebrating?"

"Nothing that would interest you, Mr. Saeati," Mallory said. "Only business."

Ishmael laughed as he poured himself a measure of something, probably brandy if Illea knew him. "How dreadful. I would offer my condolences, but I think the three of you like that sort of thing." He skirted around the sofa and sank down on the empty side of it, beside Mallory, though he leaned away from her and toward Wolfe. "Really, you're a terrible influence on the General, Illea. I think there was a time when he used to be fun."

Illea laughed. "I promise you, he was always very serious. He and my father got along well. He's had those frown lines as long as I can remember."

Nathaniel sighed at both of them like they were children, shifting in his seat to rub his thigh. "Is your household ready for the arrival of the Queen?" he asked, his not-so-subtle change of subject. "I understand she'll be arriving tonight."

"In the morning, actually. I received a message that they're delayed, but the Queen likes to keep her schedule whenever possible, and the banquet is still scheduled for the day after tomorrow. Mallory, should I bother trying to find a seat at the table for Langston, or will he be skipping this banquet too?"

Mallory sighed, shaking her head and taking a sip of the whisky as if it could offer some comfort. "He's been complaining about his freedom, so I expect he'll refuse to go."

Ishmael snorted. "Rich for your brother to complain about his freedom."

"Will you be the only Imburleigh at the banquet, then?" Nathaniel asked.

Another sigh, and Mallory drained her whisky. She forced a smile at Nathaniel, shaking her head at the servant who moved to refill her glass. "Alistair is still in Obisza, with the boys. They're quite pleased with the factory and watching it grow. I think I've lost them all to Obisza for the foreseeable future."

How nice it must be to live in a marriage where you miss your husband. Illea's eyes drifted across the yard again, to the stone. The sun sat at such an angle that it lit the grave, making the granite glow. The grass in the yard was verdant green, though the forest had turned all the shades of autumn. It was too easy to picture Amias alive, running through the woods with his dogs, maybe right alongside

Ishmael. They'd known each other well enough, before—Amias was only a year younger and their energy went well together.

"What about Mairead?" Illea asked, forcing herself to look at Mallory instead of Amias's gravestone, dragging herself back into the present instead of some fantasy that she couldn't have. "Is she with the boys in Obisza?"

Mallory shook her head. "No, she's up in Cruinnich still."

Ishmael drained half his glass in a single swallow. "I would think the eldest Imburleigh child would be more active in the Imburleigh Armament Company by now. Preparing to take a board seat and all that. She isn't being disinherited, is she?"

"Disinherited?" Mallory echoed, turning to Ishmael. "No. Of course not. She's quite capable. She prefers staying up in Cruinnich over being down in Yaelsmuir, when she has the choice. With her father's family."

Ishmael took a long, deep breath, draining the rest of his glass. "Yes, of course. With her father's family. Why else would any sane person like Cruinnich, if it weren't for family?"

"What about Obisza, Ishmael?" Illea asked, leaning on the arm of her chair toward him, forcing herself to focus on him rather than letting her attention wander back to the gravestone. "You like it up there, don't you? I know General Wolfe has sent you there more than once to charm the Miran Governor. What sort of attractions are up there that might draw some crowds from Yaelsmuir?"

"Obisza has excellent vodka," Ishmael said. "They sweeten it and infuse it with grass, which sounds strange, but it gives a fantastic herbal tone. They distill mostly rye, I think. Oh, and beef. They raise excellent beef."

Mallory sighed, shaking her head. "Honestly, Mr. Saeati, do you take anything seriously?"

Ishmael scoffed, spreading his hands. "What do you mean? Illea asked me what might draw the people of Yaelsmuir to Obisza, and you can't honestly tell me that you don't know that people of this city *love* to eat and drink."

"Perhaps your impression of the city is filtered through your own interests."

Ishmael pushed both his hands through his hair, trying again to smooth the waves. "Perhaps your impression of the city is filtered through your lack of interests. If you want people of this city to go anywhere, tell them about what they can eat and drink. You know I'm right. What is Karra known for?"

"Olives and grappa," Illea supplied. "And fruit orchards."

"Exactly," Ishmael said. "What's Dür known for?"

"Fresh sausage and beer," Illea said. "Not to be confused with Lida, who is known for cured pork and wheat beer."

"Thank you, Illea," Ishmael said. "And Cruinnich and Glad-wydd both are known for whisky, but not food because it's all so bloody bleak no one can imagine anyone having anything to eat. Shall I go on, General Imburleigh? We can do this for every city on the continent proper, and every Dominion holding, too. You ask anyone in Yaelsmuir the first thing they think of when you name a city, they will tell you a food or an alcohol or both."

"Will people be interested in Obiszan beef when we have Wolfe beef?" Illea asked.

Ishmael shrugged. "Just tell people that Obiszan beef is different and they'll want to try it. And it is different, for the record. Beef raised in Yael is fed a lot of grain and it changes the flavour. Obiszan beef is almost entirely raised on pasture."

"There you are, then," Illea said. "It's time to invest in Obiszan beef and vodka, and start building a service economy for all the tourists heading west."

Mallory sighed again, glancing at Ishmael before pushing herself to her feet. "I suppose I should go, then. Apparently I need to speak to the board of investors about the cost of iron and steel."

Illea and Nathaniel both stood to see Mallory off, but Ishmael sat firmly in place, ignoring Mallory's exit with all the air of a toddler sulking. Nathaniel sighed at him once Mallory was gone.

"Honestly, Ishmael, perhaps you could be a bit more civil."

"She fired the first volley, General," Ishmael muttered, pushing himself to his feet and moving to the sideboard to refill his glass. "I was merely responding in kind."

"That's a very elegant way of saying 'she started it', which is exactly the excuse I got from Amias whenever he and Elysia were fighting," Nathaniel said. "Back when they were children."

Ishmael shook his head but bit back whatever comment was tempting him.

"Where've you been this time, Ishmael?" Illea asked. "Your tan is making me quite jealous, with winter coming early this year."

"I don't remember exactly," Ishmael said with a shrug. "All this fucking rain makes my brain foggy."

"Oh yes, it's all very secretive, isn't it, that diplomatic division of yours," Illea said, smiling at him as he made his way back to the sofa. "One day, you'll tell me your little secrets, won't you?"

"Illea," Nathaniel said, "leave him be."

9

STELLA
DAY 6

The boy's mother sobbed when they came to gather him from the Facility, covering her face with a kerchief and struggling to master herself. The father was more stoic at first, blinking in surprise at every step it took for him to get back to his son, from the paperwork on the main floor to the long stairwell up to where the boy was still in his bed.

The boy was rather fidgety, sitting on his cot bed and staring at his stump of a leg. Stella had washed his clothes, helped him to dress, and pinned up the cuff of his trousers so it wouldn't hang so uselessly. He waited quietly for his parents, looking at the space where his leg used to be rather than at his fellow patients.

When the boy's father stepped into the room and saw his son sitting upright and looking healthy, if rather skinny, the man's blinking finally crumpled into emotion. He staggered to his son's side, sitting beside him and hugging him so tight that the boy squirmed to get away.

"I don't understand," the man gasped. "He was dying. How could he have recovered?"

"He's stronger than anyone imagined, I suppose," Stella said. She'd practised this lie a while, knowing they'd ask. "His body fought off the infection. After that, the fever broke and he was well again."

"I can't believe it," the mother wailed, hiding her face in her kerchief. "I can't believe it. Sweet North Star, I can't believe it."

"The North Star was tainted," Stella said, the words escaping before she could stop them.

"Excuse me?" the woman breathed, turning her wide, blood-shot eyes on Stella. "What was that?"

"The North Star. You invoke her name, as most of the rest of us do. And yet she was, by modern standards, tainted. She was able to change the course of the war because of her healing Talent."

"Yes." The mother wiped her face, tilting her head at Stella. "I realize that."

"I only say this because I hope, in the future, you wouldn't be so afraid to seek help from someone tainted. Most of us—especially healers—genuinely do want to help people."

Stella walked away from the startled couple before they could respond. Ceridwen was awake when Stella went to fetch her, lying on the floor with a large piece of paper in front of her and a char-coal pencil Tashué Blackwood had given her. She was sketching the big shaggy dog that lived in the Row, guarding a chicken coop in one of the shared courtyards.

"Are you ready to go, Pigeon?"

"Yes, Mam! You're late today."

"I know. I'm sorry. I was helping a boy go home to his family."

"That's nice." Ceridwen rolled her paper up and tucked her pencil away into a pocket. "Was he happy to go home?"

"I should think so." Stella didn't know how to explain to Ceridwen how hard it was to be happy about unexpected things. When you prepared yourself for tragedy, it took the mind a while to switch tracks. "Shall we go have some breakfast in the Market?"

"The Market? Yes please! I'm *hungry!*"

"Hungry? I find that hard to believe, Miss Ceridwen Whiterock. All the time I've known you, you've hardly eaten at all, like a little bird pecking away at a few seeds. How could you be hungry so late in the morning?"

Ceridwen screwed up her face, her nose wrinkling and her brow furrowing. "Mam, you're a bad teaser."

"Perhaps I'm a good teaser and you have a poor sense of humour. Perhaps my teasing is too sophisticated for you."

"Maybe you should try less 'sophisticated' teasing and then you'd be funnier."

"Well, perhaps if we get some more food into that belly, you'll be in a better mood."

The Market Quarter was a great seething mass of bodies and chaos. Tinkers and carpenters, blacksmiths and watchmakers, cloth dyers and weavers and spinners. In the centre of the quarter, a round open courtyard held a sea of stalls that all stood around the statue of Bronwynn the North Star, in the centre of a fountain. Large canopies stretched between the stalls to guard merchants and shoppers from the weather. It was always a riot of colours, of smells, of bodies shuffling, of hawkers shouting.

"What shall we have first, Pigeon?" Stella asked. "Bread? Fruit? Nuts? I think I see someone selling sausages over there by the fountain."

"I'd like to go to the fountain. But I don't want a sausage yet. Can we have something sweet?"

Stella smiled, squeezing Ceridwen's hand. "If you were made of sugar, you would eat your own hand. Let's try some fruits."

"Peaches, then? I know they're your favourite."

"Ceridwen Whiterock, I think you very well are made of sugar." Stella leaned down to lay a kiss on the girl's forehead. "The peaches are finished now, but we'll see what we can find."

Stella led Ceridwen into the maze of covered alleyways. Harvest season meant a wealth of fresh food, fruits and vegetables of every imaginable colour piled on trestle tables. There were no peaches—summer was over and the nights were too cold for the heat loving fruit—but she found soft pears the colour of the sunset, and plums that were bright, merry purple. There were baked things, too, tarts with flaky crusts, fresh-made jam oozing out of pastries, savoury pies piled high. Stella bought a jar of peach jam, thick and golden. Jam was expensive but it would carry the flavour of her favourite fruit though the winter if she rationed it well. Ceridwen used her own crowns for a bag of roasted hazelnuts, rich with their own oil and dusted with cinnamon sugar.

As they moved closer and closer to the great stone fountain in the centre of the square, a familiar figure caught her eye.

"Mr. Blackwood!"

Ceridwen went tearing off through the crowd. For a moment, Stella's heart leaped with lingering fears. She took a deep breath and fought for calm, reminding herself that Ceridwen was a child half-grown and old enough to be earning her own money, old enough to be trusted. And yet, Stella was all too aware of who might be out there, searching for her.

Tashué smiled when he saw them, lighting up his otherwise grim and serious face. He carried something, a long canvas bag, the type used to store and protect high quality clothes. "Well hello, little warrior. You've crumbs on your chin. Have you been into the sweets already?"

Ceridwen grinned as she wiped her face. "Not yet. We had fruit and hazelnuts. Those aren't sweets."

Stella scoffed. "The hazelnuts aren't, but the sugar crust on them most certainly is."

Tashué grinned. "Sugared hazelnuts, is it? Sounds delicious. What'll you have next?"

"I don't know." Ceridwen looked up at Stella. "We're making our way to the fountain. What's that you have there, Mr. Blackwood?"

"Ceridwen."

Another smile. His growing stubble almost hid the smile lines that creased the sides of his mouth. "It's fine, Miss Whiterock. I have to admit that I had more than a healthy dose of curiosity when I was a child. I have a brand-new suit, little warrior. I'm to attend a party this evening, and they expect me to look my best."

"A party? Is it to be a fancy party? With lots of food?"

"Fancy, indeed. I'm not so sure about the food, though. I thought I would load up on a good lunch, just in case."

"Would you like to come eat with us?" Ceridwen asked.

"I'm sure you two are rather busy without my intrusion," Tashué said, but he glanced up at Stella.

She couldn't help but smile at him and the eagerness he couldn't hide. "We haven't anything particular planned. If Mr. Blackwood would like to accompany us for a time, it would be fine."

"That's very kind of you, Miss Whiterock."

They made their slow way through the corridors between the stalls, stopping at a table where a man was displaying a great collection of wooden toys. There were spinning tops of all varieties, animals carved lovingly and painted with fine detail, puzzles that fit together and came apart with only the most precise movements. Ceridwen spun each of the tops on a wooden platform the toy maker had supplied for just such a purpose, watching each one spin. The toy maker, a man almost as large as Tashué but older by a decade, handed Ceridwen each top, watching her with as much joy in his eyes as there was in hers. The one Ceridwen played with most was marked with grooves that were painted red and blue alternatively, which blurred to a happy purple as the top spun.

"They're lovely!" Ceridwen gasped, clapping her hands together.

The toymaker grinned. "Why thank you. The tops are my favourite. I suppose I never really grew up. I know how to make cabinets and chairs and wooden spoons, but all I ever want to make is spinning tops."

"Mam says growing up isn't as much fun as it sounds," Ceridwen said, the crease that folded across her forehead making her look terribly serious. "She said I shouldn't be rushing it so much. So maybe you have the right idea."

The toymaker winked at Ceridwen. "Sounds like a wise woman, your mam."

Ceridwen nodded. "She is."

"Well there you are, little one." The man scooped up the top before it could topple over and held it out to Ceridwen. "You take that one there and you remember to stay young as long as you can."

"Let me pay for it, at least, sir," Tashué said, shifting the canvas bag from one arm to the other so that he could go fishing in his pocket for a few coins.

The toymaker shook his head. "No, sir, let me make it a gift." He tucked his hands into his pockets and took a half step back.

"Making gifts is a hard way to earn a living," Tashué said.

The man shrugged, smiled. "I've a military pension to keep my head dry and my belly full. Making toys is the reason I wake in the morning and it's my pleasure to give them as gifts now and then."

Ceridwen's eyebrows rose and she leaned over the table, clutching her new top in one hand. "How long were you a soldier?"

"Thirty years. I wasn't much older than you when I enlisted. I would have kept right on serving, too, but it seems the army doesn't have use for a soldier with one leg."

"You've only one leg?" Ceridwen echoed, her eyes going wide.

"Ceridwen!"

The man chuckled. "No, miss, it's quite alright. I wouldn't have said anything if I didn't want to be asked questions."

"How did you lose your leg?"

"Horse fell on it. Keeled right over. I'm big and clumsy and I wasn't able to get my fool leg out of the stirrup in time."

"You were cavalry?" Tashué asked.

"I was," the toymaker said with a nod. "Attached to the Queen's 6th."

Tashué grinned. "The 6th, is it? The Wild Southern 6th?"

"Aye, the Wild 6th. You served too?"

"Under Maddox in the 8th," Tashué said.

"Damn, Maddox, hey? You 8th kids were tough. Were you there when they held the Black Ridge with the Derccians?"

"Yes, sir," Tashué said and tension crawled across his shoulders. "Lost a lot of good soldiers on the Ridge. Lost my best horse, too."

The toymaker nodded, then smiled at Stella when he glanced at her and saw her surprise. "It's not that we don't feel the weight of the loss of the soldiers. We do. It's that those Jitabvi hotbloods don't fear death, you see. They call it a good death for a warrior to fall in battle. But they also teach us to love those horses. Those creatures don't volunteer to serve the way humans can, but they'll carry you through the fires of hell. I've known more than one soldier who was saved by a well-trained horse."

Tashué forced a smile, meeting Stella's eye and nodding. "You don't ride with the Jitabvi without learning to appreciate a good horse."

The toymaker thrust out a hand and Tashué accepted the shake. They shared something in that handshake that bore the full weight of their military service and all the mixed feelings that went along with it.

Ceridwen cocked her head to one side. "If you've only one leg, how are you standing up?"

"Ceridwen!" Stella breathed.

The big toymaker chuckled, waving a hand. "I don't mind, miss, honest. The little ones are so blunt, aren't they? I've made myself a new leg. Carved it from an old oak branch with these big hands."

Ceridwen's eyes went wide. "Can I see it?"

The toymaker glanced up at Stella first. She bit her tongue and nodded at him. He seemed genuinely pleased to be talking about it, but somehow the moment still saddened her. Perhaps the boy was still too fresh in her mind, the sight of him sitting on his cot and blinking down at the stump he was left with. He wouldn't have lost anything at all if only his parents hadn't feared the *tainted*.

"Come 'round, then," the toymaker said, shuffling to his stool, "take a look."

"Showin' off yer leg again, are ya, Božic?" said the woman at the table next to the toymaker. She had an array of wooden things, too—some toys, but also cookie presses and spoons and bowls, coat hooks and stepladders and small pieces of furniture.

"'Course I am," the toymaker said. He reached down to drag up the leg of his trouser and Ceridwen slid through the narrow gap between his table and the next.

"It's beautiful!" Ceridwen gasped.

The toymaker chuckled. "You've got good taste, little one. Got your Mam's wisdom, I think."

"It isn't finished. Everything's carved so nicely but there's a big blank spot right here."

"Ah, well, I haven't thought of the right thing to put there yet," the toymaker admitted.

"You should put the horse." Ceridwen furrowed her brow, then nodded. "The one that fell on you. You wouldn't have your wooden leg if the horse hadn't fallen on you."

"Well, I'll be damned. I think you very well might be right, little one. I never thought of it that way."

Ceridwen stood, smiling broadly. "It's the perfect horse shape, too. Was the horse alright? After it fell."

"No, she died, I'm afraid." Božic smoothed his pant leg back down. "Was a shame, too. Best horse I ever had in all my thirty years. With me the longest. You promise me you'll come visit again in a few weeks time, and I'll show you the horse."

"Yes, sir!"

"Thank you, sir. It was nice to meet you." Stella reached down, taking Ceridwen's hand. Her hands were still so small, for all that she was growing. "Shall we go see the fountain now?"

"Yes, Mam."

Tashué hung back just a moment exchanging some words and another handshake before following them away to the fountain. The statue of the North Star was faced west, toward White Crown, holding up a hand as if commanding the entire army of the God King to stop. She carried a sword in the other hand, but the point was trailing on the ground. Stella wondered if Bronwynn had ever carried weapons in the revolution against the God King, or if she had been a healer from the beginning. The sword could have been intended as a representation of the Talent she wielded so deftly, healing every man, woman and child she came across during the war, no matter which side they gave their loyalty to. It was a beautiful statue. Her face was so serene as she gazed west, but her hand gripped the sword hilt so tightly that she could have stepped down from the platform and fought against any foe. It was easy to imagine who she would have fought against if she were alive today.

"Shall we go get a sausage, then, little warrior?" Tashué asked.

"Yes please!" Ceridwen said.

Stella sat on the edge of the fountain as they wandered away, the stone cold and smooth beneath her. A fine mist of water sprayed her cheek, reminding her of autumn days on the far northern shores. Her parents would take her and her sister up to the Hand. The salmon would come up from the ocean to spawn in the streams and tributaries. Some streams were so thick with them that it seemed Stella could walk across their backs without once getting her feet wet. But Stella hadn't yet been created, she reminded herself. She was still Ffyanwy then.

Turning, she pushed the past out of her thoughts and looked for Tashué and Ceridwen instead, finding them standing together in the line. Tashué leaned in, said something, and Ceridwen laughed. Her whole body seemed to glow with joy. He had such a way with her.

They tucked into their sausages as they came walking back, lips and fingers shining with grease. Ceridwen held out a sausage for Stella, the meat smelling of garlic and fennel and the sharp tang of hot peppers.

"Here, Mam. We got you one, too. A spicy one!"

"Thank you, Pigeon."

The meat was delightfully spicy, a hint of lemon and rich herbs balancing out the heat. She ate carefully, the juices threatening to drip down the sides of her hands, but the freshly cooked bread was hearty and thick and caught most of the fat.

Stella looked up at Tashué, at the canvas bag that he kept draped over his shoulder. As he shifted the weight of it, she caught sight of the logo stitched carefully into the canvas. It was a subtle logo, the thread almost the same colour of the fabric. "Is your suit from Bellmore's, Mr. Blackwood?"

"It is." He sucked grease off his knuckle. "Illea Winter arranged for it. The Winters are hosting a dinner for the Queen and I'm to attend."

Stella's eyebrows rose. "How does a tinman find himself invited to dinner with the Queen?"

"I'm not entirely sure," Tashué admitted. "I've received a couple of promotions."

"What's a promotion?" Ceridwen asked, wiping her face of grease and bread crumbs with a kerchief.

"It's when you receive more responsibilities at your work," Tashué said.

"What are your new responsibilities?"

"I'm taking command of my station house. Otherwise, I'm not sure exactly what I'm expected to do. Other than dine with the Queen, of course."

"Do you have someone to help you dress?" Even as the words escaped, Stella cursed herself. It was no business of hers. Why would she insert herself into a tinman's life? All she wanted was to fade into the background of the Dominion, invisible and forgotten. And yet, it was the sensation of fading that scared her, the feeling that she didn't know who she was anymore. Standing in a room with Tashué Blackwood, alternating between infatuated and annoyed and attracted and afraid, her heart beating faster every time he moved, she felt like Ffyanwy again for the first time in years.

Tashué scoffed. "Help me dress? I've been dressing myself for a *few* years. Why should I need help now?"

"The clothing of the wealthy aren't so simple as that. They're generally designed to require help, since the wealthy have so much help on hand. It's a status symbol."

"Well… I'm afraid I haven't the status to have someone on hand to help me dress."

Ceridwen grabbed Stella's hand, pulling hard. "You could help, Mam! You said you should always help a neighbour in need and Mr. Blackwood is our favourite neighbour!"

Stella almost told her no, but she clamped her mouth shut. She couldn't meet Tashué's eye and deny him, not when he stared down at her with all that eagerness, not when Ceridwen was looking up at her with her open, joyous face. There was no way to get out of the moment without disappointing Ceridwen, embarrassing herself, and rebuffing Tashué. She didn't want to stand out in the world, perhaps, didn't want to put down roots that could trap her when she needed to go. But neither could she bring herself to turn him down, not when he was looking at her like that.

"When is the dinner?" Stella asked softly.

"Tonight."

"Is the Winter house sending a carriage for you? To deliver you to Highfield?"

"No, I have another stop to make first. I'll leave at five o'clock, which should give me plenty of time to get to the Winter house."

"Very well. I'll be at your apartment at four."

"Four?"

Stella smiled at him, at the way he shifted, at the way the flush returned. "You need plenty of time in case it's a particularly complicated suit."

Tashué scoffed again. "What on earth could be so complicated in a suit that it will take me an hour to get dressed?"

"One never knows what the latest fashions entail, Mr. Blackwood. There was a time when it was fashionable for men to wear a corset to give them a more triangular shape. I believe they also wore padded jackets, so as to make their shoulders look more muscular. Though you don't look like you need any enhancement in that area."

Tashué took a deep breath, the flush deepening. "I hope I haven't agreed to wearing a corset."

Stella grinned at the panic in his eyes. "You would know if you had been fitted for a corset. A professional like Mr. Bellmore would expect you to try it on before sending you away with it. Precise fit is quite important."

Tashué shifted the weight of the suit over his shoulder as if he meant to dump it on the ground and flee.

Stella laughed, the sound bubbling up in her chest. "Oh, Mr. Blackwood, I'm sorry! Male corsets went out of fashion while I was still in Cruinnich, and I haven't heard any suggestion that they've returned."

"You are a vicious tease, Miss Whiterock. You had me near convinced that you would be lacing me up."

"Mam likes to tease," Ceridwen said, the serious crease appearing on her forehead again. "She isn't very good at it."

Tashué let out a long breath. "Well, I should go before she gets a mind to tease me about something else. Will I see you at four o'clock, then, little warrior?"

Ceridwen smiled. "I hope so. I want to see your nice new suit!"

Tashué laughed, reaching down and patting her shoulder. "Let's hope it's not too complicated!"

Stella watched him go, moving through the press of the crowd with an easy confidence. She tried not to admire the curve of his broad shoulders and the sheen of his hair. It really had been too long since she had felt the touch of a man on her skin. She had thought that such things didn't matter, that such pleasures were too small, insignificant, distracting. But there was something about him, something about the resonance of his voice, about the scent of his skin that made her belly tight. She couldn't help but watch him and wish he would come back.

10

TASHUÉ

DAY 6

"What happens to them? The children, I mean."

Jason sighed and the way his body slumped made him look like some discarded doll. Tashué ached to reach through the grate and hug his son, to crush him close like he used to when Jason was young, when his prodigious energy was spent and he was so tired that he couldn't settle himself. Tashué would cuddle Jason into submission, trapping him in his arms so he couldn't wriggle anymore, and then Jason would finally sleep. But Tashué couldn't do that now. It was a strange feeling to be so surrounded by people that he wanted to touch but couldn't. Somehow a wall had been built between him and the people he cherished most and there seemed to be nothing he could do to break through.

"What's with all the questions you know the answers to?" Jason asked. "Children are too young to be registered, so there's none in the Rift."

Tashué emptied his pockets on the table between them, dragging up the grate. The grate in this room was stiffer than the others, as if it hadn't been moved as much. The sausage rolls were wrapped in muslin to contain the crumbs and he unwrapped them to squeeze them through the gap, using the muslin to protect his fingers as he dragged the metal up as high as he could so it didn't crush the delicate pastry. Jason's whole body was tense as he ate them, his eyes closed, as if he was struggling against his instinct to gobble them up. He forced himself to savour them, his hands almost trembling with the effort. The figs were easier to get through the gap and Jason scooped them up, twisting off the hard stems and flicking them back.

"I know," Tashué said. "I mean… Remember last time, you mentioned that sometimes babies are born here. It happens when men and women live together. Do any of the mothers get to keep their babes after they're born?"

Jason leaned forward, elbows on the table, resting his hands on either side of his face as if he was hiding from someone. "Women don't have babies here. That's the official statement. Doesn't matter what we think we see, who might be getting a swollen belly, there isn't any copulation here and there most certainly aren't any babies."

"I'm sure."

Jason's eyebrows raised and a strange smile quirked the corners of his mouth. "What, you don't trust the word of the Authority? You, of all people? Aren't you Chief Administrator yet?"

"Jason."

"*Captain.*"

"You're in a fun mood."

Another smile, but it faded and Jason looked down at the table. He still had one fig left and he reached down to it, turning it over onto its side and then righting it again. It was too easy for Tashué to forget how old he was. Jason wanted so badly to be grown-up, back when he was young. And he certainly was 'grown-up' in the eyes of society. By the time Tashué was Jason's age, he'd served in the military already for seven years and was thinking about retirement. Looking at him from the vast space of age between them, Jason still seemed little older than a child. Was it because everyone in their twenties seemed so terribly young to him now, or was it because he remembered what it was like to hold this particular twenty-year-old in his hands? Jason was so small when he was born, and Tashué's hands were so big that he could hold him with one hand, cradling Jason's head in his palm and supporting the rest of his tiny body across his forearm.

"The women disappear before they come due, then appear again twenty pounds lighter. Or whatever a baby weighs. They aren't allowed to talk about them, the babies. But we all know what they've lost."

"What are the rumours, then?" Tashué asked, leaning in. "Where do people say they go?"

Another pause. Jason glanced over his shoulder, listening to the hum and bustle of the place. Jason turned back to his fig, knocking it over the other way. Tashué reached out to the grate, starting his fight to smooth it back into place and turn the screws back into the surface of the table.

"I'm sure it's all shit," Jason said finally. "You know how people talk."

"Indulge me. Tell me anyway."

Jason sighed so hard that his whole body heaved with the effort. "What's this all about?"

"The child I found. Remember I told you? I can't figure out where she's come from and I can't let it go."

Jason looked at Tashué for a long time, chewing the inside of his lip. "You think she's one of ours?"

"I don't know, Jason. That's why I'm asking you. Tell me what you've heard."

"All kinds of ugly shit. The one they say the most is that they grind the babies up for meat to feed us so the guards get to keep more of the beef. I don't believe it for a second. I mean—I wouldn't put it past the Authority to grind up children to save a copper crown, but not *tainted* children. They'd be too valuable. Some of the people here are strong. Their children would be put to work some-where, I'm sure."

Tashué took a deep breath, resisting the urge to argue. There was no point bickering about whether or not the Authority would grind up children for meat. "What else do they say?"

Jason sighed, scooping up the fig. He still didn't eat it, turning it over and over in his hand. "We have chores. I'm down in the gardens, but I have a friend who cleans. He goes up into the top floors. We don't use the top floors, but he has to clean them. He's not the most reliable storyteller. So I don't know, alright? I don't know if what he's saying is true. But there's no reason for me to ever go up there. If I go up there and they catch me, they'll fucking kill me. So don't ask me to go."

"Alright, Jason, I won't ask you to go," Tashué said, keeping his voice calm and measured. "Just tell me what you heard."

"He thought he saw… experiments. He says he saw meat-mongers from the colleges. They were experimenting on them, but they weren't babies anymore, they were children. I don't know how old… He said he never had children of his own so he doesn't know how old they looked. He said they were cutting them up, the kids. He said they were still alive."

"Fucking hell, Jason."

"I know, alright? I know. It sounds insane. But the look in his eyes when he said it?" Jason shuddered. "I think he really believes it."

Tashué wanted to buck against the rumours, to reject them completely. But the images of the girl passed through his mind, of her scars and her gaping wound.

"What were they cutting?" Tashué asked. "What part of the children's bodies?"

Jason scowled. "I don't fucking know. I didn't ask for details. That's not exactly the sort of thing I want popping into my head when I'm trying to stroke one out, you know?"

"Would he tell you if you asked?"

"Shit," Jason breathed, leaning in again, a hand turning into a fist around the fig. "Do you believe it? Could it be true?"

"I don't know, Jason. But I found a dead girl downriver from here and someone had cut *her* up while she was still alive. So who fucking knows?"

Jason met Tashué's eye for a long, quiet moment, searching for something. What was he looking for? It wasn't clear if he found it or not, but he looked away first, opening his hand and staring down at the fig. He'd crushed it a bit, pushing some of the gummy seeds out the top where he'd broken off the stem. He popped the fig in his mouth, scraping the seeds off his palm with the back of one nail.

"You've changed."

"What do you mean?"

Jason shrugged, but his eyes came up again, searching, searching. "There was a time that you would have insisted that the Authority wasn't capable of a thing like that." He sucked the last of the seeds off his nail, crossing his arms over his chest. "You would have gotten all angry with me for even suggesting something like that. But now... what? You almost believe it? You're wondering if it's possible?"

"I just want to know what happened to her. I'm willing to consider all possibilities."

"That's it? After all these years, and one little dead girl changes everything? Makes it so you don't trust your precious Authority anymore?"

Tashué sighed. His hands went for his pockets by habit, but of course he'd left his cigarillo case behind. He ran his fingers across his jaw instead, feeling the scrape of his stubble beneath his palm. "I don't know. Maybe I'm just getting old."

Jason looked up again, finally meeting Tashué's gaze. "Maybe you're right. Is that grey I see in your beard?"

Tashué scowled, folding his arms over his chest to resist the urge to fiddle with his stubble any more. Jason grinned at his father's discomfort, but again the smile didn't last long. He spread his hands on the desk in front of him, looking down at the scars and bruises there.

"Sometimes, inmates disappear," he said. "When inmates are executed, they make sure we all know about it. Keeps us in line. But sometimes, they don't tell us where someone goes. They're just... gone, and they won't tell us why. My friend, he says he's seen them, upstairs. And the meat-mongers are working on them too. Trying to figure out where their Talent comes from. Making them do things. They're trying to understand us. My friend, he thought it was so they can eliminate us. But I don't believe that, not for a second. The Dominion wouldn't run without Talent. Trams, ships, foundries… If they didn't have us, everything would grind to a halt. If it's true, and they're trying to figure out our Talent, I would wager it's to control us better. Or breed us better."

"There's a way out, you know," Tashué said. "Out of here."

Jason sighed, sagging down again. He shook his head, but it was slow and without his usual energy. "I won't do it. I'm not registering."

Tashué sighed back, leaning closer. He reached out, aching to touch his son, but the back of his knuckles scraped against the grate instead. "Jason, look at me. I love you. I miss you. You need to get out of here before this place kills you."

"I'm not registering."

"Then what do you want me to do with your ashes?"

Jason's head came back up and Tashué saw the spasm of pain across his son's face. It made his whole body weak, that look.

"If you die in here, whether they execute you or beat you to death, they'll have you cremated and I get your ashes." Tashué leaned closer to the grate, clenching his fists to resist the urge to start pounding on the metal. "Back when we were together, your mother used to tell me that she wanted to go in the Brightwash so the river would wash her ashes out to sea. What do you want me to do? Bury you somewhere? Bring you up to the mountains, like the Kaadayri? Cast you into the wind? Send you out to sea?"

"Fuck you."

"I'm not trying to be cruel," Tashué said, and his voice cracked, forcing him to pause and collect himself, "it's just reality. If you aren't going to get out of here by registering, then you'll probably die here. A few years is optimistic. Look at you! They'll keep starving you and beating you and one day I'll come to visit and I'll walk out of here with you in an urn. So please, tell me, what do you want me to do with your ashes?"

Jason shook his head, wiping his eyes with the heel of his palms. "Fuck you. These people won't kill me. I'm a fucking Blackwood."

He shot to his feet and stomped to the door, pounding on it until a guard came to escort him away. Tashué sat at the desk for a long time, holding his head in his hands. His son was going to die in this place and there was nothing he could do to stop it. Instead of making Jason see reason, Tashué feared he'd only made it worse.

11

JASON

DAY 6

Fuck him. What does he know? Asshole.

Jason stomped through the halls of the Rift, his whole body still trembling. What was it about his father that always twisted him up so damned much? He always seemed to hit every raw nerve Jason had. What the fuck did he know about what it was like in the Rift? Bastard.

Part of Jason wondered if his father was right. He *was* going to die here, if he didn't come up with some way to get out. He wouldn't register though. He wouldn't let them call him bad meat and point him in whatever direction they wanted. Bad meat kept their fucking empire running. The Dominion would collapse without all their *bad meat* working for them.

The guard abandoned him once they climbed the stairs to the second floor, heading off to find the next inmate that had a visitor waiting. Jason headed to the gardens, where he could take out his frustrations on plants. Getting his fingers dirty and contributing to growing food had been calming in his years here. Gardening was good therapy. Not many inmates had the fortune of having jobs in the Rift that were actually enjoyable.

As Jason stomped through the halls, he became aware of

someone following him. And then someone else following. And someone else. He stomped faster. He didn't like the idea of a three-on-one fight, but if he made it to the garden before the fight started, they might back off. Gardeners stuck together.

A fourth person cut him off, standing in the middle of the hallway. Fucking Verrit. Verrit loved to fight and he got away with it because he was one of the proxies. There weren't enough guards to actually *guard* everyone so some of the inmates were trusted with the dubious honour. Everyone else called them rats, but 'proxy' was the official name.

Verrit was the Rat King.

He stood with his legs spread and his arms crossed, taking up as much space in the hallway as possible. Jason was forced to stop, but his whole body was tense and wound and ready. Fuck Verrit. It took a real special coward for someone Verrit's size to bring three men to pick a fight with someone Jason's size. But then maybe they hadn't been looking for Jason specifically, maybe they'd just been roaming the hallways looking for anyone to harass. Sometimes people walked away from visiting with goodies in their pockets and they were vulnerable until they had a chance to hide their contraband away.

"What the fuck do you want?" Jason snapped.

"What's wrong Jason?" Verrit laughed. "Dear ol' Daddy still isn't helping you pay your debts?"

"I don't have any fucking debts, you wet turd. I don't owe you a single bent crown and you know it. You can't just invent debt."

"That's the thing, Jason," Verrit said, stepping closer. He unfolded his arms, holding them out at his sides like he was getting ready to catch Jason. "I can. I did. Your piece of shit father put me in here, and he's going to pay for that, one way or another. Either he pays me, or you do."

"Well, that's too fucking bad, 'cause I don't have anything."

"I don't believe you."

Verrit's thugs were closing in, a ring of bodies. Jason tried to take a step back, but someone grabbed him by the arm and someone else pushed him forward at Verrit so that he swung like a door on bad hinges. He knew what was coming. It was going to be ugly. If he didn't resist it would be over with faster but he was so viciously angry and tired of just *taking* shit all the time.

"Let's search your pockets, just to make sure."

"Fuck you," Jason hissed.

Verrit grinned, grabbing Jason by the hair. "Is that an invitation?" He leaned miserably close, taking a deep breath in through his nose. "You smell like you've been snacking, Jason. Sausage rolls? What else did dear Daddy bring you, huh?"

Jason horked and spat. Mucus and spit slapped against Verrit's face. Verrit staggered back, then gave a howl and sent a fist cannoning into Jason's ear. It cut Jason's knees out from under him, the pain hitting him so hard he couldn't see. He didn't fall to the floor because someone had him by the arm still, but he was left trying to blink away the white spots that drifted through his vision.

"Search the little shit!"

More hands rustled through Jason's clothes. Jason kicked and bucked but someone else grabbed him by both legs and lifted him right up off the floor. Brutish fingers grabbed at his pockets, at his limbs, searching for hidden things.

Don't fight it. Leave it. Don't fucking fight it this time.

But those hands found something and Jason's heart leapt at the sound of shuffling paper. He watched Verrit pull the letters out of the hidden pocket. It was the only personal property he had, his only precious belonging. Letters from his mother. The only contact he'd had with her since that day, when the Authority dragged them out of their home. Jason bucked and twisted, trying to get any limb free.

"No, not my letters!" he howled. He twisted again. "Give those back!"

"What's this, then?" Verrit asked, stepping back. "Love letters? How sweet!"

"Give them back, you fucking ape bastard! Give them back!"

Someone laughed and Verrit sneered, kicking Jason in the side, knocking all the air out of him. "Who's the wet fucking turd now, huh?"

"Verrit, I'm sorry," Jason gasped, fighting to fill his lungs again.

"I'm sorry! Please, give them back. Please. Don't take them! They aren't worth anything!"

"They aren't worth anything?" Verrit echoed.

"No, no, they're just letters. Please, please don't take them! I'll pay you, please, I'll pay you what you want, just give them back. Please!"

"Well, shit, if they aren't worth anything, why do you even have them?"

Jason knew what was coming before it happened and a howl ripped from his chest. The vicious pleasure on Verrit's face at the sound was a terrible, primal thing. He lifted the first letter and tore it in half. The ripping sound hit Jason right in the heart and he started his thrashing again. He almost kicked someone off, so they dropped him to the floor and then they were piling on top of him to keep him still. Verrit ripped those halves and the pieces of the letter started to fall out of the envelope and onto the floor.

And the rage. It boiled in him, pushing on his skin from the inside out. No, not rage—his Talent. It was pushing and forcing against the layer of suppression that kept him separated from it, building in his veins like steam. It started to escape, a little trickle at first that coiled up and away from him, but the pressure kept building, building, building.

And then it burst out of him, an explosion of energy that knocked his attackers off their feet, scattered like detritus all around him. Jason rolled over, grabbing the paper that Verrit had dropped, the torn pieces and the unmarred letters alike, stuffing them back into his pockets. And his Talent ran through his veins, heady and intoxicating and filling his whole body with strength to do whatever the fuck he wanted.

Get the fuck out of here!

He left a shred of his Talent behind, weighing his attackers down, pinning them to the floor. He hoped if he pushed hard enough he would crush them, popping their skulls and turning their guts to jam. They all started howling, writhing, fighting against the pressure he laid on their bodies. Fuck them.

He ran.

The gardens were just ahead and his Talent was swirling, writhing, a vicious bull that had finally broken free of its pen. He'd jump into the Brightwash and his Talent would protect him from the current and the bitter cold of the water until he could find his way to shore. He'd go to the Bay and he'd find Lorne. And then where?

Doesn't matter. Lorne will know what to do. Just go!

The heavy door to the garden gave its familiar squeal and the fresh air hit Jason's lungs, cold and brittle, wet with spray from the river. And freedom was so close. The pair of guards that watched over the gardens saw him coming, but maybe they also felt his Talent and they stood rooted in place, blinking at him in surprise. One of them elbowed the other and they both shuffled closer. Jason ignored them, turning toward the fence that kept them in, reaching out with his Talent to bend the metal out of his way. If they came close, he'd fucking kill them.

But the people in charge of the layer of suppression—whoever they were—recovered themselves. Their Talent snapped down on Jason like an overstretched elastic, smashing into his senses with all the weight of a ton of bricks. Jason skidded to a stop, clutching his head. The pressure of it felt like it was going to smash his skull. His bones were going to buckle under that much weight. They were going to crush him into the stone of the island and no one would find a trace of him.

Someone was screaming. Howling. Sweet North Star, it was a terrible sound. Who was screaming like that?

Him. It was him. The sound was ripping his throat raw and making his ears ring—or did the ringing come from the force that lived in his skull with him, the force that beat his Talent back into his body?

And then the pressure was gone finally, subsiding to the same grinding headache that he lived with every day, but instead of standing in the gardens, Jason was lying on the ground. Something hit him in the leg. In the chest. In the back. Feet. Verrit and his thugs had followed him out and they were kicking him, stomping him. He felt something snap in his chest, a rib maybe, the pain so hot and vicious that he almost vomited. He curled around the wound instead, tucking his legs up tight against his chest, covering his head with both arms. And he retreated into the hollow place that he'd found in his soul, the place that protected him from pain.

He had his letters back, at least. He could feel them, rubbing against his skin under his clothes where they poked out of the pocket that they didn't quite fit into. His mother's words, the only thing he had of her. He wondered if the ripped one would still smell like her, or if tearing it up would make it smell like Verrit's sweaty hands. Bastard.

I almost made it out, Lorne. I was so close. So fucking close.

His father's voice skittered across his brain, threatening to drag him out of his hollow place to feel the pain of the fists and the feet that were still raining down on him. *What do you want me to do with your ashes?*

Fuck you. These people won't kill me. I'm a fucking Blackwood.

12

STELLA

DAY 6

It felt strange to step into the same set of rooms as the ones she lived in and see different furniture, a slightly different view out the windows. There was a small table near the stove with only two chairs, and none of the pieces matched. There was only one couch and one high wingback chair, both covered in silk brocade that was faded and torn at the corners. The horsehair stuffing peeked through each hole.

Tashué was smoking when Stella arrived. He was stripped to his shirtsleeves, suspenders shrugged off his shoulders and hanging around his hips. The sight of him took the air out of her, freezing her for a moment. His beard was coming in with more red tones than his hair, which was a deep, rich auburn. With dark hair and reddish beard and those hot amber eyes, he looked like an earth spirit, built of clay and loam.

"Hello, little warrior," he said, grinning at Ceridwen. "I bought a snack for you. It's there on the table."

"For me?" Ceridwen asked brightly.

"Yes, you. Go on."

Ceridwen sat at the table, eyes wide and round as she stared at the golden-brown pie waiting for her. The top was scored with an X and the deep red filling had bubbled out the hole.

Tashué stepped over to her, handing her a fork. "Sour cherry pie. It's my very favourite thing. My mother used to make it every year."

Ceridwen beamed with excitement. "Thank you, Mr. Blackwood!"

Stella smiled at Tashué. "You didn't shave?"

"Shave?" His hand went to his cheek and Stella could hear the scrape of his stubble beneath his palm. "I just shaved yesterday. Or was it the day before?"

"That's impressive stubble for a day or two."

He shrugged, dropping his hand to his side. "Maybe it was longer, then."

"However long it's been, you should polish yourself as best as possible. You're headed to see the Queen, Mr. Blackwood! Do you have a razor? You could clean up the lines of your cheeks and neck a bit, at least, to present yourself well. Do you keep any fragrance?"

"No…"

"I thought that would be your answer," Stella said, reaching into the pocket under her skirt, pulling forth a little vial. "I brought you a gift, then. I found it in the market, after you left. I thought it would be a good blend for you. It's mostly oils of citrus and mint, which will have a freshness that I think will suit you."

She dropped the vial in his outstretched hand, but he stared at her for a long moment after, a bit of a smile pulling up the corner of his mouth. Flush climbed up her neck, to her cheeks. The longer he stood there, staring and smiling at her, the hotter her cheeks burned.

"I'm sorry," she breathed. "I was babbling. It's the gentlemanly thing, a well-groomed face and a good fragrance. Moustaches are popular at the moment."

"I know." He closed his hand around the vial. "I never gave much thought to beards and trends. I just let it grow until it's too itchy and then I shave again."

"Highland men never pay much attention to the trends either. At least not in the winter. The air's too cold and they can use all the insulation they can get. I was envious, as a child, of my father's beard when my cheeks were so cold."

The grin spread wider. "Why, Miss Whiterock, I must say you would look most handsome with a beard. All those red curls would make you look a proper mountain man. Mountain woman?"

Stella laughed. "It's you that looks like a proper mountain man." She reached for his beard before she could think to stop herself, fingers sliding through all that thick red-brown hair. "You must have ancestors from the north, to be so red."

He didn't back away when she touched him. He turned his face toward her hand, eyes closing for a moment, leaning into her touch. The look on his face caught Stella's breath in her throat, the simple pleasure making her tremble on the inside. She pulled her hand away. His eyes searched her face for what felt like a long time, before he seemed to shake himself out of the moment. He cleared his throat.

"My father's family came down from the north, a few generations back. He was like me, brown hair and a red beard. The colours were lighter than mine, I think. I don't remember exactly, not anymore. I do remember that my mother used to tease him, about his red beard. Said it was where he got his temper from."

"You don't remember what your father looks like?"

He shook his head, but he reached for his beard, sliding his fingers across the rough stubble. "I have photographs of my mother, but not my father. He hated the idea. Thought it was a waste of money, to get a photograph of himself." He shrugged, as if to dislodge the weight of memory. "I just remember that he was tall, and that his red beard made my mother laugh."

"He was taller than you?"

"Oh, I don't know." He shrugged, looking away and taking a deep breath. "It's just that he died before I finished growing. I was thirteen, I think—right before I enlisted. It's funny, the things we think when we lose someone. I remember being angry that I would never know if I grew up to be as tall as he was. I probably did. I don't know."

Stella reached for him again, sliding a hand along that red hair, moving with the grain so that it was smooth beneath her palm. His eyes searched her face, his body tight and rigid. She smiled at him, wishing she could think of some way to offer comfort. She kept taking pieces from him, pieces that she didn't think she was entitled to. He was so honest with her, opening his chest and bearing the weight of past pain to her, but everything she had told him was a lie. It made her ache. She didn't know how to make it right.

He turned his face toward her hand again and his mouth pressed against her palm, just for a moment. When he turned to look her in the eye again, he seemed to be leaning in, like he was going to kiss her. And she stood, rooted in place, waiting. He had looked at her like that before, like he was going to kiss her. But he never did.

And—just like every time before—he took a deep breath and stepped back. "The cheeks and the neck, you said?"

"Yes," Stella breathed. "You can leave the beard if you tidy up the lines some."

He kept his straight razor and his shaving brush in the kitchen and Stella stood back and watched him. He opened all his buttons with one hand, just the left. He was watching her out of the corner of his eye as he pulled his collar back, showing the line where the sun had darkened his skin considerably, his neck below the collar a few shades paler. Was it all that redness and strength that made her so fond of him, perhaps, reminding her of highland men from home? It had been so terribly long since she had been at home.

"Why do you have a bottle of whisky on the counter, and another up there on the shelf?" Ceridwen asked. She ate the pie slowly, scooping the cherries out one by one, but her eyes were on the bottle in question.

"That was my father's," Tashué said. "He kept it up there for special occasions."

"What kind of whisky did your father drink on special occasions?" Stella asked.

Tashué shrugged, glancing up at the bottle as he worked his soap into a lather with his shave brush. "The expensive kind. Why?"

"Mark me curious," Stella said. "I'm a highland woman, after all. I know a thing or two about whisky."

"Of course, Miss Whiterock." He spread the soap on his neck and cheeks, then stepped away from the basin, stretching an arm up to pull the bottle off the shelf. "Maybe your highland knowledge could tell me a few things about my father, through the whisky he drank. Is that what you're saying?"

"Perhaps," Stella said with a smile as she took the bottle from him, though he stepped back to the basin and turned his back on her. There was a bit of dust on the bottle, but not much—Tashué must have taken it down now and then to clean it. The label was still in good shape and Stella's eyebrows rose. "This is eighteen-year-old Ladovaugh. Cask strength! Oh yes—this would be the year Ladovaugh put out 120 proof. This is some whisky, Mr. Blackwood."

"I didn't realize," Tashué said. He turned to Stella again. He'd shaved his cheeks and his neck, making the lines of his emerging beard sharp and clean.

"Where did your father get eighteen-year cask strength whisky?" Stella asked. She handed the bottle back and he looked at it differently than before. "It would have been very expensive."

"I'm not sure," Tashué admitted. He looked down at the label, but his eyes were distant. Looking into the past, no doubt. "I... seem to recall someone gave it to him as a gift, when he married my mother. He gave some to her, on her wedding day... The joke was that she didn't like it, but he married her anyway. He said he had another drink when I was born, and a few others. The rest he wanted to share with me—so he gave me a dram when I turned thirteen. He said we'd have another when I got married, and that would leave enough for us to finish the bottle when I made him a grandfather." His eyes focused on Stella, coming out of the past. "Like I said, I don't remember what he looked like. Whenever I think of him, I remember smells. Stone dust and sweat, and the smell of whisky. The peat smell—say it again. The name of the whisky."

"Ladovaugh."

He repeated it, mimicking the gh sound well. "This is the

brand he always drank, just the regular stuff. Ladovaugh. I still remember the smell of it, the sound of him pouring a glass when he got home from work." He shook himself, turning and replacing the bottle on the high shelf. He pushed it a few times, as if there was a particular spot it needed to be to appease his nostalgia, then grabbed a cloth to wipe the last of the soap off his face. He forced a smile, fighting to break through the weight of memory. "What about you, Miss Whiterock? Are your parents still up in Cruinnich?"

"No," Stella said, the weight of that pain somewhat lessened by the fact that it was a true thing she could tell him, finally. "They died. Three years ago. I tried to keep in touch, but I've missed them, since leaving."

Tashué nodded, sensed her hesitation to talk about it, perhaps. He took the vial and cleared his throat as he seemed to test the weight of it in his hand. "Citrus and mint, is it?" He pulled off the cork stopper, the smell effervescing immediately. "The Jitabvi cook with a lot of citrus and mint. Add a clove or two of garlic and some onions and I'll smell like a good camp meal."

"I hope I didn't cause any offence, Mr. Blackwood."

"No, not at all." He forced a smile, gave a shrug. "I just find it amusing. They wanted their war hero to parade around for them." He upended the bottom over his fingertip, adding a dab of fragrance to his neck and his chest. "Seems fitting that I would parade while smelling like a Jitabvi camp."

Stella took a deep breath, trying not to let her eyes linger too long on the skin of his chest, where the buttons were still open. "Where's the suit, then? Let's see what the Jitabvi camp will be wearing in the Governor's house, shall we?"

Tashué laughed. Sweet North Star, how she liked the sound of his laughter. It cut so easily through the heaviness in the room, making her feel warm and light again. He turned away, to the door of his bedroom, where the suit hung in its canvas bag. At Stella's direction, he gathered it up and laid it across the couch. Stella opened it, shifting carefully through the contents. The wool and silk was soft against her hands and she wondered at how long it had been since she had handled such fine material. She had left so much when she fled Cruinnich.

"It is a very nice suit." Stella slid a hand down the sleeve, relishing in the softness of the high-quality wool. "It doesn't look nearly as complicated as I'd thought. Rather straight-forward, actually."

"So, you scared me for nothing. I think that was a ploy to watch me dress, Miss Whiterock."

Stella felt the heat rise in her face, her cheeks burning. Tashué grinned at her, one eyebrow arching.

"I was teasing, but I think I've hit close to the truth."

"You shut your mouth, Mr. Blackwood. You, sir, are a trouble-maker. Go on, then. Start dressing and if you need help, call out to me."

Tashué's chuckle was deep and throaty, a caress that drifted in the room between them. A shiver passed through Stella's body and she bit her lip, fighting against the warm feeling that spread through her skin. He gathered up his suit and retreated to his room. Stella dragged the second chair closer to Ceridwen, sitting beside her. Tashué's had his table closer to the stove and the dry heat of it crawled across her body. Ceridwen was suspiciously quiet, staring down at the pie with careful intensity. Perhaps all the talk about fathers sat heavily on her shoulders, too.

"Can I try one?" Stella asked.

Ceridwen nodded and scooped up another cherry on the tine of her fork, handing it across the table. The cherry was delightfully tart, cooked in sugar and plump with its own juice.

"Delicious."

Ceridwen smiled, nodding. "They are. I like sour cherries."

Sitting was a mistake. Now that she'd stopped moving, the weariness caught hold of her. She'd slept a little after returning from the market, but now it didn't feel like enough. It never felt like enough.

Her eyes wandered across the room, taking in the little details, the points of difference. He didn't seem to keep much food at all, but that wasn't unusual, especially for people who lived alone. There was so much food available in Yaelsmuir, vendors who sold from the streets day and night. He kept plenty of coffee, though, a great canister of coffee beans sitting within easy reach, a grinder clamped to the counter, a pot sitting beside it, waiting for its purpose.

Something that did surprise her was the wooden shield hanging over the door, round and wrapped in birch bark, ochre paint making familiar symbols on the bark. Cedar twine kept the birch bark in place and wrapped around the nail above the door, hanging the shield in place. It had been a long time since she had seen any Pashibé art, which suddenly struck her as odd. Pashibé, after all, came from the area, the city of Yaelsmuir standing on their ancestral ground.

Tashué stepped out of his room, though he hadn't gotten very far in his efforts to dress. He wore the trousers, woollen plaid with all the colours of autumn—rich reds and burnt sienna, pale yellow and russet brown. The silk shirt was the very purest white, draped across his body but still open. He hadn't buttoned the shirt yet, nor affixed the stiff collar or cuffs, which he brought out with him in one hand. The whiteness of the shirt only accented how deep and rich the colour of his skin was.

"I've been defeated by buttons. I haven't much feeling in this hand." He stretched out his right hand, showing the scar that ran along his wrist and through the fleshy part just below his thumb, a little canyon that had almost faded with age. "Usually I manage on my own, but these buttons are so bloody small."

Stella stepped closer to see the buttons, and of course they were tiny. Carved from mother of pearl, they were round, the faces each bearing intricate carvings. They showed various weapons, swords and guns and curved daggers, a small inventory of the weapons used by the Dominion military.

"Why don't you have feeling in your hand?" Ceridwen asked.

"I have an old wound that did some damage to the nerves. I didn't see a healer in time for them to fix the damage completely."

"Can I see?"

Tashué shrugged. "There isn't much left to see but the old scar."

"Is it a big scar?"

Tashué held out his hand. "Come see then, if you're going to ask me a dozen questions."

"Wipe your face first, messy little beast. You'll get cherries all over Mr. Blackwood's nice new suit, and he'll make a bad impression on the Queen."

Ceridwen wiped her face quickly and slipped off the edge of her chair, bouncing across the room to look at Tashué's hand. She stared at the scar with such intensity that she seemed to be trying to peer right into his flesh. Stella felt it, just for a moment, the stirring in the centre of Ceridwen like the breeze across old coals, whipping up dust and the suggestion of heat. Even as the whisper of it passed through Ceridwen, Stella reached out with her own Talent, her mind tying the restraining knots in place again. Tashué seemed to feel it, too, his eyes turning to Ceridwen and watching her with an intensity Stella hadn't seen in him before. How much had he noticed? How much could he sense?

Ceridwen seemed oblivious to it all, looking up at Tashué. "What happened?"

"I was trying to learn to use a sword with my right hand and the woman I was duelling with slipped past my guard and sliced me right open." Was he speaking slower than before?

Stella swallowed the rising fear. "I didn't realize people still use swords anymore."

"That was a very long time ago. I went to the Officer's Academy when I was fifteen. They expected us to be proficient with as many weapons as possible," Tashué said. There didn't seem to be any tension in him, at least no more than before. He chuckled, breaking the fear that sat in Stella's chest. "At least they gave up on trying to force me to fight right-handed."

"Left-handers are pure poison. Harder to fight when your opponent is your mirror image."

Tashué raised an eyebrow at her. "Oh, and how might you know that? Since swords are so out of date now?"

Stella shrugged. "Guns are still hard to come by in the north. At least they were when I left."

"Who were you in Cruinnich that you knew about high fashion

and sword fighting?" That smile again, pulling his mouth up on the left side.

Stella smiled back. "Cruinnich is a greatly nuanced place. Go finish your pie, Pigeon, and I'll help Mr. Blackwood button up his shirt."

Ceridwen skipped back to the table and sat down. "It's very good!"

Stella took a deep breath. The fragrance was a good one, the bright smell of citrus and mint playing in delightful contrast to all the rich smells of him naturally. She reached out to him, easing the first button into place. It wasn't easy, for the newly-stitched hem on the hole was still tight and narrow, the rough surface of the button catching. It seemed a silly thing to struggle with, a button. Stella could feel Tashué's rising discomfort. He was leaning back, she realized, his face turned away, but as the backs of her fingers brushed his chest, she thought she could feel his heart pounding against his ribcage.

"You have a nibu," Stella said, desperate to fill the tense silence between them with something, anything. "Above your door."

Tashué's eyes went up to the shield, and he nodded. "It was my grandmother's."

"Oh, your grandmother is Pashibé? You don't have your ishani tattoos."

Tashué looked down at his hands, and the spasm of pain that flashed across his face made Stella regret her words instantly. "No, my mother never learnt what it meant to be Pashibé. And so she never taught me, either. My grandmother kept a few things, a few tokens like the nibu, but we only found them after she died. We had to ask around to find out what they were. How did you know what it was?"

"There's always been a large Kaadayri population in and around Cruinnich."

He stretched out his arm to her, letting her affix his cuffs. His cufflinks were the same mother of pearl set in rose gold, the right hand carved with the insignia of the 8th division, the left carved with the crest of the Authority.

"You'll have to lean down for your collar," Stella said. "You're too tall for me to reach otherwise."

His chest swelled with the deep breath he took as he leaned down. Stella stood on the very tips of her toes to reach around to the back of his neck, struggling with the button there. Her chest touched his shoulder as she leaned in, his hair tickling her cheek. The fragrance lingered around him, bright and fresh like she'd hoped. His breath was hot on the side of her neck. It made her skin go tight all across her body and her heart started pounding again. It was hard to separate the earlier flash of fear from the thrill of plea-sure her body twisted with now, the two sensations so terribly simi-lar. She moved to the buttons beneath his throat, biting the inside of her lip, hoping the pain would help to clear the fog that settled on her mind.

She thought he leaned even closer, just for a moment—she felt his rough stubble scraping across her cheek, his breath swift and shallow in her ear. But then his buttons were fixed into place and he took a step back.

"Thank you." His voice croaked and he cleared his throat as he tugged at the collar, taking another step back. "I think I'll manage from here."

Stella took a step back, but something held her in place. "It's not too late, you know. To get your ishani tattoos. I know they're thought of as a coming-of-age ritual, but it's more... a way for your Pashibé family to lay claim to you and for you to give your life to them in return. So you could still get them, if you wanted to. You would need to track down your grandmother's family and see if they want to lay claim to you."

"I wouldn't know where to start. She didn't tell us anything... Who would I even ask?"

Stella shrugged. "All you have to do is start asking. Pashibé believe that all the children of their family will find their way home, if they want to."

Tashué took a deep breath, taking the waistcoat off the arm of the couch where it lay behind him, pulling it over his broad shoul-ders and fumbling with the buttons. They were larger, but the button holes were still stiff and his hands were still clumsy. Stella stepped in again, pushing his hands away and doing up the buttons one by one.

"Are you afraid they'll reject you, if you go looking for them?"

"I don't know."

"I admit, I'm not Pashibé, so I can't speak *for* them. But in my experience, they're happy to reclaim their own. All the Pashibé I've known in my life have felt that their people have been stolen from them by the Authority and by the Dominion, and everyone that comes back to them feels like a victory. So, if you want to know, you should look for answers."

He smiled at her, but he still looked sad. "You are a woman of constant surprises, Miss Whiterock. You know everything from the trends of high fashion, to sword fighting, to cask strength whisky, to Pashibé traditions."

She stepped back again, smoothing out the front of his waistcoat. The silk was deliciously soft, the brocade thick and intricately detailed, but the colours were muted and subtle. "Do you have your pocket watch?"

He reached into the pocket of his trousers, producing the timepiece he carried with him. She took it, unbuttoning the centre button of his waistcoat to thread the delicate chain through the hole, attaching the end to the button before closing it again.

"I listen," she said finally. "People give me their stories, and I listen."

He took his timepiece from her hand, tucking it into his pocket. Was he leaning closer to her again? She could feel his breath in her hair, the sensation of it making her scalp tight, making the skin on the back of her neck tingle.

"We met someone, back when we were trying to understand the things my grandmother had. He was just passing through, on his way to the western legacy territory. He explained that the nibu was like a charm, a wish. You hung it over your door, on the way out, to bless anyone that left your home. The wish is that, no matter the reason a person came into your home, you would settle your differences and they would leave as a friend. So, Miss Whiterock, did the nibu work on you? Will you leave my home as a friend?"

Stella smiled back. "Of course, Mr. Blackwood."

He nodded, reaching out and catching her hand, lifting it. He kissed the back of her knuckles for just a moment, but the warmth of him made her whole body tight. She took a deep breath. Tashué scooped up the suit jacket next, pushing his arms into it. It was a lovely reddish brown, complimenting all the hues in the plaid of the trousers. He seemed to have relaxed some, his body losing the tension it had before. "Thank you for your help, Miss Whiterock. Can I walk you home?"

Stella smiled. "Yes, thank you Mr. Blackwood. It is such a long way."

He laughed at that. North Star preserve her, she loved the sound of his laugh, so rich and deep. He was a dangerous man, with that beautiful laugh and that ugly tin badge.

13

TASHUÉ

DAY 6

The memory of Stella's body, so warm and so close to his, sat on Tashué's skin like a blanket as he made his way through Cattle Bone Bay. The oldest part of the city, the Bay was still the place where most of the river traffic docked, riverboats and barges all sidling into the Hive—a great labyrinth of docks and high platforms that allowed barges to be loaded and unloaded with unmatched efficiency. Warehouses had been built high above the river, to hold goods short term while merchants dickered over the cargo that came and left from the Bay. Nestled in the centre of it all, Powell Iwan's fight house. He ran his stage fights matches in a never ending cycle of blood and pain.

The ring was little more than a raised stage. The crowd pressed right up against the wooden platform during a fight, leaning in, pounding on the wood. If the fighters weren't careful, they would fall right into the press of bodies.

Men glowered at Tashué as he settled at the bar, sneering at his badge and his fine suit. His tin badge was pinned to the front of his jacket, as requested by Elsworth. It hadn't caused a problem before, but maybe the combination of the Bellmore suit and the badge made him stand out too much.

"I can't say I've seen a tinman so well dressed before," said a young man, sitting a few stools away. "It isn't often we host Regulation Officers. Especially ones in Bellmore suits."

Tashué shrugged out of his brand new coat—also from Bellmore, with sleeves that actually fit—and looked down the bar at the young man. His wild shock of blond hair was barely contained by hair oil, and his suit hues of blue and rich brown. He smiled at Tashué, which took the hostility out of his words. For all that he commented on Tashué's suit, the young man was wearing high-quality clothes himself, certainly much more expensive than anything any of Powell Iwan's patrons could afford. No doubt this man was Iwan's grandson, the old man's only successor and thus dangerous in spite of his friendly smile and his young face.

"Are you here on behalf of the Authority, sir?" the young man continued. "There aren't that many tainted here in the Bay. We have more than enough Officers to supervise them all."

"No, I'm here on personal business," Tashué said. He unpinned his badge, sliding it into his pocket. Little good it did. Everyone who cared had already spotted him and made up their minds.

The crowd started howling again, and Tashué looked toward the platform. He finally caught a glimpse of the young man he'd come to see, Lorne Coswyn. Stripped to the waist and standing on the stage, his body was covered in a thin sheen of sweat. His black hair stood on all ends, giving him a wild look, blue eyes piercing and sharp. He swung his arms in slow, measured circles, walking back and forth in his corner. The crowd shifted on the far side of the stage, and soon another fighter climbed up onto the platform. The man was shorter than Lorne, but broader across the chest and shoulders. His warm-up routine consisted of an elaborate series of jumps and kicks that set the crowd into a wild frenzy. The ringmaster lifted his arms and both fighters walked to the centre of the platform, squaring off. The crowd howled, a wild animal on the verge of devouring itself. The ringmaster dropped his arms, stepping back. And the shorter man attacked.

A roundhouse kick hurtled toward Lorne's face. Lorne sidestepped, caught his opponent's leg and smashed his elbow into the tender spot just above his opponent's kneecap. Lorne dragged him closer, striking with a vicious head butt. Lorne let go of the man's leg as the head butt connected, sending his opponent spilling to the platform. Blood sluiced from the man's nose as he hit the wood floor hard, the back of his head striking with a sickening crash. He coughed and spluttered, sending blood everywhere as he struggled not to choke on it. The ringmaster started counting. The man struggled up to his feet. As soon as he had both feet under him, Lorne hit him again, his fist coming down from above and snapping his opponent's head to the side, sending a spray of blood and spit across the crowd. The smaller man's legs went to jelly and he started to sink back down. Lorne hit him again, full in the face. The shorter man fell hard. Lorne stepped in to hit him again, his blood too hot for him to see his opponent was finished. The ringmaster forced his way between them, pushing Lorne back as he counted again. Lorne stepped away and Tashué could see him taking deep, gulping breaths, walking in a tight circle around the empty side of the stage. Tashué couldn't even hear the ringmaster, but the crowd was echoing his count. The other fighter rolled onto his side, a pool of blood spreading around his face from his smashed nose. The ringmaster reached ten, and the crowd roared. Lorne rolled his shoulders a few times, then clambered down from the stage and disappeared into the crowd.

"How did a Regulation Officer come to know the Lledewydd Lightning? He isn't registered—is he?"

Tashué shook his head, glancing down the bar at the young man. "No, he's not registered. He knows my son. They met on the streets some years ago."

The eyebrows went higher. "Why was your son running with Bay kids? You're not from here."

Tashué shrugged, reaching for his cigarillo case and flicking it open. "My son had his own ideas about how to live. I told him he could follow my rules or he could leave. He left. Spent about six weeks in the Bay before he decided my rules weren't that bad."

"Six whole weeks! Well, good for him. I don't think I'd last six hours with the street kids around here."

Tashué grunted as he struck a match. "He's always been stubborn, my son. Hasn't changed much since then."

"Has there ever been a more contentious relationship than the one between fathers and sons?" The young man nodded to the barmaid as she drifted close. "Will you let me buy you a drink, sir?"

Tashué nodded. "Thank you." This day, this shit day, seemed to be all about reliving the hardest parts of his life. Talking about his parents with Stella was almost a warm memory, at least, because of the way she looked at him, the way she leaned so close, the way he *wanted* to give her every shred of himself, even the pieces that hurt. Talking to a stranger about his strained relationship with his son, in the wake of remembering his own father, sat sour in his mouth.

"A pint?"

"No, I can't stay much longer. Just the copper whisky is fine."

"I'll have the same, Ollia, if you please."

The barmaid nodded and turned away to pour out two servings. She set the glasses down in front of the young man, who slid one over to Tashué and raised his glass to toast. Tashué forced a smile and raised his own glass. What would his father think of him, drinking this shit? Still, he threw it back with his usual expertise, but the young man grimaced, his whole body wracked with a shudder.

"That's fucking awful. Why would you drink such terrible whisky? A tinman's salary can't be *that* bad. Did you spend all your wages on that fancy suit?"

Tashué slid the empty glass back to Ollia. "I didn't have to pay for this suit, fortunately. I definitely couldn't afford it. But no, my wages aren't *that* bad. I hate the copper whisky—that's why I drink it."

The young man chuckled. "You'll have to explain that."

"I love a single malt whisky, from Cruinnich or Gladwydd. On a bad day, I could sit and drink bottles of it. But the copper whisky goes down like acid and I'll burn a hole through my gut before I can get through a bottle, so it's easier to stop."

The young man laughed, shaking his head and pushing his glass away. "I would love to sit and drink a bottle of single malt whisky with you. Ollia, I'll have a proper whisky this time. Let me buy you a good dram, sir."

"Thank you, but no. I have other places to be tonight."

The young man shrugged. Ollia served out a measure of whisky and moved away.

"Did your son learn his lesson?" the young man asked.

Tashué took a deep breath. "Excuse me?"

"Your son. He lived on the streets because he didn't want to listen to you. Did he learn after that?"

"I'm afraid not," Tashué said slowly. "He's in the Rift now."

The young man winced. "Shit. What did he do to get himself there?"

"He refused to register."

"Sounds like a conflict of interest for a man in your position."

"No conflict at all," Tashué said, standing up a little straighter, smoothing the front of his jacket. "The law has been followed in Jason's case."

"Yes, of course. I didn't mean to imply otherwise. It's just—one might wonder where your loyalties lie, with your own son taking a stand against the very organization you represent."

Tashué swung to the young man, anger coming hot and fast. "Are you accusing me of something specific, or are you just making general statements?"

"Accusing you?" the young man echoed, raising his hands. "No, I'm not accusing you of anything, sir. Families can be complicated, can't they?"

Lorne finally made his way through the crowd, stepping between the young man and Tashué. He was dressed in his worn rags, holes darned and patched so many times there barely seemed to be an inch of the original cloth left. A smaller man followed him, his face deeply etched by age and weather.

"Lemme buy ya a drink," said the little man, smiling his gap-toothed grin. "Ya made me a pretty crown tonight."

Lorne laughed, looking over his shoulder at the man. "That's very kind of you, Tam, but it's not necessary."

"Hush, boyo, don't ever say no to a free drink." Tam held up two fingers to Ollia, who set to pulling a pair of pints from a keg of stout. "When do you fight again?"

"End of the month, unless Mr. Iwan asks for me sooner," Lorne said. "You smoke, Tam? Mr. Blackwood shares."

"No, no thank you. Just the pint is enough for me."

"Suit yourself," Lorne said, dragging Tashué's cigarillo case closer and flipping it open. Tashué passed him the box of matches. "You're dressed up nice. What's the occasion?"

"I'm dining with the Queen tonight," Tashué said. "Needed to look my best."

Lorne snorted. "With the Queen, is it? Am I invited?"

"Sure," Tashué said with a shrug. "We'll make quite the pair, you and I. Do you have any clothes without holes in them?"

"Queen Leony is for the common people. I'm sure she'll forgive me my rags if I tell her how hard life is in the Bay."

The young man slid from his stool, stepping around Lorne and offering a hand. "It was a real pleasure to meet you, Mr...."

Tashué leaned in and accepted the handshake. "Blackwood. It was a pleasure to meet you, Mr. Iwan."

The young man shook his head. "Please, call me Vasska. Or if you must *Mister* me, I took my mother's family name: Czarny."

"My apologies, Mr. Czarny."

Vasska grinned, tilting his head. "You pronounce it surprisingly well. Most people fumble on the rolled r. I think you're a man with a lot of good stories, Mr. Blackwood. One of these days, you and I will have to sit and share a bottle of Cruinnich whisky."

Before Tashué could say anything, Vasska moved away. Tam slid up onto the stool that Vasska had vacated, turning to watch the next fight as it started on stage.

Tashué turned to look at Lorne after Vasska had gone. "Are you busy?"

Lorne shook his head, blowing out a line of smoke. "I'm done here for the night."

Tashué pulled out his notepad, holding it tight between two hands for a long moment. He couldn't do this alone, that was becoming clear. He might have found time before, but now? With the campaign shit and a promotion headed his way? "I need your help."

Lorne furrowed his brow at the notepad. "I didn't think you were taking on any new cases."

"This isn't Authority business."

"Do we need to step outside?"

"No, nothing like that." Tashué took a deep breath as he flipped through the pages, pulling the photographs out of the way to give Lorne the sketch of the girl's face. "I'm looking for any information about this girl."

Lorne reached past the notebook and dragged the ashtray a little closer so that he could flick his cigarillo into the heavy glass. Taking the notepad next, he studied the girl's face for a long time. He flipped the page and studied the numbers with the same intensity.

"Who is she?"

"She washed up on the riverbank. I thought she might have come from the streets around the Facility of Rest."

"The one Stella Whiterock works at?" Lorne asked. "Did you ask her?"

"I did." The ache set in Tashué's chest again, the memory of the shock on Stella's face when she looked at the photograph. "She doesn't recognize the girl or her wounds."

Lorne flipped back to the girl's face. "What makes you think she came from up that way?"

"Her arms and legs had been removed at some point. The infection in one of the incisions could have been what killed her, though I don't know for sure."

Lorne grimaced, blowing a cloud of smoke up over his head. "And the numbers?"

"They were tattooed on the back of her neck."

"Fuck me. Where was she found? Exactly."

"At the end of Murne, where the old bridge used to be."

Lorne grimaced. "You know what else is upriver of the old bridge?"

Tashué nodded. "The Rift. The same thing occurred to me, but she was too young to be registered and they tattoo differently."

"Can't be a coincidence, though, can it?" Lorne pressed, leaning closer. "The Rift tattoos inmates and this girl is also tattooed... who else might do something like that but the Authority?"

Tashué took a deep breath of smoke from his cigarillo, pulling his notebook closer to look at the numbers again. "They all have the same mark at the Rift; name and number. If the Authority is tattooing people like this, Jason hasn't seen it at all."

Lorne shrugged, shaking his head. "I'll go around the Facility in the morning, see what I can find."

"Hey, boyo," Tam said, leaning over Lorne's shoulder. "Seems like trouble's coming."

Tashué followed his gaze into the crowd, watching the knot of bodies starting to come together. "Are you going to be in trouble with Iwan if we get into a fight here?"

Lorne shook his head, glancing over his shoulder at the trouble makers. "No. He'll make money out of it somehow."

"What's crawled up their trousers, then?" Tam slid off his stool and dropped his voice to something like a whisper but considerably louder. "Ain't no problem with the fight, is there? Was a good fight, that one."

"No, they aren't looking for trouble with me," Lorne said, crushing out his cigarillo. "It's my friend Mr. Blackwood they have a problem with."

"Oh. What did Mr. Blackwood do?"

"He works for the Regulation Authority."

"I bet they're especially pleased about Winter's Provincial Police Force," Tashué muttered.

"Say it louder. I bet someone will throw something at you."

The knot of men were trying very hard not to appear to look at him. They were arguing. He couldn't hear them over all the other noise, but he could see them working themselves up. One man shoved another and a third swung to glare at Tashué as if he caused the conflict.

"Are we fighting then?" Tam asked. The little man seemed to be vibrating with excitement.

"I don't know, Tam," Lorne said. "It's up to Mr. Blackwood. Although he hasn't left yet, so I'm guessing that means he's waiting for the fight to come to him."

Tam nodded, turning to Ollia and waving her back as he fished a few more coins out of his pocket. "I'll take one of those wheat beers. The kind from Lida, that you serve in the big heavy glass with the thick bottom."

Ollia nodded and moved away to pull a fresh pint for Tam, finding exactly the glass he was asking for. Tam's grin was wide, showing the gap where he'd lost a tooth. He leaned against the bar to watch Ollia fill the pint, the white head frothing over the top of the glass.

"You're not usually the type to go looking for a fight," Lorne said, glancing up at Tashué. "One of the things I like about you."

Tashué turned long enough to flick the ash into the heavy ashtray. "They're never going to let me out of here. If I try to go around them, they'll follow me and try to hit me from behind before I leave the Bay. Better here, where there's enough light I can see them."

Lorne nodded, stepping away from the bar and rolling his shoulders, loosening up the muscles again. "I know these idiots. They like to think they're fighters, but they aren't. The one with the thick neck there, he's always the one to lead trouble. If you put him down ugly, the others should back off. And then maybe he'll stop causing fucking problems around here."

Tashué nodded, shifting and unbuttoning his jacket. "I was thinking the same thing."

The three that had started the trouble stepped from the crowd. Tashué made a good show of ignoring them at first, pulling on his cigarillo and breathing out the smoke in long, measured breaths. He stood with one elbow on the bar, turned to Lorne, his back almost to the crowd. Tam eased closer, slurping the head off the top of his wheat beer, knobbly hand clutching the heavy glass.

"Time to go, tinman, or we'll drag you out by your balls," the lead man said.

Tashué took a last drag from his cigarillo, breathing out the big cloud of smoke as he crushed it out in the ashtray. "But I'm not finished here. I think I'll stay. Have another drink."

The bull-necked man cursed and stepped in again. He had massive fists, strong and wiry, covered in the long scars of a man who worked with something sharp. He didn't strike Tashué as a fighter, as Lorne said. His stance was all wrong. "You must be stupid, tinman. You're not welcome here. Get the fuck out or you'll be walking out with your teeth in your hand."

Tashué furrowed his brow. "My teeth? There isn't anything wrong with my teeth. Why would I have them in my hand?"

At Tashué's shoulder, Lorne snorted. The bull-necked man cursed so loud and fast that it was drawing attention. His companions, though, seemed to be shrinking. Maybe seeing the Lledewydd Lightning standing at Tashué's shoulder gave them pause.

"Are you fucking daft?" the man growled, baring his teeth like a dog with its hackles up.

"I'm just trying to enjoy a few drinks, sir," Tashué said smoothly. "You're the one that isn't making sense. Maybe you should sit down? You're looking flushed."

The bull-necked man snapped and swung. Tashué turned and the fist only glanced off his shoulder, setting the man off balance. Tashué grabbed the heavy ashtray and swung, smashing the thick glass against the side of the man's face. The man's head snapped to the side and his knees went to jelly, his whole body tilting as he started to fall. Tashué caught him by the front of the jacket and hit him again—skin split along his cheekbone and there was a pause before the blood came. Tashué struck him again, the blood spurted in a wide arc. Another hit snapped something. Tashué let go of him, letting him fall to the floor.

"Huh." Tashué turned his back to the crowd, looking at the ashtray. "I thought this would break."

Lorne laughed, leaning an elbow on the bar. He held out a hand and Tashué passed him the ashtray, waving for Ollia. It took every ounce of self-control not to throw himself into the crowd and start hitting people with whatever he had. There were still too many of them for that. He turned to the crowd. The bull-necked man was still where he had fallen, groaning softly through his own blood. The other two stared at Tashué. The bull-necked man lay directly in their path, like a shield of flesh.

One of the men took a deep breath and charged. Lorne snatched the ashtray next, springing forward in a fast and ugly moment, and swung hard. The man's cheekbone crunched and he fell back, into the crowd. Lorne took another step and the third man flinched.

"That'll be enough of that." The voice trembled with age, but there was enough force left to freeze the crowd. Powell Iwan moved to the bar, steadily, albeit slowly. There was never any need for him to rush. The world waited for him. He scowled, his big grey brows knitted together. "If any of you fools want a fight, you can step into my ring like everyone else."

"No sir," the third man said, taking a big step back. "Sorry, sir."

"You'd best be picking up your idiot friends. Or at least roll that one over so he doesn't drown in his own blood. And when they wake up, you can tell them that none of you are welcome in my establishment anymore. I see the three of you in here again, I'll be sure someone rearranges your fucking organs, you hear me?"

The last man standing sprang forward, grabbing the bull-necked man by his arms. "Yes, sir, Mr. Iwan, sir."

The old man stood silently as he watched the man struggle. The bull-necked man was heavy and rolling him onto his side was a challenge. Powell waved at the two unconscious men, and more of the crowd came forward, helping to drag the pair away.

"Someone clean this shit up," he muttered, waving at the blood.

Someone came rushing forward with a bundle of rags, dropping to his knees to wipe up the drying mess. Tashué stepped aside, looking down at his clothes. There was blood on the front of his jacket, on the vest he wore beneath, on the grip of his pistol.

"Ah, fuck." Tashué huffed, shaking his head. Of course, of

course, he would get blood on the Bellmore suit on his way to dine in Highfield with the Queen. "I'll take one of those rags."

"Blackwood, isn't it?" Powell said, watching Tashué struggle with the stain. "The same Blackwood I read about in the papers? The same Blackwood that's off to see the Queen tonight?"

"Yes, sir." Tashué shuddered as the energy of the room started to shift. He hadn't met Powell Iwan before, in all the times he'd come to the Bay to meet Lorne. For Iwan to take an interest in him now, it must be because Tashué had fallen under the attention of the Queen. *Please, don't ask me any favours.* "The very same."

Powell's big eyebrows rose as he shifted his weight. "It's nice to meet you, Mr. Blackwood. It's not often we have guests of the Queen in our fine establishment."

"I don't see why not," Tashué said smoothly. "You run the best fight house in the city, Mr. Iwan."

"Ah, Mr. Blackwood, I'm immune to flattery. You're right, of course, but it doesn't gain you anything to say it. You never bet on my fights, after all."

Tashué shrugged. "I'm not a gambler. I prefer to spend my money on whisky."

"You should place a bet next time. Come see me and I'll give you the best odds."

"Yes sir."

Powell nodded, reaching out and patting Tashué's shoulder. "Wise man. It's nice to see."

14

TASHUÉ

DAY 6

Illea Winter's manor was a massive, sprawling estate, backing onto the cliff that overlooked the Brightwash. It was strange, hearing the river so far away, muted by the height of the cliff that set Highfield apart from the rest of the city. Down in Brickheart or the Bay or even the Market, the river was so immediate, so inescapable. Highfield, quite literally, stood above the rest of Yaelsmuir.

The hired carriage rattled right up to the front door. Tashué unfolded his long limbs from the back of the carriage and stepped down. He spotted a familiar face almost immediately—Ishmael Saeati was sitting on one of the carriages with a driver, swathed in winter clothes. He stood when he spotted Tashué and patted the driver on the shoulder before leaping down. He landed easily despite the rough cobbles and smoothed out the front of his coat.

"Well, aren't you looking fancy," Ishmael said, with his lopsided grin. "Illea really had you dressed up, hey? Bellmore and everything."

Tashué shrugged. "You're looking like you just got back from somewhere sunny. You're far too tanned for Yaelsmuir rain."

"Ha, yes." Ishmael grinned and ran a hand over his cheek, as if he could feel the warmth from whatever sunny place he'd left behind. "I hate coming back when it's fucking cold here."

"Cold?" Tashué said with a scoff. "The cold hasn't started yet. Hasn't even started snowing."

Ishmael scowled. "Don't remind me. You ready to head in? Or do you want a smoke?"

"Oh, you were sent to be my guide, were you?"

Ishmael nodded as he reached out, hand sliding into Tashué's jacket pocket and pulling out his cigarillos. "The General thought you would appreciate a friendly face." He flicked the case open, taking out a cigarillo and putting it between his lips. "Which pocket do you keep matches in again?"

Tashué found his matches in his trouser pocket, tossing them to Ishmael. "Do you get to tell me where you were this time?"

Ishmael headed up the big front steps and leaned against the wall. Beside the doors, tucked away into an alcove. "I was in the Commonwealth. Down in the southern countries. Where all the best fruit trees are."

Tashué lit his own cigarillo as he followed Ishmael up the steps. He leaned into the alcove beside Ishmael, blowing out a line of smoke and letting the wind pull it away, up the road, toward the forest. "Sounds nice, especially this time of year. Little tight in here, isn't it?"

"That's the fucking point, Captain," Ishmael muttered. He pulled his coat closed against a strong gust of wind that found them even in the alcove. "I'm hoping I can leech some of that body heat of yours. You make so damned much of it."

"You just need a thicker coat. You've been gone less than a year? You can't possibly have forgotten how to dress for winter in that time."

"Maybe it's just wishful thinking," Ishmael said with a shrug. "Maybe if I stay away long enough, winter will just fuck off. Not the Governor, of course, the season. Actually the Governor can fuck off too."

"Why not settle somewhere else, then? If you hate the cold so much. You wouldn't even have to leave the Dominion. You could go down to Khurya or Corradan. Fruit trees aplenty down there."

Ishmael sighed, blowing a line of smoke out his nose and watching it swirl away on the wind. His whole body shuddered, his shoulders hunching, making him look smaller, which was no easy feat for someone usually so dynamic. "Everything I care about is here. Keeps pulling me back, no matter how much I hate the fucking cold."

Tashué reached out, sliding his arm across Ishmael's shoulders, dragging him in closer. Ishmael laughed, leaning into the warmth of Tashué's coat.

"Shit," Ishmael muttered. "You smell like dinner."

Tashué chuckled, all the tension fading away. If General Wolfe had sent Ishmael out here because he hoped their history would help the whole experience feel more comfortable, it was working. Everything about Ishmael's company was easy. "I know. Like a Jitabvi camp meal, right?"

"Actually, I was thinking khafreh. Remember? It's the pie with lamb and mint and olives and lime."

"Are you saying I smell like meat?"

"And mint and lime." Ishmael took another drag of his cigarillo, though his shivering had relaxed. "Suits the occasion, I guess. Illea's planning to make a proper meal out of you."

A proper meal. It was hardly a surprise, considering how she looked at him at the fitting. Would it really be the worst thing? "How long does shit like this usually last, then?"

Ishmael snorted. "You've had that cock forty-two years and you're trying to tell me you don't know how long it lasts? Although I'm flattered that you think I remember. It's been a while."

"I thought you didn't forget anything."

Ishmael smirked. "Fine, you're right. I remember. But I'm disturbed that you don't."

"You're funny. I meant the banquet."

Ishmael rolled his eyes, his shoulders sagging. "Fucking hours. Light chatting, fourteen courses, and then smoking after."

"Don't tell me eating and drinking wears you out."

"It's not the food or the booze, it's all the godsdamned politicians."

Tashué took another drag of his cigarillo, the tension crawling back, bit by bit. "Fourteen courses?"

"Fourteen," Ishmael said with a nod. He elbowed Tashué. "Relax—don't let me get you all worked up. It shouldn't be that bad. It's just a very long meal with way too many fucking rules. Leony is about as laid back as you can get in a member of the royal family, and I expect she'll like you."

Tashué glanced at Ishmael instead, cocking an eyebrow. "My, Ishmael, on a first name basis with the Queen of the Dominion, are you? Look at you, from Cattle Bone Bay to banquets with dear Leony."

Ishmael grinned again, taking a drag from his cigarillo. "Queen of the common man."

Tashué stifled a sigh, flicking his cigarillo away. "You going to lead me up to the abattoir, then?"

Ishmael laughed, stepping out of the alcove. "You're so melodramatic."

Tashué followed Ishmael through the big doors, into the foyer. Servants were waiting to take their coats, and Tashué tucked his arm against his body, hiding the vague shape of the stain. At least his jacket was almost the same colour as the blood, giving it some camouflage. They wiped their wet boots on a rug before stepping up onto the elaborate smithed-stone, the sort of thing his own father used to do. Colours and patterns blended together, granite that had been crafted by Talent to look just so—but Illea Winter kept massive, sprawling rugs over the floors that hid most of the craftsmanship.

Ishmael led him through the house, to a massive room where the bodies were already milling. Tashué could hear them, the chatter spilling out into the hallway. A servant stepped into the room ahead of them and announced them both. There was only a slight pause in the conversation, and then the room was filled with chatter again. Ishmael led Tashué through the room, plucking a pair of glasses off a passing tray and handing one to Tashué.

"Smile, Captain," Ishmael said, elbowing Tashué again. "And drink. Helps loosen things up."

Tashué took a deep breath, sipping whatever Ishmael handed him. Brandy, maybe, or sherry. General Wolfe peeled away from a knot of people Tashué didn't recognize—all of them adorned in jewels and silk and all manner of glittering things—and made his way across the room. Wolfe always leaned more heavily on his cane in the cold, wet weather of autumn and winter, and Tashué understood it, how deep the aches went when the air was thick with the promise of rain and snow. Wolfe stepped close, offering Tashué a handshake.

"It's good to see you, Captain," Wolfe said. "I understand how busy your schedule keeps you, so I appreciate you taking the time to do this for Rainer."

"I wouldn't say I'm doing it for Mr. Elsworth, General," Tashué said.

Ishmael snorted, hiding another grin behind a sip from his glass. "Not the type to inspire loyalty, is he?"

"Ishmael," General Wolfe huffed. "This isn't the time."

"That's what you get for bringing him back so soon," Tashué said. "He probably still has left over energy from whatever highly secret project you sent him away on."

"Yes, I like that," Ishmael said, grinning. "It's your fault, General."

"Yes, fine, all my fault," Wolfe muttered, waving a hand. "It's not as if you're a grown man who should be capable of managing your own behaviour."

"Where's the fun in that?" Ishmael asked.

"Oh, General—how's the hospital coming along?" Tashué asked, turning to Wolfe. "I keep meaning to come by to see, but like you said, I'm so damned busy."

Wolfe nodded. "It's going very well. Slow, but these things take time. The first two floors are nearly finished, and we'll have the grand opening on schedule. For Myron's campaign, of course, because heaven forbid something good should happen in this city without him taking credit."

"You chose to enter into politics with the man," Ishmael muttered, draining the last of his glass. "I don't know what else you expected."

Wolfe scowled, but his eyes shifted focus over Tashué's shoulder and his face relaxed. "Ah, General Imburleigh, it's good to see you!"

Tashué swung, stepping out of the way. Mallory Imburleigh was the latest head of the Imburleigh Armament Company, and Tashué's breath caught in his throat at the thought of meeting her. She was dressed as finely as anyone else, a gown of crushed blue velvet that caught the light as she walked. She took Wolfe's hand when he offered it and leaned in close, planting a small kiss on Wolfe's cheek before turning to Tashué.

"This must be the Captain I've heard so much about," Imburleigh said, offering a smile. "Blackwood, is it?"

"It is, General."

Imburleigh smiled. She stood apart from the group, leaving a bit of distance between them. "Who did you serve under, Captain Blackwood?"

"I was under Maddox in the 8th," Tashué said. "Cavalry."

Imburleigh's eyebrows climbed up. "You wouldn't be the same Blackwood who held the Black Ridge, would you?"

Here it goes. "Yes, I would be, General."

"Heavens," she breathed, glancing at Wolfe, "Rainer left that bit out when he was talking about you. My brother will be quite jealous to learn that he missed meeting Blackwood of the Ridge. Was it as bad as they say, on the Ridge?"

As bad as they say, shit. Nothing Tashué had faced in his entire life was like those long months. "I don't know—I haven't paid attention to the gossip about it. I retired not long after that."

"Yes, I can understand why," Imburleigh said, nodding. "The gossip is... Well, I'm sure you know. Even if you don't listen to the gossip about the Ridge, you've heard about how soldiers talk about other big moments like that."

"Yes," Tashué admitted. "Hard to tell the truth among the wild exaggerations. I should say, though—those Imburleigh repeaters probably saved our lives. We'd just gotten them before marching to the Ridge, and the Ibeh we were fighting still only had single shot rifles. The ten-round repeaters gave us a fighting chance."

"Oh—thank you, Captain. Such stories are always good to hear."

"Don't you still have it?" Ishmael asked. "He showed it to me a few years back, and I have to admit I thought of you, General Imburleigh. I thought you'd like that story."

"I do have it," Tashué said. "My Lieutenant still has hers, as well."

Imburleigh's eyes widened as she took a deep breath. "You have a first-run repeater, which you had with you on the Black Ridge? Captain Blackwood, if ever there was a reason you wanted to find a new home for that rifle, I would greatly appreciate it if you brought it to me. I would pay you handsomely for it. Pieces of history like those are exactly the sort of thing we like to have in our private collection."

"I expect I'll be keeping it, General," Tashué admitted. "I never know when it might save my life again."

Tashué felt rather than saw the shift in the crowd and he glanced over his shoulder to see Rainer and Myron approaching. Tashué took a deep breath, feeling like he was bracing himself for some assault. Interacting with Illea at Bellmore's had been a welcome distraction. Interacting with Rainer Elsworth at the station house, however, had set a tension in Tashué's chest that he hadn't forgotten. The easy answer was to call himself a hypocrite—Illea, a beautiful woman, wanted to objectify him. Fine. Maybe it would evolve into something physical, and maybe he needed exactly that. But really, the physical distraction was incidental. Rainer Elsworth was the Chief Administrator of the National Tainted Registration Authority, and he was using Tashué to... what? To help Myron's career?

Ishmael leaned closer, grabbing Tashué's arm. "Hey," he whispered, as Imburleigh and Wolfe all but collided with Myron and Rainer, entering in their greeting ritual. "Relax."

Tashué took a deep breath, glancing down at Ishmael. Maybe

he understood. Or maybe they just knew each other well enough that he sensed Tashué's spiralling mood.

"This is your man, is it?" Governor Winter asked. He kept his distance from Tashué, one hand in his pocket and the other clutching a half-drained glass. "The new face of the Registration Authority?"

"Yes, Governor," Rainer said with a grin. "I'm so glad you made it, Mr. Blackwood. I see Illea made sure you were dressed quite well."

"Yes, sir, Mr. Elsworth," Tashué said. "Mr. Bellmore is very detailed."

"That's what it takes, to be the best," Ishmael said with a grin. "Attention to detail."

"And what are you the best at, Mr. Saeati?" Imburleigh asked, swinging to Ishmael. Her eyes were hard and she leaned away from him, just a little. "Drinking?"

Another of Ishmael's crooked smiles, but one hand slid into his pocket and he swirled the contents of his glass around a bit, that restlessness of his trying to break through. "Yes, General Imburleigh, and I pay great attention to those details. This nice dry sherry, for example," he tilted his glass toward Imburleigh, "is a great drink for before a big meal, or something bitter like that anise liquor from the south opens up the pallet. Wine goes well with dinner, but each course requires different things from a glass of wine. I believe Miss Winter has brought up some of her first bottles of their Salt Isles red. She'll pair it with a roasted beef shank which will play off the spiciness of the grape quite well. After dinner you have your harder spirits, of course, a good highland whisky perhaps to go with cigars and all that. Or something sweet, if you prefer, to pair with dessert."

Imburleigh sighed at Ishmael, shaking her head. "Honestly, Mr. Saeati."

"You asked, General," Ishmael said. "Please, ask me what else I'm an expert on. I'll give you whatever details you want."

"Hey, don't be an ass," Tashué said, biting back a laugh. Best not encourage him by laughing. "Not everyone wants those kinds of details from you."

Ishmael scoffed, putting a hand over his heart, all innocence and sincerity. "I didn't mean it like that."

"Ishmael," Wolfe grunted. "Behave yourself for an entire hour, as a gift to me."

"A whole hour?" Ishmael said. "Why even bring me along, then?"

"Yes, why indeed?" Myron muttered.

Some signal that Tashué missed drew everyone else's attention. Myron and Rainer turned, heading toward the massive staircase that fed down into the room from the floor above. Illea and the Queen stood at the top of the stairs. Queen Leony wore gentle shades of grey, but Illea wore a gown of pastel yellow, bright and attention grabbing, forcing the eye to her. Tashué took a deep breath, feeling tension climb up his spine, and into his shoulders. Tension at meeting the Queen. Tension at remembering the way Illea's hand felt in his.

They came down the stairs arm-in-arm, trains of their gowns trailing behind them. The crowd stood frozen for a while, until Leony and Illea reached the bottom of the stairs. Myron peeled away from Rainer to meet the Queen, taking her hand and bowing low. Tashué couldn't hear the exchange, but something made Illea roll her eyes and pull Leony away, into the centre of the room.

"How is the new factory progressing, General Imburleigh?" Wolfe asked, shifting his attention back to Imburleigh.

Ishmael plucked another pair of glasses from a passing tray, trading one for Tashué's empty glass. "This is the anise spirit I mentioned. The bitterness pairs well with rich people talking about how they spend and make money."

Imburleigh smiled at Wolfe, but it was tight and tense, like she was trying to ignore Ishmael but failing. "Things are progressing again. We had stalled, with some supply issues. There was some mix up with our order regarding the stone for the foundation. But of course, the Rhydderch family is most accommodating."

"I understand it's only the younger Miss Rhydderch now," Wolfe said softly.

"Oh gods, enter the very subtle judgemental portion of the evening," Ishmael said, shaking his head dramatically. "Wherein rich people discuss the personal lives of other rich people and sigh pointedly and make loaded statements. I'm embarrassed for you, General. Usually you're above such petty sniping."

Wolfe huffed at Ishmael. "I'll have you know we're both quite fond of the younger Miss Rhydderch." He swung back to Imburleigh. "Have you seen her since her parents passed?"

"I haven't been up north much in the years since, no. Although I understand that Miss Rhydderch has kept herself busy. I think she was working with Illea on that rail line up through Riguan."

Rainer and Myron circled back toward them, and Tashué took a sip from his glass. The anise spirit was bitter and dry, like Ishmael said, but the warm flavour of the anise sat like a furnace in his chest.

"You'll have to forgive us, Mr. Blackwood," Rainer said. "A social event like this has so many needs of a man! I trust Mayor Wolfe is keeping you comfortable?"

"Yes sir, very comfortable," Tashué said.

"I take it you'll have Captain Blackwood accompany you on various political functions, Governor?" Imburleigh asked.

"Yes," Myron said, glancing at Rainer. "I understand that's the intention. For the campaign. Most especially, for the Provincial Police Force."

"Perhaps you could arrange for a better guide for him in the future," Imburleigh said. "Our Mr. Saeati is a terrible influence."

"General Imburleigh, I'm wounded," Ishmael said. "Who better to guide our Captain than a fellow common man, risen through the social hierarchy of this fair city?"

"Perhaps someone who isn't so crude," Imburleigh said with a smile.

"Mr. Saeati is an old friend, General Imburleigh," Tashué said. "And anyway, we agreed years ago that we're a bad influence on each other."

Myron gave a long sigh, turning to Rainer. "This is the one you settled on, then? What happened to the other one? Isn't this the one with the tainted son in the Rift?"

The words, and the casual scorn they were delivered with, froze Tashué. Froze him, then ignited him with an anger so sharp he couldn't breathe. So this was it, then. It wasn't about the Black Ridge or the medal he got for it, or the fact he looked good in a fancy suit. It was about Jason.

Look, he imagined Rainer saying, *the man is so loyal to our ideals that he allowed his own son to be processed for refusing to register. An exemplary Officer, truly.*

Wolfe reached out, squeezing Tashué's shoulder. Whatever he meant to say, though, was killed by the frisson of excitement that passed through the crowd. Illea approached, leading the Queen. Even across the room, meeting Illea's eyes set a heat in his chest that burned hotter than his anger. Her mouth pulled into the smallest of smiles, something private, something warm.

"Mr. Blackwood, you look most excellent," Illea said.

She clove easily through the crowd around Tashué, putting a hand on his arm and standing on the tips of her toes to kiss his cheek. It took the breath out of him, that kiss, the familiarity and the warmth feeling so out of place here, with everyone but Ishmael and Wolfe standing at arm's distance from him, like he was some curiosity that they didn't dare touch. But Illea, what was she doing? Laying some claim? Forcing the rest of the room to accept him?

One glance at her husband made it clear what she was doing. The man had turned deep red, his hands clenched at his sides. And Rainer shifted a little closer to Myron, putting his shoulder between Myron and Illea. With those words echoing in his head, *the one with the tainted son*, Tashué put a hand on Illea's waist and kissed her cheek, maybe a little too close to the corner of her mouth. Myron made a strangled noise in his throat that filled Tashué with savage joy.

"You look positively radiant, my Queen," Ishmael said, his voice as warm and smooth as honey. Hard to tell, with him, if he was flirting with Leony or stealing the attention from Tashué and Illea. Bless him, either way, because the Queen blushed at him and the tension drained away. "How were your travels? I understand you were in the Commonwealth?"

"I was, Mr. Saeati, and thank you," the Queen said. "I was asked to negotiate a peace treaty between the southern countries. They were able to come to decent terms, so we'll see how long this peace lasts."

"Peace in the Commonwealth is a mystical beast indeed," Myron muttered. "Nearly as rare as peace in the Derccian Empire."

"Peace is a matter of perspective, Governor," Ishmael said smoothly. He drained his glass in one long swallow. "Simply because there is no obvious fighting doesn't mean one nation or another isn't facing strife or hardship. And sometimes, some things are worth fighting for."

"And what might you know about fighting, Mr. Saeati?" Myron sighed, rolling his eyes. "Other than fighting the pull of the bottle, that is?"

Tashué felt his neck go tight—again, that dismissive tone. Ishmael gave so much to the diplomatic division, to the Dominion entire, and these people spoke to him like his presence was an offence to their sensibilities.

Ishmael, however, laughed. "I never once fought against a bottle, Myron." He tossed his empty glass at Myron, a friendly, under-handed toss that sent Myron scrabbling to catch it. "Neither have you, I should think."

"Honestly, Governor, that's not fair," Imburleigh said, and her voice cut the outrage out of Myron before he could get going. Bless her, at least she understood, her and Wolfe. "For all his flaws, Mr. Saeati served his country."

"I didn't realize, Mr. Saeati," Leony said, leaning in closer to Ishmael. Queen of the common man, indeed—of all the people in the room, the Queen stood closest to Ishmael, leaning in as if she was drawn to him. "You served in the Dominion Army?"

"I do, your Majesty," Ishmael said. "In the diplomatic division. I was never a warrior like our fantastically decorated Captain Blackwood."

"Yes, Rainer—you didn't mention the part where the man had a

White Shield," Mallory said. "You went on and on about the new face of the Authority, but you neglected to mention the man was a decorated hero."

Myron flushed again, but forced a smile and stepped closer to the Queen. "I'm informed that our meal is ready for us, my dear friends. My Queen, would you do me the honour of joining me at the table?"

"Of course, Governor Winter," Leony said with a smile.

"Excellent," Myron said. "If you'll follow me, my Queen."

The crowd made another shift, heading for the dining room, but Myron seemed frozen by something, meeting Tashué's eye. His fidgeted in place, working himself up to—something.

"Do you know how to behave at a formal dinner party, sir?" he asked. "You've been told what is expected of you?"

"Why?" Tashué asked, glancing at Ishmael. Was Myron serious? "Do rich people have a particular way of eating dinner?"

Myron forced a laugh, eyes going wide and wild, lips pulling back in a sneer. "So uncultured, our Mr. Blackwood. He will have to be educated in proper meal etiquette if he's to dine at my table."

"Excuse me, Myron," Illea said, a slow and dangerous smile spreading across her face, even as she hooked her arm in Tashué's again. "I thought I heard you say *your* table."

Myron's eyes bulged as he looked between Tashué and Illea, Wolfe and Mallory, and lastly at the Queen. "Of course, my dear, I misspoke. It's just that the man needs to be educated. Our Mr. Elsworth named him as an honoured guest, and I won't have him making a fool of us in our house, especially tonight, with our beloved Queen at our table."

"Your Majesty, surely you'll forgive our Mr. Blackwood for any rough manners," Ishmael said, leaning closer to Leony. "He is a hardworking member of our city and probably came here directly from an honest day's work."

"Of course," Leony said swiftly.

"Very well, then." Illea smiled at Myron. "Let's take a moment before we sit, shall we? Mr. Elsworth, please take the Governor around the room to let him charm his beneficiaries. Meanwhile, we can brief our Captain Blackwood on the etiquette expected of him. Who better to teach him than our beloved Queen?"

"Can I leave you unattended, Ishmael?" Wolfe asked. "Or will you manage to stir up some other trouble if I walk away?"

"General, I have been on my best behaviour," Ishmael said.

"I'm afraid that's true, General Wolfe," Imburleigh said, hooking her arm in Wolfe's and leading him away. "This really is the best behaved I've seen him in some time. Perhaps your Captain Blackwood is a good influence after all."

Ishmael grinned as the crowd shifted again, winking at Tashué. "Illea, darling, I think your husband accused me of being an alcoholic."

Illea huffed, rolling her eyes. "Honestly, for him to judge anyone else's drinking defies belief."

"You're to explain the rules of the evening to me, Miss Winter?" Tashué asked. Best get this shit over with. "I didn't realize dinner etiquette of the wealthy was so important."

Illea smiled, leaning against Tashué. "We shroud ourselves in these frivolous little rituals as a way to establish ourselves as somehow better than the working classes. Since we are fortunate enough to be dining with the Queen, our usual rules are slightly different. No one eats until our Majesty begins. It shows respect. Of course, you mustn't stare at her overtly, since that would be unsettling, wouldn't it, your Majesty?"

"Indeed it would be," Leony agreed. "I've never loved formal dining to begin with. It's much worse when everyone is staring at me."

Tashué shifted, trying to swallow the rising panic. How many courses did Ishmael say? "I will promise not to stare at you, your Majesty."

"Never finish everything served to you," Illea continued.

Ishmael gave a dramatic sigh that heaved his shoulders. "My least favourite rule. The people of high society are above petty things like hunger and demonstrate their mastery of the base instincts by leaving food on their plates."

"Never use your fingers to touch your food while sitting at the table, if you please," Illea said. "We mustn't be eating like street urchins. You must avoid excusing yourself from the table if you can, but if it can't be avoided, wait for the pause between courses. It would be rude to stand while the Queen is eating."

Tashué took a deep breath. "Are any of those rules jokes, or are you serious?"

"Proper etiquette is no joking matter, Mr. Blackwood!" Illea gasped, laying a hand on her chest and taking a deep breath. She leaned even closer, until her shoulder pressed against Tashué's chest. "You heard my dear husband. We can't be having you making a fool of us all in front of the *Queen*."

"I promise not to think ill of you, or even notice, if you finish all the food on your plate," Leony said. "Mr. Saeati certainly does and I must admit, I find him quite charming."

"Shit, I'd lick my plate if I thought I could get away with it," Ishmael said with a grin. "But that might be a step too far, even for me."

"Oh, heavens, please do," Illea laughed. "Myron would have a fit."

Ishmael shrugged at her. "While I would dearly love to antagonize your husband, there's only so far I can push General Wolfe's tolerance."

"Oh yes, heaven forbid you should incur the wrath of General Wolfe," Tashué chuckled, looking down at Ishmael. "If you push him hard, he might make very stern faces at you."

"Oh, but then he really scolds me once we get home. Although somehow, we've gotten sidetracked, talking about me."

"Don't lie, you love being the centre of attention."

Ishmael laughed, reaching out and pushing Tashué back, just enough to set him off balance. "Ass."

"It certainly seems Captain Blackwood knows you exactly as well as he said he does," Leony said.

Ishmael glanced up at Tashué with the sort of grin that made Tashué's face flush. It wasn't that he was ashamed of *just* how well he knew Ishmael Saeati, it was just that he didn't expect to be talking about it in front of the Queen of the Dominion. But Ishmael didn't press it.

"Our Captain needs his education, Illea," he said instead, "so we can eat."

"Of course, forgive me, Ishmael," Illea said, reaching around Tashué to lay a hand on Ishmael's arm. "I know how hard it is for you to be patient when food is waiting for you."

If Ishmael was bothered by Illea basically calling him a poorly trained dog, he didn't show it. Tashué bristled, though, the tension returning.

"Mr. Blackwood, you must never leave the table without our Queen's permission," Illea went on. "We are all here at her pleasure and it would be absolutely scandalous to leave without her consent."

"I wouldn't want to cause a scandal," Tashué muttered. "At least not on my first formal dinner party. I should ride this out and make sure my scandal is as interesting as possible."

Ishmael's laugh was loud and maybe a little forced, and he patted Tashué on the shoulder. "That's the spirit!"

"I officially give you consent to leave whenever you need to, Mr. Blackwood," Leony said quickly.

Illea gave an exaggerated gasp, laying her hand on Tashué's arm. "Don't listen to either of them! They're giving you terrible advice, Mr. Blackwood. You can't rest your reputation on such open-ended permission. If you require a break from the table for any reason, please ask permission from the Queen. However, you mustn't draw attention to yourself, nor give a reason or interrupt the Queen if she's speaking."

Myron shuffled closer, but the way the four of them stood facing each other meant there was no way for him to break into their group. "Are you finished preparing Mr. Blackwood?"

"I have done my best," Illea said, squeezing Tashué's arm. "However, our dear Queen has kindly passed an all-inclusive forgiveness should Mr. Blackwood make any mistakes in etiquette."

"Yes, exactly," Leony said, offering Myron a stiff smile. "I hereby absolve you and your household for any embarrassments due to your honoured guest's lack of experience."

Leony sat at the head of the table. Illea kept hold of Tashué's arm, guiding him to his spot. She sat closest to the Queen, and Myron sat across from her, to the Queen's right. Instead of looking at Illea with her arm looped around another man, Myron looked down the table as his guests gathered. He tugged at his collar and clenched his fists and no one would look him in the eye. Wolfe was settled beside Myron, and Ishmael beside him—and the faces bled into the many, many people Tashué didn't recognize from there. Mallory Imburleigh sat beside Tashué, and then Rainer Elsworth beside her.

The servants burst into movement, pouring the first course of wine and then setting bowls at each place. The seating was such that Tashué was almost, but not quite, comfortable. Ishmael and Wolfe, his familiar faces, were well within reach on the other side of the table. But Myron glowered and seethed beside them. And Illea leaned just a little too close to Tashué, the bare skin of her arm pressing into his; even the layers of his suit didn't block the warmth of her body.

"Rainer, you'll have to explain your vision for this 'face of the Authority'," Leony said. "I heard some mention of it, and I must admit I'm curious to know your plans."

The doors to the kitchen opened and the first wave of food arrived, filling the dining room with the smell of tarragon and garlic.

Rainer nodded as the servants moved away. "The Authority needs a new public face. We need to be seen for the work we are doing on behalf of the Dominion entire. We provide safety, stability, and security. The tainted can be unpredictable and dangerous, yes, but under proper management, they can be an asset, as you yourself saw. I was quite inspired by your experiences, Majesty."

Tashué took a slow, deep breath. Here it was, the part he'd dreaded. *If anyone so much as mentions the Rift...* Illea touched his arm before he could complete the thought and picked up one of her spoons—so many damned spoons. She'd misread the rush of tension in him, maybe, as something to do with the first course. He picked up the same spoon she did and tried to eat, but the soup was like ash in his mouth. What had he let himself get dragged into? He didn't have time for any of this, no matter what the General said. He almost, almost, resented General Wolfe for pulling on his loyalty like he did, but no, he pushed that thought away. If General Wolfe asked him to do it, there had to be a reason, and the reason had to be bigger than *to parade you in front of rich people for politics*.

"Perhaps you could share a little more context than that," Illea said, glancing down the table.

"Yes, some context, Rainer!" Myron said but he was watching Tashué still, as if he thought Tashué would start hurling dishes the moment anyone stopped supervising him. "I know you had some plans for the man, but I didn't realize they come all the way from our beloved Queen."

"Well the Queen didn't give me the orders, exactly," Rainer said, "but I was inspired by her experiences abroad, particularly in the Commonwealth. Perhaps the Queen would like to relay her experiences herself. Your Majesty?"

"Yes, I think I know what you're referring to," Leony said, smiling. "I was so impressed with how the policies of the Commonwealth allow their tainted citizens to reach their fullest potential. They haven't any registration or legislation in the Commonwealth regarding the tainted, but rather a 'job placement' program. Tainted are matched to various companies based on their latent skills. It's the responsibility of each company to manage their tainted employees as they would for any other employee. Mostly the tainted are matched to trades, where their skills are used to make things of better quality and in a faster time frame than regular employees."

Every word hit Tashué like a fist. Queen of the common man, maybe, Queen of the 'regular' people, but even she clearly believed that people with Talent were people apart. To be *managed*. Jason had it, all along, back when Tashué still thought the Registration was for safety, to help people. Tainted, bad meat. *Jason, I'm so fucking sorry.*

They were still talking, Leony and Rainer, batting the conversation back and forth, but Tashué could barely hear what they were saying because his ears were still ringing, *allow their tainted citizens to reach their fullest potential, manage their tainted, of better quality and in a faster time than* regular *employees.* Queen of the common man, but not Queen of the tainted.

Rainer said something about the Dominion having an 'unusually large concentration of tainted citizens' and Myron said something about statistics, but damn him, he looked so fucking smug, like the statistics were something he could be responsible for, and Tashué's veins seemed to be quivering, his blood boiling with the heat of his fury.

Ishmael caught Tashué's gaze, across the table. He cocked his head toward Myron, just a little, and rolled his eyes with all the drama he so deliberately cultivated. Lifted a hand off the table, made a fist, jerked it back and forth a few times.

And the motion was so crude, so ridiculous, that it released some of the tension in Tashué's chest. At the table, with the Queen, all these people talking about etiquette and leaving food on their plates because they were above hunger, and there was Ishmael. Holding Tashué's eye contact, making his very pointed suggestion that Myron was stroking himself with his smug little comment about statistics. A laugh escaped Tashué before he could stop it, abrupt and short, a release of the anger as much as it was any show of amusement. Beside him, General Imburleigh sighed.

"Mr. Saeati," she whispered, her voice soft because Rainer was talking again, "honestly."

"What?" Ishmael whispered, but it was hardly quiet, cutting over Rainer's voice. He put his hand over his chest—the right hand, the same one that had made the jerking motion, and that was almost too much for Tashué, that almost made him laugh again. That Ishmael would pair his act of sincerity with the very motion that had broken through the tension to begin with. "I'm still on my very best behaviour, I swear."

"Perhaps your 'best' could have some room for improvement," Wolfe muttered.

Myron shook his head, waving Rainer's talk away. "Excuse me,

Rainer, all this talk of shipping lanes and fresh fruit is quite fascinating, but I'm struggling to grasp how it relates to our Mr. Blackwood. Are you indeed a fruit merchant, Mr. Blackwood?"

"I am not." Tashué reached for his wine, draining the glass. "I am a Regulation Officer for the National Registration Authority."

"Well, that is no longer accurate, Mr. Blackwood," Rainer said with a nod. "You are actually a Station Commander for the National Tainted Registration Authority."

"Not yet. I'm to receive my promotion at the Imburleigh event."

Rainer laughed. "That sense of exacting standards is the very reason I knew you were the man I needed."

Myron snorted. "For Station Commander?"

The derisive snort made Tashué clench a fist again—or maybe it was just the reminder that Station Commander was coming to him, a brass badge to replace the tin one, coming from the man that said *that sense of exacting standards* as if he was talking about Jason in the Rift.

"No, for the public face of the Registration Authority," Rainer said. "We are hoping to make a shift in our public relations, your Majesty, so that we might bring a little peace to the Dominion. We'll start with a local campaign here in Yaelsmuir and if it meets with positive feedback, we'll take the campaign to a provincial, then national level."

"That's wonderful, Mr. Elsworth," Leony said with a smile. "What are to be your responsibilities, Mr. Blackwood?"

Slow breath, in and out. "I'm not exactly clear on that yet, Majesty," Tashué admitted. Provincial, national? What were they going to do, trot him across the whole damned continent?

A servant hovered at Tashué's shoulder, too close. It made the skin on his neck tight. There were so many damned *people* in this room. Sure, some nights at the *Pint Under* were just as busy, but Tashué understood the flow of the *Pint*, he understood what he had to do to get his space, what he had to do to get service. Illea rested a hand on his arm and Ishmael met his eye; they were both trying to tell him something, but Rainer started up again.

"Mr. Blackwood will be standing beside Governor Winter

during his campaign for re-election to show an alignment between Governor Winter and an interest for national peace and security. He is to signify all the strengths and qualities of the Registration Authority. He has an excellent record of following the law to the letter,"—*fuck, there it is, Jason*—"but also a deep-rooted sympathy for the tainted. We would like to highlight both of these aspects going forward. Our desire to adhere to the law of the Dominion is tied to our sympathy for the tainted overall."

Tashué shook his head. The words were so viciously empty. "But you write the law."

They were simple words, out before Tashué could stop them, but he felt the whole room go still. Ishmael half-choked on his wine, clapping a hand over his mouth to cover his grin or hold in whatever comment he wanted to add. Wolfe swung to look at Rainer, those blue eyes intense and... amused? Tashué turned to look at Rainer over Imburleigh's head, though Rainer was studiously avoiding meeting his gaze.

"What do you mean, Mr. Blackwood?" Imburleigh asked.

Tashué took another deep breath, choosing his words carefully. "Mr. Elsworth is trying to imply that his main consideration is adhering to the law, as if it's some kind of sacrifice for him. But the National Registration Authority was given the power to write its own laws and you, Mr. Elsworth, have the power to change those laws as you see fit. Perhaps if you chose me for my 'deep-rooted sympathy' you could write language into the law that would allow me to be more lenient with my cases. But don't try to imply that upholding the Registration laws is a challenge. Those laws are literally the reason the Authority exists."

"Well," Illea said, lifting her glass and smiling at Leony, "there's that exacting character."

"I don't like the truth to be misrepresented, Miss Winter," Tashué said. "Especially when regarding a large percentage of the Dominion's population, most of whom live in poverty." *One of whom is my fucking son.*

Myron snorted again, draining his glass. "They live in poverty because they can't manage their own lives very well."

Tashué swung to Myron, his whole body tight, his legs aching as if they were begging him to stand, to reach across the table. "That's offensive, sir."

"Offensive?" Myron scoffed. "How so, Mr. Blackwood? Is this untrue? These people make poor choices and as such, they live in poverty and squalor. How could such a simple truth be offensive?"

"Shit," Ishmael breathed, speechless for once.

"I find it amusing that you would look so unfavourably on people who are trapped in cycles of financial strain," Illea laughed. "After your failed endeavours with—oh bless me, I can't even recall all your failed ventures! Lucky for you, you have considerable family wealth to fall back on, even if it isn't the wealth of *your* family."

The silence left in the wake of Illea's statement was smothering, spread all the way down the table. Tashué cursed himself for saying anything. Now everyone was looking at them, and he had become the spectacle he didn't want to be. Myron's mouth worked but no words came. Illea smiled brightly at him, leaning forward to retrieve her wine. Tashué looked to General Wolfe, trying to read the man's face. *Is this what you wanted?* he wanted to ask. *Is this what you chose me for?*

Rainer shifted and cleared his throat. "I must agree that it is a more nuanced issue than you're trying to portray it, Myron."

Leony lifted her chin again. "Indeed it is, Governor. In fact, it is a matter that I take quite personally. I would think that the Governor of the people of Yael would also take it seriously."

"Yes, my Queen," Myron said, his face flushing again. "Please forgive me. I misspoke, your Majesty."

"Perhaps think more carefully about your words before you speak in the future," Leony said.

"Sir," the servant finally whispered, leaning low over Tashué's shoulder, "would you like more wine?"

"Yes please," Tashué said.

He plucked the empty glass off the table and twisted into the narrow space between him and Illea, holding the glass up to have it refilled. Beside him, he heard Imburleigh gasp, then choke, and the table dissolved into chaos. She rose out of her chair and

Rainer rose with her. He caught her arm and patted her on the back.

Leony half-rose too and nearly everyone else at the table shot to their feet, sending chairs clattering back. "General Imburleigh, are you alright?"

"I'm fine!" Imburleigh gasped, waving Rainer away. "It's just that I noticed—Captain Blackwood, you have blood on your jacket! Are you injured?"

Oh fuck. "Ah—no," Tashué said. He'd forgotten about the bloodstain, about the fight in the Hive. He cleared his throat. "I was in a fight, earlier."

Imburleigh took a deep breath, grabbing her napkin to dab at her face in an attempt to recompose herself. "That looks like a lot of blood, Mr. Blackwood."

Ishmael laughed outright this time, a hand slapping against the table as he leaned back in his chair. "General Imburleigh, are you telling me that the owner of the Imburleigh Armament Company and former General of the Imburleigh Division is squeamish over the sight of blood?"

Mallory turned to Saeati, shooting him a withering glare. "Excuse me, I served my time with blood on my hands. You'll forgive me for being surprised to see blood on a man while I was sitting for dinner with our Queen!"

Myron's face had turned deep red and he shot to his feet. "This is too much! Please forgive me, Miss Imburleigh. You're absolutely right. This is obscene! You, sir, will not sit at my table covered in another man's blood!"

Illea smiled at her husband, rising smoothly. "Not to worry, Myron, the solution is quite simple. We have extra clothes upstairs— some of the hunting tweeds might fit him. Perhaps not formal enough for this setting, but fortunately our Queen has already forgiven us for any mistakes made this evening."

Myron's face drained of all its colour. His hands were still clenched at his sides, but Tashué could see the slow retreat in his eyes. Myron couldn't tell her no. He wanted to, so badly it made his hands tremble, but then she would defy him and shame him even more.

Myron cleared his throat, looking away from Illea, searching the faces of the servants all around the table. "Someone please show Mr. Blackwood upstairs so that he can change."

Illea smiled, hooked her arm in Tashué's again, dragging him to his feet. Tashué fought the urge to shrug her off. He hated all the attention landing squarely on him, all these people staring. But pushing Illea away would only make it worse. Maybe stepping out of the room was the thing he needed. Fourteen fucking courses of this shit, he couldn't do it. They were still only on the first one. Fucking soup.

"Not to worry, Myron, I'll make sure he is well dressed."

"Illea, please…"

Illea turned to Leony, smiling. "Would you excuse us, my Queen? It won't do to have a man with bloody clothes at the table."

Leony smiled back, though the blush returned to her cheeks. "Of course, Miss Winter. I understand completely."

Illea bowed her head. "As ever, you are most generous, my Queen. Follow me, Mr. Blackwood."

15

TASHUÉ

DAY 6

"I must admit, Mr. Blackwood, I can't say that Rainer himself could have designed a better beginning to a political career," Illea said as she climbed slowly up the stairs. "No one will forget the name Blackwood, not now. Once Wolfe steps back from the Mayor's office, you'll snap it up without much effort at all."

Tashué followed Illea up, making sure to leave space between them so he didn't step on her flowing silk train. She crested the top of the staircase then paused and looked back at Tashué as he caught up. The neckline of her gown scooped low across her back. Her hair had been piled in a mass of braids and beads atop her head and a single lock sat like a black feather down the back of her neck —not corkscrew coils like Stella, but a thick wave.

Tashué shook his head. "I am not even remotely interested in the Mayor's office."

"We hope you'll reconsider. The General won't be running again and he wants to have someone loyal to him and to the common man run in his stead."

"Is that what all this was about?" Tashué wasn't sure if he was angrier still, or relieved. At least now he knew. "I thought I was here for Myron and Rainer."

"Oh, heavens, no. I mean—yes. When Rainer was looking for someone for his little project, Nathaniel and I seized the opportunity and recommended your name. But really, we've been looking for something like this for some time, now."

"Something like what, exactly?"

Illea glanced up at Tashué, giving him one of her liquid smiles—a smile that he'd enjoyed a couple of days ago, at Bellmore's. But now he wasn't so sure. "Something like you. To come in and disrupt Rainer's stranglehold on politics here. Nathaniel will want to explain it all to you himself."

"I am very sincerely not interested in a political career."

"Well, there's time to think about it. Don't discount us yet, Mr. Blackwood. We can be very charming and persuasive when we decide we want something."

"Is this supposed to be part of the charm, then?" Tashué snapped. "Dinners like that?"

Illea laughed. "I can't say that dinners at my home are always quite so interesting, though I wish they were. We'd give the prudes down in White Crown something to whisper about, wouldn't we? And while they were whispering and tittering about the dinner tables of Yaelsmuir, we would take the power from their fingers, one little grain at a time, until all they had left was dust. Although I'm curious why it makes you so angry. You held your own remarkably well. I think you'd fit in quite well to Yaelsmuir's political landscape."

"You don't understand why I might be upset by watching a close friend make an ass of himself to distract attention away from the tension in the room—which was only caused by my presence?"

Illea snorted. "How much do you know about Ishmael Saeati?"

"Plenty."

"Does it please you to know that he always behaves like that at functions like this?"

Tashué stopped walking, looking down at Illea. "Why do you think that is, Miss Winter? Why would an intelligent, articulate, highly capable man act like a court jester for you people? Could it be because he knows nothing he'll ever do will be good enough because his parents are from Qasan and he was born in Cattle Bone Bay instead of Highfield?"

"Mr. Blackwood, I can't speak for everyone else. Perhaps you're right, perhaps he behaves that way because he knows what people expect of him... but he also does it to hide things, to camouflage what he's capable of. And I promise you, I don't care a wit for who his parents were or where he was born. I can tell you the same thing: I don't care who you are, or where your son is. I care what you can do."

Tashué took another slow breath, forcing it into his chest. "And what might that be, exactly?"

"That remains to be seen, doesn't it?" Illea headed down the hall again, stopping at one of the doors. She leaned against it, but the bustle at the back of her dress made a curve of her body, her hips tilted toward him. "I must admit, if it weren't for the fact that I found it so attractive, I would be terribly annoyed that you got blood on that suit. He bled a lot? The man you fought with?"

"Yes," Tashué said. It wasn't the first time in his life he'd met someone attracted to him for the blood on his hands—or on his jacket, as the case may be. "He bled a lot."

"Let me see."

Tashué pulled the front of his jacket closed, lifting his arm. Illea's eyes roamed the shape, studying the borders of the stain with the same hungry intensity she had when he was being measured by Bellmore. It was a primal thing, to be proud of blood spilt, to be excited by it, drawn to it. He wondered if she took soldiers to her bed often, asking them to whisper stories of battle in her ear as their bodies pressed together.

"How did you get so much of another man's blood on your jacket?"

"I broke his jaw with an ashtray."

A shiver passed through Illea's body, the skin of her neck and exposed shoulders going tight with gooseflesh. "Where did the blood come from, then?" she asked. "If you only broke his jaw."

"I had to hit him a few times to put him down. The impact

sliced up his face." Tashué shrugged. "I'm losing my touch, I suppose."

Illea smiled and leaned toward him. "I find that hard to believe."

She opened the door, turning into the room. The back of her neck was still tight with gooseflesh when she turned away from Tashué, the long black lock of hair drawing the eye down all that olive skin that was exposed by the low scooping hem of her bodice. He took a deep breath again and followed. To say that talk of her attraction didn't have an effect on him would be to lie, but it mixed with his anger and made something ugly.

The door opened to a suite of rooms that was larger than Tashué's entire apartment. The first room they stepped into was adorned with enough seating and side tables for a dozen people. The large window at the end of the room caught his eye. Night had settled on the city, but once he reached the window, he could see the other windows of the manor lit from within. It gave the manor the appearance of a constellation, spread along the horizon instead of up in the sky.

How had he come to be here? He'd never set foot on this side of the river until he went to Bellmore's. Rainer Elsworth had never given him the time of day in all his nineteen years of service to the Authority.

And Illea Winter. He could feel her gaze on the back of his neck, making his heart beat faster.

"Are you attached to someone, Mr. Blackwood?"

He turned from the window, shuffling through his pockets as he looked at her. She wasn't looking at him as he'd imagined. She was tucked away into a smaller room off the sitting room he stood in. The wardrobe she shifted through was a massive piece of hardwood furniture, oiled to a smooth polish. Her bright yellow gown made her shine like a beacon of light among dark furniture and wood-panelled walls.

"Attached?" he echoed.

"Yes." She turned to him again, taking a half step away from the wardrobe. The step made her body appear longer somehow, the train of her dress staying where she had been standing and her body arching up away from it. He felt the intensity of her eyes even from the distance between them, the way they seemed to be cutting into him and shuffling through him, trying to figure out his inner workings. "Is there a woman in your life that you're attached to? Or a man perhaps? Is that why you're so concerned with Mr. Saeati?"

Tashué looked down at his case rather than stare at her anymore, busying himself with the ritual of lighting a cigarillo. Attached? Yes, he was attached. His heart was attached. His mind was attached. Every breath he took was attached. To Stella Whiterock. But he wasn't meant to be with Stella.

"No, Miss Winter, I'm not attached. Not to Mr. Saeati or anyone else."

"Is it my husband, then? Does it comfort you to know that we haven't touched each other in nearly ten years?"

"Why would it comfort me to know of your mutual misery? What kind of man do you think I am?"

She watched him a while, her head cocked to one side. It was a slow look, the way she took his measure. "Clearly I have no idea the kind of man that you are," she finally said, turning back to the wardrobe.

She drew out a suit, closing the door and hanging it on the hook on the front of the wardrobe. Her movements were quick and sharp as she smoothed out the jacket, picking off a few pieces of lint. It was hunter's tweed, hues of brown and green, the jacket lined with bright green silk. He'd never seen so much silk in his life as there was in the Winter estate. Who wore silk to go hunting?

"This should fit you," she said, stepping back. "The Queen's brother wore it once or twice and he was almost as tall as you."

The prince of the Dominion wears silk to go hunting. Tashué took another drag of his cigarillo and looked around for an ashtray. There was one on a nearby table, small and delicate and brass.

Illea turned to him, meeting his eye. "I can't be rid of him—Myron, I mean. His father was an excellent attorney, you see, and built a contract around our marriage that I can't escape. If I throw him out of my house, he gets a stake in my businesses and a chunk of the estate. My family has been building the Winter name for generations... He doesn't deserve it, not a single bent copper crown. At least if he's here, I can fund his damned political career to keep him busy."

"Why doesn't he just leave, then?" Tashué asked. "It sounds like it would be lucrative for him to simply walk away."

She smiled, but it wasn't the bright, beaming thing that Tashué had become accustomed to. Some of the weight of the years of her bad marriage settled on Tashué's shoulders as he tried to imagine what it must have been like. "Ah, but my father wasn't completely addled in those last months. He insisted on a clause that made sure that Myron wouldn't get a thing if he initiated the dissolution of the marriage."

"You're trying to drive him away?"

"Absolutely."

"Why do you hate him so much?"

Illea sucked in a deep breath, baring her teeth and glaring at him. "How can you ask that? I saw how angry he made you. Would you like to live with him for the next ten years?"

Tashué shook his head. "That's different."

"How?" Illea snapped, and the snarl that curled her lip was probably the most genuine moment he'd seen from her since he met her. "How is your righteous rage different than mine?"

"You have power over the man, don't you? How many lovers have you trotted in front of him? In front of his peers—*your* peers. It's all just a game to you people, up here. The whole fucking city is just the field for you to play your games with each other, isn't it?"

"Is that what it comes down to?" She leaned toward Tashué, taking a few steps toward him. "I'm a bad wife so that makes my life a game. But you, sir, you're the down-trodden common man from Brickheart, so you get to burn incandescent with fury? Please. Why did you come here, then, if you were so busy judging all of us for the crime of being born wealthy?"

"I came because General Wolfe asked me to." The way she leaned in, it dragged Tashué closer, and he was stepping toward her without thinking about it, even though he was so viciously angry. "I was under the impression that I was here for some good reason, not just for you people to gawk at me like I'm a trained ape."

Closer, closer, until he could have touched her if he reached out. But she glared at him, her fury making her tremble. "If you didn't want to be perceived as an ape, why did you behave like one?"

Tashué's breath hissed from between his teeth, the tension draining out of him. Not because he wasn't angry anymore, but because it shifted to something colder. "Sure. I'm the ape here. This was a mistake, clearly."

Fuck these people, every one of them. Illea and Myron and Rainer, fuck them for being so predictably awful, but fuck Wolfe especially for dragging him into this shit. No, he wasn't going to play this game; he didn't have the time, or the energy, or nearly enough patience.

He stalked away from her, toward the door. He dragged it open, slammed it behind him—the solid wood gave a satisfying *bang*, and the whole frame rattled. The sound only stoked his anger. He stomped down the hall to the stairs. How would he even get out of this fucking place? It was a maze of big rooms and small ones and bending hallways. Hadn't he seen another staircase on his way in? Fuck this place.

He stopped at the top of the stairs. The sound of the diners bubbled through the house like some distant, babbling stream, but it was an ugly sound that made his gut clench. He was missing some piece still, something that might make it all make sense.

He spun on his heel and stalked back, pushing the door open and slamming it again once he was through, giving another satis-fying smash. Illea stepped out of the other room to meet him, like she was ready to fight with him some more, like the whole vicious thing gave her a thrill.

"Why me, then, Illea?" Tashué asked, stalking closer, closer. She didn't give any ground, meeting his eye as he closed in. "Why fucking me? Myron—he said something about my son. Is Rainer planning on holding my son over my head if I don't play his little game?"

Illea gave a lazy shrug. "I haven't the slightest clue what Rainer plans."

"That's a fucking lie—you have every clue, don't you? That's what *you* said. You put on this act to distract people, just like Ishmael. So why me?"

Illea's lip curled and her nose wrinkled, but still she held his gaze. "I expect Rainer knows your son is a weakness, yes. He'll be hoping you get it in your head to start asking for favours, and he'll keep giving them to you so long as you keep dancing for him."

Tashué took a deep breath. Jason. That thought pierced through his anger. How much was Rainer willing to give him if he 'kept dancing'? "But it wasn't Rainer's idea, was it? You said it was General Wolfe's. So why me?"

No snarl this time—a smile instead. Illea leaned forward, coming up on her toes like she was coming in for another kiss, but she stopped short. "Why, that incandescent fury of yours, Captain Blackwood. It really is quite delicious. The people of this city will lap it up when you hit the campaign trail. Nathaniel will put his hand on your shoulder, and he'll use that calm, paternal voice that he does so well. But you can't be soothed, can you? And whatever snivelling crony Rainer puts up to oppose you can't possibly survive in your shadow, because you'll have Winter money and Wolfe's approval and Blackwood righteousness. You're perfect for the job."

"I don't want it."

"Yes you do. Look at you. You love to be the hero. And maybe you don't like duelling wits with Myron and Rainer, and I don't blame you. But your campaign won't be about them. It will be about Brickheart and the Bay and In the Tracks. And all the many ways you get to be their hero."

Tashué shook his head. There was no point telling her anymore that he didn't want it. She wouldn't believe him.

But he didn't walk away—Jason kept him rooted in place. Would Rainer really do it? Would he let Jason out?

"Ah, there it is," Illea said. "The decision to stay. I won't bother asking what changed your mind. You'll probably lie to both of us and say it's for your son. You'll need to get changed, though. Can't have you wearing a bloody suit at the table with the Queen."

"Perhaps I could have some privacy then, Miss Winter."

Illea cocked her head to her side. "Why, Mr. Blackwood? Are you bashful? Colour me surprised. You seemed so comfortable the last time you were undressing in front of me."

"I liked you more the last time I undressed in front of you."

Her hand came up so fast that Tashué didn't have time to react. The slap echoed like a thunderclap in the room, made his face burn, made his chest tight. Another slow breath, in and out. He clenched his fists, focusing on the ache in his hands instead of the fury that was making it so hard to breathe.

"Who are you to judge me?" she snapped.

"No one," Tashué said. "Is that what you want to hear? I'm no one."

"If that's what you think I want to hear, you aren't listening to me. I don't care *who* you are, I care what you can do. But look at you —how old are you? The Black Ridge was twenty years ago, so you must be in your forties now, or near to it. Where's your wife, Tashué Blackwood? Your only son is in the Rift, and you drift through the world alone. Where are your roots, what is your legacy? What have you built for your son? Nothing. You're a man of nothing. So who are you, with your nothing, to judge me for trying to honour the legacy my father built for me, and fight against Myron and all the ways he tries to tarnish it?"

"Where's *your* legacy, then, Illea Winter? This big house that you didn't build? The lumber yards in the Dunnenbrahl that you didn't buy? Where are your children?"

She lifted her hand to slap him again, but this time he saw it coming, this time he knew how she breathed in right before she swung and he knew that her arc was high and fast—he caught her wrist before the slap could connect. She clenched her fist, glaring across the short gap between them, but even still she leaned closer.

"Whether or not I have children has no bearing on whether or not I leave a legacy for the future."

Tashué shook his head, leaning closer. "I didn't say it did. You did, though. You asked me where my wife was, why I only have one son."

"I'll have children when I'm rid of Myron. Having you here was supposed to help with that. He won't stay, not if he loses this election. He won't announce his candidacy tonight." She shook her head and she smiled, the tension draining out of her as her eyes sparkled. "He can't, not after what we've done. He's made such a fantastic ass of himself in front of the Queen. She's really quite fond of Ishmael, and now you, too, by extension. He'll have to wait until after she's gone back to White Crown or risk her voicing her disapproval, but Eirdis Redbone will be starting her campaign tonight. It all went better than I could have hoped, you and Ishmael together like that, and you with blood on your suit so I could bring you up here to let everyone know I intended to have you."

A deep breath came easier this time. It was all so fucking ridiculous that it was almost funny. He let go of her wrist and she dropped her arm to her side. She turned away quickly, heading back to the second room, where the wardrobe stood, where the silk-lined hunting tweed was waiting. And Tashué followed, cursing himself for following her so eagerly, following her with the memory of her body so close that he could feel her chest heaving with fury, the memory of her wrist in his hand, pulse pounding beneath his fingers. He closed the second door behind him as he followed, another slam, but this time it didn't rattle so dramatically.

"Well?" she asked, stopping beside the wardrobe and turning to him. "Are we wasting time with more fighting, or are you going to take off your clothes for me? Do you need an order, is that it? You military types usually like that. Captain Blackwood, I command you to take off your clothes."

Tashué shrugged out of the jacket, but the sleeve caught on the cuff-link and he had to wrench his arm free, frustration returning. He tossed the jacket aside, starting on his waistcoat next—at least the buttons were easy enough to undo with one hand. Illea stepped in closer, reaching out to him, to the silk, her finger sliding around the edges of the blood stain like she wanted to memorize the shape of it. He had to unhook the chain of his timepiece to get out of his waistcoat, and that slowed him, just a little. No matter how angry he was, he couldn't bear to damage it. He put it into his trouser pocket instead, to keep it a little bit safer. The waistcoat came off more easily and he tossed it aside, but there wasn't enough weight to it for it to go far.

He shrugged out of his suspenders next, letting them fall around his hips. The buttons of his collar, the buttons of his shirt. Harder, these ones, and opening them made him remember Stella, in his apartment, her breath on his face, her hand on his beard. Leaning close to button his collar, so close that it made him weak because all he wanted was to reach out to her and crush her against him and kiss her, but he didn't dare. But Illea, she was right there, almost as close as Stella was, and he had no power over Illea.

Illea reached out, grabbing the front of his shirt and dragging it up out of the hem of his trousers so he could finish unbuttoning the front. He fought out of his shirt, cuffs tight because he hadn't opened them. The loose undershirt was last, and she reached out, sliding a single finger down his chest, down his navel, to the hem of his trousers. And the trail she left, the trail she scorched across his skin with nothing but a finger, wound him even tighter.

"Keep going," she said, meeting his eye again. "You can't wear autumnal plaid like that with the hunter's tweed. They don't match."

Tashué reached out, grabbing her by both arms and dragging her closer. The bodice of her dress was rougher than he'd imagined, the boning and the embroidering digging into his chest. But she leaned in, even as he pulled her, leaned in and let him kiss her. He slid his hands up, up to her shoulders, touching what skin was available to him, along her arms, her shoulders, that line of her back. Slid his fingers up the back of her neck, until they found her hair, thick and silky and bundled so fiercely atop her head with combs and pins. She jerked away from him, slapping his hand.

"I don't have time to fix my hair if you make a mess of it."

"Yes ma'am."

She scowled. "Don't call me ma'am, you ignorant ass."

Tashué scowled back—*ignorant ass*—but he still kissed her again.

There wasn't anywhere to lay her down in this fucking room, just a dressing table and a few chairs that were way too small for him to be comfortable in, and the wardrobe. He pushed her toward it, just a few steps away, pushed her until her back hit it and the whole thing rattled. The suit, the stupid hunter's tweed, fell off its hook and over her shoulder and he flinched away to avoid the hanger hitting him in the face. She huffed and pushed against him, getting away from the wardrobe. Grabbed the hunter's tweed and threw it on the floor, kicking it out of the way. Threw her arms around his neck, pressing her back against the cold wood and dragging him in again. She kissed him so hard that he had to put a hand on the wardrobe to steady himself. The bustle at the back of her dress was pushing her hips forward again, pressing her against him. He reached down, dragging all the layers of skirts up, but there was no skin to be found under there, only her drawers and her stockings.

A frustrated noise rumbled in Tashué's chest, all the barriers making him burn with impatience. "How do I get you out of this fucking dress?"

"If I don't have time to fix my *hair*, what makes you think I have time to get undressed and dressed again?" Illea said. She kissed him again before he could respond, reached down to drag her skirts up further, then broke away, just enough to speak. "Take off your trousers, Captain Blackwood."

Tashué kicked off his boots as he reached for the buttons of his trousers, pushing them down with his drawers. He stepped away from her long enough to fight out of every last shred of clothes, watched her chest swell with her deep, fast breaths, watched the flush settle in her cheeks, watched her eyes as they scanned his body. She had such dark eyes, dark and beautiful and hungry, and they drew him back in so easily. She lifted a leg to hook it around his waist and he leaned down, grabbing her other thigh and bracing her waist to heft her up. Her back slid up the wardrobe so easily and he stepped between her legs, long and elegant and strong.

She kicked off her shoes once she was off the floor, pressing her stocking feet into the back of his thighs. The split drawers she wore gave him access without having to undress her. He pushed deeply into her. She gasped in his ear, letting her skirts fall against his chest so she could wrap her arms around his shoulders, her fingers sliding down his back and running across the deep canyons of his old scars. Her face was above him now that she was up so high and she had to lean down to kiss him. He tilted his head up to meet her. She gasped every time he pushed into her, and it made him tremble, that sound she made. Made him tremble, the feeling of her. The gasps were getting louder and she leaned away from him, pressing back against the wardrobe. Louder, louder, every time he moved, every time his hands squeezed her thighs, just to feel the warmth of her. He leaned in, pushing his face into her neck, feeling the sweep of her collarbone beneath his lips, tasting the first sheen of sweat that emerged on her soft olive skin.

Her hands shifted, sliding up his neck, into his hair. She nipped the skin just behind his ear, teeth scraping, breath hot and fast. She pulled his hair, dragging his head back so she could look him in the eye.

"Slow down," she breathed. "Don't finish yet."

He groaned against her mouth when she kissed him and groaned again when she bit his lip. Another shift put her hips at a different angle and he took a deep breath. The angle let him push deeper and her legs trembled, even as he forced himself to go slower. She still had him by the hair, holding his head in place, watching him. And she was so beautiful, so primal and raw, still so *angry* but not with him, not anymore. She kissed him hard. Her fingers relaxed, sliding through his hair. Every part of her trembled. He could feel her toes curling, digging into his thighs. He went faster again, he couldn't help himself, not when she was trembling like that, not when she was kissing him so hard, not when she started to gasp again. He broke the kiss because he couldn't focus, couldn't think, couldn't breathe. Couldn't breathe until he finished, and even then it was just a single strangled breath, a groan that forced its way out.

Illea sagged back against the wardrobe, chest still heaving, eyes still locked on his. She smiled. Tashué leaned in to kiss her neck and taste her sweat again before resting his forehead on her shoulder.

"Pull yourself together, Captain," she breathed, patting his shoulder. "We have a dinner to attend."

He let her down, holding her until she had her own weight on the floor again. She stepped away quickly, to the dressing table, where she retrieved a bell and rang it just once. Tashué barely had time to get back into his drawers before a hidden door opened at the back of the room and two women in Winter livery stepped through. The first went for Illea, fixing her hair and the back of her dress, smoothing the creases and adjusting the bustle, making sure everything was as it was before Tashué pinned her to the wardrobe and fucked her. The other came at him like she was going to help him dress, shit, but he waved her away and grabbed the hunter's tweed himself. The second servant made herself helpful by emptying the pockets of the Bellmore suit instead, laying everything in a neat line on the dressing table while Illea watched. Tashué winced when the notepad hit the desk, the corners of the photographs sticking out and faded, creased by his pocket and starting to fade. But Illea didn't touch it.

"Whatever Myron says to you, don't get angry anymore," Illea said, watching him dress. "If he's drunk—which he might be—he'll throw a little tantrum, maybe say something vicious about your son. Don't give him power over you. Don't let him see that he can needle you. Whatever he says, just think of him as a toddler, one who's up past his bedtime and is lashing out. If it helps, remember which one of you will be sleeping in my bed tonight."

"Oh?" The servant was hovering, watching him struggle with the damned buttons. He nodded at her, dropping his hands. "And which one of us will that be?"

"You, of course," Illea said, the smile making a return. "If it were up to me, we wouldn't waste time going downstairs at all, but it would be disrespectful to the Queen not to return. He might not throw his tantrum, though. Rainer might have told him to settle down. Sometimes he listens to good advice."

The waistcoat of the tweed was a little snug, and when he pulled on the jacket, the arms were predictably short. The servant took the collar and the cuffs from the Bellmore shirt and affixed them quickly. It felt strange to mimic the same motions that he had done with Stella, the leaning down, the holding out his hands. Another reminder of the person he *wanted* to be with.

He filled his pockets with all of his belongings, and the servant followed to help him thread the chain of his pocket watch through the buttonhole. He almost asked her to stop fucking helping. He wanted to catch her hands, to push her away. What had been intimate and beautiful when Stella did it seemed obscene now with the taste of Illea's sweat still on his lips. The servant ran her hand down his waistcoat, smoothing it out.

"That's sufficient, Beatrice," Illea said.

"Yes, Mistress."

The servant gave a curtsy and retreated, out through the little hidden door at the back of the room. Tashué took a deep breath, resisting the urge to light another cigarillo. Illea leaned in, reaching up, sliding her fingers through his hair. Smoothing it, after making such a mess of it. She grinned, something small and friendly.

"I sent Beatrice away too soon. You've some of my lip rouge on your face. It's not your colour, I'm afraid." Her hand plunged into the hidden pocket in her skirt, retrieving a kerchief. "Don't forget. Whatever he says, it doesn't matter. You have the power over him, now. But don't be boastful or crude. We won't mention it, none of this, not even if Ishmael makes one of his jokes. We don't need to. Everyone knows."

She led him out after he'd wiped his face, down the hall. She hooked her arm in his elbow as they made their way down the stairs, back to the dining room. A servant was waiting for them, his hand on the door. He pushed it open just a crack, just enough for them to hear that the Queen was speaking. Illea held Tashué's arm, waiting until the Queen was done, and when someone else started speaking, the servant pushed the door open and let him through. Rainer was speaking, of course.

Everyone did their very best to ignore them as they approached. Except Ishmael. He sat with his elbow on the table, his chin on his knuckles, plate empty and glass full, eyes looking distant and tired. Or bored. Until Illea and Tashué stepped into his line of vision. His eyes flicked up to Tashué's face, just for a moment, but settled on Illea. Illea wasn't looking at him, though. She was whispering something to the Queen as she sank into her chair, so Illea didn't see the expression that crossed Ishmael's face. Dark, angry. Ishmael sucked in a deep breath and glowered at Illea for just a moment, a blink, and then let his breath out and forced himself to relax. He reached for his glass and looked at Tashué.

"Cheers, Captain," he said, lifting his glass and giving Tashué a nod. "The tweed looks good on you."

———

D awn hadn't yet arrived when Tashué was woken by his own restlessness, his need to be moving. Illea didn't stir as he rolled from the four-post bed, as he started to dress. He fought with the buttons of the tweed. They weren't as small and frustrating as Bellmore's suit and he was able to manage on his own. He paused beside the bed, looking down at her as she slept. Should he wake her to tell her he was going? Would she care?

He laid a hand on her shoulder. She stirred, rolling toward him.

"I have to go back to Brickheart."

"Yes, of course," she said, rolling away again.

He stepped out of Illea's room, trying to remember the maze of hallways and stairwells that led him here. It was worse even than the dressing room, where they first had sex, because at least that room was within view of a staircase. He headed for the end of the hallway, where a window was lit by the moon. Maybe if he could see where in the house he was…

A soft whistling stopped him. Ishmael came sauntering down the hall, a lazy grin spreading across his face. "Good morning, Captain."

"Well, Ishmael," Tashué said, shuffling through unfamiliar pockets to find his cigarillo case, flicking it open and offering one to Ishmael. "You stayed the night too, did you?"

Ishmael grinned as Tashué tossed him the box of matches. "Who am I to deny the Queen? I am just a humble citizen of the

Dominion, serving at her Majesty's pleasure." He took his first breath of smoke as he shook out the match, nodding down the hallway. "You're going the wrong way to get out. Follow me."

Ishmael led him out a different door than the grand entrance he had come in, this door smaller and around the back of the property. They emerged looking out over the Brightwash, the cliff falling sharply somewhere not too far ahead of them.

"It's a long walk to the tram station in Boardwalk Market. Do you want one of the General's carriages to take you?"

Tashué reached for his timepiece, flicking it open. Dawn was on its way soon, but the sun was late to rise with the steady decline of autumn. If he was going to be promoted to Station Commander, he should update as many of his files as he could so they would be ready for whichever Officer took over his cases.

Tashué nodded. "Thank you."

Ishmael perched his cigarillo between his lips, stepping closer to Tashué and taking the timepiece from his hand. He leaned over, holding the timepiece to his ear for a moment. "Your timepiece is slow. Do you wind it regularly?"

"Of course."

Ishmael took a long drag of his cigarillo, turning the timepiece over in his hand. "How old did you say this was?"

"Shit, it must be thirty years old now. My father bought it for me. Right before he died."

"So my father made it himself... Maybe I even helped. Can I fix it? It's going to irritate me, knowing one of my father's pieces is out in the world, not keeping time properly."

Tashué unbuttoned his waistcoat where the chain was tucked through unhooked it. Ishmael pulled the chain free, his movements slow and reverent. Neither of them needed to mention how much emotion was in this one little timepiece, with both of their fathers laying their hands on it. Fathers that had been gone too long.

"I'll get it back to you in a few days," Ishmael promised, flicking his cigarillo away. He tucked the pocket watch into his breast pocket, buttoning his overcoat closed as if to protect it further.

"Thank you."

Ishmael nodded and turned, heading up the street. He shuffled through his pockets again, finding a handful of candy and popping one in his mouth.

"That was an experience I don't want to repeat," Tashué muttered as the distance between them and the Winter estate grew.

Ishmael laughed. "But Captain, you did so well. Invited to stay the night and everything."

Tashué stopped, reaching out to Ishmael and grabbing his arm. "Why do you do it? Why do you let them talk to you like that?"

Ishmael shrugged, popping another candy in his mouth. It smelled of lemon and sugar and he rolled it back and forth with his tongue a few times, looking back toward Illea's manor. "What do you think I would achieve by throwing a tantrum, demanding they treat me with respect? That makes it worse. Then I'm asking something of them that they won't give me, and I'm left looking like a limp cock."

"Then why make it worse? Why act like that?"

Ishmael snorted again, looking up at Tashué. "Like what? Like myself? Fuck them and their manners and their etiquette. I won't diminish myself for their approval. I am who I am and I'm sitting at their fucking table anyway, aren't I? And when the Queen wanted company last night, she sent for me. Not a single other person in that room could ever have a chance with her, and there isn't a damn thing they can do about it."

"That's enough, is it?" Tashué asked. "Getting fed and fucked, that's enough payment for letting them laugh at you?"

"Captain," Ishmael said, the grin returning, warm and mischievous, dark eyes shining in the light of the brights, "that's all there is. We eat and we drink and we fuck, and then we die." He shrugged again, turning away from Tashué and heading down the street toward Wolfe's manor. "Besides, it's good, letting them think I'm a drunken idiot. Then they don't notice everything else."

"I thought you didn't do 'everything else' while you were home in the Dominion," Tashué said, glancing down at Ishmael. 'Everything else,' the things the diplomatic division had trained him to do.

Ishmael stopped again, turning to Tashué. His teeth clamped down on the candy and Tashué heard it shatter. "Things change."

Tashué leaned closer, the distance between them suddenly feeling too open. "What does that mean, Ishmael? What things are changing?"

Ishmael shook his head, but he took Tashué's arm, squeezing hard. "I can't tell you this part. I'm sorry, but I can't."

"Don't you think I have the right to know what the hell I'm getting into?"

"No, it's not like that. This stuff isn't connected, not really. I'm just helping Wolfe with his political shit because he's finally had enough of Rainer. And I'm helping you because you're about to be caught between them."

"That's not comforting in the least."

Ishmael grinned. "It should be. Means you've got me on your team, and the team I'm on never loses."

The wind was cold and sharp off the river, and Ishmael cursed, pulling up the collar of his coat. Tashué followed him up the slope of the hill that climbed to General Wolfe's estate. Again, Ishmael avoided the front door, leading Tashué around the back of the manor. As they walked through the grounds, familiarity ticked something in Tashué's memory. He had been to Highfield once before—for Amias's funeral. He remembered that awful day in bits and pieces. Remembered Illea, her body splayed on Amias's casket, weeping so openly and with so much pain that it made Tashué's throat tight with emotion. He remembered General Wolfe, his face grey with pain and grief, leaning on his new cane because his broken leg still hadn't healed quite right but he was determined to stand for his son's funeral. He couldn't remember who had taken Illea by the arm and led her away. Maybe it was her father.

He met Ishmael that day. He'd gone wandering through the house to get away from all the weight of grief out in the gardens, and found himself in the kitchen. Ishmael found him there, cravat gone, hair mussed, eyes distant. Tashué remembered that Ishmael's suit was very fine, but too big, hanging off him like he was nothing but bones, a suggestion of a man.

"Do you want something?" Ishmael asked, pulling Tashué out of the past. "The kitchens will be ramping up for breakfast."

"I could use coffee. Lots of coffee."

"I see it's still just tobacco, coffee and whisky for Captain Blackwood. Do I have to start forcing you to eat again?"

"I ate more at the Winter's house than I have all month, I think."

Ishmael snorted. "I'm sure you did."

Tashué sighed. "How are you thirty-five and *still* immature about sex?"

"Excuse me, Captain, I'm thirty-*six* and I have cultivated my immaturity very carefully. What did I tell you? Eat, drink, fuck."

Tashué shook his head, trying to tell himself not to be surprised. He'd known Ishmael a long time now, and he knew enough to recognize that some parts of him, drinking and sex especially, were a shield against the ghosts floating around his head. "You're missing something, though. Probably the most important part."

Ishmael paused at the door, cocking his head at Tashué. "Which is?"

"Family."

"Well, that comes from the fucking, doesn't it?"

"Does it?" Tashué asked. "You and I, we've done plenty of fucking in our lives. Don't have much family to show for it, do we?"

The smile disappeared from Ishmael's face and Tashué cursed himself for saying it. What would family even look like for Ishmael? He was away more than he was home and certainly the diplomatic division wouldn't let him bring a wife and children along with him on those postings he wasn't allowed to talk about.

Ishmael shrugged at him again, opening the door and stepping right into the kitchen. The heat was thick and welcoming, sliding around Tashué's body as he stepped inside. There were near a dozen people working already, a kind of organized chaos as they made breakfast. It seemed like too much work, just for breakfast. Nathaniel was the only Wolfe living in the massive house, after all. There was so much about life on this side of the river that Tashué didn't understand.

Ishmael, on the other hand, folded into the chaos so effortlessly. There was water already boiling on the massive wood stove and Ishmael found the coffee beans, passing them through the burr grinder clamped to a counter. Tashué stood back and watched him, how easily he laughed and joked with the various staff that populated the kitchen. He existed so naturally, everywhere he went. How did he do it? Tashué envied him the ability to fold so well into any moment when Tashué seemed to spend his life bouncing off people, grinding against the world. Never quite fitting anywhere.

Ishmael found a pot to steep the coffee, and poured over the grinds, laughing with one of the bakers all the while. He sent someone off to wake a driver. A tray of rolls came out of one of the ovens and Ishmael snatched a roll, tossing it between his hands as steam wafted from it. He grinned and threw it at Tashué, and Tashué had to react quick to catch it. It smelled of cinnamon and sweetness. In spite of not thinking he was hungry, he broke it open. Cinnamon sugar had been swirled right into the crumb, which released a puff of more steam. The bread was warm and buttery and sweet, a good breakfast while waiting for coffee. But even as Ishmael poured their cups, General Wolfe came into the kitchen, cleaving through the chaos instead of folding into it.

"Good morning, Captain. Will you come speak with me a moment?"

Tashué met General Wolfe's eyes, trying to read him. No one had mentioned what Tashué and Illea had done when they returned to the table. These people were so careful, their faces like masks, concealing what they really thought. Illea Winter should have been Wolfe's daughter-in-law. Did he care who she took to her bed, since it couldn't be Amias?

Tashué cleared his throat. "Of course, General."

"Shall I come, General?" Ishmael asked, plucking another roll off the tray.

"Please." Wolfe led Tashué out of the kitchens, into a fresh maze of hallways. "I would welcome you to my home, but I suppose you aren't staying for a social call. You'll be waiting for one of the carriage drivers to take you back to Brickheart?"

"Yes, sir."

Wolfe nodded as he put more distance between him and the kitchen, heading out into the open air. The courtyard that they stepped into housed a half dozen horses, and Tashué watched a pair of stable hands lead a big dun coloured mare out of the stables to dress her in draft tack.

"You don't have to look so guilty, Captain. I'm not going to scold you. Illea Winter is a grown woman and it's no business of mine who keeps her bed warm." Wolfe settled on a bench and stretched out his leg. He grimaced, his fingers digging into the muscle just above his knee. "I suppose Miss Winter spoke to you about our hopes for your political career."

The anger that returned was hot and ugly and unexpected. He thought he'd worked through it all with Illea. "Why didn't you tell me sooner, General? I would have liked some warning that you'd pulled me into this to derail Myron's campaign."

Wolfe winced, glanced up at Ishmael.

"I told you, didn't I?" Ishmael said with a shrug. "Comes from getting fucked by the Dominion military one too many times. They go in dry, without any foreplay to get you ready. Makes a man want to know what's coming at him."

"I'm sorry, Captain. I wanted to say something, but I wasn't able to find time to speak to you privately. It was important that Rainer didn't know the idea came from me and Ishmael, or he wouldn't have chosen you."

"I'm not interested, General," Tashué said, trying to breathe through the frustration. "I'm sorry. I'll dance for Rainer, but I don't want the Mayor's office."

Wolfe sighed, leaning back on the bench. "I hope you'll reconsider. I won't be running again next term. The Queen's voting council has taken advantage of my busy schedule in Yaelsmuir and they like to hold meetings when I can't possibly make it. If I run for election again, I fear all the work I've done in the voting council will be pulled apart. But I don't want Rainer to install another of his lackeys in my place. Yaelsmuir has had enough of Rainer Elsworth's influence. This city is in crisis, and we need real solutions."

Tashué took a deep breath. "Sure, excellent. I believe you. Every word, I'm with you. I don't trust him either, especially after meeting him. I'm with you, General, I really am. But I can't help but remember what Myron said, when he was talking about me as if I wasn't even in the room. 'Isn't this the one with the tainted son in the Rift?' And Myron, he didn't really understand what he was revealing, did he? He really is as much of an idiot as Illea thinks he is. But you know, it makes me wonder what might Rainer do to my 'tainted' son in the Rift when he realizes that I'm not playing on his team."

Wolfe shook his head. "I'm sure he wouldn't—"

"He would, General," Ishmael interrupted. "He absolutely would."

Tashué watched the shock pass across Wolfe's face, and it dissolved some of his anger. Wolfe was a rare man, with his long service in the military, his ties to Highfield, and his honest belief that people were better than they really were. He spoke of distrusting Rainer but was still surprised that the man was capable and willing to further threaten Jason's safety. Surprised, because such a thing hadn't even occurred to him. It was what Tashué had always liked about Wolfe. That he still had the capacity to be surprised by the darkest parts of human nature.

"That's why you're in such a sour mood, hey?" Ishmael asked. He blew the steam off the top of his coffee and took a sip, not even flinching at how hot it must be. "You're worried now, about Jason. About how fucking Illea has inadvertently put Jason in some kind of danger."

It hit like a punch, right to the gut. It was hard to breathe again, in the wake of those words. "Yes. That's exactly what I'm worried about."

Ishmael shook his head. "No, this is still fine. All you have to do is plead ignorance. You weren't trying to interfere with the campaign—how could you have known? Illea is very persuasive, isn't she? Rainer knows all about how persuasive she is."

"That's not a detail I cared to know, Ishmael," Wolfe said with a sigh.

Ishmael shrugged. "Those days are a long time gone. He still remembers them, though. He'll understand."

Wolfe shook his head, fingers digging hard into his thigh. "I say it's none of my business who warms Illea's bed because I truly, genuinely hope that you will stop telling me the details."

"I would try, General, but Miss Winter passes a lot of politics through her bed, and you asked me to come home to help with politics."

Tashué sighed, watching the stable hands guide the dun mare backwards to affix her tack to the carriage. "I don't know what you think I can do. Why me, then? Illea seemed to think it was for all my righteous rage, but that doesn't sound like something you'd care about."

"You're the hero of the Black Ridge, Captain," Ishmael said, sipping his coffee again. "Army manual teaches the Ridge as part of the curriculum now. They put it in five, maybe ten years ago. They tell a good story about the plucky young Captain Blackwood, who executed a textbook entrenchment on the Ridge, so that he and his Jitabvi savages could hold it long enough for the 12th to come rescue them with their artillery."

"Don't fucking start with that 'savages' shit, Ishmael," Tashué snapped. "I'm so sick of hearing it."

"I know, Captain." Ishmael reached out, grabbing Tashué's arm, maybe trying to anchor him, to save him from his own anger. "Look at me. We Qasani, we usually aren't as dark skinned as most Jitabvi, and our culture isn't quite as wild, but we get the same shit from people around here. Trust me when I say that I know exactly how sick you are of hearing it. Every bit of it and more." Ishmael leaned closer, meeting Tashué's eye. And he was burning, too, the anger smouldering in those dark eyes. So maybe he wasn't trying to save Tashué from his anger, when he held onto Tashué's arm. Maybe they were just going into the vicious heat of it together. "That's what the manual says. That word, exactly. A textbook entrenchment by Captain Blackwood and his Jitabvi savages, holding the Ridge until the 12th artillery could rescue them."

Tashué took a sip from his coffee, fighting the current of all those memories. "Me and my savages held the Ridge with a text-book entrenchment, did we?" His voice trembled when he spoke and he sucked in a deep breath. "Why'd I get fucking flogged for it, then?"

Ishmael snorted. "Wouldn't that be because you defied a direct order to pull off your nice little textbook entrenchment?"

"Men with small minds are responsible for your flogging, Captain," Wolfe said. "It wasn't right, what they asked of you on that ridge, and it wasn't right that someone wanted to punish you for it for trying to stay alive. Your death would have accomplished nothing. Your survival turned the tide of that battle. It fills me with shame that the military, who I gave my life to, sent so many soldiers onto that ridge to die, because they were Jitabvi and they were expendable."

Tashué shook his head, looking down into his cup. He tried to breathe through it, the anger, the bitterness. He might have been able to move past it all, if he had been able to come home and his regular life had been waiting for him. But his mother had died while he was trying to survive the Ridge, beaten to death in the streets, a man calling her a *filthy Kaadayri whore* while Tashué entrenched when he was supposed to attack. Attack downhill, on terrain that would kill their horses on a charge, down into a position that the Ibeh soldiers had well fortified.

"How many lashes did they give you?" Wolfe asked. "I've heard the stories, but…"

Tashué looked up at him, his hand clenching on the cup so hard that his knuckles were white. The mug was still hot, the coffee inside still steaming, and it hurt to grip it like that instead of holding the handle, but the pain kept him here in the courtyard even as parts of him were returning to that moment when Keoh looked at him with tears in her eyes and told him, *I'm sorry, I'm so sorry, your mother is dead.* "Fifty. Maddox wouldn't let them hang me, but I think they'd hoped I'd die from the lashes."

Ishmael squeezed Tashué's arm again. "Fuck them."

"That's what I said," Tashué breathed. He shook his head,

swinging back to Wolfe. "I don't see how getting a flogging and a medal qualifies me to be Mayor of Yaelsmuir."

"It doesn't help you in the office, no," Wolfe admitted. "But it does help you get elected. That's the important part. It's hard to find a candidate enticing enough to pull on the voters in the Bay, Brickheart, In the Tracks. Either they don't care enough to be bothered, or they vote how their employers tell them to—and since most business in this city is owned at least partly by someone in Highfield, they vote how Rainer tells them. But a man like you? With your Shield, and your service, and, yes, your energy and your fury and all the things that make you so memorable, you could pull people in. If you agreed, you wouldn't have to think about this sort of thing. Illea, Ishmael and I will take care of all the political subtleties. Once you're in the Mayor's office, you can keep all the staff I've collected over the years. They're all very good—they'll know what to do. Through you, I could continue funding projects like the hospital in Brickheart, while still being available for the Queen's Voting Council."

"I would be a figurehead?"

"Truthfully? Yes. The alternative is one of Rainer's figureheads, and I daresay that's worse."

Tashué took a deep breath, but General Wolfe rose, patting Tashué's shoulder again.

"Don't say no just yet. There's two years still for you to decide. I know it's a big change, but think of the good we can do for this city."

Tashué took a deep breath. "What about Jason, General? I'm not agreeing to anything until he's safe."

"Well," Wolfe said, glancing up at Ishmael. "We'll just have to find a way to make him safe, won't we?"

Ishmael threw back the last of his coffee, giving a shrug. "I suppose we will."

16

TASHUÉ

DAY 7

Stella sat on the front steps of her building when Tashué made it back to his apartment. She wore her uniform for the Facility still, but she'd pulled the combs from her hair, leaving it loose over her shoulders. Ceridwen played among her gang of friends, kicking a ball made of rags—a new one this time; they were masters at improvising fresh balls. They dodged carts and horses and pedestrians as they played, their squealing laughter pealing up around them.

"Good morning, Mr. Blackwood."

Her voice was soft, tired, but when his eyes met hers she smiled warmly and his chest felt hot and tight. Guilt tore through him. The memory of Illea sat like a hot stone in his memory. He felt as if he'd betrayed Stella. But what was there to betray?

"Good morning, Miss Whiterock."

"That isn't the suit I helped you into," Stella said, her head cocking to one side.

"Miss Winter lent it to me. I went down to Cattle Bone Bay before I went to Highfield and I got blood on the Bellmore suit."

"Blood? How?"

"I was in a fight in the Bay."

Stella stared at him for a long moment. "You were given a suit made by the finest tailor in Yaelsmuir so that you could go sit at a banquet with the Queen, but before you went to Highfield you stopped in Cattle Bone Bay and got in a fight?"

"Yes."

She laughed, and the sound was so beautiful. It pierced him and all the anger left him, draining him like a knife to a water skin. He wanted to press his face into her neck and feel that laughter, feel the warmth of her. "That's too bad. It was a fine suit."

Tashué nodded. He never seemed to know what to say to Stella, because all the things he wanted to say were wrong.

"Are you alright, Mr. Blackwood?" she asked.

"Yes," Tashué said swiftly. "It was a long night." Heat crept up his collar and he regretted his choice of words instantly. Long night, indeed.

"You should sit with me," Stella said. She sat up a little straighter. "For a little while. Watch the children play. Enjoy the warmth of the sun."

She slid closer to the edge of the steps, leaning against the banister. She patted the step beside her and his body was drawn to her. As he settled on the steps, the door behind them swung open and someone emerged from the building. Tashué slid closer to Stella, so close that their bodies pressed together, her shoulder digging into his arm. The wind pulled her hair across his cheek, the strands getting caught in the stubble. He closed his eyes. It was as if he'd been holding his breath all morning, lungs aching, body buzzing, blood boiling in his very veins. But sitting here, beside her, her hair caught in his beard, he could finally exhale. He remembered the feeling of her hands against his chest, her breath on his neck as she struggled with his buttons.

"How was your dinner, then?" She tucked her hair over one shoulder to stop it from blowing in Tashué's face. The wind had other ideas, and soon the long strands were flying through the air between them again, curling over his shoulder. "With Illea Winter and the Queen."

The heat returned. "The food was very nice."

"And the company?"

Tashué almost laughed. Had she heard the rumours? Was she asking if they were true? "Rich people have a lot of rules."

Stella smiled, closing her eyes and turning her face toward the sun to catch its warmth. He wondered how she would react if he leaned in and kissed her. On the neck, just below her jaw, to get her attention so that she would turn to face to him again. And then he could kiss her on the mouth, taste her lips.

"They do have a lot of rules," she said with a nod. "It must be worse here in Yaelsmuir, with the royal family so close. Cruinnich wasn't so... judgemental."

"They had a lot of alcohol, too, which helped."

She laughed, opening her eyes and turning toward him. Meeting her eye made him ache, the memory of Illea turning from a shield to a burning pit of shame. *You can't have Stella*, he reminded himself. *You haven't betrayed her because you can't have her.*

But then, belatedly, he realized what she had said. "Were you wealthy in Cruinnich?"

She didn't hesitate, turning her face toward him and smiling. "The life of a stevedore and his wife is not one of wealth," she chuckled. "My neighbour was a maid at one of the big houses, and she had all the best stories. Besides, you don't need to be wealthy to know the gossip of the city."

Tashué searched her face. He couldn't tell what exactly had bothered him about what she said, just that something crawled across his skin. Like when she said, *Mother expected us to help in the kitchen.* It didn't fit the timeline that he understood for Ceridwen to ever have helped in the kitchen—she was just over a year old when Stella left.

Stella smiled at him, tilting her head to one side. Was there fear in her eye or was he imagining it?

"You seem especially tired," she said.

He sighed, all the tension flowing back out of him again. "I am."

She nodded. "I keep hoping that if I sit in the sun long enough, some part of me will bloom and grow. Like a flower."

"The sun probably isn't warm enough for that anymore," Tashué said. "It's too close to winter now."

She shrugged. "There are plenty of flowers that bloom in the autumn. Some even in the winter."

"Then maybe you aren't meant to be a city flower. You're meant to have more room to grow and fresher air."

"Aye, maybe that." Stella turned her face back to the street. Ceridwen was on her knees, tying a length of fabric back together so that the ball would stop unravelling. "She's a city flower, I think. Seems she was meant to grow in the crags between all these stone places, with so many people to talk to."

"I've seen Ceridwen's like before," Tashué said. "She'll bloom no matter where she is."

"You're probably right. Perhaps I'll take her somewhere else, far from all the cobblestones and factories."

Tashué felt breathless at the suggestion, like the moment was slipping away from him. Her body was so close that he could feel the rhythm of her breathing, but he also felt so very far away from her. Was she joking about leaving, or was it something that she actually considered?

"Would you perhaps come with us, Mr. Blackwood?" she asked. "If we were to find some open space where we could grow like wild flowers?"

Yes, his mind screamed. *Yes*, his body howled. He wanted to say, *Stella Whiterock, I will follow you anywhere.* Instead of his affections being distracted by Illea, it had only made him burn for Stella all the hotter, a reminder that no other person was right when Stella existed. His hands ached to reach out to her, to take her in his arms, to press his face into that beautiful hair, to feel her skin against his body. He stuffed his hands into his jacket pockets instead, leaning back on the step behind him.

"I've always been one for the city myself."

"Oh."

The silence between them made him ache.

"That reminds me," she said, sitting up straighter. "I have a gift for you. Do you have a moment? I know you're always busy—could you wait here?"

"Of course, Miss Whiterock."

She smiled and stood, putting a hand on his shoulder to lever herself up before stepping around him to head into her apartment. A gift? Sweet North Star, that sliced him open. He'd spent the night with Illea Winter, and Stella had gotten him a gift.

He reached for his cigarillo case, trying to comfort himself with the familiar motions of lighting one. Trying not to remember how good it felt to sleep with Illea, how miserable he felt after because he still hated her a little. But then, she probably hated him, too. Or she liked the chaotic energy, the fury and the passion, the anger that crawled through both of them because neither of them could have exactly what, or who, they wanted.

It took Stella a while to go up and then come back down, letting Tashué smoke and watch the children to calm his nerves. She sat beside him again, squeezing her body into the gap she'd left, leaning closer still when she handed over the bottle of whisky. The label hit him hard, knocked the air out of him. He recognized it so completely that it made his ears ring, made him feel small and young again. Ladovaugh, in simple print, the black ink silhouette of a bird in flight nestled between the d and the h, the silhouette of a man harvesting peat at the bottom. It made his chest tight again, but there was no room for anger, not anymore. Just memory. Pain, but the old and distant kind. The kind that you had learnt to live with, the kind with dull edges.

"It's not any of their fancy vintages, just the regular," Stella said. "Blended, I'm afraid. Their single malt goes for a pretty crown down here in Yaelsmuir. What's your father's name? Is it Blackwood?"

"No," Tashué breathed. She was leaning so close that their shoulders pressed together, her face inches from his. He looked into her green eyes and he ached. "No, ah—Blackwood was my mother's name. I signed Blackwood when I joined the military, because I was angry at him, for dying. Sounds so stupid, but I was just a boy and being angry was easier than hurting." He cleared his throat. "My father's name was Guinne."

"Guinne," she said, nodding. "I was thinking, about that bottle of yours, the cask strength. I think your father's family came from Ladovaugh."

"The distillery?"

"The island. A lot of whisky distilleries up in Fuar exist in these small rural communities—or rather, small rural communities spring up when some crazy person decides to start brewing whisky in the middle of nowhere. Ladovaugh is the big island north-west of Riguan's Valley. They grow the barley on the biggest islands, harvest the peat from the fens on the smaller islands. Takes longer to grow peat on the fens than it does on the bogs, so they have to manage their harvest carefully."

Tashué cleared his throat, trying to dislodge the emotion that sat so heavily there. He put the bottle on the steps between his feet because he couldn't bear to hold it anymore, to look at that label. "What makes you think that? I'm sure plenty of people drink Ladovaugh and have no idea where it comes from. It's very good."

"It is, you're right. But someone gave him a bottle of their cask strength whisky on his wedding day." She pushed some of her hair out of her face, but the wind was relentless. "The thing about the rural distilleries is they often fail. They're always balanced on the knife's edge between survival and shutting down. And usually when a distillery fails, the people in the village make due, until someone new comes along to revive the business. But when Ladovaugh shut down, over a hundred years ago now, it was so hard for those people on the islands, to make a living. They didn't have much in the way of livestock, because every-thing was about whisky—all they had was barley fields and peat fens. Back then a clan called Duncreek was scooping up land that didn't belong to them, and they were trying to get up onto the islands. But the Duncreeks have always been trouble makers and I expect the island folk didn't want to work for them. So families left. Some went to other distillery towns, some just went down into the Dominion… But then, about sixty years ago, someone started making Ladovaugh again. Laid their first good batch in old oak casks for eighteen years. And the story goes that it came out of the casks so beautiful that they couldn't bear to water it down, so they sent it out at 120 proof. Those bottles trickled down into the Dominion and it was very emotional for the families that left. It was a signal to them that Ladovaugh was alive again. A lot of descendants went back. Ladovaugh has been open ever since."

Tashué turned to her again. She was leaning so close, her weight resting completely on his shoulder. The wind had her hair and it was swirling all around her face, all around him. A copper curtain, shielding them from the world, so that all he could really see was her. What was it about her, then, this one woman who left no room in his mind for anyone else? *Everything.* It was the sound of her voice and the smell of her hair and the freckles on her cheeks. It was that she knew that left-handed swordsmen were harder to fight and what a nibu was. It was that she was so tired, but also so quietly strong, lovely and resolute, turning her face to the sun so that she could bloom. It was that she knew where his father's whisky came from, that somehow she looked at him and knew *him* better than he knew himself.

A lock of hair caught on Stella's lip and he reached up before he could stop himself. Slid his fingers across her cheek to catch the silken copper curl, and pull it away from her face. She was breathing faster, leaning closer, her mouth free of that curl, of any barriers that might stop him. She met him in the middle of the small gap between them, her breath hot and shaky against his mouth, but her lips were so beautifully soft. Tashué leaned back, sliding his hand across her cheek so that he could look into those beautiful green eyes again, to see himself reflected in them. To see himself how she must have seen him. She didn't leave the distance between them; she leaned in, against his hand, and he kissed her again. She took all of the sadness out of him, all the weight of the old grief. It was just the two of them, hair and skin and the cold wind that pushed them together, and a bottle of whisky.

But it's not right. You're her tinman and none of this is right.

He broke away, taking a deep breath. Took his hand off her cheek and grabbed the bottle of whisky instead, closing both hands around the cold glass and the paper label. Another deep breath, try to calm that racing heart.

"Thank you. I didn't know any of that." He cleared his throat, looking down at the label again. His father had told him what bird it was, but he couldn't remember. "What happened to the Duncreeks? Did they get a foothold on the islands?"

"The Duncreeks," Stella echoed, but something had changed in her voice. It had gone quieter and she shifted her weight so she sat up straighter. Not leaning on him anymore. "Um, no. No, there wasn't anything on the islands for them, not once the people started to leave. Didn't know how to harvest peat or grow barley or turn it into malt." She cleared her throat. Why had her face drained of all colour? She pushed her hands through her hair, gathering up all the stray curls and twisting it into a braid so it stopped swirling around them. Something had been lost, some-thing precious, their togetherness shattered by... what? "They just have their land now, up in Riguan. The Duncreek and the valley around it. Still troublemakers, though, the lot of them. Still petty and vile."

"Do you know them?"

She turned to him, tension crawling up her whole body, so that her shoulders hunched up around her face. She folded her arms over her chest, like she was hugging herself, like she was suddenly cold. Her eyes met his and he felt she was searching for something, but he couldn't imagine what. He wanted to reach out to her again, but... Was she upset that he'd kissed her? Shit. That was exactly what he didn't want, exactly how he didn't want to make her feel. The ringing settled in his chest, like he was a bell and his own sound was reverberating back into himself, ringing with shame.

"No," she said finally. "No, I don't know any Duncreeks. Their reputation precedes them."

"Mr. Blackwood!" Ceridwen came skip-running through the crowd. "Mam is making sour cherry pie after supper today. She wanted to try making it because you said it was your favourite."

A deep blush climbed along Stella's neck, settling on her cheeks. But her hands were shaking and she clenched them into fists, pinning them under her arms to hide it. There was no hiding it, though.

"I can't stay, little warrior," Tashué said, looking up at Ceridwen. "I'm sorry."

"Oh." Ceridwen's shoulders slumped. Again, that *oh*, the secret weapon of the Whiterock family, a tiny syllable that contained all the weight of their disappointment. "Alright."

"Go play, Pigeon."

Ceridwen turned and ran away again, finding her friends and folding back into the game. Tashué looked back at Stella again. She took a deep breath, her chest filling, her back straightening, losing some of that deflated hunch that made her look so small.

"Stella, I'm sorry," Tashué said. He didn't lean closer, didn't try to touch her. He gripped the bottle tighter to keep his hands busy, because if she was upset that he'd kissed her, touching her now would be no comfort to her at all. "This is a wonderful gift. The whisky and knowing where my father's family might have come from. Thank you."

She unfolded her arms, just long enough to reach out and touch his beard again, fingers sliding with the direction of the grain. Her fingers felt so good, but it made the shame burn hotter still. He shouldn't have kissed her. He pushed himself to his feet, smoothing out the front of his trousers with one hand and tucking the bottle of whisky beneath his arm.

"Thank you," he said again. "I should go. Change and… perhaps do my job for a few hours."

"Yes, of course," Stella said. Her voice was so distant now. "Have a good day, Mr. Blackwood."

"You as well, Miss Whiterock."

17

STELLA

DAY 7

Kissing Tashué Blackwood had made Stella's body feel more alive, more vibrant, more beautiful, than she had felt in a terribly long time. The way he touched her cheek, the way he looked her in the eye, the way the warmth of him leached through his clothes, it all lit something in her that she'd thought was dead. It didn't even matter that he'd probably slept with Illea Winter the night before—gossip travelled fast and she'd heard the rumours already, of how the pair of them behaved at the banquet. Stella had laid no claim to him and he owed her nothing. All that mattered, really, was how perfectly easy it was to sit with him, to lean against him, to offer him her theory of where his father's family came from and bear witness to the emotion passing across his face. To let him kiss her. Big hands and rough stubble and soft lips, everything about him was so…

She would fall in love with him, if she let herself. If she stayed in Yaelsmuir much longer, she would fall in love with him.

But talking to him about Fuar and the Duncreeks was the timely reminder she needed that she couldn't stay in Yaelsmuir. She was running, after all. Running and hunted. She'd become so tired in the last years, so exhausted that she'd forgotten the sharp edges of her fear, forgotten how precariously she was balanced in this life she had fabricated. If Tashué found out… No, best not think of that. And he was the least of her problems. Siras Duncreek was after her, and she'd been in Yaelsmuir too long.

She waited for the inevitable *Mam, can I…* from Ceridwen. She asked to visit with her friend Gill for lunch because his mam was making something special.

"Yes, Pigeon, that sounds fine."

"Really?" Ceridwen gasped. "Thank you!"

"Ceridwen, I've some errands to run," Stella said, pushing herself to her feet. "You stay with Gill until I come back."

"Yes, Mam!"

To the Market, then. She didn't want to go down into the Bay, even though there was more river traffic there. She walked fast. She wasn't tired, not anymore. She tried to pinpoint the moment when she'd lost her fear, but it must have been a gradual thing. A wearing away, bit by bit. The exhaustion took the place of everything, forcing everything out, but Tashué…

That made her falter, thinking of him. Leaving, it meant leaving *him*. How long had they known each other, drifting in each other's orbit, coming to know each other slowly? Stolen moments, talking about pocket watches and the weather and Ceridwen. She liked how he shared sweets with Ceridwen, how he played in the street with the children sometimes, especially in the summer when it was so hot that it was hard to be serious about anything and the days were so long that it seemed like the sun was begging you to play. She liked everything about him except his tin badge. And maybe, with a bit more time, she could come to understand him well enough to know why he wore the badge when otherwise he seemed to be a kind and compassionate man, but there was no more time left to her. She had to leave. Take Ceridwen and go.

The Wharf in the Market saw considerably less traffic than the Bay. The barges there mostly carried perishables, fruit and vegetables from the farm lands to the north. It would be easy enough to book passage on one of the barges. She needed a few days. Time to gather what she needed to make another trip, to start another life.

Ceridwen, oh Ceridwen. She would be so heartbroken. All the other times Stella had moved them, Ceridwen had been too young to know what she was leaving behind. Not this time. This time she had so many friends. Stella tried to think how she might soften the blow, but her imagination failed her. Just the anticipation of Ceridwen's grief made a tight ball of emotion in Stella's chest, made her eyes water.

"Can I help you, Miss?"

Stella blinked through the tears, to the kind and earnest face of a man. He carried a bushel of carrots under one arm, greens still attached, orange roots still covered with earth. "Who might I speak to about booking passage south?"

"South, is it? To White Crown? Not many go down that way, not from here."

The man rubbed his chin, leaving a smear of dirt on his stubble as he turned from Stella, scanning the faces of the many people crowding the Wharf. She almost asked him what it would cost to go north. How far did they go, all the way up past Northern Garrison? She could go back to Fuar, maybe, the home of her heart and her soul. She didn't have to go to Cruinnich. She could find some small settlement in the mountains and stay there, somewhere quiet, the sort of place where you didn't see your neighbours unless you actually wanted to, somewhere craggy and remote. Could she survive up there, all by herself? Farm a little patch on the mountain, hunt for meat. Would anyone even question her up there?

But would Ceridwen ever be happy in a lonely place like that?

Would people in Fuar recognize Stella's face?

"Ask Gilda," the man said finally, pointing across the Wharf. "See there, she wears the scarf over her hair. She'll go down to White Crown now and then, she brings up the dried fruit, doesn't she? Go see when she's headed down that way again."

"Thank you, sir."

Gilda smiled and nodded when Stella asked her if she was going down to White Crown. The thought that she was really leaving made her throat tight and she wiped her eyes. Damn it all, she was making a fool of herself.

"Have family in White Crown, do you?" Gilda asked.

"Yes," Stella lied. "My father, he hasn't been well. Mother worries this is the last midwinter we'll get with him, so I'd like to go. Are you leaving soon?"

"Next week. Is it just you travelling?"

"Me and my daughter."

"Aye, I fancy I could make room for you. Don't take passengers much, but, well. This sounds important."

"Thank you," Stella gasped. "Thank you so much."

18

TASHUÉ

DAY 7

E ven though it had been less than a week, the tide of the Brightwash was getting higher, with autumn rains swelling the banks. The water was too deep for Tashué to stand in the spot where the girl was found. He crept as close as he could, the near-freezing water sliding over the toes of his boots as the rocky bank shifted beneath his weight. The bank was lit by brights, casting his shadow into the water, the form of him crossing the spot where she had lain. Tashué could still see her in his mind's eye, small and grey and so terribly broken. Returning to the bank with the long shadows of night crawling across the city, Tashué felt guilty. He'd spent the night before feeling entirely too comfortable. But he hadn't yet fulfilled the promise he'd made to that little dead girl, so wretched and small.

With a curse, Tashué kicked at the stones and turned away from the water, trudging back up to the street. *Pint Under the Rails* was an inviting place as he bucked against his own guilt. What else could he have done? Refuse to attend the banquet? *Sorry, General Wolfe, I can't attend the banquet. I found a dead girl and I can't do anything else until I find out how she died.* And how long would that take? Would he ever know?

And now they wanted more from him. Mayor Blackwood. The thought made him cringe. He hadn't thought about it all day, trudging through the city to update as many cases as he could.

He'd thought about Stella, though. Thought about her plenty. Thought about the rise and the crashing fall of his own emotion, of the moment between kisses that he looked into her eyes and felt so incredibly close to her, and the moment where the distance between them opened like a yawning chasm. How had he read the situation so badly?

He stepped into the *Pint Under* as a tram passed overhead. The whole building shuddered with the passing energy and the misery bled from the Talented operator in the front car, sitting all across Tashué's skin like a fog.

All the familiar faces were at the bar, each leaning over their own bowls of the stew and the hearty dark bread. Pallwyth saw him coming first, lifting his head from something he was doing behind the bar and offering a smile and a nod.

"Evening, Mr. Blackwood. Are you looking for dinner?"

Tashué settled beside Kazrani, trying to shake off the heaviness in his shoulders. The girl from the Brightwash, the Black Ridge, his mother, his father, Stella, it all blended together in a muddy mess in his head. "Yes please, Mr. Pallwyth. And a pint."

"No whisky?" Kazrani asked. "You must be in a good mood."

Good mood, shit. He couldn't bear to drink the acid, not with Illea Winter's smooth whisky a memory on his tongue, and not with his father's Ladovaugh bringing back the scent of all that peat smoke to his nose. "I had plenty of whisky yesterday."

"How was it then?" Beckett asked, leaning on the bar to see around Kazrani. "Did you really meet the Queen?"

"I did," Tashué said. "She was lovely."

Duskan snorted. "I'm sure she was. And Illea Winter? How lovely was she?"

Tashué rested his elbows on the bar, leaning forward to look across Kazrani at Duskan. "I very much enjoyed Illea Winter's company, Mr. Hillbraun. Thank you ever so much for asking."

Duskan scowled. Pallwyth delivered a pint of stout first, then disappeared back into the kitchen.

Kazrani leaned closer to Tashué, as if there was any privacy to be had at the bar, or anywhere in the small pub. "Is it true, then? You spent the night?"

Tashué let out a long, slow sigh. Of course the gossip had spread beyond Highfield. What else could he really expect? And of course Kazrani would want to know—there were no boundaries between them, not after all these years. They'd broken through all of that with khat and sweat and their bodies on the plains of the Hadia more than twenty years ago. "Yes. I spent the night."

Kazrani's eyebrows went up and she sank back again, pushing the last of her stew around her bowl with her spoon. She waited until Pallwyth delivered Tashué's meal and then leaned in again. "Are you sure you want to get yourself involved with Illea Winter, of all people?"

Tashué snorted. "If you met her, you would know that what I want has very little to do with anything."

Kazrani scoffed. "Tashué Blackwood, you had better not be trying to tell me that Miss Winter took you against your will."

"Sweet heaven, is there anything you won't complain about, Blackwood?" Duskan huffed. "Was it a great trauma for you, then? Must be because you couldn't keep up with her."

Tashué laughed, but it was a short and bitter sound, all the anger bubbling in his chest anew. "Judging from what I've heard at the station house, the only one here unable to keep up with women is you. Disappointing Duskan, they call you."

Beckett laughed, too, sharp and fast, and then he clamped his hand over his mouth. "Sorry. I shouldn't laugh. Happens to the best of us."

Duskan's face went deep red and he shot to his feet, his barstool clattering behind him. He stomped around Kazrani to come in behind Tashué's stool, his fists clenched at his sides. "Say it again, you fucking asshole."

Tashué clenched his teeth, grinding them together until his jaw ached. He turned on his stool to face Duskan. He didn't stand, but his face was level with Duskan's, looking him in the eye. Duskan wore his fury like a shield, his whole body writhing with the energy of it. And with the memories of the Ridge dragged back to the surface, Tashué wasn't as calm as he would have liked to be. He took a deep breath. Duskan was his colleague, soon to be his Officer if the promotion went through and the station house became his. Another breath, and he reminded himself that Duskan wasn't responsible for all the things that made him so angry about the Ridge. About what came after. About Highfield, and all those damned people. Duskan was just a man with something to prove and not enough sense to see that he was looking for a bigger fight than he could handle.

"Go sit back down, Hillbraun," Tashué said, forcing a calm that he didn't feel. "Before someone gets hurt."

"Fuck you, Blackwood! You think you're so much better than the rest of us, going to fucking Highfield. But while you were up in Highfield like some street whore summoned by Illea fucking Winter, the rest of us were here working."

Tashué leaned forward, even though he knew he shouldn't. Even though he was older, should have been more mature. Reached out and grabbed the front of Duskan's jacket, dragging him in so close that Tashué could smell the beer on Duskan's breath. "You think you're insulting me by calling me Illea Winter's whore? I've been called worse, by better men than you. You want to get up on your hind legs and yap at me a bit, that's fine. Go yap over there, at your spot, so I don't have to smell your shit breath anymore. But if you think you're over here for a fight, to prove you're the tough guy, I suggest you give it some close fucking consideration. Because unlike you, I don't need to prove myself in front of an audience. I know exactly who I am and who I can hurt. And son, you aren't man enough to hurt me."

"Better listen to him, Hillbraun," Kazrani said, using a finger to swipe the last of her stew from her bowl. "Even I don't fuck around with him when he's in a mood like this. I'll bet it's the Ridge, rattling around his head again. And the Ridge usually makes him want to break things."

Tashué grinned at Duskan, letting go of his jacket and shoving him back. "So, what are we doing? Are you yapping, or am I hurting you?"

"Fuck you," Duskan hissed, and he tensed like he was really going to take his chances.

The door stopped him—it swung open and Pallwyth cleared his throat, drawing both of their attention. A young woman paused in the doorway, no doubt waiting for her eyes to adjust to the dark interior of the pub. She was a small woman, inky black hair pulled back into a thick plait, a few strays hanging around her face, and a massive satchel hanging off her shoulder.

"Morning, miss," Pallwyth said. "Will you take some dinner?"

"No thank you, sir." She took a step in, scanning the faces at the bar again. "I'll take a pint of amber if you have it."

Pallwyth nodded, stepping to the keg. Beckett righted Duskan's stool, dragging Duskan away.

The woman paused a moment, looking between Duskan and Tashué both. "Am I interrupting something?"

"Nothing important," Tashué muttered, turning back to his stew.

The woman was still watching him, warm brown eyes taking measure of him. She settled at the bar beside Tashué, lifting her satchel and resting it between them. It hit the wood bar top with a heavy thunk and Tashué wondered what she was carrying around with her.

"You look the part, don't you?" she asked, cocking an eyebrow at him. "I can see why you're the talk of the city now."

"Excuse me?"

"You're Tashué Blackwood, aren't you?"

"I am."

She nodded at Pallwyth when he delivered the pint, dropping a few coins on the bar. "The gossip isn't exaggerated much, I see. You're taller than I expected."

"Is there something particular I can help you with?"

She stuck out a hand, her fingers stained with ink. Tashué accepted the shake. "Mr. Blackwood, my name is Allie Tei. I am a reporter for the *Highview Times*. Would you come sit with me for a bit? I have some questions for you."

Duskan groaned. "Fucking hell, he's getting interviewed. You make sure you tell her that you weren't man enough to keep Illea Winter happy and she had to take you against your will."

Her professional face wavered for only a moment, her lips curling inward as she tried not to smile, but her eyes never left Tashué's face.

"No, thank you," Tashué said, turning away from her and reaching for his own pint. "I'm not interested in an interview with the social pages."

"I understand that, Mr. Blackwood. A gossip rag like the *Highview Times* isn't for everyone. And although our readers would *love* to know about what you have to say about last night, that's not why I've come to find you." She paused to sip her beer, reaching for her satchel with the other hand, but she didn't open it yet, just pulled it a little closer. Her eyes flicked across the faces again. She cleared her throat. "I had hoped you would be willing to talk to me about the girl you found."

That made Tashué's heart skip a beat. *The girl you found.* No one else was interested in the girl he'd found. But when he looked down at the woman again, she couldn't hide the eagerness behind her mask of professionalism.

"Will you come sit? I understand if you're busy, of course, since you're a Regulation Officer. But I could start with some questions and then maybe we could set an appointment for a time that would suit you better."

"No, I can make time." He stood so fast that he almost knocked the stool over. "Come, there's somewhere to sit out back."

Allie shot to her feet, dragging her satchel off the bar and snatching up her pint. He led her to the back of the pub and out the door to the small patio Pallwyth kept back there. Eternally shaded by the elaborate structure that kept up the tracks, it was a cool place to sit in the heat of the summer, if you could learn to ignore the roar of the tram when it passed overhead. Tashué dragged a chair out of the small storage shed, tucking it up to one of the tables. His hands shook as he went for the second chair. *The girl you found.* Finally, someone else knew. Someone else cared.

"How did you know about the girl?" he asked, setting the second chair by the table and sinking into it. "How did you find me?"

Allie sank into the chair opposite him, setting her satchel beside her leg. "How did I find the only man in Brickheart ever invited to a banquet with the Queen? That part was easy."

"And the girl, then? How did you know about the girl?"

She bit her lip. She leaned down, opened her satchel, and drew something out. It looked like a small scrap of paper. As she reached across the table, Tashué could see that it was an article, clipped from a news page. "I know what it is to look at a face like that and wonder how something so terrible could have come to a child so young."

Tashué took the article. It may have been a tiny scrap of paper, but the words seared across his soul as he read.

What Happened to the Boy Beneath the Bridge?
by Allie Tei

Everyone surely remembers the baby boy found beneath Park Bridge three weeks ago. He was very young and wounded, but no information has been found as to his identity or what happened to him. He has since been interred at the cemetery of the Sisters of the White Veil. The sisters have procured a headstone, which reads "Park Bridge Baby Boy," and only the date that he was found. It seems a shame to let him be forgotten.

If you know anything about the Boy Beneath the Bridge, please contact the Highview branch of the City Civilian Patrol.

Tashué read the article five times. When he looked up, Allie wouldn't look him in the eye. She looked at his hands, at the lapel of his jacket, at their pints. Hers was mostly drained. She watched the foamy head slide back down the inside of her glass.

"What is this?" Tashué asked. "What does this have to do with the girl?"

"My editor wouldn't publish any more than that. The readers of the *Times* have no desire to be rattled by such sordid details as the wounds of a dead child. If they wanted crime statistics, they would send for the *City Watch*, or perhaps for a thrill they would read *Yael's Yells* from down in the Bay. And yet I can't help but wonder, if they had published more, would you have known to come find me when your girl washed up on the bank? We might be closer by now to finding out what happened."

"Tell me what happened to him, then," Tashué pressed, leaning closer. "Tell me what you know."

"He was found with his arms and legs removed. He had been dead some time, before he was left beneath the bridge. He had a tattoo on the back of his neck. Some kind of code, some series of numbers. I can see by the look on your face that all of these things sound familiar. Your girl, she was in the same state, wasn't she?"

The tram came rattling down the track, the vibration of the whole structure silencing them for a moment with the hum and the vicious tingle down Tashué's spine. He rested the article on the table in front of him, smoothing the wrinkles and the dog ears out of it.

"She was." The now familiar weight pressed down on his shoulders, but at least he was finally talking to someone who cared. "Except one of the wounds hadn't healed. I thought maybe the infection killed her. It was so deep that the bone was exposed."

Allie nodded. She reached down again, retrieving a notebook and a fountain pen. "If you'll bear with me a moment." She flipped through the pages, settling about halfway through the notebook. All her notes were written in a tight shorthand that Tashué couldn't decipher. She made a few checks on the page, looking up at Tashué again. "When was your girl found?"

"A week ago," Tashué said. "Maybe a little more than that, now."

Her pen glided across her notebook, continuing the shorthand. "Where, exactly? She washed up on the bank, you said?"

"Yes, up in Brickheart, at the end of Murne Street, where the bridge used to be."

"Did she bear any other marks or memorable aspects that someone might recognize her by?"

Tashué shook his head. "Only the tattoo."

"Had she been in the water long, do you think?"

"At first I didn't think it had been long, maybe only a few hours. Long enough to wash her clean." Tashué reached out to his pint, hand settling around the glass. Wind howled somewhere above the track, trying to reach down into the courtyard but failing. Tashué cleared his throat. "But it occurred to me that the Brightwash is so damned cold this time of year. It could have been much longer than that."

"Have you a lot of experience looking at dead bodies, Mr. Blackwood, that you might be so certain?"

Tashué took a deep breath, meeting her eye. "I served in the Foreign Deployment Army."

Allie nodded, making more notes. "I imagine that's experience enough."

"When was yours found? Your boy?"

"Nearly a month ago now. I've been searching for some word about what happened but there isn't much. Until I heard of one Mr. Tashué Blackwood, who bullied some hapless Patrollers when they found the body of some street urchin on the bank of the Brightwash."

Tashué felt his mouth pull tight, felt his shoulders tense. "Is that what they say? That she was a street urchin?"

"It is. Patroller Bowman was adamant that the girl was probably from the Bay, some vagrant. It was the other one, the young boy." She flipped through her notes. "Kiplar, that's it. Young Mr. Kiplar was considerably more imaginative. Seemed sceptical that a girl from the Bay could have washed upriver to Brickheart. I was inclined to agree."

Tashué nodded. "Kiplar did his best. What about your boy? Was it clear how he died?"

"No, it wasn't. Aside from his scarring, there were no other wounds or marks on his body." She took a deep breath, steeling herself against something. "I walked past him on my way to my office to type up a report about the Queen stopping in Yaelsmuir. I still don't know how I possibly walked past him. I must have thought he was an old doll or something." She paused, squeezing her eyes shut and shaking her head. "I only noticed as I was walking away, because other people had stopped and were staring."

"It can be hard for our minds to understand things that we don't expect to see."

"My mother said the same thing. And yet I still can't believe I walked past him." She shook herself, scanning the notes she'd taken. "I'm not usually so emotional. This boy has been haunting me. You are the first person I've met that seems half interested in these children."

"I could say the same about you. I'm afraid I don't have much to add."

"That's quite alright, Mr. Blackwood." She looked down at her notes, flipping through the pages a few times. "It seems we have somewhat of a pattern. Which is information in itself, isn't it? Perhaps if we could discover where these children are being... removed from their limbs, we would have some understanding as to why. And what happens to them after."

"I wouldn't even know where to look for those answers," Tashué admitted. "I've heard some disturbing rumours about what goes on in the Rift, but I have no jurisdiction there at all. The only other thought I had was that the girl might have been turned away from the Facility of Rest for the Critically Ill—it's also upriver from where I found her. But the staff there have never seen wounds like hers. Nor have any charities near the Facility."

Allie nodded, making another note. "My boy, he was a redhead. With freckles. Your girl?"

Tashué reached for his own notebook, flipping it open to the page where he'd drawn the girl's face. He slid it across to Allie and there was some relief in not needing to explain why he carried the girl's likeness and photographs around with him. "Black hair. A Sittami girl, I thought, with the shape of her features. Although I can't be sure. It's just that she reminded me of someone I knew."

She studied the face for a long time before she flipped to the next page, where the tattoo was scrawled out. She copied it down in her own notes, under the line of numbers that must have been from the boy. She handed the notebook back and sighed. "So, what do a little redhead boy and a Sittami girl have in common, aside from their tattoos and their missing limbs? The search continues, I suppose." She gathered up her notes, bit by bit, tucking it all away into a leather satchel she kept at her feet. She replaced her pen reverently, setting it in a case that kept it upright in her bag. "Thank you so very much for your time, Mr. Blackwood."

"Will you tell me if you find anything?"

"Yes, I think I will. Will you do me the same courtesy?"

Tashué nodded. "I will."

"Thank you, sir."

She stuck out her hand again and he shook it. The still wet ink on her fingers left two little black marks on the heel of his palm. She tried to smile, but it seemed a hollow thing. He didn't know what to say to comfort her. What comfort was there to have in a world where children had been abused so horribly and then discarded, and no one else seemed to care? He finished his pint as she put everything back in to her satchel. She reached for her empty glass, but Tashué stood, waving her off.

"It's alright, let me take it."

"Thank you," she said, wiping at her eyes. It left a bit of an ink stain, on the top of her cheek, a smudge of black that only made the faint freckles stand out more. "If ever you change your mind about the interview for the *Highview Times*, I hope you'd come find me. It would be a boon for my career."

"That's extremely unlikely, Miss Tei."

"Ah, well, maybe you'll change your mind once you get to know me better. You'll find I'm quite likeable."

"I'm sure that's true, but I have no interest in having my life in the social pages."

Allie smiled and shrugged, heading for the door. She held it open for Tashué as he followed with the empty glasses. "I'm afraid you chose the wrong company if you like your privacy, Mr. Blackwood. The exploits of Miss Winter and the Governor are particularly popular at my paper. People will be writing about you whether you sit for an interview or not."

19

LORNE
DAY 9

The Hive was as buzzing and active as its name suggested, three barges sitting docked beneath the towering warehouses and another two coming down the river. With another storm threatening to come in off the ocean, everyone was working faster to get their loads clear before it arrived.

Lorne walked down on the docks instead of heading up into the Hive. After what happened the last time Tashué came up into the Hive, Lorne thought it was better to stay on the docks for a while. Getting more attention from Powell Iwan didn't seem wise.

He could feel the vibration of the river and the docks through the wood as he walked, feel the spray of water on his face when the water got really rough. Sometimes, he missed being close to the ocean, but whenever he was tempted to think too fondly about living on the coast, he remembered the grey rage of the sea, cold and unforgiving, so strong it could rip apart the rocks of the shore. He'd lived through more than one hurricane in Lledewydd. The river was better. All the charm of waterfront property without the vicious winds of the Western Sea.

"You hungry?"

Lorne glanced over his shoulder. Ishmael Saeati had managed to catch up to him. He held a paper bag filled with smelt—tiny fish coated in batter and fried right on the docks. Ishmael offered the bag, and Lorne plucked one off the top of the little pile. The fish were still steaming, the batter turned crispy by volcanically hot frying lard. Lorne broke the fish in half, watching the steam curl up from the creamy white flesh.

"I brought your wages," Ishmael said, reaching into his pocket and pulling out a small coin purse. "From the last two weeks."

Lorne popped the half fish in his mouth to free up one hand, breathing in through his teeth to try to cool the steam as he chewed. He took the coin purse, feeling the familiar weight of it, finding an empty pocket to stash it away. Powell Iwan knew that Lorne ran spies for General Wolfe, and allowed it, but it still felt strange taking Wolfe's money while he stood on the docks of the Bay.

"How's Jason?" Ishmael asked.

"Fine," Lorne grunted, putting the other half of the fish in his mouth. The grease and the salt was massively satisfying when it wasn't burning his tongue. "What does the General want me to do now?"

"Nothing in particular, just business as usual. Anything of interest, send it up the line."

"Cut the shit," Lorne said. "You only come down into the Bay when the General wants something special. So, what is it?"

Ishmael didn't respond right away, taking a fish off the top of the pile and popping it into his mouth. He seemed mostly unconcerned with how hot they were and he met Lorne's gaze for a while, as if he was picking his words carefully. But Ishmael never needed that much time to decide what to say. His words were always ready on the tip of his tongue. A long pause like that was for dramatic tension, the bastard, and it was working—Lorne felt the frustration building through his shoulders, crawling up his face, his very skin alive.

"The General isn't after anything specific. I'm just being proactive. So. How's Jason?"

"I told you, he's fine. Still very much in the Rift. You can go visit him, if you want. You have your military paperwork still? That's enough to get you in. What does being proactive have to do with Jason? You don't need him."

"Do you visit him?" Ishmael pressed. "Did you hear what happened?"

Lorne grimaced, looking back up the river. The bridge that carried the tram over the river blocked the Rift from view, but he knew exactly where it was. Yes, he'd heard. He'd hoped it was wrong, a rumour, a lie. Someone used their Talent in the Rift. Someone in there was so strong they broke the layer of suppression, if only for a moment. He hoped it wasn't Jason. "How do you know it was him?"

"Aren't you the one in charge of spies and runners?" Ishmael countered. "How do you *not* know it was him?"

Lorne shook his head. "Everyone is talking about Blackwoods now. Because of Tashué. So, of course they would say it was Jason on the same day Tashué fucked Illea Winter. That doesn't mean it was actually Jason."

"Wow, Coswyn. I'm surprised. I didn't expect you to be so good at self-delusion."

Heat crawled up Lorne's neck, down his shoulders, into his fists. It took every ounce of self-control he had not to lash out. Could he take Ishmael in a fight? He wasn't sure. Ishmael was taller, had a better reach. Lorne was younger. Ishmael was uncomfortable on the docks, and Lorne knew how to use the swaying of the river to his advantage. But Lorne had never seen Ishmael fight, didn't know Ishmael's style—he couldn't see it, the way he usually did when he pictured how a fight would go. He did know that Ishmael was trained by the diplomatic division, same as Lorne, and he knew everything that came with that. Ishmael had an effortlessness about the way he moved, a total understanding of his own body that was built into him by all that training.

And Ishmael watched him too closely. He was still eating his fucking fish, but his eyes were locked with Lorne's. He wasn't tensing up for a fight—he was going loose, muscles relaxing, ready to react without needing to think. That was worse than someone going tense. That showed just how deeply he *knew* what he was doing.

Lorne took a deep breath. "Jason has enough problems in his life, he doesn't need you involved."

Ishmael cocked an eyebrow. And grinned. "I'm hurt. I've always thought of myself as a problem solver."

"The fuck you are," Lorne snarled. "A problem solver for who? The highest bidder?"

Ishmael's movements slowed as he put another smelt in his mouth. "No need to get personal."

"You made it personal by getting Jason involved. How about you ask his father if he's heard the rumours? No? Could that be because you know that Tashué would sooner burn Yaelsmuir to the ground than let Jason get dragged into whatever shit you have in mind for him?"

"And yet Tashué 'let' the Authority lock Jason away in the Rift."

"That's between him and Jason."

Ishmael nodded, but the tension hadn't passed. "You're very defensive of the Blackwoods."

Lorne took a deep breath, turning away from Ishmael to look down river. He couldn't keep eye contact with Ishmael anymore or he'd just go on imagining how their fight might happen and he'd get himself into real trouble then. He watched the river traffic instead, but the water didn't soothe him. What was it about him that he was always drawn to water, even though he hated it a little?

How could he explain that the Blackwoods were the family he'd always longed for as a child? Jason, who saw him so clearly because he also knew what it meant to compete with opium for his mother's love. Tashué, who seemed to love him as a son, even when Lorne's skin felt like it was crawling right off his body, rage and restlessness making him feel a little insane. He didn't know how to explain how deeply he loved these two people who had found him on the streets of Yaelsmuir and never once asked him why he was so damned *angry* all the time. And even if he could explain it, would Ishmael even care?

"Yes," was all Lorne could think to say. Why was it so damned hard to say the same words that floated so clearly through his mind? "I am very loyal to the Blackwoods."

"Just so we understand each other, I'm very fond of the Captain, and so is General Wolfe."

"Yes, and I'm sure Illea Winter is 'very fond' of him too, but that will only last as long as he serves her purpose."

"General Wolfe and Illea Winter are not the same person."

"What's the expression?" Lorne asked, looking at Ishmael again. "They're cut from the same cloth."

"Why? Because they have old money?"

"Of course because they have old money," Lorne snapped. "You of all people must know how different life is on this side of the river."

"There you go making it personal again."

Before Lorne could answer, he spotted Tashué coming up the docks. Lorne took a deep breath, trying to slow his racing heart. It was the same feeling as when he stepped off the stage in Iwan's fight hall, except he didn't know if he had won this bout.

A small knot of dockworkers came stomping along the pier, heading for a barge that was tying itself to one of the pilings to wait for a spot inside the Hive. Tashué arrived just ahead of the knot of men, and Lorne and Ishmael had to shuffle to get out of their way. There was a moment, a brief and delicate moment, where Ishmael was off balance, his body heading too close to the edge of the dock, toward the water. But Tashué reached out, catching Ishmael by the arm and hauling him back before he lost his balance.

"Fucking hell," Ishmael muttered. "Fuck the docks. Why are we standing here in the way?"

"But you were born here in the Bay," Tashué said. "I would have thought you were used to the docks."

"I was born on dry land, thank you very much. Right up there, overlooking the stockyards. Everything always smelled like cow shit, no matter how much my poor mother cleaned."

Lorne snorted. "You grew up in the Bay and you're still afraid of the docks?"

Ishmael shook his head as he offered the bag over to Tashué.

"Only the kids of the dock workers played on the docks. I never could get in with the dock kids. And then there was an accident one winter when an ice breaker hit the Hive and dozens of people died. Mother wouldn't let me anywhere *near* the docks after that. And then we moved across the river to the Boardwalk Market."

"And now you're back down in the Bay," Lorne said.

"No, I'm not back in the Bay, I'm just visiting."

"That's not what I heard," Lorne said. "I heard you fought for Powell a few years back."

"It's true, he did," Tashué said. "Long time ago though, wasn't it? Back before I knew you. Ten years ago or so?"

Ishmael rustled around the bottom of the bag for the last of the smelt. "More than that, now. Fucking time, where does it go?"

"And yet here you are still," Lorne said with a smirk. "Down in the Bay. Once a Bay rat, always a Bay rat."

"Hey, fuck you," Ishmael laughed. He was so completely different now that Tashué had arrived, his banter easy and playful. Gone was the predatory readiness, the intense stare. "I'll push you off the dock, right into the Bay, and then we'll see who the rat is."

Lorne shrugged. "People say it as an insult, but it doesn't need to be. We carry a bit of home with us, no matter where we go. It shapes us, changes how we see the rest of the world, doesn't it? Nothing wrong with it."

Ishmael's smile faded. "What do you bring with you then? I get to walk around with cow shit from the Bay. What do you have?"

Lorne pushed his hands through his hair, trying to shake the way his skin felt too tight, the way his arms ached with pent up energy. He didn't want to have to start smashing things to calm down. He wanted to be able to command himself, the way they taught him in the diplomatic division. Best thing they taught him, that control. The only good thing. "What do I carry? Other than coal dust, you mean?"

"Everyone talks about the coal mines and the slate mines," Ishmael said, nodding. "But there's always a dark side to trade, isn't there?"

"Sure. If you carry cow shit from the Bay, I'm carrying opium from the Western Sea."

Ishmael wiped his fingers on the outside of the empty bag, smirking at Lorne. "I'd ask how that colours your vision of the world, but I've been to my fair share of good parties, so I already know."

Deep breath. "You're funny."

Ishmael grinned, turning to Tashué. "What about you, Captain? What are you carrying?"

"From Brickheart?" Tashué shrugged. "Probably the rage of the lower class working family. Maybe the dregs of empty kegs. Brickheart has the most breweries of any of the quarters, doesn't it?"

"Don't they call it Prickheart because of the high population of brothels?" Lorne asked.

Tashué snorted. "That too."

"Aren't you part Kaadayri?" Ishmael pressed. "You've got the amber eyes."

"There is no 'part Kaadayri'," Tashué countered. "You're either accepted by a nation or you aren't. And not all Kaadayri have amber eyes, you ass. That would be like me looking at you and saying 'Aren't you Derccian? You have the nose.' Sounds fucking ignorant, doesn't it?"

Ishmael scowled before he could master his expression. "I'm not fucking Derccian, I'm Qasani."

"Exactly."

Ishmael nodded. "Fair enough. You didn't answer my question though."

Tashué sighed at him. "I don't know why we're talking about this. I don't know, alright? My mother didn't know what it meant to be Pashibé and she had nothing to teach me. Does that make you happy?"

"No, Captain," Ishmael said softly. If Lorne didn't know how manipulative the bastard was, he might have thought Ishmael sounded contrite, but the very idea was entirely too ridiculous. "The thought that you don't know your own family's culture doesn't make me happy at all."

"I thought your mother was a healer," Lorne said. "Don't most healers live in the nice neighbourhoods, where the hospitals are?"

Tashué shook his head, shuffling through his pockets to find his cigarillos. "Back then, the hospitals only employed people who were willing to take up residence on hospital property, and they didn't allow children. So my mother worked at one of the factories, patching up people who injured themselves on the machinery. Didn't pay very well. Wasn't until I had enlisted that she took a job at the hospital, since she was alone when I left."

He stemmed his own stream of words by putting a cigarillo between his lips, finding his matches next. Lorne glanced across at Ishmael, who was in turn watching Tashué go through his ritual of lighting the cigarillo, studying him like Ishmael could glean some deeper meaning from the way Tashué moved. The moment was heavy with old pain.

A barge came against the dock too fast, knocking into the far corner and sending the whole dock jostling in the water. Tashué had Ishmael by the arm again, holding him steady until the ripples of movement subsided some, but the structure started bobbing again when someone jumped from the barge to the dock.

Ishmael huffed, balling up the empty paper bag and tossing it into the water. "I've had enough of this fucking dock for one day."

With that, he was headed back to shore, walking in that stiff, swift way that people did when they weren't comfortable with the sway of the dock. Lorne wanted to tell him that the stiff knees made it more likely for him to pitch right over the side, but he was gone too fast, disappearing into the crowd so quickly that it was like he had never really been with Lorne. It made Lorne think of the stories his grandmother told him about the cyrw, who lived in the sprawling grasslands between the Ghost Mines and the Black Mountains. They took the form of attractive, smiling humans, and lured children out of the settlements with sweets and snacks.

Don't trust the cyrw. You're so tall and plump, they'll eat you up for sure.

Ishmael was like a ghost when he wanted to be, stepping into a crowd and all but disappearing from view. General Wolfe's own personal cyrw, drifting across the world to lure people from safety with his smile and his pockets full of snacks.

Swallowing his unease, Lorne looked up at Tashué. He had his cigarillo case out again even though he was still smoking the one he'd just lit, turning it over in his hand. Lorne wondered if Tashué even realized how much he fiddled with that thing. He watched Tashué flick it open and then closed.

"You're really pushing your luck, you know."

Tashué cocked an eyebrow at him, eyes coming back from whatever distant place they'd been. "What luck is that?"

Lorne motioned to the badge, pinned to Tashué's chest for all to see. "Not even the tinmen who work here wear their badges in public. After last time, the Bay doesn't like you."

"The Bay doesn't have to 'like' me." Tashué stopped fiddling with the case finally, tucking it away into his pocket. "Powell Iwan says I'm welcome here."

"That shouldn't be comforting. It should be fucking terrifying. You should be asking yourself why he's interested in you and what he's going to ask you to do. Especially since you're apparently so close to Illea Winter now."

Tashué's mouth pulled tighter at the mention of Illea Winter, but he shrugged it off. "Has Iwan asked you to do anything other than fight for him?"

"Not yet. And I ask myself every damned day what he wants from me and when he'll try to take it."

"Why don't you leave, then?"

Lorne scowled. "You fucking know why." Jason was why. Tashué was why. And there was nowhere else in the world for Lorne if it wasn't with the Blackwoods.

Tashué sighed, shaking his head as he exhaled a particularly large cloud of blue-grey smoke. He unpinned his badge, sliding it into his pocket. "I don't know how to talk to him anymore. I don't know what's left for me to say. He's going to die in there and I don't know how to stop it."

Lorne shifted, jamming his hands into his pockets. He wondered if he should mention that Ishmael was asking about

Jason, but the very thought set his teeth on edge. "Jason's tougher than you think."

"I know he's tough," Tashué sighed. Took another long drag of his cigarillo. "I tried to raise him, remember? I know exactly how tough he is. Do you visit him?"

"Of course I do."

Tashué nodded, flicking his cigarillo into the river. "That's good."

Lorne looked upriver, toward the Market Wharf, toward the mountains. The Ammuilghur chain stood like a line of massive soldiers, looming in the distance. It was easy to see why some of the Kaadayri brought their dead to the top of those mountains, the flanks of which pierced the clouds. Sometimes, when Lorne got restless, when his skin felt like it was crawling off his body, he entertained the thought of climbing those mountains and finding the dead resting there. It would be like touching the past. The North Star was up there somewhere, her body wrapped in a burial shroud and tucked away in a cave. She wasn't Kaadayri, but sometimes they made exceptions. And the Ash Child was with her, his whole body turned to stone by the Wrath.

Lorne wanted to say something comforting to Tashué, something helpful. *He'll be alright. He'll figure out a way to get out. We'll see him again on this side of those walls.* But none of those things felt true. And he couldn't think of anything better.

"I have something for you," he said instead, "about one of your cases."

"Which one?"

"Forsooth. The brightman."

Tashué sighed heavily, cursing under his breath. "Let me guess."

Lorne nodded. "He's been seen with Gianna Tarbrook again, twice since the last time. Once near the Rift of all places, and again in Drystone Park."

"Damn his foolish, stubborn head," Tashué muttered. "I'll take him as soon as I can. Put someone on him to watch for anything suspicious."

"Like him running?" Lorne asked.

"Yes, like that exactly."

"Off to the Rift with the pair of them, then?"

Tashué sighed, pushing his hand through his hair. "It seems so."

"Seems like such a little thing," Lorne said. He cringed when he realized what he'd said. He hadn't meant to say it out loud, but the words drifted from his mind to his mouth too fast for him to stop them.

Tashué sighed again and Lorne felt his body go tense for the fight that was coming. But Tashué's shoulders slumped and the big man forced a smile. "It does, doesn't it? But it's my job to uphold the law of the Authority, even the little ones."

"Shit," Lorne breathed. Had he heard right? "I'm surprised. It seems like not that long ago, following the letter of the law was something that got a bit more passion from you."

Tashué closed his eyes, taking a long, slow breath. He cursed under his breath, shook his head. "Things that used to be clear and important to me seem like small things these days."

"Well that's good, then. There's someone that wants to see you."

Tashué looked down at Lorne, brow furrowed. "Who?"

"Just come with me. I don't think I could possibly explain it if I tried."

20

TASHUÉ

DAY 9

Rain misted them as they made their way through the streets, the storm edging ever closer, driven by the wind that howled in off the ocean. They stopped at a small stall jutting out from the corner of one of the great, sprawling buildings, a slaughter house for processing cattle. Lorne ordered three cups of deep, rich broth made of offal and bones. Tashué dropped a few copper coins on the narrow counter to pay for them.

Lorne led him to a tenement building. The roof leaked and the brickwork on one wall had begun to fall apart. They climbed to the topmost apartments, which overlooked the stockyards. The whole building smelled of blood and shit and death. The air was thick with it, so pungent and raw that Tashué had to breathe slow and shallow. He lit a cigarillo to cloak the smell, but it didn't help much. Ishmael had grown up in a place like this?

The room was tiny, enough space for a cot. The window that looked out over the stockyards had been bisected by one of the hastily built walls, leaving only a sliver of visibility.

Most notably, however, the little room was empty.

"Shit," Lorne muttered.

"If you needed some time alone with me, you could have just asked. But maybe you could have picked a nicer spot for us to go."

Lorne huffed, pushing a hand over his face. "I know you think you're funny. You aren't."

Tashué grinned and moved to the small sliver of the window. Rain left tracks on the pane of glass, making the world behind it indistinct and blurry. The cattle below became only vague brown shapes, lowing and snorting as they milled in the yard. In their own shit, waiting for the death that would feed the city. "Who is it?"

"I don't know, not really. What she told me... I don't know if she's telling the truth, but she *believes* it."

Tashué opened his mouth to ask more, but then the door swung open and the woman stepped inside. She was tall, her shoulders broad and suggesting strength, but hunger or sickness had stripped the flesh from her bones and her joints were knobbly and protruding. A great nest of brown hair almost obscured her face. Her clothes were dripping wet, and she hugged herself to try to keep some of her warmth. She froze in the doorway, and the way her body twisted and her legs bunched, Tashué knew she was about to run.

"Hey, it's alright." He offered the second tin cup to her, his voice low and gentle. "Come inside, have a drink."

Lorne stepped across the small room, closing the distance between them and resting a hand on her arm. She flinched when he touched her, but she didn't run. "Remember me? And this is the man that I told you about. I told you I would find him, and bring him to you, because you wanted to tell him what you knew about the children."

"A tinman," she said. She wasn't looking at Tashué, but at Lorne, leaning close like she was hoping to hide from Tashué. "You said he was a tinman."

"I am." Tashué rested his cup of broth on the thin windowsill. With his free hand, he reached into his pocket to retrieve his badge, offering it to her. "My name is Tashué Blackwood."

She took the badge, touching the engraved tin. She traced the edge of the Authority insignia, slid her finger across his badge number. "I don't trust tinmen."

"I know," Lorne said. "I don't trust them, either. But you can trust this one. He wanted to know about the little girl, remember? He was there when she was found and he wants to know what happened to her. Hey, look at me. I trust this man with my life. Alright? You can trust him."

She eyed Tashué and as she handed the badge back, her movements painfully slow as if she was still fighting the urge to run. He retrieved the cup of broth from the windowsill again and offered it to her.

"You look like you've been out in the rain. It's getting heavier, isn't it? Are you cold? The beef broth is good and it's still warm."

She edged closer and Tashué handed her the cup. He backed away again, as far as he could until his back was pressed into the corner.

"What's your name?"

She shook her head. "No. I won't tell you that."

"That's fine," Tashué said quickly. "What would you like to tell me, then?"

She looked at Lorne, and he nodded at her. She wrapped both her hands around her cup and leaned her face into the curling steam. Tashué could almost hear her heart hammering in her chest and he definitely *could* feel her Talent, coiled in the centre of her. She kept a firm hold over it, even with her fear.

"I know about the little ones," she said softly. "The children."

The silence that stretched after those words was taught and ugly. Tashué felt his heart beating faster, his body gathering tension like it did before a fight.

"Which little ones?" Tashué pressed when he couldn't wait anymore.

She glanced at Lorne. When he nodded at her, she gulped back most of the broth, then took a deep breath. "The little ones from the Breeding Program. I was in the breeding house, with the other women."

Tashué took a deep breath, trying to calm the erratic pounding of his heart. He bit his tongue, fighting against his own instinct to press, to ask questions. She would run if he pushed her too hard. He leaned back, pressing his body against the wall as if he could sink into plaster and make himself smaller. But she wasn't talking, wasn't saying anything else, and he twisted with his need to know more.

"You escaped the Breeding Program?" Tashué asked.

The woman nodded. And with that nod came the ugly realization that it was now his responsibility to arrest her and drag her to the Rift. Or was he supposed to take her back to the Breeding Program? He wasn't even sure—he'd never encountered an escapee from the Breeding Program in all his years working for the Authority. But he looked into her wild, haunted eyes and he knew there was no law in the world that could make him bring her back there.

"I gave the Authority five. The Authority took them all. We aren't supposed to use our Talents at the breeding house, but I found a spot where I could." Tears pricked the corners of her eyes then, her lip trembling. "They let us keep our babes for the first year. Let us name them. Only the first year, that's all we get. Some women won't take with another pregnancy if they're still nursing." She drained the last of her broth, wiping her mouth with the back of her hand. "After a year, they take them to the creche. It's right there, in the walls with us, but we aren't allowed to visit. They only want us making more, always more. I wanted to watch them grow." She squeezed her eyes shut. "I shouldn't have looked. I didn't believe it at first. I didn't think it could be true. I thought my mind was twisted by that horrible place and it was playing tricks on me. But it's true. Another woman saw the same. Sweet North Star preserve us, it's true."

The tears came in earnest now and she pressed her lips together. Tashué reached out to her, moving slowly. She seemed to lean toward his hand. Her shoulder was thin when he laid his hand there, bones pressed against her skin as if she was nothing but sticks and paper.

"Tell me what you saw."

She opened her eyes, searching his face. Her cheeks were wet with her tears. She looked so tired, so bone-weary that it made Tashué ache for her. "What will you do? Will you send me back?"

"No, I don't think I will."

"Why not? It's your job, isn't it?"

Tashué slid his hand down her arm, struggling to offer her some comfort. "You're right, it is, but…" *But what? I'm not sure I believe in this job anymore?* "I came here to learn about this girl. I want some justice for her suffering."

"You'll punish whoever is responsible for her death?"

"I will try my very best."

"It was the Authority. The Tainted Authority. They killed your girl."

Tashué flinched. "You'll have to explain to me how you came to that conclusion," he said, letting each word out slowly, trying to sound calm even though his heart was hammering in his chest.

"You smell like tobacco." She wiped the tears from her eyes, collecting herself again. "Do you smoke?"

Tashué offered his cigarillo case to her. She slid one beneath her nose, taking in a deep breath before placing it between her lips. Tashué struck a match with his thumbnail and she leaned in toward him to light her cigarillo on the little flame. He tried to be patient, but something in him was grinding, churning, anxious to hear more. How did she come to make such accusations? Had she been driven mad by her time in the Breeding Program? Five children, borne to the Authority and taken from her. Did she know the fathers that put those babes in her belly, or was it a different man every time? Did they get the chance to know each other first? How many children had Keoh brought into the world for the Authority to take away?

The woman moved a little further into the room, sitting on the edge of her cot. It creaked as she settled her weight on it and tucked her legs beneath the edge. Tashué glanced at Lorne, who was leaning against the wall next to the door, his arms crossed over his chest. He was watching Tashué instead of the woman.

Tashué drained the last of his broth, leaving the empty cup on the windowsill. He leaned his back against the wall and sank down, crouching a few feet away from the woman, so close they could hold hands if she reached out to him. She breathed in smoke from the cigarillo with a hungry desperation.

"I watched them," she said finally, dropping the end of her cigarillo into the tin cup. The ember fizzled as it hit the last bit of broth. "I looked with my Talent and I watched my little ones. They raise them in the creche until they graduate, and then they march them out of the Program. They're so small when they walk out those gates, four and five. Still plump with baby fat. I used my Talent and I watched them ride through the city in their little parade, down to the Bay. They take a barge out of the city and then…" Her lip trembled, her eyes filling with tears. "I watched the procedure when the Authority removes their arms and legs. I watched the Authority break their sweet little minds, so that they quicken before they're old enough. Then the Authority can meld the children to whatever foul machine they're meant to run. They feed them with a tube down their throats. And the little babies just sit in the bellies of their machines, throwing their Talent out, oblivious to everything but their purpose." Her voice trembled and she squeezed her eyes shut. Tears gathered in her lashes, then rolled down her cheeks. "I prayed that I was wrong, that my imagination had turned foul in that cursed building. But when I looked at my next baby, they did it again. All five of them. I kept them for their first sweet year, taught them to walk, listened to their first words. And then the Authority took them from me and sliced away their limbs and broke their minds so that they'd never walk or speak or even live another day."

She fell silent then, breathing deep but fast. Her whole body shook. When Tashué reached out to her, she flinched away from him. He sank back, turning to meet Lorne's steady gaze. He could imagine the questions that flitted through Lorne's mind—he was asking himself the same things. *Could it possibly be true? Could her Talent work that way? Do you believe it? What are you going to do now?*

"Where are they?" Tashué asked. "Your children? Do you know where they are now?"

She whimpered, shaking her head. "Three are dead. They didn't survive long."

"The other two?"

"One lights the foundry fires for Imburleigh. The other runs a transcontinental ship across the ocean. What will you do?" Her eyes flared open and she leaned toward him, reaching out and grabbing his wrist. "What will you do? The Authority killed your girl, as sure as the bastards killed mine. What will you do now?"

"Where is this procedure done?" Tashué asked. "Where are the children taken for this horrible thing?"

"I asked you what you'll do now," the woman breathed, taking her hand away from Tashué.

"I don't know," he admitted, his mind whirling.

She made a strange noise, an animal sound in the back of her throat. "You don't believe me!"

"I do believe you. I do."

"I've made a mistake. I've made a terrible mistake." She stretched out her legs and shot to her feet, dropping the cup. "I shouldn't have spoken to you. Not a tinman."

"Wait!" Tashué stood, his knees protesting, his head light as the blood drained down to his feet.

He tried to grab her, but he was too slow—she was already running. Tashué cursed. Chasing her through the Bay at night wouldn't help her trust him any. Lorne didn't stop her, either. She slammed the door behind her as she fled into the hall and Tashué could hear her footsteps fading away.

"Follow her," Tashué breathed.

Lorne's body bunched to go, but he paused. "Then what?"

"Let her calm down. But I want to know where she goes."

"Will you send her back?"

"Not a fucking chance."

21

TASHUÉ

DAY 9

The *Pint Under* was entirely too inviting these days, the familiarity and the warmth helping to chase the bitter cold from his bones as the rain lashed the city. It was quiet in the little pub, too early for the day shift to be released from their factories, too late for the night shift, who would be on their way around to the Industrial Quarter. Tashué nodded at Pallwyth as he took a seat down at the far end of the bar and a pint met him there. Sucking back the foamy head, he tried to organize his thoughts before he went into the station house.

The woman and her terrible visions—was it true? Lorne was right. There was no deception in her when she spoke. She believed that ugliness. But her believing a thing didn't make it true.

He would have to add a note to Glaen's file, once he went back to the station house. Glaen left him no choice—Tashué had to process him, send him to the Rift. The law was entirely too clear for Glaen. Tashué sighed, running a hand through his hair, trying to squeeze out the water, but he was soaked. It was an ugly thing, that thought. Jason sprang to his mind. Glaen wasn't as tough as Jason, didn't have the wildness. Would that make him better suited to surviving the Rift? Or would it hasten his unravelling?

It's not your choice. It's the law. Glaen broke the law and these are his conse-
quences.

That woman broke the law, too. Are you going to arrest her?

Why one and not the other?

Kazrani found him when he was halfway through his pint, Beckett trailing behind her. Even though it was cold and miserable, Kazrani smiled when she saw him, her face so bright and energetic. She somehow hadn't changed, in all the long years he'd known her. There was grey in her thick black hair and the sun had taken its toll on the skin of her hands and face, but her eyes were still bright and young and he didn't think she had stopped moving in all that time. Were it not the fact that he had *seen* her sleeping, he wouldn't have been sure that it was possible for her to be so still for so long.

"Just some bread and butter if you please, Mr. Pallwyth. I'll be back later for a proper meal."

"Of course, Lieutenant," Pallwyth said. "And you, Sergeant Collstone?"

"I'll have the same, thank you," Beckett said.

"You look surlier than usual," Kazrani said, sinking down on the stool beside Tashué and elbowing him on her way down. "Which is quite a feat for you, Captain."

Tashué sighed again, sliding the bottom of his pint glass back and forth through the ring of condensation on the bar. "I'll have to process one of my brightmen. The damned fool won't see reason."

Kazrani nodded as Pallwyth delivered some thick slices of bread, warmed on the oven and dripping with butter. "When will you process him, then? Tonight?"

Tashué shook his head, drinking the last dregs of his pint. "He'll be out lighting the brights already, with night coming on. No. I'll take him during the day, when he's at home."

"You need help with him?"

"I don't think so. He isn't a violent man."

"Procedure says two minimum, *Commander*."

Tashué scowled. "Don't be an ass. I know the procedure." He looked past Kazrani, to where Beckett was chewing mechanically on his bread. "How are Minna and Lenora?"

Becket's smile lit his entire face, chasing away the shadow of fatigue. "She's sitting up now, all on her own. Minna says she'll be crawling soon, and then we're in real trouble. She hasn't quite figured it out, yet. She gets herself up on her hands and knees and just yells at the floor." He grinned, but even as he did, he rubbed his eyes. "Hard to imagine we were all so small once, isn't it?"

"Ha, that's because you're young still, Collstone," Kazrani said. "Once you're old like us, everyone under twenty-five looks like a wee baby."

"Did you have many children, Lieutenant?"

"Just one, just my fool boy," Kazrani said.

"You seem so experienced with children," Beckett said. "I'd always imagined you had a whole bunch of them."

"Ah, well, I only had the one of my own, but I had a hand in raising every child born in my ashrab. It's our way. A child is born not only to the parents, but to the whole ashrab. To the whole Jitabvi people."

"Is it true that the children ride with the cavalry?" Beckett asked.

"Your division didn't have Jitabvi cavalry?"

"No, I marched with the 14th. They had regular cavalry."

"I started in the 14th," Tashué said. "That's where I was assigned when I enlisted, and I learnt how to ride with them. Did you still have Lazure when you served?"

Beckett nodded. "Lazy Lazure, yes, I had him."

"Ah, that's not fair," Kazrani said. "Lazure was always a solid General, if a little cautious."

Beckett shrugged. "The consensus was that he was past those days, when I served. I think he retired right after I did. Anyway, you didn't answer me. Do the children really ride with the soldiers?"

"The whole ashrab rides with the division," Tashué said.

"No—not the whole ashrab," Kazrani said, shaking her head. "A lot of coldbloods stay behind in the Hadia. But yes, the Jitabvi units are allowed to keep more camp followers with us, since it's our culture. When we march, our families march with us, and take care of the camp and the horses and the cooking and all the little things that keeps us well provisioned for battle."

"I'm sorry to tell you, Kaz, they don't let the coldbloods march with the unit because it's your culture," Tashué said. "They let you do it because your people are more efficient than anyone they ever try to send along with you, and your self-reliance cuts down on equipment costs."

Kazrani laughed. "Well, I can't say I'm surprised. Army efficiency is a rare beast."

"Did your son ride with you, then?" Beckett asked. "I can't imagine it. Having a baby on the march? I love my girl, but she's hard enough to manage, and we hardly try to take her anywhere!"

"Honestly, it's raising a child in the city that sounds impossible to me," Kazrani said with a shrug. "Being out in the open, constantly on the move, with many people willing to help take care of the littlest ones when they're fussy and hard to manage? That's all I know. All I ever wanted to know. Raising children is easier when you have the whole ashrab—or even just the unit—to lean on."

"I remember when I got there, Tevir preferred to sleep during the day, in the saddle," Tashué said. "How old was he then?"

"Two, by the time you were assigned to us. He turned two right after our last Captain died."

Tashué nodded, draining the last of his beer and leaning back to find his cigarillos. "Right, two. And you and his father would take turns with him at night. Whoever had him at night slept with him in the saddle during the day."

Kazrani smiled and nodded. "I remember. And when that idiot got himself killed, you took over. At first you just took him in the saddle, remember? That's when I knew you were a keeper. Not many of the Captains give two shits about how we did things, let alone participated. But you took him in your saddle with you, and talked to him until he fell asleep, and I knew you were one of the good ones."

Tashué laughed, lighting a match with a flick of his thumb. "And then you laid claim to me so that everyone knew I was officially part of the ashrab."

"No, it was before that," Kazrani said, shaking her head. "Before we even left the Hadia. Remember?"

"Ah yes, of course. How could I possibly forget?"

"How did she 'lay claim' to you?" Beckett asked, his head cocked to one side.

"Well, there are a lot of ways for Jitabvi to lay their claims, I understand," Tashué said, grinning at Kazrani when she rolled her eyes at him. "There are some smoke ceremonies, and of course a wedding leaves no room for doubt. A hunting ceremony too, I think."

"I chose the quickest and most effective ceremony," Kazrani said, wiping the crumbs off her hands. "Sex."

Beckett snorted and coughed, just about choking on a mouthful of toast.

"I really didn't have time for a smoke ceremony, and I *definitely* didn't want to be married to this ass for the rest of my damned life. I just wanted the rest of the hotbloods to start listening to him before we were deployed again and we got into another bad scrape."

"I never really thought of the two of you like, ah, that," Beckett coughed, and a blush climbed up his cheeks. Sweet North Star, he was still so young—like Kazrani said, anyone under twenty-five seemed little more than a child to Tashué now.

"We're long past those days," Kazrani laughed. "But it worked, didn't it?"

"It did," Tashué agreed, dragging the ashtray closer and flicking in the first bit of ash. "Shit, that was a long time ago, wasn't it?"

"Twenty-four years, Captain," Kazrani said, her voice soft and heavy with the weight of each of those years. "Nothing quite turned out the way we expected, did it?"

Tashué shook his head, exhaling smoke through his nose as he watched the last of the foam slide down his empty glass. Being like a father to Tevir had filled something hollow in him, even at that young age. Watching Tevir and all the other Jitabvi children grow up in a world of blood and death was something deeply profound, something he still thought about. They were all so joyous, resilient, energetic and full of love and life. It seemed impossible when they watched their parents fight and die in wars they couldn't possibly understand. But it was true. It didn't matter that the world was chaos around them. Those children were loved so deeply and grew up knowing who they were so acutely that they existed to the full breadth of their potential. Having such an active role in raising Tevir had fooled him into thinking that raising Jason would be easy. How miserably wrong he was.

The door smashed open behind them. A young Patroller staggered in the door, winded and dishevelled. "Officer Mahalouwan?"

Kazrani sat up straighter, the weight and fog of the past disappearing from her shoulders in an instant. "Yes, that's me."

"We've one of your brightmen with us, out on the streets. Said his name is Moore. He's asking for you and he's quite agitated. He's assaulted someone and he's raving about being allowed to go to work."

Kazrani was on her feet in an instant, almost knocking her stool over as she rose. "Shit. I'll need your help with this one. I think the fool has the Wrath!"

Tashué cursed, shooting to his feet and following Kazrani, Beckett one step ahead of him since he was closer to the door. "Why didn't you process him sooner?"

"Fuck Captain, you know how it is. I have so many of these people…"

Tashué bit back the angry retort that tried to escape. *These people.* He followed her through the streets, the Patroller ahead of all three of them. They came on the knot of Patrollers ahead, a cluster of black wool uniforms.

"I have to work! The sun's setting. It's getting dark. I have to work! I have to go light the brights! It's my job. I have to do my job, or they'll send me away! You have to let me work!"

"It's alright, sir, your Regulation Officer is coming. She wanted us to tell you that she's coming to talk to you. Just wait right here, and she'll come in no time at all."

Tashué recognized one of the Patrollers—Kiplar, from the riverbank. He stood a little straighter now as if he had finally found his spine.

"Here she is now, sir," Kiplar said.

"Miss Mahalouwan!" the brightman shrieked. "Please, tell the

Patrollers that I have to work. I know I have to work. They won't let me work!"

"It's alright, Mr. Moore. I'm here now. These fine Patrollers will leave, and you and I will have a talk. How does that sound?"

"No, I don't want to talk. I want to work!"

He turned, trying to run, but Kiplar sprang forward and grabbed his arm. Moore howled, spinning around. Tashué didn't see the gun in Moore's hand until it was too late. It boomed and Kiplar folded, falling like a crumbled newspaper. Beckett jumped in fast, catching Kiplar before he hit the ground, easing him down. Blood coated Beckett's clothes by the time his knees hit the cobbles, his hands scrabbling on Kiplar's chest, searching for some way to stem the bleeding.

Moore spun again and bolted. Kazrani darted after him. The Patrollers stood uselessly around Kiplar, staring down at the youth. He was gasping for breath, blood flecking on his lips. Tashué grabbed the nearest Patroller, shaking the young woman until all the shock melted out of her face.

"Get a fucking healer! Now!"

"Yessir!"

She darted off. Tashué dropped to one knee beside Kiplar and Beckett, looking into the young Patroller's wild eyes.

"Hang on, Kiplar. A healer will be here in no time at all to help you. I have to go, but you hang on."

"Yes, sir," Kiplar gasped

More blood came from Kiplar's mouth when he spoke and he was breathing hard and fast like a man who had just tried to sprint for miles.

"Get him on his side," Tashué said, taking Kiplar by one shoulder and turning him. "Wounded side down, so the blood can drain instead of pooling in his lungs."

Beckett shifted, keeping Kiplar's head up but his body turned, and the blood came even faster, spreading across both of them in an ugly red tide. It was too bright, that blood. Bright blood was carried by the arteries, and arteries bled fast.

"I'm going after Kaz," Tashué said, grabbing Beckett's shoulder and meeting his eye. "You stay here, with Patroller Kiplar. Keep him up, keep him talking. A healer is coming."

"Yes, Captain."

Tashué nodded and bolted after Kaz, his long legs eating up the distance. The streets gave him the trail to follow—the gun, dropped on the cobbles ahead, a knot of people, helping someone back to their feet, someone else cursing after Kazrani somewhere ahead.

And Kazrani, stalled by a crowd—patrons of a pub spilt into the street in a great knot of flesh. Some of them still had pints in their hands, looking down the street to find the source of the excitement. Kazrani ploughed into them. A yelp from the crowd, the tinkering smash of glass shattering on the street. Beer and glass shards flew everywhere.

"Oi, that was a full fucking pint!"

The crowd churned like it was going to dissolve into a brawl, and the mass ejected Kazrani back the way she came. She took a deep breath and plunged back in.

"Move!" she howled. "Get out of the damned way! Move!"

Tashué caught up to her, using his size and his elbows to clear a path through the milling bodies until they burst out the other side like a pair of bullets through flesh.

But the brightman had gotten away.

"Shit," Kazrani gasped. "Shit. Shit shit shit."

"You didn't tell me he kept a gun!" Tashué snapped.

"I didn't fucking well know he kept a gun, did I?"

"That's a big thing not to know when you need to process a man, Kaz!"

She bared her teeth in a primal snarl, but didn't say anything—probably because she knew he was right. They were supposed to know things like that.

"How's the boy?"

It was Tashué's turn to snarl. His hands were still sticky with Kiplar's blood. "Dead by now if they didn't find him a healer. Maybe dead, even if they found one."

"Shit!"

A scream echoed from around the corner and Tashué burst into a run again, following the sound. Kazrani followed. Up the street and around the corner, they found a man lying at the mouth of an alley, holding his face as he howled with pain. Burns turned his skin into angry red weals and blood seeped from split flesh. A woman knelt beside him, trying to pull the man's hands away so she could see his wounds—as if that would help.

"What happened?" Tashué asked.

"I don't... I don't know," the woman gasped. "That man was muttering about doing his work and then Bryn was screaming. I don't know what happened!"

"Which way did he go?" Kazrani snapped.

The woman's arm flung out, pointing down the alley. They took off again, jumping over a pile of shit that hadn't yet made it to the gutter.

Buildings gave way to the riverbank and the rocky ground shifted beneath Tashué's feet. The vague shape of a running man moved upriver, half-lit by the brights on the docks. Tashué's feet skidded on the rocks as he made his turn, arms pinwheeling to catch his balance again. Kazrani pulled ahead for a moment, but then Tashué overtook her again. Fatigue threatened his long limbs, his heart pounding too hard in his chest. But he pushed himself on, on, ignoring the pain. His eyes locked on the man's back. The brightman was starting to slow, the distance between them closing.

The Market Quarter was up ahead, the Wharf jutting out into the river. The brightman staggered and almost fell, arms flailing, somehow catching himself before he smashed to the ground. He turned, heading back into the streets, where the cobbles were a bit more sure and the buildings offered places to hide.

The brightman ducked into a warehouse, leaving the door open behind him. The darkness swallowed Tashué first, so thick and murky that he couldn't see. He had to stop, to give his eyes time to adjust. Kazrani stepped in behind him, filling his ears with the sound of her heavy breathing. Slowly, the details came to him— bolts of cloth and bags of grain and ingots of metal. The warehouse seemed silent, but the way his pounding heart roared in his ears, he couldn't be sure. He took a deep breath and held it, closing his eyes scanning the warehouse, ears straining for any noise that might signal where the brightman had gone.

"Where the fuck did he go now?"

"I don't know, Kaz," Tashué hissed. "You think I would be standing here if I knew that?"

Kazrani eased forward, placing her feet softly, but something tickled across Tashué's senses—was that the brightman's voice? Tashué's caught Kazrani by the wrist, freezing her in place. And in the silence when she stopped moving, Tashué finally understood what he was hearing. The brightman was sobbing, but his voice seemed to bounce around the cavernous space.

"There!" Kazrani breathed, darting deeper into the warehouse.

Tashué bit back a curse as she disappeared among the boxes, turning toward the stairs that stretched up to the catwalk above. It seemed a better option than staggering blindly through the alleys and crannies the stacked boxes made. Maybe, from above, he could figure out where the brightman was.

The whole structure felt too flimsy to hold him up and his every footstep sent a vibration of movement through the wood. Up and up he climbed. As he went higher, he realized that the sound of the sobbing was getting louder. When he reached the catwalk, Tashué could finally see the man, sitting in one of the corners of the intricate web of platforms that hung above the warehouse floor. He was curled so tightly that Tashué mistook him for a discarded pile of cloth at first, but he shook with his sobs.

"Mr. Moore," Tashué said, easing closer.

The man shot up, staggering over his own feet and lurching toward the guardrail of the catwalk. Tashué's breath caught in his throat, but the man caught himself before plunging over the side.

"Leave me alone!" the brightman shrieked. "I have to work! Why won't anyone let me work?"

"Yes, I know," Tashué said. His eyes scanned the catwalk. It was a maze, platforms and thin walks and another set of stairs on the other side of the building. "It's dark outside and it's time to light the brights. Come with me, won't you? Where's your patch? Which lamps are yours?"

"Along the river," the man gasped. "I light the riverbank. It's important. Don't want anyone falling in the water!"

"No, we don't want that," Tashué agreed. "That's good work you do. A few months ago, I pulled a little boy out of the river. He was playing with his friends and went too deep. I wouldn't have been able to find him if it weren't for those brights. Come with me, sir. I'll walk you to your patch and you can start your work."

The man blinked at Tashué. He took a half-step closer and Tashué held out his hand to him. He could feel the man's Talent, writhing and angry, a miserable force. Tashué felt it like a heat crawling up his chest, settling on his shoulders. The brightmen weren't supposed to use heat on the brights, only light, but something had gone wrong. The Wrath, like Kazrani said—using his Talent had twisted something in his mind, turning the ability to light the brights into a compulsion. A compulsion to burn.

"You're a tinman?" the man asked.

"I am."

"I didn't mean to hurt anyone."

"I know." Tashué nodded. "I know."

"If I don't work, they'll send me to the Rift. I don't understand why they won't let me work!"

"Everything's fine now, Mr. Moore. Come with me and I'll escort you to your patch. There's no need to make things worse."

The brightman made a low, keening sound from the back of his throat, reaching up and pulling at his own hair. The motion was so much like what Jason did to cope with his frustration that it made Tashué's heart skip a beat. The brightman looked up at Tashué with wide, searching eyes and Tashué felt the moment slipping away from him.

"I've the Wrath," the man whined, a wheezing, pained sound.

"We don't know that, not for sure," Tashué said slowly. "I know you didn't mean to hurt anyone, Mr. Moore. There's no reason to think it's the Wrath."

"I can feel it. It burns my mind. They taught us to make light without heat but now the heat is in me and I can't get rid of it! I can't make it go away. I'm burning. Everything is burning. I tried to tell her I was burning, that I had to stop, I had to stop making light without heat because it was driving me *mad* but she wouldn't let me stop! She said I had to work or I'd go to the Rift but now I've the Wrath and you're going to kill me for it."

"That's not for me to decide. But Mr. Moore, if you come with me now, I promise you I will do everything I can to help you."

"How will you help me?" the brightman snapped, some mixture of rage and fear turning his face deep red and bringing tears to his eyes. "There's no help for me, not now... North Star preserve me, there's no help for me now. They'll make a spectacle of my death in front of the whole city. They'll send me to the gallows, even though it's their fault I'm going mad!" He took a step closer to Tashué, reaching out, hands plucking at Tashué's sleeve. "But if you kill me, then I don't have to die in front of everyone. Would you do that for me? You said you would help me, didn't you?"

Too much of what he said was right. The Authority did send people with the Wrath to the gallows. And yet, Tashué couldn't help but hope there was still something to be done, some way he could help. He reached out to the man, offering his hand. "I don't want to kill you, Mr. Moore. That's not my decision to make."

Moore glanced once over his shoulder, down the catwalk, something like peace coming to his eyes. "Maybe she'll do it."

Heat spread through Tashué's chest like a good shot of whisky, warm and comfortable and radiating out into his arms, down his legs. But then the heat built, turning to pain, a searing, ugly thing. Tashué took a step back. Something in him stirred in response, a sleeping beast that threatened to wake, pushing against the chains that held it in place. Talent, long locked away, long ignored, thrashed against the heat, against the Talent that invaded.

A gunshot echoed through the warehouse and the brightman howled, staggering. He charged, forcing himself past Tashué. Tashué staggered, but tried to grab him, some part of him, his arm or his sleeve—but he was away so fast and Tashué felt so removed from his own fingers. He staggered, catching the railing of the catwalk.

"Are you alright?" Kazrani had him by the arms and dragged him back up to his feet.

"Yes, I'm fine," he breathed, shrugging her off. He took a deep breath, pushing back against the force in his chest, smothering it back down into the crevices of his being. "You shot him?"

"Of course I fucking shot him, he was trying to kill you! I could feel it! Couldn't you feel his Talent? Why didn't you do something?"

Tashué bit back another curse, turning to the stairs. How could he explain that the brightman couldn't hurt him without explaining the great, sleeping power that sat like a boulder in his chest?

He ran down the stairs, seeing the splatter of blood on each step, deep red droplets that smeared into the wood. The door was still open, another smear of blood on the handle, on the frame. He stepped out into the night, out into the brittle cold and the howling wind that swept across the city. Kazrani came up behind him, and then she was ahead of him, following the trail of blood. Stepping out of the cluster of buildings, to the riverbank, Tashué found the brightman ahead, on the docks, the form of him lit by brights that someone else managed. A pair of barges bobbed at the end of the docks, a third was making its way against the current, heading north.

The explosion knocked them off their feet.

22

STELLA

DAY 9

Walking to work at night was an unpleasant experience that only got worse as winter took hold on the city. The breeze that came in off the river was cold and vicious. Ceridwen pulled her shawl tight around her shoulders and up to her rosy cheeks. Her wild hair was plaited for the night, but the wind tugged at the curly locks, working them free.

Daphne was working already as Stella led Ceridwen up the stairs. Daphne seemed to have a bit more of a spark in her, her movement crisp and lively.

"Good evening, Miss Whiterock."

"Good evening, Daphne. How's the spread tonight?"

"Not so bad. We haven't too many patients."

Stella nodded as Daphne headed down the hall. Stella led Ceridwen all the way up to the top, setting her in the cot bed. Ceridwen's eyes were glazed and distant, and she settled easily into the warm blankets.

"Stay here, Ceridwen," Stella said, just like every other day. "I'll come check on you to see if you need anything."

"Yes, Mam."

Stella kissed her on the forehead, feeling her warm soft skin. Ceridwen settled in the cot and Stella headed back down the steps.

The blast rattled the whole Facility, rumbled so low and loud it shook her whole body. The air turned thick—was that ash in the air? No. Dust, knocked from every crevice by the rumble, floating in the hallways. She turned and headed back up. She had to set eyes on Ceridwen. Had it been an earthquake? She didn't think so. She'd felt an earthquake before, the long, slow vibration that rattled her bones up through her feet. She'd felt explosions before, too, the way they scythed through you with their concussive force, turning your whole body into a drum.

Peeking into the room, she was relieved to see that Ceridwen was already sleeping, the blast having not woken her at all. The child could sleep through anything.

Back down, then. Daphne was in the stairwell, her boots sliding on the stone floor with her panic. "What was that?"

Stella swung to Daphne. It was strange, to look at Daphne's panic and not feel any of it herself. She often felt like this when she was at the Facility, as if her Talent recognized the place and started cutting her away from herself the moment she set foot in the building.

"I'm not sure, Daphne," Stella said, squeezing Daphne's arm. "But it seems no one here was harmed by it, so we can relax."

Stella left the stairwell on to the closest floor, past the patients and the cots heading to the window. Daphne followed, standing at Stella's shoulder. She could see upriver from the window. Fire raged somewhere up near the Market Quarter, a seething ball of flame. The inferno made the clouds above it glow dark and orange. Was the fire on the water? In the quarter? It was hard to see anything, as if the fire sucked all the light from around it and made the city darker by its existence.

"What happened?"

Sweet North Star, how many people lived in the Market Quarter? Stella stepped away from the window, her heart beginning to race. The distantness was fading away, dissolving as she imagined the carnage that must be down there. She headed for the door. "Daphne, would you do something for me?"

"Of course, Miss Whiterock. Anything."

"Watch Ceridwen. She's sleeping already. But please, don't leave her long, keep an eye on her. Please?"

"Where are you going?"

"I'm going out there! Don't leave Ceridwen alone long, please? It might not seem like much of anything, but I like to know she's watched."

Daphne nodded and Stella was away. She went down the stairs so fast she felt like she was falling.

"Miss Whiterock, where are you going?" Tarren Bayside—the director of the Facility—was standing in the hallway.

Stella stopped with her hand on the door. "I am going to help. Daphne said we aren't busy tonight. You can spare me. Write the paperwork and we can charge the Mayor directly for my time."

Tarren, to his credit, hesitated only a moment. "Yes, you're right. Go."

Stella turned and burst out into the night, into the vicious wind. Was the fire growing, blown by that wind? She couldn't tell. But she hurtled through the streets toward it, letting the chaos of it pull her ever closer.

The air filled with ash and smoke, but there was something strange about it. It left a metallic taste on her tongue. What kind of fire tasted like metal in the air?

People were running from the Market Quarter, deeper into Brickheart as if the stone buildings there would protect them. There was so much wood in Yaelsmuir. If the fire really got hold, the whole damned city would burn. And Dunnenbrahl, on the other side of the river, that could go up too. If the forest went up there would be no refuge for anyone. Was it too much to hope that the autumn rains had left Dunnenbrahl damp enough that it could resist the hold of the flames?

Only when she was close enough did she realize that the fire *was* in the water, a bright ball of flame at the Wharf. And the wind was blowing it, sending embers and tongues of flame skittering across the docks and up to the streets. The market stalls had caught next, the waxed wool receiving the flames as surely as a candle wick.

Voices came echoing through the chaos—people screaming in pain, screaming for help, screaming in their desperation to get the fire under control. So much screaming.

A woman staggered toward Stella. Her hair had been burned away and her face was hot and blistered and bleeding, split in some places, charred in others. Stella caught her, cooing in her ear. The woman smelled too much like meat and bile rose in Stella's throat. At least meat had the luxury of dying first.

"It's cold." The woman drew a shuddering breath, tears cutting trails through the soot on her face. "I'm so cold."

"Let me help you," Stella said, but her Talent was already slipping through the woman's body reaching for the burns.

The joining was too fast, too clumsy, and the woman's pain raged through Stella's scalp as hot and fierce as if she was on fire. Parts of the woman's nerves were dead, seared away so completely that it left spots of emptiness across her body. She didn't even see the woman's memories like she normally did when she joined with a person to heal them—there was no room for anything but pain. Stella didn't have the benefit of shock to protect her from the rest of the burns, from the hot agony that seared across her mind. She swallowed her own screams as she poured her Talent into the woman's body, healing what damage she could.

The woman's knees buckled, dragging them both to the ground. She was sobbing now, clutching at her own face. The healing hurt more than the wound. The woman's skin must have felt like it was writhing as the wounds knitted shut and the new skin pushed to the surface. Just enough to close the wounds, to protect her from ugly infections. There was nothing Stella could do to prevent the scars. Stella pulled her Talent out of the woman and struggled to untangle their limbs, rising again.

"What happened?" Stella asked, trying to help the woman to her feet.

"I don't know," the woman gasped. "I don't know. There was just... fire. So much fire."

"Do you have somewhere to go? Someone that can help you?"

The woman looked around, eyes wild and unseeing. Stella couldn't blame her. The darkness had only gotten thicker, and the smoke drifting through the streets turned the buildings into indistinct beasts that pressed in entirely too close. Stella reached out, grabbing another woman as she passed.

"Help this woman," Stella said, pushing them together. "Help her get home. She's been wounded, you see? Help her get somewhere safe."

Stella pushed deeper into the smog. What was that metal taste? It was familiar somehow, tickling the back of Stella's mind, but she couldn't place it.

The fire crews had arrived, men and horses dragging massive wagons that carried great vats of water. People used buckets to attack the flames. Some parts of the city saw the crews descending into brawls as the fire spread through great swathes of the neighbourhood, but in the Market Quarter, the fire crews were well organized and disciplined. They knocked one stall into the flames, dousing the next stall in water in the hopes that it would stop the inferno's advance.

A man lay on the cobbles in front of her, his burns so terrible that Stella didn't think he was still alive. He couldn't possibly be alive. But a rasping groan came from his throat and Stella fell to her knees beside him. How had he come so far from where the fire raged? Had he run, his body burning with every step, his speed only fanning the flames? She tried to take his hand, but the skin peeled away from muscle and the man gave a piteous wail. Stella reached out her Talent to him, slicing away his pain. He wouldn't live long, not with burns like that. She reached out, putting her hands on either side of his face, touching skin that was less burnt. His chest spasmed a few times as she met his eyes, brown and filled with tears. Stella stroked his hair. This, at least, was familiar. Bearing witness to a person's last moments had been her life since coming to Yaelsmuir. At least he could go to the Keeper of the Keys free of pain. He let go slowly, his breath rattling in his chest, his eyes fading.

She staggered to her feet and she wiped her hands on her heavy skirts, trying to dislodge the feeling of greasy ash that clung to her fingers. There was so much fat in the human body.

She fought through the smoke, choking on the ash filling her mouth. The heat from the fire made the skin on her face feel dry and brittle. Made her chest hot. She healed those she could, knitting skin together wherever it could be salvaged, cutting people away from their pain when there was no hope. She never seemed to run out of patients, people dragging themselves from the wreckage, people carried by others who were driven to help, people lying unconscious or helpless in the streets. The white marble of the statue of Bronwynn stood like a beacon in the smoke, the Market Square stretching around her feet. Someone had directed people here, organizing the bodies into some semblance of order as healers walked through the crowds. She scanned the healers, looking for any face she recognized. Did anyone know her? Did any of them know she wasn't supposed to be able to heal? She didn't think so.

She helped another half dozen people before she saw a familiar figure moving through the ash and the smoke. Tashué. His body was smudged with ash and the sleeve of his jacket was burnt, smouldering still. A man was over his shoulder, limp and half-conscious. A Jitabvi woman appeared from the smog—a woman that had visited Tashué at the Row or walked with him now and then. Her tin badge was smeared in ash and almost imperceptible from the mess that had become her clothes, but Stella knew that shape anywhere. Tashué and the woman lowered the injured man to the ground, nestling him beside another body as a healer came through the chaos to help.

Tashué paused when he set eyes on Stella.

How had he picked her out of the chaos and the crowd? But then, she had just done the same. There were some people in your life that you searched for constantly, praying that they would appear just so that you could know they still graced the world. She hadn't seen him since the day he'd kissed her. How long ago was that? A few days, maybe. An eternity. Part of her didn't want to see him again, now when she was trying to leave. Why did it have to be him, a tinman of all people, a man who stood for the values of the very organization that had seen her and people like her turned into chattel, a man that could send her to the Rift with nothing but his word that she was non-compliant. And yet...

The way he looked at her, as if they weren't surrounded by the dying and the wounded, as if the very city wasn't on fire.

The way her heart beat faster when she looked at him.

Part of her couldn't bear the thought that she would never see him again.

The Jitabvi woman disappeared into the fray, but Tashué stomped through the chaos toward Stella. He reached out to her— but stopped short, biting his lip. Were it not for the fact she was looking at his lips when he did it, she would have missed the gesture completely, with the murky darkness hiding his features and his beard growing scruffy. But she saw it—and remembered the slow dawning anguish that crossed his face after he kissed her but said the name Duncreek, reminding Stella of all the things in the world that she was afraid of.

There was blood on his face, on his hands. Was it his blood? Yes —there was a lump above his eye, his eyebrow split. He'd wiped the blood away and packed ashes into the wound, an old soldier's trick. The ash had stopped the bleeding. Stella pressed her fingers against the wound, prodding the edges of it, feeling the swelling. And her Talent reached out to him, searching his body for other wounds, anything that might threaten his life.

"What are you doing here?" he asked.

"What am I doing here?" Stella echoed. "I'm helping. There are people in pain here. What are *you* doing?"

His lips pulled back in a grimace. He shook his head, turning his face away from her as he looked back toward the water—toward the fire. "We were trying to arrest a brightman and he blew up the fucking barge." He looked at her again, searching her face. What was he always looking for when he looked into her eyes like that? "Were you here? Where's Ceridwen?"

"She's safe. We weren't here. I just came... I couldn't stay away."

He nodded. He understood that, perhaps, not being able to stay away when there was blood in the streets.

A hand grasped at Stella's, dragging her away from Tashué. A man whose face was smeared with blood too, his body bathed in ash. "Help me," he gasped. "Please! Help my son. I think he's going to die!"

A boy lay on the edge of Bronwynn's fountain. His blood swirled in the water where his hand dipped below the surface, a dark stain against the white marble. The angles of his body were all wrong, his clavicle making a bend that shouldn't have been possible, his ribs caved in. Blood was coming out of his mouth, out of his ears. As Stella took his hand, the pain of all the wounds struck her so hard that she vomited, leaning over the poor stricken boy and voiding her stomach into the fountain. His memories, scattered and weak, flitted through Stella's mind. Always a bad sign, when a person's memories were so indistinct.

"Help him," the man was whimpering. "Please. Please help him."

"What happened?" Tashué asked.

"They knocked over our store," the man wailed. "We were hiding in the cellar—thought that would keep us safe from the fire. What is *wrong* with them? They didn't even give us the chance to get out. They just started smashing through the walls!"

"Who?" Tashué asked.

"The fire crews!"

"That's how they stop the fire," Tashué said. "They knock down buildings in the fire's path so that there's less fuel."

"But they didn't even give us time to get out!"

The sheer number of broken bones in the youth's body was staggering. Blood haemorrhaged from so many organs... The liver —that was bleeding badly, filling his abdomen and putting pressure on everything else. She knitted that flesh back together, just enough to stop the bleeding—but then the boy's heart stopped. Memories faded. Stella turned her attention to his chest. There was so much pressure around his heart. She needed to drain some of the blood and fluid to give the heart more room to beat, but how? She pushed some energy into the tired muscle, sending a prayer to Bronwynn.

"Are you helping him?" the man breathed, tugging at Stella's arm. "Are you healing him?"

"She can't heal, sir," Tashué said and the words clawed at Stella's mind. "She hasn't that much Talent. She can help ease your son from his pain, but she can't heal."

"But I saw her," the man pressed. "I saw her helping that woman. She can heal my boy! Tell him, tell him that you can help my boy!"

"You're mistaken." Stella sent her Talent into the youth's brain. The pressure there made Stella's skull ache and her vision swim. She squeezed her eyes shut, clenching her teeth against the fresh wave of nausea. If she could hold the boy in some state of survival, long enough to figure out what to do—or for another healer to come. But every time she healed something, some other part of the body failed. There was so much damage everywhere. She shook her head, trying to clear it.

"No! You must help him!"

"Get someone else," Stella gasped, pushing Tashué away from her. "Another healer—I can't—"

Even as Stella began to heal the brain, the heart stopped again. She sent a fresh surge of energy there, but the organ didn't respond. The pain slipped out of Stella's body as the connection between them faded—she couldn't be connected to a body that was no longer alive. She sent another surge of energy, but it dissipated through the boy's whole body, leaving no effect.

Stella opened her eyes. The man behind her fell to his knees, howling and tearing at his hair. Stella fought to catch her own breath, looking down at the youth. Was it her fault? She should have tried harder, moved faster. To hell with Tashué Blackwood and his damned Authority. Their vicious rules weren't worth the life of this innocent boy, crushed by his father's store for the sake of taming the fire. Stella closed her eyes again, plunging into the boy's body. She sent another wave of energy at the heart, trying to coax it back to life. It stirred for only a moment and then fell still again.

"Stella." The sound of Tashué's voice pulled her back. Had he come back? Or had he never left? He pried her fingers from the boy's hand. "You've done what you can. Come away. There are others that can use your help."

The emptiness of the boy's body lay like a shroud across Stella's mind, leaving her numb, staggering, and delirious as Tashué led her away from the fountain. She pictured the wounds in her mind, the few scarce moments turning over and over again in her thoughts. What could she have done differently? She needed to drain the spent blood, to pierce him somehow to relieve all that pressure. What had stopped her? Tashué Blackwood, at her shoulder? Or her own lack of practise, making her forget all that she knew?

"Captain!"

The Jitabvi woman stood cloaked in smoke. Her clothes were smeared with blood, wet and gleaming in the night. It wasn't hers— Stella could tell that much, even over the distance. There were hand prints in the smear, and the woman stood too straight and strong to have bled that much.

"Come, quick! I need your help!"

Tashué glanced at Stella and she waved him away, heading back into the chaos.

"You liar! I saw you! I saw you heal that woman! Stop walking away from me! Damn you, you lying tainted bitch, look at me!"

Stella walked faster, trying to put more space between them. But he was closer than she thought—he grabbed a fistful of Stella's hair and dragged her back. Pain seared through her scalp and she fell, tripping over her own feet. She twisted as she went down and her knees hit the cobblestones, sending hot pain through her kneecaps. The man dragged her back toward the fountain. Stella thrashed, trying to get her feet under her, or even around toward the man so that she could kick him, but he was moving so fast. How could such a slight man have so much strength? Her instinct was to reach for her Talent, but what good would that do? Take away her pain? His? Could Talent heal the wounds of the soul?

"You have to heal him!" the man wailed. "You have to help!"

The man slowed as he reached the fountain. Stella kicked

against the ground, her heel catching the cobbles and giving her some traction. She got both feet under her, her shoulder crashing against the man's chest. He cursed, grabbing her by both arms. She kicked again, a boot catching him in the shin, then stomped, smashing against his toes. He yelped—

—and Tashué hit him. The man staggered, but still held on to Stella and they were both falling. Stella hit the pavement face first, pain flashing like white light in front of her eyes. But the man wasn't so easily dazed. Rage fuelled him. He was up again, swinging at Tashué, and all Stella heard was the grunt and shuffle of fabric as they fought. Stella pushed herself up, trying to shake the fog from her mind. The side of her face was somehow both hot and numb. Red splattered against the cobblestones around her hands. Her cheek was bleeding. Blood pooling in the ash on the ground. The gash must have been bad to bleed so much. *Why don't I feel any pain?*

Something gleamed in the man's hand. He pointed it at Tashué's chest. Stella's breath caught in her throat. A gun. Tashué grabbed him by the wrist. A shot exploded. Flash of the incinerating gunpowder, more white in Stella's vision. Tashué kicked the man back, sending him staggering toward the fountain.

The man tripped and nearly fell, but still tried to point his gun at Tashué again. Tashué pulled his own pistol and Stella saw it, every moment drawing out before her. She was so distant from it all, so far away. Tashué fired once, his Imburleigh giving a ferocious roar. The man grunted, a breathless sound, folding over the red spot that spread across the front of his jacket. He lifted his pistol to shoot back, but Tashué stepped in and kicked the gun from the man's nerveless fingers. The man's gun went off as it skittered across the cobbles, the bullet smashing next to Stella, sending up a spray of broken stone that sliced at her face, leaving more hot tracks on her forehead, on her cheeks. Tashué cursed, his own pistol still pointed at the man.

But the man couldn't hurt anyone anymore. He was deflating, sagging against the wall of the fountain—sobbing, one hand trying to cover the wound on his chest, the other covering his face. He shook his head, then twisted, pushing himself back up. Tashué stiffened as if he might fire again, but the man turned away from him. Even through the gloom of the advancing night, Stella could see the ragged hole punched through his back, all blood and muscle and torn cloth. He whimpered, the sound wet and gurgling. He dragged himself up. Groped for his son's face. He kissed the boy, leaving a smear of blood across his cheek, before sagging back down. He died there, slumped against the base of the fountain, one bloody hand grasping his son's cold fingers.

Someone touched Stella's shoulders and she flinched away.

"Stella," Tashué breathed. "Are you alright?"

She looked up at his face, at those hot amber eyes that she loved so much. "I think so."

He sank down beside her, rather than forcing her up to her feet. He lay the Imburleigh on the ground between them, the barrel still emitting a tendril of cordite smoke, and he took a deep breath. His whole body was shaking. Tashué slid the heel of his palm across her cheek, doing his best to wipe the blood away.

"It doesn't look bad. The face bleeds a lot."

Stella looked down, watching the blood splatter on her skirt, spreading in a dark stain. Her uniforms for the Facility were all so filthy, but they had never been stained with her own blood before.

"Is she alright?"

Stella looked up at the sound of a new voice. The Jitabvi woman had joined Tashué, was looking down over his shoulder, her face so smeared with ash that it was hard to even see her features.

Tashué glanced up at the Jitabvi woman. "I don't know—I think so."

He pressed a cloth into the wound, soaking up the blood, using his other hand to push her hair out of her face. So beautiful, those eyes of his. She remembered what he said, about his mother. *And my mother was killed by the husband of one of her patients. She tried to save a woman, but it didn't seem to matter what my mother did, the woman died anyway.*

"I just… drift sometimes," she said. She wanted to say anything to make him stop looking at her like that, so hurt and scared, some flash of his younger self showing through the ash and scars and many years between him and the death of his mother. "I can't seem to…"

"Because of your work as a whisperer?" he asked.

Sure, that was most of it. Because her Talent was stretched to its very limit, making her so weary that sometimes she wasn't even sure she was awake. Because she had been running and hiding so long that she forgot who she used to be. Until she met him. She wanted to tell him that it wasn't him that upset her, that day on the steps, with the bottle of Ladovaugh and a lovely, gentle kiss. It wasn't him that made her whole body cold. But if she told him that, she would have to explain the gripping terror at the thought of Siras Duncreek, and she had no good answers for that unless she was willing to expose her lies.

And it all felt so ridiculous, so selfish. The Market was burning and people were dying. It was so distant, so far away, like she couldn't grasp it. She couldn't hold on to anything except the feeling of his hands on her arms, the heat of his amber eyes.

He lifted the cloth, looking at the wound. "It will take a few stitches, I think. To help it stop."

She nodded. She reached out and grabbed his sleeves with both hands, clutching them tight. He was so solid, so sure. Holding him made it feel less like she was floating away. The Jitabvi woman crouched beside them both, scooping up Tashué's Imburleigh and pulling open his jacket to slide it back into its holster. They were so intimate, the pair of them, sometimes existing as one person, their movement in such harmony that they could have shared the same mind. Stella used to wonder how they knew each other, how they got to be so close—surely they were lovers, for them to understand each other like that? But no. Tashué didn't look at the Jitabvi woman that way.

He looked at Stella that way, though. She was sure of it now. He looked at her *that way* as he sat across from her, holding the cloth against her face to catch her blood, like he would just as soon kiss her again.

A tremble started deep in Stella's chest, spreading out into her skin, down to her hands. Thinking about kissing Tashué Blackwood and thinking about being dragged across the cobbles by her hair warred in her mind. The pain in her face came to her distantly, the numbness fading away and replaced by more heat, more deep ache, and suddenly even her Talent knew it was there. She felt the contour of the tear too vividly, the skin ragged and ripped, blood rushing from the capillaries, the same blood that made her blush when Tashué Blackwood looked her in the eye and said *I think that was a ploy to watch me dress.* The same cheek that he'd touched, between kisses.

Tashué slid his arms around her body, pulling her close. He was so strong, so warm, smelling of soot and ash and smoke and sweat.

23

JASON
DAY 10

The winter greens were coming in well, mustard and beet, spinach and radish. They were good for stews, and it was good to have the gardens producing as long as possible. Jason picked tender leaves from the plants as he shuffled between the garden beds, filling a basket with freshness that the foul guards didn't deserve. It was better than the other jobs, though. Better than slaughtering chickens and scrubbing the water closet. Or mopping the floors upstairs! He shuddered at the thought.

What if there was a way out of here?

He tried not to think of that question too much as he made his way through the garden beds. The air was thick with smoke and ash from the Market fire, but Jason kept his back to it. There wasn't anything he could do to help those people—all those people—from here. As he picked, he wondered why the city used fire crews with buckets of water when it would be easier to have someone with Talent fighting the flames. But then, maybe that required too much trust. Can't have *bad meat* being the hero.

He was all the way to the far end of the gardens when someone came looking for him. He heard the door open and shut, heard the stomp of guards. And another man, someone he didn't know. Had an Authority badge, though, pinned to his chest. A Regulation Officer, then? What was a Regulation Officer doing in the Rift? He knew they were coming for him, the way they watched him from across the yard, staring while they stomped.

Jason looked down at the garden instead of staring at the guards and the Authority man, acutely aware of the massive fence at his back. There was nowhere for him to go, if they were here to arrest him. But where would they take him? He was already in the fucking Rift. Were they going to hang him, then? For what he'd done? He'd been waiting for this, if he was honest with himself. Talent strong enough to break through the suppression that lay on them all? Surely they weren't going to leave him to rot in here, waiting for him to break through the suppression again.

"Jason Blackwood."

Jason was glad he was already kneeling. He wouldn't want them to see how his knees trembled when they came to stand in front of him and said his name like *that*. He took a deep breath, looking up. "Yes?"

The Authority man crouched on the opposite side of the garden bed, resting his elbows on his knees and looking Jason in the eye. Trying to be friendly, almost? It felt strange, for someone wearing a badge to approach him so casually. Jason looked up at the man, noting the deep lines on his face, the ashy grey in his hair. The man tried to give a friendly smile, but his eyes were too cold and empty for the smile to work. "How would you like to get out of here, son?"

Jason almost laughed, but he bit it back. "I'd love to, but I'm not registering."

"Oh, I know, that's been a sticking point for you. I thought perhaps I could change your mind. You have incredible Talent, Mr. Blackwood."

Jason cringed. "My father is Mr. Blackwood."

"Young Mr. Blackwood, then. Your Talent is immense, and we could use someone like you. I have the very best of assignments, if you're interested."

"I'm not registering."

"Ah, but son, you haven't heard my offer yet. I would like to bring you to the Breeding Program."

"That's supposed to entice me, is it?" Jason laughed. "The Breeding Program? The place that imprisoned my mother, that's supposed to be my big lure? Thank you, but no. I'm not interested in registering so that I can be shuffled from this prison to a bigger prison."

"It doesn't have to be a prison, son." That grin again, a vicious, ugly thing that made Jason's skin crawl. "Think of the good you'll do in the Breeding Program. A Talent like yours—it can make generations with incredible skill. You would be doing the Dominion a service. And the men of the Breeding Program are afforded certain freedoms, you see. The women, they have to be closely guarded because their bodies carry the next generations, of course, but the men's contribution is considerably less time-consuming. And, honestly, what man can really complain about doing such *important* work?"

Jason laughed, the sound escaping before he could stop it this time. He sank back, sitting on the ground instead of kneeling, resting his basket behind him. "That's—oh, honestly, men are disgusting. That's how you want to convince me to register? You're trying to convince me to register by promising me sex in the name of the Dominion?" He shook his head, pushing his hands through his hair. "Sweet North Star. Do people really go for that? Do men really sign on when you say shit like that? Come empty your sack for the Dominion." Jason shuddered. "That's horrible. I should inform you that none of the things I like to do sexually involve women."

The man tilted his head to one side, but the smile never wavered. "I understand. Perhaps I used the wrong tactic here. You mother is in the Breeding Program, yes? Wouldn't you like to see her again?"

"You mean, if the Breeding Program doesn't kill her before I get there?"

"And your father—did you know that the Breeding Program is more relaxed with their visitation policies? You could hug your father again. How long has it been, young Mr. Blackwood? Since you hugged your own father? And the other one that visits you, Lorne Coswyn. I suppose he's the one you like to entertain sexually, is he? He could be visiting you, too. And all you have to do is spread your seed for the Dominion. Seems a small price to pay to touch the people you love again, doesn't it?"

Jason closed his eyes, his heart skipping a beat. To touch Lorne again, to kiss him. He'd been in the Rift for three years, three fucking years of taking beatings from Verrit and the guards, of getting swallowed by fights, of trading his body for blankets and food. Three years of a grate sitting between him and the people he cared about. Longer than that since seeing his mother. He didn't even remember what she looked like. All he had was the smell of her, imbued in the letters she'd sent him over the years.

"In case that still isn't enough to sway you, perhaps you could think of this opportunity as our way of expressing our gratitude," the Authority man continued. "What you did, it exposed a flaw in our system. We're very grateful, believe it or not. It's good to know where your weaknesses are. We brought in more energy units to make sure that sort of thing is never possible again. And, just so you understand, your time here is likely to get harder. Your presence, it's making the guards nervous. You see—they insisted I bring three of them here with me, simply to speak with you. Even though I assured them I'm quite capable of taking care of myself. Even though it's not possible for you to use your Talent here again, the guards all know what you did, and they appreciate the danger in it. In who you are. So, really, what are you giving up, by going to the bigger prison? Not very much, I don't think."

Jason opened his eyes. The man had stopped smiling, the stone hardness coming across his whole face. *So it comes down to threats, then. Of course it does.*

This was the part he was expecting, but somehow it made him angry instead of afraid. He tried to breathe slow and even, like Lorne taught him to do when his heart started to race and his hands started to shake with fury. Something they taught Lorne in the army. Control your breathing, and it can help you learn to control your heart. But Jason had never mastered it. His heart pounded in his chest and his hands felt like they were trembling, so he clenched them into fists and pushed them against the tops of his thighs. It was always threats and violence with the Authority. Register or we'll imprison you. Register or we'll kill you. Do what you're told. Follow the laws. Except it wasn't *Follow the laws and you'll be safe*, like his grandmother apparently thought. It was *Nothing you do will ever keep you safe, but follow the laws anyway.*

What if there was a way out?

The question that haunted him since the day he'd used his Talent, since he'd taken the vicious beating from Verrit and his men. Since the day one of the other inmates came to him and put that question in his mind.

She looked him in the eye, and asked him, *What if there was a way out?*

I don't know, Jason had said. *What if?*

She only shrugged. *Be nice to get out, wouldn't it?*

"Well, young Mr. Blackwood?" the Authority man pressed. "What do you think? Are you going to the Breeding Program, to see your family again, or are you going to stay here? Maybe to die here?"

"Can I have some time to think about it?" Jason breathed. He had to force the words out through the tightness in his throat.

The Authority man tilted his head to the side again. "What is there to think about?"

Yeah, idiot, what is there to think about? "I don't know if the idea of raping women in exchange for my own comfort sits very well with me."

The man blinked, spreading his hands. "Who said anything about rape?"

"You can't honestly expect me to believe that they're all willing, every time. I don't think I can perform under circumstances like that."

The smile came back and it made Jason's spine tingle. Something like fear, but colder and sharper, spread through his chest. As if the thought of 'willingness' was amusing to this man—but of course it was. He was Authority. And the Authority was used to getting what it wanted.

"Don't spend too much time in the thinking," the man said, pushing himself to his feet. He smoothed out the front of his trousers, adjusted his coat. "I would hate for something terrible to happen to you in here, and have all that Talent wasted."

Fuck you, too, asshole.

24

STELLA

DAY 13

Tashué was lying by the fountain when Stella spotted him again, three days later. The fire was finally out—the efforts of the fire crews had contained it, and a steady day of rain extinguished it. Now that the fire was vanquished, she thought it would be safe enough to return, to bring Ceridwen during the day, to find some way for them both to help. It was good for Ceridwen, she thought, to step into a great need and find her purpose, to help a community that they both loved.

But the sight of Tashué Blackwood froze her. He was stretched out on the cobbles with his head in the Jitabvi woman's lap, his arms crossed over his chest. The woman sat with her back to the fountain, one hand tangled in Tashué's hair, the other holding a tin cup that sent steam curling into her face.

It seemed strange that the most noticeable thing in the midst of all the chaos was Tashué Blackwood, lying on the ground with his head in a woman's lap. Everywhere there were signs of the toll of the fire. People wounded. Dead bodies, stretched out on the ground. People sobbing, people so shocked and tired that their eyes were empty of any emotion. Was Tashué wounded? It took her a moment to catch her breath and think clearly. No, he was probably fine. Sleeping, or at least resting. The woman was entirely too relaxed.

She squeezed Ceridwen's hand, but the girl had noticed Tashué too and she jerked her hand away. Her skirts and the long hem of her coat trailed behind her as she tore off through Market Square.

"Ceridwen, wait!"

She didn't listen, the stubborn girl—weaving through bodies, dodging people, charred wood, and puddles made thick with blood and ash, clothes still damp from the rain.

"Mr. Blackwood!" Ceridwen cried, skidding to a stop in front of the woman. "Is he hurt?"

"No, girl, he's just having a rest," the woman said, smiling up at Ceridwen.

Stella marvelled that the woman had any smiles in her. Her whole body was covered in ash and blood. Still.

Ceridwen shifted in place, wringing her hands together. Stella weaved through the crowd to catch up to her, dodging the jostling bodies that filled the courtyard.

"How do you know the Captain?" the woman asked.

"He's our neighbour," Ceridwen said, shuffling a few steps closer. "And our friend. Are you sure he's alright?"

The woman nodded. "I promise you, he's fine. He's been working hard, now he's just having a sleep."

Tashué stirred then, reaching up and rubbing his eyes with the heels of his palms. Stella tried to grab Ceridwen, to drag her away again, feeling terribly like they'd intruded on something. But Ceridwen jerked out of Stella's grasp again and she sank down on the ground, sitting nestled against Tashué. Her arrival made him stir even more and he opened his eyes finally, looking at Ceridwen. He smiled at her and pulled her down so that she rested against his chest.

"Well, hello there, little warrior." He melted again, perhaps falling asleep for a moment, his head resting so naturally in the woman's lap.

How Stella longed to sit with Ceridwen and lean against him like that, bury her face in his wool clothes and breathe in the smell of him. He probably smelled of ash still, of sweat, of rain-drenched wool. In the few days since he'd held her like that, she'd thought of little else. The feeling of his arms around her, the smell of him, the rhythm of the rise and fall of his chest. He'd held her until she felt well enough to stand, until she had pulled herself back together. She went back to helping people, whispering for those the healers couldn't save, and Tashué went back to fighting the fire.

The woman's hand returned to stroking Tashué's hair, her fingers teasing through the auburn locks, the motion mindless and incredibly intimate all at once. "Your face is looking better, Miss Whiterock. It should heal well enough."

Stella reached up, touching the stitches on her cheek. The wound was still tender, but it had scabbed well. How had the woman known Stella's name? "It'll scar, I think."

"A person without scars is a person who hasn't lived much."

Stella nodded. "That's true."

Tashué grunted and opened his eyes again, shifting so that he was flat on his back. He ran both his hands over his face, fingers lingering on the split above his brow. The swelling was gone; it was trying to heal. "I feel like I could sleep for days."

"You've earned it, I'm sure," Stella said. "Have you even been home since the fire started?"

The woman shook her head and Stella could see the weariness all across her shoulders. She hid it well, her fatigue, but Stella had noticed it. She could almost feel it herself, that weariness—or perhaps being tired was ingrained permanently into her.

"Everyone's been working hard." Tashué grunted. He shifted again, sitting up, then leaned back against the wall of the fountain as Ceridwen nestled herself in the crook of his arm. "It's nice to see you, little warrior. How've you been keeping?"

"Mam said we should see what we can do to help."

Tashué nodded. "It's good to help. I should be getting back. There's still so much to be done."

Ceridwen didn't argue and stood up when Tashué did, her eyes scanning the chaos all around her again. She looked a little calmer now, and Stella blessed Tashué Blackwood and the effect he had on Ceridwen.

Tashué's eyes found Stella's face. He stood still for a long time. He reached out. His fingers whispered against her cheek, and then found a lock of hair. He twisted it around his finger. Leaned a little closer. He might have kissed her again, but he leaned away, shaking himself.

"I'm glad you're alright," he said.

Stella nodded. "The same goes for you."

The Jitabvi woman sprang to her feet next, draining the last of the broth in her cup. "We're off again, then?"

Tashué nodded. "We're off again."

Stella caught his hand before he left, squeezing his fingers. He paused, meeting her eyes. Forced a tired smile. And then he was away. Stella couldn't help but watch him go, until he disappeared down the street. Ceridwen squeezed Stella's hand with both of hers. She stared at something through the crowd and Stella followed her gaze. A woman sat on the cobbles. She seemed to be bathed in blood, her clothes gone dark with it. There was a gash across the bridge of her nose and on her cheek that had been closed with stitches, but it hardly seemed enough of a wound to account for all the blood.

"Shall we help her first, Pigeon? She looks like she needs it."

Ceridwen nodded, but she was trembling. Stella stepped away from Ceridwen, forcing her to follow. She cut through the crowd, straight toward the woman. Stella crouched beside her, touching her shoulder gingerly to pull her back into the present. The woman turned only slowly toward her, her eyes scanning Stella's face but not connecting to anything.

"Are you alright?" Stella asked. "Are you hurt?"

"Am I…" Her hand went to the stitches on her nose. "No, I'm not hurt. Not badly. They said I didn't need a healer. Said stitches would do."

Stella nodded, reaching out with her Talent just to touch her, looking for any other wounds. There wasn't anything hidden beneath her skin, no lurking nightmares that would kill her while she sat here, only a few bruises and strained muscles.

"It's not my blood," the woman said, but she had drifted away again, staring off toward the Wharf. "My Da bled so much and I couldn't make it stop."

Ceridwen made a small noise in the back of her throat and Stella glanced up at her. Ceridwen's eyes were brimming with tears, her whole body trembling.

"Ceridwen, you see that man over there?" Stella said, pointing back toward the centre of the square. "Over by that table there? He has broth and bread for people. All you have to do is ask. Go fetch a cup of broth and a slice of bread for our friend. I think she could use something warm in her belly, what do you think?"

Ceridwen blinked through the tears to see where Stella was pointing. Her confidence was returning slowly now that she had a task, her hands relaxing.

"Off you go, Pigeon."

Ceridwen darted through the crowd. Stella sat on the ground beside the woman, turning her body so that she could watch Ceridwen at the same time. She reached out, taking the woman's hand in both of hers.

"He was dying anyway. We saw a healer a few months ago, 'cause he was coughing blood. Healer said she couldn't help us, said he had a cancer in his lungs. We were selling things off and saving our crowns to see if we could find a better healer. I didn't want to lose my Da. I have two whole silver crowns. Ain't never had two whole silver crowns before. What should I do with them, do you think?"

"Save them," Stella said. "For the right day."

"Do you think if I give them to one of the charity houses, the North Star will send me my Da back? That's all I want. Just my Da."

"It isn't up to the North Star, is it?" Stella said softly, reaching out and brushing some matted hair out of the woman's face. "It's up to the Keeper of the Keys, and once he takes someone, he doesn't give them back."

The woman's lip quivered and her eyes filled with fresh tears, but a deep breath straightened her spine. Stella could feel the swirling eddy of the woman's emotions as she battled hard against the grief.

"Do you have any other family?" Stella asked, stroking her hair. "Anyone at all?"

"Na, no family. I had a husband once, but he was a drunken wretch, wasn't he? Couldn't even give me a child, the gin-soaked bastard. I sent him out years ago. Now it's just me and my Da. Or... I guess now it's just me. I don't even have a home anymore. Fire took that too. What am I supposed to do now?"

Ceridwen returned with a tin cup and a slab of bread. Stella squeezed the woman's hand again, forcing a smile.

"Right now, you eat some bread, drink some broth. Perhaps find a place to lie down and sleep. Have you slept at all since the fire started?"

"I don't know." She blinked for a long time and then shook her head. "No, I suppose not."

Stella nodded to Ceridwen, motioning for her to sit with them. Ceridwen handed over the cup and the bread and the woman drank deeply. When the bread and broth were gone, Stella helped her climb slowly to her feet, walking her out of one knot of chaos into another. The fountain, at least, seemed a safer place.

Someone approached them with a wool blanket and the woman draped it over her own shoulders, pulling it up around her cheeks as if she meant to bury herself into it.

"Marinne!"

The woman looked up, her lip trembling again. The big toymaker, Božic, came barrelling through the crowd, leaning on a crutch instead of his wooden leg. His empty pant leg was tied into a knot to keep it from dragging on the ground, but of course he was as filthy as everyone else. He closed the distance between them, catching the woman around the shoulders with his free hand and pulling her in so completely against his body that he looked like he was trying to crush her. The woman didn't fight it, burying her face in Božic's barrel chest as her body started to tremble.

"I thought you were gone too. Thank the North Star, you're alright. Where's your old man, then? Did he make it out of that damned store?"

"Da's dead, Božic," the woman wailed. "I tried to stop the bleeding myself but I couldn't."

"Ah, girl, I'm sorry. I'm so sorry. Come on with me then and we'll get you cleaned up." His eyes shifted to Ceridwen for a moment and his face cracked into a weary smile. "Thank you, wee girl. Thank you for finding my friend."

Ceridwen nodded but didn't say anything, frozen by the woman's grief. Božic turned away, leading the woman through the crowd back the way he'd come.

"There now, see?" Stella squeezed Ceridwen's hand, forcing a smile for the girl's sake. "Sometimes all it takes is to help someone get to their feet and then the North Star guides them to where they're meant to be."

"Is she going to be alright?" Ceridwen asked, her voice so small that Stella could barely hear her over the chaos of the square.

"She isn't hurt badly, and she has friends to help her through her grief."

Stella couldn't think of any better words, for who could say how a person recovered from a thing like this? There was so much death and destruction in the Market Quarter. Stella knew enough about loss and grief to know that you never really *recovered*, so much as you learnt to go on living even though you were falling apart.

———

S tella approached the man who seemed to be in charge of it all, who stood in the centre of the chaos like a man defying a storm and telling it how to behave. His bright blue eyes fell on them and Stella felt Ceridwen quail again, her hand trembling as she clutched Stella.

"We'd like to help," Stella said.

His grey-white beard almost hid his smile, but not quite. "Excellent! We need all the help we can get." Merry blue eyes, made brighter by the black soot smearing on his face, fixed on Ceridwen. "Do you know how to make soda bread, my dear?"

"What's soda bread?" Ceridwen asked.

"It's bread without yeast or sourdough culture. Can you believe that bread without yeast can still be light and fluffy? I didn't believe it until I tasted it myself, but I can tell you that it's delightful. And no need to proof the bread before baking! What's your name, girl?"

Ceridwen glanced at Stella first, but the calm warmth of the man was easing her back to her usual self. "Ceridwen Whiterock. And this is my mam."

"It's a pleasure to meet you, little Miss Whiterock. My name is Mr. Wolfe."

He extended a hand and Ceridwen shook it, her little body swelling with pride. Stella breathed a slow sigh of relief. She'd worried about bringing Ceridwen into the blood and death and ash that had fallen on the Market Square, but she believed it was right to teach Ceridwen to respond to a crisis by helping.

"Come with me, little Miss Whiterock," Wolfe said, leading Ceridwen and Stella away, "and we'll find someone who can show you how to make bread without yeast."

It was only after the man set them up at one of the tables that Stella realized he was the Mayor of Yaelsmuir, General Nathaniel Wolfe. She turned back to say something better, to thank him perhaps, but what could be said? Everyone was doing their best.

Someone brought them water to wash their hands, and a woman talked them through the steps of making the bread. A sticky dough was made with flour, a sharp smelling white powder and sour milk, and mixed only minimally. Stella's instincts pushed her to knead the dough and make it smooth, but the woman stopped her. They dumped the ragged dough ball into an oiled cast iron pot, and the woman helped Ceridwen use a wickedly sharp knife to score a long X in the top of the ball. The lid closed over the pot and then someone with a strong arm carried the pot away to nestle it into the coals.

"Did you hear about Illea Winter's man?" someone said. "Blackwood?"

Stella looked up, but the speaker wasn't addressing her. A pair of the people cutting fresh loaves were standing close to each other.

"I heard he carried a whole family out of one of the shops. Six of them or some such. Kept going back through the flames to get them."

Illea Winter's man was what people called Tashué now? Something ugly wormed through Stella at the thought. *Illea Winter's man.* It was silly to be upset about it. She wasn't staying. She wondered what had happened to Gilda, the woman that wore the scarf in her hair and promised to take Stella to White Crown. Had her little barge been docked at the Wharf when everything exploded? If she wasn't, where would she dock now? Down in the Bay? Stella wasn't sure she'd ever find the woman again, not in the chaos of the Hive. She'd have to find some other way out of Yaelsmuir.

The mindlessness of the bread making brought Ceridwen back to herself. She started peppering the people around them with questions, even though the other volunteers were so weary that most only gave single-word answers.

Someone fished some onions out of the broth pots and brought them to the bread tables. They were too soft to cut, so the woman had Ceridwen mash them into a thick onion paste, and the next dozen or so loaves got a scoop of the savoury onion mush.

A man approached them, stripped to filthy shirtsleeves that showed the vague form of the tattoos that peppered his body. He cut right through the crowd, straight to Ceridwen. A flash of fear cut through Stella's numb fatigue. But the man was moving toward the pile of cooked bread beside Ceridwen, which more people were cutting into thick slices.

"Hullo there, little baker." The man grabbed one of the fresh loaves off the top of the pile, tossing it back and forth between his hands as the steam twisted out of the crust. "Did you make all of these?"

Ceridwen blinked at the man, looking at the loaf in his hands and then at the people slicing around them. "I think you're supposed to wait until they're cut up."

The man scoffed. "My people call it shameful to take a knife to bread. It's entirely too violent for something so sacred. My people break bread with their hands, and share it with their hearts." As if to demonstrate, the man broke the whole loaf in half, releasing a large puff of steam.

Ceridwen shifted. "I think the bread is supposed to be for everyone."

The man laughed and winked at Ceridwen, pushing both pieces of bread back together and tucking them under one arm. "Very well, then, what if I trade you?" He fished around in his pocket, pulling a small paper bag out and tossing it a few times. "I'll trade you this bag of licorice allsorts for the loaf of bread. What say you?"

Stella bit her lip against the laugh that tried to bubble in her throat, watching the battle in Ceridwen's eyes. Candy was a grave temptation for her indeed, but even at such a young age, she believed in rules and order. The bread was to be sliced and distributed to everyone.

The man chuckled, tossing the bag up and catching it a few times. "Ah, I see you are a young woman of upright character, immune to such petty bribery."

"You should find out if he has anything else," Stella said, fighting to keep from smiling. "If he had a bag of licorice in his pocket, he might have other things hidden away."

The man grinned at Stella. "You're driving up the price of bread in such difficult times?"

"She's right," Ceridwen said, lifting her chin. "I don't like licorice allsorts. I don't like the flavour. Do you have any other kind of candy?"

"The pair of you are regular profiteers. I hope you're quite proud of yourselves. Fine then. I have..." he made a great show of searching through his trouser pockets, as if there were nooks and crannies that couldn't be reached under ordinary circumstances, "...about a dozen nectar drops. Do those meet your exacting tastes, Miss Baker?"

Ceridwen's chin went higher. "My name is Whiterock."

"A pleasure to meet you, Miss Whiterock. My name is Mr. Saeati. Do we have a deal?"

"There's no deal until we see the nectar drops, sir," Stella said before Ceridwen could say anything.

Saeati grinned at Stella, trying to make it look like a grimace or a glare but failing. He pulled out the bag of nectar drops and tossed them onto the table, the bag giving a satisfying thunk. He snatched back the bag of licorice drops and shoved it into his pockets, shaking his head. "The pair of you drive a hard bargain."

"Check the bag, Pigeon. Make sure they're nectar drops and not something else."

"Questioning my honesty! I'm offended, lady."

"You can be offended all you like, sir, but we're still checking to make sure the payment is what was agreed," Stella said.

Saeati laughed and Ceridwen snatched the bag, unfurling the paper to peek inside. She left a smear of flour and wet dough on the paper, but the beaming smile that spread across her face was plenty confirmation.

"We have a deal," Ceridwen said brightly.

Saeati thrust out a hand, undaunted by Ceridwen's sticky dough fingers. Ceridwen grinned as she shook his hand, leaving a smear of dough on him too. "It was a pleasure doing business with you, Miss Whiterock."

He took one of the halves of the loaf from beneath his arm and broke it in half again. He whistled, the sound short and sharp, then tossed one of the quarters to Mayor Wolfe. The Mayor caught the bread deftly before he stomped away to deal with some new issue.

A shiver seemed to pass through the crowd in the square, some fear that turned all the chaos to stillness and quiet. And then Stella heard it, a voice, drifting through the crowded square. She could feel the urgency in the voice, even if she couldn't hear the words right away, and it sent a shiver through her whole body.

"Help! I need help here! Someone help!"

Saeati was first to react, dropping the bread and bursting into a blistering run across the square and disappearing into one of the alleys. There was a slow trickle of people following him, and then a rush as the shouting grew louder and more urgent. Stella felt something tug on her, as if something had caught her by the guts and was pulling her to the sound of that desperate voice. It was familiar. Or was it her imagination?

"Has the fire started again?" someone asked.

Stella looked up over the roofs of the buildings, searching for plumes of smoke that might herald a second fire. It wasn't uncommon for wind to stir the coals back to life, for the rescue efforts to uncover too much heat that set things ablaze again, but there was no hint of new smoke.

"Stay there, Ceridwen," Stella said as she stepped around the table. "Keep making bread. Don't go anywhere."

"Mam, where are you going?"

"I'm going to go see if I can help. Stay here, Pigeon!"

25

TASHUÉ

DAY 13

A voice drew Tashué to the pile of rubble. At first he thought he was imagining things, driven half-mad by grief and guilt and exhaustion, the voices of the dead rattling in his skull. Sleeping by the fountain hadn't helped. It only left him more exhausted.

Help.

I'm sorry. This is all my fault.

Help.

So many dead because I couldn't catch him.

"Somebody! Is there anyone there? Help! Help, please!"

The next thing he knew, he was battling a fallen tin roof. The remains of a large building were scattered around the tin. It looked like the building had been knocked over by the fire crews, but the fire had claimed half the building anyway. So much fucking tin. Tashué hated tin now, but unlike his badge, this tin was viciously sharp. A hot rush of blood spread across his hand, dripping from his fingers. He looked down at his hand, at the deep cut that started up the side of his smallest finger and then travelled up the heel of his palm and to his wrist. His mind was slow to realize how badly he'd cut himself, but the ache came eventually. Settled deep.

"Help! Help! I'm here!"

He kept digging. He was so tired that the pain in his hand couldn't get a good hold on him. He didn't feel the strain in the muscles of his arms, shoulders, back. He only felt his heart, clattering in his chest. And the desperation, the urgency.

He was stopped by a solid wooden beam. He dug through the debris all around the beam. One side was charred down to the core, but the charring faded halfway through until the other side was solid and unmarred. The tin had protected the youth beneath the beam from the other falling rubble, bricks and wood and from the rest of the building. But Tashué saw also that the beam was resting on a pile of bricks, allowing it to hover above the boy instead of crushing him completely. The boy blinked against the afternoon sun, his eyes watering. His lips were so dry that they were bleeding, and his face had a greyish pallor. Was the boy as good as dead already?

"Well hello there, young man," Tashué said, crouching down to reach out and take the boy's hand. Blood covered both of them, splattering on the boy's sleeve. "Can you move now? Can you make your way out?"

The boy tried to lick his lips, but there was no moisture left on his tongue. "I can't move my leg."

"Your leg, is it?" Tashué eased through the rubble. The fulcrum bricks were resting on the boy's pelvis and thigh. Tashué moved a few of them, leaving a smear of blood behind. But he couldn't move any that were carrying the weight without sending the whole pile collapsing. "Just a few bricks here. We'll move the beam and then you'll be out in no time. They have bread and broth in the Market Square. How's that sound? It must be a while since you had something to eat."

"I don't know. I was trying to get some things out. The fire wasn't close yet. But then the far side did catch and the fire crews came and I think they knocked this side of the building over. Is the fire out now? Did they stop the fire?"

"We did," Tashué said. He moved around the beam. The other side was still covered in tin. He ripped away the next panel. His hands were bleeding so much that they were trembling now, weakness spreading slowly through his body. He drew his old cavalry knife, using the blade to scrape charcoal dust off the burnt side of the beam. He packed the dust into the wound to slow the bleeding, but his hands were clumsy. The exhaustion coming to him would hit him as hard as those bricks.

Under the beam, on the other side of the brick fulcrum, a woman hadn't been so lucky. Her long black hair was clotted with blood, which seemed to have leaked from her mouth and her nose and her ears. Tashué took a deep breath and returned to the other side, looking down at the boy. "Or the rain did. Last night. Did you hear the rain last night?"

"I don't know. Can you get me out? I can't move my leg. It hurts! Please, can you get me out?"

"I'll see what I can do," Tashué said, resting a hand on the beam and testing the weight of it. "I'm going to try to move the beam and then I'll get you to the Market Square. They'll have everything you need. How does that sound? I had some bread myself and it's quite good. I heard Mayor Wolfe is going to have some proper beef brought up too, and he'll turn the broth into soup soon."

"Soup sounds nice," the boy gasped. "With beef you think?"

"Of course. What else would you expect from the Wolfe family?"

The boy smiled, his eyes distant. "They trade pork too. Everyone always talks about Wolfe and beef, but they trade just as much pork. My mum, she smokes pork. Bacon, ham. Sausage. Buys it all from Wolfe butchers. Says she always gets fair dealing from Wolfe butchers. Other butchers try to raise the price, or sell her lower quality meat. Not the Wolfe butchers."

Tashué made his way around to the boy's head, testing his grip on the beam. "I'm going to try to lift this beam, alright? Just a little, just enough to loosen the weight so that you can get out. Are you ready? As soon as I lift, try to pull yourself out."

"Yes, sir."

"Ready?"

"Yes, sir!"

Tashué planted his feet as firmly as he could, reaching down and getting his hands under the beam. It was worn smooth by age and Tashué's bloodied hands slipped and slithered as he tried to lift it. Tashué cursed, stepping back a moment and wiping his hands on his pant legs. The ash had helped some, but the wound was still oozing. Tashué dug his heels into the rubble and tried to push the beam to one side, hoping that he could slide it right off the pile, but as it shifted, the bricks only seemed to spread across the boy's body and the beam sunk lower, closer to him.

"Shit. I can't lift it, not on my own." Tashué took a deep breath, reaching for the last shred of strength he had. "I'm going to get some help, alright? I just need a few more people to help and then we'll get you out."

"No, wait, don't leave!" the boy cried. "Don't leave me alone again! I can't be alone anymore."

"I'm coming right back, I swear," Tashué said, stepping carefully around the boy's head. "I just need to find someone to help me lift this damned beam and then we'll have you out in no time at all."

"No, please, please don't go. Please! I'll try again, I'll pull myself out!"

The boy started scrabbling at the rubble, trying to drag himself out. The pile of bricks spread further and the beam kept sinking.

"Stop!" Tashué howled, leaping closer, scrabbling for purchase on the beam but it had settled itself already. "Stop, boy, stop moving! This thing is going to crush you if you keep moving. Just stay still. I won't leave, alright? But just stay still!"

Tears welled in the boy's eyes and his lip trembled, but he nodded. "I'm sorry," he gasped. "I didn't mean to."

"It's fine," Tashué breathed, sinking down to his knees. He was so damned tired. "Just stay still now."

The boy nodded. Tashué reached down, patting his shoulder. He lifted his fingers to his mouth and whistled, hoping the sound was piercing enough to get attention. He didn't hear anyone coming, not right away. He tried to remember how far he was from the Market Square, but he couldn't be sure. How long had he been wandering through wreckage? The fact that the rubble was only half eaten by fire meant that he had reached the perimeter, but where was that? He whistled again. Waiting. Did he hear voices somewhere in the distance, or was that his imagination playing tricks? Where was Kazrani? They'd parted ways at some point. She went back to the Market Square to get water but she hadn't come back. Or had he wandered too far for her to find him? He cupped his hands around his mouth and took a deep breath.

"Help!" he cried. "I need help here! Someone help!"

A pause. The moment seemed to stretch for an eternity. He took a deep breath to call again but he heard footsteps—Ishmael. He sprinted down the alley, dodging the rubble. How could he possibly have so much energy?

"I need help moving the beam," Tashué said, forcing himself up to his feet. "I can't get him out from under it unless we lift it off."

"Alright, Captain, not a problem," Ishmael said, patting Tashué's shoulders with both hands and pushing him back down. "Have a seat, catch your breath. That beast looks too big for the two of us to lift anyway so let's wait for more help." He turned back the way he came, giving another whistle, though his was louder and carried better. He put his hands on his hips and his face broke into a wide grin, looking down at the boy. "Hullo there, son. What's your name?"

"M-my name?"

"Of course, lad. Have you forgotten it?"

"No! My name's Edwin. Everyone calls me Eddie."

"It's good to meet you, Eddie. My name's Ishmael. I haven't got any good nicknames, I'm afraid. Oh—that's not true. My mother used to call me Kishleh, and that's when I knew I was going to catch hell."

"Why?" Eddie asked, blinking up at Ishmael. "What does Kishleh mean?"

Ishmael grinned. "Means 'trouble'. So, what was this big mess, Eddie? Was this a warehouse?"

"No, sir, it was my home," the boy gasped. "We live in the big row house, the only one in Market Quarter, everyone called it the Hook cause it was shaped like a fisherman's hook—can you see my mum? She was with me. She was talking yesterday, I think. It was before the rain, maybe, but then when the rain came I couldn't hear her anymore. And then she hasn't said anything since."

"Alright, Eddie, calm down," Ishmael said. He crouched beside the boy, finding Eddie's hand and squeezing it. "We have you now. Take a few deep breaths for me, that's a good lad. The Captain and I are going to get you out, and then we'll look for your mum."

Ishmael glanced at Tashué, but Tashué shook his head, gesturing to the body he'd found on the other side of the fulcrum.

"For now we're going to worry about getting this big log off you, hey?" Ishmael went on. "Here comes Mayor Wolfe himself. Not many people can say they got rescued by the Mayor, can they?"

"Mum will be so happy," Eddie breathed. "She voted for Mr. Wolfe. She told everyone the story of the time she met him at one of his butcher shops and shook his hand. Do you think he'll help rescue her, too?"

Ishmael nodded. "He'll be happy to help however he can."

General Wolfe herded a group of helpers up to the pile and around the beam. Tashué pushed himself back up to his feet, wavering. He found himself staring down at his own hands, at the deep and ugly gash along the side. The ash had almost stopped the bleeding. He packed more in, gritting his teeth against the hot ache of angry flesh.

Tashué's legs plodded forward mechanically and he took up a place beside the boy's head. Eddie, he reminded himself. Tashué didn't dare ask if the boy had any other family because he was terrified the answer was 'no.'

"Maybe you should sit down."

Tashué looked to his left to see that Kazrani had joined them. She had him by the sleeve and she was trying to tug him away from the beam but he shrugged her off. "Have to get him out."

"On the count of three, we're going to lift," Wolfe said. There was something soothing in his firm voice, in following the orders instead of making decisions. "Everyone ready? One. Two. Three. Lift!"

Tashué put all his strength into it and this time the beam moved the right way—up. Even with so many hands lifting, the thing was damn heavy. Tashué's muscles ached and strained, his arms and back and shoulders all screaming. Everyone shuffled slowly across the pile, placing their feet carefully. It was a long stretch for Tashué to step over Eddie but of them all, he was the only one with legs long enough.

"Down to the bottom of the pile, if you can make it," General Wolfe said. "You all are doing excellent. Just a little further."

Rubble shifted beneath Tashué's foot and he staggered. The weight of the beam came down too hard on his right, the worst of the two hands, and blood oozed from the wound again.

"Ah fuck—I can't hold on!"

And his hands let go.

The other people fought with the beam, trying to hold it, but the weight of it had shifted too much and there was a mad scramble of people getting out of the way. The beam hit the pile of rubble and sent up a cloud of dust and ash, the wood giving a low resonance as it hit some piece of stone, and then it was tumbling down the pile. It hit the cobbles with an ugly crash that shook the whole thing, bouncing and rolling a little further before it was still.

"Anyone hurt?" General Wolfe asked.

Tashué turned back to Eddie, staggering along the pile and sinking down beside the boy. The cobbles around Eddie were still wet from the rain and the cold seeped into Tashué's trousers. The rest of the volunteers had scattered across the pile. Ishmael must have told General Wolfe that they were standing on the Hook and they were off to search for more survivors. Ishmael came back into the hole, digging through the bricks, tossing them away.

"Wait!" Stella. She had followed, too, pulled in by the chaos, and she staggered into the crater. "Wait, stop! Don't dig him out yet!"

Ishmael froze, one brick still in his hands, most of the pile still sitting on Eddie's body. The boy probably could have wriggled free now, but he had frozen too, his eyes on Stella.

"We need a healer before you dig him out," she gasped. "We need someone here, ready to help, or he could still die. The release of pressure could kill him if there's no one here to help him once the bricks are gone."

"Can you do it?" Ishmael asked, breathless and tired.

Stella paused—Tashué wondered what made her hesitate. "No, I can't. I'm not a healer. I'm only a whisperer."

"There's value still in a whisperer," Wolfe said, laying a hand on Stella's arm. "Perhaps you could help by removing the lad's pain while we find someone."

Stella nodded, hefting up her skirts to pick her way through the rubble. She settled beside Eddie, but her eyes were on Tashué. Tashué could feel her Talent, touching the boy so tenderly, and Eddie's whole body relaxed once his pain was gone. Stella's eyes drifted down to Tashué's hands. The right one was still bleeding. He watched the blood slide down the heel of his palm, bead on the end of his smallest finger, then fall into the rubble. He was surprised to see that his hand wasn't shaking, because his whole body felt like it was trembling.

"How old are you, son?" Ishmael asked. He stood beside the brick pile, ready to spring into action.

Stella squeezed the boy's hand when he didn't respond. "I know you're tired. You must have been waiting for help for a long time, but you have to stay awake a little longer. Look at me."

The boy's eyes drifted over to her, but they were bleary and distant.

"After the healer comes and we dig you out, you can sleep then," Stella said. She brushed the hair out of Eddie's face, smiling. "But for now, I think you should stay awake. So why don't you tell us how old you are?"

"I turned fourteen last week," Eddie said. He was shivering, his teeth clacking together. "Mum said I was a real man now and she was going to take me to buy my horse."

Ishmael smiled—and it made Tashué ache. He knew the toll all of this would take on Ishmael, but of course he was here to help. "What kind of horse were you hoping to get?"

"I was hoping—I was thinking I would like a black horse. All the heroes have black horses, in the stories? So I thought black."

"Ah, well, I'm afraid I don't know much about horses, so I couldn't help you," Ishmael said. "Captain Blackwood here was a cavalryman in the military. What say you, Captain? Were your best horses indeed black ones?"

Tashué dragged his head up, blinking through his bone-deep fatigue. "My best horse was a dapple grey. She was a brave, vicious beast. Took a chunk out of a soldier's arm during a charge, once. Probably saved my life that day. The soldier had a gun pointed right at me, but I didn't see him with everything else going on."

"I thought the Jitabvi ponies were little shaggy brown horses," Ishmael said.

Tashué shook his head. "I couldn't ride the Jitabvi ponies. I'm too tall. Anyway, my best advice is not to worry too much about the colour of your horse. Better to have a healthy animal with a character that matches what you're looking for. If you want to join the Dominion cavalry, you need a horse that is strong and brave and well trained. But if you are looking for a first horse as a pet, better to go with a horse that is friendly and gentle. You wouldn't want your arm bitten half off."

Eddie's eyes widened to big white saucers. "I didn't know horses could bite."

Tashué nodded. "They bite hard if they have a reason to."

Someone's Talent spread across the rubble, a slow, creeping warmth that was beautifully familiar. Tashué felt his own strength return, just a bit, pulling him back from the brink of his exhaustion. He rose to his feet, looking out over the rubble. Rhodrishi Kheir moved through the chaos. He didn't live in Yaelsmuir, but in the legacy territory to the east. Tashué stepped over the boy's prone form to help Rhodrishi down into the hole. He wasn't a young man, his face deeply lined with age, his thick grey hair pulled back from his face in a tight ponytail. His hands seemed older even than his face, his joints swollen and his knuckles rent with deep wrinkles. Tattoos swirled across his hands, the ink well faded with age. He grimaced at the wounds on Tashué's hand, at the blood that was dripping onto his boot.

"I've put so much work into keeping you alive, Captain,"

Rhodrishi said. "I would appreciate it if you put a little effort in yourself."

"It's good to see you, Colonel," Tashué said, and it was so good that he felt the relief in his bones. "Colonel, this is Eddie. He was pinned by that beam there, but the bricks saved him. Miss Whiterock didn't want us to dig him out until there was a healer here to help him."

Rhodrishi nodded, his eyes sweeping across the whole scene and drinking in the details. His eyes lingered on Stella, but then settled on Eddie. "Miss Whiterock was right. But don't you worry, son, I'll make sure these fine rescuers get you out now. Are you able to help your patients sleep, Miss Whiterock? It might be easier for our Eddie."

Stella nodded. "Eddie was falling asleep when I took his pain, so I think it will be easy enough. What say you, Eddie? You rest and when you wake up, you'll be wrapped in a blanket with a meal waiting for you."

Eddie nodded, but there were tears in his eyes again. "Am I going to die? I don't want to die not knowing that it's happening. I've heard the Keeper of the Keys doesn't take people if they die without knowing it and then they're stuck here."

Rhodrishi reached for his Talent, and Tashué felt it, the pooling of strength and energy. "I will do my very best to make sure that doesn't happen."

Eddie didn't have a chance to respond, his eyes sliding shut as Stella gently stroked his hair. Tashué could only stand and watch, and feel Rhodrishi's Talent. Was it possible that the healing force was spreading out of Eddie's body and into his own? He looked down at his hands. Clots formed in the ugly wound, finally stemming the flow of blood. His hands were so beaten up by digging through the rubble. The long, clean slice from the tin was only the worst of the wounds.

A chunky, round sound of bricks smashing together pulled Tashué up out of his stupor, and he looked to see Ishmael tossing the bricks away, revealing Eddie's body. His clothes hid the wounds, but still Tashué could see how terribly flat his hip looked, his thigh twisted at a strange angle so that his foot pointed the wrong way.

Rhodrishi reached out, gripping Ishmael's arm. "I need a clear space to lay him down, but I need to stay close to the rubble. Hopefully there'll be more survivors and we're likely to see more crush injuries. I'll need to be close at hand."

Ishmael nodded and he was away in an instant. Rhodrishi turned to Stella next, offering a hand to help her to her feet.

"Perhaps you could help guide the rescuers to find survivors? Can you do that? With your Talent?"

Stella nodded, but she didn't move away. Why did she hesitate again? Her eyes wandered to Tashué, looking at his hands and then up to his face. And Tashué, as tired as he was, wanted to reach across to her, to bury his face in the crook of her neck and breathe in the scent of her, to pull her body against his. And sleep. Maybe for the rest of the year. But at least he could be sleeping with her in his arms. He clenched his fists instead, focusing on the pain. Reminding himself of the look on her face when he kissed her a few days ago. He didn't ever want to make her feel like that again.

"I can't stay, sir," she said. "I have a shift at the Facility of Rest and I should be heading there now."

"It's no problem, Miss Whiterock," General Wolfe said, stepping closer. "Your help here is invaluable. I'll sign the paperwork for the Facility. I seem to recall signing paperwork for you once already."

"Thank you, sir, but it's more than that. I've my daughter with me—back at the bread tables. She's too young to be here all night. Usually she sleeps at the Facility while I work, but certainly everyone there is too busy to keep watch over her. If I'm here, I'm afraid I don't have a safe place for her to sleep tonight."

"Kaz can take Ceridwen," Tashué said. "She was saying she's going to go home to sleep tonight. She's spent, though she won't admit it. If she brings Ceridwen to my apartment, they can both sleep there. And then you'll know where to find her come morning."

Stella looked at him a while before she answered. She always seemed to need a moment to think before she answered anything he said. Was it because he was her tinman now? He cursed himself again. Was she worried he'd be offended if she declined the offer? How could he tell her that she didn't need to fear him? He couldn't ever lift a finger against her.

She nodded, breaking the moment of stillness. General Wolfe burst into motion, tracking down Kazrani to introduce her to Stella and set them off with their marching orders—fetch Ceridwen, bring her to Tashué's apartment. Kazrani paused on the pile, looking at Tashué first. Maybe resisting the urge to insist he go home, too. She gave a weary nod and followed Stella back to the Market Square.

"Captain," Rhodrishi said, pulling Tashué's attention back, "would you lift the young man, please? My back isn't what it once was."

Tashué crouched down, scooping the boy up. He was so little, so light. The bones of the boy's pelvis shifted and crunched, the skin feeling taut like a drum skin pulled too tight. Tashué made his way down the pile, where Ishmael had cleared a space for the boy. Someone had thought to bring blankets and they stretched one out, folding another to be a pillow. The boy whimpered in his sleep but didn't wake. Tashué rested on one knee to lay him down on the ground, pushing his hair out of the boy's face and leaving a smear of half-dried blood and ash.

"You should go home, Captain. Get some sleep. You look half-dead yourself."

How could Tashué possibly explain to Rhodrishi how responsible he felt? He had his hands on that brightman. Both hands, grasping at the brightman's coat, at his sleeves. But then the man had slipped through his fingers and was down the stairs. If only he'd been faster, stronger, his legs less tired, he could have stopped all this. If he hadn't flinched away from his own Talent, so many people would still be alive.

But did he even need to explain it to Rhodrishi? He didn't really understand how Talent worked, or indeed why it seemed to work so much better for the Kaadayri specifically. Could Rhodrishi look into his eyes and know what he was thinking?

"I can't stop," Tashué said, and the weight of the words only added to his weariness. "I have to help. It was a row house. I have to help them find survivors."

The gathering dark only made it harder to dig through the rubble and find people. Tashué returned to where he'd found Eddie, looking down at the woman crushed by being on the wrong side of a pile of bricks. He pushed the mess of hair from her face, trying to see if there was a familial resemblance between her and the boy. They both had dark hair, but it was a tenuous link at best. The rest of her face was too damaged to be able to tell. It was hard to imagine this woman talking, as Eddie had said. Was her shattered face even capable of speech?

"Is this Eddie's mum, then?" General Wolfe asked.

"I don't know, General," Tashué breathed. "I can't tell."

"I'll help you lift her."

What a mess the pair of them must have looked like—Tashué covered in his own blood, General Wolfe with his limp. Tashué lifted her by her knees and Wolfe hooked his arms under hers. Ishmael had set up a different area for the dead, and they brought her there, laying her gently among the growing pile of bodies. A child, a man, another woman. A few bodies so charred or so crushed that it couldn't be known what they were. Tashué watched another body arrive, and another. And Rhodrishi was still only helping Eddie.

He felt something brush against his hand and looked down. Fingers, gingerly probing the edges of the largest wound. He followed the fingers up the arm and found the familiar copper curls that haunted his every thought, the bitter autumn wind lifting the locks of hair. Stella was looking at him so intently. It made his knees weak, meeting those bright green eyes.

"You should rest."

She twined her fingers in his, undaunted by the blood. His other hand reached for her, acting without his consent, and he found a stray curl, wrapping it around his finger. The lock picked up some of his blood and some of the grime, turning a darker shade of red. She was so still and so strong, a pillar of stone undaunted by the chaos. It had been a long time since his world had so much blood in it.

"I can't stop."

She nodded and he blessed her for accepting it instead of arguing. He wasn't sure he could resist her if she pushed her will on him. He uncoiled his finger from her hair, but he didn't have the strength to untangle his fingers from hers. So much for not touching her anymore. Had she taken his hand, or had he taken hers? He couldn't remember. His hand was warmer now that Stella was holding it, the heat spreading up his arm and into his chest. Was she using her Talent on him, somehow separating him from his exhaustion like she separated people from their pain? Or was it Rhodrishi, channelling him a bit more energy to fuel him through the oncoming night?

She let go of his hand, stepping away. He took a deep breath, and plunged back into the chaos.

26

STELLA

DAY 14

With so many hands helping, they sifted through the rubble of the Hook by dawn. With Eddie, there were only six other survivors.

Stella didn't know what the official tally was, the number of wounded and dead. It was still growing, with new pockets of people being found as the rescuers pushed deeper and deeper into the borders laid by the fire. But there weren't many survivors among the ashes and the sodden charcoal. Stella had been to enough fire rescues to know the pattern of it. In the first days, there were lots of survivors. Smoke in the lungs, burns on the body, cuts and broken bones. The longer it raged, though, the fewer were found, even with healers on hand.

Stella found Tashué again, sitting on a pile of rubble, watching over the wounded. He sat and stared at them, his eyes so blank and empty that she was scared for him. Pulled to him again, as she ever would be, she sank down beside him. Eddie's bones were so smashed that Stella wondered if Rhodrishi's massive Talent and skill would be enough to save his ability to walk. Talent could only hasten things that would happen naturally, especially when a living body was involved.

Stella sank down beside Tashué and took his hands gingerly, turning them over to inspect the wounds. They were worse still than when she saw him last, more cuts and shredded flesh, a fingernail smashed and bloody. Ash clogged most of the wounds, but some of them still oozed. She resisted the urge to touch him with her Talent again. She'd funnelled him a little strength, as much as she could spare, but Rhodrishi had been using his Talent in the same moment on Eddie and she didn't think Tashué had realized that she was using hers at all.

"Are you intending to steal my patient, Miss Whiterock?"

Glancing up, Stella saw Ishmael approach. He had a flagon of water in one hand, and an aid pack tucked under one arm. Mallory Imburleigh had arrived with crates of aid packs, needles and twine for stitches, muslin for bandages, a few pieces of wood for splinting small fractures and breaks, and small scissors for trimming the twine and the bandages.

"I found your patient unattended, Mr. Saeati," Stella said, letting go of Tashué's hands as Ishmael passed the flagon down to her. Someone must be boiling the water from the fountain, to make it clean and safe. She drank deeply, trying to wash the taste of ash from her throat, but it wouldn't let go. "You should have staked your claim better if you meant to keep him all to yourself."

"Ah," Ishmael said with a wistful smile, "but how can I presume to keep him away from you?"

Ishmael sat on the other side of Tashué, handing the aid pack to Stella. She handed the flagon back, unrolling the aid pack to find a needle. Ishmael drank deeply, then poured some water over his head, rubbing the soot and sweat and dried blood off his face. He had such fine features, long limbs and fluid movements. He could be a dancer, with all the endless grace that he had.

Ishmael elbowed Tashué, motioning to his hands. Tashué stretched them out. Ishmael poured water on them and Tashué cupped his hands together, catching as much water as he could, then rubbing his palms together. He stopped when one of the wounds reopened, the skin peeling back, the blood starting to ooze again. Ishmael poured more water, washing the fresh blood away.

Stella pulled Tashué's hand onto her lap. He hissed as the needle went into his skin, baring his teeth. She could feel the tension in his arms, but he didn't say anything as she added a line of stitches, holding the flap of skin closed. She wondered if he would notice her using her Talent. She could knit some of the wounds, just a little more, just enough to make sure they would all close. Surely he didn't care about the scars, but she didn't want them to become corrupted with infection. She couldn't bear to see that, to watch him wither away, to watch his fingers turn black and green, the decay crawling up his big arms. Strength didn't matter when a wound went bad.

When the last stitch was snipped, she turned his hand, finding the long gash down the side of his hand and up to his wrist, the one that had dripped blood for so long. The skin was swollen and tender, the wound so deep.

He cursed as the needle pushed through his skin, leaning away, but Ishmael pushed back against him.

"Quit whinging," Ishmael said. "You've taken worse wounds than this. I've seen the scars."

"Fuck you."

Ishmael laughed. "There's that fire. Had me worried with all that quiet."

Tashué squeezed his eyes shut, sucking in a deep breath. It took near a dozen stitches to close the long gash, from his wrist to his palm. She moved slowly, methodically, making a neat little line of ties, like soldiers on a ridge. How long had it been since she had tended to a wound like this with her hands? Perhaps not since Cruinnich had she needed to use twine and a needle on anything but fabric.

"Let me see the other hand," she said.

He reached out, and she was entirely too aware of how close their bodies were. His breathing was so slow and deep that she wondered if he was sleeping while sitting up, and she had to look up at his face a few times to see if his eyes were open. He was watching her, watching her hands, looking at her hair as it was caught by the breeze. And Ishmael, sitting beside them both, watched them.

With her hands busy in the important task of stitching him closed, it was easy enough to resist the urge to kiss him on his very serious mouth. She would taste ash, probably, and sweat, but maybe it would make his lips turn in a smile and bring a little light back to his eyes. The pain and the fatigue must have drained him of all his emotion, turning him as numb as Stella used to be. She wanted to return him the favour that he had given her, to drag him back to himself and save him from the empty void of numb despair he was staring down into. She replaced the rest of the twine and the needles and the little scissors into the aid pack, rolling it back up. She didn't think he would let her wrap his hands in the bandages.

"Are you hiding any other good wounds from us, Captain?" Ishmael asked, prodding Tashué again.

Tashué shook his head, reaching up with his newly stitched hands to wipe his face. "Is there anyone else?"

"No, no one's found any bodies in a while. It's time for you to go home, and get some rest. You hear me? General's orders. He doesn't want to see you here anymore, not until tomorrow morning at least. Should I walk you home, or can I trust you'll make it there without being tempted by any other disasters?"

Tashué huffed at Ishmael, turning and reaching out to the flagon of water. Ishmael handed it over and Tashué drank, nearly draining it. The last of it, he poured over his head, rinsing some of the soot and ash and blood away.

"Come, Mr. Blackwood," Stella said, rising to her feet and taking Tashué by the arm. "I'll walk you home and collect Ceridwen. She'll be hungry."

Tashué stood with her, taking a deep breath. Stella thought for a moment that he was about to plunge back into the wreckage of the Hook, but he looked down at the wounded instead. "Did you find his mum?"

Ishmael shrugged, reaching into his pocket and pulling out a heel of bread. "Don't know. The Colonel's kept the wounded sleeping all night. He wants us to move them today."

"Let me know," Tashué said, his voice raspy and brittle. "If you find her."

"Eddie can tell you himself, next you see him. We'll take good care of him."

Tashué nodded and Stella tugged his arm, guiding him away. He walked with the slow, plodding steps of a man on his last reserves of strength. She walked so close to him that their hands brushed together, the prickly ends of each stitched knot of twine scraping Stella's skin. She reached out to him, her fingers lacing in his again. Touching him made her heart beat fast.

"You've been working hard," she said, breaking the strange silence between them. "I've heard the stories about you."

Instead of lightening the mood or making him smile, it made him scowl. "I've heard them too. They're idiotic stories. Carried six people out of a burning building. Dug out a whole family. As if I was the only one working to save people."

"Not the only one, just the most recently famous. It's easier to talk about someone when people are already gossiping about them."

"I don't like it."

Stella shrugged. "It won't last. People will find someone new to talk about. Illea Winter seems to lose interest quickly and cycles through her lovers to keep the gossip fresh. I can't help but wonder, though—if you didn't want your life gossiped about, why did you stay the night at the Winter house? Surely you must have known what people would say."

Tashué sighed and stopped walking, turning to look her in the eye. He looked sad, she thought. She cursed herself for bringing it up. What business was it of hers?

"I wasn't thinking about what people would say. I was only thinking…" He sighed again, shaking his head and looking away, down the road and back toward the Market Square. "I was only thinking that it had been a long time since I'd been with someone, and it's not easy to say no to Illea Winter."

"No, I imagine it isn't." She could understand that, the emptiness that lived in your gut when it had been too long since another person touched your body. What was it about him that made her ache so badly? Was it just that it had been so long for her as well? "She's very beautiful, isn't she?"

"Yes," he said. His eyes came back to her, drifting down to her hand as if he only just realized that their fingers were laced together again. He ran his thumb along the back of her knuckles, and she felt the scrape of his callus. He reached for her hair with his other hand, finding the same corkscrew curl that he'd twisted around his finger the night before. "So are you, Miss Whiterock. I think you're the most beautiful woman I've ever seen in my entire life."

The words made her whole body burn but she shook her head. "You flatter me, Mr. Blackwood." She took her hand from his, hooking her arm around his bicep instead and tugging him along the road. "Come, I should get you home before you collapse in the street."

His plodding steps continued on, straight down the main road that clove through the city from Highview to the Market Square. It was strange to watch the transition to normalcy as they moved into Brickheart, the bustle of human traffic only somewhat thinned by the chaos in the Market Quarter. While standing in the midst of the destruction, it felt like the whole city had been sucked into the efforts to save lives and shift through the rubble. But the further away they walked, the more people were going about their daily business. So it always was. No matter how miserable things were somewhere, life always managed to go on everywhere else.

K azrani was busying herself in the kitchen when they stepped inside, a slab of bread sitting on the top of the potbelly stove to toast as the fire crackled. She turned to them and took stock of Tashué in one long sweep of her eyes.

"You look fucking terrible, Captain."

"Fuck you, Lieutenant."

The exchange had a familiar feel to it, a comfort that contrasted the harshness of the actual words. Kazrani plucked her bread off the surface of the stove, flipping it over to toast the other side. "Your daughter is still sleeping, Miss Whiterock. She had a hard time settling last night." She shrugged. "It's a new bed and I imagine she had a hard day. I taught her an old Jitabvi lullaby and that seemed to help. I hope you don't mind."

"Not at all, Miss Mahalouwan. Thank you for looking after her."

Kazrani smiled as she plucked the bread off the stove again, taking a big bite from one corner. "It was nice to use that song again. Reminded me of when my boy was little. He never slept well. As if lying still for all those hours was too big of a challenge."

Tashué snorted. "You say that like you can't figure out where he got that trait from."

Kazrani waved her bread at him, scowling. "I'm not the one who stayed in the Market for four days straight. That was you, sir."

"At least the fire's out."

The scowl fell away from her face and she looked down at the floor. "True, at least the fire's out." She took a deep breath and seemed to shake herself. "I'll see you at the station house later?"

"You're going back to the station house?"

"Of course I am," Kazrani said, throwing her hands up. "I have *paperwork* to fill out. Khosran will be crawling out of his skin by now, wanting to know where we've been. As if he can't imagine. Heaven save me from men of little imagination."

"But there's still people trapped in the rubble!"

"That may be the case, but there are plenty of able and willing volunteers to get them out. The Governor will show his face eventually and then the cleaning crews will start in earnest. But there probably aren't many people left alive, Captain."

Stella's heart skipped a beat. It wasn't Kazrani's words—it was something she had suspected herself, and she was no stranger to death and disaster—but it was the way Tashué went completely still except for the sharp intake of breath. Kazrani wasn't so daunted by the rage that seemed to emanate from him like heat waves, squaring off as if the pair of them were about to brawl.

And then, just as suddenly and viciously as the anger came, Tashué took another deep breath and stomped off to his room.

Kazrani sighed. She reached out, brushing the crumbs off the surface of the stove with movements so quick that she didn't get burned. "Don't worry about him. He's angry because he blames himself. Or me. Or both of us, I suppose."

"How could it possibly be his fault? I thought it was a barge explosion."

Kazrani nodded, crouching down to add a few more logs to the fire. "It was my brightman that blew up the barge. He had the Wrath, poor sod. We were trying to arrest him, but he got away from us."

The words sat like sour stones in the pit of Stella's gut. A brightman with the Wrath. Tashué would have arrested him and sent him to the gallows.

"These things happen, of course," Kazrani went on, "but not usually with such a heavy death toll. It's a shame he got away from us." She paused in her constant movement long enough to look Stella in the eye. "He's too stubborn to say so himself, but he's got himself all twisted into knots over you. I wanted you to know, because I thought it might be good for him. A little company, you know? If you're interested."

Blush leaped immediately to Stella's face, but before she could answer, Kazrani stomped away and knocked on his bedroom door.

"I'm leaving, you stubborn ass. I'll see you at the station house tomorrow."

The door swung open. He'd changed his shirt to a fresh one, which hung open still as he fought with the buttons. Stella could see the black lines of another tattoo, half-hidden by his shirt. Kazrani made a noise from the back of her throat, pushing his hands away. He scowled at her, but let her help.

"I don't know why you're getting dressed." Kazrani only closed two buttons, just enough to hold the shirt closed over his chest, but nowhere near enough to be considered decent. "You're supposed to be going to sleep."

"I still have a guest in my home, Kaz."

"Well, she can help you unbutton your shirt when you're done being a stubborn ass."

Another scowl from Tashué but Kazrani seemed to be a curator of the last word—before he could say anything she was off in a flurry of bread crumbs and confidence, a woman so completely in control of her world that Stella wondered if she even knew what doubt felt like. Tashué and Stella were left in her wake, staring at each other across the apartment, neither of them able to think of the right thing to say.

He's got himself all twisted into knots over you...

He's a tinman, you fool. He holds your entire life in his hands. What happened to hiding? You could have any other man, but not a tinman. If he knew all the things you're lying about, would he still look at you with that devotion in his eyes?

"I should go," Stella said, taking a step closer to the second room. She'd have to pass him to get to the room where Ceridwen was sleeping, but she took a deep breath and steeled herself.

"No, stay," Tashué said quickly. He reached out, but stopped himself before he touched her again. "Don't wake Ceridwen. Let her sleep as long as she needs. If you want."

Stella nodded, turning so that her back was pressed against Ceridwen's door and Tashué's chest was a few inches away. He couldn't step out of his room with her where she was, not without their bodies pressing together in the tight space. She wanted to reach out, to pull the buttons open and strip his shirt away, to reveal his body and his scars and the lines of his tan and find out what the tattoo on his chest looked like, if there were any more. Her heart was beating in her throat and she tried to swallow it back down because it was choking her. She wanted so badly to touch him.

He's a tinman. Find any other man but him.

But there's no other man quite like him.

"You should sleep, then," she breathed, her voice barely above a whisper. "Don't stay up because of me. You look so tired."

His shoulders relaxed, all the tension and anger draining out of him. Biting the inside of her lip, she reached out and eased open the button above his navel. Tashué's hands came up but froze in mid air. She could almost feel it, his desire to touch her warring with whatever made him decide not to. She unfastened the next button and his shirt was open, baring his body to her. She slid her hands up his abdomen, up his chest. His skin was so hot that she wondered if he was feverish, or maybe the heat in his eyes always burned in his whole body. Up, higher, until her fingers brushed over the lines of ink of the tattoo. A long ridge with a single horse and rider at its highest peak. Stella grabbed the front of his shirt and pulled him closer. When his mouth met hers, she thought her whole body was going to melt against him. He wrapped his arms around her shoulders, pulling her closer, pressing their bodies together. It would be too easy to fall into him completely, to follow him into his bedroom and never come out again. But instead, she broke away. Took a step back, pressing her body against the door to Ceridwen's room. It was cold compared to his body, the solidity of it anchoring her back into reality and helping tear her mind away from Tashué's mouth.

"Sleep well, Mr. Blackwood."

He exhaled slowly, clenching his trembling hands into fists for a moment and then forcing them into his pockets. "Thank you, Miss Whiterock." He cleared his throat, stepping back into his room. He opened his mouth to say something else, but second guessed himself and clamped his teeth shut, biting off whatever he wanted to say.

But he was still staring at her, eyes boring into her. And she couldn't move away from him.

He stretched out an arm, catching just her fingers. He lifted her hand to his mouth and kissed her fingers, her palm. The feeling of his mouth spread like heat up her arm, making the hair on her neck stand on end, making her belly twist. His lips were so warm and his beard tickled her skin. And then he let go.

Stella didn't drop her hand. She reached for him instead and wrapped her arm around his neck, pulling him down. Another kiss. This one deeper and urgent, filled with all the things Stella wanted to say but couldn't. *It's not you,* she hoped her kiss said. *Thank you for bringing me back to myself. I'm sorry I can't stay.* He tasted of ash, like she'd thought, and smoke was trapped in his beard. He wrapped his big arms around her and pulled them together. Her whole body was lit by the heat of him. His hand slid around her back as she opened her mouth to him. Hands slid down, fingers tangling in her skirts and starting to drag them up. She could feel the swell of him, stirring in his trousers and pressing against her thigh, even though he must have been so exhausted. Stella slid her hands along his shoulders, pushing his shirt open even more, down off his arms. He let go of her long enough to fight out of the fabric, but he didn't break the kiss. The shirt fell away. Stella wrapped her arms around his waist, sliding her hands up his back, but the skin there wasn't smooth as she'd imagined—there were ridges and canyons, lines that didn't follow the natural shape of his muscles. Were they scars?

Ceridwen stirred in her room—her feet thumped on the floor. Tashué broke the kiss, taking a step back as the bedroom door swung open. He breathed fast and deep, his whole chest heaving. Stella turned away from him, smiling at Ceridwen as she emerged from the borrowed bedroom, rubbing the sleep from her eyes.

"Morning, Mam. Is there any breakfast?"

Tashué cleared his throat. "I don't keep much in my kitchen, I'm afraid—just coffee. Would you like a pot of coffee, little warrior?"

Ceridwen's brow creased together. "No thank you. Coffee isn't breakfast."

"We'll go home for breakfast, Pigeon," Stella breathed, smoothing her skirts. "Go get your boots on."

"Yes, Mam."

Ceridwen shuffled away and Stella turned back to Tashué. She wanted to say something, but couldn't possibly think of what. His mouth quirked into a smile and he took another step back, leaning down to pick up his shirt. He turned away from her to hang it back in his wardrobe, showing her his broad back. The scars she'd felt were a mess of ragged, criss-crossed stripes of a military flogging. He seemed to be just a collection of scars, tissue cobbled together with twine, knitted together by sheer force of will. He continued pretending to ignore her as he opened his trousers, pushing them down off his hips and kicking them away. He left his drawers on, the pale off-white linen making the rich hues of his skin stand out more. He still didn't close the door as he turned, climbing into his bed. She couldn't quite see him in his bed from where she stood, but when she closed her eyes, she could imagine herself following him in and stripping off those drawers, climbing onto his body and chasing all the numb places in her soul away once and for all.

Will he send you to the Rift when he finds out you're lying?

The thought turned her body cold again. It didn't matter how much she longed for him. He was a tinman. She was a fool to trust him, a fool to yearn for him. The barge she meant to take may have been lost to her, but that didn't mean she was staying. She needed to find another, needed to get out of Yaelsmuir. She'd been here too long, now.

27

LORNE

DAY 15

B*reathe.*
Don't hold your breath.
In and out. Slowly.

The Hive was hot. The Hive was always hot. There were always so damned many bodies in here.

Holding your breath again. Stop it.

Lorne forced himself to release the breath, emptying his lungs as completely as he could before letting himself take in any more air. His bones felt like they were quivering beneath the layers of flesh that sheathed them. It had to be his bones that trembled when the rush of an impending fight made him feel so wild, because it couldn't be his muscles. As quivery as he felt, his hands were always steady.

He swung his arms back and forth, then up and over his head, back down again. He crouched and stood, stretched his legs. His eyes drifted across the crowd until he found a familiar face. Ijaz was watching him, leaning against the back wall. So, he knew that Iwan wanted to put them in the ring together. And he studied his opponents, too. Was he worried about standing against The Lledewydd Lightning? It seemed an uneven match. Ijaz was twice Lorne's size.

Lorne was tall, but not *that* tall, and life on the streets left him hungry and a bit too thin. Ijaz the Derccian Hammer was bulk and muscle and height and brute strength. Lorne was almost certain he would lose that fight when it came. But damnit if he wasn't going to make Ijaz bleed first.

Not fighting Ijaz today. Doesn't matter.

He felt rather than heard or saw the excitement that passed through the crowd. His opponent had finally appeared, stalking through the audience toward the platform. This one had been around long enough to have a nickname, too. What was it again? Billy the Bruiser. His name wasn't Billy though. Lorne couldn't remember what it was, but definitely not William. But what was accuracy when faced with a snappy fight nickname?

Billy scrambled up onto the platform and Orix, the fight organizer, yelled at him for being late. Billy raised his hands and made some excuse, but it wouldn't be enough. He'd been late too many times before. Someone who fucked with the schedule got their pay docked.

Billy stripped down to a bare chest, and Orix checked his pockets quickly for weapons. No parts of the body were off limits, but using weapons or trying to shield your tender bits with padding was considered bad sportsmanship. Orix shoved Billy into the centre of the platform, and the ringmaster waved Lorne over.

"Lorne the Lledewydd Lightning!" the ringmaster announced. "And Billy the fucking ugly Bruiser! Odds three to one for the Lightning, ladies and gentlemen, make your last bets to the house now!"

A pause. Bets went to the house before the fight, but plenty of patrons ran bets as the ebb and flow of the fight changed things. Lorne couldn't imagine the sheer amount of money that changed hands on a big fight. A bell rang somewhere in the hall, signalling the end to the house bets, and the fight was on.

Billy had both fists up, knuckles facing Lorne. He shuffled back and forth, back and forth. *Fucker.* His fist snapped forward and he was so damned fast that he caught Lorne in the lips. Pain, the iron taste of blood. Lorne caught Billy by the forearm and dragged him closer. Smashed his knee into Billy's guts. Billy folded over Lorne's knee. Knee up again, hit Billy on the chin. Billy's teeth clacked together, *snap*.

Billy swung with his left. Pain in Lorne's ribs. Lorne held him. Knee up, in Billy's face, crunch of cartilage, rush of blood down Lorne's leg. Falling—Billy had Lorne's leg and they both went down. Hit the wood hard. Lorne twisted, trying to get away. Billy had him. Flexed the knee so hard that pain spasmed up through Lorne's leg, hot and ugly.

Billy's bloodied face loomed over Lorne. Lorne swung hard with his left, catching Billy in the ear. With his right, hit Billy in the jaw. Billy listed to one side, his eyes going distant. Lorne kicked. It threw Billy off balance. Lorne scrambled away. Billy threw his weight forward again, trying to catch Lorne, the pair of them scrabbling and clawing and kicking. Lorne's foot smashed against Billy's teeth. Billy fell back. Lorne sprang up, but his knee spasmed with pain and he almost fell right back down. Threw himself forward, fuck the pain, came down on Billy with fists flying. Billy tried to get out of the way and he was still fast and Lorne's fists missed but his weight hit Billy and knocked him down and Lorne was straddling his chest. Lorne's fists didn't miss with Billy pinned in place. Lorne hit him again and again and again and—

—the ringmaster dragged him off.

Lorne staggered back, his chest heaving. The ringmaster counted. Blood spread around Billy's head from his smashed nose, smashed lips. The vicious, trained part of Lorne's mind told him that the fight wasn't over yet because his opponent was still breathing—choking on his blood—and a breathing opponent could still get up and fucking kill you. Lorne's legs bunched, ready to launch himself back in, but the ringmaster leaned a shoulder against his chest and held him back. Still counting. Eight, nine, fucking ten. He grabbed Lorne by the hand and dragged him further away while a bell rang and the fight was over.

The bell echoed in his chest. His body wasn't ready to quit.

Orix caught him by the arm and dragged him off the stage, handed him his clothes. They knew, they all knew. It wasn't that Lorne wanted to hurt people, especially not once they went down.

But once the army put training into you, especially training like the diplomatic division, it was hard to get that kill-instinct out. He shouldered through the crowd, not seeing faces but just bodies in his way. To the bar. Waiting for his heart to slow its hammering. Waiting for the pain to hit him. It always took a while. Usually a dull ache that grew and grew until he wanted to tear his own skin off to let the pressure out. This one would hurt his knuckles, all that pounding on Billy's skull. They were swelling already, except the one that split. Oozed blood.

Ollia served him a pint and he sucked the head off the top, fighting his arms back into his shirt. His shoulder hurt. Must have hit it hard when he fell.

"How do you do it?"

Lorne looked down the bar. Tucked his shirt into his trousers, pulled his suspenders up. Fuck, that shoulder hurt. Didn't have a waistcoat, just a jacket. Vasska was perched in his usual spot, the one where he could see the fight and just about the whole hall without moving much. He had a waistcoat. Looked like silk.

"Do what?" Lorne asked.

Vasska nodded to the platform where the other fighters were already getting ready. Lorne's quick fight meant they were almost on time again. "You make the whole thing look so easy. Just in and out, stop for a pint after, like anyone else doing business."

Easy? Every shred of him got so hot in a fight that he was convinced part of his soul burned away. And in the quiet moments after, when he was trying to sleep and his whole body ached, his mind flashed him through all the fights he could still remember. But instead of clear pictures and rational thoughts, it was just a jumble of pain and blood and guilt. Because the fights in Cattle Bone Bay ended with a count and the ring of a bell. The fights before ended in graves.

Lorne shrugged. "I guess it's just easy for some people."

Vasska snorted. "Of course it is."

Lorne sucked back near half his pint, letting the beer sit cool in his stomach and make his body feel a little slower. His bones would stop trembling soon, especially if he kept drinking.

"Do you have a minute?" he asked, moving down the bar so he could be a little closer to Vasska. "To talk?"

Vasska cocked an eyebrow at him. "Talk? What do you want to talk about that we can't do it here?"

Lorne took a deep breath. "Well... I wanted to talk about some things that might contrast with your image. You know, how you sit on your stool? And pretend to be a spoilt rich kid who doesn't have a thought in his pretty head except how to spend grandad's money, when actually you are watching fucking *everything*. And you know as much about what's going on as your dear old grandad does."

Vasska's smile never wavered. It was perfect, the way he cocked his head like he didn't know what Lorne was talking about. Ollia stepped a little further away to make it very clear that she wasn't listening. Vasska reached for his glass, throwing back the contents in one swallow.

"Let's take a walk then."

"Excellent," Lorne said, scooping up the half-empty pint and draining it. "Thank you."

Instead of going down to the docks, Vasska led him further up the Hive. Up and up, until they were close to the top and standing on the walkway. The Hive was the only part of the Bay lit with brights, the glow giving the dock workers enough light to see by to work all through the night. A gap of darkness held the rest of the Bay until the tram tracks, and then the brights dotted the riverbank all the way up to the Market Square, where the stone piling of the wharf still jutted up from the river, scorched and smoke-stained, all the wooden planks devoured by the fire. Beyond the Market, the river was swallowed by the night.

Vasska sat on the edge of the walkway, his legs dangling out over the drop. Lorne joined him, leaning forward to test the way his gut clenched when he looked down. The Hive's pilings kept the bottom-most levels firmly planted in place, but the whole structure was so tall and rickety that you could feel it swaying in the wind. Would a strong gust knock them both off? How survivable was the fall?

Depends on how much shit you hit on the way down, I guess.

"I like you, Lorne, so I'm going to assume that wasn't a threat."

Lorne glanced at Vasska. The young man was watching him now, looking for fear maybe. But Lorne had been convinced he was going to die so many times while he served the Dominion fucking Army that he didn't think he knew what fear was anymore.

Lorne drained his glass, sucking back the dregs at the bottom. Shrugged. "No, not a threat. I just wanted to skip all the shit where we pretend not to know what the other person is talking about. You know?"

Vasska laughed. "Alright, we've skipped that. You know I'm not as vapid as I try to appear and I know you might be crazier than you let on. What do you need, then? A favour? If you want a favour you can ask Grandad. He adores you. You make so much fucking money for him, you could ask for a slice of the Bay and he'd give it to you."

"No favour, I just have some questions." Alright, maybe he did fear some things. He very much feared being *liked* by Powell Iwan. "I was wondering about the Red Dawn."

"The Red Dawn has no official presence here in Yaelsmuir," Vasska said but the way he laughed when he said it showed just how much he believed it.

"Sure, no official presence," Lorne muttered. "They're ghosts. Very mysterious and all that shit. How many of them are here? A dozen? A hundred? I know they're hiding in the Bay. Iwan just… lets them stay?"

Instead of answering, Vasska reached into his pocket and found his own cigarillo case. It was nicer than Tashué's, and certainly newer. Tashué Blackwood's cigarillo case may well have been older than either of them. He handed the case to Lorne and they went through the ritual together of striking matches and taking the first deep breaths of tobacco smoke.

"What do you want with the Army of the Red Dawn?" Vasska asked finally.

"I was looking into something for Tashué Blackwood," Lorne said, flicking the first line of ash off the side of the Hive. The wind took it before it went far, disappearing into night. "Things led me to the Red Dawn."

"What things? What 'something'? Does it have something to do with his 'face of the Authority' nonsense? He wants to arrest some rebel bad guys to make Elsworth and the Governor look good?"

"No, nothing like that." Lorne took a deep breath of smoke, trying to organize his thoughts. How much should he even say? "I was looking for information about a dead child and someone said I should ask about what the Red Dawn has been up to. I'm tired of chasing this shit around. I want to give him something, but I don't have anything. Except the Red Dawn. But what would they have to do with a dead child?"

Vasska kept smoking, looking out over the river. It would be his empire one day, the Hive and the Bay and the never-ending barge traffic. Those barges went to White Crown, and up into the mountains. It was a long reach for the poorest quarter of a city that was scorned for being *common*. As if having connections to the Crowne was the only thing that could make a thing special or civilized.

"Who is he to you?" Vasska asked. "Blackwood, I mean."

"Fuck, everyone's interested in him all of a sudden," Lorne muttered. "You know he's lived here all his life, right? I guess not when he was stationed abroad, but he was born here and he'll probably die here, the stubborn bastard."

"Attending a banquet for the Queen and sleeping with Illea Winter has that effect on a person. So who is he to you?"

"He's Jason's father."

"Thank you for the hereditary lesson. I did actually know that. Jason Blackwood, the tainted son in the Rift. Who are these men to you, that they keep you in Yaelsmuir when you clearly hate it here so much?"

"Why do you want to know?" Lorne snapped. "Are you just stalling, or are you looking for something specifically?"

"The Blackwood family strikes a nerve in you, does it?" Vasska asked, turning to look Lorne in the eye finally. "And why is that?"

Because Jason's life is fucked up enough without you interfering with it. "Tashué Blackwood is stubborn and self-righteous and maybe a little arrogant, but he's a good, honest man and he's surprisingly naive considering the shit he's seen in his life. I don't like the idea of you people drawing him into your fucking webs."

Vasska laughed. "'You people'? I've never been so scornfully clumped together with Illea Winter before. 'You people.' Who else has been asking, then? Was it Saeati, asking on Mayor Wolfe's behalf? I'm sorry to tell you, Lorne, Tashué Blackwood landed himself in these webs all by his damned self and you can't save him from the choices he's made."

Vasska slid back, giving himself enough room to stand and flicking his cigarillo butt out over the river. Lorne watched it tumble, the glowing red end twisting through the darkness until it hit the river and died.

"You don't want to chase the Red Dawn, Lorne. Leave it be. Those people will fucking kill you."

"What am I supposed to tell Tashué, then? Does his dead girl have anything to do with them?"

"I don't care what you tell him, that's between the two of you. But remember that I told you that I like you, and I don't want the pair of you to get killed over this. You think Illea Winter and Mayor Wolfe have pulled him into a web? Fuck them. They're playing child's games. You two don't want to get wrapped up in the Army of the Red Dawn."

"What do you know, Vasska?"

"Too fucking much."

28

TASHUÉ

DAY 17

Allie Tei was surprised to see him when he turned up at her office in Highview. He hadn't gone back to the station house since the fire, sleeping away the exhaustion and forcing himself to eat something now and then. And, if he was honest with himself, he drank too much whisky, trying to chase the victims of the fire out of his head. But the girl from the river and the woman from the Breeding Program were not patient, chewing at the corners of his mind, demanding attention.

Allie had ink smeared on her cheek again and her hair was held back from her face with ivory hairpins. She half-stood from her desk, leaning forward to offer a hand, but she drew back when she saw the mess that his hands were, Stella's stitches still holding his flesh together.

"You're in rough shape, Mr. Blackwood."

He looked down at his hands, but shrugged. "It was another long week."

"Did you find something about the children, then?" she asked, sinking back down. She shuffled through the clutter on her desk, finding her pen.

"Maybe. I spoke to a woman from the Breeding Program who

said she used her Talent and saw her children being mutilated by the Authority."

Allie's eyes went wide. "That is a startling accusation. Where is she? Would this woman be willing to speak to me?"

"I hope so," Tashué sighed. "She doesn't trust me very much, though. Someone I trust is trying to convince her to talk to me again. If I hear from her, I'll bring you."

"Where is she? In Brickheart?"

"No, she's staying in Cattle Bone Bay."

"I can't say I've ever been to the Bay," Allie admitted, tapping her pen on her notebook, cap side down. Wishing she had something worth writing, maybe. "I hope she'll speak to me. It becomes very difficult for me to write an article if all I have is the word of a Regulation Officer that he has spoken to a woman who has opinions but not actual proof. I'm assuming you would like to remain anonymous?"

Tashué shook his head. "No, not at all."

Allie's eyebrows rose at that, her head cocking to one side. Hair fell across the side of her face and an unconscious flick of her head moved it out of the way again. "Are you not receiving a promotion? Are you not standing elbow to elbow with Illea Winter and the Queen and the Chief Administrator of the Authority?"

Tashué grimaced. They almost sounded like accusations. Was that the way she asked the question, or his own frustration, coming to life any time someone mentioned any of those things? "Yes to all of that."

"And you want me to run your name in an article that accuses the Authority of mutilating children?"

"If it's true…" Tashué wondered if he should say more, that in fact Illea Winter and General Wolfe would be delighted with him for dismantling Rainer Elsworth. But Jason. Wolfe said he would find a way to make Jason safe, but how? "If it's true, I won't be wearing a badge anymore."

"And I can run your name? As a witness and a source?"

Tashué sighed at her eagerness. *Jason, what about Jason?* "Let's find some proof first. And then we'll see."

"Well," Allie said slowly, nodding to herself. "Yes, you're right. Let's try to find some proof."

Tashué nodded, drifting toward her single window, the bridge across the Brightwash catching his eye. It spanned to Park Island and Highview, sloping high and wide to crest the river without interfering with water traffic. Allie joined him as he lingered at the window.

"That's where he was, the boy," Allie said, laying a finger on the glass to point to the pilings where the bridge started its arc upward. "I often wonder how many other people must have passed him, before someone noticed him. This street is busy, especially in the morning, with all the office buildings here. No one really knew how long he'd been there."

"Had he been in the water, your boy?" Tashué asked. He could almost see it, the flow of the traffic, the first people lingering, the crowd growing. "Could he have washed up there from the river?"

Allie sighed. "I don't know. The river was low then, before all this rain started. I can't remember if he was wet. But there was other debris around him, so maybe? Sometimes the barges go through here pretty quickly, especially if they're tainted-powered, and the wake they leave in the water pushes debris high up the bank." She scowled, shaking her head. "He wasn't debris. He was a child. A dead child."

Tashué stepped away from the window, trying to picture the city in his mind, sitting as it did on the curve of the Brightwash. "Do you have a map of the city?"

"A map of the city…" She stepped away from the window, heading for her desk. She opened a few drawers before she found the right one, pulling out a map and unfolding it. It was too big to fit on the space she had, the edges of it hanging off, and the side that held Highfield and Highview were propped up on her typewriter. "What are you looking for?"

Tashué reached into his pocket. He had to pull out the notepad to find his charcoal pencil. The photographs, the girl's face and the tattoo on her neck, slid from between the pages of his notepad. His eyes lingered on the girl's face before he handed them to Allie. She took them reverently, examining them as Tashué unwound the twine on the end of his charcoal pencil.

"Your boy was here, under the bridge." He made a small smudge, a black mark beside the bridge. "If the river washed him down here, he would have passed all the structures of the Hive, but somehow hit the shore here, where the river runs fast because of Park Island."

"He might not have come from the river, though," Allie said. "He might have been dumped there."

"But my girl *did* come from the river," Tashué said. He left another mark where the street died at the riverbank because there *used* to be a bridge there. "She was still wet."

"Right downriver from the Rift, and the Facility of Rest. Could she have come from either of those places?"

Tashué shook his head. "There are some ugly rumours in the Rift, about what happens to children born to the inmates there, but nothing that mentions tattoos on the neck and removed arms and legs. And the people at the Facility would remember a child in such a terrible state."

"You've asked?"

Tashué nodded. "My son is in the Rift, and one of my cases works at the Facility. Neither have seen anything."

"Your son—"

"Yes," Tashué interrupted. "I know. The tinman with the tainted son in the Rift. I didn't put him there, if that's what you're going to ask next."

"No, I wasn't going to ask that," Allie said. She stared at Tashué for a long time, her lip curling in as she chewed it. She wanted to ask something, maybe wanted to ask that stupid *conflict of interest* question that people threw at him. Of course it was a conflict of fucking interest, it was his *son*. But she took a deep breath, shaking herself. "What else is upriver, then?" She cleared her throat, looking down at the map. "Brickheart and the Market…"

"When the Breeding Program children graduate creche, they're marched through the city and loaded onto a barge in the Bay," Tashué said. "Have you ever seen the graduation parades?"

Allie nodded. "I have. I never liked them very much. They're all so young, those children. It seems impossible to fathom the amount of Talent they must have, and yet they all run some of the most important structures of the Dominion, don't they?"

Tashué nodded. "They're designed to quicken early, and have more Talent. They're put on a barge and brought somewhere upriver for training. If the woman I spoke to is right, they could have both come from there."

"How far upriver is it?" Allie asked, her eyes tracking the line of the Brightwash until it disappeared off the edge of the map. "And why would they be dumping their children in the river? Aren't they awfully valuable? Even if they died, wouldn't they have a better way of disposing of them, rather than tossing them in the river? Seems risky, doesn't it, to have mutilated children washing up on the riverbank?"

Tashué sighed at the frustration building in his skull. They were all good questions, and none of it quite made sense. "And if they went into the river outside the city, how likely is it that your boy made it through Cattle Bone Bay without getting caught on anything there, but washed up right there, under a bridge, right beside a street with heavy traffic on a daily basis?"

"So… either there have been numerous other children that have washed downriver that no one found, or these children were placed on the riverbank with the intention that they would be seen."

Her words sucked the air out of him. It took a moment for him to catch his breath. "Neither of those are good options."

She made some attempt at a smile, but it was a sad expression. "I know. I don't want to think that there have been other children that no one knows about, but… Why would someone want us to find them? Did someone else find them, dead already, and place them to be found? And… wet doesn't necessarily mean she came from the river. This time of year? Had it rained, the day you found her?"

Another good question. Tashué sighed, pushing his hand through his hair—and wincing at the way his hair scraped across his open wounds. "I don't remember."

Allie shook her head. "We're missing something."

Tashué nodded. "I was thinking the same thing. I'll try to keep looking. See if I can find any proof of what the woman from the Breeding Program said." He sighed and reached for his timepiece—but it wasn't there. Ishmael still had it. He stifled a curse, picking up his notepad and his pencil. "I have to go."

"You have your big Imburleigh event today, don't you?" Allie asked, looking up at him. "Where you receive your promotion?"

Tashué nodded. "To Station Commander."

"You don't seem terribly excited."

"I'm just tired."

"Is it true, then, that you were in the Market for four days, fighting the fire and rescuing survivors?"

Tashué shook his head, gritting his teeth. "A lot of people were there, doing all the same things I did."

"I know that, Mr. Blackwood." She sighed at him, folding up the map. She picked up the photographs, offering them to Tashué. "Did you want these back?"

"No, keep them. I don't know how much time I will have to be looking for her anymore, with everything. I think they'll serve you better."

She opened her satchel, tucking the photographs away. "I'll try to find out if there are more bodies that we've missed."

Tashué held out a hand to her—the left, the least wounded. She accepted the shake, her hand small in his. "Good luck, Miss Tei."

"You're going to make us *late*."

Kazrani stared at him from the top of the stairs, her arms folded over her chest. She looked good, wearing her old military dress uniform, the leaf green reminding Tashué of when life was both infinitely harder but also so much simpler. She had more lines on her face since then, and some grey in her hair—hell, they both did—but that uniform suited her. He wondered if she ever would have retired, were it not for him needing her.

"Sorry," he said, heading for the door to his apartment. "I had to see a reporter."

"The one from the *Highview Times?*" Kazrani asked, following him into the apartment. "Are you honestly talking to reporters now?"

"Just about the girl," Tashué sighed. "Miss Tei found a child too. Don't worry—I haven't turned into a socialite."

"Thank everything holy for that. Hurry up, then! The carriage is waiting for us already."

Tashué first stopped at the table in the little sitting room to fill his cigarillo case from the pile he'd made that morning when he couldn't sleep anymore. Kazrani chased him to his bedroom, pulling his dress uniform out of his wardrobe. She had to beat the dust out of it, pick lint off the jacket. He didn't have the occasion to wear it as much as he used to.

"Are you watching me strip down, Lieutenant?" Tashué asked, snatching the uniform from her hands. "Or can I have a moment of privacy?"

"It's not like I haven't seen it before, Captain."

"Kaz."

She huffed at him and stomped out of his room. Tashué took a deep breath, trying to force down his own agitation. He wasn't sure what bothered him the most—the promotion that he didn't want, the dead child that he still had no answers for, the brightman and the Market fire, or the lingering memory of Stella Whiterock kissing him. Feeling her body against his, hearing the soft sounds she made in her throat when she pulled him down against her, the way his skin tingled and his body lit on fire when she pushed his shirt off his shoulders. He took another deep breath. That was three days ago now, and he hadn't seen her since.

He tried to dress quickly, but his hands were still so damned sore. The stitches pulled tight at every little movement, and if he wasn't careful, the long, deep gash on his hand would split open again and ooze. His struggle with buttons was only getting worse. *What a stupid thing for a grown man to struggle with.*

Kazrani came wandering back in. She sighed at him and pushed his hands out of the way. She buttoned up the shirt, turning up the collar so it wouldn't get crushed by the remaining layers.

"How long are we going to pretend you aren't angry?"

Tashué scoffed, reaching for his waistcoat. "You're the one fucking snapping at me. I haven't said anything at all!"

"All night, then," Kazrani muttered. "Pretending we're not fighting will be harder once I start drinking. I'll probably drink a lot too—everything's free and you know how I like to bury my frustration in a good spiced rum."

Tashué sighed, pushing his arms into the waistcoat. His body was still sore, the muscles aching. "Kaz…"

"No, no, I understand. It's been a lot of stress, fighting that fire and digging through the rubble. Better to let things sit so that you'll explode later, instead of having a conversation like a pair of grown adults."

"You should have known better!" Tashué snapped, swinging toward Kazrani. "Why didn't you do something sooner? You, of all people, should have known how terrible the Wrath could be, left unchecked."

"Why's that, Captain?" Kazrani hissed. "Because my father killed my mother and my brother when the Wrath took him?"

The silence that hung in his room was a bitter, angry thing. Kazrani's eyes burned as she glared up at him. He knew how much it hurt her to even mention her father—all those wounds lay like festering sores across her soul, unable to heal. She'd lost so much on that night. Her father's descent into madness still haunted her nightmares.

And yet, she *should* have known better, for exactly that reason.

"Why didn't you do anything?" Tashué pressed.

"I didn't realize what was happening," Kazrani snapped. Still, she reached out, helping with the buttons of his waistcoat next. Her hands trembled. "I didn't know! All he said was that he didn't want to work anymore. He said he was 'tired.' I told him we're all fucking tired. How was I supposed to know that 'tired' meant 'going mad?' He didn't tell me what was happening!"

"How could you not know?"

"How could I not know? Tashué, I have forty-three cases! Can you honestly tell me that you know *everything* about every one of your cases? Does Stella Whiterock have a gun? Does she feel a little overwhelmed by her responsibilities, like she's starting to lose herself? That's what happens to those whisperers, most of the time. They just stop feeling anything at all. Isn't that what she said, in the Market? That she just drifts sometimes?"

"Miss Whiterock has nothing to do with this."

"Oh no, of course not. Not Miss Whiterock! She's perfectly innocent, isn't she? Couldn't possibly be capable of a thing like *this*."

A low growl rumbled in Tashué's throat before he could stop it. "Are you implying something specific, or are you just making random accusations to make me angry?"

"I'm making a point!" Kazrani snapped. "We don't know them. We can't ever *know* them and what goes on in their minds! We don't understand them—you and I never will because we aren't built the same. The tainted aren't inherently evil, no, but they are *different*."

"You can't honestly believe that."

Kazrani scowled. "You can't honestly believe otherwise. Just because you're smitten with one of them doesn't change the fact that they're *tainted*."

Tashué sucked in a deep breath, feeling his heart hammering in his chest. Did he used to think such ugly things about people? He couldn't remember. He thought back to Keoh. Their relationship was mean and hot and almost as chaotic as a battle. *I never want to see you again* to *I miss you so much* in the span of weeks. And he was away so much, they could never quite spend enough time together to sort through the mess of their emotions. They were both so angry at other things, both so young and desperate. Keoh had quickened late in her life, or maybe she'd hid her Talent well at first. Had he thought her *less* after that? He'd pushed her to register. He'd thought it was the right thing to do, the honest thing to do.

"I don't want to fight with you, Kaz," Tashué sighed. "Not today."

She sighed back, reaching out to straighten his medals and fix his collar. "Too late for that, isn't it? You can't lay this at my feet."

She shook her head, her mouth twisted into a hard line. "It's not my fault. A lot of people died and the only one responsible is the man that blew up that barge. I couldn't have possibly known that he would do such a thing."

Tashué caught Kazrani's hands to stop her from fidgeting with his medals, giving her fingers a squeeze and taking a deep breath. "He didn't want to be publicly executed. That's what he told me, before you shot him. He knew the Wrath was on him and he didn't want to be dragged in front of a crowd and executed for the crime of being driven mad by his own Talent. He wanted to stop because he could feel it coming and he tried to tell you."

"Even if he told me—and I'm telling you, he didn't—what would you have liked me to do? The manual is clear. A tainted that refuses to work goes to the Rift, non-compliant. A tainted with the Wrath who is exhibiting dangerous behaviour goes to the gallows, because there's nothing to be done about it. Tell me what you would have done differently. Would you have sent him to the Rift? Or the gallows? Or told him to keep working so that he could stay alive? And then when your choice was the wrong one and he blew up a fucking barge, would you have blamed yourself for all the people he killed, or would you have told me that you did your best to help him and you didn't know what was coming?"

How little she knows me, after all these years, to think that I'm not blaming myself right now.

He found his cigarillo case and lit one, hoping that the familiar motion would be enough to chase the pain away, as it had been so many times before. But he looked down at Kazrani, feeling the echo of the pain in her eyes, ringing in his chest. It had been many long, hard years for both of them. Everything went so differently than they both imagined, when they were younger.

"Why are you still here?" he asked.

She scowled, glaring up at him. "You don't have to be an ass. We're going to the factory together, remember?"

"No, I mean—here in Yaelsmuir. I know you miss the Hadia. Your own people. Your family. You have a granddaughter in the Hadia. A life, waiting for you."

She took a long breath. She touched the Shield, sliding her fingers over the white enamel, over the silver ribbon. "You've always looked good in the uniform. It suits the shape of you very well."

"We're long past the days when you could distract me with flattery."

Kazrani laughed, stepping away. "Those were the days, hey? You were such an arrogant cock back then. If you were Jitabvi, you would be hotblood. You and Jason both."

Tashué turned away from her, flicking his cigarillo in the ashtray on the windowsill. "I wonder how things might have been different, if I had listened to you. If I had taken Jason out of Yaelsmuir, and followed you and Tevir back to the Hadia. Honorary hotbloods, the pair of us."

"Oh, Tashué," Kazrani sighed, "of course it would have been 'different. Every choice we're faced with makes things 'different.' But don't convince yourself that 'different' is the same as 'better.' You tried your best with Jason. It was good for him, to stay here and know his grandparents while he still had them. It's good for a boy to know there are people in the world who love him unconditionally."

Tashué nodded. "Keoh's parents were good to us... Why did you come back here, after Tevir asked you to bring him back to the Hadia? I know you never loved this city. Why did you stay, all these years?"

"For you, you idiot. Tevi went back to the Hadia and he had family to guide him—he rode with his father's family and he made his life for himself. But you and Jason? You didn't have anyone. Keoh's parents, maybe, and they loved you plenty, but it wasn't ever going to be enough. I know you never felt like you could tell them what you'd been through. I was afraid of... Of what demons might get ahold of you, if there was no one around who knew what it was like. The Ridge, and everything. I couldn't bear it, the thought of leaving you alone in this giant city, with no one to tell you that you were being a stubborn ass. No one to tell you that you were going to be alright, no matter how badly you were hurting. I lost so much when the Wrath took my father, but of everyone, I missed my brother the most. And when you were assigned to us, it felt like the gods—or the North Star, or whoever—were giving me a second chance."

"Why didn't you put down roots here, then?" Tashué asked. "You're worse than me, sleeping with someone for a few weeks before discarding them again. You never met anyone you wanted to try to build a relationship with?"

Kazrani shrugged and shook her head. "I didn't think I needed roots here. My roots are in the Hadia. I always thought this would be temporary, that I would go back. None of the women here understood what I was, or the men for that matter. They all saw a Jitabvi hotblood, and maybe they thought that was exciting. But I'm not some ornament, some circus show for people to entertain themselves with."

"The girl you met at the pugilist gym seemed nice enough," Tashué said.

Kazrani laughed. "Which one?"

"Alright, the blond one, then. With the big eyelashes, always batting them at you when she wanted something."

"See—she's the perfect example. She seemed nice enough, sure, and she was fun, for a few weeks. But she was just curious. Heard Jitabvi were wild. Wanted to see what all the fuss was about, I suppose, and then when it turned out I was just human, same as her, I think she was disappointed. There was nothing there and what we had was empty and maybe even a little ugly. And then it was over. It's the same, with everyone here. They don't see me, they see the braids in my hair and my brown skin and they assume I'm some other creature."

Tashué took a deep breath. He wanted to tell her that people with Talent would say the same of her, and others like her—people that saw them as 'different' simply because they could change the very fabric of the world. But he didn't want to fight with her anymore. He took a few drags of his cigarillo instead, watching her drift through her own memories, trying to think of something to say that might bring them closer together again.

"We should try to make time to go back to the pugilist club,"

Kazrani said. "We both need it. We'll dig out the practise swords and bash at each other a while to take out our frustrations."

"When do you think we'll have time for that?" Tashué sighed. "I'm only getting busier."

Kazrani sighed. "That's true, isn't it?" A smile crept across her face. Leave it to Kazrani to find something to smile about when the pair of them were battered and bruised by old pain. "Do you remember teaching Tevi how to fly?"

Tashué laughed, the warmth of the memory spreading through him. That boy, that little Jitabvi boy, so small and so incredibly brave. Tashué threw Tevir in the air over and over, *again, higher!* No matter how high Tashué threw him, he always loved it. He could go all day, up, again, higher, until Tashué's whole body burned with fatigue and he couldn't lift his own arms anymore.

Don't forget to flap your arms, Tevi. You'll stay in the air longer that way.
Did I do it? Did I fly?

"Of course I remember."

"Most of the other Captains we got—especially the young ones like you—took themselves too seriously to play with Jitabvi children. That was beneath them. But watching you play with him like that, I knew you were made for us, to be a part of our family. Part of the ashrab. So even though it hurt me to leave Tevir with his grandparents, and come back here to live in this fucking city instead, it was the right thing to do. Because you're my family. And you're right, about Jason. It doesn't matter if everything's shit and you don't know what you're doing. You do whatever you have to for family."

Tears welled in Kazrani's eyes. Tashué sighed and pulled her close. She wrapped her arms around his back, burying her face in his jacket, avoiding the ribbons and the medals as best she could. She took a few long, deep breaths, then shook herself and stepped away.

"I know you blame us both for what happened." She smoothed out his ribbons again, one by one, instead of looking him in the eye. "But he was going to kill you. I felt it. I couldn't let that happen. That's all I was thinking about. My friend—my brother—is going to die. So I shot him. I'm sorry for everything I did up to that moment, that led us there, but I'm not sorry for shooting a man to protect you."

"You don't have to protect me, Kaz." Tashué sighed. "I'm a grown man. I can take care of myself now."

Kazrani snorted, shaking her head. "When you start eating three proper meals, every day, I'll believe that. Until then, someone has to take care of you. I'm happy to do it, at least until you find someone better for the job. Let's go, already! We're going to be late."

29

TASHUÉ

DAY 17

The Imburleigh Armament Company was among the top employers in the Dominion, and their largest factory sat on the outskirts of Yaelsmuir. It was a massive building, a sprawling compound that seemed large enough to be a small city. Smoke billowed from its chimneys constantly, a rotation of employees working day and night. Imburleigh guns were the most sought-after in the world and they had to keep up with demand.

Inside, a stage stood against one wall. A banner hung above the structure, painted with carefully formed letters: *A Vote for Winter is a Vote for Peace.* No one was up there yet, but a podium was waiting. The wall closest to the hallway was lined with a long bar, where a small army of Imburleigh-liveried staff were serving drinks to the growing crowd.

"What happened to the girl from the brewery?" Tashué asked as Kazrani followed him to the bar. "The one that always smelled like sour mash."

"Oh, are we doing this now?" Kazrani sighed. "Are you planning to go through the whole list, then?"

Tashué grinned down at Kazrani as they settled at the bar. "If there's time before the speeches start."

"Fine, so long as I get to go through your list, too."

"Ladovaugh single malt," Tashué told the bartender. "And she'll have your most expensive spiced rum, the darker the better."

The bartender poured them each a generous measure, sliding an ashtray over as Tashué lit another cigarillo. Tashué looked down at Kazrani expectantly, waiting as he pulled the ashtray even closer.

"Well?" Tashué pressed, turning to the crowd and scanning the faces. Uniforms mingled with finer clothes. It was telling that a gathering made up of Regulation Officers involved so many veterans. Or perhaps what was telling was how many veterans were among the Dominion's population. Service wasn't mandatory, but the draft rates were high to keep all the branches of their various foreign units well populated. It was better to enlist before you could be drafted. "What happened to her, then? The one that kept asking you what Jitabvi wedding ceremonies were like?"

Kazrani huffed at Tashué, throwing back half her rum in one swallow. "I think she's married now. For the second time? Third? And Miss Whiterock, then? Since we're talking about our sex lives tonight. How is she?"

Tashué took a deep breath, his smile fading. Seeing Stella dragged across the square by the man had lit a fear in him that he hadn't felt in years. A gripping, crippling fear that left his nerves raw and his limbs shaky. But that kiss... Her hands, on his body, pushing away his shirt, touching his scars. "I haven't seen her since she walked me home."

"What?" Kazrani scoffed. "Really? I thought for sure I'd said the right thing."

Tashué swung on Kazrani. "What the hell does that mean? What did you say?"

Kazrani shrugged, spreading her hands. "Just that I thought the company would be good for you. It didn't work?"

"I don't know what happened," Tashué muttered. He took a deep breath before sipping the Ladovaugh, bracing himself for the familiarity of it, for the smoky heat and the long, lingering burn. It was twice the memory now, once of his father, once of Stella Whiterock explaining the history of the island. "Anyway, I told you—I'm not going to take advantage of my position."

"Sweet North Star, you're so infuriating. I can't fathom why you always fight so hard against the things that are good for you. What do you mean, you don't know what happened? It should be pretty obvious, I would think. It's not like you lack the practise."

"She kissed me, but then she left."

"That's fucking tragic, Captain."

"It's for the best," Tashué sighed. Why had she kissed him, then? Because she thought it was what he wanted? Because she wanted to? But maybe the fact that he hadn't seen her since was all the answer he needed. She'd kissed him for reasons he didn't see—but then she regretted it and now she was trying to put the distance between them again. Another sip of whisky didn't do enough to wash the ashen taste of his own regret from his mouth. "Your turn. What happened to the Qasani man you were seeing a few years ago? He can't have thought you were a circus show. He would have understood what it's like, to come from somewhere else and live in Yaelsmuir."

"Sweet North Star, the Qasani man," Kazrani breathed. She drained her glass, sliding it along the bar and waving to the bartender. "No, that was different. It was serious, but... No, we weren't a good match, no matter how good the sex was."

"Shit, that sounds familiar." Ishmael leaned on the bar beside Tashué, grabbing Tashué's cigarillo case and helping himself to one. Tashué tossed him his box of matches. "Jitabvi and Qasani never mix well. Both entirely too passionate in all the wrong ways, and too stubborn."

"What's wrong with two passionate people coming together?" Tashué asked. "Passion is good."

"Sure, it's great," Ishmael said, draining whatever was in his glass—probably brandy, knowing him. "Right up until the two passionate people eat each other whole."

Tashué swung to Kazrani, raising an eyebrow at her. "I hope this isn't the point that you tell me that *he* was your Qasani lover."

Kazrani laughed. "And, so what if he was? When did you

become the man that judges me for my bed partners? Besides, he has a good reputation, doesn't he? Maybe I wanted to see what all the talk was about."

"Captain, I promise she's teasing you," Ishmael said, reaching behind Tashué to tap his cigarillo in the ashtray. "I've had my fair share of Jitabvi lovers, but Lieutenant Mahalouwan remains yours exclusively. And anyway, I learnt my lesson years ago. It went the same way every time. It was fantastic, and brutal, and violent, and delicious. I loved every minute of it, and each time, it very nearly killed me."

"You're not a healthy man," Kazrani said. "Even by my standards."

Ishmael grinned at her, nodding to the bartender and drawing him over. "I never once said that I was. Are you having another?"

"Please, yes," Tashué breathed, draining the last of his whisky and sliding his glass over to the bartender. "I need it to scrub that image from my mind."

Ishmael snorted. "Don't be a prude, it doesn't suit you. Or is it the idea of sharing that bothers you?"

"He's sulking because he's sexually frustrated."

"Kaz!"

"How could you be frustrated already?" Ishmael scoffed. "I just helped you sneak out of Illea Winter's house a week ago. Was it more than a week ago, now? I can't fucking remember anymore."

"Oh, yes, that's my fault for not being specific enough," Kazrani said. "He's frustrated over a particular woman."

"Ah," Ishmael said, nodding. "Understood. That would be Miss Whiterock, then? The whisperer who stitched up your hands? She was something, shit. I don't blame you."

"This is not a conversation I want to have with either of you," Tashué muttered, throwing back the next measure of whisky. Maybe a little too fast. "Not tonight."

"Pace yourself, Captain," Ishmael said, elbowing Tashué. "These events can go on for fucking hours, and you don't want to be drunk on stage." His glass, though, was empty too, and he waved the bartender for another.

"Shit, is that what pacing yourself looks like?" Tashué asked. "I'm behind, then."

Ishmael laughed. "I'm not the one climbing up on stage, am I?" He shifted so he could reach into his pocket. "Here, before I get really drunk and I forget, I thought you would want this back. I know I've had it longer than I meant to, and I'm sorry it took me so long. But, you know, sometimes the fucking Market explodes."

He produced Tashué's timepiece, freshly cleaned and polished. It was a relief, to have it back. Tashué hands were too damned sore and whisky-numb to fight with the buttons of his uniform. He tucked it away into his breast pocket instead.

"I replaced some springs," Ishmael said. "One of the gears looked a little worn so I replaced that, too. It should work like new. If ever there's an issue with it, please bring it to me. It's an honour to work on one of my father's old pieces."

"I'll remember that," Tashué promised.

Ishmael drained the last of his glass, sliding it closer to the bartender and nodding for another. "I'd best be finding General Wolfe. He has me on a short lead these days."

"Did you get yourself into trouble again?"

Ishmael grinned as he scooped up the glass, newly filled. "Not yet. It's still early, though."

Tashué watched Ishmael go. It was easier to focus on him and how he folded so naturally among the suits and the gowns and the dress uniforms than it was to let himself think about Stella or the Market. The fucking campaign or the Mayor's office. Ishmael didn't have a uniform, being in the diplomatic division, but that didn't stop him from pausing to talk with the other veterans, chatting with them with easy familiarity before making his way back to Wolfe.

"What about him, then?" Kazrani asked, but her voice had gone soft. "What happened there?"

Tashué shrugged, dragging the ashtray closer to crush out his cigarillo. "What we were doing wasn't ever going to work. We collided when he was home and needed a distraction. We fucked around to distract ourselves from all the things we were angry about, and when we were tired, we were still angry, so we drank.

Too much." He nodded to the bartender, sliding his glass closer for a refill. Maybe the last one—Ishmael was right, he was headed up on that stage to get a brass badge when he didn't even think he wanted the tin anymore. "It was like when you and I started up again, remember? When you came to Yaelsmuir and Keoh was gone and you hated the city, but you wanted to stay. So we took all that frustration out on each other."

Kazrani winced. "Of course I remember. That was... not good."

"Excuse you," Tashué muttered. "I was excellent."

Kazrani laughed and shook her head. "Alright, sure, but I can't say many other sexual encounters have left me with scars."

"What, where did I leave you with scars?"

"On my fucking thigh, you ass, where I touched the wood stove by accident."

"Shit, I don't even remember that."

"Of course not, because it was all a blur of sex and whisky and self pity," Kazrani muttered. "And you're not the one that got burnt."

"Exactly." Tashué motioned to Ishmael, who was leaning on the stage and talking to Illea, Wolfe a few feet away like he really was supervising Ishmael's behaviour. "Him and I, that's what we did. Except we were both burning." Tashué shook his head, looking down at his whisky and taking a slow sip. "We decided it was better for our health to put some distance between us. We fit better as friends."

A different familiar face caught Tashué's eye, cleaned of the ash and blood of the Market Quarter—Rhodrishi. He too was dressed in his military uniform, the deep blue of a healer, the Colonel's stars on his shoulder showing that he'd been in charge of a regiment of healers a thousand strong. He wore medals for bravery, for loyalty, for dedication. He wore the Hands of Bronwynn, the medal that was given when a healer had personally tended to a million wounds.

"Go, go see him," Kazrani said, giving Tashué a push away from the bar. "I'll catch up. You think they have coffee here?"

"I don't fucking know, Kaz, ask the bartender."

"Go, I said!" She gave him another shove, sending him out into the crowd.

Tashué took a deep breath as he plunged through the milling bodies, heading straight for Rhodrishi. He hadn't seen the healer since that day at the Market, either.

"Good afternoon, Captain." Rhodrishi gave a wide, warm smile. "You're looking much better than the last time I saw you."

"Thank you, Colonel. It was good to have you on the Hook. How's the boy?"

Rhodrishi shrugged. "I'll try to see him walking again, but I don't know if it's possible. The bone is dust. If the injury was lower, I would recommend amputation, but the pelvis contains too many vital functions. I may still recommend someone take the leg off. At least then he'll have less weight to carry around." He reached out, patting Tashué's arm. "I'm sorry to disappoint you, old friend. I know it's easy to believe the myth that a Kaadayri healer can fix any wound, but we're still only human. We aren't gods to wave our hands and solve any crisis."

"I know that," Tashué said softly, looking down at his glass and draining the last of it in one swallow. He was far too sober to talk about Eddie and the Market Square.

Kazrani rescued him from having to continue the conversation, appearing at Tashué's shoulder with coffee, bless her. "Colonel Kheir! It's good to finally see you again under better circumstances. Where have you been? I was hoping to see you sooner."

"I was pulled into service at Mayor Wolfe's new hospital, where the wounded from the Market were transferred. The rescue crews did well. There were a lot of survivors. And you? I thought you were going to head back west after you retired. Back to the Gift Lands to be with your people."

"Kaz thought she needed to keep an eye on me," Tashué said.

Kazrani shrugged. "Someone has to take care of him. Fortunately for me, you were on hand to look after him in the Market, since he wouldn't damned well listen to me. You're serving the Authority now, Colonel? I thought you were going back to your land when you retired, too."

"The Authority expects me to keep gainful employment in exchange for free movement across Dominion lands," Rhodrishi said slowly. Tashué knew why he was hesitant to talk about it. The Dominion was strict about how any Kaadayri moved outside of the legacy territories, and Tashué's accounting of Rhodrishi's movements hadn't been honest in the least. "I work for them directly now. I help to organize and assess their healers so that they might be assigned to appropriate positions. Captain Blackwood keeps my case file updated for me."

"I didn't realize you lived so nearby." Kazrani elbowed Tashué in the ribs. "Why didn't you tell me the Colonel lived in our jurisdiction?"

"The nature of his position means he doesn't stay in one place for long," Tashué said. He wished he could tell Kazrani more about the life of their dear friend, but he knew she wouldn't understand. She held to the laws even tighter than Tashué did. He didn't think he could explain to her that there was a debt that needed to be paid. Some loyalties ran too deep, some rightness superseded the rigid structures of the law. To Kaz, there was nothing higher than the law. He understood that. His mother was the same. If only he'd come to question things sooner, maybe Jason wouldn't now be dying in the Rift. "I keep his file up to date when he's in Yaelsmuir."

"Are you in Yaelsmuir long after this?" Kazrani pressed. "We should get a meal together."

"I'm here as long as the hospital needs me," Rhodrishi said. "Whenever you have time, come find me."

"And here is our most valued healer." Rainer's voice cut into the conversation, silencing the three of them.

The crowd shifted around them and Tashué turned toward the voice. It was a strange thing to feel a sense of familiarity with these people, the very richest people in all of Yaelsmuir. Even if it was an ugly familiarity, borne of resentment and anger. Rainer had a knot of people around him again, or maybe all those people were following Illea. She looked right at him, giving him a smile across the room that made him feel like they were naked together again, in her bed, her thighs so warm and strong around his waist.

He took a deep breath. This was a bad time for thoughts like that. And though she was very beautiful and very enthusiastic, she wasn't Stella Whiterock.

Mallory Imburleigh was dressed in her uniform as well—sky blue of infantry, the black sash of an artillery attachment. She smiled at Tashué, too, and at Rhodrishi. Maybe Tashué hadn't made as bad of an impression as he thought.

"Only a few dozen Hands of Bronwynn have been awarded in the history of the Dominion military, and Colonel Rhodrishi Kheir is the only one still active," Rainer continued. "He has retired from the military, but now he serves the Authority, like many of this nation's veterans. In fact, he joined in the rescue efforts after the Market fire, and even now he has been working with the wounded in Mayor Wolfe's new hospital."

"I didn't realize your hospital was finished," Imburleigh said, laying a hand on Wolfe's arm.

Wolfe shrugged. "It isn't, not quite, but it was the best place to house the wounded of the Market fire. We had the space and the beds. We're most fortunate to have Colonel Kheir with us in the meantime, as he's been able to suggest some changes to help improve our efficiency."

Myron Winter gave a long-suffering sigh, looking down at his brandy as he swirled it in his glass. "I still don't understand why you chose Brickheart for your very best hospital when there were excellent building sites available in Highview and Drystone. And indeed, Highfield."

Tashué saw the spasm of frustration that crossed Wolfe's face, a tightness that pulled on his mouth that was mostly hidden by his beard. But he smiled, turning to Myron. "All of those places have excellent hospitals already. More than enough to serve their population. Brickheart is stuck in the past, with nothing but apothecary stores and lone healers who work out of their front parlours. Brickheart and Cattle Bone Bay and In The Tracks are our most densely populated quarters, and the residents there deserve modern healthcare."

Myron shrugged, shaking his head, giving the impression that this was an argument they'd had more than once and he still wasn't interested in the answer. "They have the Facility of Rest, don't they? That's in Brickheart."

"The Facility of Rest is hospice care," Rhodrishi said. "For people with no options left but to die. I would hope that the Governor of this great province would wish for more for his citizens than to die of wounds and ailments that are perfectly treatable by people with the right skills."

Myron forced a smile. "Well, I bow to your expertise, Colonel Kheir."

His smile plastered expertly in place, Rainer reached out to Tashué and put a hand on his shoulder, pulling him closer. "And of course, we have Officer Blackwood with him. You all remember our Officer Blackwood."

"Of course everyone remembers," Ishmael said brightly. "Captain Blackwood has certainly been the most memorable of dinner guests, especially since he missed so much of dinner."

Myron's face turned a deep shade of red, and Tashué felt Rainer stiffen, his hand turning into a vice on Tashué's shoulder. Everyone turned toward Ishmael, varying shades of amusement and frustration across all of their faces. Ishmael seemed positively delighted with himself.

"That's rich, coming from you of all people," Tashué laughed. "Whose company have you been keeping these days?"

"Hey now, you don't want to be the kind of man that spills my secrets," Ishmael said, but his grin belied the threat. "Don't worry— I wasn't criticizing you. In fact, I'm sure that every man in this room is envious of you. Some of the women too."

Myron made a strangled noise in the back of his throat, his eyes bulging. "Excuse me, Mr. Elsworth, I think I need a little more time practising my speech."

Rainer sighed. "Of course, Governor."

Myron turned and stomped away. Rainer pointed his steely glare at Wolfe, who did his best to ignore the glare completely.

Ishmael's grin only widened and he winked at Tashué. Ishmael pulled a wrinkled paper bag out of his pocket. "These formal events. You have to bring provisions or they'll starve you half to death."

"Thank you," Tashué said, reaching into the bag and pulling out a handful of sugar coated hazelnuts.

"The Captain is quite adept at starving himself on his own accord," Kazrani said, elbowing Tashué out of the way and reaching into the bag. "This is a good idea, though. I should keep snacks in my pockets so I can feed him when he gets cranky, like I did for my son. When he was a toddler."

Tashué snorted. "Excuse me, I kept the snacks for Tevir. My pockets were always sticky because of that boy."

"I heard you and Lieutenant Mahalouwan were down in the Market when the barge exploded," General Imburleigh said. "In fact, the pair of you worked very hard in the early days when the fire was still burning. Is that how your hands were so wounded, Captain Blackwood?"

"It is, General Imburleigh," Tashué said, stretching out his fingers. The scabs and the stitches pulled at healing flesh. He'd dreaded this conversation. He could feel the flow of it already, these people with their expensive clothes and their glittering jewels telling him how heroic he was, asking him how it had all happened, gasping and sneering at the foul tainted brightman who had killed so many people—and all Tashué wanted to do was ask Rainer to fix it. Give him and Kazrani and all the other Officers an option other than the Rift or an execution for people who couldn't trust their own minds anymore, couldn't use their own Talent. He couldn't help but remember the woman that he had spoken to in the Bay, the one that said that they broke the minds of children. He wanted to ask Rainer if it was true.

Illea smiled, reaching out and plucking a piece of lint off Tashué's arm. It was such a subtle moment, but it seemed to Tashué that she was laying claim to him in front of anyone. "You're being very modest, Mr. Blackwood, pretending it's nothing to mention." She left her hand on his arm, even as she turned to look at Kazrani and Rhodrishi. "The three of you do this city a service."

"Thank you, Miss Winter," Kazrani cut in. "But there were lots of people trying to help."

"Of course!" Rainer said. "Would that we could thank them all."

"I heard that it was an attack by the Army of the Red Dawn," Imburleigh said. "It seemed too terrible a thought to contemplate, but if it's true—"

"No, Miss Imburleigh, there's no evidence that the Army of the Red Dawn is even active in Yaelsmuir," Rainer interrupted. "Never mind perpetuating an attack within the city. The answer is far more mundane than that, I'm pleased to inform you."

"Are the other rumours true, then?" Wolfe asked. "A brightman caused it somehow?"

"How could a brightman have that much strength?" Illea asked. "I was under the impression that brightmen are trained to do that job because their abilities are weak, and they can't do much else but make a few lamps glow."

Tashué bit his tongue at her dismissive tone. Making a few lamps glow was no small feat. It didn't take much Talent perhaps, but it was relentless work, which had driven that particular brightman mad.

"It seems that the particular barge he targeted was carrying a load of thermite," Rainer said. "The whole situation was unfortunate, of course—the barge shouldn't have been carrying so much thermite, and the sheer volume of it meant that the blast had considerable power."

"What's thermite?" Kazrani asked.

"It's an incendiary powder, which burns so hot that it's used to weld train tracks together," Illea said. "It seems Cruinnich is building a rail line and a merchant was looking to supply them as quickly as possible."

"Why would a brightman do such a thing?" Imburleigh asked. "I don't understand…"

"He had the Wrath, General Imburleigh," Kazrani said. "Driven mad by his own abilities."

"And so, this madman went around the city starting fires?" Illea asked. "Why wasn't he stopped?"

"Lieutenant Mahalouwan and I were trying to arrest him," Tashué said. "He knew what was coming, and he said he didn't want to be publicly executed."

Another stretch of silence as the knot of people all looked at each other, trying to absorb Tashué's words. Tashué watched Rainer, wondering what went through the man's mind. Had he known these things already?

"You must be excited for your promotion, Mr. Blackwood," Rainer said. "Will you miss your work once you move into the office? Many Regulation Officers say they enjoy working on the streets."

Tashué took a deep breath, wondering if Rainer realized how ridiculous he sounded. He scanned the faces around him, looking for some ally. Wolfe looked annoyed, at least. Maybe he understood. Of them all, he and Ishmael were the only ones who came down to the fire. He and Ishmael had wounds on their hands, too, and Ishmael had that distant look in his eye.

"Though I could use a break from the streets, I won't be leaving them behind quite yet," Tashué said. "There aren't enough Officers at the station house to take my caseload so I'll be working my cases until I can find an Officer to replace me."

"Yes, I recall you mentioning that your station was shorthanded," Wolfe said. "You haven't received any new Officers since that time?"

Tashué grinned in spite of his sour mood, looking at Rainer. The man had mastery of his face, only flinching a little—a bit of tightening around his eyes, the thin lips pulling back into a grimace for just a moment—but Tashué revelled in every moment of it.

"No," Tashué said. "We haven't received any Officers yet. In fact, I understand that many of the station houses are struggling under high capacities."

"If anything, it's a sign of the success of the Authority," Rainer said swiftly. "We have a high concentration of *compliant* tainted, who are registered. Yes, our Officers are struggling under the weight of their responsibilities. We will allocate funds for the establishment of more station houses to help lighten the burdens all across the city."

"How many station houses are there in Yaelsmuir? How many Officers at each one?" Wolfe asked.

"Twenty station houses," Rainer said. "Housing thirty Officers on average."

"Managing how many cases each?"

"On average, thirty-five, I would say," Rainer said.

"Everyone at House 15 has forty or more," Tashué said. "But then we aren't fully staffed."

Wolfe nodded. "So, it could be said that there are over a thousand tainted managed per station house—and if there are twenty houses, that is over twenty thousand cases. Twenty-two thousand, actually, if we take the averages at face-value." Wolfe's eyes were on Rainer as he spoke, boring into the side of Rainer's face as Rainer avoided eye contact. "That's a lot of people. Close to a tenth of the population of the city."

That was a sobering number. The gathering was still for a moment as they absorbed the thought. A tenth of the population, compliant and registered. Tashué grimaced at 'compliant'. It *was* an ugly word. How many weren't compliant? How many were in the Rift or killed in the streets or hanged with the Wrath? How many weren't registered at all? And the Breeding Program—who supervised their care, all the babies created under the Authority's supervision? How many were there?

Would he have access to that information as a House Commander?

Rainer smiled, reached out to pat Tashué's shoulder. "We'll have your station house sorted in no time, Mr. Blackwood, so that you can focus on your various new duties."

"Yes, sir."

Tashué took a deep breath as they moved away, trying to release the knot of tension. Where had his life taken him that he was starting to hate the man in charge of the organization he thought he believed in?

"Good evening, ladies and gentlemen!" Mallory Imburleigh stood very naturally on the stage, commanding the attention of the room. "The Imburleigh Armament Company is honoured to host such a fine crowd of men and women, and I would like to thank you all for coming. It was easy to decide the sort of guests that I wanted to invite when Governor Winter came to me with the idea for this function. The Governor's proposed police force is a revolutionary idea, set to forge a new age of peace and safety. With a united, organized police force, Governor Winter hopes to investigate criminal activity to a degree that isn't yet possible and bring resolution to violent crimes more efficiently than ever before."

Imburleigh paused as someone started clapping. She smiled.

"Thank you, my friends, thank you. It's clear that Yaelsmuir craves peace and stability. Our Governor will give it to us. A hundred years ago, when our people were threatened by lawless tainted who used their dark abilities to bring death and violence, a wise man saw the path to pacification. And so the National Tainted Registration Authority was created, forged in fires of violence and strife. The first brave men and women who took the tin fought a war within our borders against those that would tear our civilization to pieces. You, my friends, are the descendants of those first Officers. Perhaps you are not related by blood, but you are brothers and sisters nonetheless."

Kazrani seemed to be bursting with pride, her chest swelling as she was swept up by the applause that rippled through the crowd. Tashué crossed his arms over his chest, taking a deep breath. Even though the applause made some primal part of him shiver, he felt no pride. Imburleigh's speech seemed to highlight all the things he disagreed with. He couldn't applaud for the idea that people like Stella and Jason and Rhodrishi were 'lawless and violent'.

"And so, when Governor Winter seeks to create a force of men and women who must stand against violence for the safety of the people, he looks to you," Imburleigh continued. "He will model his police force after you. Remember that you now have two roles.

Firstly, you are Regulation Officers, trusted by the Dominion entire to protect them from the tainted. And secondly, you stand as an example for the police force to come, as something to emulate for the next wave of courageous men and women who are willing to take up the fight against crime and violence in this city, in this province and eventually, in the Dominion entire."

Kazrani elbowed him this time when another applause broke out but he kept his arms crossed. *Trusted by the Dominion entire to protect them from the tainted.* Forcing a man like Moore into madness rather than giving him an opportunity to save himself from the Wrath.

"And so Governor Winter asked me to invite you all here today," Imburleigh went on. "He wants to honour you. And he wants you all to bear witness to my pledge."

Imburleigh turned, and a youth rushed forward, handing over a leather-wrapped folio. She flipped it open, holding it up to the crowd as if anyone could read the words from the distance.

"My friends, this is a purchase order. Governor Winter and I have come to excellent terms. Imburleigh Armament Company will supply Governor Winter with every gun he needs to arm his new Provincial Police Force with the very best guns in the world!"

More applause. Tashué found himself wishing that he was anywhere else. He didn't want the brass badge. He didn't want the responsibility. He didn't want the weight of a thousand registered people on his shoulders.

Imburleigh stepped back to the small podium. She took a fountain pen and signed. Imburleigh handed the pen to Myron, who leaned down to sign, too. They shook hands and the applause only grew louder, the military men and women cheering with such force that Tashué could feel the rumble of it in his chest. Imburleigh held up the folio again and showed the fresh signatures, the wet ink glistening in the light.

Rainer went to the stage next. "Ladies and gentlemen, it is my considerable honour to run these promotions. I have met the most hardworking men and women I've ever known through this organization. First allow me to introduce you all to our newest Station Commander—Tashué Blackwood."

Tashué took a deep breath and headed up to the stage, his legs plodding on even though his mind screamed at him not to. The crowd parted for him as he made his way and he couldn't go anywhere but forward. His body was flushed with energy as if he was plunging into battle, the room going quiet around him as his ears rang. Rainer stood in the centre of the stage, waiting for Tashué to come to him. Tashué unpinned his badge and handed it over. Rainer replaced it with brass that had been polished so it shone like gold. The revulsion Tashué felt at the thing was powerful and he almost refused it. But he couldn't, not in front of all these people. He would wait until Rainer was done with him and he would retire quietly. He would find a way to get Jason out of the Rift and he would leave Yaelsmuir. He found himself holding his breath as Rainer pinned the badge to the front of Tashué's jacket, opposite the medals and ribbons that told the story of his service.

"A moment, if you please, Commander Blackwood," Myron announced, stepping forward from the back of the stage and blocking Tashué's exit. He gripped Tashué by the arm, squeezing so hard that his knuckles went white. Tashué fought the urge to shrug him off. *Fuck, what now?* "My friends, as you all know, our beautiful city was struck with tragedy last week. It is fortunate for us, therefore, that our citizens are so brave and involved in their communities. So many of our excellent citizens did their part to help fight the fire and find survivors, and I wish that I could thank them all personally. But, even as Governor, there are only so many hands I can shake in a day!"

He paused for the polite chuckle that passed through the crowd, nodding and smiling. It reminded Tashué of a rictus, exaggerated and wild. His hand clamped down on Tashué's arm even harder. Tashué tried to clench a fist, but the stitches pulled too tight and he forced himself to relax.

"It's in that spirit that I have decided to establish the Blackwood Medal for Exceptional Bravery. The medal is intended to honour the very best protectors of the province, men and women who step into the storm in order to protect their fellow citizens. The Medal will be intended especially for my Provincial Police Force, for I dearly hope that the men and women who volunteer to serve in the force will look at the bravery and the dedication and be inspired to serve their province."

Tashué stared down at the many faces that watched him, sweat crawling across his body. He wished he'd been warned of this moment, but then, he might not have come up on the stage at all. He clenched his fists again, focusing on the pain in his hands as the stitches pulled. So many people had participated in fighting the fire and in the rescue efforts, and Tashué hardly felt that he, specifically, deserved any accolades for it. The fire was his fault. If he had managed to stop Moore, none of the carnage would have happened at all. Eddie and his mum would still be smoking pork. Božic would still be selling toys. The destroyed lives weren't limited to those killed or wounded. Everyone who lost their store, their stall, the stock that their livelihood depended on, the coin they left stashed under their floorboards for hard days. How many businesses in the Market would be bankrupt by the fire? By the crews that burned buildings or knocked them over to try to contain the spreading flames?

"Smile, Commander!" Rainer chuckled, giving Tashué a jovial shove with one elbow. "It's not every day a man gets a medal named after him."

"Yes, sir," Tashué said, because he didn't know what else to say.

Myron presented the medal to Tashué in its velvet case, an eight-pointed star made of the kind of knotwork that was typically associated with the North Star. Tashué's badge number was scrawled across its centre. The whole damned thing was made of rose gold, making it the single most valuable thing Tashué owned. But he didn't want it.

Myron handed him the box, taking the medal out to pin it to Tashué's jacket, just above the military medals he already had. Above the White Shield they'd given him for the Black Ridge. At least on the Ridge, he'd been protecting his soldiers from the angry, churning death that waited for them. At least on the Ridge, the dead were someone else's fault.

Myron was grinning still, but some of the tension had melted out of him and his chest swelled as if he had accomplished something. He pulled a kerchief from his pocket, wiping the fingerprints off the front of the medal and then stepping back to admire it. He stuffed his kerchief away in his pocket, grabbed Tashué's hand, and forced him into a shake, squeezing Tashué's wounds a little too hard.

"You do this city, and this province, a fine service, sir. Thank you."

"Thank you, Governor."

Illea Winter caught him when he finally stepped down, leaning up to place a kiss on each of his cheeks, dodging the rough stubble. Her smile was so warm and bright that Tashué was tempted to believe she was genuine. Of them all, she was the best actor.

Kazrani caught Tashué next when he returned to his place beside her, pulling him in for a hug. "I'm proud of you."

Tashué shrugged, unable to meet her eye. How could he tell her how miserable he felt about the whole thing when she believed in it so completely? She was the best friend he'd known in his entire life, a sister that he had found in the service, an ally through his darkest days. She and Tevir had come to stay with him after Keoh left with Jason, because living alone when he had come home to be with his family had been too ugly a thing to bear. How could he make her understand how things were changing so completely for him?

There were a dozen or so promotions for the night. Tashué caught Rhodrishi's eye, motioning to a doorway that led to some hallway. Rhodrishi nodded and they shuffled through the crowd, heading back toward the bar. They each took a beer before making their way around the crowd and finding the hallway. The noise of the gathering faded as they moved through the hall, putting distance between them and all those bodies. Tashué sucked the foamy head, letting it soothe the angry parts of his soul, all the jagged places that didn't fit together anymore.

"You didn't tell me you were being promoted," Rhodrishi said softly, his voice pitched so quiet that Tashué could barely hear him.

"I'm sorry, I only just found out. And at the Market, I was thinking of other things," Tashué said. He took a long sip of the thick porter, resisting the urge to pull off his badge. At least it was easier for him to breathe, now that they were outside. "We don't have enough Officers for me to start moving files around. I'll keep you as long as I can, but maybe it's time to consider what you would do once I have to transfer your case."

"I've thought about that more than once."

The courtyard was shaded from the sun, and without the warmth of its rays, the air held a deep chill. Tashué could hear the wind howling over the courtyard. The nights were almost cold enough for snow, the days not far behind.

"What will you do?"

Rhodrishi stepped into the centre of the courtyard, tilting his head toward the sky. "I'm tired." He sighed, sipping at his beer, a red ale that sat like ruby liquid in his glass. "I've given the Dominion so many years. I asked you to do this thing for me because I wanted freedom. But freedom... I don't know. It isn't such a great thing. Or perhaps there isn't such a thing as freedom at all?"

"Maybe not," Tashué agreed.

Rhodrishi nodded. "We're getting old, you and I."

"You're getting old maybe," Tashué muttered. "I'm just over forty."

"Your soul is old. I suspect you've been a vicious old man since the day you were born."

Tashué chuckled. "That's probably true."

That got a smile from Rhodrishi, folding the deep creases around his mouth. "However did you come to have a Pashibé name?"

Tashué reached for his cigarillo case, balancing his beer and the case long enough for him to put a cigarillo between his lips. "I don't know. I wasn't involved in that conversation. Being still in my mother's womb when the decision was made." He shuffled for his matches next. "My grandmother was Pashibé. She didn't teach my mother what that meant, but somehow I got a Pashibé name anyway." He sparked a match with his thumbnail, lighting the end with a few deep breaths. "What does it mean?"

"One who sees," Rhodrishi said. "It's usually paired with the word for 'past the horizon', which then comes to mean *One who sees what is hidden.*"

One who sees what is hidden. If only. "Is it a prophecy?"

Rhodrishi shrugged. "It depends who was responsible for the naming. How did she feel about you working for the Registration Authority, your mother?"

"I don't know how she would have felt. She was dead by the time I took the tin. But she always insisted that I should follow the laws, to stay safe, so maybe she would have approved." Tashué sighed, watching the smoke curl up from the end of his cigarillo. "I wanted to retire from the military so that I could stay home and raise my son, but I didn't see many options. I didn't think I had any skills except fighting. The Authority recruiter came to the barracks to talk about salary and signing bonuses… It seemed like a gift so that I could see my son grow. I had such a short time with him, a furlough to see his birth and the first few months of his life, and then I had to go back. I hated leaving him, leaving to serve the military that flogged me for the crime of not wanting to throw my life away. All the other floggings, I deserved, but that one…" He shook his head, draining the last of his beer. "I often think that everything I did with Jason was wrong, except my decision to come home to him. That was the only good step."

"I think that our children grow into their personalities and decisions in spite of our efforts, not because of them," Rhodrishi said. "Jason was made with parts of you and parts of his mother and those parts came together no matter what you did. I don't know his mother—but I know his father. His father is a stubborn man who stands by his beliefs, no matter the cost. Jason inherited that. And he believes that the Authority is an evil entity that will strip his humanity from him, so he defied them and got himself sent to the Rift. You *used* to believe he was wrong. What changed?"

"I don't know," Tashué said with a sigh. "Everything."

Rhodrishi held out a hand and Tashué knew immediately what he wanted. Tashué reached into his jacket and pulled out the notepad, flipping it open to the face of the child. Rhodrishi peered through the darkness at the face that Tashué had drawn with his charcoal lines. He looked for a long time, eyes scanning carefully, as if he could read the story of the girl by studying Tashué's rendering of her.

"So young," he said.

"Yes."

"You have your suspicions then? About who killed her?"

"I have some wild, unsubstantiated accusations and I have horrifying rumours. I don't know how to go about finding real answers." Tashué closed the notepad, tucking it away into his jacket. "Can you feel other Talented when they're near?"

"I can."

"Can you feel the Talent that's running the foundry? They smelt their own metal for the guns here."

"Of course I can feel it." Rhodrishi nodded to the far end of the courtyard, into the shadows that lurked there. "I hate this quarter. I can feel all the misery here." He shuddered. "Even with all I know about the Authority, I can't imagine what they must be doing to these people."

"Let's go find out."

Tashué stalked across the courtyard, to the door there tucked under an awning. It was locked—it didn't matter how hard he turned the handle, it wouldn't give. Rhodrishi stepped in behind him and put his hand on the door. The unfolding of his Talent was like the warmth of a familiar hearth fire as it tickled across Tashué's senses. The lock slid and thunked.

"Well, that's helpful," Tashué said. "How does a healer know how to open locks?"

"People who use their Talent for a single purpose is a construct of your Authority," Rhodrishi said with a sigh. "Talent is not the ability to light a lamp or heal a wound. Talent is the ability to touch the world around us and change the flow of energy. Healing wounds is merely lending the body the strength it needs to do what comes naturally, and speeding the process. Opening a lock is merely shifting the weight of the locking mechanism."

"I didn't know that," Tashué admitted, leading Rhodrishi through.

"Of course you didn't. Your understanding of the world has been shaped by the Authority, and it's always been in the Authority's best interest to reduce people with Talent to singular tools, to be used and discarded to serve the Dominion."

It was dark, but somewhere in the distance Tashué could hear the clatter of voices and work. It was far away and indistinct, filtered through more doors and hallways. Rhodrishi tapped his shoulder and led him away down another hall, which opened to yet another courtyard. Back in through another locked door that Rhodrishi opened. Had this place been built as a maze on purpose, to make it impossible for the uninitiated to make their way through? A warehouse stretched out in front of them where ingots of steel were stacked and waiting. The air was thick with the smell of dust and iron. Beyond it, Tashué thought he could feel the heat of the foundry fires and the Talent of whoever was working for the factory. Rhodrishi was right; it was an ugly, angry energy, like the Talented that ran the trams.

"Excuse me, sirs, you aren't supposed to be in here."

Tashué stopped advancing, turning to the voice. A group of Imburleigh employees had followed them into the warehouse, or perhaps they had been here all along. Their hands were dirty and their clothes the rugged uniforms of people who worked hard, stained with sweat, blood, and soot, darns and patches and new seams decorating each uniform differently.

Tashué used his widest smile, stepping closer to the group. "I was looking for the guns," he laughed. "I thought I would get to play with guns when I was invited to the Imburleigh factory. Someone told me there was a shooting range in here somewhere."

"There's no shooting range here, sir," the largest of the employees said, stepping forward to meet Tashué. "You need to go back to the warehouse."

"Alright, fine, it's fine," Tashué said. He looked down into his empty pint, grunting and lifting it up so that he could drink back the last dregs. "I guess we should go back, Colonel."

"I guess we should," Rhodrishi agreed.

"Are you sure there isn't a firing range in here?" Tashué pressed but he allowed the group to lead him back to one courtyard, and then another.

"You'll have to speak to the organizers at the function, sir. That isn't my job."

"Thank you, sir," Tashué said. "You folks do good work here. Imburleigh are the very best guns. Those guns saved my life in the service. When the enemies' guns misfired or jammed, Imburleighs shot true."

"Thank you, sir, that's very kind. Enjoy your evening."

The man left them in the first courtyard they'd found, nothing but their empty glasses and the sound of a few hidden crickets to keep them company.

30

ILLEA

DAY 17

Myron stayed on the stage, drinking and grinning and shuffling. As if he was in any way responsible for anything happening. It all had Rainer's mark, every piece of it, from the promotions to the damned medal. Myron didn't even have the sense to quit drinking while he was up there, sending Imburleigh staff off for gin, and his eyes were starting to look rather dull and empty. At least his eyes matched his brain.

Once the promotions were over and Myron stepped forward to give his second speech, this time about the election, Illea knew it was safe to slip away. That she didn't much care about her husband's political career would surprise no one at all, and if it did, they weren't paying attention anyway. Rainer met her at the bottom of the stairs, giving his tight smile and a bit of a bow of his head, hooking his arm in hers.

"Will you walk with me, Miss Winter?"

Illea forced a smile. "Of course, Mr. Elsworth."

She cast her eyes through the crowd quickly, looking for someone to drag along with her, but no one was close enough. The days when Rainer Elsworth was a potential partner for her were long gone. She had come to learn that Rainer was entirely too self-serving, and that not all men were so oblivious to their partner's enjoyment. Her lack of interest, though, hadn't yet deterred him from trying.

He led her away from the party. There was something stiff about the way he moved, a little bit of a stomp as he walked. Not a tryst, then.

"The election is almost over," Rainer said, once they left the crowd behind. "Did you have any more plans for our Mr. Blackwood, or will you allow us to use him as we intended?"

"Oh?" Illea asked, smiling. "Am I interfering with your political campaign, Mr. Elsworth? That wasn't my intention. I was merely taking him on a pleasurable diversion."

"Yes, yes, and it was very entertaining and memorable and I'm sure all of White Crown has been gossiping about it endlessly. You promised me that you wouldn't interfere with Myron's career, Illea. You looked me in the eye and you swore that you would stand aside while I made him Governor this year. This is the election I need from him."

"Please, keep him in the Governor's office as long as you like," Illea said. "So long as he's in that office, he spends less time in my house."

"How am I supposed to do that, precisely, when you are making a mockery of him during his campaign?"

Illea took a slow, measured breath, fighting for the appearance of a calm she didn't feel. There was a time, early in their marriage, when she tried to forgive Myron for not being Amias. Those days were long gone, destroyed by years of Myron's foolishness and ineptitude. Soon, she would be free of him, free of financing his campaigns, free of paying his debts, free of conversations about his 'career.'

She smiled. She nudged Rainer's arm playfully, looking up at him. "What do my leisurely activities have to do with Myron's campaign?"

The tension melted out of Rainer as he smiled back at her. "Ah, dear Illea, nothing about your activities can be described as 'leisurely'."

Illea laughed, leaning against him. "Be that as it may, I don't understand how it affects the campaign. A vote for Myron is a vote for the name Winter, and I seem to remember on the last campaign, you requested that I be as gregarious and charming as possible. You said it was good for people to be talking about the Winter name. Well, what could be better than to show the bond between the Winter name and the Authority?"

"I understand the attraction—honestly, I do," Rainer sighed. "Blackwood is a fine specimen. That's one of the reasons we selected him, isn't it? But I think you could perhaps show your bond and your support in a different way. At least until the campaign is over."

As if summoned by the sound of his name, Tashué came around a corner with the Kaadayri healer. He looked very fine in his dress uniform, the green cavalry wool sitting so naturally on him. She felt Rainer go tense again, his pace slowing as if he was trying to hold Illea back. What did he think she was, some trained bitch on a lead for him to direct as he saw fit? She slid her arm out of his, walking a little faster and forcing him to choose between matching her pace or being left behind.

"Mr. Blackwood, what a pleasant surprise!" Illea said, closing the distance between them and kissing his cheek again. "You've been caught exploring, have you? What have you gone looking for, instead of enjoying the well stocked bar?"

"I'm at the Imburleigh Armament Factory, Miss Winter," Tashué said. "I was hoping to find the firing range."

"And you, Colonel?" Rainer chuckled, catching up to Illea and standing beside her again. "It seems a hard thing to imagine a healer with the Hands of Bronwynn searching out firearms."

Kheir shrugged, glancing up at Tashué. "I have an appreciation for skill and craft, Mr. Elsworth. It's not every day that a man gets the opportunity to see the production of the finest arms in the world."

"Mallory would be most pleased to hear you say so, Colonel," Illea said. She liked this Kheir fellow. Watching him dress down Myron about the hospital had been a real pleasure.

Kheir turned his startling amber eyes on Illea, and she was swept away for a moment by the intensity of him. He seemed so calm and composed as he stood at Tashué's shoulder, very dignified in his dark healer's blues and his Colonel's stars. But meeting his eyes, Illea was aware of the depth of him, roiling and dangerous. Was it his Talent that made him seem so intense? Did Talent work that way? He smiled and the tense moment passed, leaving Illea feeling a little off-balance.

"Mr. Blackwood, I'm disappointed," Illea said, recovering the moment. "I would expect you to know to look to your friends when you have a desire to get behind locked doors."

Tashué swung to Illea, stepping a little closer. So much about sleeping with him was exactly as she'd hoped it would be—angry and frantic, like a storm that swept her away. She could see him remembering the same thing, and it made him take a deep breath. "I was concerned that I hadn't made a very good impression on General Imburleigh and she wouldn't be interested in giving me a tour."

Rainer scoffed. "And you thought that exploring her factory uninvited would somehow endear you to her?"

Tashué's smile never wavered, and he turned to Rainer. "You're right, of course." He looked at Illea next, lifting her hand to his lips to kiss the back of her knuckles. "I should have come to you. But I have to admit, it's still incredible to me that I can count myself as friends with Illea Winter. Do you forgive me?"

Illea cocked her head and smiled up at him. She saw the effect her smile had, even in this strange moment when everyone was so tense. "Of course, Mr. Blackwood. How could I hold a grudge against a man for having an adventurous soul?"

He smiled and kissed her hand again, squeezing her fingers. She let him hang on to her, his hand so warm, the calluses now so familiar. She could almost hear Rainer hissing like a boiling kettle behind her, his feet scuffing on the floor of the courtyard as he fought for calm.

Tashué looked over Illea's shoulder at Rainer. Those burning amber eyes locked on Rainer and froze his anxious shuffling for a moment.

"What about you, Mr. Elsworth?" Tashué asked. "Can I count you as a friend?" A fast learner, after all, for all that he said he hated it, that he didn't want it. Give Rainer a bit of power, take something in return. Eventually, he would come to learn how to get things from men like Rainer without giving anything away at all, if he was as smart as Illea thought he was.

"Why, yes, of course," Rainer said too swiftly, perhaps before his mind had the chance to catch up with the moment. "But such a friendship is a knife that cuts both ways, Mr. Blackwood. There needs to be trust between us. Knowledge that what is asked will be given. This afternoon was good for your career, with your promotion, but it is also for the Governor. He's making a big promise to the people of Yaelsmuir with his police force, and I'm sure he would appreciate your support. Especially after how... disruptive the banquet was."

Illea almost laughed at the concept of Myron appreciating Tashué's support. Still, Rainer was smart to appeal to the man's honour. Tashué glanced at Illea as if he was looking for her approval. *Good man. You know who's in charge here.* She squeezed his hand, giving him a little nod.

"Of course," Tashué said. "I would ask something of you, if I may. Just a small thing, but I would be deeply grateful."

Rainer smiled, his chest swelling. "Of course you can ask, Mr. Blackwood."

"I would like to see Keoh. I've tried to get access to her but the paperwork defeated me."

Rainer blinked a few times, his smile frozen in place. "Keoh?"

"Yes, sir. The mother of my son. She's been housed at the Breeding Program for a number of years, and my son has been asking about her."

"Ah, a visitation to the Breeding Program. It can be rather hard to get past those walls, but of course you understand; it's important to keep close eye on who is coming and going. Can't have any accidental breedings, can we?"

Standing pressed against Tashué as she was, Illea was able to feel him stiffen—and not in the way she'd enjoyed so thoroughly. His hand twitched and there was a fraught moment when Illea thought he was about to lash out at Rainer.

"Thank you, sir," Tashué said, his voice gone mechanical and stiff.

Rainer nodded, no doubt pleased with himself in that way he was when he toyed so easily with Tashué's emotions. "I'll have the paperwork waiting at your new desk come morning, Commander."

Illea squeezed Tashué's hand, hoping to anchor him in the moment before he did something stupid. He seemed to shake himself, looking over at Colonel Kheir, who had stood as a silent observer through the whole exchange. Illea almost forgot about him, but not quite. The memory of meeting those eyes wouldn't leave her any time soon.

"Well, then, Colonel, shall we return to the festivities?" Tashué asked.

Kheir nodded slowly, scanning Illea's face and then Rainer's. "Lead the way, Captain."

31

TASHUÉ

DAY 17

Ishmael had that look in his eye, the one he got when he was drinking and he still had too much energy from being away and all the things he was angry about were starting to get a hold of him. It might have looked like distance to someone that didn't know him. Like boredom. Tashué should have known it was coming, with all the talk about sexual partners with Kazrani, with the way he seemed to have fewer smart comments as he followed Wolfe around the room. The brandy would be sitting hot in Ishmael's chest by now but the energy would be crawling up his spine as he avoided eye contact with everyone so that he wouldn't start hitting people just to get his body *moving*.

Tashué gave Rainer three fucking hours of chatting at people. Kazrani rescued Rhodrishi, but Tashué hung on for three miserable hours and tried to eat the food that staff carried around on silver trays, but it all tasted like ash. He didn't dare drink too much or he'd start hitting people, too, he'd start swinging because he couldn't bear how people remarked on his new medal and his Shield. He knew he was finished when he started asking people where they were when the Market was burning.

"I heard you fought the fire for three days, Mr. Blackwood."

"I did. What were you doing for those three days? Was it important?"

"Are you the same Blackwood that was on the Ridge? Manual says that was a textbook entrenchment."

"Sure, textbook entrenchment. That's what you do when you've got the high ground. You hold it. I don't know why they sent the cavalry in for that."

Rainer started moving him from one person to the next so fast he didn't catch anyone's name. And Myron had drifted off, standing at the edge of the crowd because it was closer to the bar. He had the flushed face, loud voice, the distant eyes of too damned much gin. Rainer had given up on him.

"Captain Blackwood, it's good to finally meet you, sir."

Tashué shifted his attention back to whoever was standing in front of him.

"I'd shake your hand, but it looks like your hands have seen better days." The man grinned, leaning closer. "I hear from my sister that I missed all kinds of gossip-worthy things when I declined to come to Illea's banquet. I really have the worst luck!"

"Commander, this is Langston Imburleigh," Rainer supplied.

"Yes, the *other* Imburleigh," the man said, grinning. "I'm sure you've heard the stories. At least half of them are true."

Tashué tried to recall if he had heard any stories at all. Most of the gossip he heard was about Illea. Or Ishmael. Or himself, now, which was a uniquely uncomfortable experience. "Our city does love to tell stories, doesn't it?"

Langston gave a wicked grin, raising a glass to Tashué. He certainly looked like Mallory, the same chestnut coloured hair, the same friendly brown eyes. "It's half the fun, isn't it, giving them all something to talk about?"

Fucking hell, who would think this is fun? "Is it?"

"Is it true, then, that you were at the Market fire? Three days, that's the smallest number. If you believe some of the gossip, you're still there! Lucky for Yaelsmuir there are two of you so that you could come get your shiny new medal while you also help the poor sods of the Market rebuild."

Even Rainer flinched. He put a hand on Tashué's shoulder, leaning closer to Langston. "The fire lasted three days and Commander Blackwood was there for the duration, and then longer than that to find survivors. How have you been, Langston? Has your health improved since the banquet?"

"Oh yes, I had a bout of... something, didn't I?" Langston said, winking at Rainer. "I'm quite improved, thank you for asking. You'll have to let me know ahead of time if you plan on bringing your Captain Blackwood with you to any more events. I'll want to see that."

"The hope is that Commander Blackwood will continue to represent the Authority for some time," Rainer said.

"Hey, good for you, sir. What does Miss Winter think of your representation?"

Tashué sucked in a deep breath. "Maybe you should ask her what she thinks. She's quite capable of speaking for herself."

"Yes, she is, isn't she? She's delightful."

"I hear the Crowne approved the rail line from Yaelsmuir to Obisza, Langston," Rainer cut in. "Will the Imburleigh company be bidding on the contract with Miss Winter?"

"Have mercy on me, Rainer, you can't honestly expect me to know any of that."

Tashué let his eyes drift across the crowd. How much longer did he need to stay here and let people drag him through the Market and the Ridge? Sober, no less. Because he'd asked to see Keoh and Rainer's price for that was that he floated around the room for Myron's campaign, even though Myron couldn't seem to care less. He saw it all too clearly while he was sober—three days fighting the fire, hauling buckets, running into buildings, and feeling the vicious heat of the flames. All those burnt bodies, smelling too much like meat, people still alive and half-cooked anyway.

And the Ridge—the Ridge was worse, the Ridge smelled of death in the hot Derccian sun, bodies bloated and rotting as they piled up at the bottom, the endless stack of dead Ibeh soldiers that they kicked down the cliff's edge. Smelled of fire, too, because Tashué's company burnt their dead every night, burnt everything but a lock of their hair and a shard of their bone to bring back to the Hadia. And he smelled his own fucking body rotting as he made his way up the Brightwash on a barge, rotting because they'd dragged him to the military prison in White Crown, given him fifty lashes, and sent him home to die.

Tashué let his eyes drift across the crowd, trying not to think about what came next, what pain came after getting home. *I'm sorry, I'm so sorry, your mother is dead.*

There were fewer people in the event hall now, many of the Officers having drifted away to... somewhere. Ishmael was still there, leaning against the stage again, turned half liquid by all the brandy in his veins, elbow propped on the wooden structure. The other hand held a cigarette, smaller than the cigarillos Tashué rolled for himself and wrapped in thin paper instead of a tobacco leaf. Whoever stood beside him was smoking cigarettes, too, which was probably where he got it. He tilted his head back to exhale the cloud above the heads of the people he was talking to. But even though he appeared to be made of liquid, so relaxed that his bones were brandy, he was tapping his foot, the anxiety in him building and building. The pair of them were going to start burning soon, burning from the inside out.

Ishmael met Tashué's eye as he took another drag of his cigarette, glancing just once at the hallway. The same one Tashué had led Rhodrishi into, maybe thinking of the courtyard. Where were Kazrani and Rhodrishi, anyway? Tashué nodded. He needed to get away.

He turned his attention back to Rainer, laying a hand on Rainer's shoulder and squeezing. Maybe squeezing a little too hard, judging by how Rainer tensed, how his lips pulled back in a grimace but he tried to hide it with a smile.

"Excuse me, Rainer, I'm going to get some fresh air," Tashué said.

"Yes, of course, Commander," Rainer said, nodding. "Thank you for your time this evening, you've been very helpful. I'm sure Myron appreciates it."

Tashué didn't say what he thought of Myron's appreciation—

telling Rainer where he could put Myron's appreciation probably went against the terms of their agreement. He could hear Myron laughing at something, laughing too loudly. Tashué looked at Langston again, forcing a smile. "It was good to meet you, Mr. Imburleigh."

"And you, Captain Blackwood, I hope I'll be seeing you again at one of these dreadful functions."

Tashué peeled away rather than trying to say anything else, pushing through the crowd. He could still smell it, the too-sweet smell of rotting flesh filling the cabin of the barge, the copper whisky burning in the wounds. He should have circled around to the bar on his way to the hall, for another measure of the Ladovaugh. Maybe the smoky scent of peat could have saved him from the smell of his on body dying, too close to the smell of decaying Ibeh soldiers on the Ridge. Better to sink into the kind of old and dull-edged pain that lived with the ghost of his father in a bottle of Ladovaugh than *this*.

He made it to the hallway, the cool air spreading from the courtyard. A big knot of Regulation Officers were in the courtyard already—Kazrani was there, Tashué could hear her. Laughing. He didn't want to see her, not now, not with this vicious and angry tension crawling through his body. He couldn't bear the way she looked at him when he felt like this, a mix of sympathy and sorrow.

Footsteps, behind him. Coming fast. He turned, hand clenching, ready for a fight, but it was Ishmael. Ishmael walking fast to catch up, pulling the knot of his tie loose, opening the buttons of his collar and taking a deep breath. He winced when he looked up at Tashué's face.

"You alright?"

"No I'm not fucking alright," Tashué growled, turning back and heading down the hallway. He didn't know where he was going. He didn't care. "If one more person says something idiotic about the Ridge, I'm going to start hitting people. This was a fucking mistake. I never should have agreed to this."

"You're going the wrong way."

"What?" Tashué snapped.

"Well, I suppose I don't know what you're looking for exactly, but I thought maybe you'd want to find somewhere to relax, in which case you're going the wrong way. Unless we're just stomping around for a while, then don't mind me and my advice."

Tashué sucked in a deep breath, forcing himself to stop walking. He didn't know where he was. He'd taken turns and he wasn't sure he could make it back to the event hall if he wanted to. Ishmael stood at his shoulder and waited. Hands in his pockets, body loose. Waiting.

"Lead the way," Tashué said.

Ishmael nodded, turning and heading back the way they'd come toward the main hallway. "I saw you talking to Langston Imburleigh. What did he say, then? That set you off?"

"It wasn't just him, it was everyone." Tashué tried to breathe good and deep, like Ishmael always did when he was fighting a thing like this. But his heart was pounding too hard, so hard it hurt, his chest feeling too tight. He couldn't fill his lungs all the way. Change the subject, then, stop thinking about *everyone* and how viciously ignorant they all were. "I got the impression that Langston Imburleigh fancies himself the next Ishmael Saeati."

Ishmael snorted. "Captain, I'm offended that you think anyone could follow my act."

"I didn't say *I* thought so."

"Thank the gods. I was about to be really upset."

They stepped into another warehouse. This one smelled of wood instead of iron, great stacks of raw planks sitting in piles. Oak, cherry, walnut. Darker, more expensive woods against the far wall. The whole room was lit dimly with Talent-powered brights, as if someone could walk in at any moment and start choosing planks to be cut and milled.

Ishmael led him to a stack of boxes towered next to one wall, furthest away from either of the doors that led into the warehouse. Standing behind the boxes, they were out of sight of either door, giving them some illusion of privacy. Tashué wasn't sure how hidden they would be if someone came into the warehouse and started pulling wood planks off the various piles, but maybe that didn't matter. Maybe just standing in the silent warehouse was enough, free from the bodies and the buzzing noise and sound of Myron's laughter.

"You're bleeding, Captain. Your hand."

Tashué looked down. His hands were clenched into fists so hard they were shaking. He tried to unclench them but that hurt somehow, like the muscles were locked in place. All the tension had split open the scabs of the deep wound on his right hand. Blood dripped. Tashué tried again with a deep breath. Ishmael pulled a kerchief from his pocket, handing it over. Tashué pressed it against the split places, catching the blood so he wouldn't get any on his dress uniform. It was hard to clean blood from wool and the cavalry greens seemed to show blood especially well. All the Dominion uniforms were such light colours. For visibility on the field, that was the official answer, so the Generals could watch the ebb and flow of battle. But maybe they wanted their soldiers to be a mottle of stains, blood and dirt and sweat and more blood, decorating their bodies with proof of their service as obvious as their medals and their rank symbols.

Ishmael opened his jacket, reaching into his breast pocket and pulling out a cigarillo. Leaned forward and slid his hand into Tashué's trouser pocket, finding his box of matches. Sparked a match with a flick of his thumb and touched the flame to the end. Tashué recognized the smell of hashish immediately, rich and oily and thick. Ishmael took a long drag, leaning his head back against the boxes and exhaling a great billow of smoke. He held the cigarillo out to Tashué.

Tashué sighed. "I thought we weren't doing that anymore, Ishmael."

"Why the fuck not?" Ishmael lifted his head off the box, leaning a little closer. "You look like you're going to burst all the blood vessels in your face, the way you're so tightly wound. Especially my favourite one, down the centre of your forehead. You need to relax before you give yourself a heart attack."

Tashué huffed. Anything to stop feeling like this, to get the smell of death and rot out of his nose. The smoke was thick and familiar and too comforting, too easy to like. He leaned forward, still holding the kerchief against his hand. Ishmael put the cigarillo between Tashué's lips and Tashué closed his eyes as the smoke curled up over his face, crawling across his eyelids like it knew he needed it to wash himself clean.

Breathing deep was easier with the comforting taste of tobacco and hashish billowing down into his lungs. Ishmael took his hand, turning it over to look at the wound, at the cracks in the scabs that were still oozing. Just a little now. Ishmael took the kerchief from Tashué, dabbing the blood away.

"Looks survivable, Captain," Ishmael said. "I think you'll recover."

Tashué exhaled the first lungful of smoke and took in another. He could feel his heartbeat slowing down, his own pulse still loud in his ears but at least it was a little slower now. At least he could breathe without smelling death.

He took the cigarillo from his mouth and handed it back to Ishmael. Ishmael smoked a bit more, then licked his fingers and crushed out the ember, the red hot tobacco sizzling between his fingers and dying. He tucked it away into his breast pocket again, but his hand wandered up to his throat, opening more buttons of his shirt like he still couldn't quite breathe.

"You alright?" Tashué asked.

Ishmael ran both his hands up over his face, fingers pushing into his hair. "Excellent. I'm excellent. Happy to be home and all that."

Tashué turned, leaning against the boxes. He took a deep breath, the smell of the hashish lingering around them, the smell of dust, the smell of wood. He closed his eyes and kept breathing. Ishmael leaned against him, their shoulders pressing together. Tashué knew what came next, even before it happened, because it always went this way.

Ishmael pressed against him, that long body of his fitting so well against Tashué's chest. Hands on Tashué's neck, in his hair. Tashué leaned into it, into the kiss. Ishmael's mouth tasted of brandy and tobacco and hashish, the flavour of all of their encounters, the flavour of their desperation and the bone-deep ache that lived in both of them. Ishmael had shaved just before the event, and his skin still smelled of shave oil, the expensive kind that had some sort of fragrance in it, something spicy and almost sweet at once.

And even though the familiarity of it was comforting, stripping away the tension and the anger, Tashué reached out and put his hands on Ishmael's shoulders and gently pushed him away.

"I thought we agreed we weren't doing *this* anymore, either."

Ishmael sighed. "That's what you said last time. Didn't stop us though, did it? What's different this time?"

"Everything."

"Everything." Ishmael ran his hands over his face again, pressing his shoulder against the boxes. "Shit."

Tashué closed his eyes for a while and just let himself feel his heart beat.

"Is it Illea, then?" Ishmael asked. "You're holding out for her?"

Tashué dragged his eyes open. "Is that why you looked so angry at the banquet?" He grinned. "Are you jealous?"

Ishmael rolled his eyes. "Fuck you, I don't get jealous, I just get someone else." He took a step back, and then another, until he reached the stack of boxes that was only half as tall as the others. Ishmael sprang up easily, sitting on the edge and looking down at Tashué from his perch. His hands were shuffling through his pockets again, looking for something for him to eat, no doubt. "I don't trust her."

"Then you'll be happy to know I don't intend to sleep with her anymore." Tashué stretched out his hands, looking down at his knuckles, at his fingers. His hands looked terrible and it was strange to have wounds only there. He couldn't hide them, couldn't get away from them. Couldn't bandage them and forget them. Everyone saw them and he kept opening the scabs. "I'm tired of shit like that."

"It's too late."

Tashué looked up at Ishmael, trying to figure out if Ishmael had said something else and he'd missed it. "Too late for what?"

Ishmael shrugged, shook his head. "I'm sorry I dragged you into all this, is all. It seemed like a good idea, you for Mayor. I think you could do it, for what it's worth. You'd be good at it, and Wolfe could keep building good things through you. But sometimes I forget how stupid people are. How people who didn't fight think it's all such a glorious game. How people want their heroes to shine with some blessed glow, like they've been touched by their precious North Star." He sighed, lifting his legs and pulling off his shoes, tossing them over his shoulder so that they clattered on the box behind him. Peeled off his socks, too. "You coming up or what?"

Tashué pulled himself up onto the box, wincing at the pressure in the sore parts of his hands. He unbuttoned the front of his jacket, pushing it open. He was tempted to take it off, go down to the green waistcoat and the lighter green shirtsleeves. The jacket was so heavy now, with the rose gold medal and the brass badge. Ishmael pulled the cigarillo out again, putting it in his mouth and working it back and forth a few times like he was about to start chewing on it. He mustn't have had anything left in his pockets to eat.

"How's your whisperer, then?" Ishmael asked. He found Tashué's box of matches in his own pocket, shaking it to listen to the matches rattle inside. "The one that's got you all wound up."

Tashué shook his head, rubbing his eyes with the heels of his palms. "She's not 'my' whisperer."

Ishmael paused long enough to strike a match and relight the cigarillo, sending up a cloud of smoke between them. He lay back, stretching out on the box, his legs hanging off the edge. "Why not?"

"Because she's a fucking human being, not a possession for me to put in my pocket and walk around with."

Ishmael huffed at him. More smoke, drifting between them. "I know that, Captain. And you fucking well know that's not what I meant. That's never what I mean."

"Fine, then she doesn't want to be 'mine'."

"Hang on, no, we're coming back to this, because fuck you," Ishmael snapped, the anger rising again. He sat up, twisting to face Tashué, cigarillo clamped between his fingers. "You're all self-righteous these days, burning with the fires of some kind of fucking higher understanding, good for you! But you keep pointing your self-righteousness at me like you still think I'm garbage after all these years."

"When did I ever say you were garbage?" Tashué scoffed.

"When you lectured me about that whisperer not being yours because she's not a possession. I know that, damnit, and it makes me really fucking angry that you think I don't. And when you got all righteous about the Army calling Jitabvi hotbloods 'savages'. I know how shit that sounds! I know! I've lived this shit all my fucking life, Tashué. My earliest memory is of walking with my father in the Bay and someone calling us horse fuckers because he thought we were Jitabvi. And my father pretended he didn't speak the language well enough to understand and asked the man to explain what 'horse fucker' meant. But you, you got to hide, didn't you? Born in fucking Brickheart, and you got to blend in because it's only your eyes that sets you apart, and I'll bet most people don't notice what colour they are until they get up real close, but by then you've had a chance to make a good impression and maybe that person will decide it doesn't matter."

"I didn't choose to hide!" Tashué snapped. "I didn't fucking choose that, Ishmael. That choice was made for me and I never even got a chance to wonder what it meant, not until I was old and grown and fucking *alone* and there was no one left for me to ask questions."

"You think I chose to stand out? You think as a child I wanted to be the frontier of the Qasani presence in fucking Cattle Bone Bay?"

Tashué threw up his hands. "Of course not! So if neither of us made these choices for ourselves, why are we fighting about it?"

"Because I've only been gone a year and suddenly 'everything' has changed," Ishmael said. Another lungful of smoke, a scowl as he exhaled. "And now you're talking to me like you think you've gotten better than me somewhere along the way."

"No, I never said I was better than you. Never once." Tashué reached out to him, taking the cigarillo from between his fingers and taking a long drag before handing it back. "If that's what you think I said, you're not listening. I just said I'm tired."

Ishmael sighed, leaning back and resting his weight on one

hand. "Everyone's tired, Captain. Everyone is just bones and exhaustion in this city." He took a long drag of the cigarillo, filling his lungs so completely that he seemed like he could burst. He closed his eyes and he exhaled. "What makes you think your whisperer doesn't want you?"

Tashué sighed, shaking his head. He leaned forward and rested his face in his hands. His weight was hanging too precariously off the edge of the boxes, with his elbows on his knees like that, his legs dangling. He opened his eyes and looked down at the floor, so far away, but it couldn't really be that far because he'd climbed up here with so little effort.

"I don't want to argue about this with you. Kaz *loves* to argue about this with me."

"I'm not arguing, I'm just asking," Ishmael muttered. "Her body language suggested otherwise, when she was stitching up your hands. So I'm just wondering if something happened."

Tashué shook his head, searching for the right words, but they were drifting too slowly through his head. He didn't want to think about kissing Stella. Didn't want to think about her 'body language' or how good she felt in his arms. Was there anything safe to think about anymore? Anything at all that didn't lead him spiralling down into vicious cycles of anger and pain?

He sat up, slowly, leaned back, slowly, except he couldn't put his weight on his hands because they hurt. Even if they only hurt distantly, with the smoke swirling through his body. He leaned back on his elbow instead, taking the cigarillo from Ishmael's mouth. He really shouldn't smoke anymore. But he did, the pull of the tobacco and the familiar motion making him put the cigarillo between his lips and take another long drag. He blew it out through his nose. At least it wasn't opium.

"Your father made some asshole explain what 'horse fucker' meant?" Tashué asked.

Ishmael laughed, snatching the cigarillo back. "Yes. He was something. He always seemed to know how to suck the moment away from people, without actually giving them what they wanted."

A door opened, squeaking on its stiff hinges. Stomping feet, clattering into the warehouse.

"Honestly, Langston, I don't know why it's so hard for you to be civil." Mallory Imburleigh, of course.

"Oh for fuck's sake," Ishmael muttered, laying back on the box and running his hand over his face.

"I don't hear you telling Illea Winter to be civil!"

"Of course not!" Mallory snapped. "She's not my responsibility! Her behaviour doesn't reflect on our name and our company!"

"And I'm your responsibility, am I?"

"I would like you to be your own damned responsibility, but that's clearly too much to hope for!"

Tashué sighed, leaning forward again, rubbing his eyes with the heels of his palms. He wondered if his impression on Mallory Imburleigh was doomed. Did she hate Ishmael, as her barbed comments seemed to imply? Was it because Ishmael was from the Bay, like Tashué thought at first, or was it simply the way he acted? She didn't sound too impressed with Langston's behaviour, either. The pair of them were still arguing, still stomping, getting closer, louder. Coming right for the stack of boxes and the smell of hashish.

"Oh, for heaven's sake, Mr. Saeati," Mallory Imburleigh sighed. "Honestly."

"Honestly, General Imburleigh," Ishmael said. Another lungful of smoke, another big cloud out. "*Honestly*."

Langston laughed. "Are you going to lecture him on being civil, too?"

"I'm not sure it's possible for him to be civil," Mallory muttered.

"I didn't realize you were friends with Mr. Saeati, Captain," Langston said. "I'm surprised. Usually my sister doesn't like Mr. Saeati's friends."

Tashué tried to sit up a little straighter, looking down at Ishmael. Ishmael grinned even though the Imburleighs couldn't see him. He looked up at Tashué and gave him another wink. As if it was all his doing, this entrance into high society. Mallory Imburleigh liking him. But what had he said? *I'm sorry I dragged you into all this.*

"I'm surprised to hear General Imburleigh likes me, if I'm honest," Tashué said. He looked down at his hands again, at the black twine stitches that hugged the gashes. His fingers acted without him, pinching the stitches on his left hand and tugging. Twine pulled on his skin, pulled on something in the centre of him, in his chest, maybe or deeper than that—in his soul. He patted his pockets, finding his cigarillo case to light a cigarillo without any hashish in it, to help him stop smoking Ishmael's cigarillo. The Imburleighs were watching him, as if they were waiting for him to follow up on that statement. He blew the first breath of tobacco smoke out his nose, shaking the match to kill the flame. "I thought I'd made a bad impression."

"How could she not like the Hero of the Black Ridge?" Langston said. "One of these days, I hope you'll tell me about it. Was it as bad as they say?"

"The Ridge was shit and I don't tell it like a fucking campfire story," Tashué said and maybe his voice rumbled a little too low because Langston winced. "With all due respect. Mr. Imburleigh."

"I told you, Langston," Mallory said.

"Ah—forgive me, Captain Blackwood. My enthusiasm outpaced me."

"Well," Ishmael said, sitting up and sliding off the boxes, "I think it's time for us to go. General Imburleigh, if you'd be so kind, would you tell General Wolfe that Captain Blackwood and I left. Tell him I was quite inebriated and Captain Blackwood did the natural thing for decorated war heroes to do and made sure I made it home safely."

Mallory shook her head. "I'm not lying for you, Mr. Saeati."

"For heaven's sake, Mallory, pull the stick out of your ass, would you?" Langston huffed. "Let the poor sods go. Myron's so blind drunk that Captain Blackwood couldn't help him anyway."

Mallory sighed. She looked between Ishmael and Tashué, meeting Tashué's eye for a long moment. Or was it just for a heart-beat, Tashué's heart beating so slow now that he couldn't tell how long a *moment* even was? He wanted to say something nice, that he appreciated how honest she was, that he understood the desire for it, how he wasn't hiding back here from *her*. She seemed like the sort of General Tashué always imagined she would be, since hearing she'd taken the Imburleigh Company—upright and honest, honourable, and intelligent. But he didn't say anything. His mouth was dry and his mind was foggy and Ishmael was still smoking, sweet North Star, that man could take in so much, so much alcohol, so much smoke, trying to keep up with him had knocked Tashué flat more than once. What was it about him? He was smaller, lighter. Maybe his body processed it all faster. Maybe all that energy he had burned through things like food and brandy and hashish faster than everyone else and that's why he was always eating or drinking or smoking *something* when he was home.

"Yes, you're right," Mallory finally sighed. "It was a pleasure to see you again, Captain Blackwood."

"There we go, Captain," Ishmael said, nudging Tashué with an elbow. "Take me home. I'm so very inebriated and all that."

"Oh yes, look at you, you can barely walk, you poor thing," Tashué said, putting an arm around Ishmael's shoulders. "Such a spoilt brat you are. Are you putting on your shoes, then?"

"Fuck shoes," Ishmael muttered, leaning against Tashué. "Shoes are overrated."

"It's cold outside. Almost winter."

"Hmm. That's true, isn't it? Alright, shoes aren't so overrated."

Tashué dragged the shoes off the boxes and dropped them onto the floor in front of Ishmael, pushing them so they faced the right direction. Ishmael pushed his feet into his shoes without his socks. He took one last drag from the dwindling cigarillo, dropping it to the floor and crushing it beneath his heel. His hands searched his pockets.

"Shit," he muttered. "I'm all out of snacks. It's a fucking tragedy. I'm not going to make it all the way to Highfield without something to eat."

"Dig deep, soldier," Tashué said, stepping away from the boxes. "Find the will to go on."

Ishmael led him out the other door, through different hallways, and for a while Tashué wondered if Ishmael had smoked so much that he didn't know where he was going. But maybe Tashué didn't care. Maybe walking through hallways with Ishmael was all he wanted. All the things that were pulling him apart—Jason and Stella and Keoh and the girl from the river and Moore and the Market and his new brass badge and everything, fucking *everything*—were so distant now. Hashish and Ishmael and whisky. Everything about Ishmael was so easy except it also hurt. Hurt because they were so much alike. Hurt because you couldn't hide from the things that were pulling you apart forever, they just kept on pulling even when you weren't thinking about them and when you turned your mind to them again after you were done hiding, they had done more damage when you weren't paying attention. And that's why he didn't do it anymore, because it got harder and harder to get himself together again, harder and harder to brace himself for the way things would hit him when he was done hiding.

32

TASHUÉ

DAY 18

Commander Khosran's office didn't belong to Khosran anymore. The little man was in there when Tashué arrived in the station house, packing up his various belongings. The desk he kept was a maze of drawers and shelves, all needing to be emptied. Rainer was in there with him, sitting in the large plush chair that Khosran kept tucked against the desk. He was smoking, his fat cigar sending up a coil of blue smoke. He looked bleary-eyed and tired, but pleased. Winter's campaign was going well, in spite of the gossip Tashué and Illea had started. The police force was coming and he would have the entire city in the palm of his hand. Looking at him, and his self-satisfied smirk, Tashué understood everything General Wolfe was afraid of.

"Mr. Blackwood, please, come in," Khosran said, looking up from his desk as he clambered around Rainer to get to another drawer. "Don't just stand there in the doorway. It's your office now!"

Tashué took another step in, looking around. It was too small of a space for him to ever feel comfortable in it, especially with Khosran and Rainer in the room with him. He wondered how long it would stay a place where he sat and disagreed with Khosran, or if the room would ever feel like *his*.

Rainer's eyes brightened when Tashué stepped in and he rolled the chair back, rising and stretching over the desk to shake Tashué's hand. He clamped his cigar between his teeth, reached into his breast pocket and pulled out an envelope, sealed with stamped wax. "Good morning, Commander! As promised, I've arranged your access to see Miss Gian Ly. Take this to the desk where you applied to visit, and they'll see you through without any more problems."

"Thank you, sir," Tashué said, and this time the enthusiasm was genuine. He took the envelope in both hands, running a hand across the wax seal. He wondered if he could open the letter without breaking the seal. Surely someone out there knew how to remove the wax from the paper, how to forge Rainer's signature contained within. What else could he gain access to if he wanted to? "Thank you very much, Mr. Elsworth."

Rainer gave a beaming smile, nodding to himself and taking a few puffs of rich blue smoke. "What does the first day for my newest and most favourite Station Commander look like? I suppose you're still managing cases."

"I need to process a brightman," Tashué said, the heady joy of the moment draining out of him so fast he almost felt dizzy. He'd forgotten about Glaen, in the midst of everything, but it was past time to process him. Tashué had felt guilty, the night before, for going home when Ishmael still had that prowl in him, that need to move and get his energy out. But Tashué's new brass badge was heavy and the realization that he was taking this station house pulled all the urge to roam out of him. He was glad of it, now, of the decent night's sleep he'd had. It was going to be a longer day than he'd thought.

"Excellent!" Rainer said, and the man's beaming smile made Tashué's skin crawl. "Give me the morning to organize a photographer, would you? This will be excellent press for the whole program, especially considering the Market fire. We take our jobs very seriously, and all that. I'll organize other Officers to attend the processing with you. Does this one have the Wrath too?"

"No, not the Wrath. He's non-compliant for fraternization." *Non-compliant* made him wince.

"And the other tainted? One of yours?"

Tashué winced at the word 'tainted,' too. "No, sir. Her name is Gianna Tarbrook, registered over at House 6. A healer, I understand."

"You'll process them both this afternoon?"

"It's not our jurisdiction to process Tarbrook," Tashué said, the hollow feeling in his gut growing into a yawning chasm. "Standard procedure is to notify her Regulation Officer and process Forsooth ourselves."

"You don't need to explain standard procedure to the Chief Administrator of the Authority, Mr. Blackwood," Khosran said with a screechy laugh that grated on Tashué's nerves like nails down his spine. "I suspect the man wrote the standard procedure."

Rainer chuckled. "One of my predecessors wrote it, not me. But as the Chief Administrator, I can authorize deviance from those procedures. The timing is most excellent."

"Do I have a say in all this?"

"No, I'm afraid you don't," Rainer said, but the jovial tone had disappeared. "You are, after all, my employee, and should you wish to remain as such, you will cooperate. I thought we understood each other. I need to be able to trust you, Mr. Blackwood."

Tashué took a deep breath. Khosran froze. And Rainer sank back into the chair, putting the cigar back in his mouth and taking a few long puffs. He was nodding to himself, some conversation still passing through his mind, but he watched Tashué as if he was waiting for some sign of obedience.

"Is there a problem, Mr. Blackwood?" Rainer asked, cocking his head. "Some issue in the way that I have missed?"

Tashué let out the breath slowly, trying to release the tension. He couldn't even begin to explain the very many *issues* that stood in his way. Glaen Forsooth didn't deserve to go to the Rift because he was in love. Moore didn't deserve to die for using his Talent the way he was told and going mad because of it. The Authority asked too damned much.

But Jason...

"No sir," he said finally. "No problem at all."

"Excellent! I look forward to reading about this matter in the newsprints."

Jason looked worse. The worst Tashué had seen him in a long time. His face was a mottle of bruises, his steps slow and hesitant, like someone with a deep ache haunting his every movement.

Tashué slid him another handful of figs. "I didn't have time to get anything more than that. I'm sorry."

Jason shrugged, then winced. He reached out, sliding the figs closer and standing them all up in a row. "Thanks."

"What happened this time? Fall down another flight of stairs?"

Jason's eyes widened and he grinned. "You aren't going to believe this. They offered me a way out of here, can you believe it? They told me they want me in the Breeding Program." He snorted and started laughing, the sound so maniacal and wild that it made the skin on the back of Tashué's neck go tight. "They want me in the fucking Breeding Program! Isn't that hilarious? I told them none of the sexual things I like to do make babies, or even involve women, but they didn't think that was funny. Do you think they'd let me bring Lorne in there with me? He could be like my concubine, for after I do my duty for the Dominion. I can make sure he promises not to touch any of the breeding women. Can't have him making untainted babies, can we? You think he'll agree to it?"

Some bit of hope flared in Tashué's chest, but it died away as fast as it came to life. Jason could be out of here—but then they would put him behind higher walls, in that place that he could only get to with Rainer's signature on heavy parchment. How long would Rainer's good will last? Until Winter was elected? Would he continue to have access to Keoh and Jason once Rainer forgot about him?

What if he was Mayor of Yaelsmuir? Would he have access to them then?

But, most importantly, would Jason be safer in that place?

"I bet they don't throw their breeders down flights of stairs," Tashué said softly. "Or let the guards beat them. Did they break anything this time? Some ribs, maybe?"

Jason grimaced, shaking his head, but Tashué knew it wasn't a denial. "I told you, I'm not registering. I told them to fuck off right back to their fucking Breeding Program. I'm not doing it. I'm not playing their disgusting game." He looked down at the figs, all lined up in front of him. His bluster began to slip, his face relaxing and making him look younger.

Tashué pulled the letter out of his pocket, turning it around so Jason could see the thick wax seal. Jason shrugged at him.

"What's that?" Jason asked, crossing his arms over his chest. "Your invitation to the next banquet?"

"No, it's signed permission to see your mother. This gets me around the bureaucracy and the paperwork and I go today. I'm going right now, that's why I didn't have time to get you anything better. I wanted you to know that I haven't forgotten. What do you want me to say to her, when I go? I can't tell her that you're doing well, obviously, but I could tell her that you're coming to see her. That you're getting out of the Rift, finally, and you'll come live with her. I know you want that so badly, to see her yourself after all these years, and put all your fears to rest. How long has it been since you saw her, Jason?"

"I don't know," Jason said softly, his eyes misting with tears. He folded in on himself, slumping down low. He wouldn't look at Tashué anymore, instead staring at the figs and blinking back tears. "How old was I when they arrested her? How old was I when the Authority tracked us to the Cya delta and dragged us out of our home? We lived in a real house outside Roa, in one of the rice paddies. She was happy there. She said no one there cared she wasn't proper Sittam and they treated her just like everyone else. She said it was because they knew what it was like to be born in a different country than your parents came from. It wasn't Sittam, but it was theirs and they knew how to survive and evolve and they didn't resent her for doing the same, the way her own parents resented her for it."

"Jason, do you really believe all that?" Tashué breathed. "That her own parents resented her—for what? You remember them, don't you? They were always so good to us. They loved you just for being alive. Can you really imagine them *resenting* her for being born here—when they're the ones that came here to give her a better life? Where did you get this idea?"

"She writes about it sometimes, in the letters she sends me. About how those were the happiest days of her life."

Tashué shook his head, fighting against the old anger. How easily those old fires could be rekindled. "Nice that she is able to rewrite history so efficiently."

Jason looked up at him again, blinking through the tears. "What do you mean?"

"The Authority didn't 'track her down'. They went to process her because she was using her Talent for money to spend on opium. Telling fortunes and making charms was one thing, but charms and fortunes didn't get her enough money to feed her habit. She started hurting people. She would pretend to lay curses on people, and she would stalk them and use her Talent to hurt them until they paid her to stop. She broke one man's arm. Crushed it with her will until it was nothing but dust. It wasn't until a meat monger amputated it that anyone knew what was happening, because people were too afraid of her to say anything. The meat monger told the Authority what he'd found. They were going to execute her, did she tell you that? They wanted to hang her for her crimes, but they found the missive that was sent out by House One saying that they wanted her alive."

"You're lying," Jason gasped.

"I'm not. Why would I?"

"Because you hate her. You can't stand the fact that I love her and you're fucking lying about her to make me stop loving her."

"Jason…" Tashué rested the letter on the table in front of him, reaching up to rub his eyes with the heels of his palms. "I don't hate her. I don't like the person she became when she was smoking that fucking opium. She wasn't herself. She wasn't the woman I knew when we were young." He lay his hands flat on the table, looking down at his wounds and scars. It had been so long since he lived so firmly in the past, but everyone seemed to be dragging him backward these days. He tried to reach back, past the day he'd come home with his discharge papers in hand, only to find his home empty, past the day he came home half-dead because the lash wounds were infected, past all the fighting and the opium smoke. To the first day. For Jason. "I was younger than you are now when I met her, did you know that? I think I was fifteen. I was in a military parade in Zuri. They sent me out with a recruitment team to sign new kids for service."

"I thought she was born here, in Yaelsmuir."

Tashué nodded, leaning back in his chair and folding his arms over his chest. The warmth of the memory was sullied by all that came after and he hadn't thought about it much. But the trajectory of his life had changed so much in that day. "She was. She was there with her parents. I don't remember why. She found me with the recruitment team and she kissed me. I ditched the recruitment team the first chance I got to sneak away with her. I got flogged for that, five lashes for 'dereliction of duty during a peacetime action'. I figured it was worth it, though. She was so…" He sighed. Shrugged. "I'd never met anyone like her. I was sent to White Crown after that, to the Officer's Academy. I didn't think I'd ever see her again, but I did. I saw her in Yaelsmuir, right after I graduated. I was waiting for my first posting. The rest…" He shrugged again. "I don't hate her, Jason. I hate all the destruction that opium brought to our lives, but I don't hate her."

Jason finally dragged his eyes up, looking at Tashué through the grate. His brow was split, Tashué realized, the wound almost hidden by the contour of his eyebrow, black hair almost camouflaging the long gash. If his face looked that bad, Tashué could only imagine what his body looked like.

"Do you regret it?" Jason asked. "Knowing her?"

"How could I?" Tashué asked. "Knowing her got me you. I've never regretted you a day in my life."

Jason bowed his head, covering his face with both his hands. His shoulders heaved. The tears that leaked between his fingers made

Tashué ache. He wished he could reach out and take his son in his arms, but wishing was a wasted effort. Wishing hadn't gotten Jason out yet.

Jason took in a few deep breaths, his whole chest spasming and sending a fresh grimace of pain across his face. "What if—what if there was another way? Another way out?"

"What do you mean?"

"If there was a way for me to get out of here, without registering. Would you still love me if I did something like that?"

Tashué shifted forward, perching on the edge of his chair. He pulled at the grate, wishing he could get it higher so he could get his hand through, but of course he had the stiff one again. "Jason, I'll love you no matter what, but whatever you're thinking, please don't. Just don't do it."

"You were right though." Jason's voice trembled and his face twisted with pain. He pressed his hands into his rib like it might help ease the pain. "I'll die in here. I need to get out before they kill me."

Tashué pressed his hand on the mesh instead of trying to get under it. He wished Jason would reach out and press on the other side. Their skin would press together through the open gaps and Tashué would be able to feel the warmth of his son for the first time in years. Three years, how could it have been three years already? Somehow all the days and weeks and months blurred together into a mess of emotions and stone and headaches and that damned wire mesh.

"Give me more time, please?" Pressure built in Tashué's muscles and he desperately wanted to do *something*, anything, but there was nothing. He thought maybe he could tear the whole mesh right off the wall if he was really determined, and they could walk out of here. But how far would they get before guards gunned them down? "Give me just a little more time. Look at this." He pulled up the mesh and slid the letter through the gap, pushing it forward until it touched the figs standing in their little sentry line. "Open it."

Jason snuffled as he picked up the letter and ran trembling fingers across the seal. The letter slid out easily from the side of the envelope, where Tashué had torn it open. Jason spread it flat in front of him, reading Rainer's brief note inside. Tashué already knew what it said. *Tashué Blackwood, House Commander of NTRA Station House No. 15, badge number 15-44072, is hereby granted visitation access to registered breeder Keoh Gian Ly.* Rainer's signature at the bottom was an elaborate swirl of pure black ink, and a second wax seal sitting beside it.

Jason looked back up at Tashué, turning the paper around so Tashué could see. "So, what, you're friends with the Chief Administrator now? Fantastic. How the fuck does that help me?"

"Maybe I can get you out of here. Elsworth wants me to do his little fucking song and dance, fine. I'll do it. I'll dance for him. But maybe, if he was willing to give me *that*," he gestured to the letter, "maybe I can get you out of here. Maybe we can come to some kind of agreement, since he wants his police force so damned much."

"How many favours do you really think he'll be willing to grant you?" Jason asked, folding the letter carefully and replacing it in the envelope again. "You act like you're doing him some big favour, but you aren't, are you? If you don't play his game, someone else will. That's the thing about the Authority. If we don't march in line, they throw us aside and find someone else to fill the gaps. It doesn't mean a damned thing to them when we don't do what they want. We're all disposable."

33

TASHUÉ

DAY 18

Tashué had almost forgotten what opium smelled like. Sweet and ashy, pungent and filled with so many emotions. Surely he must have encountered it as he made his way through the city—especially Cattle Bone Bay. The import and export of opium was one of Powell Iwan's most lucrative businesses. It came in for medical purposes, to be refined into morphine, but the importers paid Powell in pure opium rather than money, accepting the loss of stock in exchange for Iwan's good will. But then Tashué didn't much care about opium smokers in the Bay.

The years hadn't been kind to Keoh. Her skin was papery-thin, her eyes ringed with bags so deep they almost looked like bruises. Her thick black hair had gone thin and brittle, more grey than black now. Her wrists were even skinnier than he remembered, like she was nothing but crepe-paper over bone. He never remembered her being so insubstantial. Was that the opium that stripped the life out of her eyes, or was it this damned place? The woman he'd met in Cattle Bone Bay had more frantic energy, and she blamed the Breeding Program for her madness. He recognized the sleepy shuffle that carried Keoh into the room. Maybe the madness would take her later when the opium wore off.

She stood in the doorway for a long time, staring at Tashué. She blinked slowly at him. Did she think he was a fever dream, come to haunt her? Shit—had that happened to her before?

"You look terrible," she said. "I haven't seen you with so many stitches since you came back from the Black Ridge. What happened to you?"

Tashué took a drag from his cigarillo while he tried to think of what to say. Arguing that this was nowhere near as bad as when he got home from the Ridge seemed like a pointless exercise in dragging up old pain. He was so fucking tired of talking about the Ridge. Pointing out that she looked like a mess didn't seem conducive to a conversation, either. "I was digging people out of the rubble at the Market fire."

"Of course you were. You love being the hero, don't you?"

Tashué stifled a curse, shaking his head. "Keoh, I didn't come here to fight with you."

"Why did you come, then?"

"Your son sent me. He wanted me to check on you."

The bluster fell out of her and she hugged her body, tucking her hands under her arms. "How is he? My boy? I miss him so much."

Another curse bubbled in Tashué's chest, trying to escape. He tried to smother his roiling emotions with another cloud of smoke, but it wasn't helping. He'd honestly fooled himself into thinking he'd forgiven her after all these years, but sitting here in this room he knew that it wasn't possible. Some wounds were too deep, some scars so brittle they split and started bleeding again.

"He's not well." Tashué sighed, shaking his head. "He's been in the Rift for a few years now and I don't know how much longer he's going to last. Something happened, last week maybe, and he's the worst he's looked since the beatings he took when they first sent him there. Whatever happened, though... They want him here, in the Breeding Program. He doesn't want to come, but I was hoping maybe you would encourage him. He'll die if he stays there any longer."

Her eyes went distant as he spoke, staring at the wall over his shoulder instead of looking at him. Tears welled in her eyes and then rolled down her cheeks. Tashué took the last pull from his cigarillo, crushing it out on the stone windowsill behind him. He watched the tears, waiting for some answer. The years hadn't dulled the ache he felt at watching her cry. Whatever went so wrong between them, he'd never meant to cause her so much pain.

"Let's go for a walk," she said swiftly, wiping her eyes and then folding her hands back under her arms. She looked around the room with wild eyes, then down the hall. "This way. Don't look at me like that, you ass. Just come."

Tashué sighed and pushed himself to his feet, following Keoh out of the room. Once visitors made their way through the massive gates of the Breeding Program, they were given somewhat more freedom than those in the Rift. Keoh led him out, between the cluster of buildings where the breeding men and women seemed to be housed. The whole place felt almost homely, if it weren't for the massive stone walls and the staring, dead eyes of the women shuffling through the hallways. There were few men, or perhaps the building was a woman's dormitory. The guard who marched Tashué into a visiting room hadn't been particularly interested in answering questions.

"I heard you got a fancy medal for what you did at the Market Quarter. Made me right pissed, that. Do you ever get tired of being the centre of attention?"

Tashué sighed. "I wasn't trying to be the centre of attention, Keoh. I was just doing what I thought was right."

"Oh? Were you doing what you thought was right when you fucked Illea Winter, too?"

Tashué stopped walking, turning to Keoh. But she wasn't angry, as her words had suggested. She was staring up at him with wide eyes that were gleaming with fresh tears. Was it the opium, making her emotions so changeable? She'd always been mercurial, but this seemed worse than he remembered. Or maybe she was fighting against the weight of memory, too.

He took a deep breath, fighting back the anger, the confrontation that was building across his shoulders and down his back. *You aren't here to fight. You have questions. And you need to do something to help Jason.*

"It's a little cold for a walk in the garden, isn't it?" he said instead and he knew how petulant he sounded, but it was better than starting a fight.

She nodded down the path, ducking her head against the wind. "There's a spot to sit, over there in the rose bushes. Blocks the wind, at least."

Tashué nodded and let Keoh shuffle on. She walked stiffly, hunched forward and still hugging herself. Their feet crunched on dry, fallen leaves and rose petals, the blooms all fallen away and replaced with swollen, vibrant-coloured rose hips, though they too had shrivelled away. The oldest of them had rotted on the stem. They found a small gazebo, the roses trained up a sturdy trellis. She was right—the thick tangle of the rose bush shielded them from the wind, but also from the weak sun. It was cooler in there than outside, and Keoh hugged her ragged green shawl closer to her body, fighting against shivers. Before he could think much about it, Tashué found himself shrugging out of his heavy wool coat, offering it to her. She hesitated only a moment before pushing her arms in, gathering the collar up about her face and sinking onto a bench. He sat beside her, finding his cigarillo case again and offering her one. They were quiet through the routine of lighting and taking the first puffs, the rose bush trapping the cigarillo smoke for a moment before the wind took it away.

"Jason says you're pregnant again," Tashué said, breaking through the silence.

Keoh scowled. "Not anymore. I lost it, again. That's it for me. They won't waste anymore time on me, not after losing four in a row." She shook her head, balancing the cigarillo between her lips so that she could hide both hands inside the jacket. She tilted her head back, watching the curl of smoke on the way up. "They're going to kill me rather than house me any longer."

"Kill you? Keoh, why would they kill you? You have immense Talent. They'll find a job for you, in the Industrial Quarter somewhere."

She laughed, but it was an awkward thing with the cigarillo clamped between her teeth. She took the cigarillo between her fingers to turn and stare at him. "How have you managed to stay so fucking naive? They won't 'find a job' for me. They won't ever trust me. Don't let Jason come here. It's just as bad as the Rift. Worse. He won't survive this place. They won't like how wild he is, and they'll wear him down until he is nothing but a ghost. When they're done with him, they'll kill him, too."

"They're killing him in the Rift," Tashué muttered, flicking his ashes onto the hard-packed dirt floor.

"So, get him out of the fucking Rift."

"It's not that easy. I'm trying to figure something out. But it will take time, and I don't know if he has it." Tashué reached up, rubbing the back of his neck, where the headache clamped on the base of his skull. The fucking suppression—did anyone ever get used to it? "If he comes here, maybe they can train him for the directed work program. The men here do that, don't they? They work with the stonesmiths and such, working outside the Authority."

Keoh shook her head as she took another drag from the cigarillo, the puff of smoke drifting up around her head like a shroud. "They'll never let him work out. He's been in the Rift too long. They won't ever trust him. Besides, even if he gets transferred here, I won't see him." Her hands plunged under his coat, shifting through her own pockets. "I told you, they're going to kill me."

When her hand came back out of her pocket, Tashué thought his heart would stop. She had the little piece of opium wrapped in a scrap of paper. The thick black lump stuck to the paper as she peeled it away.

"Looks like you're doing your best to kill yourself," Tashué said before he could stop himself. "How are you getting that shit in here if they don't trust you?"

She laughed again, pinching off a piece and putting it in her mouth. She'd keep a little piece tucked in her cheek to suck on, to help her float on a cloud of oblivion until she could lay down to smoke again. "They give it to me. The bastards. They leave it in my room. They know I can't resist it, can I? I think I have opium in my bones instead of marrow. They'll just keep giving it to me until I smoke myself to death and then I won't be their problem anymore."

"Why don't you just stop, then?"

"Fuck you, 'just stop.' It'll kill me if I 'just stop.' You know what it's like, even if you have a little. You used to smoke with me. Remember? Back before Jason. You would come home with your stitches and your bloodstains and we would smoke until you didn't feel the pain anymore." She reached out to him, grabbing his right hand, dragging it into her lap like Stella had when she was setting stitches into his wounds. Keoh's fingers were cold as they slid along the contour of the new wounds, traced his old scar. "Remember when you came home with your shoulder all messed up? Right before you were assigned to your precious Jitabvi company. They wouldn't let you report for duty again until it was healed and your mum wanted you to see a healer. But you couldn't do it. You bought the lies that the Dominion told and you didn't trust healers, not even your own mother. Didn't trust *the tainted*. Even though you're tainted too. You could never quite forgive yourself, or me, for being tainted, could you? How about now, Commander Blackwood? Do you still hate yourself for being tainted?"

Tashué shook his head, feeling the old waves of anger trying to drag him down. "You're so good at revising history, aren't you? I didn't want my mother to see my memories. I'd lost count of how many battles I'd been in already. Of how many people I'd killed. You always liked those stories, didn't you? We'd chase the poppy dreams together and you'd make me tell you what I'd done. But my mother hated it. I told her about one battle, about how close my whole company came to death, and what we'd done to survive, and it made her cry." He pulled his hand away from Keoh's fingers, tugging again at the stitches. Part of him wanted to rip them right out, to tear at his own skin and make himself bleed again so he could focus on that instead of remembering everything. He'd been running from so many memories for so long, he thought he'd outpaced them, all those painful days. He thought twenty years and more would be enough to leave it all behind. But maybe he hadn't been running at all, maybe he'd only been hiding. And now the memories had found him. "I never hated myself. Or you. I hate that fucking tar that rotted your soul but I don't hate you."

"Liar."

Tashué took a deep breath, looking down at his feet instead of looking at Keoh, instead of letting her drag him into another argument. "Why don't you escape, then? Run away."

Keoh snorted, leaning back against the support beam of the trellis, pulling the collar of Tashué's coat up around her face again and closing her eyes. "No one ever escapes."

"No one?" Tashué asked. He met her sleepy eyes. The woman he'd spoken to—did Keoh know her? "Not a single person?"

"Oh, well there was that one woman. The Lidan girl, a few weeks ago. She slipped out in one of the graduation parades. Dumb horse broke its leg, and the Lidan girl walked right out the gates, people say."

"Tall, with thick brown hair," Tashué said. "And a scar across the bridge of her nose, like maybe she'd broken it once before."

"Mmmhmm. One of the other breeders did that to her. Fighting over boiled sweets. How did you know?"

"I met her."

Keoh dragged her eyes open with some effort, her eyes drifting across Tashué's face and struggling to focus.

"Did she ever tell you what she saw?" Tashué asked. His heart was racing suddenly. If it was true that the woman had escaped this place, could it also be true that she had seen her children? "She told me she used her Talent and watched her children after they graduated from the creche. Did she ever tell you about it?"

"Oh, it's Talent now, is it? Maybe you have changed."

"Keoh. Did she tell you what she saw?"

She shook her head, closing her eyes again. "I didn't know her well. She was on the fourth floor. I'm on the third."

Tashué took a deep breath, shaking his head. "What about you? Have you ever wondered what happened to them? Your children?"

"Of course I wonder. I wonder every day. I gave my son six siblings, and off they went into the Dominion, to spend their days feeding industry. I wish he could meet them. They all looked like him, when they were born. So little. So strong."

"What are their names? The children. The woman I saw, she said the program lets you name them."

She opened her eyes, blinking at him a few times. Her hands went back into her pockets and she pulled out a folded piece of paper. It was worn and wrinkled with age, and as she unfolded it, Tashué saw the dark ink scrawled in her messy hand. There were six names, and between them there were three X's, then four of them in a row at the end of the list. Her miscarriages, then. Seven in all.

"Could you find them?" she asked. "My children? Can you find them for me, and tell me where they are? And if ever you get Jason out of that place, maybe he could know his siblings."

Tashué pulled out his notebook, flipping for a new page. He paused only a moment to look at the girl's face. To remind himself what he was looking for. It was painful, how much she looked like Jason. Like Keoh. But if she was a child from the Breeding Program —in theory the most valuable asset the Authority had—how did she end up dead on the bank of the Brightwash? He flipped past her face, past her tattoo, finding a blank page. He scribbled down the names, one at a time. Lizanne, Petrik, Gwinnith, Benjin, Dex, Valen. Two girls. Four boys.

"How old are they?"

"Valen is still in the creche," Keoh whimpered, her forehead creasing even though her eyes were still closed. "I wish they'd let us see them. I don't understand why we can't see them. They're just right there." She opened her eyes, turning her head and looking to the maze of buildings that sat in the distance, looming and ugly on the well manicured lawn that lay around it. "So close we can touch them. Sometimes at night, when it's quiet, I swear I can hear them. Maybe it's just my imagination. Maybe it's the opium, rattling around my brain. Or the ghosts of the ones I've lost."

"And Lizanne, the oldest?"

Keoh turned to look at him and Tashué knew she was losing the ability to follow the conversation. "Hmm?"

"Lizanne, the oldest of the children you gave to the Authority. How old is she?"

Keoh nodded. "She's just turned eleven. Her birthday was the same day I miscarried. Seemed a funny thing, bringing two babes into the world on the same day. First and last for the Authority. One living and screaming, one dead." She blinked a few times and tears slid down her cheeks, but her eyes were so far away that Tashué wasn't even sure she knew he was still sitting with her. "Don't let my boy die in there. My son, my sweet son. I missed his whole life. I missed every life I made. Get him out of that terrible place."

"I'm trying," Tashué said softly. He stood, looking down at her. He knew what it felt like, that drifting. As much as he'd hated the opium now, he'd smoked with her before. When they were young, and convinced themselves it was harmless. After the Ridge and he came home to learn his mother died, and he thought he was drowning in pain. After Keoh left with Jason, and he would have rather died than live in that little empty apartment. But every time he slipped down into the sweet smoke, he always dragged himself back up. What was the difference, between them, that he could just make himself stop and she never could? But maybe he was lying to himself, thinking that he knew how to stop something that took the pain away. How many times had he smoked hashish with Ishmael? How many gallons of shit whisky had he drank, since his flogging? Even after those wounds healed, he kept on drinking copper whisky, wishing it would extinguish the fire of rage and pain in his soul—but the thing about whisky was there was so much alcohol in it that it didn't extinguish the flames—it fed them. "Keoh."

"Hmmmm?" She dragged open her eyes and they focused on his face a moment.

"Why did you go to Roa?"

"What do you mean?"

"When you took Jason," Tashué pressed. "When you left Yaelsmuir. Why did you go to Roa? You used to get so mad at your parents, when they wanted you to learn Sittami customs. They just wanted you to learn where they came from so that you could under-stand who they were, but you always hated it. So why did you go to

Roa? To the Delta, where everyone was trying to hang on to Sittami culture?"

Eyes drifted open again, shifting up to search his face. He used to love looking into her eyes, so dark and wild. Even when she was thunderously angry with him, when she was throwing things at him and cursing him, he convinced himself that they were just two passionate people who didn't know how else to be. Maybe Ishmael was right. Maybe passionate people didn't belong together, for their own safety.

"Aren't that many tainted in the rice paddies," she said, her eyes drifting closed again. "No use for them, not when oxen can do the job. Not enough money in rice, anyway. So I thought there wouldn't be that many Regulation Officers, either."

Tashué sighed, feeling parts of himself collapse. He wasn't sure exactly why he was disappointed. "You told Jason it was so you could be with people that understood you."

She shrugged. The silence stretched between them and he wondered if she'd finally drifted away, off to sleep the poppy dreams.

"No one understands me," she said finally. "I don't understand myself."

34

TASHUÉ

DAY 18

The trip from the Breeding Program to the Row was cold and miserable, with his coat left behind on Keoh. He stopped at home, where his only other overcoat was from Bellmore. It seemed a waste to wear such an expensive coat for work at the station house, over a suit that had seen far better days, but it was thick and warm and the easy way it fit was comforting.

"I trust you were able to see Miss Gian Ly?" Rainer asked.

"I was," Tashué said. "How is she able to get opium in the Breeding Program? I thought that the men and women of the breeding program are highly valued by the Authority, so it seems a shock that they would have access to such a deadly drug."

Rainer made a face. Tashué watched it carefully, trying to read it. The crease of his brow, the way he bore his teeth. It almost looked like a smile but then he frowned, shaking his head. "Of course it's not our policy to *allow* the men and women of the program to so injure themselves with opium abuse. We do our best to control things like morphine and laudanum for strictly medicinal purposes, but unfortunately there's been some issues with guards smuggling the pure opium into the facility to trade for favours and crowns from the residents. Would that we could all be so upright as you, but humans are rather more vulnerable to corruption than any of us would like to admit."

Tashué took a deep breath, trying to process everything Rainer said, but his mind stuck on that last statement. *Would that we could all be so upright as you.* What was Rainer trying to say, exactly?

Rainer reached out, gripping Tashué's shoulder. "If it helps to ease your mind, I'll see what I can do to help Miss Gian Ly. We can move her to another floor, perhaps, and assign her a personal guard."

Somehow, that didn't sound better.

"What about my son, then?" Tashué asked. "I went to see him this morning, and he's taken a beating recently. How am I supposed to focus on all my new duties if I live every day fearing that my son is going to die in the Rift?"

Rainer's smile faltered. "I thought we understood each other, Mr. Blackwood."

"We do, Mr. Elsworth," Tashué said, filling his chest with a slow, deep breath. "We understand each other very well. You want Myron elected so that you can have your police force, and you're using me to show people how successful the Authority has been. And I am the face of that strength. Fine. But my son, he's going to die in the Rift, and I'm not sure I can be the man you need if that happens."

Rainer's smile was stiff when he met Tashué's eyes, searching, calculating. Tashué thought he could see it, the way Rainer weighed his thoughts, the way he came to his decision slowly. Finally, he gave a little nod. "Of course, Mr. Blackwood. I understand. A father's love is a powerful thing, even when our children make the wrong choices. I'll see what can be done. I hope that puts your mind at ease long enough for you to see your work done today?"

"Yes, sir," Tashué said. "I think it does."

Though it was standard procedure to send two Officers to process non-violent non-compliants, Rainer made some speech about the safety of the city and sent four. He had managed to rope in Kazrani, Beckett and Duskan, sending them off with the photographer and the modified omnibus to transfer the prisoners to the Rift.

The photographer asked them to stand in a line on the front steps at Glaen Forsooth's building. She placed Tashué front and centre, the rest of the Officers splayed around him. He refused to hold one of the long rifles Rainer insisted they bring along. It reminded him of the days when he served; someone was always on hand to photograph the various companies with rifles and bayonets glistening in the sun, standing on any ridge or hill that could fit them all. *For the war effort,* they'd say. Sepia photographs of grim-looking soldiers on foreign hills would recruit more young people who couldn't possibly know better.

Tashué heard the photographer's flashbulb go off again as they filed in the front door, the pop of the bulb following Tashué up the stairs. The boots of four people thumping up the steps of the stuffy tenement building were stiflingly loud, their bodies throwing off so much heat and humidity that Tashué could feel the temperature rising. Sweat beaded at his collar. A child poked her head out into the hall, her eyes as wide and round as an owl's as she tried to peer through the gloom.

"Go back inside," Tashué said, his voice echoing in the hall. "Keep the door shut."

The girl leaped back behind her door and slammed it. They climbed up to the top, stopping at Glaen Forsooth's door. Tashué waited until all his Officers were bunched up on the door with him. He looked at them all one by one, catching each of their gleaming eyes. One by one, they nodded at him. Ready.

Turning, Tashué pounded his fist against the door. He listened for any sound, the scrape of cloth or the thump of boots on the floorboards. There was nothing. He knocked again, the sound echoing through the whole building. The very door frame shivered with the force of it.

"Glaen Forsooth, open your door for the National Tainted Registration Authority." He pounded again. "Open the door, Mr. Forsooth, or I'll break it down."

"Alright!" Glaen's voice was thin and panicked on the other side. "I'm coming. I'm coming!"

He could hear the soft slap of bare feet. The lock thunked in its mechanism and the door swung in. Tashué stepped forward as the door opened, putting his body in the way in case Glaen tried to close it again. When Glaen's gaze fell on the Officers at his door, all the colour drained from him. His eyes went wild, searching for some escape, but of course there was nowhere for him to go. The door was blocked by bodies and guns and grim determination, the window dropping six stories to the hard, unforgiving cobblestone street.

"Let us in, Mr. Forsooth," Tashué said. "We don't want any trouble today."

Forsooth staggered back from the door. The four of them pressed into the apartment, shuffling close together. Forsooth was dressed in his nightclothes, his feet bare, his hair tousled by his pillow.

"Glaen Forsooth, you are flagged non-compliant by the National Tainted Registration Authority." Fuck, Tashué hated it, hated the words and how they felt in his mouth.

"No!" Forsooth gasped, a bit of colour returning to his cheeks, a bit of rage glimmering in his tired eyes.

"You are non-compliant for continuing an unsanctioned fraternization with another registered tainted." How many times during his career had Tashué done this exact thing without flinching at those horrible words? How did he not see sooner how vile they were, how they seemed designed to strip away all humanity from *the tainted*.

"No, damn you!" Forsooth growled.

"You've been issued your final warnings but still refuse to comply." Tashué hadn't flinched at those words in sixteen years of service, not until he heard them being said to Jason, to his son, to his flesh and bone, to the embodiment of his beating heart. "You are hereby transferred to the Residential Institute for Feral Tainted and Non-Compliants indefinitely, or until you are deemed willing to comply."

There were tears in Forsooth's eyes, and Tashué burned with shame.

"Why is it a crime to want to be with people you can relate to?"

"Because you're tainted and you can't breathe without Authority permission!" Duskan snapped, edging forward and thumbing back the hammer of his rifle as if he actually meant to use it.

Forsooth turned on Duskan with wild eyes, all the colour draining from him when he saw the rifle. Tashué stepped forward, pushing the rifle down so it pointed at the floor.

"Dress yourself, Mr. Forsooth," Tashué said.

Forsooth turned away, shuffling past the narrow partition and into his bedchamber. Tashué swung to Duskan, hissing a deep breath through his clenched teeth.

"Uncock your rifle or get out."

Duskan was breathing hard and fast, eyes a little too wild. His hand shook as he rested his thumb on the hammer, shook as he squeezed the trigger. Tashué held his breath, half expecting the shot that would go through the floor when that hammer dropped too hard, but Duskan guided it back to its resting position and Tashué could breathe again.

There was no privacy to be had in the small room, but Forsooth did his best to keep his dignity while he dressed. The fight had gone out of him as they escorted him down the stairs, the hallway just wide enough for two people to walk down side by side. Tashué walked beside Forsooth, holding him by the arm. There wasn't much to the man, little more than the bones that kept him upright.

"Haven't you any manacles for him?" the photographer asked.

"We don't put the manacles on the ones that come peacefully," Kazrani said.

"But do you have any? It makes a better photograph that way. Easier to tell who's who and all."

Tashué clenched a fist, focusing on the tug of the stitches and the healing wounds. "You can tell just fine without."

"Very well," the photographer said, lifting her chin, "if you could all stand as you were before, then, with the tainted in the centre. Mr. Hillbraun, could you point the rifle at the tainted?"

Duskan swung the rifle down in front of Tashué's chest to point the muzzle at the side of Forsooth's face. Tashué's arm snapped forward, grabbing the barrel and pointing it at the ground. He could feel his blood rise, his chest going tight with frustration over the whole ridiculous ordeal.

"We don't point loaded rifles at men unless we intend to shoot them," Tashué snapped. "Get this fucking rifle out of my face, Duskan, or I'll shove it up your ass!"

"Try it!" Duskan snapped back.

Duskan tried to jerk the rifle out of Tashué's grasp, but Tashué held firm. Tashué gave it a hard yank and a twist. Duskan staggered, off balance. His grip on the rifle slipped and Tashué twisted it again, pulling it out of Duskan's hands. Tashué swung the rifle by its barrel, the buttplate catching Duskan just behind the knee. His whole leg buckled and he fell hard, tumbling to the cobblestones below.

"Fuck you, Blackwood!" Duskan barked, scrambling to his feet.

"That's salty language to be throwing at the man holding your rifle," Kazrani laughed.

"Keep the rifle." Duskan spat at Tashué's feet, his face deep red, the veins in his thick neck bulging at his collar.

He stormed away, but didn't go far, climbing up beside the omnibus driver. Tashué took a deep breath, trying to cool his blood. He handed the rifle to Beckett, who quickly came to stand in Duskan's place beside Tashué.

Tashué swung on the photographer. "Will you take the damned photograph *now*?"

The pop of the flashbulb made Tashué's skin crawl. They loaded Forsooth into the back of the omnibus, the windows replaced with wood boards, the bright paint replaced with grey, gold lettering on each side proclaiming it as *National Tainted Registration Authority Prisoner Transfer*. There was another pop of the flashbulb as Tashué helped Forsooth up into the back. He felt like smashing the camera on the steps of the tenement building, turning it into shards and splinters so that it could never be used to dehumanize another person again—but he didn't. He stepped into the omnibus and settled beside Forsooth. Kazrani took the seat closest to the door and Beckett sat on the other side of Glaen. Tashué knocked on the ceiling. The driver flicked the reins, and the horses leaned into their traces.

There was silence in the omnibus, Forsooth staring blankly out the barred window at the back. He seemed almost lifeless as he sat on the bench, jostling and bumping as the big wooden wheels thumped along on the cobblestones. But something changed in him, maybe when he realized that the omnibus wasn't heading to the station house or even the Rift, but east to Drystone.

"Where are we going?" he asked.

"I warned you, didn't I?" Tashué said. "I told you—it's your business if you don't care about your life and where it goes, but there are two of you to think of. She's non-compliant, too."

"No," Forsooth gasped, surging to his feet.

Tashué caught him by the back of the shirt and dragged him back down. Forsooth twisted, his thrashing a wild and animal thing. His flailing limbs struck Tashué in the face, sending a flash of pain through his mouth. And then Glaen twisted around, one foot striking Tashué in the chest, forcing the wind out of him and almost knocking him off the bench. But Tashué threw himself down, crushing Forsooth beneath his bulk before he could wriggle away. Beckett was on his feet, grabbing Forsooth's hands and snapping manacles around his wrists before he could cause any more trouble.

"Let's not try anything else, sir," Kazrani said, swinging the rifle to point at his chest. "This is a tight space and you wouldn't want to get yourself hurt."

"Please," Glaen whimpered. "Please, just leave her out of this. She's a healer!"

"It doesn't work that way and you know it," Tashué grunted, sitting up but holding Forsooth's arms. "I warned you."

Gianna lived in an Authority-run boarding house, which was in a wide four-story row house. Gianna's room was on the second floor, making escape a consideration unlike Forsooth's tiny room. He sent Duskan around to the back, along with Beckett.

"Keep an eye out in case she tries to run," Tashué said. "But don't hurt her if it can be avoided."

Tashué stepped into the boarding house first, where an old woman came to the door with a scowl.

"Excuse me, sir, this is a private boarding house!" she snarled. "There are no men allowed here without prior arrangements!"

"Sorry for the intrusion, ma'am, but we're here on Authority business," Tashué said.

The woman's back straightened at the sight of the badge. Her face went harder, if that was even possible. "Which one is it, then?"

"Miss Tarbrook."

"Aye, she's here, in her rooms. Second floor, to the left. We shan't be disturbing any of the other girls, shall we?"

"Not unless necessary."

"Best not be necessary, then."

Kazrani followed, her rifle at her side and pointed at the floor. Tashué didn't knock at Gianna's closed door, pushing it open instead. The breeze hit him immediately, curling around his body. The window gaped open, the light curtains billowing in the wind.

"Runner!" Tashué bellowed, darting to the window.

Beckett gave a yelp and there was a hard thump as flesh hit the thin, rocky grass in the courtyard, and the furious roar of the rifle discharging. The great boom echoed up between the buildings, leaving an ugly silence in its wake.

Cursing, Tashué leaned out the window, trying to peer through the branches and the dried autumn leaves. He couldn't quite make out anything below the tree, but he saw something blue—cloth maybe? And red. Red and wet. *Oh no. Please no.*

His limbs moved without any decision from him and he was only distantly aware of climbing out the window, onto the nearest branch. His boots scraped across the bark as he clambered down. Gianna lay splayed on her back. Her skin had gone pale already as the halo of blood spread on the ground around her. Her legs were tangled with Beckett's arms; he lay in a heap beneath her, dazed and groaning.

Tashué dropped to his knees beside the tangle of them both, pressing his hands into the wound, trying to stem the bleeding. Her blood was too hot, pumping too fast, sliding between his fingers no matter how hard he pressed. And her Talent swirled around her, weak and fading.

"What the fuck happened?" Tashué roared, swinging to Duskan.

Duskan stood at the mouth of the alley, rifle in his hands, smoke still swirling from the barrel. His face was drained of any colour and his hands were trembling so much that the rifle shook. He breathed fast and shallow like he couldn't quite fill his lungs.

"It was necessary," he said, his voice trembling as badly as his hands. "She attacked us."

The sound of Glaen Forsooth's anguish would haunt Tashué for the rest of his life.

They'd waited near two hours in the courtyard of the boarding house, waiting for a runner to make their way to the nearest Patroller house to request the blackwagon. Forsooth apparently saw the blackwagon roll up through the bars at the back door of the omnibus, watched as they loaded Gianna into the wagon, congealed blood dripping in dark, ugly clots from the canvas wrapping around her body.

The cries the man made were inhuman as both vehicles trotted through the streets. Tashué sat with Gianna's body in the black-wagon. He could still hear Forsooth, the sound like a scythe cutting through him. Forsooth's pain echoed in the core of his being, ringing in his ears even when the blackwagon and the omnibus parted ways.

He left Kazrani in charge of bringing Glaen to the Rift. He went to Gianna's station house—House 6—and filled in the paper-work for her death, giving as many details as he could. His hands were still covered in Gianna's blood when he sat with the House 6

Station Commander, stains on the cuffs of his shirt, ingrained in the calluses on his palms, embedded under his fingernails. The artery that ran below the collarbone was a vicious one, bleeding so fast that even healers often couldn't stop it. That she was still alive by the time he made it down to the courtyard was a shock. Her Talent must have slowed the bleeding some, keeping her alive longer than the few seconds it usually took for such a wound to bleed out, but it still wasn't enough—the strength of her Talent leeched out of her with her blood and putting pressure on the wound did nothing. He could only look into her eyes and watch them go dark.

When the paperwork was complete and signed, Tashué left the Drystone station house. He climbed back into the blackwagon and rode with Gianna to the crematorium.

Rainer Elsworth waited for him at his station house, taking residence in his office. Duskan and Kazrani and Beckett were all crammed in there with him, the blood cleaned off Beckett's face, but still staining his jacket and his coat. Tashué wondered how much of that blood was Beckett's from the gash to his head, and how much was Gianna's. They'd been so tangled when Tashué made his way down to the courtyard.

"Commander, please come sit with us!" Rainer said, standing in the door to the office. "I hear there was some sort of incident."

"Some sort of incident?" Tashué scoffed. He swung an arm to Duskan, pointing at him across the small office. "That idiot shot an unarmed woman. Does that clarify things for you?"

That stiff grin again, like it had been carved onto Rainer's face. "Let's keep things calm and talk about this behind closed doors."

"No," Tashué said. "I filed my report with Gianna's station house. My statement is there."

"Mr. Blackwood!" Rainer snapped. His voice thundered through the station house like a man who was used to getting his way, but Tashué wasn't cowed by him, not with his hands still coated in Gianna's blood, not with Duskan sitting in that chair and looking like a sullen child instead of a man who actually felt some shred of guilt for the death he'd caused. "Come into your office and we'll deal with this properly."

"Fine, let's fucking deal with this, then," Tashué sneered, charging into the office and slamming the door behind him. The glass rattled in the frame, but it held. "Let's deal with the death of an unarmed woman properly. Duskan Hillbraun, you no longer work here. Get the fuck out of my station house!"

"What!" Duskan howled, rising to his feet, eyes wild as he turned to Elsworth. "He can't do that! He can't fucking sack me over some tainted bitch!"

"Sit down, Mr. Hillbraun!" Rainer snapped. "Let's not be rash, Captain." Why did everyone call him *Captain* when they wanted him to settle down, like they could tug on that old title like reins, reminding him of his place. But when the word came out of Elsworth's mouth, it only made Tashué angrier because the bastard hadn't even served, he didn't have the right to use Tashué's rank on him like a bit and bridle on a runaway horse. "There will need to be an investigation regarding the death of Miss Tarbrook."

"What's to be investigated?" Tashué asked. "Gianna was unarmed. Duskan Hillbraun shot her. I want him out of here, damnit! You wanted me to take over this station house and improve the Authority's relationship with our people? Fine. This is what my station house needs—that man shot an unarmed woman and he doesn't deserve to wear a badge!"

"I told you, there's going to be an investigation. There needs to be due process."

"Beckett, did you see what happened?" Tashué asked.

"No, sir, I'm sorry. I was heading for the tree and then she just hit me and I don't remember anything after that." Beckett's hands trembled as he reached up, touching his head where a few stitches had been thrown to pull the wound closed. "I'm sorry. I shouldn't have gone so close to the building. I don't remember anything else until the healer had me up and moving around."

"Lieutenant, did you see what happened?" Tashué pressed.

"No, Captain, I didn't," Kazrani said softly. "I was behind you. I heard you yell 'runner' and then I heard the shot. Next thing I knew, you were climbing out the window yourself."

"What about you?" Duskan snapped. "Did you see what happened, *Captain?*"

Tashué swung on Duskan. "I saw an unarmed woman dying on the ground because you fucking shot her, you piece of shit."

Duskan flung an arm toward Beckett. "She attacked him!"

Beckett's eyes widened and he leaned away from Duskan. "I don't think that's true…"

"She attacked you!" Duskan breathed.

"I don't know," Beckett said, throwing up his hands. "I don't remember!"

Duskan turned to Beckett, leaning closer to him. "She attacked you! She jumped out of a fucking tree and she attacked you! That's what I saw, damnit!" He turned away, his eyes wild as he searched the room for some sympathy. "Lieutenant Mahalouwan, you understand. After what happened at the Market, you know what it's like. These people, there's no predicting what they'll do!"

"That's enough, Mr. Hillbraun," Rainer cut in. "I'll file the paperwork today at House One, and everything will be cleared up in a few weeks."

"I want his badge while the paperwork is being processed," Tashué pressed.

"Captain Blackwood, that's not an option," Rainer snapped. "It's not possible for this station house to manage its cases if you lose another Officer."

"Then give me someone to replace him!"

"There is no one else!" Rainer snapped. "There's no one else. We have Officers in training, but there's no one ready to fill the gap. Give me time to sort things out and I will make this right."

"How?" Tashué pressed, stepping closer to Rainer, leaning against the desk between them. "How will you make it right? Will you get rid of him?"

"That depends on the findings of the investigation."

Tashué shook his head and stepped back, reaching for the door. "Unbelievable. This whole organization is unbelievable."

"Commander Blackwood, where are you going?"

"Oh, it's Commander now, is it?" Tashué snapped, yanking the door open. "I'm going to file my paperwork. This whole fucking place runs on paperwork, doesn't it? And then I'm going to go get a copy of the report from House 6, because if there's going to be an investigation, I want my statement filed with House One. That man shouldn't have a badge."

"Fuck you, taint-loving bastard!"

Tashué spun, slamming the door shut again and stalking closer to Duskan. "You've got big fucking balls whenever I have my back turned, don't you? You want your fucking fight with me? Fine. Stand up and look me in the eye and say it again, you weaselly fucking coward."

Rainer stepped between them, so close to Duskan's chair that if Tashué took another step, he would push Rainer right into Duskan's lap. "Commander, go file your paperwork."

Tashué took a long, deep breath. He looked down at his hands. He could still feel Gianna's blood pumping beneath his fingers, her body going cold even as he tried to stem the flow. He could feel her collar bone, broken and jagged and buckling beneath the pressure he put on her. His whole world seemed to revolve around blood again, just like it used to when he was a soldier. Everything that mattered was blood and death and he couldn't fix all the broken pieces of people.

He turned on his heel without another word to any of them, opening his door and stepping out into the main room. Everyone had frozen, looking at him, but as he stepped out, they averted their eyes and pretended to go back to work. He waved them out of the way, stalking to the typists. Miss Weir had Glaen Forsooth's file waiting for him already, bless her. She had the paper threaded into the typewriter, her fingers at the ready.

Tashué stopped in front of her, but didn't sit down. "Glaen Forsooth, processed for noncompliance—fraternization. In the custody of the Residence for Feral Tainted and Non-Compliants indefinitely."

35

STELLA

DAY 18

S tella wasn't sure exactly what possessed her to make the sour cherry pie. Perhaps it was how empty Tashué's kitchen was, nothing but the means to make coffee and a few pieces of cutlery just in case some food lost its way and found itself on his table. Perhaps it was just an excuse to see him again. Before she left. She'd seen him wearing his cavalry dress uniform, and wanted to ask him where he was going, but he was away too fast. With Kazrani, the pair of them looking so good together in their sharp green uniforms.

She found sour cherry preserve at the Market—she tried to go more often now, to support those who were still selling—and bringing the jar home brought her thoughts of seeing him again. Of standing so close that she could feel the warmth of him. Of his lips.

No, not that. Don't be a fool.

She didn't have to work tonight—her one night off in eight nights on. She set Ceridwen on the front stoop to watch for him. The pie came out of the oven, crust golden with a dust of sugar, the bright red cherry sauce bubbling out of the vent in the top. Setting it on her table, she watched the steam curl up and she waited. No matter where life took her from here, the smell of sour cherries would forever make her think of Tashué Blackwood.

She heard Ceridwen coming, the smash of her boots on the stairs as she ran up each flight. Tireless. Did Stella have so much energy when she was young? She couldn't remember. Her sister, though, definitely had energy like that, ever since she was wee.

The door swung open and Ceridwen burst in. "He's home!"

"Go watch at the window, wait 'til he's settled in."

"What if he leaves again?"

"Then we'll have to wait until tomorrow, Pigeon."

"But you have to go to work tomorrow night!"

"We'll catch him in the morning then. Off you go!"

Ceridwen dashed off to Stella's room, to the window that faced Tashué's apartment. "He's got his lamps on! Is he settled now?"

"Just a little longer, Pigeon. He's had a long day, I'm sure."

"If he's had a long day, we should go over quick to give him his pie. Before he gets too sleepy!"

Stella took a deep breath. Her hands were shaking suddenly, at the thought of going over to his apartment. It wasn't late yet, but the shortening days meant that the sun had set. Looking deep into herself, she tried to ask what her motivation really was for going over there. But it couldn't be that mysterious, could it? Lately she felt like a ship without a rudder or a sail, drifting aimlessly in an ocean without a breeze. She used to *feel* more. Anger, joy, bitterness, passion, it all burned so hot and sharp in her that she used to think she would be burned alive by the fire of her own emotion. She couldn't even pinpoint the moment when her emotions left her, when the things that she knew about herself became less true. But she *could* pinpoint the moment they started coming back—a summer day, the air so hot and humid that it felt wet, Tashué sitting in his bedroom window to catch the breeze on his skin, cigarillo smoke curling away from him.

She could almost feel the warmth from that day. It chased the chill from her, that day. He chased the chill from her.

Stella pushed herself to her feet, fetching her coat before gathering up the pie. The cast iron pan was still hot, but the towel she kept wrapped around it was enough to shield her hands from the heat.

"Alright, Pigeon. Let's go, then. Come open the door for me, would you?"

"Yes, Mam!"

Ceridwen came running across the small apartment so fast that Stella could feel the air swirling behind her. The girl was nearly vibrating as she pulled on her coat, closing the door behind them both and running off down the stairs again. The children were still playing in the street as the darkness turned everything into shadows and the buttery light of the brights, enjoying the last precious weeks before snow and ice cloaked the city and playing got even harder. For once, Ceridwen wasn't tempted to join them, not even for *just one game, Mam, I'll catch up!*

Ceridwen ran all the way up to Tashué's floor, but waited at the door instead of knocking. She stood, shifting her weight from one foot to the other, wringing her hands together, until Stella caught up. Stella nodded to her and Ceridwen burst into motion again, her fist hammering on the door and her face breaking into a wide smile when Tashué opened it.

Tashué didn't look happy to see them.

He stood in his doorway, looking dazed and surprised. He looked at the pie, and at Stella, and at Ceridwen, one by one. He was stripped to his shirtsleeves again, and there was blood on his shirt. Had he hurt himself? Torn some stitches?

"We made you a pie, Mr. Blackwood!" Ceridwen beamed, oblivious.

Stella shifted from one foot to the other as Tashué's gaze tracked up to her face. She forced a smile, feeling the moment rapidly slipping away from her. This wasn't what she'd expected. Had she indeed misread him completely? Where had the fresh blood come from? "I thought—" she cleared her throat, trying to chase away the tremble there. "I thought we should bring it over while it was still warm. Pies are best when they're warm."

"They are," he agreed.

Tashué stepped aside. Ceridwen darted past him, into his

kitchen. He reached out to Stella, his hand taking the weight of the pie pan. "Come in, Miss Whiterock."

Biting the inside of her lip, Stella eased past him and into the apartment. He set the pie on the table, but didn't seem to know what to do next.

"Where are your plates, Mr. Blackwood?" Ceridwen asked. "Would you like to have a piece? It's very good. It's the same as we made yesterday, and we did a good job. Even Mam said it was good and Mam doesn't usually like her cooking. I don't know why. I like Mam's cooking."

"I'm not hungry at the moment, little warrior," Tashué said. "But you go on and help yourself. Plates are right above the sink."

"Yes, Mr. Blackwood!" Ceridwen turned, but she wasn't quite tall enough to reach the cupboard. She climbed up onto the counter.

Stella watched Tashué stand there, so off balance. He was worse than when she walked him home from the Market fire. Then at least it was obvious he was exhausted, a slackness in his every movement that told a story of the work he'd done over the course of those days. Now he was both distant and tightly wound.

"Mr. Blackwood, are you alright?"

Tashué turned to her, his eyes finding her face. He took a deep breath. "Yes, yes." His hands wiped at the stain, as if some part of him thought he could still clean it away, but it was long dry. "I'm fine. It's not my blood. Excuse me. I should change my shirt."

He stepped away before Stella could say anything, disappearing into his room and closing the door behind him. Ceridwen swung to look at Stella, hanging precariously on the edge of the counter.

"Is Mr. Blackwood alright?" she asked.

"I'm not sure, Pigeon," Stella whispered. "I think we should go."

"But he said I could have a piece of pie!"

Stella took a deep breath, but nodded. "Hurry up, then, get a plate and have your one piece."

Ceridwen grabbed one of the two plates sitting on the top shelf and climbed back down. "What's wrong with him?"

"I'm not sure. He's had a hard day, perhaps."

Ceridwen pursed her lips, her whole face screwing up as she thought hard about it. "Well, it's a good thing we made him his favourite pie, then. It's good to have your favourite sweets if you've had a hard day."

She set her place on the table, then found a knife on the counter. Ceridwen watched Stella as she measured out a piece, but Stella's motherly stare made Ceridwen cut the piece in half again before she served herself.

A pot of water steamed on the wood stove. Ground coffee sat on the counter, waiting to go into the water. Stella stepped closer to the oven, watching the first little bubbles float to the top of the water, waiting for it to get hot enough to steep the coffee.

Tashué emerged from his room again. He was in a new shirt, one made of silk. It didn't fit him, though, the shoulders too tight and the arms too short. The blood had been splattered on his arm and chest, but Stella couldn't see any fresh wounds on him through the silk. His eyes lingered on Ceridwen as she sat at the table, kicking her feet while she ate, scooping up the cherries one at a time.

"Your water is ready for the coffee," Stella said, drifting over to the counter and gathering up the cup he'd used to store the freshly ground beans. "Do you really take coffee this hour of the evening?"

He nodded. "I always take coffee. There's enough there for both of us, if you'd like some."

Stella nodded back, dumping the coarsely ground beans into the almost-boiling water and lifting the pot off the stove to steep on the counter. He was still standing, frozen in place, watching the pair of them.

"Were you hurt, Mr. Blackwood?" Ceridwen asked once her pie was cleaned away.

"No," Tashué said. "I'm alright."

"Where did the blood come from?"

"Ceridwen," Stella breathed.

Ceridwen bit her lip, looking wounded. She'd been rather more sensitive since Stella had brought her to the Market Quarter. Part of Stella regretted laying such a heavy burden on her, but the world lay its burdens on everyone. Better that she see the ugly things while Stella was available to help guide her through the emotions that followed such trauma.

"Perhaps we should go," Stella said softly, but she couldn't bring herself to move toward the door. Everything seemed so delicately balanced. Whatever had happened, she wanted to help, but she didn't want to intrude if he needed his privacy. "We'll leave you to your evening in peace."

"Are you on your way to work?" Tashué asked, shaking himself a little, some life coming back to his distant eyes. "I could walk you to the Facility. I wouldn't want you to be late."

"No, I haven't a shift tonight."

"Stay, then. Please?" Tashué reached out to Stella, his fingertips brushing along the outer edge of her palm, just a whisper of a touch that sent a shiver through Stella's body. "It's a joy to have you both here. If you want to stay, that is."

Stella smiled, reaching out to catch his hand when he inevitably withdrew. "I would very much like to stay." How could such a tiny touch communicate so much? A longing, a loneliness. That little touch brought the memory of his whole body to the surface of her mind, the feeling of those big hands on her, of one finger twisting in her hair. Of his lips on hers and the scrape of his beard and the heat of his skin. "You should have some pie, at least. Ceridwen said that it's good to have your favourite sweets if you had a hard day, and I think she's right."

"I see Ceridwen is as wise as her mother," Tashué said, pulling over the big wingback chair from his little sitting room so they could all sit at the table together. "Thank you both. It smells delicious. I see you've cut a second piece for yourself, Ceridwen. Are you going to have that now or are you saving it for later?"

Ceridwen's eyes widened and she looked at Stella, who nodded. Ceridwen took a deep breath, trying to look demure and mature, and Tashué smiled. It was a beautiful thing, his smile. It was Ceridwen's special gift, to bring so many smiles to people.

"Yes, I think I will have a second piece."

She served herself, then cut two more pieces for Tashué and

Stella. He poured himself his coffee and ate quietly, listening to Ceridwen chatter on about the whole story of finding the preserve in the Market and cutting both butter and lard into the flour for the best pie pastry. Stella watched him relax, one measure at a time, the tension melting out of him.

Eventually, the stream of words began to slow, Ceridwen's eyes looking heavy-lidded. The decision to set her to bed in Jason's old room wasn't discussed, but came naturally. Stella put Ceridwen's hair into the rolled plait that kept it almost neat when she slept, and Ceridwen stripped out of her dress down to the linen shift she wore beneath, which served fine as a nightgown. Tashué showed her to Jason's bed and Stella stood in the doorway, watching how tenderly he plucked an old toy off the shelf above the bed. Of all the things he'd brought home for Jason, he explained, this one old fox he bought in the Derccian empire was Jason's favourite. The toy seemed to have strange proportions, the ears much too large for the size of the fox's head. Tashué sat on the floor beside the bed, looking cramped and crunched in the small space between the bed frame and the wall. He explained that the massive ears helped to keep the foxes cool in the desert heat, like rabbits. Ceridwen cradled it tenderly in her hands, staring at its face as Tashué spoke, firing questions at him any time he paused for breath. He answered each one, outmatching her energy with his patience, and eventually she ran out of questions. Tashué stood, but Ceridwen caught his sleeve before he stepped away.

"If it's his favourite, I'd like to put it back," she said softly. "I don't want to drop it while I'm sleeping."

Tashué replaced the toy in its spot, pausing a moment to consider the array on the shelf. Stella marvelled at it, realizing how clean they were. The whole apartment had a thin layer of dust and soot—hardly surprising, since dusting was an ever losing battle even for the most diligent of cleaners—but Jason's room was immaculate. It was like Tashué was keeping Jason's room ready for his return, as if he expected it at any day now.

He gave a bashful smile when he caught Stella watching him,

easing toward the door. She stepped out of the way to let him out and he pulled the door closed behind him.

"You didn't have to supervise me. I've put children to bed before, you know."

"Of course," Stella said, heading back to the table and settling down in one of the chairs. How could she explain to him how afraid she was for Ceridwen without letting it slip that she was lying about nearly everything? "It's just that... She's only ever with me."

"It's good to take care of them," Tashué agreed, sliding into the wingback chair across from Stella. "You never know where life will take them and they're only little for such a short time."

Somehow, the words took the wind out of her. Watching Ceridwen grow was a joy, and yet it seemed to happen faster and faster these days, time sliding away from her before she could grasp it. And the older Ceridwen got, the more scared Stella was that she would lose her delicate hold on protecting her.

Stella wiped at the tears that threatened to gather in her eyes, fighting for a calm she didn't feel. She forced a smile. Had he seen her, and her tears, and how deeply his words shook her?

"How old is your son?" she asked.

"Jason?" Tashué paused, perhaps adding up the years of his son's life. "He's twenty. He'll be twenty-one in the spring."

"You still have his toys in there. It made me think he was younger than that."

"Some of them are his, some of them are mine, from when I was a child. My father made mine and my mother kept them, so that she could pass them down to my children one day. He kept such good care of them all, even the ones I bought... Most of them, I bought before he was even conceived, thinking one day, I would be a father. He's the one that asked me to build that shelf. I had hoped he would come back and see them there and know that everything would be alright. But... I don't know if he'll ever come back."

Tashué sighed, sinking down at the table again. He found his cigarillo case, flipping it open and clicking it closed again a few times. Stella knew the distant way he stared at his own hands, the emptiness in his eyes that of a parent who was staring back at his choices and wondering if he could have done something better. She reached across the table before she could stop herself, her fingers lacing with his. She avoided the stitches and the smashed fingernails, one of which had gone black with its bruise and was threatening to fall off. He stretched out his fingers, letting her touch him without actually touching her back. His knuckles were rough, scarred like the rest of him.

"I wasn't prepared for how hard it would be, raising Jason by myself," he continued. He turned his hand over and Stella's fingers slid across the lines of his palm, the natural creases and the scars. His fingers curled toward her like he wanted to hold her hand, but he stopped himself. Still. "When he came back to Yaelsmuir, he didn't know me at all. He'd spent the first four years of his life with his mother, until she was arrested by the Authority, and brought back here. He was so angry—and who could blame him? As far as he knew, he was just living his life in Roa, and then the Authority dragged both of them out of their home and they were separated. I thought I could handle it. I was so close to Kaz's son, Tevir. His father died not long after I took the company, and Tevir and I... I don't know. He was so easy. But there was always something happening, always someone to take care of him when Kaz and I couldn't because of course we were fighting in wars." He shook his head, his eyes drifting up to the nibu above his door. Then back down to Stella's face, searching again. "I guess this is what you meant, about people giving you their stories. And you listening."

Stella smiled, taking his hand, sliding their fingers together. Carefully, to avoid all the injuries. "It's good, to share our stories. Even the ones that hurt. Perhaps especially the ones that hurt."

"It seems almost obscene to say it, but life was simpler when I was riding with the Jitabvi. A lot of it was blood and death in wars I didn't understand, but at least I knew my purpose. I knew who I was. I knew what was right, and what I was meant to do. Follow orders. Stay alive. I even managed to convince myself I would be a good father." Tashué laughed, a bitter and empty sound. "What an arrogant fool I was."

"Struggling as a parent doesn't make you a bad father," Stella said. "If struggling was the only bar, I don't think anyone could call themselves a good parent."

"What is the bar, then?" Tashué asked. "That our children go into adulthood healthy, with the opportunity to make a life for themselves? I've failed there—he's in the Rift."

She took her hand away from his. She flipped open his cigarillo case and took one for herself, then slid it back to him. He shifted to find his matches in his trouser pocket, letting their hands brush together as she took the box. She lit her cigarillo, leaning back against her chair and watching as he did the same. He favoured his left hand. Even the simple act of turning the matchbox over in the right hand lacked precision. Perhaps she was staring at his hands too much that she had come to notice these little things, but it was better than looking at his face and thinking about his mouth and the way his beard felt against her skin when she kissed him.

"How did he end up there?" she asked.

"He refused to register," Tashué said, shaking his head. "I begged him to register. On my fucking knees in front of him, begging. He has such incredible Talent, that boy—it's so strong." He leaned forward, holding his head with one hand. He shook his head again, bringing his cigarillo to his lips for a deep drag of smoke like it would clear the pain away. "It didn't matter how much I promised or demanded or begged, he refused. Wouldn't register as 'bad meat.' That's what the word 'tainted' reminds him of. Bad meat. I told him I would handle his paperwork, try to get him a good assignment—I thought I could get him into the directed work program, and he could be a stonesmith like my father, but no. None of it was good enough. He just kept saying 'I won't call myself bad meat.' He didn't fight it, when other Officers came to process him. Didn't run. I think he thought he was making a stand, making a point. Like he could change something by refusing to play their game. But they're winning, if it's a game. They're winning, and he's going to die, and there's nothing I can do to save him."

"Maybe it isn't your job to save him," Stella said, reaching out again. She slid a finger over his knuckles, one by one, then back across them the other way. "Maybe it's your job to bear witness when he saves himself."

Tashué shook his head. "I should have done more, before. I should have done something different, to keep him out of that place."

"It's easy to say 'should have' once it's already too late, isn't it?" She reached out to the ashtray, tapping the ashes in and taking another drag. "Will you tell me what happened today? Whose blood was it, on your shirt?"

Tashué groaned as if she'd twisted a knife in his guts, squeezing his eyes shut. "A woman died today. A Talented woman. She died because she was in love and the Talented are forbidden from feeling such human emotions. They mustn't be allowed to be human, lest we face the reality that we're exploiting other humans for little conveniences like brights and trams."

"Such thoughts aren't generally spoken by employees of the National Tainted Registration Authority," Stella said. "Seems rather counter-productive to your job of ensuring the tainted are kept compliant."

"And yet, here I am," Tashué sighed. "Protecting the fine citizens of the Dominion from the likes of you."

Stella flinched, leaning away from him and hiding the twist of her mouth behind the cigarillo, taking a long puff of the smoke. Tashué grimaced, reaching out to her again, catching her hand before she leaned back too far.

"Shit, Stella. I'm sorry. I'm angry and I was being sarcastic. I begin to wonder what I'm doing." He started to let go of Stella's hand, but she caught him, sliding her fingers across his palm. She found the old scar that made his fingers so clumsy and traced it a few times. "It's hard to imagine what threat you pose to the Dominion. Gianna Tarbrook was a healer, at a hospital in Drystone. Glaen Forsooth is a brightman. And even the brightman that *was* dangerous, the one that started the fire—he was driven to his madness by us, by the Authority. If we had helped him sooner, none of that would have happened. And Jason... And you... You heal people."

"I don't heal anyone," Stella breathed, shaking her head. "I'm a whisperer. Whisperers only take the pain away so people can die in peace."

Tashué sighed, scooped up his coffee cup, and drained it in one sip. It was cold, no doubt, having sat there for so long. When he set it down again, he stared into the bottom of the empty cup. Stella found herself watching his face closely now that he wasn't looking at her—at the way his jaw flexed as he clenched his teeth, the way he scratched at his beard and then smoothed it back down. There were faint freckles on his bottom lip, just a dusting of them, and more on his cheekbones. She hadn't noticed them before. It was a hard thing, watching him struggle with his emotions.

"What happened to her?" Stella asked, crushing out the spent cigarillo in the ashtray. "Gianna Tarbrook, the healer."

"We killed her," Tashué said. "She was running from us."

Stella took a deep breath, the words striking her hard. She let go of his hands, leaning back into her chair. Tashué gave a long, slow exhale, his shoulders slumping and his head sinking down. He ran one hand over his face, fingers pushing up into his hair and then grabbing a fistful of it like he was going to start tearing his own hair out.

We killed her.

Sweet North Star, those were ugly words.

"What happened?" Stella asked.

He shook his head. "I don't know—I didn't see it. She climbed out her window before I got to her room, and jumped down. It seems she landed on one of my Officers, and one of my men shot her for it. I shouldn't have trusted him. I should have known that he was shit. He's so... They're all mine, now. My house. My Officers. And I should have known better than to send him into that alley."

"You were there to process her, then? For fraternization?"

Tashué nodded. The storm broke across the city, rain and ice splattering on the window. He rose from the chair, moving across the small room. He grabbed a rag from the pile he kept, stuffing it in the gap where the warped window frame wouldn't close. He stood there for a while, taking in breaths of smoke and watching the rain and the ice chink against the glass pane.

We killed her.

Somehow, he wasn't the man she expected him to be. Or perhaps he was exactly the man she thought he was, and being a tinman didn't fit him.

"If you weren't there when she was shot, how did you get so much blood on your hands and your shirt?" she asked.

Tashué took a deep breath, looking down at his hands. "I tried to save her. I put my hands on the wound to try to stop the bleeding, but it wasn't enough. Even her own Talent wasn't enough." He dropped his hands at his sides again and let out a long sigh, the breadth of him deflating. "I would have given anything to save her. I would have traded my life for hers in a heartbeat, if such a thing could have been done."

"Would that we could save them all," Stella said. "But the Keeper of the Keys comes for us eventually." The decision came to her suddenly, her whole body warming at the thought. "What would happen if your colleagues found me here with you?"

The words seemed to take him by surprise, rousing him from his stupor. He turned to stare at her. "What do you mean?"

"Would you be arrested for fraternization? Would I?"

"No," Tashué said. "I'm not registered."

"So, a registered tainted can't 'fraternize' with another tainted without some kind of permission, but it's fine for us to 'fraternize' with regular people?"

He shrugged, spreading his hands. "I suppose it is."

Stella nodded. "An old friend of mine thought that it was because of the Breeding Program. That the Authority didn't want the valuable Talents—like healers—to dilute their Talents by having children with weaker Talents. It's not true, is it? Or else we would be forbidden from taking up with people without Talent. So, what is it, exactly? What's the Authority so afraid of?"

"I think that's partially true," Tashué admitted. "You, for example, would have to apply to the Authority if you wanted to get married. Regulation Officers don't handle cases like that, but it seems to me that you would be permitted to marry someone with little or no Talent. But someone stronger—like Gianna—wouldn't be permitted to marry a whisperer." He shrugged again, this time an agitated movement, sharp and filled with frustration. "It started before the Breeding Program, though. The language of the fraternization law implies that it's to prevent Talented from coming together and organizing a rebellion." He laughed. "Gianna and Glaen weren't organizing a rebellion. They were just trying to feel alive. And now Gianna's dead and Glaen is in the Rift."

"You've Talent, though, haven't you?" Stella said.

"I have," he admitted. "A little. Never quickened, though. Never needed to register."

"That's good, then," Stella said, the chair legs scraping across the floor as she stood. "I'm glad that, in this at least, we aren't breaking any laws."

Stella took great joy in watching the shock pass over his face. She walked closer, her heart beating so hard she could feel it all through her body. Wind rattled the loose pane, filling the silence in the room as Tashué stared down at her. He reached out, his hand trembling as he reached for her hair. But he dropped his hand, clenched both fists. Stella wondered if it hurt when he did that. The wounds hadn't healed, after all.

Stella sighed at his hesitation. "Are you honestly going to make me kiss you first twice now?"

He took a step back, shook his head. "Stella, I can't. This is inappropriate."

"Inappropriate? Why?"

"Because I'm supposed to be your tinman. I thought..." He huffed, running his hands over his face. "I kissed you once already and something changed between us. I don't want you to..." Tashué pushed his hands through his hair, more agitated than she'd ever seen him. He took a deep breath and reached for Stella again, hands sliding up her arms, but he was as far away as he could get while still being within reach. "I don't want you doing anything you think you have to do in order to stay safe. I won't... I can't..."

Stella sighed, leaning into his hands and looking up at his open, earnest face. How pained he looked, how conflicted. She needed to give him something, some explanation for that day. Something that could close the gap that had opened when that old fear had taken hold of her.

"I lied before," she said quickly, throwing the words out before they could catch on the fear in her throat. "When you asked me if I knew any of the Duncreeks."

Tashué furrowed his brow, shaking his head. He dropped his hands to his sides, but he leaned in. "Why? Why lie about that?"

Stella shrugged, biting her lip. "I knew Siras Duncreek at a time in my life that I don't like to think about." She didn't fight against the emotion, letting the tears gather in her eyes. "They are not happy memories. The weight of them took me by surprise, when you asked. That's what changed, that day. It wasn't you, or that hateful tin badge you wear."

Tashué opened his mouth, but didn't say anything for a long while. "It's a brass badge now."

He flushed after he said it, no doubt realizing how ridiculous he sounded. Stella laughed, stepping closer and sliding her fingers through his beard. He hadn't shaved since the banquet, and it was getting thick and bushy, starting to curl. She wrapped her arms around his neck, meeting those eyes she loved so much. How terribly she would miss looking into those eyes when she left.

"I can assure you that your brass badge is no more alluring to me than the tin was," she said, leaning closer still. "In fact, I am attracted to you *in spite* of you wearing that damned thing."

Tashué slid his hands across her hips, up her waist. His touch turned her to butter, melting beneath the heat of him. She let her gaze track across his face, his mouth and his beard and his amber eyes that stared into her and past her at the same time. She waited for him, letting him come to his decision. Something ugly took root in the back of her mind, a fear of rejection, a fragile, delicate thing that cursed her for laying herself at his feet to accept or deny as he saw fit, for allowing herself to be so desperately vulnerable in a time when all her mind seemed to be crumbling away to nothing.

The woman she used to be tried to tell her that she didn't need to seek validation and acceptance from a man. But the woman she used to be didn't know how lonely the world could be, how a city so full of people could feel so empty. This man was the only one who looked into the crowded mass that was Yaelsmuir and *saw* her. He breathed life into her simply by looking at her, his eyes so filled with hunger and passion and longing that she remembered what it was to be alive.

And if he turned away?

Tashué didn't.

He kissed her, crushing their bodies together. His lips were soft and warm, tasting of coffee and sugar and sour cherries. She leaned into him completely. She slid her hands between them, finding the buttons of his shirt.

She broke the kiss long enough to look down, to undo the buttons. The silk shirt was high quality, the holes small—not as small as the Bellmore suit, but it must have been a challenge for him to do the buttons himself. She slid her hands up his body again, feeling the taut skin of his abdomen and the swell of his chest like she had the last time. Tashué pulled her back to kiss her again, but he rolled his shoulders as she pushed his shirt away, letting go of her long enough to wrench his arms, one at a time, from the ill-fitting sleeves. His shirt got tangled in his suspenders and hung around his hips and he fought with it, trying to drag it up out of the hem of his trousers. It was almost absurd, how a man so self-possessed and confident had become so clumsy. So beautifully flushed with energy and desire that Stella could feel it coming from him like the heat from a stove.

Stella peeled her own clothes away while she watched him. She stripped off her bodice and the first layer of her skirt, reaching behind her back to open the clasps of the petticoats next. He reached for her as she pulled them up over her head, catching her around the waist with trembling hands and kissing her again as she tossed the petticoats away. One of his big hands reached for her hair, his fingers pushing into the wild tangle of it. The other hand went down, finding the hem of her linen drawers, pulling the fabric up, his fingers roaming across her thigh. His rough calluses scraped across her skin and the sensation sent a hot shiver through her, making every inch of her tight and warm. She went for the ties of her corset next, the ribbon knotted in front of her from tightening it herself. Once the ties were open, his hand slid along the front, where the hooks and bars kept it closed. Those hands would never get them open. She broke the kiss, leaning away from him, her hands turned clumsy too, as she fought against hooks that should be familiar. And he was still holding her, still kissing her throat, her face, the sweep of her collarbone, any inch of skin he could reach. The corset finally fell away and she reached for him again, dragging their bodies back together.

She slid her hands up his back. The uneven skin of his scars and the corded muscles made a map for her to explore, but she realized that she was trembling too. The air in his apartment was so cold and his body was so beautifully warm against her, and it had been *so* long since the last time a man put his hands on her in desire. So much of her had been lost in the long years since she had left Cruinnich, falling by the roadside as she searched for a safe place. A safe life. A home? No, she'd never thought she would feel like she was *home* ever again. Home was Cruinnich and she couldn't go back.

You aren't staying here, either, said the hunted part of her, the part that had kept her alive even as the other parts of her fell away. *This is only a distraction.*

Tashué broke away from the kiss to lift her shift over her head. One big hand slid across her breast, a low groan coming from his throat, as if the very sight of her naked skin in his sitting room burned him with pleasure.

She ran her hands down his chest, finding the buttons of his trousers. It was easy enough to open them, one by one, until she could slide her hand inside and feel the hot hardness of him. If it was to be a distraction, let it be properly distracting.

He gasped. Took a deep breath. His broad chest filled against her, pushing their bodies together even more.

Stella took a step back. Tashué followed—with her hand in his trousers, how could he not? She retreated all the way to his bedroom, never letting him catch up to her until her calves were pressed against the frame of his bed, and there was nowhere else for her to go. Tashué had her then, wrapping those big arms around her and laying her down. He kissed her again, so tenderly, even though his whole body was trembling, the hardness of him pressing against her but blocked still by his trousers.

Why was he being so slow and gentle with her? Did he think her something delicate, liable to break? She wanted to tell him that no man could break her. Men before him had tried. And failed. And maybe she was tired, maybe she was drifting away from herself and into the storm of pain she saw every night at the Facility, and maybe she was stretched to the very edge of her stamina, but he, of all people, could not break her. He, of all people, had made her whole again.

She slid her hands down his back again, finding the hem of his trousers. They were loose now, with the buttons open, and she pushed them down off his hips. He stood again, fighting out of his boots. Stella laughed, watching him.

"What are you laughing at?" he muttered.

"In all the time I've known you, I've never seen you so clumsy."

Tashué grinned, resting one knee on the bed beside her. "You have a very particular effect on me, Stella Whiterock." He lifted her leg, pulling off her boot and tossing it aside. It went clattering out of his room, thumping on the floor and bouncing off the wall. "I can't seem to think straight when I look at you." The other boot came off and he threw it harder.

"Stop throwing things, you brute," Stella laughed. "You'll wake Ceridwen."

"Is she a light sleeper?" he asked, fingers on the hem of her stockings, teasing them down.

"No, she sleeps very heavily, but you're being especially loud."

He bit his lip as he dragged her stockings further down, baring her skin. He leaned down and kissed her knees, her thighs. He stood again and pushed the door closed to give them some shred of privacy. Stella wriggled out of her drawers, so that there wouldn't be a single scrap of cloth between them, so that she could feel him against her whole body.

Tashué slid his hands along her legs as he returned to the bed, kneeling between her thighs. The sight of him took the breath from her—how long had she been watching him, imagining a moment just like this one, feeling the heat return to her body to chase the numbness away? He leaned over her. His hands trembled still as he slid his fingers up her torso, pausing at her own scars the way Stella was always drawn to his. They could read the stories of each other's lives by the scars—the one across her ribcage from when she fell from a tree and ripped open her skin on a branch, another on her hip from her days learning to use a sword, and the mottled skin of the stretch marks she earned as her child grew within her belly.

Stella reached down, running her fingers through Tashué's beard and dragging his face up so that she could kiss him again. Everything in her was trembling. He shifted his weight on the bed, a hand sliding along her thigh, adjusting both of their bodies so that they fit together just so. She gasped as he slid into her, breaking away from the kiss so that she could look at his face. He made a soft groan from the back of his throat and she loved the sound of it, the sound of him enjoying her as much as she enjoyed him. He moved slowly inside of her, but his heart was beating so hard that she could see it, fast and wild in his throat. She arched up so that she could kiss him there, feeling his pulse beneath her lips.

Tashué moved faster, pushing harder, and Stella had to bite his shoulder to keep from crying out. He groaned again, pushing his face into the crook of her neck, his beard scraping her, his lips finding her skin. It was so easy to let herself believe that there was nothing else in all the world but the two of them, that all she needed was the strength of him to shield her from the weight of her past.

It's a lie, said the hunted woman. *You'll never be safe.*

That took the breath out of her, too. Tears escaped before she could stop them. They must have found his face—his head came up. His body slowed, and then stopped, a hand reaching up to wipe the tears off her cheek.

"Stella…"

"No, don't stop," she gasped, catching his beard again, so rough. She pulled his face back down toward hers, into another kiss, only breaking it when she needed to catch her breath. "Everything about you feels so good. Please, don't stop."

Calluses scraped her cheek as he slid his hand up, pushing those big fingers into her hair. "Are you sure?"

"Yes," she gasped. Pulled him into another kiss and wrapped her legs around his hips, pulling him back into her. "I'm so incredibly sure. I've never been so sure of anything in my life."

He shifted his weight, keeping himself up so that he could watch her face as he started moving his hips again. Tashué kissed the tracks on her cheeks that her tears had left and his beard tickled her face. The movement of his body against her, inside of her, built the heat of her pleasure and her trembling only got stronger, making her heart pound, making it hard for her to catch her breath. His whole body shuddered and he slumped against her, finding her mouth for another kiss. He was back to kissing her tenderly, slowly, his hands finding her hair again.

With his body so relaxed, something uncoiled in the centre of him, pushing against the bonds of his iron will, the Talent trying to break free of the prison he had built around it. She squeezed her eyes shut, reaching out to that beast. She didn't dare try to unknot it, but she wanted to feel it, wanted the force and the strength of it to wash over her. It was easy to believe that he could save her, with that Talent.

36

TASHUÉ

DAY 18

"You have more than 'a little' Talent."

Stella's voice dragged Tashué back out of the sleep that ate at the corners of his mind. It seemed such a natural thing to stretch out and let Stella tuck herself against his body.

"I can feel it," she continued, her finger tracing lazy circles on his chest, "in the core of you, like a sleeping giant. It's true that you've never quickened, but the Talent in you is not a small thing."

Tashué felt her in his chest and in his mind, as if her hand had reached right into him. Distant memories that didn't belong to him flitted through his thoughts. The winds of Cruinnich, howling across the plains and crashing against old stone. A face like Stella's but so much younger, her hair darker. Ceridwen, maybe a year old, wrapped in a blanket of shaggy fur and highland plaid. Another face—a man, with a thick blond beard—her husband perhaps? But this man was too well dressed to be a stevedore, his coat too black and his shirt too white for a poor working man.

"A great Talent," Stella whispered. "In Cruinnich, they would call you a man who moves mountains."

The storm rattled the bedroom window and howled through the

streets, pelting rain and ice across the glass. Her words left a cold fear in him. He reached down, catching Stella's hand and drawing it to his lips. He kissed her knuckles, her wrist, her palm.

"Are you afraid of the notion that you've Talent?"

"Of course I am," Tashué breathed.

"And yet you don't use the word 'tainted' anymore. Every time the word comes to your tongue, you flinch."

Tashué stifled a sigh, turning to look at Stella. She was examining his face, waiting for his answer. "Everything I believed... The sacrifices I made, the losses I've suffered, all seem for nothing. A fool's choices, bringing nothing but despair to the world."

Her hand returned to his chest, tracing those circles again. "Are you talking about your son?"

"Jason. Keoh. Gianna. You."

"You don't bring me despair, Tashué Blackwood." She rolled to lie on top of him, her body stretching across him. Stella seemed such a little thing, but her skin was so warm, a strength so deep. She laid a kiss on his mouth, looking into his eyes. "You are a beacon of hope in a life of darkness and pain."

Tashué reached up, trying to push his fingers through her hair, but the curls were even messier now and they caught him, held him. "Are you sure?" He eased his fingers free of the tangles as carefully as he could, wincing as strands of hair dragged at the healing wounds. He settled his hands on her hips instead. "I've never made a woman cry in my bed before."

She sighed, turning her face away from him. Her gaze drifted to the window, the same one that looked into her own apartment, where he sometimes caught her watching him. In the heat of the summer especially, when he sat in the window to catch the wind that howled between the buildings, letting it cool the sweat on his body. He waited for her, feeling the emotions that ran through her. She was so distant most of the time. But maybe now he knew her better and he could sense what lay beneath all that.

"I don't think I realized how long it's been," she said softly. "I love Ceridwen. She fills my heart with joy in a way I can't describe. But it's a lonely thing, drifting through this world. And working at the Facility..." She closed her eyes, and shrugged, but Tashué thought he saw tears glistening in her lashes again. "Sometimes I forget who I am."

"Do you feel their pain, when you take it from them?"

"All of it," she gasped. "Every broken bone, every wasting disease. There are days when I feel my body could buckle beneath it all, as if it would crush me and I would cease to exist. I would only be a storm of pain, like a hurricane drifting across the ocean."

Tashué slid his hands along her back, trying to find the words that might bring comfort. He found the scar on her ribs, the one that had healed ragged and puckered, the flesh still pink and knotted even though it seemed to be years old. He traced it with his finger as she had traced his and he wondered if she really could read the stories of his wounds by touching his old scars.

"What can I do?" he asked, sliding his hands along her back, feeling her skin go tight, the fine hairs standing on end. "To help you?"

A small smile pulled at the corners of her mouth and she slid up his body so that she could reach him for another kiss. She pushed her fingers through his hair, then down along his shoulders, across his chest. The lamplight was weak and cold, washing the colour from the room so he only saw the vaguest of shades, the copper of her hair only a suggestion, the hues of her skin turned as pale as bone. The sight of her atop him made his blood stir and she smiled again, rocking her hips against him.

He sat up and wrapped his arms around her so that he could kiss her as she slid onto him. She broke the kiss, gasping, leaving him hungry for more of her. He kissed the hollow above her collarbone, the curve beneath her jaw, the spot where the dimple appeared on her cheek when she smiled. She caught his face with both hands, fingers curling in his beard again, leaning back so that she could look him in the eye. Her chest was heaving against his, her eyes bright and wild.

"This is plenty help."

And she kissed him again.

S tella slept on her side, the blankets pulled up over her face so that she seemed to be only a lump of a quilt and a great mass of curls. Tashué rolled toward her, pulling the blanket down just long enough to kiss the side of her neck. She shifted but didn't wake. He tucked the blanket back into place, up around her cheek, resisting the urge to slide his fingers through her hair. He'd tried that a few times already and it wasn't as he imagined. His fingers got trapped in hidden tangles and it was some challenge to get them out without hurting her. She hadn't minded so much, not when he was deep inside of her, when her breath came out in rapid pants and her whole body was trembling. But now, she was so still and peaceful that he didn't dare disturb her.

For a moment, looking at her and the mess of her hair made him think of Gianna Tarbrook, dying as he watched, her blood pumping beneath his hands no matter how hard he pushed down on her wound, and her hair tangled with moss and leaves from the oak tree that she had jumped down from.

He pushed his face into Stella's hair, breathing in the scent of her, letting himself drift across the darkness of sleep. He saw hazel eyes and tears sliding down Gianna's cheeks, which had gone grey for lack of blood flow. But now when he saw it, he could taste the salt of Gianna's tears as he watched her die, just as he had tasted Stella's tears when he was inside her.

He woke with a curse, his heart hammering in his chest. Beside him, Stella shifted but didn't wake, a soft noise coming from the back of her throat. He reached for her body under the blankets, finding her warm skin, so soft beneath his callused hands. Part of him feared that this was some cruel dream, too. But the smell of her was so real, the tangles catching in his beard when he moved, the warmth of her body leaching from the covers.

When he convinced himself that she wasn't a dream, he slid carefully from the bed, finding his trousers and sliding them on. The suspenders were still attached and he let them hang loose around his hips. He drifted out of his room, where most of their clothes had been abandoned, and he went to find his cigarillos. He lit one and stood in the darkness with nothing but the tobacco smoke to keep him company. It was raining again, sleet pattering on the glass. The rhythm was almost a song, rising and falling to nature's own tempo. What would come next for him and Stella? What did she want from him? He knew what he wanted, felt the ache of it too keenly in his chest.

Best not think about what he wanted. But what was left to think about, if not Stella? Keoh, and Jason, and the woman he met in Cattle Bone Bay. A Lidan woman, who had her nose broken by another resident at the Breeding Program, who snuck out when a horse fell and broke its leg. He wished he knew her name. Illea Winter and Rainer Elsworth and their endless webs. Could he do what General Wolfe wanted? Run for Mayor? Suddenly, unseating Rainer Elsworth seemed like a noble cause. Illea and General Wolfe would take care of everything. He needed only to cooperate with them. But Jason... What had Wolfe said? *We'll just have to find a way to make him safe.* Did General Wolfe have that kind of reach? He cursed, shaking all those questions out of his head. Better to spend the rest of the night trying not to think at all.

He heard rustling from Jason's old room, heard Ceridwen mutter in her sleep. He pushed the door open, gently so the hinges wouldn't squeak. The bright outside cast only a thin sliver of light through the room, sitting across Ceridwen's torso. She was shifting around, trying to make herself comfortable, but she wasn't awake. It was good to have a child in that bed again, the sight of her there acting like a plug in a wound to stem the bleeding. The wound would probably never fully heal, at least not while things with Jason were still so uncertain. But at least Ceridwen helped him survive a little longer.

She settled on her stomach, one arm stretched up under the thin pillow and another dangling off the edge of the bed. Her hair was dishevelled, one of the plaits pulled free from the low bun so that it hung loose over her shoulder. There was something, Tashué thought, some darkness on the back of her neck, but it was hard to tell the shape of it in the dimly lit room. Like a birthmark, perhaps, or...

Before the thought even finished, he heard footsteps padding gently behind him. Stella slid her arm through his, planting a kiss on his shoulder.

"Is everything alright?" she whispered, tugging him out of the doorway. She stepped inside through the gap he left to see for herself.

"Everything's fine," Tashué said. "She sounded unsettled, but it was nothing."

Stella turned to him, offering up a wide, warm smile that clove straight through his chest. "She talks in her sleep sometimes." She edged closer, guiding him out the door. "You should come back to bed."

"Well," he said, reaching for her. She was in her shift, the fabric light and thin and hugging the lines of her. Her nipples rose to hard peaks in the cold air and he brushed one with his thumb, watching the gooseflesh rise up her neck. "It's hard to argue with that."

She leaned up, nuzzling under his neck so that she could plant a kiss on his throat where the line of his beard ended. Even as her lips touched him, her hand was pulling Ceridwen's door shut behind her.

37

TASHUÉ

DAY 19

Rhodrishi and Kazrani sat at the bar when Tashué stopped at the *Pint Under* on his way to the station house, tucked over bowls of stew and fresh pints.

"There you are!" Kazrani said. "You're late. Where have you been?"

"I was in my bed," Tashué grunted. "You know, those things that people lie down in when they're tired? I know you don't actually use one. You Jitabvi sleep standing up, like horses, but the rest of us need to be more horizontal."

"You don't look like a man who's had a good night's sleep." She leaned over, making a show of smelling him. "At least you don't smell like you've bathed in whisky. In fact, what *have* you been bathing in?"

Tashué smirked but he couldn't stop the blush that climbed up his neck. "You're hilarious, honestly."

Kazrani laughed. "I'm right, aren't I? Good for you, Captain. Who's the lucky one this time? Is it Miss Whiterock, finally?"

Instead of rising to the bait, Tashué settled on the stool and turned to Rhodrishi, stretching out a hand. "It's good to see you, Colonel."

"And you, Captain," Rhodrishi said, accepting the shake gingerly, avoiding Tashué's stitches. "Or should I call you Commander now?"

Tashué touched his badge, shrugging. He fought the urge to unpin it and slide it into his pocket. "Captain is fine."

"Hey, look at this, Captain," Kazrani said, holding out a fresh sepia photograph. "I just got it this morning. That's my grand-daughter, can you believe it?"

Tashué took the photograph. He recognized Tevir immediately, the grin the same as he remembered from the last time he saw the boy. Sweet North Star, he had grown so much. Had it really been nearly ten years since he'd seen Tevir, the boy who was like his first son? Tevir stood beside a Jitabvi pony, and a child sat bareback on the pony. Her features were indistinct because she'd moved when the photograph was being taken, making her a blur of black hair and a big smile that looked like her father.

"What's her name?" Rhodrishi asked.

"Dahlia." Kazrani took the photograph back. "She's already five, can you believe it? How do they grow so fast?"

Tashué didn't want to tell her that they grew faster when you didn't see them. The days slipped away without you even noticing when you didn't get to watch and marvel at their every develop-ment. One day, they had just been born and they fit in your one hand, the next they were almost five and they didn't know who you were and wanted to know where their mother was. But then, Kazrani knew that already. She'd given Tevir up when he was thir-teen, taking him back to the Hadia to take up life as a Jitabvi hotblood with his grandparents. The same age Tashué was when he signed to enlist. Tashué and Kazrani had blinked and Tevir was a man grown now, with a daughter, a career. Captain's bars.

"He must be an old man now," Tashué said, because he didn't want to say the other things that were drifting through his head.

Kazrani scowled. "Twenty-six is hardly old, you bastard."

Tashué shrugged. "He would have been ancient compared to the children he went to the Academy with."

"I didn't think the Jitabvi were allowed to go to the Officer's

Academy," Rhodrishi said, handing the photograph back. "The Dominion deemed you rabble too unruly to get higher than Lieutenant."

Kazrani laughed at that. "What Tevir wants, Tevir gets," she said, tucking the photograph away. "He won't be deterred from anything, that boy. He petitioned the Queen directly, with a letter about all he'd accomplished in his career already and how he longed to serve the Crowne to the very extent of his ability. She granted him entry to the Officer's Academy herself. He's the very first Jitabvi to take the Captain's bars. He hopes this will open the door for more Jitabvi to follow him. He was given Iris Company, in the 8th."

Rhodrishi's eyebrows rose. "Your old company?"

Tashué nodded. "That's the one."

"Tevi said they still call it Mad Maddox's 8th, even though old Maddox retired. I don't remember who has it now, but Tevi says he's good. Says the new General signed his letter for him."

Rhodrishi nodded, reaching for his pint. "I always thought that boy would change the world."

"So did I. Did I tell you, he graduated with the gold bars?" Kazrani asked. "What is it, the top five percent of all graduates get gold bars instead of the silver ones?"

"Top one percent," Tashué said. "Good for him. That's not easy, getting the gold bars. Can't say I'm surprised, though."

"Morning, Mr. Blackwood," Pallwyth said, approaching. "Whisky or a pint this morning?"

"A pint, thank you Pallwyth."

"Feed the man, Pallwyth. He worked up his appetite last night."

Tashué sighed at her. "Where's Tevir stationed now?"

"He's in the Derccian Empire, to help in some border skirmish. He's annoyed because so far his company is stationed at the rear, but I told him to be patient. He's the first Jitabvi Captain ever, and now he's supposed to fight for the very Empire our people were running from all those years ago. It will take time to earn the Crowne's trust. But my son is not a patient man."

"You say that as if you find it surprising," Rhodrishi said. "As if a young man raised by you and Captain Blackwood should be anything but tempestuous."

Kazrani laughed. "Are you saying that the Captain and I are not even-tempered, Colonel? How shocking."

"Perhaps the pair of you have mellowed with age, but not by much."

"Is this mellow?" Pallwyth asked, delivering a pint and a bowl of stew. "Heavens, I'd hate to imagine the pair of them before they mellowed, then."

Rhodrishi nodded at Pallwyth. "You should have seen them when they were both young. I think they aged me by a decade, just being near them and all the energy they had."

"That's not entirely fair, Colonel," Kazrani said softly. "When I brought the Captain to you, he was nearly dead."

"That's true," Rhodrishi admitted, turning to Tashué. "Do you remember it?"

Tashué shrugged. It was something he thought of often, but his mind only had bits and pieces. He remembered the wound on his calf, from a bullet that passed through him and killed his horse. It hadn't seemed that bad, at first, just a wound that went straight through the muscle. But their healer had been killed in the same action and there was no one around to stop the infection that ate through him slowly. His first experience with a wound going bad... he hadn't known it was so serious until there was nothing he could do to stop its advance. He didn't remember Kazrani having him tied to his saddle, though she'd told him about it plenty of times. He didn't remember the long journey to the nearest healer's camp. He didn't remember the healers that tried to help him but failed.

"I remember hearing your voice," Tashué said. "I was dreaming —I don't remember what. It was all just darkness and pain, I think. But you said, 'Don't leave yet. You still have time here.' And then, I drifted for a while, but it seemed that you were always there, hanging on to me so I didn't slip away."

Rhodrishi nodded. "You did try to die a few times. I was very frustrated with you."

"Sweet North Star, I didn't know that," Kazrani breathed. "He almost died, even after you had him?"

"Just because I'm Kaadayri doesn't mean I can fix every body that comes beneath my hands," Rhodrishi said. "He was very ill when you brought him to me."

All the colour drained out of Kazrani's face and she leaned back like she was reeling. Tashué reached out to her, catching her hand and looking her in the eye.

"Hey, stop that. This was more than twenty years ago. I survived. I'm still here."

"I know, I know," she said, waving his hand away. "It's just— shit. Can you imagine? How different everything would be?"

"I don't have to imagine," Tashué said. "I'd be the one dead. And you would have been assigned a different Captain and your life would have gone on. More importantly, it didn't happen that way."

Kazrani shook herself, reaching for her pint and taking a long swallow. "How is it with the General at his hospital, then? He must be a decent man to work with."

"He is, and he's built a good facility," Rhodrishi said. "Best I've seen in some time. He will serve the people of Brickheart well with it, once it opens fully. We've discharged quite a few of the Market survivors, I'm pleased to say. General Wolfe asked me to stay until the dedication ceremony, which I suspect will be turned into a Winter campaign event." He shrugged. "I'll go, but I'm anxious to return home after that. I wasn't intending to stay at all after the Imburleigh event." He reached out to Tashué, the way he did when he wanted Tashué to pay attention. "I want to talk to you after, about retirement."

"Retirement?" Kazrani echoed. "You're the only active Hands of Bronwynn in the whole Dominion!"

Rhodrishi nodded. "And I've had the pleasure of training many young men and women who have the potential to do great things for the Dominion. But I'm tired. It's time for me to go back to my people."

Before anyone could say anything else, the door swung open again, Duskan and Beckett stepping past Kazrani to sit by the fireplace. Beckett still had a black eye, the lump he took on the head hidden now beneath his bowler hat. Tashué sucked in a deep breath, battling hard against the anger that crawled up through him.

"Did you see what happened?" he asked, swinging back to Kazrani. "With Gianna?"

"No. I was behind you, remember? Why are we talking about this again?"

"Because he's my fucking problem now," Tashué muttered, gesturing down the bar to where Duskan sat. "I shouldn't have put them together. I should have known Duskan would have asked for the gun back, and I should have known that Beckett wasn't strong enough to resist him."

"You can drown yourself in all your 'should've's'," Kazrani said. "It's tempting to wallow in all the things you could have done differently, but it helps no one. Learn from it, certainly, but leave yourself room for forgiveness, hey? Besides, he can't exactly be blamed for being afraid. After Moore and the barge, who can blame him for thinking that Tarbrook could have been a threat?"

Tashué stifled a sigh, searching for the right words to explain how things had so shifted. "Do you ever wonder if we're right?"

"Right about what?"

Tashué motioned to his badge. The brass gleamed, polished to a high shine. "Right about everything we're doing."

"What are you talking about?" Kazrani asked, swinging to him with her brow furrowed. "About what who is doing? You and I? Or the Authority?"

"The Authority. Do you ever wonder if what they ask us to do... is right?"

"Of course it's right. We're upholding the law. The law is right."

"But what makes them right?" Tashué pressed. "Simply that they're laws? Who made them? And for what purpose?"

Kazrani scowled, her eyes flicking back and forth between Tashué and Rhodrishi. "The Authority made the laws to protect the people of the Dominion. And the tainted for that matter. Some countries are still chasing their tainted down in the night and tossing them into bonfires. And after what happened in the Market Quarter, it's little wonder that they do. The Authority is doing their best to keep *everyone* safe."

"Even Gianna Tarbrook?"

Kazrani shook her head. "Tarbrook tried to run. If she had surrendered to you, she would still be alive."

"In the Rift."

"Of course in the Rift," Kazrani scoffed. "Where else would you suggest she go?"

"But what was her crime?"

"Fraternizing."

"Falling in love," Tashué pressed. "Her crime was falling in love."

"Captain, surely you're joking. The fraternizing laws are in place to keep the tainted under control. It gives us a tool with which we can separate rebels and insurrectionists when they are trying to start trouble."

"You think Glaen and Gianna were plotting an insurrection?" Tashué asked. "Were they doing that before or after they made love, do you think?"

The door swung open again before Kazrani could answer. Five people entered this time, five tin badges that Tashué didn't recognize. Their clothes were too nice for them to be Brickheart residents, but they had the hard faces and the clenched fists of people spoiling for trouble. They stood in the door for a long moment, eyes scanning the growing crowd. One spotted Tashué and his face flushed.

"Trouble's come looking for us," Tashué said, elbowing Kazrani.

"For us?" Kazrani swivelled around to the door, taking measure of the knot of tinmen there. "Why?"

"I'm not sure."

Kazrani turned to face them, leaning her elbows on the bar and grinning at the whole group. They were all so terribly young, probably still believing the lies of their own invincibility. Well dressed, too, their badges stamped with House 6—Drystone. Tashué turned away from them, reaching for his pint. Rhodrishi shook his head at the whole thing, heaving a tired sigh.

"You're Tashué Blackwood?" the leader of the knot asked.

"He would be Commander Blackwood to you, son," Kazrani said.

"I don't care if he's King fucking Blackwood," the man hissed. "What's the matter, Blackwood? Afraid to look me in the eye?"

"I couldn't care less about looking you in the eye," Tashué muttered.

"You led the idiots who shot Gianna Tarbrook."

Tashué's heart skipped a beat, the anger turning cold. He turned to the group, searching their faces one by one. "What do you care about Gianna Tarbrook?"

"She was my damned case," the man snapped. "Mine! And you and your Prickheart idiots shot her. A healer! Do you have any idea how hard it is to come by healers? She was a good one, worked her shifts at the hospital and didn't cause any trouble. You had no business processing her and no business fucking shooting her!"

Everything drained out of Tashué, all the tension and the frustration and the anger. "I'm sorry. I didn't see what happened. I've advised that the Officer responsible be fired, and Rainer Elsworth has filed paperwork for an investigation."

The young man froze, blinking at Tashué a few times.

"Your precious little healer was fraternizing," Duskan snapped, sliding off his stool and stepping closer. Beckett followed, pulling at Duskan's sleeve as if he was trying to hold him back. "Your precious healer was non-compliant and Elsworth himself sent us after her."

"You're *the* idiot, aren't you?" the man snapped, turning to Duskan, his chest swelling. His friends edged in closer. "You're the idiot that shot her. You're Duskan fucking Hillbraun and you shot my healer."

"Your healer was running from us!" Duskan howled. "Your healer climbed from her window and dropped from a tree branch. She hit Beckett so hard that she knocked him unconscious. What would you have done differently? After what happened at the Market, tell me what you would have done differently after a tainted bitch dropped out of the fucking sky!"

"You had no right! You had no right to arrest her, and you had no right to shoot her!"

"What the hell do you care, anyway?" Duskan asked, coming so close to the other Officer that he could probably smell the man's breath. Could probably smell the alcohol that made him so bold and so angry. "She was tainted."

"We have the best stats in the city," one of the other Officers growled. "House 6 has the best stats in the whole city and you fucked them up."

"That isn't what this is about, Boyd!"

"He fucked up our stats, Stephens!"

"He didn't belong in Drystone!" someone else shouted. "He had no right to come to our Quarter and kill our healer."

"Your fucking 'healer' almost killed our man!" Duskan shouted back.

Tashué reached out, grabbing Duskan by the scruff of the jacket. "That's enough, Hillbraun."

Duskan twisted around, swinging with his right—the hand that still clutched a glass half-full of beer. Glass shattered against the side of Tashué's face. The impact staggered Tashué, made him blind, made him dizzy. One elbow rested on the bar and for a moment it seemed the only thing keeping him up, because his legs and the floor seemed so far away that he wasn't even sure they were still there. He tried to blink through the muddy pain, but then his vision went red with his own blood.

Ears ringing. Blood hot. Still, he heard the chaos erupt around him, bodies and fists, jostling and angry and swinging.

"Come out of the way, Captain," Rhodrishi said, taking Tashué by the arm. His voice was anchoring, dragging him back to himself. "That looks deep. You'll need a few stitches, I think."

Rhodrishi led him to the door and Tashué staggered after him, blind on his left side with all the blood making his vision a curtain of burning red. The pain wasn't in his eye—at least he didn't think so. It was higher, across his brow, across his forehead. Fucking hell, he hoped Duskan hadn't cut his eye. He wouldn't be able to see at all if that was the case, would he? Maybe seeing all the blood was a good thing.

Rhodrishi pushed the door open and Tashué grabbed the banister outside. The air was cooler, damp with the ever-looming autumn storms. Tashué sucked in a few deep breaths, but he was still dizzy, nausea clawing through his gut and threatening to bring up whatever beer and stew he'd had.

"Sit down, Captain, before you fall over," Rhodrishi said, tugging Tashué's arm.

Tashué sank down on the front stoop, leaning his head down between his knees. Blood kept dripping, pooling between his feet. But the fight followed him—he heard Pallwyth shouting for them to get out. Duskan and Stephens went tumbling down the steps together, still swinging, the rest of the Drystone Officers behind. Kazrani next—no, she wasn't following the fight. She'd left Duskan to fend for himself and stood behind Tashué.

"Just puke and be done with it," Kazrani said, patting his shoulder. "You'll feel better after. Pallwyth won't mind. You pay him entirely too much for the copper whisky for him to mind anything at all."

"Shut up, Kaz." Tashué reached up, trying to wipe the blood out of his face. There must have been some glass still in his skin—he felt it, cutting, scraping, tearing, and more blood, blood from his hand now too.

Rhodrishi sighed as he sank down onto the step and reached into his pocket. "The two of you are drawn to trouble like a pair of lodestones. One day, Captain, I won't be here to save you anymore and then what will you do? Lift up your head, let me see it."

Tashué leaned back and rested his elbows on the steps behind him. The door opened again and Pallwyth stepped out with a few towels. He eased down the steps, handing the towels to Rhodrishi who set about mopping up some of the mess. Beckett was behind him, looking pale.

"Is he alright?" Pallwyth asked. "That looks like a lot of blood."

"A few stitches will do wonders, and he'll have another scar,"

Kazrani said. "Won't make his face any prettier, though. He's to be old and ugly soon, I'm sure."

Patrollers were on the street, pulling Duskan and Stephens apart, dragging them away from each other. Rhodrishi pulled the glass out of the wound with a pair of tweezers he retrieved from his pocket, pressing the towels against the side of Tashué's head to help stem the flow.

"Commander," Beckett said, easing forward. "If Duskan's to be fired, I think I should be fired as well."

Tashué's eyes opened and he struggled to focus on Beckett, who stood over him. "What? Why?"

"Duskan shot her, but it was my fault, sir. I shouldn't have gotten so close. You sent us back there to monitor the alleys of escape, and I put myself in harm's way by stepping under that damned tree. It was an idiotic thing to do. If I hadn't been there, she wouldn't have landed on me. Duskan wouldn't have shot her. She'd still be alive."

"You didn't kill her, Beckett," Kazrani said. "You aren't responsible."

"And yet I feel like I am."

Kazrani huffed, shaking her head. "You keep your badge. If good men like you walk away, all that's left on this force are idiots like them. Keep your badge and make the Authority proud."

Stephens came back, bloodied and dishevelled but looking pleased with himself. "You should get your house in order, Commander! I guess it shouldn't be a surprise to anyone that Prickheart is full of shit, though."

"Get the fuck out of here," Kazrani snapped. "Maybe if you were monitoring your own cases more closely, your healer wouldn't have been fraternizing with a brightman from In the Tracks. Lay off the ale and maybe do your actual fucking job."

Beckett headed down the stairs, shouldering past Stephens. Stephens gave him a shove, but Beckett stepped in, fist cocked.

"Lay another finger on me, you fucking Drystone prig," Beckett snapped, teeth bared in a primal snarl.

Kazrani went down the stairs next, like she'd charge into the chaos if Beckett started swinging. But the Patrollers were chasing the other Drystone Officers away and Stephens was suddenly alone.

"Run off back home to Drystone, son," Kazrani said. "Pretty young thing like you isn't tough enough for Brickheart, not without your friends to watch your back."

Stephens threw a few more curses, but he stalked off after the rest of the Drystone Officers. Kazrani stood like a sentry at the bottom of the stairs, watching him go. And Beckett went to Duskan, walking away with him.

Kazrani lay a hand on Rhodrishi's shoulder. "Colonel, forgive me, but I have to work. Can you handle him?"

"Of course, Lieutenant. It's an old trick for me now, patching up our wayward Captain."

Kazrani nodded, but she didn't move away just yet. Tashué looked past Rhodrishi's hands to meet her eye. Something was holding her, her face pinched with worry. What was she afraid of? Rhodrishi glanced over his shoulder at Kazrani, offering her a smile. He had a warm smile, but it was tired.

"I have him, Lieutenant. You're dismissed."

Kazrani smiled back. "Yes, sir."

38

TASHUÉ
DAY 19

Tashué knew how terrible he must have looked, covered in blood and smelling of beer, fresh stitches applied to his brow and his cheek where the glass had sliced through his skin. They were deep cuts, but clean enough that they would heal given time. He'd waved away Rhodrishi's offer to help the healing along. He'd never gotten used to the feeling of someone's Talent sliding through his body and knitting skin together. It hurt, more than the actual wound. It burned and itched, the skin feeling like it was writhing with all that forced energy.

In spite of the blood and the stitches and the growing headache, he shook the broken glass from his coat and went back to his station house.

"How's Eddie?" Tashué grunted as they walked, going only as quickly as his dizziness would allow him.

Rhodrishi shrugged at him. There was blood on his cuffs and some in the creases of his fingers. The towels were too soaked with blood for him to clean himself with them and Pallwyth had cast them into the fire rather than try to wash them. It was incredible how much the face could *bleed*.

"He's grieving for his mother," Rhodrishi said with a tired sigh, "but he's determined to get out of bed somehow. He would like to rebuild the shop and continue smoking pork. The General has pledged to donate meat to the boy, and Illea Winter has promised lumber to help rebuild. The General is a good man."

Their talk was interrupted by the little man that stood on the steps of the station house. He had his hat in his hands, turning it around and around. His eyes searched Tashué's face from beyond the spectacles that sat precariously on the end of his nose.

"Mr. Blackwood?"

Tashué paused at the base of the stairs. "Yes."

"Are… are you alright, sir?"

Tashué reached up, touching the stitches. "I'm fine. How can I help you?"

The man shook himself, pushing his hat back on, but it sat crooked on his head. "My name is Tarren Bayside and I am the director of the Facility of Rest for the Critically Ill. You introduced yourself to me a few weeks ago, when you took over monitoring one of the Facility's tainted."

"Yes, I remember," Tashué said, stepping closer, entirely too aware of all the other bodies buzzing around them, in and out of the station house, back and forth on the street. And Rhodrishi, at his shoulder. Rhodrishi had an incredible skill for going still and silent in moments like this, melting into the background so that he could listen without disturbing the flow of the conversation. "Is there a problem?"

"Not a problem exactly, sir. It's just that I wonder if there was some mistake in Stella Whiterock's Talent assessment, sir."

"What kind of mistake?"

"It seems to me that a rather large amount of our patients are healed under Miss Whiterock's care."

"Healed?" Tashué shook his head, trying to shake the foggy feeling. "Isn't that a good thing?"

"Oh, yes, of course it is!" the man said, nodding, removing his hat again. Around and around in his hands, flexing the brim. "At first I thought it was luck. Sometimes our patients aren't as sick as their families fear and so a little bit of time and tending and food is all they need to recover. Many of our patients come from poor families, you see. It's rare, though. Lately, there has been a steady increase in recoveries. When I noticed, I started keeping track. Miss Whiterock's patients are the ones that return to health most often."

"What's the problem with that, exactly? I'm still not sure I understand why that would involve me."

"The Facility is for people who are dying, and the tainted we employ aren't strong enough to be proper healers. If Miss Whiterock is strong enough to be a healer, she should be trained properly and transferred to a hospital, where she could truly be of help to people."

Tashué nodded slowly. He reached for his cigarillo case, offering one to the little man. Bayside bobbed his head in gratitude, taking a cigarillo and putting it between his lips. Tashué offered him a match and lit his own.

"Thank you, Mr. Bayside," Tashué said. "I'll see what should be done."

"Should I come inside, sir, and make a report?"

"No, no report is necessary here. Thank you again. I'll see to everything."

"Yes, sir. Thank you, sir."

With that, Bayside was away and Tashué watched him go, turning to look at Rhodrishi. He felt the desperate need to explain, to say something. But Rhodrishi wasn't standing alone anymore—Kazrani was with him.

"Stella Whiterock?" she asked. "She isn't who she says she is?"

"We don't know that yet," Tashué said, forcing a shrug. "It might be a coincidence."

Rhodrishi's face went so blank that he seemed to be a statue.

Kazrani only grunted in response. "If she's meant to be a healer, that's good. We can use all the healers we can get. Are you going to make a note in her file?"

"I'm sure it's all just a misunderstanding."

"Is it a misunderstanding or a coincidence?"

"Fucking hell, Kaz, would you just leave it?" Tashué snapped.

"She's my case. I'll handle it. Don't you have enough of your own cases to manage without telling me how to manage mine? I thought you had work to do!"

"I forgot to file my notes this morning!" Kazrani snapped back. She sucked a deep breath between her teeth, shaking her head. "I was right, wasn't I? You're sleeping with Whiterock. You don't have to hide it from me. Unless you're planning on treating her favourably just because you're bewitched by her and all her tender places, in which case you're a fucking idiot. She's tainted. If she's a healer, she should be assigned to a hospital. Hell, she could go to Wolfe's hospital and then she would have to leave Brickheart, if that's what you're worried about. But you need to deal with it, Captain. Do the right thing."

She stomped past Tashué, up the stairs, disappearing into the station house. Tashué was rooted in place, his stomach twisting. He thought he was going to do the right thing, and he couldn't imagine how painful it would be to tell Kazrani that they had very different ideas of what that 'right thing' was.

He pushed his trembling hands through his hair, burning with the shame of it all. What could he even say to the Colonel? Rhodrishi reached out slowly, taking Tashué by the arm and squeezing it.

"We should talk, Captain. You must have an office now?"

Tashué nodded. Turned. Headed up the stairs, his limbs feeling leaden and distant. Lian sensed his dark mood and let him through without any banter. The top floor was filled with bodies and he felt everyone's eyes on him—Kazrani's especially—as he stalked toward the office. His office. Khosran's name had been scraped off the door and a woman was painting Tashué's name on it instead. She stepped aside long enough for Tashué and Rhodrishi to slip past her.

"Do you need privacy, sir?" she asked. "I can work with the door closed as easily as open."

"Yes please. Thank you."

The woman bobbed her head, smiled. She walked backward as she closed the door, careful not to get paint on the wood. There was a box of stationary on the desk, heavy paper with his name printed at the top. *National Tainted Registration Authority House no. 15, Commander Tashué Blackwood.* There was a box of business cards there too, the same words printed in the centre, with the street address of the station house. He tried to imagine what he might need the business cards for, but his imagination failed him. Had he ever seen Khosran hand the things out? He hadn't paid much attention to Khosran, in retrospect.

There was one extra chair and Rhodrishi settled into it, looking down at the dried blood on his hands. Tashué sat across from him, the chair squeaking as he settled in it. The desk was too short, and his knees banged against the bottom of the drawer that stretched beneath the centre.

"You said you wanted to talk to me about retiring?" Tashué asked, scanning his desk. He had a letter to write, for Keoh. To ask about her children. He reached into his jacket and pulled out his notebook, flipping open to the page with their names so he wouldn't forget.

"Actually, I wanted to talk about Stella Whiterock, but I see you're doing your very best to pretend that didn't happen at all."

Tashué froze again, his mind whirling. He'd bled too much this morning for so much thinking.

"I don't judge you," Rhodrishi said. "Or her. I'm sure she does what needs doing. I, of all people, can sympathize with her desire to hide her true self from the Authority. It's not an organization built on pillars of compassion and understanding. I wasn't going to say anything about her, but the Lieutenant said you've taken up with her. You should know that she isn't what she seems."

"Is it possible that she hasn't quickened?" Tashué asked. "That her Talent is simply stronger than she knows?"

Rhodrishi sighed, long and slow. "My friend, would you like me to be honest, or would you like to continue living in self-delusion?"

Tashué sighed, his shoulders sagging. "Honest, of course. I would hope you are always honest with me."

"Then in all honesty, what you're asking is not possible. The healing skill is not a thing that someone stumbles on accidentally. Healers undergo years of training, especially for the healing of diseases and infections. It's a dangerous thing. An inexperienced healer risks taking on the disease themselves, or pulling the infection into their own blood. And of course, you've been healed before by Talent. You know the incredible pain involved. The body is overwhelmed by the speed of healing and both healer and patient know they are being stretched to their limits. Perhaps it wouldn't be noticeable for patients near death, but your Miss Whiterock would know exactly what's happening."

Tashué sighed, eyes scanning his desk again. A brand-new fountain pen was filled for him already and he opened it, but the nib had leaked, leaving a splatter of ink across his hands. He cursed, wiping his hands on the first piece of paper he'd pulled off the stack. He crumpled it up, his frustration making him tense through his whole body. Pulling another piece of paper off the pile, he started his note. He didn't know how to write the kind of long, eloquent correspondences that he'd seen Khosran write. What was the point?

Writing with the new fountain pen was harder than he would have liked to admit. He'd gotten used to sketching and writing notes with his charcoal pencil. At least he was used to writing left-handed and knew enough not to rest the side of his hand on the paper. He wrote the letter three times, on three separate pieces of paper, before he was satisfied. Its contents were sparse.

To whom it may concern,

I am seeking information on children registered with the Authority through the Breeding Program. Their names are as follows:

Lizanne Gian Ly

Petrik Gian Ly

Gwinnith Gian Ly

Benjin Gian Ly

Dex Gian Ly

Valen Gian Ly

Thank you for any assistance you may be able to provide.

"Gian Ly—that's Keoh's children?"

Tashué nodded as he sat back, waiting for the ink to dry. There was more ink on his fingers, somehow, more blots of black that had worked their way down into the creases of his skin. "She's in the

Breeding Program. She wants to know where her children have gone." He looked down at his hands, at the ink stains that dried on his skin. "What am I supposed to do with this information? That this woman... This woman that owns my very soul is lying to me?"

"No, not to you," Rhodrishi said swiftly, leaning forward. "The woman you know is as true as she knows how to be. She lies to the Authority, but not to you."

"How do you know all this?"

"I saw it in her, at the Market. I can feel the knot in the centre of her, the Talent that doesn't quite breathe to its full life. And another knot, at the end of a long rope, connected to her child."

"Ceridwen?" Tashué breathed. "Ceridwen has Talent?"

"I think so, yes."

"She's so young..."

"We are born with our Talents, Captain," Rhodrishi said softly. "It lives within us, like our ability to reproduce. Waiting for our bodies to know what to do with it. If we're lucky, that Talent waits until we're ready. Some aren't lucky and the Talent quickens when the body is too young." He shrugged, shaking his head. "I worry about the children of your Breeding Program. To be imbued with such incredible power, with no training, and to be *designed* to quicken sooner. Children are resilient, but Talent is a raw and dangerous thing. It wouldn't surprise me at all if the Authority struggled with high mortality of these children they create. I would be shocked if their mortality rates were anywhere below fifty percent."

Tashué sucked in a deep breath, looking down at the list again. Fifty percent? Could half of Keoh's children be dead? How would he even tell her?

Shaking off the dread, he folded the paper and slid it into an envelope, addressing it to House One. If anyone had paperwork on where the Breeding Program children had been placed, he hoped it was House One, the foundational home of the Authority. He hoped it wasn't in the Breeding Program itself. His brass badge wouldn't gain him access to those files.

"Talk to her," Rhodrishi said softly. "And listen to whatever she says. Really *listen*. I think what she says will be something you need to hear."

"Do you know, then? What she's done? Why?"

"No, I don't know. I only felt the edges of it, but there was too much else happening for me to think about it much. Talk to her, Captain."

"I will," Tashué promised. He felt his guts had been scooped out, leaving him hollow and echoing inside. Stella was lying? "You want me to file for your retirement, though?"

Rhodrishi nodded, sinking back in his chair again. "If you're not to be my Officer anymore, I'm finished. To get another Officer as understanding as you seems unlikely. It was good to travel the Dominion, but now it's time to stop."

"Time to go home?"

Something in Rhodrishi tightened for a moment, his mouth pulling in. "Home? Yaelsmuir should be my home. My great-grand-mother was born here, my ancestors were buried in the hill where the Imburleigh factory stands. I wonder how many of their bones were dug up when Imburleigh lay their foundations or built their walls. I wonder where the bones are now. I keep coming back here, drawn here by the history of my family, hoping one day to feel as if I belong. But every time I come, I am reminded that I'm not wanted. None of my people are wanted. We wash our hands in the blood of your civilization to heal you and protect you from your own destruction, and we are called *tainted*. Lieutenant Mahalouwan calls me friend and shakes my hand, and she says in my company that anyone with Talent is inherently dangerous and evil, and the laws here are just. As if, were it not for those laws, I would be cutting a bloody swathe through this very city." He shook his head. "The legacy territory is not my home, Captain. But at least there I can be with people who understand the gift that Talent is, instead of hiding from it."

Tashué opened his mouth to deny Rhodrishi's words, but he couldn't bring himself to say anything. Rhodrishi was right. Worse, Tashué had once believed the laws just. His mother had believed it and died anyway. His grandmother had believed that the laws were so powerful that it wasn't safe for her descendants to even be Pashibé. And here he was, sitting in this office, wearing his brand-new brass badge, serving the very organization that made her believe that denying her daughter the heritage of her people was the only safe way forward.

Why can I not see her? What is the harm?

Follow the laws and you'll be safe.

What harm indeed? Gianna, I'm sorry.

"When do you want your retirement effective?" Tashué asked, instead of arguing.

"I'll play the dancing jester for General Wolfe at his ceremony, but then I'm leaving and I don't think I'll be coming back to Yaelsmuir."

"I'll file the paperwork after you leave. That way no one tries to insist on escorting you back to the legacy territory."

Rhodrishi nodded and took a deep breath. Tashué had never seen the well of anger in the old healer before, but now he was pushing it back down again, gathering his composure around him like a costume. *How little I know this man, after everything he's done for me.* The healer had saved his life more than once, and Tashué was utterly devoted to him—but he didn't know him.

"I would visit you there one day," Tashué offered, trying to reach across the chasm that had opened suddenly between them. And he remembered what Stella said, about the Pashibé thinking it a victory to reclaim their people. Rhodrishi had said that his ancestors were from Yaelsmuir. Did that mean he was Pashibé, too? Tashué's gaze drifted down to Rhodrishi's hands, to the swirling tattoos, faded by the decades. Were Pashibé the only Kaadayri people that tattooed their hands? It occurred to Tashué that he didn't even know the etiquette for asking a Kaadayri what their nation was. His total ignorance filled him with shame. "If you'd have me."

Rhodrishi nodded. "I would enjoy that. Come when you've quickened, and I will teach you what it means to have Talent."

"Isn't it too late for me to quicken now? Hell, I'm past forty."

Rhodrishi smiled as he stood and reached across the desk for a handshake. "It's never too late. It's only waiting for *you* to be ready. You should go talk to Miss Whiterock. And then, when you've the time, you should come see Eddie. It will give your heart some peace, I think, to see him."

Tashué stood, accepting the shake. "I will."

Rhodrishi let himself out, pulling the door closed behind him. Tashué stood in his office, feeling as if the ground was shifting beneath his feet. How had his view changed so much? How had he been so wrong, for so long?

Once Rhodrishi was well gone, Tashué moved to the door, making eye contact with the woman on the other side of the glass. She smiled at him and stepped back, giving him enough room to pull the door open.

"I'm almost done here," she said.

"Thank you," Tashué said, pausing long enough to look at his name. Her work was careful and precise but he didn't feel anything but dread when he looked at it. Still, he forced a smile. She had an eagerness in her young face that made Tashué's chest ache. "It looks excellent."

She smiled, nodded. If she noticed his discomfort she showed no sign of it. He turned toward the lines and the typists. Old habit almost sent him to the back of the line, but he was the Commander now. He sidestepped the line, waiting for a typist to be free. Celia was available first and Tashué stepped in.

"I need a file, if you please Miss Weir."

"Yes sir. One of yours?"

"Yes. Whiterock, Stella."

Celia nodded and sent the runner. The child was away and back again swiftly, carrying Stella's paperwork. Tashué signed the log they kept when files were removed and headed down the stairs. Lian stood vigil at his desk.

"Lian, how long have you been our doorman?"

"How long? Um... A few months maybe? Six?"

"More than that, I think," Tashué said. "There was still snow on the ground when you started."

"That's true! But we had a miserably long winter last year."

Tashué nodded. "I would like you to apply to be a Regulation Officer, Lian. I'll request that you're placed here. You would be a good addition, I think."

"Yes, sir!" Lian breathed. "Thank you, sir!"

Tashué lay the letter on the counter in front of Lian. "In the meantime, send a runner with this to House One."

He dropped a copper crown for a tip for the runner and it occurred to him that the wages of all the runners were his responsibility now. And the typists. And the Officers and the desk clerks and the guards. All of whom depended on him to see that they were paid what was owed to them in a timely manner once monthly.

Instead of leaving, Tashué headed down into the cellar. The gas lamps down there gave everything an eerie glow, an antiquated way of making light with the power of the Talented usually responsible for so much. With the thick layer of suppression across the station house, it wasn't possible for brights to keep the station house lit.

Turning, he headed further down the hall, to the door that led to the cellar. It was locked, but one of his new keys opened it. A narrow staircase led down, with steep steps cut of uneven stone, and only a small storeroom at the bottom. Boxes and boxes of paper were stacked against one wall, and ribbons of ink, and even a few spare typewriters. It seemed little more than a hallway, and at the end another door. He could feel the power of the Talented person inside. His own Talent was suppressed in this place, and here the sensation was strongest. It was like a vice, crushing his skull, grinding against bone, ugly and vicious and hateful.

He sorted through his keys. As he tried one after another in the lock, he found himself wondering why it had never occurred to him to wonder who was responsible for the layer of suppression across this building, across every station house in Yaelsmuir, across the Rift, across the Breeding Program. What Talent it must have been to achieve such a thing, to cut everyone inside away from their own Talents. People as powerful as Jason, as powerful as Keoh. What manner of Talent made such a thing even possible?

One by one, he tried every key. One by one, they failed to open the lock.

Tashué cursed under his breath. He didn't like being turned away by something as simple as a lock, and the suspicion that burned in him was an ugly, vengeful thing. Why was the Talent responsible for their safety locked away where no one could lay eyes on them?

39

STELLA

DAY 19

There was so little in Stella's apartment that she needed to take with her. She felt no connection to any of these things; each piece of furniture felt distant, like it belonged to someone else. Set pieces in the play that had become her life. *No, sir, I'm not a fugitive from the Authority, I'm just a regular working woman. See? I patched that hole in the chair myself.*

But what would Ceridwen need? She was older now, had more opinions about the world. The last time Stella fled a city with her, she wanted to bring only her favourite quilt and the small rag doll she slept with. She had a favourite teacup now, the one with the flowers painted on it, the one with the broken handle. The broken handle made it worthless, but the memory of the neighbour boy, Gill, giving it to her made it invaluable. Gill had blushed when Ceridwen kissed him on the cheek. If she was leaving that boy and his ruddy, freckled cheeks behind, would Ceridwen want to bring his teacup with her? Stella would have to be prepared to make some sacrifices, to take some things that were unnecessary. Ceridwen wouldn't want to go, so perhaps if Stella let her bring as much as she could, the going would be easier.

Easier? Tears sprung to her eyes as she imagined Tashué Blackwood, left behind. Would she tell him that she was going? *You're leaving me?* she imagined him asking. What would she say to him? Did she really have that much strength, to look him in the eye and walk away from him, when the smell, sound, and taste of him were the only things keeping her chained to the world instead of drifting away?

"Can I make molasses cookies today, Mam?"

Stella sucked down the emotion, turning to Ceridwen. She stirred oats into the pot on the stove, making their morning porridge.

Not the only thing, she reminded herself. *You made a promise to her. You have to protect her.*

Would Tashué Blackwood want to protect Ceridwen too, if he knew?

"You have your laundry today, Pigeon. And you're late already as it is."

"It was nice, spending the night at Mr. Blackwood's home. His son had a lot of toys. Do you think he misses his toys? Where is he?"

"I'm not sure, Pigeon." Lying didn't sit well with her, but Ceridwen didn't need to know that Jason Blackwood was in the Rift. "Perhaps he's all grown up now, living his own life."

"If Mr. Blackwood's son is grown up, does that mean Mr. Black-wood is going to be a grandad soon?"

"Perhaps." Stella turned to the counter, finding the canister of tea she kept on the top shelf. She pulled the lid off, the earthy smell of the strong Derccian tea wafting up to her face. She shifted the canister, peering inside. The small coin purse was still in there. She reached in, catching the drawstring and pulling the purse out. It was heavy in her hand, but not nearly as heavy as she would have liked. How many gold crowns did she have left? "That's up to Mr. Blackwood's son, isn't it? If he wants to have a wife and children."

"I suppose. Did you want tea, Mam? I'll put on the kettle."

Stella stuffed the coin purse down the front of her bodice. "No, I was just checking to see how much I have left."

"You hardly ever drink the Derccian tea. Must be lots left."

"You're right. Perhaps I'll give it to Mrs. Abernathy. She likes Derccian tea, doesn't she?"

"She likes the Kiatze tea better, I think."

Stella nodded, pushing the lid back on and returning the canister to the shelf. She'd have to go into Drystone at least to find a money changer willing to change gold for silver and copper. No one in Brickheart had gold coins, and if they did, it would become gossip as vicious as wildfire. But then, she didn't own clothes nice enough to be unnoticed in Drystone, and if someone thought she was a maid who had stolen gold from her employer, they'd send the Patrollers after her. The Market Quarter, perhaps. There was so much happening there already that no one would have much time to think about her. So long as no one there recognized her.

She forced herself to eat even though the porridge tasted of ash in her mouth and sat like a stone in her belly. She'd been in Yaelsmuir four years... Did Ceridwen even remember the last time they had moved? She remembered Miss Zee and her buffalo grass vodka. Did she remember their first home away from Cruinnich, a tiny house outside Gladwydd, on the angry western coast? Stella had liked that house, that first place that sheltered them. She liked that it was never quiet there, but neither could she hear people over the roar of the ocean crashing on the rocks in the bay.

"Do you love Mr. Blackwood, Mam?"

The question hit Stella like an ocean wave and she squeezed her eyes shut. "I don't know."

"Is he to be my da now?"

"I don't know, Pigeon." Stella turned to Ceridwen, offering a smile. "Truly I don't."

"I'd like to have a da as well as a mam one day," Ceridwen said, kicking her feet back and forth. The toes of her boots scuffed the floorboards as she kicked. Her eyes were on the porridge pot as if she wished there was another helping in there, but it was empty. "But if I can't have a da, I suppose it's a good thing that I have a very good mam."

"Oh, Ceridwen. You are sweeter even than I deserve."

Ceridwen washed their bowls before gathering up her laundry

bag and her lye soap, skipping out the door. Stella moved into her bedroom, taking stock of what clothes she had. She had three uniforms for the Facility, and two outfits for regular days, one of which she was already wearing. She had good, sturdy winter clothes, at least, cloaks and shawls and heavy blankets to keep the chill at bay. Perhaps it was because she was always so tired, but she didn't seem to have a tolerance for the cold anymore.

She dragged open her old trunk, shuffling through the extra blankets she kept. She had found a barge willing to take her from the Bay to White Crown. Once she got there, she could transfer to another barge, going down Skael Canyon to Dür, or Lida, or up the White River to Teshii. She'd always wanted to see the city built into the mountain, homes and businesses carved into the red granite. She pulled some of the blankets out, the older ones that needed darning and patching, making room for her spare clothes. For Ceridwen's clothes. It would be better if they could fit everything into one trunk. Cheaper, easier to transport. She'd keep the books she'd bought for Ceridwen, perhaps. Travelling by barge would be a good opportunity to help her sharpen her reading skills. Travelling in winter would be hard, but it was better than the Authority catching up to them. She dug to the bottom of the trunk, finding the forged transfer paperwork she'd bought, so many years ago, back in Cruinnich. She'd known she would have to run for a long time, so she bought a few blank transfer forms, to fill in as she needed. This was her last. What would she do next? Ceridwen was getting older. They would have to find somewhere better to hide this time. Maybe not Teshii, then. Maybe it was time to leave Dominion holdings completely. But where, sweet North Star, where?

A knock at her door startled her. She cursed, pushing the paperwork down to the bottom of the trunk and smoothing out the blankets over them. She knew that knock by now, so firm and sure. She pushed the lid closed and took a deep breath, trying to calm the way her hands trembled.

Tashué Blackwood had come. Of course he had. They were tied together now, a rope between them that kept them both alive when the world tried so desperately to smother them in grief. She had anchored that rope herself, inadvertently. Secured it in place when she brushed against his Talent and let him feel hers. He looked a terrible mess, fresh stitches in the side of his face, one side of his clothes crusted with dried blood. Even still, her heart beat faster still as she set eyes on him, the memory of his body pressed against her coming fast to her mind.

She thought she saw fear in his eyes, though. Surely she was mistaken, her own fear making her see something that wasn't there. He smiled at her, but it was tight. Did he know what she was planning? Was it possible that she had accidentally connected them *that* much?

"Do you have some time, Stella? I need to speak with you."

"Yes," Stella breathed. She cleared her throat. "Of course. Please come inside. What happened to your face?"

"Someone hit me with a pint glass this morning."

Stella closed the door behind him, her mind whirling. How long had it been since she walked out of his apartment after their night together? Only a few hours, at the most. Her time in Yaelsmuir had blurred together into such a formless blob of time that stretched out behind her, but now things were changing so *quickly*. Would that she could slow it down, just a little, enough that her weary mind could keep up. "Why was someone inclined to hit you with a pint glass?"

Tashué sighed. "It was an interesting morning."

The door burst open again, Ceridwen almost hitting them both with it as she came hurtling through. "Mam, I don't have any lunch! What are we having for lunch today? Oh, hullo Mr. Blackwood! It's nice to see you again already. Are you here for lunch, too?"

Tashué glanced at Ceridwen, hesitating before he spoke. He reached for his cigarillo case, taking one out, but he turned it between his fingers rather than putting it between his lips. "I come on Authority business, Stella."

Stella nodded, finding a few coins in her pocket. "Here, Pigeon. I haven't planned anything for lunch, so go to the bakery and buy a loaf of bread and maybe some sausage rolls."

"This is more than I need for a loaf and some rolls, Mam."

"Get something sweet as well. Ceridwen, only as far as Miss Muir's. No further."

"Yes, Mam!"

With that, Ceridwen was away again and Stella could hear her shoes clicking all the way down the stairs. Only when she was out onto the street did Stella close the door behind her and turn to Tashué. He had lit his cigarillo finally and offered it to Stella. She took a lungful of smoke. It still made her dizzy when she smoked tobacco since she didn't smoke very much, and the lightness that took over her head seemed a welcome relief from the ball of stress.

"Tarren Bayside came to see me this morning," Tashué said slowly. "He was concerned."

"Concerned?" Stella asked, even though it felt like she was choking on the word. Had her heart stopped beating entirely? She offered the cigarillo back to Tashué. Suddenly she was plenty dizzy on her own and didn't need the tobacco's help.

Tashué took the cigarillo, pausing long enough to take a long breath of smoke. "It seems a large number of your patients are getting better under your care. While Bayside agrees that this is good news, he wondered if a mistake had been made in your assessment."

Stella pinched her own thigh to make herself breathe.

"This doesn't seem to come as a surprise to you."

"Mr. Blackwood…"

"Tashué," he interrupted. "Please, call me Tashué. I would hope we're close enough now that we can drop the formalities."

Meeting those amber eyes made Stella weak. "I am not a healer, Tashué. I'm a whisperer. I help separate people from their pain so they can die in peace."

"I truly wanted to believe that, Stella. I did. But I remember that man, up in the Market. He saw you heal, didn't he? He wasn't mistaken. And then your supervisor comes to me with this and I put to you what little I know… I hope you're not a gambler, because your face gives you away." He edged closer, reaching out with his free hand. His fingers brushed her wrist, so gentle, asking permission to take her hand. Stella still couldn't breathe as she looked down at his hand. Moments ago, she would have loved the feeling of his hands on her skin, but suddenly he wasn't the man she was falling in love with anymore—he was Authority. All the things she feared, all the things she hated. A tin badge turned brass, the living muscle of the law that kept people like her under fierce control. "In all my years, I haven't heard of someone being wrongly assessed by the Authority. Colonel Kheir confirmed how it's quite difficult to heal another person. It takes a great deal of concentration and ability."

Stella's whole body trembled. She felt sick, her stomach clenching, threatening to purge itself of her breakfast. She was still looking at his hands, at the ink stains and stitches. They were so big, those hands of his. Never once had his hands caused her pain and yet she was afraid of them suddenly. Faced with her silence, he reached into the breast pocket of his overcoat, retrieving a rolled bundle of paperwork.

"This is your paperwork, Stella Whiterock." He lay the bundle on the table and flipped through the papers as if he needed to prove to them both that they were real, his fingers running over the long-dry ink. "Registered as tainted with weak Talent, trained with pain management for end-of-life care. But now I know this can't be true. So how did you come by this paperwork if you're a healer? Are they fake?"

It was a hard thing to meet those eyes and think. It was only vague comfort that his eyes were amber and not blue. But the colour of his eyes didn't matter anymore. He was still Authority. She forced herself to hold his gaze. "Will you arrest me, Commander Blackwood? Will you send me to the Rift for my crimes?"

Tashué flinched. He reached for her, catching her hand. Maybe it was meant to be affectionate, the way he squeezed her fingers. But it only served as another reminder of his incredible strength. "Please, Stella, if you'd just tell me what's going on, I'll help any way I can."

The door swung open then and Ceridwen came crashing in. She pushed the door shut behind her, her cheeks rosy and her breath coming out in heavy gasps. She dumped her spoils proudly on the table, turning and smiling at Stella and Tashué both.

"I got a rye loaf," she said. She lifted her second bundle onto the table more gingerly, folding back the muslin wrapper. "And six sausage rolls. And there was enough to buy a little pie for all of us. It has pears and cranberries and cinnamon!"

"That sounds lovely, little warrior," Tashué said. "Shall we have some right away?"

"I'm supposed to be doing laundry today, and I'm very late now because we stayed at your house and I had to go get lunch." She said all the right things, but she swung her eyes to Stella, eager and pleading.

Stella sighed, but nodded. Ceridwen opened the oven, gathering up the pie to slide it inside. She preferred it warm. Stella moved away, to the window. She was still trembling, still fighting to breathe. She needed to start taking deeper breaths or she was going to faint. Tashué came to her, standing behind her. He put a hand on her shoulder. She held her breath, keeping her whole body as still as she could. So she wouldn't flinch away from his touch. Some echo of old pain asked her what he might do if she stepped away from him now. He leaned down and kissed the side of her head, pushing his face into her hair like he had the night before, but this time it brought tears to her eyes. She was dizzy, still holding her breath.

"Whatever it is," he said, his voice pitched low and only for her, "I hope that you'll let me help."

Stella let the breath go slowly, emptying her chest. Stared out the window. She folded her arms over her chest, clenching her hands into fists, her nails digging into her palm. The sharpness grounded her, tearing through the fog of emotions that threatened to overwhelm her. If she looked at Tashué she would crumble completely.

Tashué leaned in and planted another kiss, this time in the hollow just behind her ear. He wouldn't hurt her, would he? He'd fought with himself so much before, about whether or not he could touch her. A man like that wouldn't turn on her now if she asked for the distance to return between them. Would he? She didn't know. Not really. And he was so tall and so strong. Just like Bothain.

Tashué stepped away as Ceridwen opened the oven and retrieved the pie, leaving Stella at the window. Stella listened for a while as Tashué carved slices out of the pie and they sat down to eat.

"Mam, are you going to have some?"

Stella didn't dare speak, feeling the sobs still clogged in her throat. If she opened her mouth, they would come bubbling out.

"I don't think your mam is feeling hungry right now," Tashué said and his voice was so gentle, a caress she could feel across the room. She felt like she was being torn in half, between her desire to trust him and her fear that he was just like Bothain. He wore that damned badge, after all. "We'll set aside a piece for her and she can have it when she's ready."

"Is she alright?" Ceridwen asked, trying to pitch her voice low, but her whisper was a loud thing indeed.

"I hope she'll feel better with time. Look, after she has her piece, we'll each have another piece later."

"Are you staying for the whole day?"

"I don't know, little warrior."

Stella finally swallowed her knot of emotion, wrestling herself back under control. There was a time before when she would use her own Talent on herself, cutting away the threads that connected her to the various pains that ached in her heart. It was tempting to do the same again now. But when she turned back to the table and looked at Tashué, she couldn't bear the thought of drifting away anymore. Fear was better than emptiness.

"If you're finished eating, you've work to do, Ceridwen Whiterock."

Ceridwen gave a sigh before she stood, casting one last longing look at the other half of the pie. But she stood anyway and gathered up their plates, bringing them to the wash basin. She glanced at the basin and the soap as if she wondered if she could get away with staying if she offered to do the dishes.

"Bring your sausage rolls down with you, so you don't need to come up again," Stella said. "You're already very late."

"Yes, Mam."

She stopped beside Tashué, her whole little body vibrating with energy. She threw her arms around his neck. He hugged her back, the motion so natural and comfortable. Ceridwen pressed her cheek against his beard, but then she wrinkled her nose and leaned away again.

"You smell like old beer."

"I know, little warrior," Tashué chuckled. "I would change my clothes, but I'm afraid this was my last clean suit."

"I could wash it for you, with the rest of the laundry!"

"That's kind, Ceridwen, but what would I wear in the meantime?"

Ceridwen laughed. "You'll have to buy more clothes, then!"

He turned to watch her go as she skipped toward the door, and Stella's whole body went rigid when she spotted the dark marks that were supposed to be hidden by her hair and her high collar. Tashué stared at the same spot. It seemed to take too long, even though it was only eight steps for Ceridwen to leave the table and reach the door, another moment to turn the handle and drag it open. The moments were immeasurably long, stretching before Stella like the entirety of her life, just Ceridwen's bouncing hair and those harsh black lines that Stella had been trying to hide for nine long years.

Stella closed the distance between them, reaching for him. Sliding her fingers into his beard, through his hair, anything to get his attention away from Ceridwen, but it was too late. He turned his face up to her, his chest expanding slowly as he took a long, deep breath. She could see his heartbeat again, the way it pounded at his throat. The last time his heart pounded like that, he was inside her, their bodies filled with heat and pleasure.

"Tashué," she breathed, because she couldn't think of anything else to say.

"That's why you're running, isn't it?" he asked. His voice was soft, but she felt the force of it echoing in her bones. He put his hands on her hips, so gentle, but those eyes were locked on her. There would be no lying now. "It has nothing to do with you, or your Talent, whether you're a healer or not. *You* aren't the one running. You're running *with* her."

Tears sprang to Stella's eyes and she cursed them for making her look weak now when she needed to look strong.

"I thought it was a birthmark last night, when I saw it," he continued. "But it isn't a birthmark, is it? It's a tattoo."

Even though Stella had known the words were coming, her heart seized, stopping so completely that her chest ached, that she thought she would faint. She sucked in a deep breath, forcing the air through a throat that felt too tight. There were so many tears in her eyes that she couldn't see him clearly anymore. She tried to blink them away but more came. She was going to dissolve into a sobbing mess if she couldn't get a hold of herself. Nine years, she'd been hiding that tattoo.

She took a step back from him, and then another. She needed some distance, away from the heat of his body and the strength of his hands. There was no more hiding and lying. She had to lay her truth at his feet and hope—pray—that he was as gentle and kind and compassionate as she had thought, before. Hope and pray that he wasn't anything like Bothain.

She tried to remember the woman she used to be, to find the last shred of heat that Ffyanwy was so known for.

"I asked you a question before and you didn't answer me." She was proud that her voice didn't tremble. *Yes, this is who you are!* "I want an answer. Will you arrest me, *Commander?* Will you process me as non-compliant and send me away to the Rift? What becomes of my daughter, if I'm to go to the Rift? All I wanted was to protect her."

"Stella…" Tashué's shoulders sagged and he seemed to melt a bit. "Do you think so little of me, that I would do that to you?"

"Then why Gianna Tarbrook and not me?" Stella pressed. "Because I lifted my skirts for you? Is your loyalty so easily bought?"

Shock and pain flashed across his face in equal measures, as visceral as if she'd slapped him. He shook his head, reaching for his cigarillo case. She watched him go through his ritual of lighting a cigarillo, blowing the first lungful of smoke out his nose. She didn't dare look away from him, didn't dare give ground. If she retreated now, she'd lose all her courage.

"You think you're the first beautiful woman to lift her skirt for me?" he asked, his voice hissing through his snarl. "I'm not so weak-minded that you letting me get my prick wet is enough to 'buy my loyalty.'"

Heat crawled up Stella's neck, into her face. Heat that could be anger or grief or more fear or all of them at once. "Oh yes, of course, how foolish of me. Illea Winter beat me to your 'loyalty,' didn't she?"

"Illea…" He bit off whatever he meant to say, shaking his head. He looked away first, out the window. He smoked fast, blowing the clouds out through his nose again. She'd never seen him smoke quite like that. He always had so much energy, of course, but she'd never seen him quite like *this*, so angry and so deflated at the same time. His whole body was jangly and moving, the tension coiling, tight, forcing him to his feet, towering and expanding, a great mass of a man with broad shoulders and big hands that he pressed against the table as if he were trying to anchor himself there. "Sleeping with Illea had nothing to do with 'loyalty.'"

"Is that supposed to be comforting? That you have the ability to sleep with a woman and feel no loyalty to her?"

Tashué sighed. His shoulders sagged. His big hands came off the table, but he turned his palms to her, like he was offering her something, or showing her how empty they were. Just ink stains and stitches and scabs. "What would you like me to say, then? You're right. I slept with Illea and I feel no loyalty to her at all. We took what we needed from each other and that was the end of it. But you?" He ran his hands over his face. "I would do anything for you. Tell me what you need me to do, Stella. Tell me how I can help, and I'll do it."

"What I need is for you to tell me why," Stella breathed. "Why help me, and process Gianna? Her crime was smaller than mine."

He shook his head and deflated, sinking back down into the chair. "I shouldn't have participated in processing Gianna. It was wrong and I should have refused. I went anyway because I was following an order, following the law, but I know better. Some orders—some laws—aren't worth the paper they're written on, or the men and women who have to pay the price for them. I know better, but I did it anyway because…" Another sigh, which he hid with a drag from his cigarillo. His hand went to his jacket, unpinning the ugly brass badge. He looked at it for a while, the new polished brass shining like gold. "I did it because I thought I owed some loyalty to this." He threw it onto the floor between them—it was heavier than she thought, landing with a thump. "The Authority bought my loyalty nineteen years ago with two ounces of tin. And it's taken me this fucking long to realize it was a bad bargain."

His hands shook as he took a few long drags from his cigarillo, and Stella realized he wasn't angry—he was terribly sad, as if the weight of those words were crushing him, breaking off shards of the man he thought he was and grinding those shards right through the centre of him.

"Please, Stella, will you tell me what you're running from now?" he asked. He had returned that hot gaze to Stella's face, searching her again. "It must be something to do with the tattoo on Ceridwen's neck?" He perched the cigarillo between his lips to reach into the pocket of his jacket. He withdrew the notepad he carried and flipped through the pages until he found the numbers. He turned the notebook to her, eyes pleading. "Is it similar to this? The tattoo on that girl from the river?"

Stella didn't need to look at the numbers again, didn't need the reminder of the child Tashué had found.

"It's a registration number," Stella said. She looked down at her feet, at the badge on the floor. The Authority insignia and Tashué's badge number. "The first number is her mother, the second her father, the third, hers. To keep track, I suppose. To judge the success and failures of their various experiments. To monitor the results of the Breeding Program."

"Ceridwen is from the Breeding Program?" He sat up straighter then, his eyes going wide. "Is that why you've run? You were in the Breeding Program and you've escaped?"

"No, not that. Thank the North Star, never that." Stella shuddered at the thought, at being locked away, being forced to submit to men she didn't know whose only qualification was that they had strong Talents.

"But if Ceridwen..." The dawning came swiftly over his face and he leaned closer. "Ceridwen isn't your child?"

The words took Stella by surprise, cutting through what strength she had gathered about herself. Tears welled in her eyes again, fell to her cheeks before she could stop them. She'd never heard the words said out loud before, because she had never been close enough to another person to reveal her secret. Lifting her hands to wipe her face, she realized they were shaking now too, her whole body trembling from the inside out. Tashué reached for her, but he hesitated, only touching her wrist with the very tips of his fingers.

"She's as much mine as if I'd carried her myself," Stella gasped, her throat feeling strangled and tight. It needed to be said.

"Of course." Tashué's voice, quiet and gentle. It was so terribly tempting to trust him completely. "Of course she is. Parenthood is not quantified by blood relation, but by love. And I know you love her as if she was a piece of your own heart."

Stella nodded but couldn't speak anymore. She turned away, to the window, pressing a hand against the glass again, wishing that the chill of it would flow through her and cool the hot edges of all this emotion. She'd been numb for so long that she didn't know how to deal with the sharpness of pain like this, of things she thought she had healed from. How foolish of her to think wounds like these could have healed. Not in a decade, not in a lifetime. She folded a hand over her mouth, trying to hold in the sobs, but there was no holding them back. They ripped her open.

Leave it be, Ffyanwy, said Bothain, springing as vividly from her memory as if he were standing beside her again, when she stood in his office, horrified at what he had done in the name of the Authority. *This is the way things are done.*

And Siras Duncreek, sneering at her in her own home, eyes laughing at her, and when she didn't *leave it be,* Bothain's hand clamped around her arm, giving a squeeze. A reminder. A threat.

She felt the movement around her, the presence of a body

coming at her, and when she opened her eyes, all she saw was a hand, coming toward her face.

She flinched. Ducked her head and stepped away and squeezed her eyes shut.

"Stella…"

She took a deep breath. Yes, Stella, and not Ffyanwy. She'd left Ffyanwy and Bothain behind years ago. She opened her eyes and saw Tashué, amber eyes instead of blue.

"Are you afraid of me now?" Tashué Blackwood asked, his voice so thick and heavy with grief that it made Stella ache. "I would never hurt you."

Stella leaned forward and pressed her face into his shoulder. He smelled of stale beer and blood, of tobacco smoke and sweat, of shaving oil and wool. He wrapped his arms around her, slowly, a hand rubbing her back, the other pushing into her hair. He rested his cheek on the top of her head and breathed deep and slow, quiet and calm as Stella trembled and sobbed. He waited, holding her in his stillness until the sobs ran out and her well of old grief started to run dry.

"How did you… Did you steal her from the Breeding Program? How did you ever manage such a thing…?"

"No, it wasn't me," Stella said. She pulled away from his chest. She wiped her eyes, trying to catch her breath, but the outpouring of emotion left her even more exhausted than before, if such a thing was even possible. "It was the Army of the Red Dawn. They took her from the Authority. I took her from them."

Tashué took another slow breath, looking down at Stella. His hands were still gentle as he held her, but she could almost see his mind working, grinding, trying to put all the pieces together, perhaps trying to figure out how it related to his girl from the river.

"I couldn't let them kill her," Stella said into the silence between them, because she couldn't bear it another moment. It seemed a terribly unnatural thing for Tashué Blackwood to be silent. "She was so wee, with little red curls… She was such a beautiful babe, my sweet Ceridwen."

"Who was going to kill her?"

"The Army of the Red Dawn."

"Why would they kill a child? An infant?"

Stella sighed, closing her eyes. There were so many memories to sift through. How much did she dare say?

"They knew about the Breeding Program, up in Cruinnich. They wanted to draw people's attention to what was happening. The Red Dawn had all these plans—all these terrible plans. There was a point that I believed in them and the things that they wanted. It's terrible, the things that the Authority have done. The things they continue to do." She searched Tashué's face, wondering if she would see the same empathy still or if he would be frustrated by her accusations, tentative as they were. He looked down at her, waiting for more. He was so eager, his eyes so bright, almost feverish. "The Red Dawn had so many ideas about what they might do to make people see how evil it all was. That all of us, by using the powers of the tainted and not asking questions or demanding better treatment for them, were complicit in the evil. They wanted people to be shocked and dismayed, to rise in the streets and change the world."

It was all so long ago, a different lifetime entirely. She was a different woman then. Ffyanwy hadn't known the meaning of being tired, hadn't known the way fear could gnaw at a person's insides and slowly diminish them until they were nothing but a dry, brittle husk of a human.

Ffyanwy knew plenty about pain, though. Knew pain in spades.

"Davik sounded like a hero," Stella continued. "He was going to start a revolution. Davik Kaine, liberator of the Talented. And I wanted to be a part of it, to be right there with them, to take part in fighting on the side of history and righteousness. And then I saw Ceridwen. I couldn't see how killing a child could possibly be the actions of a hero. Heroes don't murder children and leave them in the ditches for others to find so that *others* will rise in revolt. Heroes lead the revolts themselves on the merit of their words and their ideas and their strength, without the need to murder infants."

Another long, terrible pause as Tashué seemed to churn over the onslaught of words. He stepped back from Stella, and she could see the agitation crawling through him, the way his body moved in sharp gestures, the way his hands didn't seem to know where to be. His heel hit his badge and he turned, kicking out and sent it skittering across the floor until it hit the front door. His hands went up into his hair and then down into his pockets, pulling out his cigarillo case. He opened it, then flicked it closed, open again, closed. Pressed it between both hands, as if he wanted to still himself but couldn't quite manage. He turned to Stella, taking another deep breath.

"You were a member of the Red Dawn?" he asked finally.

"Yes. For a year or so, until they stole Ceridwen. Eight years ago. Almost nine. It was winter when I took her. It's so cold in Cruinnich, so miserably cold. I couldn't bear the thought of her out on the street in the snow, her little red curls clotted with ice."

"She's nine this year?"

Stella nodded. "Almost ten, I think."

Tashué opened his cigarillo case finally, putting another between his lips, but he didn't light it yet. The smell of the tobacco was rich and comforting. Would there ever come a time in her life when she would smell tobacco and not think of Tashué?

"I've never seen a Talented person with such a tattoo on their necks."

"They don't mark the tainted that you see."

He shook his head at her, like he was fighting with her words still. "What does that mean?"

"The tainted that receive their tattoos come directly from the Breeding Program," Stella said. "They are never meant to be seen by regular people, because they were never meant to be considered human. They are objects, sources of power, like draft horses or lumps of coal."

Stella could see the realization come to his eyes. It was slow at first, but it gathered energy and heat and force and soon his whole body seemed to be burning with rage and fury and barely-contained energy.

"They run the tram, don't they?" he said. "They run the tram and that's why the lead car is covered and locked and not a single window. They create these children with the purest Talent they can refine, and then lock them away from view."

Stella nodded. "And the foundry fires and the intercontinental vessels and sometimes even the mines. When I lived in Cruinnich, they were experimenting with using the bred tainted in the gold mines. They thought the tainted could focus in on the gold veins and dig them out bit by bit. I'm not sure how the experiments went but I can't imagine they would go back to using *regular* and *well-bred* humans when they could let the tainted die in the mines instead."

Tashué finally went for his matches, lighting his cigarillo and sheathing himself in a cloud of smoke. He smoked for a while before he answered as if the smoke could sift through his thoughts and help to clarify them.

"Ceridwen still has her arms and legs, though."

"Yes," Stella said slowly. "She does. So do I. So do you."

"The girl in the river and the boy beneath the bridge had their arms and legs removed."

"Who's the boy beneath the bridge?"

"Allie Tei from the *Highview Times* was involved in finding another body, with arms and legs missing and a tattoo on the back of the neck. Is it the Red Dawn taking off the arms and legs? Are they doing it to make the whole ugly thing more shocking?"

"No, I don't think so." Stella shook her head, folding her arms over her chest. "I don't know. The people here won't be the same as the ones I knew in Cruinnich. Nine years is a long time."

Tashué took a deep breath, stalking to the window and looking down into the courtyard. Stella followed his gaze down to Ceridwen, with her washing tub, the neighbour boy helping her. They laughed and splashed water at each other. And Stella's heart broke for the pain coming to Ceridwen when Stella told her they were leaving.

"I spoke to a woman who said she had used her Talent to see the children she had borne to the Authority," Tashué said. "She saw them amputate their limbs."

Stella looked up at him, studying his face, the way his jaw worked like he was chewing on something in his mouth, but there was nothing. Chewing on his own stress, perhaps. "A woman from the Breeding Program?"

Tashué nodded at that, picking a shred of tobacco off his tongue and flicking it away. "So the Authority is breeding children to have immense Talent and mutilating them for some reason... And the Army of the Red Dawn is killing those same children to make people ask questions about where the children are coming from," he said. "If that's true, it isn't working very well."

"What do you mean?"

His eyes shifted back to Stella. "A child was found beneath a bridge and in the river, but the only people in all of Yaelsmuir that seem to be looking for answers are myself and Allie Tei." He took out his notepad again but didn't open it. "Two dead children, and their only hope of justice is a reporter for a social paper and a Regulation Officer for the Authority. A Commander of a house now, perhaps... It still isn't much."

"Will you tell her what I told you?" Stella asked, her voice caught in her throat.

"I'll tell her some of it," Tashué admitted. "But not all. I won't tell her who you are, if that's what you're asking."

Stella let out a slow breath, trying to let herself relax.

"You're running from the Army of the Red Dawn, then?" Tashué asked, leaning forward again. "Because you stole Ceridwen from them?"

Stella nodded.

"And you think they're killing the children, don't you?" Tashué went on. "You thought that the moment I told you what I'd found, but you didn't dare say anything then because you didn't know if you could trust me to guard your secrets. Why would you trust me? I'm a Regulation Officer and you are tainted and carrying fake registration papers."

Stella nodded again. She felt the emotion boiling up, threatening to send her crumbling into a fresh fit of sobs. Tears came even though she fought them, clouding her vision as she looked up at him again. "I don't even know if I can trust you now, Commander Blackwood. How many people have you processed to the Rift? For crimes like fraternization. For non-compliance. For refusing to register."

That pain again, across his face. Tashué shook his head, reaching for her, but clenched his hands into fists. "Stella, please, what do you need me to do to prove to you that I can't... I can't possibly do any of that, not to you. Not to anyone, ever again."

"Then why did you do it for nineteen years?"

"I needed a way out of the military after Jason was born," Tashué said, shaking his head. "I needed a way to come home to him. So I bought the lies they told me about keeping people safe, about serving the Dominion with a badge instead of a uniform. I bought every word because I needed it so badly. Because..." He spread his hands again. "I needed to come home to my son. You understand that, don't you? You know what it's like to look into the face of a child and know that their whole life has fallen on your shoulders. To know you would do anything for them."

Stella shook her head, anger rising fast and unexpected. "No, don't compare what I did for Ceridwen to you taking the tin. I took Ceridwen and ran from people that would have killed her. I only endangered myself. Perhaps you took the tin for your son, and perhaps you couldn't see any better options at the time—but you sold a piece of your soul to the Authority for the benefit of your family. The Authority! The very organization that made your grand-mother so fearful of the world she lived in that she turned her back on her culture and her heritage to protect her child! And by wearing that badge for nearly two decades, you looked back at her ghost and told her she was right to fear. That she was tainted, too. And worse than that, you let her great grandson go to the Rift for the crime of being braver than his father and taking a stand against the Author-ity, refusing to submit to their vicious laws."

That pain again, still, pain that was beautiful and infuriating at once. He reached up, his hands closing over his chest, grabbing a fistful of his own clothes like he was going to start tearing the cloth from his body. Like it was strangling him. He wasn't looking at her anymore, but past her.

"What do you want me to say, Stella?" His gaze came back to her. "You're right. Every choice I've made has been wrong. But I didn't know. How was I supposed to know? My mother told me all my life *follow the laws and you'll be safe*. How was I supposed to know that she was wrong? How was I supposed to know that the entire fucking country is built on lies? How was I supposed to know that my son would be the one who had to pay for my mistakes? You think I wouldn't change it all if I could? You think I wouldn't trade places with Jason in the blink of an eye?"

"So what do you do next, then?" Stella asked, stepping closer. "Do you resign your badge, Commander?"

He groaned, his shoulders sagging. "I can't. Fucking Elsworth... I asked him to keep Jason safe in exchange for this shit with the campaign."

"So you'll keep doing it, you'll keep selling your soul?"

"Yes, I fucking will!" Tashué snapped, both hands coming down on the table, the whole thing rattling. "Yes I will. I'll carve off every piece of my own humanity if I have to, to keep him safe. Don't tell me you wouldn't do the same! If you had to sit in front of your child and see how they'd been beaten, to watch the bruises and the cuts come and go and wonder if the next time will kill them, you would do the same fucking thing. You don't know what it's like to go into that place and look at your child through that fucking grate and watch them die in front of your eyes, diminishing in front of you. Judge me for all the mistakes I've made, fine. Judge me for everything that led me and Jason to this point, fine. But don't judge me for what I do now to try to undo the damage I've done!"

Stella shook her head, tears coming back. So many tears, how did she still have any left? She took a deep breath, even though her chest was tight. Even though her heart broke for him. He was right, of course—Stella couldn't imagine what she would do if Ceridwen was put in that same place. All her beautiful energy, closed into the stone walls of the Rift, another tattoo forced onto her skin. She would do anything to prevent that.

"So if you're not going to resign your badge, how am I supposed to trust you?" she asked. "Would you trade my freedom for Jason's, if the choice was presented to you?"

He groaned, sinking down into the chair. "Stella... I won't

betray you. I'll do anything for you, don't you see? Just tell me what you want me to do, and I'll do it."

"You keep saying that."

"Because it's true, Stella!"

"Fine, then."

Stella spun on her heel, stalking away, into her bedroom. She threw open the trunk, dug down through the blankets. The papers, the last copy she had. This was the last time to run. She would have to hide well this time. *Just get to White Crown and you can figure out the rest from there.*

Back to the kitchen, where Tashué was still at the table. Holding his head in his hands. She lay her paperwork in front of him, covering the file he'd brought with him from the station house. He looked at it for a long time, like he was struggling to grasp exactly what he was looking at.

"Transfer documents?" Tashué flipped through the pages a few more times, shaking his head. "What is this?"

"I bought them before I left Cruinnich. They're forgeries, of course. All of it, a forgery. There's no husband from Fisherman's Rest, my name is not Stella Whiterock, and I am a healer, not a whisperer. I bought a few copies of this transfer paperwork because I knew I would have to run a few times."

"You're leaving." His voice trembled when he said it, his hands pressing into the table again.

"I have to. To protect Ceridwen. You understand, you said it yourself. You know what it is to look upon your child's face and know you would do anything to keep them safe. I stayed here too long, and if Tarren Bayside knows I'm not what I seem… It's time for me to go."

"Of course," Tashué breathed, nodding. "You do whatever you have to, to protect that girl. She's a gift."

Stella nodded, and the quiet weight of his grief and his acceptance took the anger from her. She wanted to reach out to him, to kiss his face and apologize for all the ways she'd caused him pain, for all the open wounds she'd prodded with her words. But not yet. Not until she knew for sure. "You say you'd do anything for me.

Prove it, then. You have all the evidence you need to process me, to throw me in the Rift for the rest of my life. I can only imagine which crimes the Authority will tattoo me with for this."

"Stella, I won't…"

"Then help me, like you say you want to. Sign them for me. Sign them so I can take Ceridwen and leave, and start again somewhere."

Tashué's hands went to his pockets immediately, but then he stopped. "I don't have a pen. All I have is the charcoal and that won't look official."

Stella found a pen among Ceridwen's schooling tools. Tashué's hands shook when he took it, but he signed the papers anyway, breathing deep and slow as if he was battling with the pain of a broken bone. He pushed the papers toward her once he'd signed in all the right places, leaning back in his chair. Stella dragged the papers closer, watching the black lines of ink dry slowly. Her freedom in those lines. That signature would make it so much easier to pass through the Dominion, and she would fill in her destination later. When she decided where she was going.

Tashué stood and moved past her, to the window. He pushed his fists into his pockets. Stella could hear him struggling to breathe, fighting against tightness that made him gasp, made him fight for air. Any relief at the freedom of this paperwork drained out of her. She'd been so wrapped up in feeling like he was saving her from her numbness and emptiness that it had never occurred to her that perhaps she was saving him, too. Not from numbness or emptiness, but perhaps from being so full of anger and agony that he was drowning.

Stella moved slowly to him, reaching out. She slid her arms around his body, beneath his arms so she could run her hands up his chest. She closed her eyes, savouring the feeling of his muscles through the coarse wool of his jacket. He took a hand out of his pocket and slid his fingers across the back of her hands, just a whisper of touch.

"It's been a joy to have a child in my life again," he said. He cleared his throat, shaking his head. "She really is a gift, your Ceridwen. It's been so long... She's reminded me the sort of man I'd hoped to be, when I was younger. How far I'd come from that person, maybe, but who I wanted to be."

"Would that we lived a different life, the pair of us," Stella said. "So that Ceridwen and I could stay here with you."

Tashué was still for a long time, looking down at Ceridwen. Stella listened to the sound of his breathing, the way he fought to breathe deep and slow. She tried to think of something she might say to file off the sharp edges of his pain. Had she not once made a choice like his? Allying herself to the Authority for her family. And even when she'd made that choice, she'd thought the Authority was an evil entity. It made her choice worse than his, perhaps. She'd known how much she hated the Registration Authority, and made her choice anyway, hoping for the best. At least Tashué had made his choice thinking it was right.

Tashué pushed his hands through his hair, turning. He touched Stella's face before trying to step around her. "I should go. I'll leave you to your day."

"No, stay," Stella breathed. She couldn't leave it like this, with his last memory of her telling him that he'd sold his soul, because of course he had, for his son. "Don't go yet. Stay with me just a while longer."

He stopped, turning back to her. His lips were pressed hard together, his body tense, but still he reached for her, his fingers catching the stray curl, the one that always escaped first. Stella leaned up to kiss him, but Tashué only let their lips brush together before he turned his face away, taking her by the shoulders and easing her back a step. He shook his head but looked down at the floor, as if he was unable to look her in the eye while denying her.

"You don't have to do this, Stella. I wasn't hoping for some payment for my loyalty to you. I gave it freely, for you and Ceridwen both."

"I know that, you fool of a man." Stella caught his face, forcing him to look at her. She kissed him again, leaning her whole body against him. "I've never met a man quite like you. You brought me back to myself, when I would have drifted away. So I give this freely, too." Another kiss, and this time he leaned into it, just a little, his breathing heavy as he opened his mouth to her, his hands trembling again as they slid across her back. "I would give you every part of me, if I could."

His smile was small and sad and he pushed a hand into her hair again, fingers sliding into the curls, into the braids. He had gotten better at it, at knowing where his fingers could go without getting caught in her tangles. Stella leaned harder against him, pushing into his chest to force him to take a step back. Another, and another, and his legs pressed against her sofa. He sank down. Stella hefted up her skirts to straddle his hips and he groaned as she rested her weight on his lap, his hands searching up under the layers of skirts and petticoats. She kissed him again, her hands pushing open his jacket, sliding along his shoulders. She needed to feel his body against hers again, feel the heat of him. The great, open world stretched out before her again, full to bursting with people but somehow so empty. This one man had given her so much and she wanted to bring a piece of him with her.

He groaned, one hand coming out from under her skirts to fight out of the sleeve of his jacket, but the other hand had found the unsewn hem of her drawers and slid along the cleft of her. She gasped, her hips tilting forward, toward his warm touch, and he slid a finger into her. Stella caught his face with both hands, grabbing his beard, pulling him hard into another kiss. His chest heaved against her as he slid his other hand up the front of her bodice, looking for the buttons that kept it closed. Not that he could undo them himself, not with his right hand, with its tight scabs and his numb fingers.

Stella broke the kiss and leaned back, fighting against the buttons herself. The attention of his fingers made her whole body tremble, made it hard to focus. Tashué followed her as she opened her bodice, his lips finding her neck and her collarbone now that the bodice wasn't keeping her skin hidden. His lips and tongue were so warm on her skin, his beard tickling, his hair soft as it brushed her cheek. She turned her face toward him, breathing in the smell of him, trying to remember every nuance of it. She wanted to strip them both of all their clothes, every last scrap of cloth that kept their skin apart, but to do it she would have to make him stop. And his fingers felt so good, strong and nimble at once.

His other hand ran up her back, fingers brushing over the ties of her corset. Then down, finding the hooks that kept her skirts tight around her waist. With his hand bracing her back, she was able to let go of him and reach back, opening the hooks, lifting them up over her head. Tashué twisted, shifting Stella's weight, resting her on the sofa. He dragged her stockings down so he could kiss her knees and her thighs, like he had the night before. So much had changed in just a few hours. The way he touched her was completely different; what had been eager and excited before was slower now, like he was savouring every moment they had. Of course he was—they only had such a small amount of time left.

Stella reached down, catching his other sleeve finally, dragging it off his arm and tossing his jacket away. The shoulder and arm of the old off-white shirt was stained with blood and beer. Stella ran a hand up his arm, to his sleeve, to his face. Her fingers slid around the contour of his fresh wounds, the new stitches tied neater than the ones she'd put into his hands. What would become of him, when she left? Had he spent his whole life as a mess of wounds like he was now? He had plenty of scars, so it seemed likely.

He turned his face into her hand, kissing her palm, but his left hand found her again, fingers searching, caressing, confident and tender at once. Stella reached up, unhooking the front of her corset. Tashué groaned, his other hand pushing up Stella's shift to her ribcage. He had to move again to kiss her hip and her navel. The air was cold on her naked skin; this time of year was always so cold and damp no matter how diligently she tended to the fire in her stove, but the chill in the air only made the heat of his mouth and his hand more intense.

Tashué leaned back, leaving her cold and exposed. He grabbed her drawers with both hands and dragged them down. They caught on the buttons of her boots, but he pulled them away. His hands hooked under her knees, pushing her legs further apart, his tongue sliding up her thigh like he wanted to taste every inch of her. Up and up until his mouth found the same place that his fingers had been exploring. His tongue was just as confident as his fingers and Stella tried to force herself to breathe, her heart beating so hard, her hands trembling as she slid her fingers into his hair. His hand went up, under her shift, pushing it higher still until his palm slid across her breast, his thumb on her nipple, the callus there scraping and it all felt so good.

He went until her whole body trembled, until she felt like she was melting. Another shift and he was up, away from her body, hands fumbling with his own buttons finally, waistcoat opening, peeling away. Stella reached out to him, trying to catch her breath as she pushed his suspenders off his broad shoulders, her hands sliding down to grab the front of his shirt and drag his shirttails from his trousers. He only opened a few buttons before he dragged the shirt up over his head, pausing just long enough to use the shirt to wipe his face, smoothing his beard back into place. Stella caught his arm as he tossed his shirt aside, pulling him into another kiss, coarse wool pressing against the inside of her thighs as he rested his weight on her.

Stella pushed her hands between them, finding the buttons of his trousers, fighting against them. His body was so warm against hers and she wanted more, wanted to feel every inch of him like the night before. How could so much change in one night? But no, the changing had come slowly. Seeing him in his window. Watching him bring snacks for Ceridwen. Walking with him in the Market Quarter, helping him with his buttons. And the Market fire, that stripped them both bare, exposing them to each other in a world bathed in blood and ash. But she had to leave him. Time to be alone again. She didn't know if she would survive it, the going out into the world. The return to the numbness that consumed her before Tashué Blackwood woke her again. Could a person die of emptiness? But she had to go. She had to run until Ceridwen was old enough to know the strength that lived in her, old enough to protect herself.

She kissed him harder, teeth scraping his lip as her hand reached into his trousers and he groaned against her mouth. Maybe she could take a little piece of that heat of him, to take with her when she went. To smoulder in the centre of her and keep the emptiness at bay.

He wasn't even fully out of trousers when he pushed himself into her, but she didn't care. She kissed him again, wrapping her arms around his chest, hands laying upon his scars as she clung to him. He moved only slowly, breathing hard against her, pulling her close, every kiss slow and lingering. Tashué broke the kiss as his breathing went fast and shallow, a hand in her hair again, his eyes sweeping her face like he was trying to commit every freckle to his memory, every line. He pressed his cheek against hers as his pace went faster, and even his breath in her ear felt good, his voice quiet from his throat, his heart beating so hard she could feel it against her chest, the reverberation of it passing through her body like they were both drums. The trembling returned to her body, sweeping her away until she couldn't think about anything but him, how good he felt in her body, how good he felt pressed against her.

His whole body shuddered for the long moment of his release. Stella caught him by the beard again, pulling him into a kiss, digging her heels into the back of his thighs so he couldn't get away from her, not just yet. If only she could stay with him and let herself fall in love.

Dressed only in his trousers and his thin undershirt, he helped her pack. He smoked as he cut up the older blankets with a sharp pair of scissors, turning them into a roll of fabric swatches that could be used to patch other things. There was only so much she could pack until it was time to go. No sense packing the pots and pans while she still needed them to cook.

"Do I go to work again tonight? If they know..."

Tashué leaned closer, their foreheads brushing together. "Yes, keep going, at least for now. Tell Bayside I've filed paperwork for your reassessment and you don't know when that will happen. That way, when you go, he won't wonder why. It's a hard time to travel, with winter coming."

She kissed him and she took the cigarillo from him, taking in a few breaths of smoke before giving it back. "I know. It's always the winter, it seems. I left Cruinnich in the winter. Went all the way to Lledewydd."

He nodded, his mouth a hard line. Worried, maybe. Worried about all the dangers the world had to offer. But none of the dangers had been enough to stop her yet. She kissed him again because she hated the thought that she only had a few days left to kiss him before her barge took her away, and he wrapped his arms around her body and pulled her hard against him. She was dressed in her uniform for the Facility and her skin was once again guarded by layers of fabric, but his was not. She slid her hands up under the thin undershirt and thought about undressing again, but Ceridwen came back up, hungry for her dinner.

Tashué put his bloodied shirt back on, his waistcoat and his jacket still smelling of old beer. His overcoat at least was clean, or so dark that it looked clean.

They ate from a street vendor on the way to the Facility and he kissed her again while they stood on the big marble steps.

"I'll meet you in the morning, when your shift is over," he promised. "Wait for me, and I'll walk you home."

Another kiss and she had to force herself out of his arms, up the stairs. Into the numbness of her job, a whisperer for a few more nights.

40

LORNE

DAY 19

Ijaz the Derccian Hammer was a great mountain of a man, hands like sledgehammers and shoulders as wide as two men. A thick, curly black beard shrouding the bottom half of his face. He fought with a cold efficiency, without temper or passion, with nothing but those massive fists and a good knowledge of how to use them to their fullest potential.

"I think you've come to the end of your illustrious career, my friend." Vasska lit a cigarillo, dragging the ashtray closer. It still had blood on it. Ollia had done her best to clean it but the crevices of the engraving were too deep and they held the stains too well. "I'll be sorry to see you go. You've been great entertainment."

Lorne scowled. "Don't discount me just yet."

Vasska leaned closer, grinning at Lorne. "Thought of a clever plan to defeat the brute, have you?"

"No," Lorne said with a shrug. "But I'm not in the habit of losing and I don't intend to start."

Vasska laughed. "Ah, well, if that's your plan. I'll bet on you even though I think you'll lose."

Stillness settled on the crowd and Lorne turned to see what he'd expected to see: Powell was making his slow way. He stopped, now and then, to exchange brief words. He didn't sit, leaning instead on his cane and the bar. He turned his eyes on Lorne, big, bushy eyebrows furrowed.

"Where are you from, boy?"

"I'm from Gladwydd, Mr. Iwan."

Powell snorted. "That's what everyone from Lledewydd says, 'cause no one here knows two shites about the west coast, do they? Me, I'm from a mining village north of the Ghost Mines, called Brower. Fucking cold in Brower, it was. Came here to get away from all that cold, but I probably didn't go far south enough. Should've kept going, all the way down to Khurya, but I liked a neighbourhood that named itself after fucking bones, so I stayed. So, boy, I'm asking you again. Where are you from?"

Lorne stifled a sigh. Powell's sudden interest in where he was from left him feeling a little cold inside. But what choice did he have? "I was born in a fishing village called Gaffryn, sir."

"That's south, isn't it? Near the Hadia."

"Yes, sir."

"Did your village deal with the Jitabvi, to graze the horses?"

"No, too much rock around Gaffryn. It was mostly fishing. And opium. The opium runners docked there first to offload their 'damaged goods' before putting in at Gladwydd. Everyone in Gaffryn smelled like opium and fish and I fucking hated it there." Lorne shook his head, trying to push those smells out of his memory. "I heard about Brower, though. It was a ghost town. Their mine collapsed and killed almost everyone. The survivors left. I heard it's still haunted by the miners that died. People say you can still get the coal cough just from walking around in the town."

Powell scowled, looking out across the fight hall, at all the people that were here at his pleasure. "That's no surprise, that. Even back when I was a boy, my father would say how the mine wasn't safe." He swung his gaze back to Lorne, his eyes gone hard, all the wistfulness gone. "I know you ain't as poor as you pretend to be, boy. You spend your fight winnings smart, and you've been investing around the city. Shares in gin, in a songhouse, in a crematorium—why a crematorium?"

Lorne shrugged, trying to hide how uneasy he felt. It shouldn't have surprised him that Powell knew where he kept his money, but to be faced with it so blatantly felt like a veiled threat. What had he done, then, to step out of line? People didn't usually survive very long when they displeased Powell Iwan. It wasn't the spies he ran for Nathaniel Wolfe, or the information he gave to Tashué Blackwood for his cases—Powell had known about those from the beginning, and sometimes even used Lorne's network to run messages to Ishmael or to General Wolfe himself. So—what, then?

"Everybody dies," he said, though even saying the words left a cold feeling in his gut. He wasn't even sure why he said it. Was it his reasoning behind investing in the crematorium? Or a reminder to himself?

Powell smiled. "Everybody dies, indeed. And in this city, everybody drinks and everybody likes a dancing girl, is that it? Clever man you are. With all that money of yours, would you take it and leave? Go back to Gaffryn?"

Lorne shook his head. "There's nothing for me in Gaffryn."

"No family?"

"No sir. Everything I care about is here, in Yaelsmuir."

"The Blackwoods, then?" Powell asked. "The son, in the Rift, and the father, the Regulation Officer? I heard he's a Station Commander, now."

"Yes, sir, I heard the same. And he's got his own provincial medal, too."

"What binds you to them, then? These Blackwood men. What draws you to them so fiercely, of all the people in the world?"

Lorne shrugged. "Sometimes it takes a while to find your true family, but when you do, you know it in your bones."

"Lucky for you to have such wise bones at a young age."

Lorne took a deep breath, the cold feeling gone, replaced instead by heat. Again, someone asking about Tashué and Jason—it made him twist, these questions, made him hate the world he found himself in. "Was there something specifically you wanted to ask me, Mr. Iwan? About Tashué Blackwood?"

Powell grinned, his eyebrows rising. "Are you growing impatient with me, then?"

"No, sir."

"Mr. Coswyn is especially protective of the Blackwoods," Vasska said at Lorne's elbow, leaning in. "He means no disrespect, Grandad."

"Oh, I know that," Powell said, waving a hand at Vasska. "Wise old bones, he has, but also no fear, not really. What was it that took the fear out of you, boy? Was it the hurricanes and the grey ocean of the Western coast? Or were you just born that way?"

"I walked the Blood Road, Mr. Iwan, when I was with the 16th infantry," Lorne said. Just mentioning that road brought the taste of dust to the back of his throat. "I thought I was going to die there, with the rest of the soldiers I knew. I've never been so scared in all my life, walking at the front of that column. And then when I survived, I knew that nothing I faced would be as terrible as that."

"Not many survived the Blood Road," Powell said, nodding.

"No," Lorne agreed, "not many survived at all."

"Is that why you think you can lie to me, boy?" Powell asked, leaning a little closer. He locked is dark eyes on Lorne's face, watching every movement. "You haven't any fear in you and you don't think old Iwan is much of a threat, since you're living this life on stolen time?"

The whole fight hall went quiet. No—they were chattering on as usual, but Lorne couldn't hear them. His mind was so blank and roaring at once that all he could hear was *is that why you think you can lie to me.* All he could see was Powell, sitting too close, watching him too hard. *Shit,* was all he could think. *Shit, shit. Fuck. Shit.*

"Ah, you're paying close attention now," Powell said, grinning. "Good. I know all that money of yours is going to Teshii, to a nice little boarding school up in the mountains. I haven't ever figured out who's being boarded up there, though. A child, maybe? Some bastard seed from your days as a soldier? You're so young, but a boy can make a child when he's still a child himself, can't he?"

The whole world seemed to get slower. *Breathe, fucking breathe.* He could feel the heat that crawled up his body right before a fight, tingling in his shoulders, settling in his mind, so hot that part of him had to be on fire. And Powell, waiting, watching. Patient, but not really.

"Are you threatening me, Mr. Iwan?" Lorne asked slowly, lest he let the words out too quickly and they lit the fuse in him that would make him start swinging.

"Threatening you?" Powell scoffed. "No, boy, if I threaten you, you won't have to ask for clarification. I'm just trying to understand you, you see. You've been fighting for me for years now, and there's still some pieces missing. You survive against the Hammer, I'll take you up to the professional fights. That'll be something, son, just you wait. All the money you've been making me has been building some real pugilist clubs down here in the Bay. And you'll be my first fighter, if you stand against the Hammer. You'll have so much money then—but I think you'll keep on sending it to Teshii, won't you? I'm putting a lot on you, and I like to know the people I'm betting on. So, a son? A daughter?"

Lorne forced his breath back out of his lungs. "A sister. My baby sister."

"How old is she, this baby sister?"

"I'm not sure, Mr. Iwan. I haven't seen her since I left."

"Can you do the maths yourself, in that head of yours?" Powell asked. "How old were you when you left?"

"I was fourteen or so, when my mother died. When I signed for the service. I guess… she'd be thirteen now."

"So you weren't signing on for an adventure, hey? Like most idiot boys who sign on before they get the chance to start fucking. You were fourteen with a mouth to feed. So who took your sister after your dear mam chased the poppy to her grave?"

"Why does this matter, Mr. Iwan?" Lorne breathed.

"Ah, so you are afraid of something, hey? Not death, maybe, but pain. Old pain. After everything you saw in the service, it's a wee baby sister and a smoked mother that haunts you. Your baby sister, was she born craving? Happens sometimes, when a mother smokes too much. They're hungry, those babes, hungry in a way they can't possibly understand, and they scream like nothing you've ever heard. Was she like that, your sister?"

"No, sir." Lorne's voice trembled and he hated it. He sucked in a deep breath, trying to still his racing heart. "My mother tried to clean herself up that year. We lived with a sailor she met. He was good to us. Wanted to take care of us. Mother tried her best to clean up for him, and for my sister once she learnt she was pregnant."

Powell cocked his head to one side, as if the recounting of Lorne's pain was endlessly fascinating. "Why isn't the good sailor taking care of his girl? He fuck off, then? Buckle under all the pressure?"

"No, sir." Lorne shook his head, fighting to breath even though it felt like a vice had clamped around his chest. "The sea took him."

"'Course the sea took him," Powell muttered, knocking twice on the bar. Old superstition, that, knocking when talking about the sea. "Jealous mistress, that Western Sea. Well then, that explains every-thing, doesn't it? Young Mr. Coswyn, fancies himself a caretaker, brother and father all at once." He nodded a few times, his eyes going distant. "That's good, then. Now I know who to settle with if something happens to you."

"Why do you think something is going to happen to me?" Lorne asked, his whole body going cold. So the old fucker *was* threatening him.

"Never know, when you step up on my stage," Powell said. "Never know when a bad punch might take you down, do you? I like to know who to settle with, when a thing like that happens. Can't exactly send your earnings to the Blackwood boy in the Rift, can I? Ah, don't look at me like that, boy. I like you, I really do. But the Hammer is a big fucker, isn't he? I like to know, is all." Powell reached out, patting Lorne's shoulder and levering himself off the bar. "I hope you come out the other side of it."

"I'll do my best, Mr. Iwan."

"Good man."

With that, Powell turned and started his slow shuffle away, retreating to the room he kept off the main fight hall, where he kept an eye on the action. Lorne fought to breathe once he was gone. He needed to swing at something, to break something, just to let the tension out. Vasska gripped Lorne's arm, squeezing hard.

"You handled yourself well," Vasska breathed.

"Really?" Lorne asked, turning to Vasska. Fuck this place, fuck this whole family. If it weren't for his sister, he would have given up fighting a long time ago. Was it too late now? "It felt like I was signing my own death warrant."

"No, that wasn't a threat," Vasska said, shaking his head and squeezing Lorne's arm again. "He was testing you, I think. Trust me, you did well." His eyes shifted over Lorne's shoulder and his face arranged carefully into a smile. "Ah, Mr. Blackwood. It's good to see you again, sir."

Lorne looked up to see Tashué approach—of course he was coming, summoned by the sound of his own name.

"Evening, Mr. Czarny," Tashué said.

"You remembered my name," Vasska said with a grin. "I'm impressed."

Tashué smiled, shrugged. It was a hollow smile, though, his whole face ragged and worn. "I served with a Czarny at the Officer's Academy."

"Officer's Academy? That must have been some years ago."

Tashué laughed at that. "I didn't realize that I was already a foot in the grave at forty-two."

"You've lived your entire life with one foot in the grave," Lorne muttered.

"That's true," Tashué admitted.

"When did you serve, Mr. Blackwood?"

Tashué sighed, shaking his head. "I'm sure you know that already, Mr. Czarny. I'm not interested in playing the game where we pretend to be ignorant of each other and what we're capable of. I've had a shit day. I have to ask to steal Lorne away from you. If you don't mind."

"Of course, Mr. Blackwood." Vasska let go of Lorne's arm, settling back in his stool. "I don't own his time."

With Tashué in the lead, they left the warehouse. It was cold outside, the air chilly and damp and clouds bunching in the sky with the threat of another storm. Tashué shuffled through his pockets as soon as they were out of the Hive, pulling out a folded page of newsprint. He unfolded it and handed it over to Lorne. "Is this what I think it is?"

Lorne sighed as he looked down at the article, and the smell of smoke returned to his mouth. He was there when the building burned, there with the fire crews as they fought over who got to claim the glory. Cattle Bone Bay's crews were largely run by the various gangs that fought for territory under Powell Iwan's watch. More often than not, the crews ended up brawling in the streets instead of fighting the fires while the buildings burned to rubble. And Powell Iwan let them. If gangs were fighting over fire territories, they had less time to fight Iwan for control over the Bay.

"It is," Lorne said, handing the article back. "It's the same building."

Tashué reached for his cigarillo case, flipping it open and closed, open and closed. Lorne wondered if he even knew that he did that when he was thinking. Open, closed. Open, closed. "How many other buildings burned?"

"The neighbours were damaged but not destroyed. Not many people seemed to have gotten out."

Tashué lay a hand on Lorne's shoulder. It was a different touch than when Vasska clung to him, like he was trying to keep them both breathing in an ugly moment. Tashué's hand was heavy and comforting. It was how Lorne used to imagine what a father's hand must feel like. But the stitches and the scabs also showed that Tashué understood exactly what it was like to fight flames and search for survivors and lift the dead from the coals. "Was she in there?"

Lorne nodded, meeting Tashué's eyes. "She came back a few days after you talked to her. I don't think she had anywhere else to go. I was trying to convince her to talk to you again but she was scared."

Tashué grimaced, finally taking a cigarillo from the case and placing it between his lips. Lorne took one too, leaning in to light it from Tashué's match. The smoke was hot as it filled his lungs. As if he needed any more heat in him now.

"I put her there," Lorne muttered. "I took her to that place and paid for her room. I killed all those people, as if I'd lit the fire myself."

"No, you didn't." Tashué turned to Lorne, reaching out and grabbing Lorne's arm, squeezing like Vasska did, pulling Lorne in, but there was something reassuring in all of Tashué's strength and stubbornness. "Lorne, look at me. Sometimes shit just burns to the ground for no reason. Especially these old tenement buildings. It just takes one stray ember, one clogged chimney, and all of this turns into kindling. You can't blame yourself."

Lorne grimaced, looking up at Tashué. "You have to be joking. You don't honestly think that this was an accident, do you? After what she said? There's no way. I can't believe this was a coincidence."

Tashué scowled. "You're probably right. But even if that's the case, you still aren't responsible. If you had known, when that woman came to you for help, that this would happen here—what would you have done?"

"I don't fucking know," Lorne muttered, taking a deep breath of his cigarillo and staring down at his feet. "Something. Fucking anything, if I thought it would have helped."

"Exactly. If you knew this was coming down on your shoulders, you would have done anything to protect her. It's not your fault that you didn't see it coming."

Lorne shook his head. Tashué's answer sounded right but he didn't like it, didn't think it sounded like enough.

Tashué sighed, heading through the streets again. Lorne followed. The tenement building wasn't far from the Hive.

But before they made it, a familiar figure came out from a corner. Ishmael Saeati, fuck him. He walked with a bottle in his hand. He had pig shit on his shoes and blood on his fingers and he seemed almost surprised to see Tashué. The surprise made Lorne uneasy. Ishmael was never surprised, was he?

"What the hell are you doing in the Bay?" Tashué asked. "I thought you hated it here?"

Ishmael shrugged, taking a pull from his bottle and falling in step beside Tashué. "There's always fucking something, isn't there? Ishmael, clean up this mess. Ishmael, take out this trash. Ishmael, do this. Ishmael, a favour for me. Ishmael, one more fucking thing. A man can't even indulge in a proper drinking binge in this fucking city anymore."

"What kind of mess are you cleaning up?" Lorne asked.

"Ah, fuck you, Coswyn," Ishmael muttered. He dragged his feet as he walked, scraping the soles of his shoes on the cobbles. "I'm not that drunk."

"Right, so I'll ask you again in an hour?"

"Why would you do that?" Ishmael scoffed. "You, of all people, should respect my privacy."

Lorne sneered, the fighting heat coming back in an instant. "Oh really? Why me, then? Why should I, specifically, give two shits about anything you want?"

Ishmael shrugged. "You and I went to the same training. Oh, but I'm forgetting something, aren't I? You couldn't cut it in the diplomatic division, could you? Washed out after a year."

"Fuck you," Lorne snarled. The fight heat climbed up his arms, itching and anxious, unresolved from facing Powell. He tried to tell himself that Ishmael wasn't any less trouble than fucking Powell Iwan, that a fight with Ishmael couldn't possibly end well. "I gave the Dominion Army my three years."

"Both of you, stop it," Tashué muttered. "You're like fucking children."

Any conversation was stopped by their arrival at the building. The neighbouring buildings were scorched and the tenement itself was burned to a hollow shell, all the stones still intact but the wooden floors, doors, furniture, all devoured by the blaze. Black tracks of soot and ash climbed out of the windows and doorways and Lorne felt again the dry heat, miserable and ferocious.

"Ah, fuck," Ishmael said, hanging back. "It's like the whole fucking city is burning down these days."

"Well, lucky for you, we have this under control," Lorne muttered. "You're not needed here."

"I said fucking stop it," Tashué snapped. "Will you wait for me?"

Ishmael's eyes settled on Tashué, and he sighed. "Sure. I guess you'll be asking something next, hey? Fantastic."

"No, not like that," Tashué said. He lay a big hand on Ishmael's shoulder too, and it was a strange feeling to see such an intimate gesture with Ishmael fucking Saeati on the receiving end of it. Ishmael seemed to relax a bit, though, leaning toward Tashué. "Just some questions."

Ishmael nodded. Tashué headed inside and Lorne followed, boots crunching on ash and coal. Lorne kept his cigarillo between his lips, letting the tobacco smoke block the lingering smell of roasted human flesh. There wasn't much to see. Rescuers had taken out what bodies could be found. Any remains of walls or furniture had been knocked over or stirred up in the wild search for survivors.

Tashué's foot turned over a pile of ash, uncovering the remains of a child's doll. It was only scorched, the yarn that was its hair half burnt, one arm almost completely gone. What had become of the child that owned that doll?

"What was her name?"

Lorne dragged his gaze away from the doll. Tashué was standing there, waiting for him. He looked even angrier than usual. Was it the fire or something else?

"What?"

"The woman. Did she ever tell you her name?"

Lorne shook his head. He reached down, plucking the doll from the ash and wiping the worst of it away. "No, she didn't. I never could get her to trust us that much."

"Does anyone know how the fire started?"

There was no repairing the doll, not really. It was too burnt, too stained with ash. "No, not exactly. Everyone agrees it started on the west side, but other than that." Lorne spread his hands. "You know how it is."

Tashué nodded. "Everyone swears on their life, but no one tells the same story. It started on the west side?"

Lorne took a slow breath, but all he could smell was smoke and ash and burnt flesh. "Right. Her room was on the west side, four floors up. She was in her room when we found her. At least, I think it was her. Now what?"

"Someone has suggested that the girl from the river was killed by the Army of the Red Dawn."

Lorne nodded, taking a long drag from his cigarillo. "I've heard the same thing."

Tashué's eyebrows shot up as he swung to look at Lorne. "From who?"

"No one I knew. I was told to look at the Red Dawn, so I asked Vasska what he knew about them. Powell knows everything that happens in the Bay. I'm sure Vasska does, too."

"And?" Tashué pressed, stepping closer. "What did he say?"

"Fucking nothing," Lorne muttered, dropping his cigarillo and crushing it with the toe of his boot. "No, that's not true... I asked him what he knew, he said 'too fucking much.' He told me to leave it alone. I don't get it, though. Why would the Red Dawn be involved in shit like this? Dismembering children and then murdering them? Why? How does that help them?"

"They want to start a revolution," Tashué said, his voice tight, his teeth clenched. "They want people to rise up in the streets and crush the Authority. They murder tainted children to incite this violence because they're too cowardly to stand up themselves." Tashué took a last drag from his cigarillo, flicking it away as he breathed smoke out his nose. "They would rather stay hidden and the Authority is happy to let them. The official stance of the Authority is that the Red Dawn has no organized presence here. Any claims made are by independents and radicals, but they are not the evidence of a militant presence in Yaelsmuir."

"The official stance," Lorne snorted. "And the Market fire? Was it Red Dawn? That's what everyone keeps saying."

"No, it wasn't them." Tashué sighed, shaking his head. "It was a desperate man who killed himself by setting a load of thermite on fire."

"Fucking hell," Lorne muttered. He dropped the doll on the floor because he couldn't stand here anymore, hanging on to the half-burnt child's toy, thinking about fires and thermite and all the children that lived here and were gone now. "I have to get out of here."

He headed for the stairs, and Tashué followed.

"You think Ishmael is still out there?"

"I hope so. He said he'd wait."

Lorne sighed, shaking his head. "I don't know why you trust him."

Tashué shrugged. "He hasn't yet given me reason not to trust him."

"That's your problem, Tashué. You wait around for people to prove how awful they are."

"What's so fucking awful, then?" Tashué snapped. "He kills people? So what? You and I have done the same. We served our years, like you said."

"It's not just that. You ever see him fight in the Bay?"

"No. I've seen *you* fight in the Bay, though."

Lorne shook his head. "Ishmael is different. Ishmael *likes* to hurt people. He likes to break them up into little pieces until they aren't even human anymore. I don't trust him. Neither should you."

Tashué scowled and Lorne could feel the anger from the bigger man, the fight coming fast to his amber eyes. "I love you like a son, so honestly, I'm telling you this with all my affection. Shut the fuck up about Ishmael. Whatever you think you know, you don't know the half of it. You don't trust him, fine. That's your business. But I know him a lot better than you do, so you can stop telling me like you think you know something I don't. I'm sick of hearing about it."

Lorne looked up at Tashué. *Deep breath.* "Yeah, alright. Understood."

"Good, now I'm going to talk to him and you're going to be civil. I don't have any spare patience tonight, I honestly don't."

Lorne nodded and Tashué stomped out. Ishmael was leaning against the building and swilling back whisky like he thought it would save him from something. From what? What was he running from? Tashué leaned beside him, taking the bottle from Ishmael and taking a quick pull.

"Looks like a shit fire," Ishmael said, taking the bottle back. "Any survivors?"

"We didn't find any, no," Lorne said.

"What did Vasska say, when he told you to leave it alone?" Tashué asked. "Does Iwan not want us involved in this?"

Lorne shook his head, trying to remember what Vasska said. He remembered the last exchange with sharp clarity. *What do you know, Vasska? Too fucking much.* Before that? "No, not Iwan. He said they're dangerous. That he doesn't want us getting killed. They must be big, if they've got him spooked like that."

"Vasska Czarny is a lot softer than his grandfather," Ishmael said.

Lorne glanced at him, at the way he melted against the building. He had the cork back in his bottle, though. He was holding it by the neck, tossing it into the air. It flipped, end over end, then came back down. How much had he drank from it? His hands weren't as clumsy as Lorne imagined they'd be. He caught the bottle easily, tossed it up again.

Tashué opened his cigarillo case again. He didn't light the cigarillo this time, snapping the case closed and then tapping it on the case's cover. Lorne could only imagine the tension and the fire that built in Tashué's body for him to be smoking so much. He knew the feeling of it, that swirling eddy of energy that screamed in the body, needing action but getting none. Could you put a fire out if you smothered it with smoke?

"Red Dawn must be bigger here than I realized if they have Vasska spooked," he said, tapping his cigarillo again. Tap, tap, tap, tap. Lorne wanted to grab the cigarillo and snap it in half, the way all that tapping made his brain itch. Taptaptap.

Ishmael reached out, snatching the cigarillo from Tashué and putting it between his lips. He held out a hand and Tashué sighed at him, fishing through his pocket for his matches and handing them over. Ishmael struck a match, the sulphur-fuelled flame lighting his dark eyes as he lit the end of the cigarillo, smoke drifting up around him.

"What the fuck are you two idiots doing messing around with the Red Dawn?" he asked, tossing the matches back to Tashué.

Tashué lit a cigarillo of his own, tucking the case away and reaching for the bottle. "Do you remember that morning, at Wolfe's house?"

"The morning after Illea's banquet?" Ishmael asked. "Yes, why?"

Tashué took a quick pull and handed the bottle back again. "What did Wolfe say? About Jason. Something about making sure Jason was safe, because I was worried about Rainer fucking me over if I didn't cooperate with his campaign shit."

"What the fuck is Elsworth going to do to Jason?" Lorne breathed. "What are you talking about?"

Tashué didn't even look at Lorne when he spoke, reaching out instead and putting a hand on Lorne's shoulder. Like the weight was supposed to be comforting, supposed to make him still and quiet, except Lorne's skin was crawling again, his heart beating too fast, his muscles bunching for a fight. But with who, fuck? Everyone. Everything. All the fucking time.

"Do you remember?" Tashué asked, squeezing Lorne's shoulder, but staring Ishmael down. "He looked right at you when he said it."

Ishmael nodded and it made Lorne's heart skip a beat. What the hell were they talking about? He didn't want fucking Ishmael Saeati anywhere *near* Jason, but what the hell was Rainer Elsworth going to do?

"I don't think I want to know the details, but was Wolfe serious?" Tashué asked. "Can he honestly keep Jason safe? Can you?"

"You're right," Ishmael said. "You don't want to know the details."

"I fucking well do!" Lorne snapped.

Tashué squeezed his shoulder, so hard it hurt. "Just leave it, Lorne."

"No, hang on. You trust him, fine, we disagree there. But for fuck's sake—Jason? What's going on? Me not trusting him means I don't fucking well want him involved with Jason."

"Why don't you come closer, Coswyn?" Ishmael said and the

way he grinned made Lorne's skin crawl. "I'll whisper in your ear just how *involved* I am with Jason."

"I swear to fuck, Saeati—"

"Stop!" Tashué thundered. "Just stop. Ishmael, please. I need to know if he's safe. Especially if everything I know is true."

"Fine, fine," Ishmael said. "I'm working on it. Alright? Things are… coming. What does this have to do with the Red Dawn and Elsworth?"

Tashué took a deep breath, in and out. "If Jason is safe… and if I knew something about Elsworth, something about the Authority and the Breeding Program, something that the people of this city might take exception to, would the General back me up?"

Ishmael cocked his head to one side, leaning in. "You're such a fucking tease, Captain. Yes. Absolutely, yes. He's always about the long game. I keep telling him to go harder, to push more, but he doesn't want to. He doesn't want people to get hurt, so he makes his little political plans and he hopes for the best. But you and I know, don't we, that hoping for the best isn't good enough. That sometimes you have to tear things apart."

Tashué nodded. "Exactly."

"What do you know?" Lorne asked. "About the Breeding Program?"

Tashué ran a hand over his face. "I don't have any proof, not yet. I'm trying to unknot it all, but I need proof. I don't know how to get it."

"How can the General help?" Ishmael asked, leaning in.

Tashué shrugged. "I don't know. He probably can't get me files from the Breeding Program, can he?"

Ishmael winced. "Maybe. It would take some time, though. You don't sound like you have a lot of time to wait."

"No, I don't think I do." Tashué shook his head, waving a hand. "I'll keep looking for now. Let Elsworth think I'm dancing for him, and maybe I can get more."

"How very anti-climactic," Ishmael muttered. "You aren't going to tell me what you think you know?"

"Is this about the girl from the river?" Lorne asked. "How is

Rainer Elsworth involved? I thought I was looking at the Red Dawn for this."

Tashué nodded. "It's all connected, I think. There's a reporter, at the *Highview Times*, named Allie Tei. She has even more than me. She found another child. If I uncover the sort of things I think I'm going to find, she's going to need protection. She wants to run the story, but I don't think the *Highview Times* will want to be involved."

"So I'm going to find Allie Tei, then?" Ishmael asked. "What am I protecting her from?"

"The Authority and the fucking Red Dawn. It's all a fucking mess."

Ishmael sighed, looking down at his bottle. "Fine, I'll go find her in the morning. I have a fuck load more drinking planned tonight. You should come along and we can stir up all kinds of trouble."

"Not tonight," Tashué said, shaking his head. "Later, when I've got all this shit figured out."

Ishmael grinned, one eyebrow arching up. "I'm holding you to that."

"Don't forget about Allie Tei. If she's getting anywhere close to the things I know, she'll be in danger by now."

Ishmael nodded, but took another pull from the bottle of whisky. "Allie Tei, at the *Highview Times*." He tipped the bottle toward Lorne. "You want to come fuck things up with me?"

"I would rather take a swim in the fucking Bay."

Ishmael laughed. "So hurtful, all the time. You don't have to take things so personally, you know."

"Fuck yourself."

"I much prefer having company for things like that."

"Lorne, leave it," Tashué said, stepping between them. "He's just stirring up shit."

"Maybe I'll go to the Hive for a few rounds on stage. You want to come test yourself out against me? I've seen you taking your measurements, trying to guess who'd win. What do you think?"

"I think I'm not like you," Lorne said. "I don't need to hurt people to feel like a man."

"That's bullshit. I know you aren't doing it for the money. You've got enough invested in this city that you could cash out and spend the rest of your fucking life in luxury. But you're so in love with your own suffering, aren't you? Poor, tragic Lorne, drifting through the city with nothing but the clothes on his back and his fists, without even his true love, who's locked away in the Rift."

"I told you to leave Jason out of it."

Ishmael grinned. "No, you told me to go visit him myself. Maybe I will."

Tashué's arm snapped out, his anger coming to life even faster than Lorne. He grabbed Ishmael by the front of the coat. "I said that's enough," he growled, hauling Ishmael in close. "That's my fucking son you're talking about."

Ishmael clamped his cigarillo between his fingers, holding both his arms to his sides and tilting his head back to blow a cloud of smoke over Tashué's head. "You going to hit me, Captain? Fine. Go ahead. I'll give you one free one, just because we're so close. Better make it good, though. You think you can put me down in one hit?"

The pair of them were so still, only their chests moving as they breathed. Shit. Tashué was so tightly wound he seemed ready to explode—but hadn't he just said he was tired of Lorne talking shit about Ishmael? Didn't he just ask Ishmael to keep Jason safe? So he was pissed about something else, then. Would he really take on fucking Ishmael to blow off steam?

"You think you're being real fucking cute, don't you?" Tashué asked, but he was still holding Ishmael close. "Talking about my son to get me all fucking worked up. Well, you got what you wanted. You happy?"

"Fucking delighted," Ishmael said. He leaned his head back again to take another drag of his cigarillo. "What are we doing, then? Hit me, fuck me, or step back. I'm not waiting all night."

Another moment of stillness and then Tashué let go of Ishmael. He took a few deep breaths, putting some distance between their bodies. Ishmael clamped his cigarillo between his teeth, smoothing out the front of his jacket.

"The pair of you are so melodramatic," Ishmael muttered. "You're so obsessed with the idea of protecting Jason that you can't see he's a grown fucking man. He can, and will, make his own choices. Besides, what has your 'protection' done for him? How have either of you helped anything? What have either of you done in the last five years to keep him safe? In spite of all your fucking help, he's still in the Rift getting killed by the Authority. Your fucking Authority, *Commander*."

"You think I don't know the mistakes I've made?" Tashué shot back. "Fuck you, Ishmael. What would you know about it? You say Lorne's in love with his own suffering, but you are too. You kill for Wolfe and you kill for Iwan and you wallow in your own self-pity when you're home in Yaelsmuir, but what have you done to change it? What future have you built for yourself? What would you know about holding your own child in your hands and knowing that you're woefully unprepared to be the man they need you to be, but you fucking try anyway, day after day, no matter how many times you fail? Until you've felt that, and faced that, you don't get to judge me. And until you've loved someone with every shred of your being, you don't get to judge Lorne either."

Ishmael took a long drag of his cigarillo, exhaling the cloud of smoke slowly. He had that stillness about him that Lorne had seen before. What could have made him angrier than when Tashué had him by the coat? Lorne took a deep breath. If Ishmael went for Tashué, Lorne would have his back. And maybe the two of them could keep Ishmael from killing them both.

"You think I've never loved anyone in my whole life?" Ishmael asked.

"I can guarantee it," Tashué said. "I know you. I've known you for years now. And maybe you've had your fair share of affairs, of people that made your heart beat a little faster, but I'm willing to bet that the minute you started to *feel* something, you stepped away. The thought of letting something like that in scared the ever living fuck out of you."

"Fuck yourself," Ishmael said. "I really mean that. Fuck. Yourself. What makes you think you know a single thing about me? If you think I don't feel things, you don't know me at all."

Tashué shook his head. "I'm not saying you don't feel! I'm

saying it scares you and you don't trust it. Because I know what it looks like—after Keoh, I turned that part of myself off. I never wanted to feel like that again. I spent twenty years being a coward and running from it. And then I met Stella Whiterock. She breathed new life into me, simply by existing. I feel like everything I've lived was shaping me, molding me to be exactly the man she needed me to be in this moment. Like I've been created, just for her. One day you'll meet someone who does the same thing to you. I hope you'll remember that I told you to lean into it. It might destroy you, but it will also rebuild you. You'll be a better man for it."

Ishmael rolled his eyes, running a hand along his jaw, knuckles scraping on his stubble. "Isn't that the whisperer who doesn't want you?"

"For fuck's sake, Ishmael." Tashué snatched the bottle from Ishmael's hand and took a long pull. "You're a real shit sometimes, you know that? I'm trying to make a point."

"Right, sure," Ishmael sighed. "Love conquers all. I got it. Thanks for the lecture. I had no idea and all that. Are you finished?"

"I guess I am, since you aren't interested in listening."

"Excellent. Thank everything holy." Ishmael grabbed the bottle back and took a long drink as he turned and walked away.

Only when he was gone could Lorne breathe again, letting it out slowly, trying to release the fighting energy from his arms. "Shit. You and him, huh?"

Tashué huffed, casting a glare over his shoulder. "I'm not interested in discussing my sex life with you."

"No, I think this time I need to know. Since you apparently asked him to keep Jason safe in the Rift and didn't fucking tell me. Because apparently, you didn't think I would want to know something like that?"

"I didn't ask him, I asked Wolfe."

"You know that's how this goes!" Lorne snapped. "Wolfe wants something, and Ishmael Saeati makes it happen!"

"And what's wrong with that? Something needs to be done! Neither of us have been able to get any good results! Have you seen him recently, Lorne? Have you been there in the last week? This is the worst I've seen him since he went in. And I don't know what else to do." Tashué's voice went thick and he took a deep breath, running his hands over his face. "If we keep doing nothing, he's going to die. Soon. Not eventually, not one day. I would be surprised if he lasts the winter."

Breathe. "But what do you really think Ishmael can do? And what do you think that's going to look like?"

"That's the thing, Lorne," Tashué said and the anger drained out of him so completely that he looked smaller. "So long as Jason is safe, I don't care."

"What makes you think that's your choice to make?"

Tashué shrugged, spreading his hands. "The alternative is that we keep doing nothing and he dies. And I know that's not what you want. You're only pissed because the solution has Ishmael's face attached to it. If it was anyone else would you even be upset about it? Or would you just be relieved that someone is finally doing something?"

Lorne felt himself deflate, too. Tashué was right, of course. Jason dying wasn't something he was willing to accept, and if it was anyone else... "Well, I guess I'm fucking praying that Jason survives Ishmael Saeati's 'help'."

41

TASHUÉ

DAY 20

Tashué couldn't sleep. He hadn't fixed his bedclothes since Stella stayed the night and he still saw the shape of her on his mattress. Some of those copper hairs he loved so much rested on his pillows. Nothing was going the way he hoped, nothing was the same anymore. Instead of laying in the spot where Stella rested her head and wishing for things he couldn't have, he dressed again.

The Market still smelled of smoke and burnt thermite—or maybe that was the memory seared into Tashué's mind. The charred buildings still stood along the river; what little of the wharf remained had been stripped back to be rebuilt. Those efforts had begun, planks of fresh timber lying in the streets in great bundles, waiting to be put to use. Illea Winter's timber, stamped with the Winter crest, donated to the survivors for their rebuilding efforts.

His feet brought him to the Market Square and he found himself looking up at the statue of Bronwynn. It was hard not to remember the sound of his Imburleigh discharging, the wails of the man as he died and fought for his son's life. So much had happened since then that he hadn't had the chance to think about it. But now there was no hiding from what he'd done in that ugly moment. Tashué knew all too well what it was to fight for a child, for a son, and he should have done more to diffuse the danger. He pushed the memory through his mind over again a few times, trying to imagine what he would do differently. He shouldn't have left Stella's side. He should have known how badly the death of a child could cut through a person. He should have listened to the man's voice, should have heard the wild desperation there. But the words the man had used cut through everything good and civilized in Tashué. *Lying, tainted bitch* sounded entirely too much like *filthy Kaadayri whore.* What world did he live in that women like Stella and his mother were reduced to such ugly words by men who saw them as tools to serve them and their needs? A man's wife died in spite of Siann Blackwood's best efforts and she became a *filthy Kaadayri whore.* A child died—had Stella given that child her best efforts? If she hadn't, did that give the man the right to call her a *tainted bitch?* She had healed people in Yaelsmuir before, that's what Tarren Bayside said. Why hadn't she saved that boy? Was it because Tashué was standing over her shoulder, oblivious? Or was it because that boy was so damaged that he couldn't have been saved? Healers weren't miracle workers after all.

He found Božic the toymaker in the square. The stallholders were setting out their goods for the coming day of sale, desperation making them stretch their hours earlier. The more people that came to the Market to spend coin, the faster they could return to something like normalcy. The big cavalry man was shuffling slowly through his belongings, pulling them from boxes or canvas wraps. The stall beside him was empty.

"Died in the fire, didn't she?" Božic said quietly, looking at the empty stall. "She lived over the pub down by the water and she was killed by the blast, we reckon. No one in that pub came out alive."

"Ah, Božic, I'm sorry."

The big toymaker spread his hands, showing his old scars and calluses. "The Keeper of the Keys comes for us all in his own time, I suppose. Naught a thing we can do to stop him when he's set his eyes on our soul."

"That's true," Tashué said. Had Božic known the man that Tashué had killed that night? It seemed likely. The Market may have been constantly evolving, but the vendors knew who was selling what on any given day. Did Božic know that Tashué had killed that man? Could Tashué see any judgement in the big toymaker's eyes?

"How's the wee soldier, then?"

"Ceridwen? She's a joy." Tears threatened him and he blinked them back, blessing the murky half-light and the fact that Božic's back was turned to him. Sweet North Star, would he never see Ceridwen again? "She has a bright mind that never ceases to amaze me. And an appetite that can't be satisfied."

Božic laughed, the sound deep and pure joy. It lifted Tashué's spirits. "My wee one was like that, she was. Always talking—and when she wasn't talking, she was eating! They grow up too fast, I'll tell you what."

"I know." Tashué stepped around the table, helping Božic unpack. He couldn't help but examine the toys as he spread them out, one by one. Wooden animals and swords and boats and, of course, spinning tops. Puzzles that fit together just so, dice carved and polished so that they glowed like gems. "My son was the same. I've never seen such a small boy eat *so* much."

Another laugh and Božic leaned forward, resting his elbows on his table. "Ah, what are they for but to bring us joy?"

"To bring frustration. Endless mounds of it, in equal measure to the joy."

"Aye, that's true. But take my word, when they're grown and gone, there are days when all you want is for them to be back in your home, making you tear your hair out."

It was so true that it made Tashué ache. What he wouldn't give to have Jason out of the Rift, stomping around Tashué's small apartment, slamming doors. At least with the stomping and the slamming, Jason was close and something like safe. And Ceridwen. What he wouldn't give to keep her in his life, her and Stella both. And they would all live together, the first time Tashué felt like he was a part of a whole and proper family since... When? Since his father was alive.

Don't be an idiot, wishing for things you can't have.

"I thought you were a woodworker," Tashué said, his eye caught by little balls of glass at the edge of his table.

"Ah, you spotted the marbles," Božic said, reaching across his table and flicking a marble. It rolled smoothly for a while until it hit a little wooden soldier's foot, which sent it careening toward Tashué. His hand shot out, catching the marble as it rolled off the end of the table. "My daughter makes them. Fun little things, aren't they? She does good work, my girl. An eye for the fine details, she has."

"She gets that from her father, I'm sure." Tashué looked closely at the marble, the clear glass holding a little star of yellow glass in the centre. "How much for them?"

"Ah, if you're giving them to the little soldier, let me give them as another gift."

"Nonsense, man. Let me pay for them. Your daughter deserves a fair pay for her work."

"You have me there, don't you? How many do you want? Need a few of them at least to play a good game."

"Give me a dozen. All sorts of colours. If she likes them I'll come back for more."

"Yes sir," Božic beamed.

The big toymaker found a little muslin pouch and filled it with a dozen glass marbles, each a different colour and a different pattern in the glass. Tashué paid three copper crowns for them all, counting it a good deal.

"If ever you'd like to take a pint and commiserate about stubborn children, you come find me," Božic said. "Helps, doesn't it? To commiserate."

"I'll remember that," Tashué promised.

He was early enough to meet Stella as she stepped out of the Facility at the end of her shift. Seeing her made Tashué's breath catch in his throat. She was tired from the night's work, her body slumped, the rings beneath her eyes as dark as bruises—and yet he had never seen a woman so lovely in all his life. But the joy of seeing her was pierced by the looming sense of loss. She wasn't gone yet, but she was going, slipping away from him, and he couldn't stop her and live with himself. She smiled when she saw him. Ceridwen saw him, too, her smile beaming and magical.

He pulled the little muslin bag from his pocket, offering it to Ceridwen. She rubbed her sleepy eyes and peered into the bag, then reached in and pulled out a fistful of the marbles.

"What are they?" she asked, her wonder stripping away the sleep that had been clinging to her mind. "Gems?"

"Not gems," Tashué said. "Marbles."

"What do you do with marbles?"

"You play with them. Roll them across the ground and make them knock together. If you've a friend with marbles, you can play for keeps—roll them around inside a circle and you get to keep the marbles that you knock out of the circle. Do you have any friends with marbles?"

"I don't know," Ceridwen said, a wide grin spreading across her face. "I hope so."

She put them all back in the bag, one by one, until she only had one left. It was mottled, red and grey flecks all pressed together to make a little opaque sphere. "This one is my favourite."

"Really?" Stella asked, holding out her hand. Ceridwen dropped it into Stella's outstretched palm. There was blood caked in her nails, pressed into the creases of her fingers like ink stains. "It's so grim. The others are bright and cheerful."

"I like it. It looks like all the leftover pieces, pressed together to make something beautiful. Like when you make cookies out of the scrap from the pie crust."

Tashué smiled, rustling Ceridwen's hair. She waited only long enough for Stella to hand the marble back and then skipped ahead. The wind swirled her skirts all about her legs, pulling at her coat, at the curls that had come free of her plait. She seemed impervious to the cold, just as she was impervious to everything else. The muslin bag clacked in her hand every time she bounced, making her noisier than ever before.

"Does she know?" Tashué asked softly, once Ceridwen was far enough ahead that she wouldn't hear them.

"Not yet," Stella said, her voice so soft that Tashué barely heard her over the wind. "I haven't told her. She'll be so sad to leave, but… I thought it better this way. I'll tell her when we're ready to go and then there's no chance she'll spoil the secret." She pulled her shawl tighter about her shoulders, up to her cheeks. "I'm tired of the wind. I would like to go somewhere that isn't so windy."

"I've been many places in my life, hot and cold and in between," Tashué said. Their hands brushed as they walked and Stella laced their fingers together. "But I'm sorry to tell you that I haven't yet found a place without wind."

"Somewhere with warm wind, then."

"You should try the Spice Isles. You can eat nutmeg fruit and drink spiced milk and let yourself get lost in the jungle."

"Nutmeg have fruit?"

Tashué nodded. "The nutmeg is the seed. The fruit is like a dry apricot but of course it tastes like nutmeg. They boil them to make jam, or wine, or juice. Or they preserve them with salt and chiles and put them in stews. Or they store them in sugar and eat them like candy."

"I should very much like to try it, then," Stella said with a warm smile. The wind howled again, slicing through them. Stella bowed her head into the wind, pulling her coat and her shawl more tightly about her body to guard what little warmth she had. "Are there mountains on the Spice Isles?"

"Plenty. Some of them so high that they're capped in snow."

"That sounds perfect. I miss being close to the mountains. And I think, as much as I hate the wind, I would miss the snow."

"Miss the snow? Stella Whiterock, you are insane."

She laughed, but burrowed deeper into her coat. "It's coming soon I think—the snow. I can taste it in the air. In Cruinnich, they'll probably have snow already."

They made their way back to the Row, where the wind screeched down their long street.

"Will you take breakfast with us?" Ceridwen asked as she bounded up the steps.

"If your mam will have me."

"We haven't much, I'm afraid," Stella said as they stepped inside. The wind still howled outside, but the stairwell offered some shelter at least, trapped some of the heat from all the wood stoves contained in the great building. "Only porridge."

"Sounds delightful."

She led him up the stairs. The coals in the stove had died through the night and Tashué busied himself by setting a new fire. He had to work not to stand and stare at Stella all day, or else he would become entranced with each copper wisp of hair. The warmth from the growing fire eased the cold from his bones. Stella set a pot on the stove top with water for the boil.

Ceridwen upended her muslin bag on the floor, setting the marbles rolling every which way. Tashué watched her scrabble for them, squeezing under furniture to retrieve them.

"Bring those into your room, Ceridwen," Stella said, once all the marbles were retrieved. "They'll have less room to get away in there."

"Yes, Mam."

And then Ceridwen was off, shutting the door behind her. Tashué heard the clatter of the marbles hit the floor again. Stella dumped a measure of oats into the pot, stirring with a wooden spoon.

"Do you know who's chasing you?" Tashué asked, watching her face. He'd sketch it later, if only he could find the time. He wanted to remember the dusting of freckles and the shape of her mouth and the faint scar on her cheek that was the shape of a birch leaf. "Someone from the Red Dawn, you thought?"

"Yes, someone from the Red Dawn."

Tashué sighed against the ache in his chest. *She's not lying to you,* he reminded himself. "Stella… I want you to know that I understand why you're running. And why you lie about who you are. For Ceridwen. I understand completely. And I understand that lying about all of it is like a reflex for you, because you've done it so long. I can see it now that I've gotten to know you, the moment when you lie. The corner of your mouth turns down, just a little, and you stop blinking for a moment too long."

She turned to him. There was so much tension in her shoulders, her bright eyes turning hot in a way he hadn't seen before. Her hands were clenched at her sides.

"Please, don't be angry," he said. "I'm only trying to untangle it all."

Still, she said nothing. Her hands weren't clenched into fists anymore; instead she wrung them together.

Tashué stifled a sigh, giving himself a long moment before he spoke. "I wish you would trust me. I'm only trying to help. I would do anything you asked, keep any secret, sign any scrap of paper. What can I do to show you that you can trust me?"

Stella reached up, wiping her eyes and turning to meet his gaze. "What makes you ask, then? Why do you need to know all these ugly pieces of my life?" Her voice was thick with suppressed emotion. But instead of retreating from him as she used to, she stepped closer.

Tashué shifted in the chair, reaching out to her and giving her a gentle tug. He pushed his face into her neck, kissed her jaw. The way she leaned against him felt so good. "I'm trying to understand. I'm still missing something. Whatever you know would help."

Stella took a deep breath, closing her eyes. "Fine, then—Siras Duncreek is hunting me. He's Authority. He's been following me, ever since I left Cruinnich. He'll kill me if he finds me."

"The Authority doesn't send Officers after the Talented."

Her body went stiff, starting to pull away turning so she looked him in the eye. "You ask me to trust you, and yet you still don't quite trust me, do you? You're still fighting with yourself about who you are, about where your loyalties lie. If I'm supposed to trust you, you can't ask me to fight with you about things that I *know* are true."

"I'm sorry," Tashué said swiftly. "You're right. Everything I thought I knew is a lie and I can't... It doesn't matter."

Stella nodded and she leaned against him, resting her face in the crook of his neck. He hugged her close, wrapping both arms about her and squeezing. There was so much tension in her—he'd once thought of her as a woman tired and deflated, but as he came to know her, he realized how he'd misread her. Her shell might have been weary, but there was a steel core to her that would never wear away. He tried to imagine what life must have been like, all these years, alone with Ceridwen and running for their lives. To raise a child was trial enough. To raise one alone was harder still. To raise one while fearing for your life at every turn, wondering if death was around the corner? He knew what it was to live in fear of death—life in the military made sure of that.

"Are you leaving soon?" Tashué asked.

"I am," Stella whispered. "A merchant barge, heading south to White Crown. A lot of the barges are running light with the wharf burned and no one buying in the Market quarter, so they're taking passengers instead."

Tashué closed his eyes, taking a deep breath. *You have to let her go.* "Where will you go after White Crown?"

"I haven't decided yet."

Another deep breath to brace himself, and then he put his hands on either side of her face and kissed her gently, just once. "You asked me, yesterday, why Gianna and not you. What I said, about arresting Gianna being wrong... That was only half the truth. The whole ugly thing was wrong and I never should have played a part in it." He fought to breathe through the tightness in his throat. With her body pressed against his, he couldn't reach for his cigarillos to soothe himself. *You can't ask her to stay. You have to let her go.* "But there's more to it than that. I think you own a piece of me. You reached into my chest and you took something, but I'm a better man for it. I won't ask you to stay because I know you can't. But I'll ask you again where you'll go. If you tell me, I'll follow you. I need to get Jason out of the Rift, somehow, but once he's out there's nothing holding me here. If you tell me where to find you, I'll come. If you don't want me to, or you don't trust me, whatever the reason—when I ask, tell me again that you don't know. I'll understand and I swear I won't ask again. If this is the moment where I have to let you go, so be it. But if you want me to follow you..." Another deep breath. In, then out. He feared the asking, because he feared that she would say it again. *I don't know.* Except this time he would know that it was because she didn't want him. But maybe she would tell him, and that chance was too beautiful a thing to let fear stop him. "After White Crown, where will you go?"

She kissed him and it was like she took another piece of his soul, holding it delicately in the palm of her hand. "I miss the mountains," she whispered. "I thought I would go to Teshii."

His throat was so tight that he fought to breathe. He smiled. He knew enough now not to run his fingers through her hair, but over it instead, feeling the curls beneath his hand but not getting himself tangled in them. "It's windy in Teshii."

"Have you been?"

Tashué nodded. "Sailed from Teshii to Uatann, when I was assigned to a Jitabvi unit under Maddox."

She leaned closer, resting their foreheads together. "Is it as beautiful as they say?"

"The city in the cliffs? It is breathtaking. I've never seen anything like it. The red granite, and the purest blue ocean of the bay, and the snowcapped mountains behind it."

Stella nodded, her fingers pushing into his beard. She was as attached to his beard as he was to her hair, the tangled mess that was growing on his face offering her some comfort that he didn't understand. Or perhaps he did understand it—one of her curls had escaped her combs, hanging down the nape of her neck and over her shoulder, one of the corkscrews that he could slide his finger into.

"Then I'll go to Teshii and wait for you there."

Finally, he could breathe. He kissed her on the cheek, on the mouth, on the neck. Not goodbye, then. It didn't have to be that. Yes, she would leave, but he would see her again. He only had to get Jason out of the Rift.

"Do you know how to shoot?" Tashué asked, pulling away from her.

"Yes. I'm better with a rifle, but I've used pistols before."

"Take this, then." Tashué shifted to draw his Imburleigh, handing it to Stella. "If you see Siras Duncreek, you put six rounds of lead in his chest."

42

LORNE

DAY 22

"You ready?"

Lorne bit back a curse as he stripped down to his trousers, handing his jacket and his shirt to Orix. He kicked off his shoes, stripped out of his socks. "Is anyone ever ready to step up there with the fucking Hammer?"

Orix laughed, and there was a nervous, uncomfortable edge to it. "No."

"Thanks." Lorne spread his arms and Orix searched him quickly, looking for hidden weapons. "Good to know."

Orix patted Lorne on the back, his hand slapping on Lorne's bare skin. "I bet on you against the Hammer, so you better be ready."

Lorne headed to the stage, pushing and jostling his way through the bodies. Climbed up.

Breathe.

Ijaz clambered up across from him, swinging his big arms back and forth to loosen the muscles. He grinned at Lorne and reached across the stage with a giant, meaty hand, outstretched as if they were business men, meeting over pints of bitter at a public house. Lorne took the man's handshake, feeling the scars and the calluses.

He half expected Ijaz to crush his hand in some show of his strength, but the shake was an honest one. The crowd loved it, howling and jeering.

The stagemaster stepped up onto his stool, raising his arms. An eerie hush fell over the storehouse. In the quiet and the stillness, Lorne found himself holding his breath again.

Breathe. In. Out. Every enemy has a weakness. That's what the diplomatic division taught you. Every enemy has a weakness—find it.

"Ijaz the Derccian Hammer, the crusher, the destroyer!"

The fight hall shook with the roar of men and women cheering for the massive fighter, but Ijaz's only response was a nod and a wave. Most fighters basked in the attention, pacing the ring like caged lions, throwing punches and roaring back, but Ijaz stood in place and kept his eyes on Lorne.

Fuck he's big.

"And Lorne the Lledewydd Lightning, the thunder, the fastest fists in the Dominion!"

Another roar. Stomping of feet. Someone had reached onto the stage and was grasping for Lorne's ankles until Orix kicked him away.

"Odds six to one for the Derccian Hammer, ladies and gentlemen, make your bets now, make 'em fast."

The chatter in the room rose to a deafening roar. He took a deep breath. *Stay calm. Breathe.* He thought of everything he'd learnt by watching Ijaz's other fights. Ijaz offered his hand every time and Lorne had never seen anyone else take it. No one had ever shaken his hand before.

Somewhere in the distance, the bell was clanging. Smashing incessantly to be heard over the din—the fight was on. Everything just got louder, the floor of the stage rattling as people smashed against it. He was a drop of water on the skin of a drum, rattling and trembling with the concussive beat.

Ijaz stepped forward and swung hard.

Lorne stepped closer instead of away, ducking under Ijaz's arm and throwing a punch into Ijaz's chest. Ijaz didn't flinch at the impact. He stepped back. Lorne stayed close, inside the reach of

Ijaz's long arms. Hit him again in the same spot. Ijaz tried to push Lorne away. Lorne rolled out of the push and darted in. Hit him again. Ijaz grunted. He backed away and swung, this time faster than Lorne could move.

Lorne's knees hit the stage. His ears rang—or maybe that was the crowd, roaring. Something hot was on Lorne's face—blood, he could taste it. From his brow. He knew that feeling, hot and numb at the same time, like his body knew pain was coming but his blood was up and his brain was dazed and the message wasn't getting through yet. The stage rattled, the tremor passing all the way up Lorne's bones. One. Two. Three. The stagemaster was counting. He'd count to ten before declaring the match over. Four. Five. Six. Lorne shook his head. Blinked away the blood. Seven. Eight— Lorne rose to his feet.

Blood stung in his eye. Dripped down his chest. Ijaz stepped in, another swing. Lorne skipped back out of range. Ijaz's fist passed so close in front of his face that he could feel the wind it made. Ijaz kept coming. A low right. Lorne stepped into his reach again. Hit Ijaz in the same spot, over and over fast as he could. Ijaz grunted, folding. Lorne swung. Smashed Ijaz's cheek. Ijaz's head snapped to the side. An angry roar from deep in his throat. He surged forward, his fist coming up fast.

Darkness. Lorne was drowning in it, the darkness. And the pain. Consumed him.

The mist of pain cleared and he realized he was laying flat on his back, blood filling his mouth where he'd bit his tongue. He rolled onto his side and spat. Blood kept coming. The stagemaster was counting, six, seven, eight.

Lorne scrambled back to his feet. Head still swimming. Only a moment to wipe the blood out of his eye and spit again—then the floor was rumbling. Ijaz charging at him. Lorne's chest caught the blow. Pain exploded. Lorne's body moved on training and instinct, stepping in even though he couldn't breathe, hitting Ijaz again and again in the ribs, both fists smashing hard so he could feel the impact all the way up his arms. Ijaz pushed him, sending Lorne staggering. Ijaz charged across the stage, both fists ready. Lorne ducked. Sprang back up, another punch landed in the same spot. This time, the rib snapped.

Ijaz grunted, staggered. Fell to his knees. The stagemaster started counting. Ijaz stood at seven, his teeth clenched together so hard his jaw bulged. He swung. The punch sailed past Lorne. Ijaz tried again with his left. Lorne charged in. Ijaz saw him coming, stepped back, one of his big fists coming at Lorne's face. Caught him in the lips. He staggered back. More blood, down his face. Down his chest.

Forward anyway. Ijaz tried to back away, guarding his ribs. Lorne didn't let Ijaz get away. Hit him again and again. Ijaz roared with pain—but his knee came up. Lorne twisted. Ijaz's knee lifted Lorne off the stage. Leaned into it so he came down on his feet. Ijaz folded himself over his injured side. Lorne snapped his head forward, catching Ijaz on the bridge of his nose. Lorne's head swam. A bloom of red. Coming from Ijaz, streaming from both nostrils.

Another roar of rage rumbled through Ijaz's chest. He swung wild. Lorne skittered aside and made a quick jab at Ijaz's face. Hit him in the nose, sprayed himself with blood. Ijaz fell to his knees.

The whole stage shook, rattling up Lorne's bones again. The stagemaster counted his steady beat. Ijaz stood at nine, came up swinging. Lorne took another fist to the chest. Worth it. Ijaz dropped his guard and Lorne hit the broken rib. Ijaz bellowed.

He lunged for Lorne, but he was slower than before, and Lorne moved to the side and kicked out at his ankle. Ijaz staggered to one side, almost falling, his knee trembling as it took his weight. Lorne kicked at the weak knee and Ijaz buckled. His knee hit the floor. And he sprang back up before the ringmaster could even count. Both fists were swinging now. Lorne stepped into the big man's reach, hit that spot and he heard another snap. Ijaz staggered past and fell to both knees this time, his guts heaving as he vomited. The stagemaster was counting again and Lorne's own head felt it would burst. The stagemaster kept counting on—five, six, seven, and Ijaz gagged and vomited again, the smell acrid and rank and making Lorne's stomach heave.

But Ijaz was up before ten. Wiped his mouth with the back of his hand. Blood from his nose. Blood from his mouth. Eyes wild. Swung hard. Caught Lorne's jaw, nearly spinning him off his feet. Lorne staggered, didn't fall. Ijaz was coming up behind him. Lorne dropped to one knee as Ijaz swung. The punch sailed over his head. The ringmaster counted one, two, and Ijaz stepped back but Lorne was already rising. Launching himself at Ijaz's bad side. He could feel the bones shift beneath his fist turning in. Ijaz howled. He staggered and Lorne pressed forward, fist catching that broken nose. Smashed it to a pulp. Ijaz fell. Gulped at the air like a fish on the dock, blood frothing from his mouth.

The stagemaster started counting. Lorne sucked in a deep breath, forcing himself to stand. If he fell before the count, they'd call no-winner. Iwan didn't like no-winners. Ijaz rolled onto his side and looked like he might rise. When he tried to take the weight on his right side, he bellowed and slumped back down again. The stagemaster reached ten. The bell rang. All the sounds of the Hive were distant, muffled by the rush of blood and the pain that rattled around Lorne's skull.

Lorne staggered. Someone caught him. Orix. People were climbing up on the stage but more of Iwan's employees had arrived to beat them back. To collect Ijaz. To spread sawdust on the puddle of vomit and splashes of blood.

Lorne shook himself, staggering to the edge of the stage, but Orix pulled him back.

"You're staying. You have to stay."

"What?"

Orix shrugged. Climbed down from the stage and left Lorne standing alone. Lorne looked up at the stagemaster and spread his hands. The stagemaster shrugged at him.

"What the fuck is going on?"

No one answered.

Lorne spotted a gap in the crowd where another man was coming through, weaving through the bodies, surging through the crush.

"Lorne the Lledewydd Lightning—your victor, ladies and

gentlemen!" the stagemaster bellowed. "Your victor that crushed the Hammer fights a marathon tonight! How many men can he take? How many men? Take a number and make your bets! Equal odds on fight one, but the odds will climb with every man down! How many men can he take?"

"I didn't agree to this!" He searched for Orix in the crowd. "Orix, I didn't agree to this!"

Orix shrugged at him, spreading his hands. "Mr. Iwan said, so that's what we're doing. Take it like a man."

"Fuck you!" Lorne spat.

Blood still dripped from his mouth, from his eye.

The bell again. His first opponent came in fast, maybe hoping Lorne was tired from his fight. Lorne rushed in to meet him. Put his whole body into the punch. His fist connected with the side of the man's head, spinning him around. The stage trembled when the man hit the boards.

The second man was on the stage faster. This one circled slowly before stepping in. He got in a good hit on Lorne's face, aiming for the split above his eyebrow but getting him in the cheek and the eye instead. Lorne got him with a knee to the chest, an elbow to the back of the neck, a heavy, downward fist to the back of the head that laid him down cold. The roaring of the crowd mixed with the roar of his own heartbeat, the rush of blood, the pain so fierce he could *hear* it. His eye was swelling fast. Soon he wouldn't be able to see.

Third man up. This one was bigger, his reach longer, his fists heavier. Maybe Lorne would just go down. Let this big one hit him in the face and just let himself drop. But Iwan didn't like it when people threw fights. Throwing a fight made it so the bettors didn't trust the fights anymore, and anyone who fucked with the bets wasn't seen in the Bay anymore.

The fighter didn't go for his face, anyway. He swung for Lorne's body instead, low and left where Lorne couldn't see. Lorne twisted. Fist found Lorne's ribs. Lorne grunted. Staggered. Twisted and kicked. He caught the other man low in the gut. Lorne kicked again, aiming for his face but catching him in the throat instead. The man fell hard, coughing, gasping for air. His hands scrabbled at his throat. After the count, someone came and dragged him away.

Another man took his place.

Lorne cursed. Spat out blood. He bit his own tongue to keep the rage up. Rage would save him from the pain. Rage and instinct would do what his mind couldn't anymore. The next man charged fast, slamming against his body with fists and chest, pushing him back and back and Lorne had to twist and stagger to keep himself on the stage. Lorne used his arms to cover his face. He kicked out, trying to hook his opponent's ankles to trip him. Lorne fell instead. Hit the stage so hard he felt his bones rattle.

"You're alright, boyo. You're alright!"

It was Tam. Leaning on the stage. Pounding on the wood. He was such a small man, almost swallowed by the press of bodies. But he stood, resolute. Clinging to the stage to look Lorne in the eye. So close that he reached out with a gnarled hand and touched Lorne's shoulder.

"Tam's got you, when this is over."

Behind Tam, Adley. If Adley was watching, Powell Iwan was watching too. Fuck him, fuck them both.

Seven. Eight. Nine. *Get up.*

His whole body screamed as he rose and his opponent rushed in. A fist knocked the air out of Lorne, but he swung. A spray of blood from the man's sharp cheekbone. His opponent stepped back. Lorne kicked out at his chest. The man stepped back. Giving himself room. Deep breath. The man charged. One more deep breath— there was only a moment to clear his head. He kicked as his opponent closed the distance, hitting the man's knee as his weight came down. His timing was off. Joint didn't pop like it usually did. Still, the man staggered. Lorne kicked again. Swept the man's feet out from under him. He fell hard, tried to scramble right back up. Lorne kicked, hard as he could. The man's jaw broke with an audible crack and he fell again, bleeding and drooling and screaming at the floorboards.

They dragged him away. Spread more saw dust. Another man stepped in. He came fast from Lorne's blind side. Big fist hit him in the face. His cheek split and his mouth filled with blood and maybe his very teeth trembled in the bone. He staggered. Fell. Head swimming. He pushed himself up. Swung. But his opponent wasn't standing where he thought—his fist found only air. Breathing hurt and punching hurt and everything hurt and he twisted to find his opponent but only found a fist, coming hard against the other side of his face, just below the eye, splitting open the other cheek. He tried to get his legs under him but they were wobbly and weak. The third hit him in the face and darkness took him.

H e dreamt of his mother, down there in the darkness. He could smell the opium she smoked like it would save her life. It was sweet and acrid at the same time, drifting around her like a perfume. But even with glazed eyes and cold fingers, she was lovely. She wore flowers in her hair in the spring, her eyes sparkling like blue stars.

He dreamt of his sister. So little, so hungry all the time. Eyes as grey as the Western Sea, like her father. Fat little cheeks and dimples on her knuckles, because that's when he got good at lying, at begging for food, at stealing. That's when he learnt to do whatever it took, to keep her fat. Since their mother was too busy chasing poppy dreams to know they were even alive.

He was bouncing and shaking when the vicious pain had a hold of him again. He lay flat on a bench, he realized, the leather pressing against his face, cold and smooth but too hard. He could still taste blood in his mouth. The sounds coming from his throat were more animal than man, like the sounds his mother used to make when she was opium sick and lying in her bed. He closed his eyes—or the one eye that still opened—and wished for the empty darkness to come back.

"There, boyo, you're alright. Old Tam has you now. Tam'll take fine care of you, don't you worry."

He felt Tam's hand on his brow and a warmth filled his mind, dulling the pain and letting him slip back into the blessed darkness.

W hen he woke again, his whole body ached, from his feet to his fists to his face and all the soft parts in the middle. He felt weak and stupid and tired. He closed his eye again and wished for more sleep.

"There, now, boyo, you'll be alright. Tam ain't a good healer, but I've done enough now that you won't die on me. There was some ugly bits bleeding somewhere in the middle of you, but they seem to be quiet now. Most your blood is like to stay where it belongs, I think."

Lorne groaned again, reaching up with shaky hands, his knuckles so split and swollen he couldn't straighten his fingers. His fingertips probed his many wounds and found stitches in the worst gashes, pulling the skin tight, crusts of blood dried over the twine.

"Let me see what I can do about that eye, hey? Hold still, now, I'm not so good at this."

Tam laid an old, knobby hand over Lorne's eye, the palm cupped carefully. Lorne felt heat, pressure, like fingers kneading into the swollen tissue. He clenched his teeth against a scream that tried to escape. The pressure spread, across his face, pushing the pain into a wide, radiating circle that chewed through his skull. His body twisted away from Tam but Tam put his other hand on Lorne's shoulder and held him still. Those old hands were stronger than they looked, clamping Lorne down against the thin, hard mattress. But then the pain started to fade and Tam took his hand away.

"There. Open up, let old Tam see those fine blue eyes of yours."

Lorne opened his eyes, both this time, the flesh feeling less tender, more like it should feel, though his eye watered and his vision was blurry. Tam's home seemed to consist of one room and two windows through which the morning sun lit the room.

"Not so bad," Tam said, tapping Lorne's shoulder. "Not so bad at all."

There was a knock on the door, a hard pounding that shook the little room. Tam cursed under his breath and took up a battered old shotgun before stepping lightly across the room toward his door.

"You leave him be, now, Mr. Iwan. You had your fun."

"Step aside, Tam," came Powell's voice. "I'm done hurtin' him, now I just want to talk to him. Hate to have to hurt you any to do it."

"Tam," Lorne croaked, rolling himself from the bed and forcing himself up. "It's alright, Tam. Put the gun down."

"You lay yourself back down, boy. You ain't in no way to be moving about yet."

"Go help the young man to his feet, Adley. Quick now. We've a carriage waiting for us."

"Stay where you are, Adley," Tam said, shifting his aim to point at the dead centre of Adley's chest. "How's about you tell me where we're all going 'fore I let you take him."

Powell grinned. "I like a loyal man, Tam, but my patience only lasts so long. The boy and I need to go have a conversation with someone he knows, and I won't be taking no for an answer. I let you get this far seeing as you work so hard at the Hive, you spend so much coin at my fights, and you never cause any trouble. Hell, I do like a man who stands his ground, but there's only so much ground-standing I can allow, you understand?"

"Fine," Tam grunted, lowering the point of his rifle. "But I'm comin', and I'm bringing my gun."

43

TASHUÉ

DAY 23

Jason was limping when he walked into the visitation room, his face tight with pain. His shuffling step was painful to watch. Tashué half-stood from his chair, reaching for his son, but of course the grate stopped him.

"What happened to your foot?" Tashué asked.

"I broke my toe," Jason grunted. "Helping another inmate to the water closet in the middle of the night. Stubbed it on the stone floor. Fucking smashed it up right to shit."

"Finally, a story that's almost believable," Tashué said. "Why did he need your help?"

"He was new. Didn't know where to go." Laughter barked from Jason's throat and he leaned forward. "One of yours, the poor shit."

"One of mine? What do you mean?"

"Glaen Forsooth. One of yours, isn't he? He certainly remembers you. He seems like a nice enough man, except he hates you."

Tashué took in a deep breath, letting it out slowly. Of course, of course. Of course Glaen found Jason. "How is he?"

Jason scowled at Tashué, sinking down and holding his head in his hands. "Are you kidding? He's fucking here, isn't he? 'How is he?' What a stupid question. His life is over and the guards will beat him into submission. What did he do to deserve it, by the way?"

"Fraternization," Tashué breathed. His chest felt so tight that he couldn't fill his lungs anymore. "I processed him for fraternization."

Jason laughed. "That's fantastic. You're really doing the Dominion a service. Regular Blaylock the Hero, you are, defending the citizens of this country from Glaen Forsooth dipping his wick. I bet you're proud of yourself."

Tashué tried to breathe, but his chest was still so tight that it hurt. "I'm not proud of myself. I'm ashamed. Does that make you happy?" He cleared his throat of the emotion that caught there, but he still couldn't quite breathe. "I'm fucking ashamed that I had any part in what happened to Glaen Forsooth and Gianna Tarbrook, and I wish I could undo it all. That's why I'm here. Jason, listen to me." Tashué slid to the edge of his chair, getting as close as he could. "I'm sorry for everything. I've been so wrong. You're right about the Authority and about this place and about your Talent. I'm sorry for everything you've been through because of me and my stupidity."

"What?"

"Wait—listen. I want you to register."

"No, but you just said—"

"Just listen, please." Tashué pressed his hand to the grate again, wishing Jason would reach out and touch the other side. "I want you to register. It won't take long—they'll have you out in a few weeks. Days, even. And then, as soon as you're out of here, we'll leave."

"Leave?"

"Yes. You and me, Stella and Ceridwen. Lorne, if he wants to come—he's always talking about leaving the Dominion. I know he only stays for you, so I'm sure he'll come, he'll follow you anywhere. Fuck the Dominion and fuck the Authority. We'll leave and we won't ever look back."

Jason's breathing went shallow and fast. He leaned back, pushing himself away from the table, shaking his head. "You bastard."

"What?"

"You fucking bastard!" Jason stood so fast that his chair clattered to the floor behind him and he slammed his fists on the table. Tashué felt the rumble of it, felt the rage coming off him like the heat waves of an inferno. "Why now? I needed you to say this to me a month ago. A week ago! Why *now*, you stubborn, righteous bastard?"

Tashué went still, biting back the anger. This would not descend into another shouting match. He took a deep breath, let it out slowly. How much could the guards hear? "What does it matter? Why not last year? Because I wasn't ready. Why not last month? I wasn't ready! I'm sorry it took so long, but it's not too late—"

"But you still don't understand, do you? It *is* too late! It's too fucking late." Jason shook his head, taking a step back. He reached up and grabbed his hair again as if the pain in his scalp was some refuge from his roiling emotions. When had he started doing that?

"Jason," Tashué said, bracing himself. "Why do you think it's too late? Why can't we just go?"

Jason shook his head and he took a step back, away from Tashué. "If I register now, they'll send me straight to the Breeding Program. Don't you understand what that means? Straight from here to the Breeding Program. They aren't going to let me out for a few weeks of furlough. This isn't the military. I'm not enlisting! If I register with them, they send me *straight* there, and those walls are higher and thicker and you won't be able to get me out of there, the same as you couldn't ever get me out of here! You can't *help* me anymore. You never could fucking help me!"

Tashué stood, leaning over the table and putting both hands against the grate. He wished he could break through, tear it apart with his hands, leap across the table to Jason and carry him out of here. "Jason, please, I'm sorry. I know. Everything I've done for you is wrong, and I'm sorry! We can figure this out. We can make this better. Jason, please, sit back down!"

Jason backed further and there *were* tears in his eyes, sliding down his cheeks. He bit his lip, shook his head, pushing himself against the door behind him. "You were right, before. I want you to give my ashes to the Brightwash, same as my mother."

"Jason, don't say that," Tashué said. "I was just trying to make a point. Please, come talk to me and we can figure out what to do."

Jason shook his head again, pulled his hair again. "No, I can't do this with you anymore. You think you can fucking fix everything, but you can't! You can't! It's not my job to soothe your delicate fucking ego. It's not my damned job!"

Jason turned and smashed the door with his palm. The whole door rattled with it, shaking in Tashué's chest.

"Come back and talk to me. Please, Jason, just let me fix it. Come sit down and we can figure this out. Jason!"

The door opened and Jason stepped out before the guard could even step inside. Tashué thought he heard the confusion in the hallway beyond, but then the door slammed shut and there was nothing in the room with him but silence.

Frustration built like pressure through his chest, and the only way to let it out was to scream. His voice echoed in the room, booming around him, his own animal sound making him angrier. He kicked his chair, sending it smashing against the wall. Wood splintered, the legs skittering across the room, the seat falling with a clatter. The door swung open and two people burst in. They paused when they saw Tashué alone, just for a second, but then they tried to come at him all at once. One person tripped over the broken back of the chair and another reached for Tashué but Tashué jerked away.

"Don't touch me," he snapped. "Don't you fucking touch me!"

Tashué stomped out. He turned the wrong way down the hall, looking for any sign of a door that might have led to Jason's side of the building. He would drag Jason out of here, saving him from this place like he should have years ago. He'd wasted so much time being stubborn and hedging his bets, hoping he was right. He was so wrong and Jason was paying for it.

The two guards scrambled after him. More running toward him. There was no doorway at the end of the hallway, no passage through. Tashué cursed, feeling something building in his veins, a pressure, a fury, a vicious power that seared him from within. The headache clamped down so hard that his vision tried to go white, a pain so fierce that it seemed as if someone had shoved a hot brand in the base of his skull.

He opened one of the rooms and found it empty, the chairs in place and waiting for the visitors. He lifted one of the chairs and smashed it against the grate, hoping to break through, but the chair shattered against the metal poles. More guards came after him and he fought them off, tempted to use the chair against some of them, but they were talking to him in low voices like he was a spooked horse. He threw what was left of the chair—just the back—into the corner. One man tried to grab him and Tashué swung before he could stop himself, a hard left that caught the guard just below the ribs, forcing the air from his lungs in a violent rush. The man staggered and half-fell, folding over himself and then the rest of the guards were rushing in, grabbing Tashué's arms. Tashué managed to get an elbow in another man's face, smashing his lips against his teeth, before the whole mass of them surged against him, pushing him back against the wall, pinning his body to the stone.

"Get off me! Get your fucking hands off me!"

"Sir, I need you to calm down." Flinn was standing in the doorway, spectacles perched on the end of his nose. "You stop assaulting my guards, sir, or I'll see you arrested."

"Flinn, you get these people off me!" Tashué thundered.

"Yes, sir, just as soon as you promise to come calmly."

Tashué clenched his fists so hard that he felt his own fingernails cutting into his palms. "Yes, fine. Alright. I'm leaving."

"Let Mr. Blackwood go, carefully now. Are you alright, Mr. Boyd?"

"Fine," gasped the man Tashué had knocked the wind out of. He was upright again, holding his stomach with both hands. "I'm fine."

"Excellent. Please escort Mr. Blackwood out of the building, all the way to the bridge if you please."

"Are you Tashué Blackwood?"

Tashué waited for Keoh in the small room with no door, just like the last time he had come to visit her. The anger that boiled in the Rift hadn't subsided. It was only made worse when he returned to his office and found the letter from House One, sitting on his desk. The letter sat now like a cannonball in his pocket as he tried to imagine the fight that was to come. Keoh wouldn't be happy. The letter itself was short and to the point, but loaded with so many questions that Tashué could barely think straight.

Commander Blackwood,

Apologies, but the following names are not registered with the National Tainted Registration Authority.

Lizanne Gian Ly

Petrik Gian Ly

Gwinnith Gian Ly

Benjin Gian Ly

Dex Gian Ly

Valen Gian Ly

We have searched our records thoroughly.

House Commander Gwllt Inmoore

But Keoh hadn't been brought to him, like the last time. It was some other woman who stood in the doorway, staring at him, waiting for his answer. She was carrying a small box. He blinked at the woman, wondering who she was and why she had come to see him.

"Yes," Tashué said slowly. "Where is Keoh?"

She stepped into the room, sitting the box on the chair that Keoh should have used. "You're here to visit Keoh Gian Ly?"

"Yes."

"Mr. Blackwood, Keoh Gian Ly has passed away."

"Excuse me?" Tashué breathed, standing. "How is that possible? I was only just here to see her a few days ago."

"Yes sir," the woman said softly. "Miss Ly overdosed on opium. She passed away swiftly, and healers were unable to revive her."

Tashué felt the tension crawl across his whole body, hot and furious. He needed to act, to move. Some bitter part of him had always known that this was how she would die, that she would float away on a cloud of opium smoke. But how, in this place, had she managed to get enough opium to smoke herself to death? "Where is she?"

"She's passed away, sir."

"Yes, I realize that," Tashué snapped, taking a step toward the woman. "Where is her body? I want to see it."

A guard stepped closer, coming from around the corner. There were so many guards in his life suddenly. So much frustration and anger and vicious hatred.

"Sir, it is our policy to incinerate the bodies of the diseased. If you would like her ashes released to you, you can fill out the appropriate paperwork."

"When did she die?" Tashué pressed. "What kind of investigation was made when she died?"

"Investigation? She took a fatal dose of opium——"

"How do you know that?" Tashué roared. "What proof do you have that this is how she died?"

"She had opium in her possession, against the policy of the Program."

"How could she have taken a fatal dose if she still had it in her possession? And how in blazing hell did she get opium in this place?"

The woman straightened her back, jutting out her jaw. She was not to be cowed by Tashué's outburst, not intimidated. "We have collected Miss Ly's belongings. If you would like to sign here we can release them to you."

Tashué reeled, looking down at the box. He grabbed the back of his chair, leaning on it or he'd keel right over. "Is the opium in there?"

"No sir, the opium was destroyed."

"How convenient that all evidence that may or may not prove this story has been incinerated."

"Yes sir, it's very convenient. In this convenient way, we dispose of all the bodies in the custody of the Program, as well as any contraband. Would you like to sign for Miss Lian's belongings, sir? If not, they will also be incinerated."

Tashué drew a deep breath through his clenched teeth. When he took the pen she offered, his hands were shaking. He read the document she presented to him, but there was nothing hidden in the text —it only stated that he received her known belongings and was entitled to no compensation for her death or for any belongings he perceived to be missing. His signature became a messy scrawl at the bottom of the page. She presented him with another paper to sign for her remains, and she waited with him while someone was sent away to fetch them. A copper urn was produced, handed over. It seemed too terribly small to contain a person, even a person as small as Keoh.

Oh, Jason... Jason, in the Rift, so filled with hate and fear churning in his gut like acid. He had started this process, asking Tashué to find Keoh and help her—and now Tashué was holding Keoh in a copper urn. Once again he had failed.

He carried Keoh and her belongings out of the Breeding Program, away from the walls that had kept her locked up for so long. How many years had it been since she was assigned here? How many summers and winters had she passed behind those high walls, overlooking the city? He didn't remember. He didn't even know, not for sure. Jason was a year old when she had taken him and run from Yaelsmuir, four when she was found again. How long after that had she been assigned to the Breeding Program?

He wanted to go back to the Rift. To take Keoh's belongings and her ashes to Jason and lay them at his son's feet and beg for forgiveness. And Jason would be angry and Jason would rage, but maybe Tashué could be able to convince him to register so that they could finally leave. And Stella could teach him to use his Talent and they would be safe together somewhere else. But he was banned from the Rift now, according to Flinn and his clipboard. Tashué Blackwood— permanently denied visitation. What about Lorne? Could Lorne convince Jason? He knew as soon as the thought passed through his mind, it wouldn't happen—Lorne didn't fight with Jason. Lorne didn't convince Jason. Lorne was perfectly happy just existing beside Jason, in the middle of whatever storm Jason had stirred up, as if his only purpose was to keep Jason company while he was in the shit.

He caught a carriage to take him to Brickheart. He finally opened the box once he was settled in the back. Keoh's belongings consisted of letters from Jason. A great stack of letters and pictures that he'd drawn as a child, some torn and creased and barely visible, some as fresh as if he'd just written them. And buried in the papers, he found the list of children that Keoh had told Tashué about, six names and tiny footprints pressed into the paper with black ink. *Lizanne, Petrik, Gwinnith, Benjin, Dex, Valen.* The feet were barely bigger than Tashué's thumb, most of the toe prints smudged. Tashué could imagine the tiny baby foot, stained with ink for days after being pressed against the paper.

He sank back against the seat, replacing the papers in the box. How had his entire life come to be such a long list of failures?

44

TASHUÉ

DAY 23

When Tashué turned his key in his lock at home, some cold feeling passed through his chest. The deadbolt hadn't made its usual heavy thunk, because it was unlocked already. He knew he had locked it on his way out that morning. He always locked his door, without fail.

He paused long enough to shift. He rested Keoh's urn in the box of letters, tucking the whole box under one arm. He turned the doorknob first, easing it open just enough to disengage the latch. He reached for his gun but of course it wasn't there. He'd given it to Stella. He drew the old cavalry knife instead, the weight of it familiar and comforting. It was a hefty blade and he still remembered how to kill with it. He'd keep the box, throw it at his opponent if they charged him, letting paper and ashes distract them long enough for Tashué to plunge the knife into flesh.

He kicked the door open and stepped in, his heart beating fast.

"Easy, now, Mr. Blackwood," said Powell Iwan.

Tashué's eyes swept the room, taking in everything. Powell and Adley had no obvious weapons. The only gun he saw belonged to Tam—the little old man had his shotgun with him. It sat across his lap, the muzzle pointed squarely at Powell's chest. Powell didn't seem to care much about the gun pointed at him.

"Let's not do anything we might regret," Powell continued. "I only want to have a few words with you, is all. Come in, have a seat. We don't need no trouble."

"If you're not here for trouble, why does Lorne look like he's been beaten within an inch of his life?" Tashué asked, kicking his door shut behind him. "You alright?"

"I'll live, I'm informed," Lorne grunted.

Tashué scowled. *I'll live* wasn't exactly comforting. "How did you get so ugly?"

"I caught a few bad fights," Lorne said. He coughed, his whole body convulsing with the power of it, his face contorting with pain. Tam scrabbled at his pocket, finding a handkerchief and handing it over. Lorne held it to his mouth and when the coughing finally stopped, Tashué saw blood on the off-white linen. "A bunch of them, right in a row. Still haven't had an explanation as to why I had to fight so many times in one night."

"As soon as Mr. Blackwood puts his big knife away and sits down, we'll have that conversation," Powell promised. "There's only so long I'll abide having weapons waved around in my face, sir, and you aren't the first to pull one on me today. My patience is wearing thin."

Stifling a curse, Tashué put the knife back in the holster around his chest. He put the box down on the table, freeing up his hands. "I need a smoke first."

Powell laughed at that and nodded. Flicking open his cigarillo case, Tashué paused long enough to offer one to the old man. Tashué sparked a match and lit Powell's cigarillo, watching the old man take a few deep breaths. Powell chuckled, putting the cigarillo between his lips and closing his eyes.

"Reminds me of when I was just a boy," he said. "I smoked cheap tobacco like this, too dry and too old. You rolled it well, though, good and tight. You roll them yourself?"

"Yes, sir." Tashué dragged a chair from the table. He took a deep breath to still his racing heart, trying not to look too closely at the box, trying to forget the sight of those tiny footprints. He couldn't match wits with Powell Iwan with so much grief clinging to his mind. "So, what are we talking about, Mr. Iwan?"

"It has come to my attention that this young man has been wandering the city, looking for information about the Army of the Red Dawn. And he does so at your request." He paused to take a pull from his cigarillo, blowing out the smoke in lazy rings. "I like this young man. He makes good money for me and he fights well and he never once complains. He's strong and he's smart. I'll make him a real pugilist, if he still wants to, and he'll make more money than he's ever dreamt of. There's a future for that boy in my mind. But he's loyal to you over me, isn't he?"

"If he's loyal to me, I don't deserve it," Tashué said.

Lorne cackled, the sound wet and wheezing. "You've fucking got that right."

Tashué shrugged. "I suspect he's loyal to my son over either of us."

"Ah, yes, of course, the tainted boy in the Rift. Jason Blackwood."

"Jason has no part in any of this," Lorne grunted.

"Oh, I doubt that very much, but I'm not finished yet, boy," Powell said, holding up a hand to Lorne. "We're here to talk about other things, aren't we? So, this foolish, brilliant young man is loyal to your son and you by extension. And you have business with the Army of the Red Dawn. He looks around for the Red Dawn because you asked him to, because you seem to think that they have some hand in business you've invested yourself in. Are we in agreement of the facts so far?"

"So far," Tashué said. "I'm looking for the Red Dawn because it's been suggested to me they are responsible for murdering children."

Powell spread his hands, as if to say that dead children were hardly something to be concerned about. "That may be, but those old rebel lobcocks happen to be partners of mine. You have an ashtray?"

Tashué nodded, pulling the small metal ashtray off the table and walking it across the room. The old man flicked his cigarillo in the ashtray, waving Tashué back again.

"Where was I?"

"You're partners with the Red Dawn," Tashué grunted, sitting back down. "I expect that's why Lorne looks like he's been in a fight with a meat grinder."

"Not equal partners, mind," Powell said, pointing up at Tashué from his spot on the big wingback chair. "Never that. But those rebel swine have their uses, you see. Them and the Authority and the Patrollers are all chasing each other in circles, like a bunch of dogs in heat, and no one takes a moment to look at old Powell. So when the rebel shits come to me and say that one of my fighters— my very favourite fighter—is poking his nose into matters where it doesn't belong and they tell me I better set him straight or *they'll* set him straight, I listen. Not so much because I care half a bent crown about what those rebel cunts want, but because I'm concerned about the well-being of my favourite fighter. You understand?"

"I can't say that I do," Lorne grunted, spitting into the handkerchief, leaving another spot of blood. "I don't understand how concern for your favourite fighter turns into *this*. Sir."

"The Red Dawn will hear about how Powell's favourite fighter got the shit beaten out of him, in front of everyone," Tashué said, looking at Lorne. There was a terrible fury in the young man, his eyes burning like coals in the fire, his whole body tense even though it must have caused him even more pain. Only the understanding of what was in the room with them kept him in his seat, kept his tongue civil. "Or they had men there to see it, even. And they'll be satisfied that Powell took care of things for them and they won't feel the need to jump you in an alley where there's no stagemaster to make sure no one hits you again after you go down."

"Exactly," Powell said with a nod and a smile. He turned to look at Lorne, smiling again. "You understand now? I'm protecting you."

"Thank you, sir," Lorne grunted.

"You see?" Powell said, turning back to Tashué. "A brilliant fool. Can't see through his anger well enough to see the favour I've done him, but smart enough to know to say yes sir when he'd rather use those fists on me. I'm just a frail old man after all."

Lorne started coughing again, the sound wet and ugly, holding the kerchief over his mouth as his face turned deep red. He coughed so hard and long he looked like he would pass out, his strength failing him and leaving him listing to one side like a ship taking on water. Powell grimaced, looking over at Lorne as Tam patted his back ineffectually.

"Don't you have Talent?" Powell snapped, turning his eyes on Tam. "I thought you'd be able to heal the boy if I let you take him."

"Talent don't work that way, Mr. Iwan. The healing is one of the hardest things 'cause it takes so much strength. I did what I could, but I don't want to be messing around with things I don't understand. I only know how to work the docks."

Powell shook his head, suddenly infuriated. His voice might quaver and his hands might shake when he spoke and his eyes may be milky with cataracts, but the old man's mind was sharp and fast. He knew everything about everyone that came anywhere near his business and the thought that he had overestimated Tam and his Talent must have boiled him from the inside. He sat in his own fury for only a moment or two, then took a deep breath and smiled again.

"I know you, Mr. Blackwood," he continued. "I know everything about you. And I realize that bringing this boy here, looking like he does, and coughing like that, isn't enough to make you give up chasing the folks that killed those little ones."

For a brief moment, the room seemed to go cold as Tashué weighed the idea of reaching for his knife and punching it through the old man's frail chest. There was some distance between them that he would have to cross, but neither Powell nor Adley had any weapons visible. If he lunged for Powell, Tam would be quick to bring his rifle to bear, putting a load in Adley before he had the chance to charge. Hopefully. If Tam didn't shoot Tashué in the confusion.

But, Tashué told himself, Powell Iwan was not the type of man to walk into a room without a way to protect himself from any eventuality. Just because Tashué didn't see any obvious weapons didn't mean the old man was vulnerable.

The moment passed and Tashué relaxed. He smiled, taking a deep drag from his cigarillo. "I would guess that means you have another card left to play, Mr. Iwan."

"Indeed I do," Powell said with another thin smile. "I like you, Mr. Blackwood. I like you very much. Should you ever need more money than the Authority pays you, you come see me, you understand? I could find a use for you very easily."

"I do alright with the Authority, thank you Mr. Iwan," Tashué said as politely as he could. "I'm quite interested in hearing about this other card of yours, though."

"Yes, of course you are," Powell said, leaning forward. "Are you listening, closely, son?"

"Yes, sir."

"The man you're looking for? The one responsible for killing those children?"

Tashué felt his whole body go tense and he found himself holding his breath.

"Edgar Hale. You can find him hiding in the Bay, much to my shame. Hale fancies himself a merchant and he keeps a warehouse near the Hive."

Tashué spread his hands, leaning closer. "Surely you know what my next question is."

"Of course I do," Powell agreed. "Why would I tell you such a thing?"

"Why indeed?"

"Put yourself in my place, if you'll indulge me. You're a man with a reputation. All your business is directly affected by that reputation, and your hold on your piece of the city would perhaps be threatened if that reputation were to slip. It doesn't seem to matter how tough you are, you just keep getting older. A group of young fools is looking for a foothold in your city and you think, yes. It could work. Gives the men with badges someone else to chase for a while, especially with all this talk about a Provincial Police force, heaven help you."

"The Authority's official position is that the Red Dawn has no presence here."

"Of course it is. Because the Authority exists on the premise that it keeps the people safe from the tainted, and if *that* image begins to slip, where will the Authority be? In Yaelsmuir, no less, the home of their Chief Administrator and the place of their birth."

Tashué nodded. "So, the Authority is lying about the Red Dawn."

"Are you really so surprised, Mr. Blackwood? After everything you've been through?"

"No, I suppose I'm not."

"Shall I continue with my little story?"

"Please."

"So, in spite of your best efforts, you're getting old. Some fools come into your city and ask for a bit of space and you decide to give it to them. To give yourself a little more room to breathe. And these fools don't understand things like respect, do they? And they ask for too much because they think they're your equal. And they go too far and attract the attention of the wrong man, and so they ask you— no, they *tell* you—that you must send warning to a man you hold dear, a brilliant fool of a fighter who is close to your grandson and who might one day be something truly special. And of course, you can't spurn them, or else they'll kill that young man and then where are you? You can't promise to protect the men and women loyal to you, not if you let that happen. And if people think you can't protect them, why would they stand loyal to you anymore in this world that's ever changing? So, you cow to them. But that doesn't sit well with you either, does it, 'cause you're not in the habit of letting foolish men tell you what to do."

"You can't allow that to stand," Tashué said. "If it becomes known that this man, Hale, bullied you into compliance, you begin to lose your grasp on the Bay."

"Indeed I do. All the gods saw fit to give me were sons, and all of them are idiots. Not a single one could have taken the Bay themselves, and now they're all dead anyway. So, I must hold it a little longer. Brilliant boy, my Vasska, but there's too much that's soft in him. His brilliance is weakened by such notions as mercy and honour. He does as I ask, but the Bay would devour him once I was gone."

"How will you make him ready?"

Powell snorted. "You must think me a proper fool if you think I'll reveal all of my secrets, sir."

"Forgive me, Mr. Iwan. I was drawn in by your story."

Powell tilted his head back and smiled, his eyes bright and mischievous. "I am an excellent storyteller."

"Yes, sir."

The smile broadened and Powell pointed a crooked finger at Tashué. "I knew I liked you. Smarter than you want people to think, you are."

"Thank you, sir."

"There it is then. Edgar Hale has outstayed his welcome in the Bay. Yes? And you, Mr. Blackwood, will do me the very appreciated favour of escorting him out."

Tashué drew deep drags from his cigarillo, giving his heart time to clatter, giving the shock time to pass through him. "How do you suggest I do that, Mr. Iwan?"

"You're a man of many resources, Mr. Blackwood. I'm sure you can think of something."

Powell started to rise, then, pushing himself slowly from his chair. It took him a long time to stand, but Adley didn't once move to help. Finally, Powell was up straight, smoothing his trousers and brushing the front of his jacket. He snatched his bowler hat from the arm of the chair, spending a moment to pick off every tuft of lint and strand of hair from the felt. "I know what you're thinking, don't I?"

Tashué shrugged. "I'm thinking that even if I brought this accusation to the Patroller, they wouldn't arrest Mr. Hale. There isn't any proof at all, save your word, and I'm willing to bet you wouldn't want me to spread your story to anyone."

Powell pointed at Tashué again, smiling. "Clever one, you are."

"What exactly are you hoping I'll do, Mr. Iwan?"

"Ah, Mr. Blackwood, if I have to make it plain to you, you're not as clever as I think you are. And you wouldn't want me thinking I've misjudged you, would you?"

"No, sir," Tashué said slowly. "I don't think I want that."

Powell nodded, motioning to his thug. "Pay the boy, Adley, and we'll let ourselves out."

The big man grunted and fished into his pocket, finding a heavy purse. He tossed it across the room. Lorne's arms shot up to catch it, but his reflexes were off and the purse hit Lorne in the chest. He grunted at the impact as the purse landed in his lap with the chink of coin.

"You did well last night, son. Made me proud, you did. And made us both a fine few pieces of silver. Here." Powell reached into his pocket, rifling around again and finding a silver crown. He held the coin out to Tashué, dropping it into his palm and patting Tashué on the arm. "Get him to a proper healer, will you?"

"Last time I saw a man as bad as Lorne looks, it cost two silvers to have him healed," Tashué said.

"You're a cheeky fucker, aren't you?" Powell chuckled. "One piece should do. He doesn't need to be pretty, just needs to stop all that damned coughing. Looks fit to burst something in his face, he does." He paused, looking at Lorne again, watching the young man seethe miserably in his seat. "Ah, boy, don't be upset with old Powell. It's all business."

"I'm not upset, sir," Lorne grunted.

"Good boy," Powell said, turning. "Come, Adley."

Tashué stayed in his seat, setting the silver piece on the table and watching it gleam in the weak light coming in through the window. Adley opened the door for Powell and the two of them let themselves out. Tashué listened as the footsteps went slowly down the stairs. Tashué focused his eyes on Tam.

"It's good to see you again, Tam."

Tam broke into a grin, so wide and happy that it seemed a strange sight considering what had just happened in Tashué's apartment. "Aye, Mr. Blackwood, good to see you, too."

"I'm glad to see Lorne has a friend who would hold a gun on Powell Iwan on his behalf."

"Mr. Iwan doesn't scare me none, sir," Tam said, resting the butt of the gun on the floor now that it wasn't needed anymore. "All he can do is kill me, and when you get to be as old as me, death isn't so bad a thing at all."

Tashué heard the door at the bottom of the stairs creak open, sticking in its frame and giving a loud squeak, then thumping shut.

"You alright?" Tashué asked, looking at Lorne.

"No, I'm not fucking alright," Lorne snapped. It set him into another fit of coughs and they had no choice but to wait for it to pass. More blood flecked the handkerchief and Lorne pushed himself to his feet as if his body was too restless to sit any longer.

"I want to leave, Lorne. All of us, Stella and Ceridwen, Jason and you. I told him, I don't care where we go."

"What do you want from me, then?" Lorne scoffed. "To talk to him? You know he won't listen to me. He doesn't listen to anyone, just like you."

"Lorne, wait. Take this to him." Tashué stood, moving to the box. He didn't take out the urn, not yet. He took the page of footprints instead, holding it out to Lorne. "This is from Keoh. It's all the children she's borne to the Authority. All his brothers and sisters."

Lorne took the page with all the reverence it deserved. "Why don't you take it to him?"

"I'm banned from the Rift."

Lorne's eyebrows arched up at that. "Banned? What did you do?"

Tashué shrugged. But the memory of the anger sat like acid in his body, making his muscles ache. "I had half a mind to break him out myself."

Lorne snorted—which set off another round of coughs. He sat back down, slumping beside Tam and gasping for breath. He held the paper carefully, looking down at the prints there. "He has six siblings?"

"In theory."

"Why did Keoh give you this? Doesn't she want to keep it?"

"She doesn't need it anymore."

"Why not?"

Tashué tried to breathe as the tightness returned to his chest. "She died."

Lorne flinched. "How?"

"Allegedly, it was an opium overdose."

The silence that stretched between them was only interrupted by another coughing fit.

"I don't suppose you told him that before you got banned by the Rift," Lorne snarled, though now his voice was shaky from all the coughing. "I bet you left that little piece of information for me to tell him."

"I didn't know. Not until today. Tell him I'm sorry, Lorne. Tell him that I'm so fucking sorry."

"You asshole," Lorne muttered.

He pushed himself to his feet again. All the colour drained out of his face and he sank back down. He sagged against the back of the couch, gulping like he couldn't breathe. Tam moved to him, cradling the shot gun in one hand and reaching down to Lorne. Tashué could feel the Talent that swirled in the air, unfolding from the old man, but it was a weak thing. Lorne pushed Tam's hand away, shaking his head.

"You said you weren't very good at this."

"Someone needs to do something," Tam muttered.

"Wait," Tashué said. He headed for the door. "I know someone who can help. Just wait. Please?"

"We'll wait," Tam said swiftly. "You hear me, boyo? You'll wait right here."

Tashué was away before Lorne could argue, down the stairs and out into the street. It was still early, just early enough. Stella would be getting ready to go to the Facility, but she wouldn't have left yet. Tashué headed up the stairs as fast as he could, up to her floor, knocking on her door. Ceridwen opened it, beaming.

"Mr. Blackwood! Mam, it's Mr. Blackwood!"

Stella stepped from her room. She was in her work uniform, her fingers twisting her hair into a messy braid. His breath caught in his throat at the sight of her, melting all the fear away for a sweet moment, leaving him just a man who stood like an idiot, staring at the woman who owned his soul. She dropped her arms, leaving the braid sitting over one shoulder and he thought maybe he could smell her hair from here.

"Stella, I need your help."

She didn't hesitate. She took Ceridwen's hand and she followed him back to his apartment. Ceridwen paused when she saw Lorne's bloody face and Tam's shotgun. Tashué took her hand and eased her in and closed the door behind them as Stella stepped closer to Lorne. She knew what was needed of her. How could she not? Lorne was leaning forward, coughing up blood onto the floor between his feet. Tam stepped aside and Stella sank down onto the couch beside Lorne.

"What happened to that man?" Ceridwen breathed.

"He was in a few fights, little warrior," Tashué said. "Your mam can help him."

"I'm fine," Lorne grunted, half-rising, trying to pull away from Stella. "I don't need any help."

"I suppose you're afraid of healers, too?" Stella said with a long sigh. "My Talent won't *infect* you. But if I don't help you, you're going to die. I don't know you, and I suppose it doesn't matter to me one way or another, but I'm rather fond of Mr. Blackwood and it seems to me he'll be disappointed if I let you slip away on his sofa."

"Lorne, please don't be stubborn," Tashué said.

Lorne sat up again, breathing deep, but Tashué could hear the rattle in his lungs, the wheeze as he struggled. "It's not that I'm afraid of you," Lorne said, looking up at Stella and fighting in a deep breath. "Is it true that healers see the memories of their patients?"

"Bits and pieces," Stella admitted. "I try not to judge people for what I see in their vulnerable moments. We've all faced dark days and I've yet to meet someone who always made the right choice. Whatever's hiding in your mind—is it all really so bad that you deserve to die on Tashué's sofa of a collapsed lung?"

More coughing stopped Lorne from answering right away. Tam reached out to him, taking his shoulder, holding him up when he looked like he was going to pass out. Lorne leaned forward and spat more blood on the floor. Shook his head.

"Diplomatic division doesn't want us to see healers. The shit they taught us..." He shook his head again, clutching his chest. "They don't want us to see healers. Heard they kill people, even after they've retired. For spilling too many secrets."

Stella knelt in front of Lorne, taking his face in her hands to look him in the eye. "I promise you, I know enough about keeping secrets that I won't be spilling any of yours. Please, let me help you?"

Lorne still didn't answer. Still shook his head.

"Lorne, please," Tashué said, stepping closer. "As much as you hate the diplomatic division, are you really willing to die for them? And then I have to tell Jason that you died on my fucking sofa because the division *might* find out that you let Stella help you?"

That made him wince, made his shoulders bunch with the anger that surely kept him alive through all the trials his life and luck threw at him. Lorne sat up straighter and nodded at Stella.

Stella closed her eyes and Tashué felt the unfurling of her Talent. He couldn't imagine how he'd ever thought her Talent was a weak thing. The sensation of it filled the room like the heavy humidity that came before a summer storm. Lorne stiffened, hands turning to knots. He bit back any sound that might give away the amount of pain he was in. Ceridwen clutched Tashué's hand and Tashué thought he felt something in her, too, some stirring. Stella had insisted that Ceridwen had no Talent, but of course that wasn't true. She was a product of the Breeding Program. Her Talent would, in theory, be stronger than anything Tashué had ever encountered, and yet he'd never once felt a stirring from her. Was that Stella's doing—the knot, that Rhodrishi had mentioned? Tashué didn't know enough about Talent to even begin to fathom how she might have accomplished such a thing.

She didn't fix Lorne's face. She left him bruised, bloodied, swollen. But the sound of his breathing got easier and the fear let go of Tashué's heart. How long had he known Lorne? Long enough that he was like family.

Stella's Talent faded from the room and Lorne relaxed, sagging into the couch again. He looked better, under all the wounds on his face.

"Thank you," he said softly, looking at Stella. "I... I'm glad to meet you finally."

Stella nodded. "It's nice to come to know the pieces of Tashué's family."

Another nod and Lorne was heading for the door, stepping past Ceridwen. Without the pain to take the air out of him, he was coiled tightly again, ready for his next fight. Tashué knew enough not to take it personally anymore, knew it was that tension that kept him alive on tough streets when his mother lacked the wherewithal to protect him.

Lorne paused at the door, casting a glance back over his shoulder. "You coming, Tam?"

Tam nodded but paused, meeting Stella's eye. "Thank you, Miss. Most kind to help the fool boy."

Stella smiled again. "It was nothing."

"I tried to do it, but I haven't the strength, you see. Haven't the skill to do what you did."

"You did fine, sir. Kept him here long enough for him to be helped."

"Keep an eye on him, will you?" Tashué said.

"I will, sir, I will." He headed for the door, then stopped, turning back to Tashué, grinning suddenly. "I ain't never seen anyone talk to Mr. Iwan with so much sauce and get away with it. Made my day, that."

"Who were those men?" Ceridwen asked, once they were gone.

"Lorne is a friend of my son," Tashué explained, squeezing Ceridwen's hand. "And I suppose Tam is a good friend of his."

"How did Lorne get so beat up?"

"He fights in the Bay. For money."

"Why?"

"I don't know exactly. Maybe he doesn't think he's good at anything else. You'll have to ask him next time you see him."

"We have to go now, Pigeon," Stella said. "I can't be late at the Facility."

"Yes, Mam. Goodbye Mr. Blackwood!"

"I'll see you again tomorrow, little warrior."

Stella kissed him on her way to the door, her lips finding his for just a moment, one hand resting on his chest as she leaned in. It took all of his self control not to wrap his arms around her and ask her to stay. Keoh was sitting in her urn on his table and if Stella left, he would be alone with his failures again. But if he went with her, he could believe that he was doing something right, just one thing.

"I'll come with you," he said. "Walk you to the Facility."

"Would you like to stop and get a sweet bun?" Ceridwen asked. "We're still early, aren't we, Mam? When we're early like this, Mam likes to stop for sweet buns."

"Sweet buns sound lovely," Tashué agreed and they headed out together.

Soon, he told himself. *Soon you'll leave this place with Jason and you'll follow her wherever she wants to go.* He wouldn't have to ask questions about dead children and the Breeding Program and burnt tenement buildings.

The very thought twisted guilt in his gut. Could he really leave? With so many things unanswered?

One problem at a time. First, find a way to get Jason out.

45

TASHUÉ

DAY 24

Rain came down on the streets of Yaelsmuir, heavy and cold, soaking through Tashué's clothes and making his skin ache. Wind sliced down from the north, only making everything colder. Ice formed in a thin sheen on the streets, making every footstep treacherous and slow. He'd promised Stella he would meet her on the steps of the Facility. She would leave him today, loading her and Ceridwen on a barge to go south. And he *wouldn't* ask her to stay. He'd help her to go, and follow when he could.

He rounded the corner to the Facility and all those thoughts fled his mind. He was blank and still for only a moment while he processed what he saw, and then he was running. People were milling around and he shoved through them, crashing through the barrier of bodies that had gathered around the front steps around Stella. She lay too still on the stairs. *No, please no!*

"Mam!" Ceridwen shrieked. "Mam! Get up, Mam! Please!"

His feet slipped on the stairs. Ice clung to the stones, but his own momentum carried him on even as his boots slithered on the steps. He tripped over his own Imburleigh and fell, but he had reached Stella and the pain that seared through his knees meant nothing. He pulled Stella onto his lap, fearing that her skin would be cold with death, but no, there was still a little rosiness in her cheeks, a little warmth left in her flesh.

"Mam!" Ceridwen cried. "Mam, please get up!"

"Ceridwen, it's alright, she's still alive," Tashué said. He couldn't believe how calm his voice sounded. Stella's eyelids fluttered against the rain that fell in her face. "Stella, what happened?"

She was so limp, so heavy in his arms. He knew what dead weight felt like. As the thought crossed his mind, his heart nearly stopped beating.

She reached up to him, one hand grabbing the lapel of his jacket. She was trying to pull herself up, trying to say something. Blood bubbled between her lips as they moved and no words came.

"I forgot my marbles," Ceridwen sobbed, "so I went back, and when I came out she was shooting at some man, and then she just fell, I don't know why! She just fell! And the man ran away, but now she won't get up. Mam! Mam, please get up! Make her get up, please won't you make her get up!"

"Ceridwen, come away, sweet girl." A voice Tashué didn't recognize, a woman, pulling Ceridwen back up the stairs. "Come inside. Out of the rain."

"No, let go of me! Mam! Mam, get up!"

"Where's the nearest healer?" Tashué asked, looking up at the woman.

"I don't know! I'm sorry. I only mop the floors!"

A cry of rage broke from Tashué's chest. He shifted his own cases through his mind, but he didn't have any healers. Forty-four tainted under his responsibility and not a healer among them. The only healer he'd come across as a Regulation Officer was Gianna Tarbrook and she was dead. The weight of that loss settled anew on his shoulders.

"The hospital!" the woman said. "General Wolfe's hospital! It isn't open yet but aren't they treating the people from the Market fire?"

Yes, of course. General Wolfe's hospital was a few blocks away, and Rhodrishi was staying there until it was time for him to leave.

Stella convulsed in his arms and he looked down at her again.

She was choking on her own blood. He lifted her upright, bending her forward, and the blood splattered from her mouth and onto his arm, onto his leg, onto the steps beside him. She gasped for breath. It was a wet and ragged sound, but at least she still breathed.

"Hang on, Stella," Tashué said, his whole body threatening to start trembling. "Come, Ceridwen, come with me. Grab my Imburleigh, there's a good girl. Let's go. We'll go find Colonel Kheir. Do you remember him? Did you meet him at the Market?"

"I don't know!"

"Never mind then," Tashué breathed. He held out a hand to Ceridwen and she passed him the heavy pistol. He tucked it away in his holster. "We'll find the Colonel and he can help your mam."

Tashué slid an arm under Stella's legs and stood, hefting her up. His boots slithered on each step, ice thick on the stone. He picked his way carefully, but when Stella went off in a fit of coughing, the shifting of his weight nearly saw his feet slipping out from under him. The wind howled and the rain turned into shards of ice. His face went numb with the cold of it. Stella's body and the weight of all the soaked wool they wore dragged him down, his legs aching with the effort to push on and stay upright. He ignored it. None of it mattered. All he needed to do was get Stella to the hospital.

General Wolfe's hospital took up an entire block, the last of the tenement buildings in Brickheart. The massive front steps were slick with ice but Ceridwen shot up them like a wight, so fast that she barely seemed to touch the ground. She pulled on the heavy doors, but they were locked. She threw her fists against the door, pounding with every shred of strength she had.

"Help! Help! Please! Someone open the door! It's my mam. Help my mam!"

Tashué followed Ceridwen up the stairs, slipping and slithering. Stella's hand knotted on his lapel again, tugging on him, or maybe she could feel how precarious each step was. Tashué bit back a curse. *Sweet North Star please someone unlock it.*

"Please!" Ceridwen cried. "Someone help!"

The hinges creaked and the door swung open as Tashué crested the top of the stairs. An attendant stood in the doorway, lit by the brights glowing inside the hospital.

Tashué pushed past the attendant and into the front hall of the hospital. "I need to see Colonel Kheir. Where is he?"

"This way, sir!"

Up to the second floor, and Rhodrishi was coming down the stairwell toward him. He was down to his shirtsleeves, his waistcoat open.

"What happened?" Rhodrishi asked.

"She was attacked."

"Shot?"

"I don't know."

Rhodrishi grimaced, but nodded and led Tashué up to the third floor. Some beds were lined up against one wall, stacked and waiting to be used. The attendant rushed ahead of Rhodrishi, dragging a cot off the stack and making room. Tashué put Stella down on the cot and stepped back. He felt Rhodrishi's Talent unfold, that familiar warmth spreading through his chest.

Ceridwen darted in to be closer to her mother. Tashué caught her, dragged her back. She was trembling, shaking so violently that Tashué feared she'd been taken by some terrible fit. Her eyes were bright and filled with tears. Tashué dropped to his knees, pulling Ceridwen into a crushing hug.

Ceridwen dissolved into sobs, pressing her face into Tashué's jacket. She clung to him so hard that it hurt, but he didn't say anything. He only hugged her, closing his eyes because he couldn't watch Rhodrishi sitting so still anymore.

"Come see your mam, Ceridwen," Rhodrishi said. "Come hold her hand."

Ceridwen broke away from Tashué, running across the wide, open room so fast that her knees struck the cot, nearly sending her falling against Stella's prone form. She took Stella's hand with both of hers and her fingers looked too small—she was still so young. She squeezed Stella's hand until her knuckles went white.

"Gently now, girl," Rhodrishi said. "Heavens, you're strong. No need to break your poor mam's hand. She's had enough troubles as it is."

"Sorry," Ceridwen said, her lip trembling.

Tashué dragged himself back up to his feet and closed his eyes, reaching out with his own senses and touching Rhodrishi's Talent. He could feel what Rhodrishi was doing, see in his mind's eye. Parts of Stella were burnt, parts were bleeding, and Rhodrishi's Talent soothed all the angry tissue. Tashué could feel the damage that had been wrought in Stella's body, burning in him in all the same places. His Talent twisted and swirled in him, rising with his rage and his fear, churning like a hurricane. He drew it away again, forcing it back down, crushing it back into his chest, his hands trembling at the very thought of it.

He opened his eyes. Ceridwen had settled on the cot, curling against Stella's side. Rhodrishi stepped back. He rubbed his hands together a few times like he was trying to coax warmth back into his fingers, his face a careful mask as his eyes swept Tashué's face. Tashué's knees felt weak. Even though he'd felt Rhodrishi's Talent, even though he'd felt Rhodrishi healing the tortured places in Stella, he'd also felt the damage. The burns.

"Is she going to survive?" Tashué breathed. "Can you save her?"

"I can. The damage is ugly, but I can fix it, with time."

Tashué's knees went out from under him and he fell to the floor, barely catching himself on the door frame. The relief had broken down the walls of strength that he'd built and every part of him was taken with the trembling he'd been fighting. His chest ached, squeezing his ribcage so he couldn't catch his breath.

"Mr. Blackwood!" Ceridwen cried, her voice squeaking as she sat up. "Are you alright?"

"He's fine, my girl," Rhodrishi said, gently stroking Ceridwen's hair. "He's just suffering from a moment of melodrama is all."

"What's melodrama?"

"I promise you, Ceridwen, melodrama isn't fatal. Are you able to stand Captain? We should speak."

Tashué struggled to take a deep breath in, grabbing the door frame and levering himself back up to his feet. "Yes, sir."

"You stay there, Ceridwen," Rhodrishi said. "I'll have Mr. Blackwood back to you in a moment. Keep your mam company for me, will you?"

"Yes, sir," Ceridwen echoed.

Rhodrishi led Tashué up another floor. This one was even less finished than the ward that Stella was lying in, alone but for the attendant and Ceridwen. The walls had their lathe but no plaster and the floors were covered in a thin coat of sawdust. They left tracks in the sawdust as they walked. Tashué found his cigarillos to try to calm the way his hands still shook. There was blood on his cigarillo case. Stella's blood, staining the silver, sitting dark and ugly in the grooves of the engraving.

"What happened to her?" Tashué asked as he fumbled with his matches. His hands shook so damned much. "You could see it, couldn't you? When you joined your Talent to her body—you saw her thoughts and her mind. That's how it works, isn't it? Healers can see the minds of those that they join with?"

Rhodrishi sighed. "Yes, that's how it works. A man came for her, a man she knew. He assaulted her with his Talent. With heat and pressure, he nearly killed her. There are burns in her body that will take me some time to heal. I worked with the most damaged places first. I will come to you this evening to continue."

"You can't do it now?"

Another sigh, a long and tired sound. "I know you don't have a great understanding of Talent and so I won't take offence. Everyone wants us to use our Talent to wash away wounds as easily as you might wipe away a spot of mud, but the body is a more complicated thing than that. Talent is, too. You have to be patient with it and give it time to work. You should take her home. I'll come to you this evening and help her along more."

"Where is Duncreek?" Tashué asked. "That's who attacked her, isn't it? Siras Duncreek? Is he in the city still?"

"I am not a soothsayer, Captain. He came for her at the steps of the Facility. She shot him, hit him in the chest or the shoulder, and then he was gone."

Tashué put his matches and his cigarillos away, finding his notepad instead. "Help me find him, then. What did he look like?"

"Square face, red beard, freckles. Curly hair, scar on his lip and another on his eyebrow. Deep set green eyes and ears too big for his skull."

Tashué paused a moment, trying to piece the description together in his head before starting to commit the lines of the face onto a page. The familiar motion of the sketching helped take the tremble out of his hands. Rhodrishi directed him through it, the mouth wider, the brows heavier, the scar bigger. It looked like a killer's face. A hard man's face. If this was Siras Duncreek, this man had stalked Stella across the Dominion, from Cruinnich to Gladwydd, to Obisza to Yaelsmuir, all for the Authority.

"Can she stay here awhile? I want to find him, while he's still close at hand, and maybe I can bring this to an end."

"Wait, Captain, before you go rushing away," Rhodrishi said, catching Tashué's arm, "there's something you need to know. You spoke to her? Like I said you should?"

"I did," Tashué said. "You were right, she isn't as she seems. She was trained as a healer, but she's running from the Red Dawn and the Authority, to protect Ceridwen."

"Yes, I know that now. And Ceridwen has a massive Talent. I didn't feel it in her before because Miss Whiterock used her own skills to turn it into a knot, hiding it from anyone's senses. It's a thing I see sometimes with Kaadayri, who would like to assimilate into the Dominion. They hide their Talent so they can move through the Dominion without fear of the Authority."

Tashué nodded, taking a deep breath. "Ceridwen's a product of the Breeding Program, so yes, of course she has massive Talent. How could Stella have hidden Ceridwen's Talent? For all these years?"

"I think you have an idea how it might be done," Rhodrishi said. "You've been doing it all your life. But Captain, listen to me now. What Miss Whiterock has done, it has pushed the very limits of her strength. To hide Ceridwen's immense Talent all this time *and* to continue using her own Talent—even the small amount of strength it took to work as a whisperer—she has brought the Wrath onto herself. Do you know what that means?"

"The Wrath?" Tashué breathed. The trembling returned to his hands, and fear churned in his gut. "Yes. It drives the Talented mad, or twists their bodies."

Rhodrishi squeezed Tashué's arm like he was trying to be an anchor to keep the fear from taking Tashué away. "It's the effect of using Talent too forcefully, or too singularly. Using Talent changes a person, bit by bit, their Talent growing like a muscle every time it's used. To use your strength evenly, across many skills, builds Talent well, without stressing any particular part of the mind or body. But when you push it too hard, it leaves behind scars. This obsession of the Authority, to force the Talented into one job so that they may be one tool, invites the Wrath. Miss Whiterock has fallen victim to it, by pushing her own strength too hard. She uses her Talent to slice people away from their pain, and little by little, she is drifting away. She needs to stop."

"What can be done for her?"

"What can be done? I don't know. If she stops using her Talent now, the damage to her mind will stop. Given time, perhaps she can undo some of it; I don't know for sure. But she *must* stop using her Talent. I will try to make this clear to her, but…" Rhodrishi shook his head, looking toward the stairs. "That child. I understand her desire to protect that child."

"She'll have to leave," Tashué said. "She was going to go, on a barge. But… It was leaving today, sometime."

"It doesn't matter. She can't hide that child's Talent anymore. It's going to unknot soon and then everyone in the Authority will sense whenever Ceridwen is near. And think, Captain, before you say what you want to say. You want to protect them both yourself, I know, but you can't. Not from this."

Tashué took a deep breath, reaching for his cigarillos again. He forced himself to move slowly, to light the cigarillo before he spoke, to give himself time to calm his racing heart and shaking hands. "What do you suggest, then?"

"I don't know. Or rather, I think I do know, but it grieves me. It will put my people in danger, and it's not fair that I should draw more burdens upon their shoulders after all the lifetimes of burdens that we have shouldered already, and yet… I can't stand idly by. That child…"

"Ceridwen," Tashué pressed. "Her name is Ceridwen."

"Yes, you're right," Rhodrishi said, nodding. "I'm sorry. She is not just 'a child,' a faceless vessel of Talent. Ceridwen Whiterock. Her Talent, when it quickens, will be immense. Its quickening may kill her. If it doesn't, the Authority will hunt her down. They will use her Talent to fuel whatever vile industrial machine they see fit, and they will use her body to breed more, and with these 'more' they will continue to dismantle the rights of people who can shape the world. She must be taught to wield her Talent carefully, and perhaps to hide it to keep her safe."

"You'll do that, then? You'll teach her?"

Rhodrishi sighed, turning to look out the window. He looked so tired. Everything about him was slumped and small. "I will."

"But not here. She'll never be safe here."

"No," Rhodrishi agreed. "Not here."

"Where then? The legacy territory?"

"That may be the best option. In a series of bad options, mind you."

"Every part of me wants to offer to go with you," Tashué said. "I would do everything in my power to protect them both, and you. But you understand why I can't leave. Not yet."

Rhodrishi nodded. "Your son. In the Rift."

Tashué nodded, reaching up and rubbing his face with both hands, as if he could scrub away the emotion and the exhaustion and all the pain. Scrub away the image of Stella, on the steps of the Facility, blood bubbling from her mouth and her nose, scrub away the sound of Ceridwen screaming.

"I need to get him out," Tashué breathed. "Somehow. Before they kill him."

Rhodrishi winced. "Are the rumours true, then? I've heard of a tainted man who used his Talent in the Rift, breaking through the layer of suppression. I've heard it said that it was the Blackwood boy, but I hoped for your sake that it was just because your name is so popular now."

"I don't know," Tashué admitted. "I heard the same thing, but I didn't ask him. I suppose it must be true, since the Authority wants him in their Breeding Program."

"First the mother, and now the son. What will you do?"

"I don't know." Tashué rubbed his face again, feeling the defeat in those words. "North Star preserve me, I don't know. But I have to do *something*. I keep hoping that if I play Elsworth's games and dance for him, I can earn enough good will from him that I can get Jason out… but the more I learn about how little the Authority values human lives, the less convinced I am that it will work. And Jason is running out of time, no matter who I ask for help." He reached for his notepad again, flipping it open to the page of Siras Duncreek's face. "Maybe if I can find Duncreek, it will make your journey a little safer."

46

TASHUÉ

DAY 24

Acrowd of Officers milled in the station house when Tashué trudged up the stairs, a mass of bodies that had been delayed in their morning routine by the ice. He waded through them, forcing himself to be gentle when he had to move people out of his way. It wasn't their fault that he had Stella's blood on his clothes. It was dry now, turning the wool stiff and dark. Wasn't their fault that his son was in the Rift. Wasn't their fault Keoh's urn sat on his kitchen table.

He shooed an Officer off a chair and used it as a step stool to get up on the typist's table. Looming over the whole crowd, he had their attention immediately.

"I'm glad to see so many of you here," Tashué said, his voice thundering in the small space. "I need your help. One of my cases was attacked this morning, by a man using his Talent. The woman attacked was seriously wounded, but she'll survive. She shot the man attacking her. I believe the man's name is Siras Duncreek, and I made this sketch based on the description of a witness."

Tashué handed the notepad down to the closest Officer, who took a look and passed it along.

"Who is Duncreek?" Beckett asked. "Is he registered here, with us?"

Tashué shook his head. "No, he's not one of ours."

"Who is he, then? Some random tainted man, attacking people?" Beckett pressed.

Tashué sucked in a deep breath, stopping himself from saying the ugly truth. Would they even believe him, if he said it? "I don't know what his reasons were for attacking my case. Hopefully we can determine all of this when we find him."

"Who was attacked?" Kazrani asked. "Was it Miss Whiterock? The whisperer?"

Tashué scanned the crowd, finding Kazrani among the milling bodies. "Yes. A whisperer for the Facility of Rest."

"Hell, he's doing us a favour, isn't he?" Duskan laughed, taking the notepad and passing it on. "If he could keep going through some of my cases, I'd appreciate it. I've too many of the fucks these days."

"Duskan!" Kazrani snapped. "Shut the fuck up."

Tashué's feet hit the floor before he even knew he was jumping down from the desk. The sheer amount of bodies between him and Duskan slowed him a moment, but he didn't move gently through the crowd this time. He was barrelling so fast that someone fell, someone else gave a shout of surprise, and then Duskan was in his reach and Tashué hit him.

Duskan staggered, blood leaking from his lips. Tashué caught him by the shirt and hauled him back up. Hit him again. Duskan's arms spun like pinwheels, his body twisting as he tried to get away. A chance blow caught Tashué on the side of the face. Rattled his skull. It wasn't enough to stop him from hitting Duskan again.

Someone grabbed Tashué by one arm, hauling him back. Someone else put both arms around Tashué's chest. Someone else had grabbed Duskan and was yanking him back, out of Tashué's reach.

"Wild fuckin' animal!" Duskan screeched, spitting blood with every word. "What the fuck's wrong with you?"

Tashué threw his strength against the arms holding him back

and broke free, closing the gap again. Duskan threw up an arm but Tashué caught it and wrenched it aside with his right hand, then sent a thundering left into the side of Duskan's head. Duskan went boneless, collapsing on the floor. Someone caught one arm and tried to haul him back to his feet, to drag him back out of the way, but a wild howl came from Duskan's chest and he surged back up. A fist caught Tashué in the mouth and blood came out in a dark rush. Tashué hit him again, and again, and all the bodies trying to help were crushing them together, so Duskan couldn't get away.

"Captain, stop!"

Kazrani stood in front of him, shielding Duskan with her own body and staring up at Tashué. Unflinching. Unafraid of Tashué and his big fists, standing in the centre of the hurricane he'd made.

He stood frozen for a moment, his chest heaving. Bit by bit, the fog of rage cleared. Kazrani reached up, taking him by the arm that was still raised and ready to strike. His fist was bloody too, his knuckles already swelling. But he let her drag his arm down, let her pull him toward the stairs.

"Let's take a walk, Captain."

"I'll have your badge, you vicious bastard!" Duskan shrieked. "You'll never work for the Authority again!"

Tashué stopped and turned, his hand reaching for his badge. Fuck the Authority. An organization that protected Duskan, an organization that sent men like Siras Duncreek after people, tracking them across the country. Tashué didn't want to be a part of it one more fucking day. Kazrani grabbed Tashué by the arm again and hauled him hard toward the stairs.

"Open the gate, Lian," Kazrani breathed. "The Commander and I are going for a walk."

"Yes, ma'am." Lian fumbled with his keys and the gate swung open. "Are you alright, sir?"

"He's fine, Lian, everything's fine. Just needs some air, is all."

"Yes ma'am."

The gate swung open and Kazrani dragged Tashué out to the street. He trembled, stumbling as he walked. It all hit him so hard, all at once, each fucking thing passing through his head at the same time. Jason, in the Rift, crying—*I'm going to die in here and you can't help me, you couldn't ever help me.* Keoh, high on opium—*they're going to kill me*—shit, was she right? Had they killed her with her own addiction? Stella, on the steps, so much blood coming from her mouth. Ceridwen screaming.

"Sit down." Kazrani's voice, cutting through it all. "You look like you're going to fall over. Again, for fuck's sake."

He sank down, wiping the blood from his lip. It didn't help. There was too much blood on his hands to clean his face. He reached down for his cigarillos instead and got blood on them, too, leaving a dark smear on the tobacco leaf as he put it between his lips.

"Who is Siras Duncreek, then?" Kazrani asked. "Why is he attacking your whisperer?"

Tashué exhaled a deep breath of smoke. "I need your help, Kaz."

"Finding Duncreek?"

"No, protecting Stella so that I can find him. In case he comes for her again."

"I knew it. You *have* taken up with her, haven't you? Finally! What are you protecting her from, then? Is that why you won't tell me anything anymore? But I know you, Tashué Blackwood. I keep telling you, I don't care what you do with her—so long as she's compliant!"

Laughter bubbled through Tashué's chest, the sound of it hot and violent and ugly. He leaned back and he held his sides and he gasped for breath. Kazrani glared at him.

"What's so funny, then?" she asked, kicking his foot.

"Everything's so fucked," he gasped, shaking his head. "I don't even know where to start."

"What did you do?"

Tashué rose to his feet. "Come with me. Please. I'll try to explain it. You aren't going to like it."

It all started with the girl he found on the riverbank. Tashué started his story there, and told her everything that had come after. He led her to General Wolfe's hospital, smoking as he walked, the story unravelling so fast that he felt like he was drowning in his own words.

"Who is she that you trust her so much?" Kazrani asked softly. He saw the struggle in her eyes, the loyalty warring with fear. "Whiterock, I mean."

"She gives me reason to breathe." The words came unbidden, his memory betraying him. Those were the words Glaen had said about Gianna Tarbrook. He understood them now in a way he hadn't before and a fresh wave of guilt tore through him.

"That's very poetic, but it doesn't say anything about how you came to trust her so much."

"If it was only her word, I might not believe it either. But Kaz, everywhere I turn, I see proof."

"What proof? A woman using her Talent to 'see' her children being mutilated? How could you know *she* was telling the truth?"

"Why would she lie?"

"It doesn't matter *why*. Maybe she had a terrible dream. Maybe her mind was addled. Maybe she had been using her Talent poorly and the Wrath had twisted her! There are a thousand possibilities and only one of them is that she saw a true vision. What else do you have? Powell Iwan? You'll take the word of the most powerful criminal in the city? Why would he tell the truth! And he didn't even say anything about the Authority—he said it was the Red Dawn who killed that girl!"

They rounded the corner to the hospital. Tashué paused, looking up at the steps. The memory of fear gripped him, and he could *feel* the weight of Stella as he carried her up those stairs. Someone had spread sand on the icy steps, making them easier to climb.

"Where are the children, Kaz?" he asked, pausing at the base of the stairs. "These children that the Breeding Program is making. Specially manufactured for the Authority's use—where are they? Why don't we ever see them?"

"They have jobs. They don't house the important ones here in Brickheart. They'd have their own apartments at the factories or on the ships that they're running."

"And the trams?"

Kazrani shrugged. "What does it matter? What difference does it make?"

"If it doesn't make a difference, why is the Authority hiding them?" Tashué pressed.

"Just because you haven't seen them doesn't mean they're being hidden."

"Damnit, Kaz," Tashué said, turning and heading up the stairs.

Kazrani followed, silent behind him, as he climbed one staircase after another.

Ceridwen ran to the door when Tashué stepped onto the third floor, throwing her body against Tashué's legs and clinging to him. Tashué knelt, pulling Ceridwen into a hug. Stella lay on her cot, tucked beneath clean hospital linens. It looked comfortable, except that she had nearly died this morning.

"Ceridwen, this is my friend Kazrani," Tashué said, leaning back to look Ceridwen in the eye. "You remember her, don't you? You met her at the Market. I've known her a long time, longer than you've even been alive. How old are you now?"

"Almost ten," Ceridwen said softly. She had turned inward, a shyness that he didn't recognize in her.

"Almost ten. I met Kazrani when I was eighteen. Damn, I've known her for twenty-four years now."

"That's a long time."

Tashué chuckled, nodding. "It is, isn't it? I trust Kazrani with my life. You can trust her, too."

"Tashué," Kazrani hissed, but she bit off whatever she was going to say next and took a deep breath.

Tashué stood slowly, looking again at the bed where Stella slept. She seemed smaller somehow, as if carrying her in his arms for so long made him realize how little space she took up in the world.

"You're here to take her home, then?" the attendant asked from the cot she sat on next to Stella. She didn't stand from the little work station she'd set up for herself, paperwork in precarious stacks all around her.

"Yes. Thank you for watching over her."

"What happened?" Kazrani asked softly.

"Like I said, Siras Duncreek came for her." Tashué glanced down at Ceridwen, at her big eyes, shining with fresh tears. He reached down to her, cupping her cheek in his hand and wiping the tears away. "It's alright, Ceridwen. Colonel Kheir is doing what he can to help her. He saved my life too, did I tell you that? He's very strong. If he said he can save your mam, we can believe his word. I'm to take her home, and Colonel Kheir will come to tend to her more this evening."

"Who is he, Duncreek? Why would he attack her?"

Tashué looked from Ceridwen to Kazrani, stifling a sigh. "I'll tell you later... Please, Kaz. *Please*. Do this one last thing for me. Protect her and Ceridwen while I can't. And then I promise I'll never ask anything from you again. I know you don't believe what I've learnt, or at best you don't understand, but please do this one last thing for me."

"Why would it be a last thing, you fool of a man?" Kazrani scoffed. "I don't keep tally. I help you because I love you, you idiot."

"I know."

The room was so still and quiet as they looked at each other. A chasm had opened between them, a distance that hadn't existed since they first met. He could reach out and touch her, but that wouldn't close the gap. He didn't know how to tell her that he was planning on leaving. He didn't know how to explain that nothing was the same.

"Will you protect them for me?" Tashué asked again. "Kaz, please."

She sighed. But smiled. "Of course, Captain. Of course."

Tashué gathered up Stella and carried her carefully down the stairs. Kazrani took Ceridwen ahead to hail a carriage to take them back to the Row. Tashué sat on the bench, holding Stella against his chest, her hair tickling his face. She seemed too terribly small. Stella stirred, making a soft sound. Ceridwen climbed in next, tucking herself against her mother's body. And Kazrani came behind her, pulling the door closed. Tashué reached down, running a hand across Stella's cheek, pushing away the memory of her cold flesh, trying not to wonder how close she had been to death. Even as he contemplated how he would find Siras Duncreek, he thought too of Jason, in the Rift, so desperate.

Give my ashes to the Brightwash, same as my mother.

Sweet North Star, those words hurt so much. Just remembering them took the breath out of him. Jason thought he was going to die in the Rift, and Stella almost died at the hands of the Authority, manifested by Siras Duncreek. He could almost feel Jason holding one hand and Stella holding the other, the two of them dragging him in opposite directions, tearing him apart. It was no fault of theirs. He couldn't seem to figure out how to be the man that each person needed without turning his back on one or the other. His loyalty to Stella being a new thing didn't make it any less carved into his bones. But Jason was his son, his blood. Tashué was the only family Jason had left.

"Tashué?"

"Yes, yes, I'm here," Tashué said softly. He brushed some hair from her face and kissed the top of her head. "I'm here."

"Ceridwen!" He heard the anxiety in her voice, felt her body coil with anxiety.

"I'm here too, Mam!" Ceridwen breathed, nestling closer.

Stella relaxed. Her eyes drifted closed again, lulled away to sleep by the rattle of the carriage. Kazrani watched them all, a silent observer as she tried to sift through her own thoughts. Tashué wondered what she was thinking. Did she think him a fool? She must. And yet here she was, beside him again even though she surely thought he was wrong. However did he come to deserve such a friend?

He carried Stella up to his apartment, where he lay her in his bed. He sat beside her, still and quiet for a moment. His favourite corkscrew curl had escaped again and he twisted it around his finger. Ceridwen looked so tired, so weary that she hardly seemed herself.

"Lay down, little warrior. Have a rest with your mam."

Ceridwen nestled against her mother again and the two of them looked so tiny in Tashué's bed. He eased his way off the edge, stepping out of the room again, sure that Ceridwen was asleep before he even closed the door behind him. Kazrani stood beside his table, looking at the urn.

"That's Keoh," Tashué said softly, easing into his small kitchen. He crouched by the wood stove, feeding in kindling and striking a match. "She overdosed on opium. Though how she got so much opium to kill herself, I don't know. I would think the Breeding Program would have tried a little harder to keep their breeding mothers alive and healthy instead of letting them smoke opium. She said they gave it to her." He shook his head. "I didn't believe her, when she said it. But how else could she get it? Elsworth said he would transfer her to another floor, put an extra guard on her. But she's dead anyway."

Kazrani sighed, reaching out and touching the urn, just once. It was a sign of respect, to touch the container of the dead. "Does Jason know?"

"I don't know. I sent Lorne to tell him, but I don't know if he's been."

"Why don't you tell him?"

"I was banned from the Rift," Tashué said. "They didn't like that I tried to break him out."

"You *what?*"

Tashué shrugged. "It's not as bad as it sounds."

"Fuck, Tashué." Another sigh. "I know you think everything you did was wrong, but you tried your best to make things good with Jason. Still—we can't go back, no matter how badly we want to. We can only go forward."

47

TASHUÉ

DAY 24

The Facility of Rest for the Critically Ill was an ugly place to be. He could almost see Stella, collapsed on the steps, and Ceridwen screaming. He headed inside, to see if he could find the woman who was standing with Ceridwen, but she wasn't there. He wandered the streets, asking people if they had seen anything, offering the sketch of Duncreek to help people remember. Some saw him, but they gave conflicting accounts of which way he'd gone. West, to the river. North, to the Market. South, into the Bay.

Most agreed that he had blood on his clothes as he fled through the streets—but the fact that he was running and no one yet had reported seeing his body suggested the wound wasn't serious. He checked the charities, to see if he'd gone to see his wound tended to. No one at the charities would say anything, anyway.

It was hard to imagine where he would go. If he was Authority, would he know to avoid the Bay? Powell Iwan wouldn't make him welcome. There was so much destruction up in the Market, it seemed scarcely believable that there would be any lodgings available there. Somewhere in Brickheart, then, or In the Tracks. There were plenty of flop houses that rented beds by the hour, and none of them were very discerning with their clientele. Surely Siras Duncreek wouldn't be the first bloody man looking for a place to rest a few hours. Would he stay near to the Facility? Did he know where Stella lived?

He needed Lorne. He needed Lorne's network of spies and informants, to find Siras Duncreek. That's what it took, to find a single person in a city like Yaelsmuir, where there were so many people everywhere, where crowds could swallow anyone. It took eyes everywhere, ever-vigilant teams searching the streets. But where was Lorne? Hiding from Powell Iwan? Hiding from Tashué?

And of course, thinking of Lorne made Tashué think of Jason.

Give my ashes to the Brightwash, same as my mother.

The day was running out, the sun threatening to set. Another storm cloud was heading in off the ocean, sliding up the foothills of the mountains. Stella was safe. Alive, thanks to Rhodrishi. Protected by Kazrani.

Jason was on his own, in the Rift.

V asska sat at the bar in the Hive, nursing a cigarillo and a measure of whisky. He smiled when Tashué approached, motioning to the empty stool next to him.

"Good evening, Mr. Blackwood. The Lightning isn't fighting tonight. I haven't seen him here since his fight against the Hammer."

"Were you here for that? You saw what happened?"

Vasska nodded, throwing back the last of his whisky and grimacing at it. "I did. I warned him. I'm sure he told you. I told him to leave the Red Dawn be, but he's so damned stubborn. I suppose you have that in common, don't you?" He sighed, pulling an ashtray closer to crush out his cigarillo. "I never liked the fights much, to be honest. It's an ugly thing, what people do to each other for sport and coin. Grandad likes me to watch, though. To keep an eye on the Hive, and watch out for people who might be important."

"Is that all you do?" Tashué asked. "Sit here and watch for who might be important?"

"Of course not," Vasska said. "But you aren't here to chat with me about how I spend my time, are you?"

"I was hoping to see your grandfather. I wanted to ask him some things."

Vasska grimaced and shook his head. "No, you don't want to see Grandad, not now."

"Oh really? And how do you know what I want?"

Vasska turned those bright blue eyes on Tashué and suddenly there was more strength in the young man than Tashué had ever seen. "Grandad asked you to do something, and you haven't done it yet. He said you'd be square with him after it's done. I like you, Mr. Blackwood. So, trust me when I say that I'm giving you this warning because I'm looking out for you. You do not want to be looking for Grandad right now, not when he's waiting for you to do what he asked. Whatever you think you want to ask him, you wait until after, and you make damn sure you don't have any other options than getting Grandad involved."

Tashué took a deep breath. "Fine. Tell me where to find him, then."

"Who?"

"Edgar Hale."

48

JASON
DAY 25

Lorne didn't come to visit often. Jason understood it, even if it hurt. Lorne was too much, too much energy, too much person, to ever feel comfortable in a place like the Rift. Too many walls in the Rift. Too many closed spaces. Jason used to be the same way. When he first came to the Rift, he felt the walls pressing in on him, trying to make him smaller. When had that feeling worn away? When had the Rift and its walls succeeded in making him smaller? In making him too tired to care that he was dying?

Lorne forced a smile when he sat across the grate. He never was very good at hiding his emotions. That's what Jason always liked about him. Some people saw a short temper, but Jason saw a man who didn't care, who didn't try to hide who he was. A man who just *was*, flawed and emotional and passionate. Afraid of nothing. Jason wished he could learn to be afraid of nothing.

Lorne pushed up the grate like Tashué did, but instead of offering food, he just stretched out his hand. Jason leaned forward, resting his head on the table between them and taking Lorne's hand with his. His knuckles had fresh wounds, though the swelling was going down. His face was a mottled mess of bruises and cuts.

"Bad fight?" Jason asked.

"Yeah, you could say that. A few of them."

"What'd you do to piss Iwan off? I thought he liked you."

"I was helping your father," Lorne muttered. "Looking for the Red Dawn."

"Powell Iwan is Red Dawn?"

"No. Maybe. I don't know. Did you hear what he did? Your father?"

"Got himself banned, the idiot," Jason said, looking down at his hands. "Everyone's been talking about it. Tried to break right through the grates with a chair. I really love how everyone's talking about him these days. It gets me so much extra attention."

Lorne pulled his hand out of the grate. "He gave me this, to give to you."

Jason lifted his head to see what Lorne had. A piece of paper, thick and long, rolled into a tube that Lorne pulled out of one of his pockets. He slid the paper through the space where his arm used to be, then sat back and held his head with both hands. What piece of paper could make him look so sad?

"What is it?"

"Open it."

Jason pulled the twine away, unrolling the paper carefully. It was old, the edges ragged and torn. It smelled like his mother, though. What was that sweet smell that always made him think of her? He breathed in the smell and it brought him back to the rice fields of the Cyr delta, to humid summer air and the ocean spray, to the lowing of the oxen that the farmers used to plough and flatten the fields in the spring.

The paper had a list of names, and footprints. They were so small, those little ink marks, the toes smudged, the heels pressed more firmly so that the lines of each heel were crisp and more defined. Jason touched each one, marvelling at how small they were, trying to imagine what a foot that tiny must have looked like, must have felt like in his hand. He hadn't seen any children since being sent to the Rift. Hadn't heard the sound of a baby crying.

He recognized his mother's handwriting, each name done in her messy hand. Lizanne, Petrik, Gwinnith, Benjin, Dex, Valen. His sisters. His brothers. Some Xs marked the children that hadn't survived. He wondered why she had never told him these names, these children that were out in the world, his siblings. She had told him about each of them, about their existence in the world, but never any details. Never their *names*.

"She gave this to me?" Jason asked. "Did he see her again?"

"No, not since the first time. This was given to him by the staff at the Breeding Program."

Jason shook his head, looking up at Lorne. "Why did they give him this? Doesn't she want to keep it?"

Lorne took a deep breath and Jason's stomach dropped. He knew suddenly what made Lorne look so sad, what he didn't want to say. Jason looked down at the footprints again, one at a time. Six siblings. Six pieces of his mother, drifting out in the world. In the city? Were any of them close enough for him to find them?

Tears misted in Jason's eyes and he bit the inside of his lip. Lorne still didn't say anything and Jason felt the fear and the sadness turn to anger. He looked up again, wiping away the tears with the heel of his free hand.

"You have to say it," Jason growled. "Don't be a coward and make me guess. If it's what I think it is, you have to fucking say it."

"She's dead, Jason. Your father has her ashes in his kitchen."

Even though he was expecting it, the words took the air out of Jason. "How?" His throat was so tight that the words were almost caught there, choking him. "How did she die? Was it the baby?"

"No, your father said it was an opium overdose. The Breeding Program gave him her ashes."

A low, keening noise came from Jason's throat. He clamped his teeth against it. He couldn't breathe. He leaned forward, clawing at his chest. Something was pressing on him so hard that he couldn't catch his breath—no, there was nothing on him, it was his own body strangling him.

He hadn't seen her in sixteen years. Not since the Officers came with their Imburleigh guns and dragged them both out of their little house. He remembered the smell of his dinner burning. He would forever remember that smell, oil turning to smoke, salted fish charring beyond anything appetizing. He'd thought of that day so much, perhaps his earliest clear memory, thought of what it would be like to reunite with his mother and hug her and tell her that he forgave her for everything that went wrong in their lives. So many of her letters asked for forgiveness but he had never written those words in reply. He'd wanted to tell her, face to face. And now his chance was gone.

"They killed her," Jason gasped, the pain turning to fury so fast that it hurt, the fire in him igniting so viciously it felt like his whole body was burning. "They fucking killed her."

"You don't know that."

"Yes I do!" Jason snapped, smashing both his fists against the table. "She told me they were trying to kill her! They were leaving that shit for her in her room because they knew she couldn't resist. She was done breeding for them so they killed her with that fucking opium rather than let her out into the world!"

Lorne shook his head. "Just because she said it, doesn't mean it's true."

"Fuck you! What the hell do you know about it?"

"What do I know?" Lorne snapped back. He half rose out of his chair, leaning closer, his lips pulled back in a primal snarl. That temper of his, as hot as anything Jason felt. "I know what it's like to be lied to every fucking day of my life. 'I'm sorry. I won't do it anymore. Yesterday was the last time. I'm going to change everything.' I've heard it all! Every single thing that your mother told you, mine told me the same garbage. It's all a fucking lie, every word of it!"

"You're wrong."

"I hope so. I wanted to believe her, every time she told me she would change. I knew she was lying but I hoped—I fucking *prayed*—that I was wrong." Lorne sank back down, his anger spent as fast as it had come. He reached through the grate again, looking at Jason with pleading eyes. "And maybe our mothers lived different lives. I can't imagine what it must have been like for your mother in that fucking place, and I don't even blame her for smoking that shit at the end, not when that place was her reality. But Jason, just because she's dead, doesn't mean *they* killed her."

"But they did," Jason said, shaking his head. He reached out, taking Lorne's hand. He looked down at the paper again, running his finger around the perimeter of Valen's foot. The youngest of his siblings, the one with the largest footprint. "They sentenced her to death sixteen years ago, when they came and arrested her. The Breeding Program was just a fucking detour."

"Jason, I'm sorry," Lorne said. "I know what this feels like and I wouldn't wish it on anyone. If I could take it and feel the pain for you, I would."

Jason shook his head, struggling to catch his breath. He wanted to say that he wanted to feel this pain. He wanted it to sear through him, hot and unrelenting, so that it would fuel him through what needed to happen. Because he knew now what that was. There was no working with the system, there was no waiting for his father to figure something out. His father was banned from the Rift. His mother was dead. The Authority had taken everything from him, and they would just keep taking humanity from people, a great maw that devoured everything good.

"Did I tell you before? Last time you were here?"

"Tell me what?"

"There's a way out," Jason breathed, and the words were soothing. He squeezed Lorne's hand, looking up at his face, at the ugly mottle of cuts and bruises, at the blue eyes that he loved so much. "I'm going to do it. I'm going to get out, and I'm going to burn it all down."

49

TASHUÉ
DAY 25

Edgar Hale lived above a warehouse he rented from Powell Iwan. The apartment was small, as the area above the warehouse was cut into a few apartments. Vasska gave Tashué a spare key, and Tashué climbed the stairs to the apartment with careful steps. The old wood creaked with every shift of his weight. The apartment was empty.

Tashué went through Hale's belongings, searching every cupboard, every drawer. There were some crowns hidden here and there, a case of bullets for a Commonwealth Imperial revolver. Tashué took the crowns but left the bullets. He'd seen enough Imperials explode in the faces of their owners to ever use them. If there was any evidence of the children, Tashué couldn't find it. But then why would Hale keep such things?

Tashué put a coil of rope down on the table. It was good rope, thin but sturdy, that he bought from a dock worker, who asked no questions for a few copper coins. He turned away from the table to look out the window instead. He could see the Hive from here, the stevedores and dockworkers swarming across the whole structure. Like ants on spilt sugar, they were an incessant grind of movement.

He heard the creak, the shift of weight on the steps. With a deep breath, he reached for the dark and angry places that lived in him. He had spent so many years trying to distance himself from the hot and violent young man he used to be, the soldier, the man trained to kill. He'd even managed to convince himself that he was a quieter, more peaceful man in these last few years. But that was so clearly a lie. The violent parts of him were only waiting. All it took was a little push to set him plummeting away from the delusion of being a quiet man and into the blood of other people.

He moved swiftly through the apartment, coming to stand behind the door. He would be concealed by the swing of it when the door opened. He waited, breathed slow, stood still. These old things came back to him too easily, no matter how long it had been.

What if it isn't Hale? But it was too late for doubt—the door swung open, stopped on the toe of his boot. And then it swung closed again and Tashué saw the man's back, the height of him, the red coat he wore with black pinstripes like Vasska described, the Commonwealth Imperial holstered at his hip like the cattle drivers of the south.

Hale paused—saw the rope, sitting on his table. Tashué stepped forward. He was too big and heavy for stealth, his boots thumping on the floor. Hale turned, reached for his gun.

Tashué was on him too fast for him to draw it. He grabbed Hale's arm and the gun fell from the holster. It discharged when it hit the floor, the sound of shattering glass splintering across Tashué's nerves. Tashué hit Hale in the face, staggering him, but Hale surged back up, swinging his head for a headbutt. Tashué stepped back and the headbutt missed but Hale was able to wrench his hand free. He charged.

Tashué stepped back in, bringing up his knee and catching Hale in the chest. Folding him in half. All the air left Hale in a breathy *oof* and Hale staggered again. Tashué swung down, his left catching Hale on the side of the face, knocking him down, onto his hands and knees.

Tashué stepped behind Hale. Looped his arm around Hale's neck and pulled him upright, hooking his wrist with his other elbow and tucking his hand behind Hale's head. Hale shot to his feet, kicking and bucking, but Tashué had him in the hold now—Hale's neck fit perfectly in the crook of Tashué's elbow and it didn't matter how much he thrashed, he couldn't wriggle himself free. He kicked out with both feet, catching the table and knocking Tashué off balance. He took a step back but his heel caught the Imperial and he was falling.

Tashué went down, flat on his back, Hale's weight driving the air from his lungs, but he hung on. Hale kept wriggling, swinging his arms, kicking his legs. None of the thrashing was enough to break Tashué's hold on him. The Imperial sat under Tashué's leg, hard metal, smooth and angular at once, and still hot from its discharge. He prayed the stupid thing wouldn't go off again.

Hale still fought, hanging on to consciousness. Tashué's grip wasn't tight enough. He took a deep breath, and with it he filled his nose with Hale's scent—sweat and shaving oil, the blood that was coming from Hale's mouth, the musky smell of his suit, which probably hadn't been laundered in a while. The spent cordite, lingering in the air from the Commonwealth Imperial hair-trigger. Filling his chest pressed Hale further into the hold. The struggles increased at first, but they got weaker, fading. And he went still, slumping against Tashué's body.

He pushed Hale away, letting him fall face-first on the floor. Tashué lay flat on his back a moment, just long enough to take a few deep breaths, enough to fill his lungs properly, enough to try to slow his racing heart. That fight hadn't gone quite as smoothly as he'd pictured. *Shit, I'm getting rusty.*

He climbed to his feet, ignoring the ache spreading across his back. Scooping up the Commonwealth Imperial, he opened the cylinder and dumped the bullets onto the floor. They clattered against the wood, bounced in all different directions. He swept his foot through them and scattered them to every corner of the room. Fuck Commonwealth Imperial. What kind of idiot had an Imperial when he lived in Yaelsmuir, where Imburleigh made the best guns in the world?

Tashué dragged a chair across the floor. It was harder than he would have liked to admit to heft Hale up and put him in the chair.

As Tashué stepped away to grab the rope, Hale slumped over, tumbling forward and to one side, hitting the floor face-first. Tashué cursed, grabbing the rope. He draped it over his shoulder before lifting Hale again. Hale's face had hit the floor so hard that his eyebrow was oozing blood.

Tashué looped a coil of rope over Hale's chest and under his arms, tying the first knot there to keep him in place. From there, he wrapped Hale's body a few times, then his legs, leaving his arms free. He used his old cavalry knife to cut the rope once Hale's body was tied firmly to the chair, then tied his arms independently of each other. He wanted to be able to get those free.

Hale was still unconscious when Tashué was finished. He stepped away, heading back to the window. He didn't go too close; he didn't want people below to see him. The Commonwealth Imperial round had sent long, twisting cracks up through the pane, fracturing the world beyond into chunks that didn't quite fit together anymore. He looked down at his hands, stretching out his fingers. When he touched Stella, they had trembled. Now, with all he planned to do, they were steady. Hale's face had left wounds over the ones made by Duskan's face. The fight with Duskan had split open the scabs left by his work in the Market. He could take the stitches out soon, if he could just stop breaking the scabs open.

How long had it been since he'd been so willing to seek out such violence? His work with the Authority—save for the occasional unfortunate processing—was mostly talking and paperwork. If it weren't for Jason, he might not have even come.

Is that even true, or are you lying to yourself?

The children. The girl from the Brightwash, the boy beneath the bridge. When had he given up on the idea of *justice*, civilized and legal? Somewhere along the way, the acid need for *revenge* had eaten into his soul.

Hale started to stir, groaning and shifting. Tashué sat on the edge of Hale's table, watching him stir. The panic came to his eyes immediately, the wild animal struggles setting him thrashing against his bonds.

"Who are you? What do you want? Let me go!"

He thrashed so hard the chair started to move and Tashué could see how poorly balanced it was, threatening to tip him over.

"I wouldn't do that if I were you," Tashué said. "You're going to fall."

But Hale didn't listen, cursing and howling and rocking his body back and forth as if he thought he could surge forward out of the ropes. When he leaned his weight back again, the chair hung precariously on its rear legs for just a moment before it fell. The back smashed Hale's hands onto the floorboards and he howled. Tashué sighed, hooking his foot on the rungs between the chair legs, dragging it closer and pulling it back up. Hale kicked out at him, yelling at the top of his lungs, calling for help.

"Scream all you want, but no one's coming to help you," Tashué said. "You're no longer welcome here in the Bay. Iwan sent me to give you your eviction notice."

"Fuck you!" Hale spat.

"Let's skip all that," Tashué growled, leaning in close. "I have a few questions for you and this whole mess can be over faster if you answer them for me."

"Fuck you and your fucking questions." Hale kicked, a foot catching Tashué in the shin.

Tashué took a deep breath, pushing Hale a little further away, the chair legs giving a screech as they slid on the floor. He regretted not tying Hale's ankles to the chair legs.

"I thought you'd say that," Tashué said, reaching into his jacket and drawing the old knife again. "So let me make it clear how serious I am."

Hale's eyes bulged and Tashué stood. Hale kicked again but Tashué stepped around him, slicing the rope away from one of his arms. Hale tried to swing, but Tashué caught his wrist and pulled it toward him. He could smell the sweat of the man again, and the shaving oil—shit, it was the same kind Tashué used when he was bothered enough to shave. He hooked his arm around Hale's elbow and then under his armpit, laying his hand against Hale's chest. Hale's sleeve was damp from outside. Everything was fucking damp this time of year.

It was an easy thing to dislocate Hale's shoulder—a bit of pressure on the shoulder and then the joint gave a wet pop like pulling off a roasted chicken leg. And Hale shrieked. He thrashed against his ropes, leaned away from Tashué and almost tipped himself over again but Tashué caught him by the shirt and hauled the chair back up. Tashué left the arm dangling at Hale's side. He lit a cigarillo, waiting while Hale screamed himself hoarse. Waiting and smoking until Hale was quiet. Waiting and smoking while all the frustration of the last few weeks simmered in his chest. The memory of that girl, lying on the shale of the river bank, cold and grey. No hair, no arms, no legs, and that ugly tattoo.

"Did they scream like that when you cut their arms away?"

"Who?" Hale howled. "Whose arms?"

"The children, you maggot," Tashué snapped. He reached for his notepad, flicking it open to the dead girl's face. He held the notepad up in front of Hale's eyes until he looked at it. "The children that you mutilated and killed and dumped in the river." He slapped Hale in the face with the pad, leaving a smear of charcoal across his eyes, over his nose, and blood on the page, right over the girl's face. "Did they scream like you're screaming when you took all their fucking limbs, you steaming pile of shit?"

"I didn't take their arms and legs," Hale gasped, swinging his head back and forth and squeezing his eyes shut. "I didn't. They were like that when I found them! They were like that when I took them!"

Tashué sucked in a deep breath. So, the woman from the Breeding Program—she'd told the truth.

"It's true!" Hale shrieked. "I swear! They were like that when I found them, I swear, I swear! The Authority did that to them, not me! It wasn't me!"

"Why?" Tashué snapped. "Why would the Authority do such a thing? What purpose would it serve to mutilate them like that?"

"Makes them easier to transport, without their arms flopping around," Hale sobbed. "Their minds are dead, killed by the Authority, to turn them into energy units. They just sit there and push out their Talents to power the trams or the ships, and their arms and legs are just dead weight. The Authority takes them off so they aren't so heavy!"

Tashué sank back in his chair, taking a deep drag of tobacco smoke. It was cold, the thing that passed through him. Too cold to be called anger, too violent to be called shock. The Authority had done it, just like the woman said. They bred the children and they sliced the arms and legs from the children so that they wouldn't be *so heavy*. He'd worked for the Authority for nineteen years because he truly believed in the lies they told. That the registration kept everyone safe. That the laws were there to bring peace. And that organization, which he had trusted, which he had believed in, cut the arms and the legs from children to turn them into *energy units*.

"I won't tell anyone," Hale breathed. "I won't tell a soul. If Mr. Iwan wants me gone, I'll go! But I didn't cut them up, I didn't. I swear I didn't."

Tashué leaned closer, taking another drag of his cigarillo. "Where did you get them?"

"What?"

"The children, you fucking twit, where did you get the children?"

"We stole them from the Breeding Program. They take them somewhere outside the city after they graduate from the creche, where they cut them up and break their minds."

"Where?" Tashué growled. "Where do they keep them?"

"I don't know!"

"Where do they keep the children, Hale!"

"I don't know!"

Tashué held his cigarillo between his teeth as he drew his knife and sliced through the rope. He cut too close to Hale's arm and the blade found flesh, freeing a surge of blood that spilt hot over Tashué's hands. Hale was howling again, rocking back and forth.

"No, please, I swear, I don't know, I don't fucking know, I don't know!"

It was harder to pop his arm the second time, because Hale was struggling, and his wrist was slick with blood, but pop it did. Hale screeched. He was crying.

"It wasn't me," he wailed, shaking his head. "It wasn't me that found the energy units! I don't know where he found them. He just gave them to me and told me what to do."

Tashué wiped his hands on Hale's coat, but the wool wasn't enough to soak up Hale's blood. "Who?"

"It was Davik, Davik found them. Davik brought them to me."

"Davik who?"

"Kaine. Davik Kaine, he's the one that found the energy units. I don't know where he found them. I don't know. I don't know!"

"Davik Kaine from Cruinnich?" Tashué asked.

"Yes, yes, that's him! Highland fucker, but he's been here eight years. He's the one that found them!"

Tashué stepped back from Hale. He took the last few drags from his cigarillo, feeling his heart hammering in his chest. Hale was whimpering, his eyes squeezed shut.

"Fucking hell," Tashué muttered, dropping the cigarillo beside the first one, crushing it out. "I believe you."

He drew his Imburleigh. Cocked the hammer. It was a big gun and when he fired it, the lead smashed apart Hale's skull in a rain of blood and bone and brain and Hale's howling finally stopped. Tashué pulled the Commonwealth Imperial out of his pocket and tossed it into Hale's lap.

It didn't fulfil anything in Tashué to see Edgar Hale dead. There was no justice in it, no revenge. It didn't bring back the children or erase their suffering or punish the Authority.

Hale was just a dead man with his brains leaking out across his dirty red pinstripe coat and Tashué was still burning with rage.

50

TASHUÉ

DAY 25

It wasn't a very long walk from Cattle Bone Bay to Highview. After Tashué left the tracks that surrounded the Bay, the road was empty and quiet, a stand of trees shielding the sensitive eyes of Highview residents from having to look directly into the Bay.

Tashué wondered if Allie would even be in her office at this hour. What would he do if she wasn't? How would he find her?

But he *needed* to find her. He needed to tell her everything Stella had said, everything Hale had said. He needed to reach out and touch the only other person that cared about the dead children and feel like he'd killed a man for some halfway decent reason. Because the alternative, that he killed Hale because he'd *liked* it, was an ugly thought.

Some of the windows of the *Highview Times* office were glowing, and Tashué walked faster. Which one was Allie's office again? The one on the corner of the building, with the view of the bridge—but was it the second floor or the third?

He stepped inside, something like excitement building. Maybe she was there, working late.

The gunshot clapped through the whole building, loud even

through the stone walls. Tashué cursed and broke into a run—once he was in the stairwell, he remembered, it was the third floor because the first floor was entirely taken up by the printing press. He bolted up the stairs as fast as his legs could carry him. His whole body hit the door to Allie's office and it burst open.

A second shot—and the impact, like a brick in Tashué's side, folding him over, staggering him.

Allie lay flat on her back, the contents of her desk thrown all around her, and an attacker writhed a few feet away from her. Tashué caught himself on the corner of her desk, folding a hand over the new wound. This time he felt his blood, as hot and sticky as Hale's had been, soaking all down his side and into his trousers. Allie swung her gun to her attacker and shot him again. This time his body went limp—no, not completely limp. His foot was still twitching and his mouth was still gaping and grey sludge was oozing from the new hole in his skull.

Allie swung the gun toward Tashué like she was going to shoot him again. *Shit.* Tashué staggered in closer and swiped the gun from her hand.

"Fuck, Allie! Why'd you shoot *me*?"

"I—" Her voice was raspy and weak. "I thought—"

Tashué dropped to one knee beside her, grabbing her by one hand and helping her up. The skin of her neck was raw and red, threatening to make deep bruises. Tashué had seen marks like that before. Her attacker had tried to strangle her.

"Are you alright?" he asked.

She took a trembling breath in, blinking at him. He realized, maybe a little belatedly, that it was a stupid question. She was alive, yes, but alright?

"Shit," Tashué grunted.

He forced himself to his feet, groaning at the pain that roared in his side, hot and vicious. He kicked the man over onto his back, peering through the darkness at his face. Tashué didn't recognize him. He'd hoped he would, so that he could know who exactly had come for her. Was it Red Dawn, or Authority? He took a deep breath, hissing at the pain, pressing a hand into the wound.

"We're leaving," he breathed. "Someone will send for the Patrollers, and I doubt you want to be here to explain why there's a dead man in your office."

"He attacked me!"

Tashué scowled. "Yes he did, but *think*. Why might a man have sneaked into your office to kill you? What sort of stories have you been investigating lately?"

Allie quailed, just a bit, fighting to catch her breath through her throat, which must have been sore. But then her face flushed and her shoulders squared. Tashué knew that look, that righteous rage that burned away fear. "The Authority?"

"Either them or the Red Dawn." Tashué walked across the floor and held out a hand, dragging her to her feet. The effort sent a fresh spasm of pain through his side. "Ah, fuck. Damnit." He pressed a hand into the wound again, but his head felt too light. He caught himself on the corner of Allie's desk, closing his eyes and praying for the dizziness to pass.

"Are *you* alright?"

"Fine." Tashué shook his head, trying to bull through the weakness that spread through his body. "I'll get a healer. But we need to leave, right now. Before the Patrollers come. If he's Red Dawn, maybe you won't be arrested, but if he's Authority? What do you think will happen to you? Ishmael Saeati didn't come to find you?"

"What? Ishmael... Why would General Wolfe's personal diplomat come to find me?"

"Because I sent him to. Because I thought something like this would happen." Tashué tried to take a deep breath, but it only made his side hurt. "Fucking Ishmael. He didn't come see you?"

"No, he didn't come see me!"

"Forget it. Let's go!"

"No—my files!" Allie pulled away heading to her desk. Her hands were trembling as she rifled through the papers there.

"Allie, it's not important now. Just trust me. We need to go before I fucking pass out."

Allie swept up the paperwork on her desk, shoving it into her satchel. "I found more. More children! There's four more, all through the city, all in the same state. I have to keep these photographs!"

More children. Sweet North Star, that hurt more than the bullet. Hit him right in the heart this time. At least he'd killed the bastard responsible, but the Authority had still mutilated them and they were still dead by Hale's hand. He stepped across to the desk and started helping her pack things away but there was blood on his hands, blood dripping from his abdomen where she shot him. He was getting blood on her paperwork.

"Step away from Miss Tei!"

Tashué spun toward the door—but the movement was too fast and the dizziness almost took the legs out from under him. He caught himself on her desk, taking a slow breath. Someone new stood in the doorway of her office with his gun out and pointed at Tashué. His hand shook so much that he could have hit Allie or the wall behind her or even the ceiling.

"There's no need for that," Tashué said, levering himself up and taking a step toward the young man. "Miss Tei shot me once already and I'm here to help."

"Who are you?"

"What's your name?" Tashué countered.

"No, sir, I asked who you are. What are you doing here?" His voice was getting shrill now, high and squealing. Tashué kept stepping closer and closer and the young man stepped back, out into the hallway. "Why is there a dead man on the floor? Allie? Allie, are you alright?"

Tashué snapped his arm forward, grabbing the gun from the reporter. The man yelped as his knees buckled and he held his arms over his head.

"Please don't kill me!"

Tashué turned, resting a shoulder on the doorframe. "Allie, it's time to go."

Allie swept up her satchel, every last paper stuffed inside, stepping over the man she'd killed to get to the door. Tashué heard the blood sticking to her soles as she stepped through it, and then again with every step she took. Tashué grabbed her by the wrist and dragged her faster, toward the stairs. His fingers were going distant and cold and he dropped the young man's gun in the hallway. He pushed on, hoping the man wouldn't scoop it up to shoot him in the back.

"Miss Tei, where are you going?" the young man called. "What should I say to the Patrollers?"

"Tell them that dead man attacked me!"

And then they were down the stairs, heading out into the street. The cold air swept across Tashué like an icy wave. He staggered, catching himself on a lamp post.

"Are you sure you're alright?" Allie gasped, grabbing his arm. "I'm sorry!"

"It's alright. I'm fine. We need to get back to Brickheart. To Stella."

"Who's Stella?"

"She's from Cruinnich. She knows things, about the Authority, about the children." He staggered again and his shoulder struck a wall. He closed his eyes again, feeling the familiar drifting lightness of blood loss. He forced himself to his feet. "I'm so fucking tired of bleeding."

Allie stepped out into the street, waving to a passing carriage. She hooked her arm in Tashué's, helping him to the curb. "Where are we going?"

"I live down on the Row."

"The Row?" the driver scoffed. "That's on the other side of the Bay!"

"Yes, sir," Allie said, "that's very perceptive."

"Miss, are you alright?"

"Fine. Take us to the Row, sir."

Before the driver could argue anymore, Allie climbed up into the back of the carriage, catching Tashué's arm again and half-dragging him in after her. Tashué hissed through clenched teeth as the carriage lurched. He sank down onto a bench, clasping his hand over his wound again.

"Tell me what to do," Allie said, reaching across the carriage to him. "Tell me how to help."

Tashué fumbled with his buttons. "I need to get a look at it—at the wound."

Allie's hands were in far better shape. She made quick work of Tashué's coat and jacket, pushing them both open. Then the buckles for the holster, his waistcoat and his shirt.

She finally had his torso bare, and her eyes locked on the wound. Her lip quivered, her eyes going wide. Tashué tried to look down, but he couldn't quite fold himself the right way, not without bending the parts of him that were fucking shot. He didn't like the way all the colour drained out of Allie's face, though.

"Don't fucking pass out on me," he breathed.

"I'm—I'm fine. It just... It looks like meat. It's weird, how it looks like meat, but it's you. What—What do I do?"

"Is it pumping or flowing?"

"What?"

"The blood," Tashué said, grabbing Allie's arm to keep them both upright. "Is the blood pumping in a rhythm, like a heartbeat?"

"No it's just... oozing everywhere. Mr. Blackwood, are you going to die?"

Oozing, that's good. "No, I don't think so. Smell the wound. What does it smell like?"

"Are you joking? It's not funny!"

"No, I am not joking," Tashué grunted. "Smell it. If it smells like shit then you've pierced my bowels and I may actually die. I don't know if a healer can fix that, even one as good as Rhodrishi. Does it smell like shit or does it smell like blood?"

Allie leaned down and took a deep breath. "It smells like blood."

"Good. That's good. If you stick your finger in it, sometimes you can tell what the bullet hit."

"How am I supposed to tell that?"

"Organs feel different than muscle. And they usually bleed faster. Stop looking at me like that. This is what they teach us in the military so we know who needs to see a healer."

Allie snapped her teeth shut, but a high, strangled noise escaped her throat. She took a deep breath and she plunged her finger into the wound. A shout ripped out of Tashué's throat as her finger went in and she flinched. Fuck, that only hurt more.

"I… I don't know. I don't know what I feel."

"That's probably good then."

She pulled her hand back, staring down at the blood on her fingers. "Mr. Blackwood, I'm so sorry."

"Allie, once you've stuck your fingers into my body, you can call me Tashué."

"I bet you say that to all the women, don't you?"

Tashué laughed at that, then groaned at the flare of pain, leaning his head back against the bench. "Help me out of my jacket. Cut off the sleeve and you can use it to plug the wound."

He shrugged out of his coat and his jacket and Allie peeled the two garments away from his body. She used his cavalry knife to cut open the seam.

"How do I plug it?"

"Just stuff the wool in. Helps to stop the bleeding until I can see a healer. Hopefully Rhodrishi will be at my apartment already, looking after Stella."

Allie nodded and cut away pieces of wool from his sleeve. She plugged the wound as best she could. As she pushed the wool, Tashué forced himself to breathe through the very uncomfortable sensation of scratchy wool forcing its way into his body.

"Is that good?"

"Fucking good enough, I hope."

"Best be covering yourself up then, Tashué Blackwood," she said, helping Tashué back into his coat. "It's indecent, a gentleman sitting in a carriage with a Highview lady and no coat on."

They came to a stop, the driver knocking on the roof of the carriage. "The Row, miss."

Allie opened the door, stepping out first. She paid the driver, who thanked her profusely and didn't ask any questions as she helped Tashué down.

The fourth floor was a long fucking climb up. His whole body was shaking by the time he reached the top, and he had to lean on Allie to reach the door. Ceridwen charged at him when he stepped inside, hitting him hard. He grunted at the pain and caught himself on the door frame, his knees wobbling and threatening to dump him on the floor.

"Mr. Blackwood, are you alright?" Ceridwen whimpered—the poor girl had been through so much. "Are you bleeding? Colonel! Colonel Kheir, Mr. Blackwood is bleeding!"

Tashué took her by one shoulder, gently easing her back lest he fall right on top of her. "I'm alright, Ceridwen."

"I'm sorry," Allie said, her voice trembling.

"What happened?" Kazrani asked, stepping from his sitting room.

Rhodrishi was at his side faster, taking him by an elbow and guiding him inside. Tashué staggered to his table. His shoulder knocked against Keoh's urn and the whole thing nearly toppled over. This little apartment was so full, bursting with people.

"I shot him," Allie said.

The room went quiet. Everyone turned to look at Allie.

"Aren't you the reporter?" Kazrani asked. "The one from the *Highview Times*? I didn't realize that reporters for social pages made a habit of shooting people."

"Why did you shoot Mr. Blackwood?" Ceridwen asked.

"I'm sorry," Allie said again.

Rhodrishi guided Tashué to a chair, pushing the coat open. "Never mind all that. It looks like you shot him clean. Did you plug the wound?"

"He told me…"

"Of course, an old soldier's trick, to help buy them some time to see a healer," Rhodrishi said, his voice calm like he was speaking to a spooked horse, and Allie took a tiny step closer. "Take all that out, then, Captain. I wouldn't want to heal you around that dirty old wool."

Tashué grunted and leaned back, pulling the cloth plug from the wound. Everything gave a sickening tug and he had to breathe deep to avoid passing out.

"Come away now, Ceridwen," Kazrani said, ushering Ceridwen back to the bedroom again. "Let's go visit your mam."

"Is Mr. Blackwood going to be alright?"

"He'll be fine, Ceridwen," Rhodrishi said. "Off you go now. Sit with your mam." He dragged a chair around the table, sitting beside Tashué and taking his hand. "I'm looking forward to the day when your Talent quickens and you can start taking care of yourself, Captain."

Tashué squeezed his eyes shut. He knew what was coming. Rhodrishi's Talent touched his chest first, a warm and comforting feeling, a moment of gentleness before the real pain hit. When his Talent reached down, Tashué grit his teeth hard, but a groan still escaped his throat. He could feel it, all the way in the core of him, his own flesh twisting and writhing, burning like Rhodrishi was cauterizing a wound but he was just forcing all the bleeding places back together. Tashué leaned away from Rhodrishi, but Rhodrishi squeezed his hand with both of his. It built, a pressure, a heat, an itching, all at once. Too much. He squeezed Rhodrishi's hand back, his fist shaking, his other hand pressing flat into the table. He was going to break it, to smash the wood, to tear his own table apart, because the healing was worse than the gunshot.

The heat receded, leaving an echo of the pain reverberating through Tashué's whole body. He took a deep breath, the first one since Rhodrishi had started. How could people do this to themselves? Did Stella heal herself, back before she was running for her life? Didn't healers feel the pain of the people they were healing?

He forced himself to meet Rhodrishi's eye. Was that why Rhodrishi looked so tired all the time? He healed so many people in his life—hands of Bronwynn, for a million wounds. A million bullets, broken bones, deep burns, slices of a sword. A million searing pains, made worse by the effort to save the life.

"Thank you," Tashué breathed, because to curse him was too damned selfish.

Rhodrishi nodded. "Maybe if you took better care of yourself, you wouldn't need to go through such things."

"How's Stella?"

"She's awake."

The relief of those words washed away every shred of pain. He let out a long breath, emptying himself completely. She's awake. She'll live. Suddenly, it was the only thing that mattered.

51

TASHUÉ

DAY 25

T ashué watched Allie take her copious notes as Stella talked, laying out the same story that Tashué had heard already. Stella looked so tired, so distant. Rhodrishi had assured him that she shouldn't feel much pain anymore, but he had taken enough wounds in his life to know that sometimes the pain lingered in the mind far beyond the healing.

"So this experience was nearly a decade ago in Cruinnich?"

Stella sighed, leaning back against the pillows. "Do you think the Authority and the Red Dawn have become any less devious in that time?"

Allie tapped her pen on her notepad. "The Authority says there is no Red Dawn in Yaelsmuir."

"Powell Iwan says there is," Tashué said.

That gave her pause. Allie played with the nib of her pen as she thought, unscrewing it a half-turn and then tightening it again. "What is the nature of your relationship with Powell Iwan?"

Tashué had never expected to have to try to define 'the nature of his relationship with Powell Iwan.' So much had changed, in so little time. "It seems we have a common enemy."

"Who?"

"The Red Dawn."

Allie shook her head, a quick movement that seemed to be a clearing of her thoughts. Her hands still trembled, though Rhodrishi had healed her throat enough that her voice was clear and the bruises had faded before they ever really formed. She unscrewed her nib again, twisted it back into place.

"You'll have to explain to me how these stories are connected. The Red Dawn in Cruinnich tried to kill a child nearly a decade ago, and that somehow proves that the Red Dawn is in Yaelsmuir and they are responsible for the children we found here?"

"It's what they wanted to do, back in Cruinnich," Stella said. "They wanted to use the wee ones to raise awareness of what the Breeding Program is doing to those children. When I took Ceridwen and left, the man who led the Red Dawn was replaced by someone else. From what I've heard they never attempted such a thing again."

"And you think that they've brought those tactics here?" Allie asked. "What makes you so sure that these are Breeding Program children, and that the Red Dawn is the one killing them?"

"The tattoos," Stella said. "The numbers, on the back of their necks. It's how the Program keeps track of their success. The first number is the mother. The second is the father. The third is the child's number. Ceridwen has the same tattoo on her neck. It was still healing when the Red Dawn took her from the Program. I remember the feeling of the scabs when I held her and imagined how much she must have cried when they tattooed her. She was just so wee."

Tashué reached out, catching Stella's hand and squeezing her fingers. Tears welled in her eyes. She took a deep breath as she wiped her face with her other hand. Something about what she said stuck in his mind, playing over and over. *The first number is the mother. The second is the father.* Maybe it was the thought of a fresh tattoo on a child—an infant—that struck something deep and ugly in Tashué's heart. He remembered getting his own tattoos, and of course that wasn't a memory of pain, not really. The one on his chest, of the Black Ridge, had been cathartic, a release of pain. All the survivors of the Black Ridge had a tattoo like it, because an assignment like that left you different. But Jason's tattoo? *Blackwood J 1.1.658753.* Tashué remembered watching that heal and thinking how ugly it was. Jason hated it so much, it had made him cry the first time he showed Tashué. He was so young when they took him to the Rift. And Ceridwen, even younger.

"She was a year old, wasn't she?" Tashué asked. "When the Red Dawn took her? That's what the woman from the Breeding Program said, that the mothers get to keep them for the first year, and then they're off to creche."

Stella nodded. "That's what I thought. About a year, but I didn't know exactly. I've always celebrated her birthday as the first day I held her." She wiped her eyes, shaking her head. "I haven't spoken of all this since I left Cruinnich. It's been a long few years."

"I can imagine," Allie said softly. She made a few more notes and took a deep breath. "What about their limbs? Is the Red Dawn doing that? For some kind of shock?"

"No," Tashué said. "Hale told me they found the children that way."

"Who's Hale?" Allie asked.

"Edgar Hale. He was with the Red Dawn. He was the one that killed the children and disposed of their bodies."

"You keep saying 'was' and not 'is'," Allie breathed. Her whole body had gone rigid and she was watching Tashué with an intensity that he hadn't seen before.

Tashué took a deep breath. "This part doesn't go in your notes."

"Why not?"

"Allie, it doesn't go in your notes."

Another deep breath and she screwed the cap back onto her pen, clutching it on her lap. "Where is Hale?"

"He's dead. I killed him for Powell Iwan."

Allie bit the inside of her lip. She was trembling harder now, her hands so unsteady that she couldn't write anymore. "Why would Mr. Iwan want you to do such a thing?"

"He feels the Red Dawn has overstepped and would like them out of Yaelsmuir."

"How nice for the people of Yaelsmuir to have such a benevolent watchman," Allie said, her lip pulling back in something like a sneer. "What does that make you, then? Some kind of hired muscle for Mr. Iwan? How does a man go from Station Commander for the Authority to death bringer for the criminal underground?"

Tashué shook his head. "I won't be doing that sort of thing again. I made an exception for Hale."

Allie snorted, pushing some stray hairs out of her face. "Everyone accuses me of being naive, but even I don't believe that. Once a man like Powell Iwan starts pulling you in, he doesn't simply allow you to walk away. I'm sure he has a purpose in mind for you even now." She took a deep breath, shaking her head. "So, help me to understand—you killed Edgar Hale on the word of Powell Iwan. He wants the Red Dawn out, and so you trusted his assertion that Hale was somehow connected to the death of those children?"

"Hale confirmed it."

"Under duress?"

"Yes."

Allie pressed her lips together and Tashué thought he could see her heartbeat, pounding at her throat. Was she afraid of him now?

"How could you…" Her voice wavered and she paused, taking a deep breath.

How could you what? Do that to a man? It was easy, Tashué wanted to say. The Dominion military made sure he knew how. And maybe he wasn't diplomatic division like Lorne and Ishmael, but killing is killing. The human body is so vulnerable to death.

"How could you be sure that he was telling you the truth?" Allie continued. "Under duress, that is. Why wouldn't he tell you what you wanted to hear?"

"I believe what he said, Allie. Do you really want the details of how I got there?"

Allie met his eye, taking a deep breath. "Tell me what he said, then."

Tashué took a deep breath. That moment was etched into his mind, but he wanted to get the words right. "He said that the Authority is the one who removed their limbs. Said that they did it because it made them easier to transport. He said that the Authority broke their minds to use their Talent sooner—same as that woman I spoke to from the Breeding Program. He said that he didn't find the children, that a man named Davik Kaine found them somewhere and brought them to Hale. He tried to justify killing them by saying they were barely even human anymore, as if it was a mercy to kill them and dump them in the Brightwash. He called them energy units, Allie. Once the children are broken, the Authority apparently calls them energy units."

"How did he know these details?"

"I didn't think to ask."

Allie unscrewed the cap, tightened it again. "Who is this other man—Davik Kaine?"

"Davik Kaine, the same man I told you about?" Stella asked. "From Cruinnich?"

Tashué nodded. "That's what Hale said. Said Kaine's been here for eight years."

Stella took a deep breath, but her cheeks flushed with colour. The tears were gone, replaced by a cold anger that Tashué had never seen from her before. She swung to Allie. "He's the man who organized everything in Cruinnich. It was his idea to steal Ceridwen from the Breeding Program. He was chased out of Cruinnich after I left."

"May I write that down?"

Tashué nodded and she unscrewed the cap from her pen again, writing swiftly. He looked down at Stella in the quiet moment, wondering what she thought of him now that she knew he'd killed Hale. If there was any fear or anger there, she hid it well. She looked up at him and didn't flinch.

"Who attacked you, Miss Whiterock?" Allie asked. "Was it someone from the Red Dawn?"

"No, not the Red Dawn," Stella said. "Siras Duncreek works for the Authority. They call people like him 'Enquiry Officers.' Their job is to track down ferals and non-compliants and kill them. Officially, they're supposed to drag people back to where they came from so they can be processed or forced into compliance, but no one ever goes back. There's always some excuse for why the person ended up dead."

Allie took a deep breath, eyebrows raising. "Enquiry Officers?"

Stella nodded. "That's what the paperwork always says. 'File referred to Enquiry Officer.'"

"You look surprised, Tashué," Allie said, leaning in. "Have you not heard this term before?"

"No, I haven't," Tashué said and his voice rumbled a little too deep. "I have never referred a file to Enquiry Officers. I didn't even know that was something we did."

"How could you not know about an entire branch of the organization you work for, *Commander?*"

Tashué scoffed, spreading his hands. He hated being associated with the Authority now, hated that he still had his badge in his pocket and his name on the door in a station house. "How am I supposed to know about a branch of the Authority that I've never filed paperwork for?"

"The only reason I know about it is because I was married to the Provincial Administrator for Fuar province," Stella said. "I saw so much of the paperwork generated by the Authority, and I couldn't let it rest. I took the knowledge I had to Davik and the Red Dawn and helped to organize the various militant actions in the city."

Allie looked up sharply, eyes wide again. "The Provincial Administrator for Fuar is Bothain Clannaugh."

Stella closed her eyes, nodding. "Yes. He drank so damned much when I was in Cruinnich. I keep hoping he'll drink himself to death, but of course fate doesn't give me such gifts."

"Bothain Clannaugh does not have a good reputation."

"I know," Stella said again. "I'm married to him. I know all about his reputation."

"Sweet North Star, that means..." Allie shook her head but leaned closer. "Your real name is Ffyanwy Rhydderch, then. The wife that went missing... Most people think your husband killed you, did you know that? That means you're a healer... How did you come to be married to a man like Bothain?"

Stella took a deep breath, sitting up again. "I understand your professional curiosity, Miss Tei, but I don't think the sordid details of my family's struggles are pertinent. I did it for loyalty to my mother and my father and Rhydderch Stone."

"You're registered in Cruinnich?" Tashué asked, his mind spinning. "And your husband is the Provincial Administrator?"

"Yes."

Tashué caught Stella's hand, kissing her fingers as his heart skipped a beat. "So he was the one who was in charge of the Enquiry Officers?"

"Miss Whiterock," Allie breathed, catching Tashué's line of thought, "did your own husband send the Enquiry Officer after you?"

Stella laughed. "You say that as if you think Bothain would have any attachment to me because we endured a wedding ceremony. As if a signature on the marriage certificate and the blessing of the Sister of the North Star could bind Bothain to any one person tighter than he's bound to himself. Bothain is not a sentimental man, Miss Tei. There is nothing more important than his personal success and nothing will stand in the way of what he wants. So yes, when I brought his secrets to the Red Dawn and fled Cruinnich with Ceridwen, he sent an Enquiry Officer after me. He couldn't bear the thought of who else I might spill his secrets to."

"What kind of secrets?" Allie pressed.

Stella shook her head, closing her eyes. "Petty things, not nearly as interesting as you're hoping. He steals money from his family's businesses. He steals money from the Authority. Enquiry Officers were his idea, his program. He took the idea to Elsworth's predecessor when he was seventeen years old and was guaranteed a career in the Authority from that day forward. He is very proud of his abrupt rise through the ranks."

Allie nodded as she scribbled, biting her lip again. "And you knew Siras Duncreek? Back when you were in Cruinnich, was he familiar to you?"

Stella looked down at her hands, folded as they were in her lap. "He was a favourite of Bothain's. They got on well, the pair of them, both of them self-serving and without souls. Near the end, I wondered if Bothain kept Siras around as a reminder to me, of what might happen if I didn't learn to *leave it be*."

Allie nodded, sitting back and fiddling with her pen again. It got ink on her fingers when she loosened and tightened the nib, but she didn't seem to notice. "And Duncreek has Talent, then? That's how he assaulted you?"

Stella nodded, wiping her eyes and sitting up a little straighter. "He took the assignment as an Enquiry Officer instead of register-ing. I heard Bothain once say that he much preferred hiring the tainted for the Enquiry positions. He said they're 'better prepared for all eventualities.' But of course, it can be hard to find people with Talent who are willing to work for the Authority to hunt down other people with Talent, especially in Cruinnich. But the Duncreeks are a different breed."

Another scribbled note, another nod, and when she was done, her eyes came up and searched Tashué's face. "And you've never heard any of this?"

Tashué shook his head. "Not a word."

"Not even once you were promoted to Station Commander?"

"No, but I have to admit that I haven't spent much time in 'my' station house."

"Do you intend to return to your post?"

"Fuck no. I hope to somehow get my son out of the Rift so that we can all leave Yaelsmuir. Allie, that part doesn't need to be written down."

Allie's pen stopped short, and she looked up again. "When are you leaving, Miss Whiterock? Can I list your name as a source when I write these articles? I mean, your real name. Ffyanwy Rhydderch. That you're alive, and that you know these things because you were married to Bothain Clannaugh, will give this article the weight it needs for people to believe it. I hope. But I know this city, and if all I have is 'an anonymous source,' people will think I'm rumour-mongering and dismiss it all as sensationalist lies."

Stella—or was it Ffyanwy—took a deep breath. The moment of silence stretched and stretched. Tashué watched her face and waited. Bothain Clannaugh, he'd heard that name before. Usually in stories about how Cruinnich had gotten rid of the Army of the Red Dawn. With brutality and violence, with lining rebels up against stone walls and shooting them instead of processing them. Bothain Clannaugh declared himself the Fist of the North, crushing Fuar and Cruinnich into submission, no small feat for a province so famous for rebels, dissent, and unrest.

"Would you wait?" Stella asked finally. "Until after I leave? He might come looking for me himself, if he finds out for certain I'm alive and have been living here. Could you give me time to get away first?"

"Of course," Allie said. "How much longer are you staying? Is there a chance I can ask you more questions before you go?"

"I don't know." Another glance at Tashué. "I don't know how much longer I'll be here. I don't want to stay long at all. Siras Duncreek is still out there and I don't want to be here when he recovers from the bullet I put in him. He won't be terribly impressed with me for that."

"You shot him?" Allie asked. "Couldn't he be dead?"

"His body wasn't at the Facility," Tashué said with a shake of his head. "I'm sure it's a possibility that he's dead in an alley somewhere, but I'm not in the habit of gambling lives on things like possibilities."

Tears sprung to Allie's eyes suddenly and she wiped them away quickly, leaving a smear of ink on her cheek. "I've never killed a man before," she said, the words rushing out of her, fast and quiet, like they were racing the sobs that were coming. She shook her head, closed her eyes. "It's not that I regret it, it's just that I can still feel his hands... on my throat... and I can't forget what that feels like."

"You never forget what it feels like," Stella said softly. "Having a man—bigger than you, stronger than you, heavier than you—use his size and his power against you. That feeling never goes away. Not for as long as you live. You learn to cope with it eventually, but the moment has changed you. For better or worse—it doesn't matter, not really. The change is still there. But Miss Tei, look at me, and listen to me when I say this part. That change is not something to be ashamed of and it's not something you should resist. You can't be the same woman you were when you woke up this morning. But it's alright to exist as this new woman, cracked by your rough handling, but still *alive*."

Allie wept in earnest then, covering her face with both her hands. The way she curled in on herself made her look so small and her shoulder trembled with the force of her grief. Tashué shifted, thinking to reach out to her, to comfort her, but Stella caught him and shook her head and he sank back down. Stella sat on the edge of the bed and leaned forward. They sat for a long time, knees touching, foreheads touching, Stella's hair turning into a red halo of pillow-mussed curls that shielded them both from the world. Allie finally broke away, wiping her face with her sleeves and taking great, gulping breaths as if she could swallow enough composure.

"Thank you for your time, Miss Whiterock."

"It was a pleasure to meet you, Miss Tei."

They didn't shake hands so much as cling to each other for a moment, lending each other strength.

Allie stood, but faltered. She pressed her lips together in a tight line, holding back a fresh wave of emotion before finding Tashué's gaze. "Where do I go now? If the Authority or the Red Dawn is hunting me."

"I'll take you to General Wolfe," Tashué said, standing. He felt the full weight of his exhaustion as he stood, the force of it making him waver. But he didn't have time. There was still too much to do. "If it's Authority, they won't come for you there. Neither will the Red Dawn."

"What about my family? My mother, my sister. Will they be in danger?"

"I don't know. Let's go see General Wolfe."

Allie nodded and she headed out, into the kitchen. Kazrani was standing in the small hallway when the door opened, her eyes wide and shining with tears. At least Tashué could comfort her. He held out an arm and she closed the gap between them, pushing her face into his chest as she clung to him.

"Tell me it's not true," Kazrani breathed. "Tell me it's all a lie, some vicious lie."

Tashué said nothing, squeezing her tighter instead. Kazrani sucked in a long, slow breath, folding her emotions back down. She pulled away from Tashué and wiped her eyes with her sleeves. She turned to Stella, her lip starting to tremble.

"I'm sorry," Kazrani said. "I'm so sorry. I didn't know any of that. That the Authority... I didn't know."

Stella sat up a little straighter, but she let the silence stretch again. Tashué could only imagine how tired she was, how hard it must be to choose her words, especially when she'd spent nearly nine years lying and hiding from exactly these things.

"More people should know," Stella said finally. "More people should be made to face it."

"I need to change, Kaz," Tashué said. "I need to take Allie to General Wolfe."

Kazrani nodded, stepping out and pulling the door closed behind her. And Tashué was alone with Stella. Her hair was still all about her face, tangled and messy and so achingly beautiful that it took Tashué's breath away. It seemed incredibly intimate to see her in such a dishevelled state, off guard and vulnerable and recovering from the brink of death. Had it made her stronger, like everyone said? Or had it made her weaker? What about his own death, looming over his shoulder? He'd been close so many times. He didn't think it had made him stronger. He was starting to suspect he left behind little pieces of himself behind every time he stared down into the yawning chasm of darkness and managed to fight his way back.

He leaned down and kissed the side of her face. She turned to him, catching his mouth with hers, fingers pushing through his beard again. It took every shred of strength he had not to lay down with her, to push his face into the tangle that was her hair and sleep the rest of the night away. But there was no time, not yet.

He stripped out of his blood-soaked clothes, dropped them on the floor, and rifled for something new. All he had left were the things Illea Winter had sent him, suits of higher quality than anything he'd owned before, save that first Bellmore suit—ruined with blood, too. Stella rose from the bed, stepping in close. Her fingers found the bullet wound, sliding around the edge of the wound, not quite touching the scabbed and crusty flesh.

"Are you going to survive long enough to come after me, Tashué Blackwood?"

"I fucking well hope so," Tashué muttered. He caught her hand, bringing it up to kiss her fingers, her wrist. He was suddenly aware of how he was naked in front of her, all his flesh and scars borne to her again—but he needed to leave.

"You killed Hale?" Stella asked.

Tashué grabbed a pair of trousers, fighting into them. All the movement in him now made him feel dizzy and distant from his limbs. How much blood had he lost? "I did."

Stella nodded. She took one of the shirts, holding it so he could slide his arms into it. He winced at the pulling in his side. Rhodrishi had only done enough to stop the bleeding, and the wound was raw and angry.

"Good," she said. She started on his buttons, her fingers deft and fast. "What will happen to his body?"

"I'm told Powell Iwan will dispose of it."

"Is it true he sells the bodies of his enemies to the pig farmers?"

"I don't know. I doubt it. Don't animals need an empty stomach before they're slaughtered?"

"I suppose," Stella said with a shrug, "but there's a farmer's auction north of the Market and they sell live animals."

"Stella Whiterock, you are a constant surprise. Or should I call you Ffyanwy now?"

She smoothed out his collar and handed him a waistcoat, helping him with those buttons next. "I haven't been Ffyanwy in near a decade."

"I know, but you don't need to hide anymore. Especially not from me."

Her hands knotted in the front of his waistcoat, dragging him down so she could kiss him again. "Ffyanwy Rhydderch is the wife of Bothain Clannaugh, and I never wanted to be that man's wife.

I'm much happier to be Stella Whiterock, whose heart belongs to Tashué Blackwood."

———————

Tashué didn't remember the route Ishmael took around the Wolfe estate to get to the smaller door that led to the kitchen, and stomped right up to the front door instead. He pounded on the thick wood, again and again, unrelenting until the door creaked open.

"I need to see General Wolfe," Tashué said to the hapless man on the other side of the door. "Right now."

"Excuse me, sir, perhaps you could return at a more convenient hour."

Tashué pushed past the man, stepping into the foyer. "Where is he? And where's Ishmael Saeati? I wouldn't mind speaking to him, either."

"Sir!"

"Are we really going to spend all our energy arguing with each other? I'm here. I'm not leaving. I want to speak to General Wolfe. If you don't send for him, I'll go find him myself."

"Alright, Captain, you can stop yelling at my servant now," Wolfe said from the top of his stairs. "Thank you, Mr. Bell, you can go back to your bed."

"Shall I send for the Patrollers, General?"

"No, no, Captain Blackwood is a friend. I'm sure there's a good reason for all this. Good night, Mr. Bell."

"Yes sir."

Wolfe made his cautious way down the stairs, leaning on his cane. "Come inside, young lady. Close the door."

"Yes, sir." Allie eased forward, dragging the heavy door closed behind her.

"Where's Ishmael?" Tashué asked. "I would like him to meet Allie Tei, who nearly died tonight because he apparently forgot that I asked for his help."

Wolfe finally made it to the bottom of the staircase, taking a deep breath to recover from the effort of climbing down. "Mr. Saeati is not currently in any shape for working. The Market fire took more of a toll on him than he would like to admit. Why did you need his help? Ah, Miss Tei, I do know you. You work at the *Highview Times*, don't you?"

"Yes, sir, although I suspect I've just given my notice there," Allie said. "I don't think the owner will be very pleased with me for leaving a dead body in my office."

"Yes, I can see how a dead body might be a hindrance for a reporter's career," Wolfe said, appearing completely unsurprised. "Shall we go sit somewhere, then? I imagine the dead body might be pertinent to the reason you're here."

They sat in a solarium. There was a sense of peace in the room. It was lit by only the stars and the moon, the furniture only vague forms in the darkness, and the looming forest beyond the flatness of Wolfe's garden. Wolfe lit a few gas lamps with a taper, turning them down low to give them just enough light to see by.

"The last time I was in your home, you asked me if I would consider running for Mayor after your term is finished," Tashué said. "You told me that you wanted to unbalance Rainer Elsworth's power. That you didn't trust him, and that he was actively harming the citizens of this city, of the Dominion entire, with his greed and his hunger for power. We served together on the Lazjar and I think I've come to know the kind of man you are. Honest, upright, fighting for the common people. Because of that, I was honestly considering your offer. I need to know if my impression is true."

"I would like to think it is," Wolfe said carefully. "But if I wasn't an honest man, would I admit it if you asked me?"

Tashué stifled a sigh, biting back his frustration. He didn't want to have a battle of words, discussing the shades of honesty and what it looked like. He was so fucking tired. The rage was burning low, the blood loss leaving him feeling half-empty and drained.

"Mayor Blackwood has a nice ring to it," Allie said, breaking through the silence. "The man that derailed Myron Winter's career. Will Illea Winter back you? That would be a statement, wouldn't it?"

"I'm hoping that it won't be necessary," Tashué said. "I'm hoping that what we now know about the Authority might be enough to start peeling people's trust away from Elsworth, without having to wait for the election."

"What is it that you think you know?" Wolfe asked.

"Over the last few months, a number of children have been found throughout the city," Allie said. She reached for her satchel, pulling out some of the papers that she'd rescued from her office. "Three boys and three girls. All of them with arms and legs removed, all of them with tattoos on the backs of their necks."

She passed the photographs to Tashué first. The photographs he'd given her were at the top of the pile, with the girl from the Brightwash and the tattoo on the back of her neck. It froze him, that tattoo. It had been a while since he'd looked at it. So much had happened since he handed Allie these photographs. He passed them over to General Wolfe, but that tattoo lingered in his head. There was something important about that tattoo, but he couldn't grasp what. Stella had explained it, hadn't she? The Authority used the tattoos to track the success of the Breeding Program. The identity of the girl's parents were coded on that tattoo, and her own number if the Authority chose her to breed new Talented children. *Energy units*, they were called. That's what Edgar Hale called them. *Energy units.*

He didn't really listen to Allie speak. She did well enough without his input, explaining all that they'd learnt together.

He reached into his pocket, finding the spent shell that had held the bullet that killed Hale. He meant to give it to Powell Iwan, to show that he had done what was expected of him. It seemed to show, also, that the veneer he wore between his wild and violent instincts—honed by ten years in the military—was thinner and more delicate than he would have liked to admit. Those instincts were still very much alive, hot and consuming, burning away all the illusions of himself that he'd built, all the ways that he convinced himself that he was a good man, a civilized man. He wasn't those things, not really. They were lies he told himself to survive.

Allie laid everything at Nathaniel Wolfe's feet, and the General listened to every word with all the intense focus that Tashué had seen from him when they were both twenty years younger.

Wolfe took in a deep breath when she was done, leaning back in his chair and looking up at the gibbous moon, hanging above the forest. "What proof do you have, then? These are... serious accusations, and I believe you. But to take any of this to a public platform, we'll need proof, or they'll be nothing but rumours. Rumours are a common part of the election cycle, and they tend to get lost beneath all the noise unless there's good, hard proof."

"We don't have proof, not yet," Tashué said, before Allie could mention Stella's real name. Let her be Stella a little longer, let Allie, Tashué and Kazrani be the only people in Yaelsmuir that knew the complete truth until she was away. "We're trying. I might have leveraged my position as Station Commander to get access to more sensitive files, but I doubt Elsworth will want a Station Commander who beats his own Officers bloody."

"I did hear about that," Wolfe said with a nod. "One of your own, was it? I can assure you, Mr. Blackwood, that there's very little that Rainer Elsworth isn't willing to overlook, so long as the overall political effect is in his favour. I'm sure, if you spoke to him, he would be able to clear up the whole mess and see you back at the office by week's end."

"General, you must be joking," Tashué said. "I would sooner eat my damned badge than go back to working for the Authority. They remove the arms and legs of children to make them *easier to transport*."

"Understood, Captain, but I agree with your instinct to work from within the Authority to get the information you need. The whole thing runs on paperwork, and if what you say is true, there's going to be some documentation of it somewhere."

Tashué shook his head, swallowing the fresh wave of anger as it rose in his chest. So he wasn't too tired for rage, after all. "No, sir. I won't go back there and pretend everything is normal. I'll find another way. I brought Allie here because I hoped you could help to keep her safe. Someone tried to kill her tonight. I wondered if it was someone from the Red Dawn, but now I don't think so. This is what they wanted, after all. They wanted someone to figure out what's happening. So, it must be someone from the Authority. But I doubt even Rainer Elsworth is bold enough to kill someone under your protection."

"If General Wolfe's protection is enough to stop an Enquiry Officer, why not bring Stella here as well?" Allie asked.

Tashué sighed, the rage draining out of him. If only General Wolfe was enough to save Stella, and she could stay in Yaelsmuir until he was ready to go with her. "There are more issues facing Stella than simply Siras Duncreek. If it was only a man, I would wait for him to come for her and put a few bullets in him myself."

"I'm sorry I can't be of more help to you, Captain."

Tashué shrugged. "Someone else will help Stella. Right now, I need to know if Allie will be safe."

General Wolfe nodded a few times, one finger tapping on the head of his cane. "How much do you know about printing presses, Miss Tei?"

"I started my career at the *Times* on the main floor, running the press. Why?"

"It seems I'll be in the market to buy one, and I would appreciate your input. And then once we have it set up, we have a few articles to run, don't we?"

"I would be honoured, General," Allie said. "Will it be enough to keep my family safe, too?"

"From Rainer Elsworth? Yes. I'll have a carriage bring you to your office to collect your belongings, and again to your home. You can all stay here if you wish, or I can have soldiers posted at your house for as long as you need."

"Thank you, General, that's very generous of you."

Wolfe nodded, easing himself back up to his feet. "I'll have a room prepared for the night. And you, Captain? Will you stay?"

"No. I still have too much to do."

"I'll get you a carriage then. To Brickheart?"

"No, to the Bay."

52

TASHUÉ

DAY 25

Vasska wasn't sitting at the bar anymore when Tashué returned to the Hive. A bartender he didn't recognize was bouncing back and forth, struggling to keep up with the demand of the crowd. It seemed that there were even more people in the Hive now, even though it was past midnight.

Tashué settled at the bar, wondering how to find Powell. It took a while to catch the attention of the bartender, to pierce through the veil of panic. The bartender pulled a few pints before he finally turned to Tashué, eyebrows up as he waited for an order.

"I'm looking for Mr. Iwan."

"Are you, now?" The man smirked. "And who might you be that you think you can order up Mr. Iwan at the bar like a pint of stout?"

"Tashué Blackwood."

"I'm not familiar."

Tashué's arm shot out, grabbing the man by the front of the shirt and dragging him forward. He came up onto the bar, hands scrabbling at Tashué's fist, twisting like a fish on a line, but Tashué held fast. He brought the man close.

"Shall I familiarize you," Tashué said, "or will you tell me how to find Mr. Iwan?"

"Yes, sir, sorry, sir, I'll send a runner, alright? I'll send a runner for Mr. Iwan if you'll just let me go and if Mr. Iwan wants to see you at this hour, he'll come."

"Thank you."

Tashué let the man go and settled at the bar, pulling out his cigarillos. When the bartender circled around again, he ordered a pint of bitter and set himself down to wait.

He drank two pints while he waited, but finally he saw a familiar face. Adley eased through the crowd. He stomped to the bar and slammed a fist down, sending a hot jolt of fear through everyone nearby. Tashué felt the collective flinch all around him.

"Hey, shitwit," Adley said. The bartender scrambled closer, dropping a half-filled pint as he fumbled with it. He ignored the way it spilt beer all over him and stood in front of Adley. Adley pointed a big, sausage link finger at the man and the bartender trembled as if he was facing a loaded rifle. "The next time this man asks for Mr. Iwan, you send him right away. This man does not wait. Clear?"

"Yes, sir."

"Now fuck off back to work."

The man scrambled away again. He slipped in the spilt beer and barely caught himself on the bar. Adley grunted at him, shaking his head. He tapped Tashué on the shoulder.

"Follow me."

They climbed up the Hive, up the scaffolding that swayed in the wind. Up and up they climbed, too impossibly high. Tashué had never realized the scale of the place, the warren of halls and alleyways and warehouse storage.

Powell Iwan was at the top, apparently, a king on his wooden throne. The room up there was small and almost warm, but the wind scythed through the walls and stole away the heat of the little wood stove. Iwan sat in a large wingback chair facing the stove, a blanket across his skinny knees. He nursed a mug of something that sent steam curling across his face. Tashué thought it smelled of alcohol but with the beer still on his tongue it was hard to be sure.

"Good evening, Mr. Blackwood. I hear you had a conversation

with my grandson earlier this afternoon. I trust that means Mr. Hale has been dealt with."

Tashué reached into his pocket, pulling out the spent shell from the bullet that killed Hale. He offered it to Powell, who took it between two arthritic fingers, peering at it for a long time.

"Are you satisfied, then?" Powell asked. "He's the man you were looking for."

"He's *one* of the men I'm looking for," Tashué grunted. "Apparently he works with a man named Davik Kaine."

"Are you here to ask after Kaine? He's next out, I assure you."

Tashué took a deep breath. "No, sir. I would ask something else of you."

"Oh you would ask something of me, would you?" Powell asked. He still had the shell pinched between both fingers and he turned his intense stare on Tashué. "We're square, you and I. But now you would ask something of me?"

"Yes, sir."

"Mark me curious. What thing might Tashué Blackwood ask of old Powell Iwan? Didn't you say that the Authority took good care of you and you didn't need the likes of me?"

"I'm finished with the Authority," Tashué said. Saying the words out loud was painful, burning across nineteen years of loyalty, nineteen years of upholding the law. *Follow the law and you'll be safe.* "My son is in the Rift and he's going to die there. One way or another, the Authority is going to kill him. Can you help me get him out?"

Powell dropped the shell into his palm, closing his fingers around it. He was still watching Tashué, nodding ever so slightly as if he was agreeing with his own thoughts.

"And what makes you think I could do such a thing?" Powell asked. "I'm just a humble merchant, running the Hive and the comings and goings of trade for this city. How could I get your tainted boy out of the hands of the Authority?"

"I come to the conclusion that you're more connected to the Red Dawn than you implied," Tashué said. "I think Kaine came here from Cruinnich and you let him in. I think you propped him up. You made it sound like you just *allowed* him to get a foothold, but

I think it's more than that, isn't it? You *helped* him survive, which means you got yourself involved in whatever he was doing. There's so much going on in the Bay, after all. No one survives here without your help."

"Ah, Mr. Blackwood, you're not as naive as I thought," Powell said. He had the shell still in his hand and was holding it so hard that his knuckles went white. He smiled across the gap between them. It wasn't a comforting thing, that smile. It was a predator's smile, a mountain lion who closed in on his prey, who already tasted blood in his mouth because the kill was a sure thing. "But you're here, saying these things while looking me in the eye, so you're also not as soft as I thought you were."

Tashué shrugged. Soft? Shit. "The part I do believe is that Kaine has forgotten his place. He's pushing you too hard, isn't he? And you're getting ready to get rid of him. That's why I saw Ishmael Saeati in the Bay, with blood on his hands. He was getting things started for you, wasn't he? But the Army of the Red Dawn will still be here, even after Kaine is gone, and there's nothing you can do to get them out. Not now. They've been here too long and there's too many of them. There will always be someone else to take his place, and you'll never really know if they'll do what they're told. Which is fine, because you have no shortage of killers here in the Bay willing to work for you, but what does one do with so many bodies? Is it true you feed them to the pigs?"

Powell laughed at that, leaning back in his chair. "To the pigs? Oh that's my favourite rumour, it really is. But animals need an empty stomach when they go to slaughter, and General Wolfe is a man of iron rules. There's no people in Wolfe's pig guts, I can assure you." He opened his hand, rolling the shell back and forth across his palm. "It seems to me that you're suggesting something, Mr. Blackwood. That you're telling me you would be willing to stand in the hole that will be created when I get rid of Davik Kaine, as if you think you can be trusted to do what you're told."

"Can you get my son out of the Rift?"

"I think I can, Mr. Blackwood. I think things are already

happening in the Rift and that boy of yours can certainly be part of it all if that's what you want."

Tashué nodded, taking a deep breath. All he *wanted* was to follow Stella across the Dominion, but his son needed him more—this was the only way he could see to get Jason out. "Once my son is out of the Rift, I'll stand wherever you want me to."

53

TASHUÉ

DAY 26

It was morning when Tashué returned to his apartment. Kazrani was awake again—or maybe still, the wood stove generating heat for the little apartment, the rich, roasted smell of brewed coffee filling the space.

"Where have you been?" Kazrani asked from her place by the window, sunk into Tashué's favourite old chair. She'd found his tobacco and was rolling some cigarillos; her work was too loose, and some of her cigarillos were starting to unroll on the small table beside her.

"Are you my mother or my wife?" Tashué muttered. He went to the kitchen first, pouring the coffee into a pair of mugs.

Kazrani scowled. "Is she safe, then? Your reporter?"

Tashué nodded, carrying the mugs into the sitting room and laying them on the table between them. "General Wolfe is officially employing her. If we can find proof, he'll have it all printed."

"Why didn't you tell me any of this sooner?" Kazrani asked, looking up at him. "All of these things that you've been dealing with… Don't you trust me anymore?"

He sank down on the couch that he never used, sighing. He

unrolled Kazrani's worst cigarillos, returning the shredded tobacco to the tin he kept and smoothing the whole leaves out again.

"You're the greatest friend I've ever known," he said softly. Could he tell her what he had done today? Would she understand why Hale had to die? Why he had to stand with Powell Iwan? "I don't know what to say. I didn't want to fight about any of it, not with you. It all happened so fast."

She avoided his searching eyes as she struggled with another cigarillo. He spread the shredded tobacco on the smoothed leaf and rerolled it. His fingers were big, but he'd been rolling his own so long that it didn't matter. Kazrani set down another. It began to unroll the moment she let go of it and Tashué plucked it up, emptying it into the tin.

"You're an idiot," she muttered.

"Yes, I probably am."

She nodded as if that confirmed something and he knew enough not to press the moment anymore. It was her way of forgiving him, of wiping clean his slate even though she was still upset with him. She kept rolling bad cigarillos, though, and he kept fixing them. He drank his coffee, but the warmth of it sitting in his belly only made him more keenly aware of how tired he was.

"Are you going with her?" Kazrani asked. "When she leaves?"

Tashué shook his head, closing his eyes. "I can't leave Jason."

"Do you need me to go? To protect them?"

"Kaz, you don't have to do that."

"That's not what I asked, Captain. I asked if you *needed* it."

Tashué shook his head, focusing on the cigarillos instead of looking at Kazrani. "You would really do that? You would help two people run from the Authority—even if it goes against everything you believe?"

"No—not everything. I may be Authority now, but first I'm Jitabvi. You remember what that means, don't you?" She reached out, catching Tashué's hand and forcing him to stop fiddling with the tobacco, probably to get him to look at her. "The company is as much a part of my identity as the ashrab and riding horses and the Hadia. And you're my Captain. It's my purpose, to do what you ask.

Even if I think it's wrong, that's not my choice to make. If you give an order, I follow it. That's how this works."

Tashué shook his head. "I don't want this to be about giving you orders, Kaz."

She gave a sad, weary smile, squeezing his fingers. "I know that. That's why I offered. I know you wouldn't ask, but I want you to understand that... maybe it doesn't sound right to you, me going because you're my Captain. But if I was doing it for the ashrab, would you even question it?"

Tashué shook his head, looking up at her. "No, I suppose I wouldn't."

Kazrani nodded. "No, you wouldn't, because you understand. It's who I am. But also... it's who I choose to be. I don't have to braid my hair. I didn't have to join a company, or ride with the hotbloods. I wanted to. I wanted to live and breathe my own culture, my own heritage. And for Jitabvi here in the Dominion, the company is a full part of our identity. Besides, the last time I disagreed with an order, it was because you wanted us to dig in instead of charge. Remember?"

Tashué would have laughed, except the Ridge was still so hot and ugly in his mind, with everyone picking at those wounds these days. He grimaced instead. "You were so angry at me. 'Cavalry doesn't entrench. Cavalry charges.'" He shook his head, forcing in another deep breath. "It wasn't that I was afraid to die, I just didn't want us all to die pointlessly. I would have done it, if I thought it was going to accomplish something. Charging down that ridge would have accomplished nothing."

"I know that *now*. And I'm glad you kept us all alive. And I'm glad you survived the flogging." She finally gave up on rolling cigarillos, leaning back in his chair and rubbing her eyes with the heels of her palms. "We don't always agree about things, but I still love you. And I'll still follow where you lead. Because I'd rather be beside you and wrong than apart from you and right. Parts of this... they don't sit right with me. So if you need someone to go with them, to protect them until they're somewhere safe, I'll do it. For you."

Tashué stood, pushing the cigarillos and the tin of tobacco

aside. He sat on the table in front of Kazrani and reached out, pulling her into a crushing hug. "Thank you, Kaz."

Kazrani hugged him back. "You should go get some sleep, you fool. You look fit to keel over."

As he stood, Keoh's copper urn caught his eye. It still took up residence on the table. It was just a little thing, that copper urn, but no one could bring themselves to set their plates beside it and eat in its company. He sighed, reaching out to it, touching her name. *Keoh, I'm sorry. I'm so sorry.*

The engraving of her name was rough beneath his thumb, catching at the whorls of his thumbprint. Not just her name, he realized. Number, too. His heart skipped a beat, something settling into place that had only been floating around his mind before. Those numbers, he'd seen them already.

Keoh Gian Ly
Registered Breeder 1693

He reached into his pocket next, fumbling with his own clothes. His hands shook too much. His notepad had blood on it now, red soaking into the paper. Whose blood was that? There were so many options. The pages stuck together as he flipped through them and he had to ease them apart carefully so they wouldn't tear. His heart had finished skipping, making double time to make up for the beats it missed. Beating so hard he could feel it across his whole body, the pulse of it, his ears ringing with it. He flipped past the page of the girl's face. To the number, tattooed on the back of her neck.

1693-0237-4494

He sagged into a chair, his chest so tight that he couldn't breathe. He felt boneless and deflated, so hollow that he could hear Keoh echoing in his chest. How she would howl if she knew. Her child, the first she had given to the Authority, dead in the Brightwash. Without limbs, without hair. Without a shred of clothes to protect her from the frigid water of the river. With an infection so deep that Tashué could see her bones.

It's better that she died not knowing. It seemed scarce comfort.

He flipped back a page, to the sketch he'd made. Blood soaked halfway up the paper, covering her shoulders, her neck, her chin. It seemed fitting. Whose blood was it? Stella's, from when he carried her, or his own? And Hale's blood, dry and dark, was smeared across her eyes. That seemed fitting as well. The details he'd so carefully rendered were smudged and indistinct now, but he remembered them too clearly. The broad, flat nose, which held only the faintest scattering of freckles. The girl must have gotten her rosy colouring from whoever fathered her, because Keoh's skin was like the colour of polished bronze.

The heat crawled up his chest, making his throat tight and his face hurt. He leaned forward, holding his face in his hands and trying to breathe deep enough to suck all the heat back, but now that it had bubbled up through the cracks in his composure, there was no forcing it down.

He wept. For Keoh, for Jason, for all the ways he had failed them both. If he was a better man, if he wasn't so foolish, so stubborn, Keoh might still be alive. If he hadn't pushed her so hard, she never would have run. If he hadn't pushed Jason the same way, he might never have gone to the Rift.

Voices came only distantly to him. Kazrani, Ceridwen, asking if he was alright. Had he woken her? He couldn't catch his breath. Couldn't stop himself. He was dizzy with the pressure of his emotions, suffocating in his grief.

Stella came to him. She wrapped her arms around him and held him. Her fingers slid through his hair and he leaned against her. This time it was her strength that propped him up, her heartbeat that kept him grounded in the world. And he would have to let her go.

He slept tucked against her body, the exhaustion of the last few days finally catching up. At some point, he was aware of Rhodrishi and the man's incredible Talent, flowing through his body and into Stella's, and the three of them were one person for a time.

He knew what it was to live in Cruinnich, to live in the legacy territory east of the Ammuilghur mountains, to travel the Dominion in
search of *something*. A safe place, or a place of belonging, or maybe
both. Maybe the three of them all wanted the same thing. After
Rhodrishi retreated, he dreamt of a red-headed child, but not
Ceridwen—a boy, a son, a finicky baby who screamed until his
whole body turned red with his rage, who defied sleep as if it was
personally insulting to him. He dreamt of a wedding ceremony, a
man and a woman promising themselves to each other and the man
wondering how he would ever provide a life for his new family when
this country didn't want either of them to thrive because of their
amber eyes and the power of their Talent.

He woke to Stella kissing him, her lips warm on his throat. He
pulled her closer, feeling her whole body pressed against his. It was
an easy thing to let himself be lost in her. For a little while, they were
only a man and a woman who had been forged together by a world
of blood and fire and pain, and there was comfort in letting themselves forget that the world was drawing them apart as sure as it had
forced them together.

"It's time for me to go," she said.

It didn't matter how long he had been preparing himself for this
moment; it still hurt to hear her say it. The words slid into his chest,
the blade of a knife. He swallowed the pain and any words he might
have said. Nothing he could say would help.

"I expect you to come find me," she said. "Don't make me wait
too long."

He kissed her face. Buried himself in her hair. Breathed in the
scent of her. "I'll come as soon as I can."

To promise anything more than 'as soon as I can' was a lie.

Ceridwen tried not to cry as they walked through the city,
through Brickheart, back to the General's new hospital. She
clutched Tashué's hand, her whole body trembling with her effort to
keep herself calm.

There weren't many wounded in the hospital. Though it had only been a few days, Rhodrishi and the other healers had seen to most of the injuries well enough to send them home. Tashué saw Eddie in a bed by the window, turned so that he could see outside. He could see the river from his window, but not the rebuilding efforts that brought the wharf back to life slowly, one plank at a time.

"Mr. Blackwood," Eddie called, stopping Tashué before he could continue his search for Rhodrishi. "It's good to see you, sir!"

"It's good to see you, Eddie," Tashué said, closing the distance between them and fighting the wave of guilt. He wasn't here to see Eddie. He should have come sooner, but life... He stopped his thoughts before he could make excuses for himself. He should have come sooner. "You're looking well."

Eddie made a grimace—or was it a smile—propping himself up on his elbows to reach up and shake Tashué's hand. "They don't think I'll walk again. Even Colonel Kheir can't fix the bone. It's dust, he says. Better than being dead though, hey?"

"Better than being dead," Tashué agreed. "I'm sorry I wasn't soon enough to save your mother, Eddie. I'm so sorry."

Tears sprung to the boy's eyes and he sagged back to his pillow. "Colonel Kheir said that Mayor Wolfe himself carried her out of the wreckage. She would have liked that, I think. Mayor Wolfe paid for her funeral, even brought me out there to see it. In my bed and everything. Must have been a sight, hey? A boy in a hospital bed, sitting in a graveyard." Eddie's voice trembled and he shook his head. "Hurts too much still to sit up. I'll get into one of those chairs one day, the ones with the wheels on them. And then I'll be back in the smokehouse, making bacon."

"Good for you, son," Tashué croaked, reaching down and rubbing Eddie's shoulder. "Good for you. I can't stay. I have to find Colonel Kheir. But I'll be back again to see you, I promise."

He found Stella and Ceridwen waiting in the hall. She was crying in earnest now, tears making glittering tracks down her cheeks.

"Was his mam killed in the Market fire?" she asked.

"She was," Tashué said, taking her hand again. "These things happen, Ceridwen. A wise woman reminded me once that the Keeper of the Keys comes for us all. Better to leave behind family that love us, and will carry our memories with them. Let's go find the Colonel."

Ceridwen nodded and Tashué led them up the stairs. The bottom floor was the only one operational, the stairs leading up to floors that hadn't yet been finished or furnished. The dedication was in a few days, but Tashué wondered if the whole hospital would be ready to receive patients by then or if the whole thing was supposed to be ceremonial. It was so hard to tell with these political functions. They never seemed to serve any purpose but to let rich people talk about themselves.

They passed the third floor, where Stella had been healed, and the fourth, where Rhodrishi told him about the Wrath. A trembling started in his chest again, threatening to set him off into another spiral of emotion. He tried to breathe deep, to hold himself together. The sawdust was gone, windows had been installed and workers were applying plaster to the lathe. On the fifth, other workers were cutting lathe and nailing it to the walls. The sixth was still bare studs, waiting for more purpose.

Rhodrishi was on the sixth floor, where a single cot bed had served as his home all this time. He had packed away everything he needed, his saddle bags coated with fresh oil to protect them against the rain and the cold that they were setting out into. His riding clothes were worn and comfortable looking, with layers of wool and leather for warmth.

"It's time to go, then?" Rhodrishi asked.

"Yes, Colonel. Thank you."

"I don't want to go," Ceridwen breathed. "I don't want to leave! Yaelsmuir is my home and Mr. Blackwood is like my da and it's not right to leave, not when I have to leave my da behind."

Stella swallowed hard at Tashué's shoulder, reaching down and taking Ceridwen's hand. "Pigeon, I'm sorry. But it's not safe here. Not after what happened."

Ceridwen turned to Tashué, turning those big hazel eyes on

him, the tears still clinging to her lashes. "Why won't you come with us?"

Tashué sank to his knees before her, fighting hard against the well of emotion. If he started weeping again, he'd never be able to let them go. He sucked it all back, fighting for a calm he didn't feel. "Ceridwen, listen to me. I love you, like you were my own. I would be honoured to be your da. But my son is still here and he needs me. You have your mam and Colonel Kheir and Kaz to take care of you, but my son has no one but me. So, you'll go with your mam and I'm going to stay here, to help Jason. Once he's safe, I'll come after you."

"Can't I stay with you? I would like to meet Jason. I bet I would like him. He can tell me about his toys, the ones in his room, and I can show him my marbles, and then we could all go together."

Tashué shook his head, catching Ceridwen's face in both his hands. She was such a little thing. Almost ten was almost grown, but she would never be a large person. But like her mother, she had such incredible strength already, such incredible presence in the world. He kissed her on the forehead. "It's not safe here for either of you. You have to go."

Ceridwen threw herself at him, locking her arms around his neck and clinging to him. He hugged her hard, wishing he could crush her against him and keep her safe forever.

He peeled her away, standing. "Stay with your mam for a moment longer, Ceridwen. I need to speak to the Colonel."

Stella grabbed Ceridwen's hand before the girl could attach herself to Tashué again and he reluctantly stepped away. Every time he walked away from them, he felt a bit of himself crack a little more.

Rhodrishi followed him to the other side of the floor. There was nowhere for them to hide, but at least the floor was big enough that Ceridwen wouldn't hear what he had to say from where she was by the stairwell.

"Has Lieutenant Mahalouwan decided to come?" Rhodrishi asked.

Tashué nodded. "She's getting supplies for the journey now.

Horses, food, enough to get you to the legacy territory. I'll follow you as soon as I can."

"You mean *if* you can."

Tashué pressed his lips together against another wave of pain bubbling up through his chest. *If.* Rhodrishi was right, of course. If he could get Jason out of the Rift, if he could settle his debt to Iwan quickly, if Jason would come with him. If not? Could he leave Jason behind? Could he accept never seeing Stella and Ceridwen again?

Rhodrishi's eyes drifted back to Ceridwen again. "Lieutenant Mahalouwan agreed to help a fugitive from the Authority escape to the legacy territory? That seems to be rather contrary to her nature."

"She's helping Stella run for her life."

"Why?"

"For me. Because I'm her Captain. Because the idea of Enquiry Officers didn't sit well with her. Officers tracking people across the continent and murdering them in the streets? It gives us all a bad name."

"And you?" Rhodrishi asked, turning back on Tashué. A little bit of anger crept into his eyes, a little bit of the fire Tashué had seen in his office. "I heard about the fight in your station house. Elsworth has asked me if I've seen you. It seems there's some question as to what's to be done with you after you assaulted one of your own Officers. He wanted me to assure you that the whole mess can be fixed. He asked me to remind you that you've a function in a few days, for this very hospital. What will you say to Rainer Elsworth, Captain? Will you dance for him so that you can have your career back? A man has to make a living, after all."

"No, I don't want my fucking career back," Tashué snapped. "I won't work for them another day. The whole organization is rotten. It *deserves* its bad name. I'm finished with them. I'll go to the General's event, but that's for General Wolfe and Illea Winter. They want to derail Rainer, too. I'll resign my badge. Everything will be about getting Jason."

Rhodrishi had his amber eyes on Tashué, as hot and intense as Tashué had ever seen them, but his face was a carefully constructed mask, neutral and watching. "You believe the whole system is rotten —so you're going to take your son and run away from it? You're satisfied to run and leave things the way they are?"

"What do you want from me, Colonel?" Tashué breathed. "You ask if I'll come, you ask if I'll stay... What do you need me to say?"

"I want to know the sort of man you are, finally. I've known you over twenty years, and in that time, I've yet to see you decide what you want to be. You came the closest to it when you stood on the Black Ridge and made a choice. You defied an order and you kept people alive when the military wanted to throw their lives away. You were very nearly a man who really stood for something, that day, but then the Army tried to kill you for it and you retreated. The moment has returned, where you must choose, but this time, there's even more at stake. You could choose to fight for the lives of the 'tainted' across the entire country, or you could retreat, and let the law make you smaller. Again."

It was hard, this time, to breathe deep, like he needed to in order to fight against the weight of memory, like a riptide dragging him down.

Follow the law and you'll stay safe.

I'm sorry, Mother. What good is being safe if the law is so wrong?

"You're right," he croaked. "I can't just run away, after everything. What they've taken from the people I love. What they've taken from people I've never met. I can't pretend to be a farmer somewhere, like none of it matters." He breathed in a lungful of smoke, blowing it out the window and watching it swirl away in the wind. "I never had the courage to be a farmer. Too much of it is left to chance. No rain, too much rain. Sun, not enough sun. Too hot, too cold." He leaned out the window, trying to catch the fresh air. Would he ever be able to follow Stella?

"Is Lieutenant Mahalouwan willing to stay with us, in the legacy territory?"

"I don't know."

"I don't want to put my people in danger by drawing an Enquiry Officer after us."

Tashué stood up straighter. "You knew about Enquiry Officers? Before now?"

"Of course I knew," Rhodrishi said. "It's an old idea, these Officers. They used to hunt down the Kaadayri when the legacy territories were first established, to make sure we stayed where we belonged. Bothain Clannaugh thinks himself very clever for selling the idea to the Authority, but it's nothing new. He merely reused old oppression for the new age, aiming his Enquiry Officers at all tainted instead of just ones with amber eyes."

"Why didn't you tell me?"

"Why didn't I tell you that the Authority was brutal and oppressive? Would you have believed me before now? Would you have understood what that meant before you had seen the evidence of it?"

Tashué sighed, crushing out his cigarillo on the windowsill and flicking it to the ground. He watched it spiral down, getting further and further away from the building until he couldn't see it anymore.

"Tell the General I'm sorry I couldn't stay," Rhodrishi said. "I don't like to break my word. But I think he'll understand why I left, won't he?"

Tashué nodded. "I told him everything I know."

"I hope he's worthy of the trust you've given him."

"I hope so, too."

"I don't want to go," Ceridwen said again, grabbing Tashué's hand. "Please don't make me go."

"I know, little warrior," Tashué said. He leaned back against the wall, which was rough stone, cold and damp. He sank down, sitting on the floor, pulling Ceridwen in his arms and crushing her against his chest again. Stella sat beside him, her eyes distant and clouded with tears. "I'm sorry. It has to be this way, my sweet girl, to keep you both safe."

"But I don't want to leave you if you're supposed to be my da."

Tashué took a deep breath, looking down at Ceridwen. "I know,

Ceridwen. I lost my father when I was only a few years older than you. He died, and that part of my heart never really healed. And Kaz, she lost both of her parents on the same day, and she was about your age. But Kaz is the strongest, bravest woman I know. I think she got to be so brave because she had to take care of herself when she was just a child. The bad things shape us, Ceridwen. Like those marbles. They were nothing but sand before, but Božic's daughter put the sand into the fire and turned them to beautiful glass."

"Glass is made of sand?"

"It is," Tashué said, nodding. "Such an ordinary thing, sand, but with fire it turns into something beautiful."

Ceridwen looked down at her bag of marbles, her eyes wide.

"Grief and loss, they're like the fire that shapes us," Tashué continued. "Turns us into something better."

"How long before I get to be glass?" Ceridwen asked, looking up at Tashué again.

"You already are glass," Tashué said. He kissed her forehead again, squeezing her tight. "You were thrust into the fire when your mam got hurt. But now you're still hot and we can't see what shape you'll take. Soon you'll cool and your beautiful new self will be revealed."

Ceridwen bit her lip, looking down at the marbles again, shifting them around in her hand. They clacked together in their little bag and Ceridwen took a deep breath. "Is that why my insides still hurt, even though Mam's healed now? Because I'm still hot glass?"

A small, wounded sound came from the back of Stella's throat. "Oh, Ceridwen."

Tashué reached out to Stella, too, catching her hand and squeezing it. "It takes a while to cool, even if things have turned out alright. The good news is that you haven't lost us. You helped me and Colonel Kheir save your mam and we still have her, thank the North Star. And me, I'm not going anywhere. I need to stay here a little longer, but I'll find you again and we'll be a proper family. The time apart will hurt and I'll miss you both so much. You'll take a piece of my heart with you when you go. But I'll find you again. I promise."

They sat there for an eternity that wasn't nearly long enough. He held Ceridwen while she cried, her tears soaking into his shirt. It was worse than all the blood he'd spilt. The blood, at least, was his.

54

ILLEA
DAY 33

Illea had never taken Ishmael Saeati as a lover. She wanted to, but the comings and goings of their lives were so erratic that she rarely had time for him, and when she did, he was gone. Or drunk.

She knew the rumours, though. She knew that people whispered about them, about how handsome a couple they made. At least people did, before the banquet. Now people talked about Tashué Blackwood instead.

Sitting in Nathaniel's solarium, Illea found herself thinking about what people said about her even more than usual. It served her, to cloak herself in so much rumour and gossip that no one could divine the truth from the lies anymore. It was good for people to think of her as powerful, rich, and unpredictable. Better still for them to think of her as vapid and spoilt, so that they wouldn't see the plans she built.

She leaned back in her chair, breathing deeply, trying to calm her twisting stomach. It was cold in Nathaniel's solarium, but still her skin felt clammy and too hot. The smell of tobacco smoke that lingered on Ishmael didn't help, but she feared that she would lose control over her stomach if she stood now. Better to sit. Bite her tongue. Hope for the feeling to pass.

Ishmael looked like a melted figure rather than an actual man. He was pooled in one of the large wicker chairs, his feet stretched out and propped up on a stool. His arms were caught on the arms of the chair, one hanging down, the other sticking straight out. He was down to his shirtsleeves again, buttons half-open, showing the tattoos on his chest, a trilby hat covering most of his face. A cat sat curled on his lap, a tight little ball of calico fur. Illea wondered if Ishmael slept so bonelessly under normal circumstances, or if the excessive brandy he had used to drown his demons had played a part in his posture.

"The two of you are a ripe pair," Nathaniel grunted, stepping into the room. "Don't tell me you let him drag you into his foolishness."

"Dear General, you should know by now that I am immune to foolishness," Illea said, as brightly as she could, but her clenched teeth belied her efforts.

"If only he was immune." Nathaniel kicked Ishmael's chair as he passed it, but the impact only roused a bit of shuffling and some incoherent mumbling. The cat's head popped up, but then she rolled onto her side and went back to sleep, stretching out along the side of Ishmael's body. Nathaniel eased past Ishmael, settling beside Illea on the sofa, moving Illea's skirt aside before settling. As he always did, he winced and rubbed his thigh, his thumb probing deep into his own flesh as if he hoped to tease loose a knot. "What has you looking so greensick, then?"

Illea reached out to Nathaniel, laying her hand on his and squeezing it. Of all the people in her life, she wanted to share this news with him the most, and yet with Ishmael Saeati snoring and smelling of stale plum brandy beside them, this hardly seemed the time. And yet, the longer the silence stretched, the more intently Nathaniel looked at her, as if he was reading the truth while she studiously avoided looking at him.

"I wouldn't have thought Mr. Saeati was in any shape to entertain guests last night."

"I wasn't here with Mr. Saeati," Illea said, shaking her head. "I stayed in Amias's room."

"It's been a long time since you stayed in his room," Nathaniel said. "Not since his grave was still fresh."

Illea felt breathless, suddenly, like when she'd fallen from a horse and knocked all the air out of her lungs. Loss was a funny thing. The weight of the pain of it had never really lessened. The only thing that time had given her was the ability to forget, sometimes, that her heart hurt so much. But when she forgot, the pain crept up on her again, took the breath from her, made her feel like it was only just yesterday that they'd put him in the ground. Everything she thought she would be died with Amias Wolfe. All the best parts of her lay in the ground beside him.

She had to breathe more slowly, more gently, to fight the fresh wave of grief. Breathing too deeply made her feel faint, as if her stomach was jealous of the space the air took in her chest.

Nathaniel leaned forward, ringing the bell that he kept on the table. He was a man that liked quiet and privacy and he had a tendency to shoo his servants away. They knew not to even bother attending to him in the solarium. The bell brought one of them into the doorway.

"I'll have my breakfast here, with Miss Winter. Bread and cheese and fruit will do, as well as coffee."

"Yes, General." The servant disappeared as swiftly as he arrived.

Nathaniel shifted, squeezing Illea's hand and giving her one of his small smiles, the kind that was hidden by his beard but made his eyes glitter. "When my wife was pregnant, being hungry was what made her feel sick, but feeling full was uncomfortable too. She ate constantly, little snacks throughout the day. By the time she was pregnant with Elysia, she had a better idea what to expect, so she had the staff leave fruit and bread at her bedside. That way she could eat before she even rose from bed."

Illea couldn't look at him, or all the emotion would run out of control. She squeezed his hand. What a gift it was to have someone in her life that knew her so well. He didn't ask anything more of her, didn't pry. But he knew. Bless him, he knew.

"Something must be done," she said. Her lip trembled and she took another slow, steady breath to compose herself. "He's taken too much from my family and my name already. He won't have this. Not my child."

The servants entered the solarium, bearing all the needs of breakfast. Bread, fresh from the kitchens, butter, and fruit jams. Dried apricots, figs and dates, apples and pears. Illea reached out, plucking a pear from the tray as it passed in front of her. The yeasty smell of the bread made her stomach twist and she couldn't bring herself to eat it.

The servants left in a flurry and there was silence behind them, once they were gone. Nathaniel leaned forward in his chair, pouring himself a measure of coffee. The mellow roasted smell of it was comforting and Illea ventured a bite of her pear. It was delightfully ripe, soft and juicy. Her stomach didn't reject it, as she feared it would, so she took another bite. Slowly, with each bite, the nausea lost some of its power.

"It's not Myron's child, then?"

"Of course it's not Myron's," Illea snapped.

Nathaniel nodded. He seemed calm and measured, but Illea could sense the excitement in him, raging below the surface. He kicked out, hitting the wicker chair so hard it rattled Ishmael from his sleep. He pushed up the brim of his hat enough to crack a bleary eye at Nathaniel.

"Wake up, you drunken ass, or I'll turn you out into the gutter where you belong."

Ishmael grunted, letting the hat fall in front of his eyes again. The General plucked an apple off the tray and threw it at Ishmael, hitting him in the chest. The apple rolled and disturbed the cat in Ishmael's lap, which went tense and leaped off the chair. Those claws woke Ishmael better than the apple or any of the kicks and he bolted upright, cursing. He snatched up the apple and hurled it vaguely toward Nathaniel's head, but it sailed harmlessly past him, exploding against the wall and showering the floor with seeds and apple pulp.

Unperturbed, Nathaniel plucked a small loaf of bread off the tray next, hurling that more gently. Ishmael caught it, scowling.

"Have something to eat and get yourself together. I've given you over a week since the Market fire. A woman almost died while you were drinking this time. Now it's time to crawl out of the bottle and get back to work."

Another scowl. Ishmael might have fought, but his eyes flicked to Illea. Sagging back in his chair, he weighed the loaf in his hand as if he was thinking about throwing it, too, and he needed to assess how much damage he might be able to do. Illea leaned forward slowly, lest she disturb the delicate peace in her stomach, and plucked a similar loaf from the tray. If Ishmael hurled his at the General, it wouldn't do much damage at all—the crust of it was hard and crisp, but when she broke it open, the crumb inside was light and filled with large pockets of air. It was a common bread down in Khurya, she recalled, a provincial favourite.

A cacophony of barking sounded from somewhere in Nathaniel's large yard, and Illea thought she heard the sound of horses in the distance.

"The Council was quite pleased with your proposal for the train lines," Nathaniel said, ignoring Ishmael and his scowls. "I suspect you'll be granted the contract, unless someone surprises us. Most of the proposals included buying the lumber from you, which of course drove up the estimated cost."

Illea smiled. "Of course. Winter lumber is the very best."

"Good gods, you woke me to talk about lumber?" Ishmael muttered, slumping back down.

"No, you idiot, I woke you to talk about business, but Rainer is about to knock on my door and demand Illea's attendance, so we'll talk about business after he leaves."

"How do you know Rainer is here?"

"I saw his carriage come down the road. The hospital dedication is today, remember? Rainer and Myron have taken it over as a political event, I'm afraid."

"You don't need me at that, do you?" Ishmael muttered,

running his hands over his face. His wavy black hair was wild, standing on all ends. He tried to smooth it out, but it was a wasted effort. "I can't listen to the prig talk about himself all fucking day, not with this headache."

"Go wash yourself up, then, if you don't think you can be civil."

Ishmael sighed with his whole body, dragging himself to his feet.

"No, wait," Illea said, before he could leave. "Come sit here with me. Excuse me, General, make room for the good man."

Nathaniel didn't question her, standing and moving to the wicker chair previously occupied. Ishmael sank down beside Illea, turning boneless again. Illea grabbed another apple off the tray, handing it to Ishmael.

"Here, eat this, and try not to look so miserable. We had a wonderful night and you're positively glowing with self-satisfaction."

Ishmael quirked an eyebrow at her, his smile becoming positively devilish. She could kiss him for it. "Yes, Miss Winter."

Illea leaned toward him so that they looked to be propping each other up. He put his arm around her shoulders, which only served to drag his shirt open even more. She hoped Myron would come with Rainer, hoped the pair of them were even now stomping up to Nathaniel's door. Ishmael's fingers started playing in her hair, an absentminded fiddling that played perfectly into the image of familiarity she wanted to create—and made her scalp tight and her cheeks flush in spite of how her stomach felt.

The stomping did come, just as she'd hoped, a flurry of noise invading the peace of the solarium. She heard Rainer's voice as well as Myron's, and she melted into Ishmael just a little more, reaching up and sliding a hand along his chest, under his shirt. His skin was soft, but clammy in spite of the cold, and Illea felt his body go tense beneath her touch.

The door to the solarium opened, a servant scuttling in. "General, the Governor and Mr. Elsworth to see you."

Nathaniel only nodded at the servant, who stepped aside to allow Rainer and Myron to stomp in. Illea lifted her eyes just enough to watch them enter, gazing at the pair of them over Ishmael's chest. The flush that sprang to Myron's cheeks was everything she'd hoped it would be, his whole face going bright red. Rainer was considerably more stoic, though she knew him well enough to spot the anger that crossed his face.

"Miss Winter, if you would be so kind as to dress yourself, we have a campaign event to attend," Rainer said, his voice brittle, his composure a thin veil across his frustration. "We're behind schedule already, I'm afraid. We expected you to be at home this morning rather than entertaining Mr. Saeati."

"Well, you asked me to stop sleeping with Mr. Blackwood, so I found myself some new sport," Illea said. "I thought you would be pleased, Rainer."

"Perhaps your sport could be restricted to evening hours, and take up less time in the morning," Rainer said. "Especially when we are so tightly scheduled for the day. If you'll please untangle yourself from Mr. Saeati, I had your servant bring a gown that would be suitable for the event, as well as some combs and what have you for your hair."

"I haven't had my breakfast yet."

Rainer went still. He was smiling, the tense smile that he used to hide how angry he was. It wasn't much of a disguise, that smile. Those flinty eyes, and the slow, measured breaths he took so he wouldn't clench his fists or grind his teeth. "Illea. You agreed to this."

Illea sighed. She stood slowly, stepping around Ishmael's long legs. He sat up before she could get away, catching her arm and dragging her back down into his lap. The abrupt fall made her stomach lurch, but he caught her, swept her back, and kissed her. His mouth tasted of plum brandy but his lips were sweet with the juice from the apple and Illea let herself melt against him. He pushed his fingers through her hair and his other hand slid along her thigh, pulling up the hem of her nightgown to show her calf, her knee...

Myron made a strangled noise in the back of his throat. "General Wolfe, how could you stand for this... this... flagrant adultery under your roof?"

Nathaniel sighed. "I have seen enough evil in this world that I can't bring myself to care much about what two consenting adults do with their own bodies."

Illea broke the kiss to catch her breath. Ishmael grinned at her, smoothing out her nightgown again to cover her. "It was a pleasure to keep your company, Miss Winter. Please do come see me the next time you think of something so delightfully acrobatic."

"Thank you for indulging my ideas, Mr. Saeati. It was better than I'd hoped it would be."

"To hell with this, Rainer, we should just leave her behind. I'm late already. Better to go without her than not at all!"

Rainer hissed, turning to glare at Myron. "We need her in Brickheart. The people there are wary of the police force, but they'll vote for the name Winter. *She* is the name Winter, not you. So she must come. Illea, you agreed to this event, you gave your word. Myron and I will go ahead, and I trust you will catch up with us as soon as you're dressed and ready. You can ride with the General. He, at least, is dressed and ready to go."

"I'll come with you, Illea," Ishmael said, his voice husky in her ear and his hand tangled in her hair. "I'll keep you company through all the dreary speeches."

Illea smiled, kissing Ishmael on the cheek, his stubble rough beneath her lips. "Thank you, Ishmael, most considerate of you."

"Perhaps you could bathe first, Mr. Saeati," Rainer said. "So as not to smell so pungently of brandy."

"Perhaps you could stay behind all together," Myron grumbled. "Perhaps your company isn't needed at all."

"Ishmael and I will get ourselves ready as swiftly as possible," Illea said, standing. "We will meet you in Brickheart as soon as we're washed and dressed. Thank you, Rainer, for understanding."

Myron huffed and spluttered, but Rainer dragged him out. They stomped back through the house. Illea's servant was waiting in the open doorway, half-buried in the dress she'd brought for Illea to wear, a formal blue and grey piece that looked to be made of ice and snow. Suiting, with winter so close, with Myron's campaign slogan splattered across the city imploring people to *Vote Winter*.

"Am I really going to Brickheart, then?" Ishmael asked, once they were long gone.

"If you would be so kind, Mr. Saeati. We can't be seen to make promises that we aren't willing to follow through on, can we?"

55

TASHUÉ

DAY 33

Approaching General Wolfe's hospital again, Tashué felt the weight of Stella's body in his arms. Would he ever forget what it was like? Carrying her through the storm, wondering if she would die while he slithered on the ice, wondering if Rhodrishi would be able to help.

This time, he carried Keoh.

Her copper urn and her ashes weren't nearly as heavy as Stella, but the weight of them was harder to bear. Stella had survived, after all. Keoh had not.

The crowd milled in the streets of Brickheart and he had to wade through bodies to get to the hospital. His patience with all the people was thin. It was probably all the whisky he'd drank since Stella left, still burning in his blood. Preparing him for what he was going to do. Nathaniel Wolfe and Illea Winter wanted to derail Rainer Elsworth, and have Eirdis Redbone elected? Fine. Tashué would give them a great show. Maybe he didn't have any proof yet, but he could do his best to get the gossip going. He'd pin his fucking badge to Elsworth's face. Powell Iwan was going to get Jason out and Tashué would make sure the whole Dominion knew what Elsworth and the Authority had done.

He found Illea first, standing with her arm twined with Ishmael's. They looked good together, the pair of them both so attractive and charming, but more dangerous than their charm ever let on. Illea turned to Tashué, stepping into his path and making a great show of laying a kiss on his cheek.

"Mr. Blackwood, you made it," she said, smiling. "You look so good in your dress uniform." She slid a hand along his chest, her head cocking to one side. Did she know, what he had planned?

"Thank you, Miss Winter," Tashué said. "Is Rainer here yet?"

"Of course. He's been waiting for you. He's around the side of the building, with Myron. Shall I bring you to him?"

"Please."

She nodded, turning. She moved so easily through the crowd, like an icebreaker to make way for Tashué. Ishmael fell in step beside Tashué, elbowing Tashué as they walked.

"Why do you have an urn?" Ishmael asked.

"It's Keoh."

"Oh, well, that explains *everything*. Are you drunk?"

Tashué took a deep breath, running a hand over his face, trying to clear the fog from his mind. "Probably."

Ishmael nodded. "Me too, I think. Didn't get the chance to sleep it all off yet."

Illea glanced over her shoulder at both of them, grinning. "Excellent. All the best scandals start with drunk men."

Ishmael grinned back at her. "We exist to please, Miss Winter."

They rounded a corner, and Tashué spotted Rainer Elsworth, standing with Myron. Tashué sucked in a deep breath, pulling away from Illea and Ishmael, charging at Rainer. He would get answers out of the smug bastard, one way or another.

"Oh, Mr. Blackwood, how good of you to join us!" Rainer said, grinning. Tashué hated Rainer's smile, the way it pulled unnaturally at his face, the way his eyes danced with smugness. "You're just in time. The Governor will begin his speech shortly."

"No, I need to speak to you first," Tashué said, pressing in close. "I'm resigning my post as Station Commander." He reached into his pocket, pulling out the badge that he had come to loathe with every shred of his being. He pushed it into Rainer's hands and the other man fumbled with it. "I'm not working for your fucking Authority another day."

"Calm down, Mr. Blackwood, no, take the badge back," Rainer said. He reached up like he was going to try to pin the badge in place, but Tashué slapped his hand away. "Surely this matter can wait a while, since we are already behind on our schedule. We will talk about this privately, another time!"

"No, right *fucking* now!" Tashué snapped. He felt the silence spread across the crowd. "Tell me where to find Keoh's children."

"Excuse me?"

"The children Keoh gave to the Breeding Program. Tell me where to find them. One of them is dead already, but I want the rest of them. I want to know where they are, damn you. Every one of them. There should be five of them left, and I want to see them."

Rainer's eyes bulged and his gaze swept the crowd. "This is not the time for such discussions."

"Yes it is!" Tashué roared. "I brought her here for you so you can tell her what you've done to her fucking children." He pulled the urn from under his arm, thrusting it toward Rainer. "Here. She's looking a little different these days, since the Breeding Program had her remains cremated. Did you know she died? After you told me you would set a guard on her, to help protect her from herself? I never did get an explanation as to how the women of the Breeding Program have access to opium, considering how valuable they must be. You know, she told me that the people at the Breeding Program gave it to her, the opium. That they left it in her room for her to find, because they knew she couldn't resist it. I didn't believe her, but I should have! Maybe that's the way the Breeding Program rids themselves of breeders that are no longer producing energy units. That's what they're called, isn't it? The children? You can't call them children because that would make them entirely too *human* for your purposes. Instead you call them *energy units*."

"Have you been drinking Mr. Blackwood?" Rainer asked, his voice gone high-pitched and screechy. "Perhaps you should take yourself home. Sleep off the whisky, sir."

"No, damn you!" Tashué thundered, stepping closer. He loomed over Rainer and Rainer flinched, taking a step back. "I should have believed her. I should have trusted her instead of letting you kill her!"

"Mr. Blackwood!" Rainer thundered back. It was a weaker thing than the rumble Tashué was able to produce.

"I have more questions for you, sir. Shall I ask them as loudly as I can muster? I've got officer's lungs still, after all these years. I'm sure I can make myself heard by the whole damned crowd if you like!"

"Perhaps you should take a walk with the poor man, Mr. Elsworth," Ishmael called. "Clearly he's not to be shaken."

"He's right, Mr. Elsworth," Illea said. "Trust me—Mr. Blackwood is not a man to be deterred when he wants something."

Rainer turned his angry grin on Illea and Ishmael both, then swung back to Tashué. "Yes, yes, you're right. Let's go somewhere more private, perhaps. Walk with me, Mr. Blackwood. You there, go find the Governor and tell him to proceed with his speech without me. Put the urn away, then, Mr. Blackwood, and we'll take a walk."

"I'll carry her for you if you like, Captain," Ishmael said, stepping forward. "I'm sorry for your loss."

Tashué whirled around toward Ishmael, his whole body vibrating with his fury. It took him a moment to process Ishmael's offer, but he nodded and thrust the urn out again. "Thank you," he murmured. "Don't fucking drop her."

"Yes, Captain."

"This way, Mr. Blackwood."

Rainer led Tashué away and Ishmael followed, holding the urn in both hands. Rainer cast another angry, wild-eyed smile back Ishmael and Illea, but led Tashué out through the crowd as fast as he could. One alley and then another, but Tashué couldn't contain his questions any longer.

"What about the fucking Enquiry Officers, *sir*," he went on. "Is it true you have an entire branch of the Authority charged with hunting people down and murdering them?"

"The Enquiry program is a vital part of ensuring the safety of the Dominion's citizens," Rainer breathed, grabbing Tashué by the arm and dragging him along faster. Did he even know where he was going? Brickheart was so crowded, surely there was nowhere for them to hide where no one would hear them. "We can't allow dangerous people to roam our country, Mr. Blackwood! Tainted that are feral and non-compliant need to be found before they harm anyone. Surely you understand. I read Miss Gian Ly's file! She was living with your son in squalor, using her abilities to assault and abuse people for opium. Surely you can understand why that can't be allowed!"

"Get your fucking hands off me," Tashué snapped, jerking his arm away. "Explain to me, then, why Gianna Tarbrook died." He grabbed Rainer by the arm instead, hauling Rainer close. "Why a healer? What are you so afraid of that a healer can't be allowed to be in love with a kind, gentle man like Glaen Forsooth?"

"Excuse me, sir!" Rainer squealed, pushing Tashué away, but Tashué was immovable. "Gianna Tarbrook died because *your man* shot her."

"Fuck you, you snivelling piece of shit," Tashué growled, hauling Rainer even closer. "You sent us after those two for your fucking campaign. Are you telling me that you didn't hope one of them would die? That's why you sent the photographers, isn't it? That's why you sent us with long rifles? That's why every fucking paper in this city had photographs of Gianna Tarbrook dead the next day?"

"You were the one that filed the paperwork! You told *me* that they needed to be processed!"

"Why did they need to be processed, then? Tell me why we couldn't just leave them alone!"

"It's against the regulation!"

"Why?" Tashué howled, shaking Rainer. He wanted the man to crack open and spill all the answers Tashué was looking for, to make him bleed and speak and settle all the demons in Tashué's head. "Tell me why!"

"She was a healer! A healer's abilities can't be *diluted* by a bright-man! We need more healers in this country! That's why there's a process, why there's paperwork to file if the tainted want to marry each other. We have to make sure they aren't wasting their abilities by creating inferior children!"

"Inferior children," Tashué said. "Yes, let's talk about the children, shall we? Tell me about the *energy units*. Is it true you have their arms and their legs cut off to make them easier to transport? Is it true you break their minds so that they serve their purposes without question? Is it fucking true that the Red Dawn is stealing them from you to start their revolution?"

"There is no Red Dawn in Yaelsmuir."

"Don't fucking lie to me! Tell me about the energy units. Tell me about Lizanne Gian Ly."

"Who?"

"Oh, do you need her registration number to know what I'm talking about?" Tashué let go of Rainer with only one hand, holding him in place while he reached into his jacket. He flipped open his notebook, showing Rainer the page with the numbers of Lizanne's tattoo. "Does this sound more familiar? 1693-0237-4494. 1693, that was Keoh. So this child must have been Lizanne Gian Ly, Keoh's first 'Breeding Program' child. She was murdered by the Red Dawn, but her arms and legs were cut off by *you*. Tell me about that program, then. Tell me about the decision to remove children's limbs. Tell me about letting a girl rot until there wasn't any flesh left to cover her bones. If the Red Dawn hadn't murdered her when they did, that wound would have killed her. Tell me why she wasn't human enough to be worthy of medical attention! Why wasn't Lizanne Gian Ly human enough to deserve her arms and legs?"

"Because they aren't human!" Rainer snapped. His face flushed so bright red that he looked fit to faint, but he fought against Tashué one last time. "They aren't! They are *assets*. Energy units are the power that run our civilization. Everything we do is powered by them, but they're never quite strong enough, are they? They need to be pushed harder and refined into something greater and they must be made efficiently!"

The words took the breath out of Tashué. He couldn't believe it, that Rainer had said it. *They aren't human.*

He reached into his jacket, pulling out his Imburleigh. Rainer's eyes went wide, his face draining of colour. Tashué leaned in, grabbing Rainer by the front of the jacket and hauling him in close, putting the gun up under Rainer's chin.

"Tell me again that Keoh's children aren't human. Tell me again that Lizanne Gian Ly wasn't human. Is that what makes it alright for you to cut off her arms and her legs? Do you stack them in some warehouse somewhere like fucking cord wood, until they're needed?"

"Stand down, Captain!"

General Wolfe's voice sliced right through the fury, making him young again, a soldier again, a man who took orders, a man who fought the whole world. Tashué shook his head, laying a finger on the trigger of the Imburleigh. Fuck that man, that young man, too stupid and naive to think for himself, so in love with his own idea of sense and order that he had taken a badge and stood for the Authority and spent nearly two decades allied to an organization that cut the limbs off children because they weren't *human*.

"This isn't how things are done, Captain," Wolfe said, and he had a hand on Tashué's arm, tugged him away. "This doesn't help anyone."

"He can't cut up children anymore if he's fucking dead," Tashué breathed.

"If you kill him now, someone will replace him, and the cycle goes on," Wolfe said. "And then you go to the gallows, and you're no use to anyone if you're hanged for this. Take a deep breath, Captain Blackwood. Take a deep breath, and a step back."

Tashué sucked in a deep breath. He looked Rainer Elsworth in the eye, and saw the fear there, but also the rage and the determination. The man was cool and still with the barrel of a gun under his chin.

"Let him go, Captain," General Wolfe said. "Put your gun away. This isn't how we solve problems in this country. This isn't how we make things better. Isn't that what we wanted, you and I? To make things better."

Tashué let go of Rainer's jacket, and Rainer staggered back. He trembled as he smoothed out his clothes, gulping in deep breaths. "Mayor Wolfe, I want that man arrested."

"There's no need for that, Mr. Elsworth," Wolfe said, pushing Tashué back, stepping between them. Whether he was protecting Rainer from Tashué or the other way around, Tashué suddenly wasn't sure. "The man is grief-stricken and drunk. He's going to walk away now, and sober himself up, and this whole mess need not have happened. Myron will give his speech, the hospital will open, and the campaign continues."

Rainer clenched his hands into fists, his face flushing and his arms trembling.

"Ishmael, take Captain Blackwood for a walk," Wolfe snapped. "Get him out of here! Don't let him do anything stupid."

"Yes, General." Ishmael stepped forward, into Tashué's line of vision. He was still holding Keoh's urn, the copper tucked under one arm now. The other hand reached out for Tashué, hooking in Tashué's arm, dragging him back up the alley. "Put the gun away, Captain, before you shoot me in the foot."

Tashué reached back into his jacket, sliding the gun back into its holster. His whole body felt numb and distant as he followed Ishmael along, not really sure where they were going. He should have just shot. He should have opened Rainer's skull, the same way he had opened Hale's skull, and Rainer would be nothing but meat and leaking brains and maybe then the churning pit of rage in Tashué's chest would finally be satisfied.

They need to be pushed harder and refined into something greater and they must be made efficiently.

"Where are we taking Miss Gian Ly, then?" Ishmael asked.

"What?"

Ishmael shifted the weight of the urn, holding it in front of him instead, so Tashué could see it again. "I'm guessing there's a reason for having her with you today."

"I wanted Rainer Elsworth to see her, and know that I saw him."

"So you hadn't planned to kill him?"

"No," Tashué admitted. "I should have, though."

"Trust me, if ever you have cause to kill a man, you should do it in private. I can help you, if you want."

"Rainer Elsworth's death shouldn't be private. It should be public and it should be messy and everyone should feel his blood on their hands."

Ishmael shrugged. "Don't take my professional opinion, then. It's just easier to clean up the mess and go on with your life if there aren't any witnesses. Are we headed for a pint? Good fucking news. I could use a pint."

Tashué looked up to see that he was heading for the *Pint Under*. It slowed him, that little pub. That place that had been warm and welcoming for so long, but now wrapped up in so many ugly memories. It was here that he was trying to have breakfast when the girl washed up on the bank.

No, not 'the girl.' Lizanne. Jason's sister. Keoh's daughter.

"Have you been to see Eddie?" Tashué asked, slowing to a stop outside the public house, watching the door swing as a patron left. "Since the fire?"

"No. I haven't. I've been spending my time with brandy and gin and rum instead."

Mention of gin and rum and brandy reminded Tashué of Allie Tei and the rage went hot again in an instant. He spun toward Ishmael and lashed out, his left fist catching Ishmael in the jaw. Ishmael staggered, but righted himself, his face going deep red as he leaned forward. Even as his whole body went loose and ready for a fight, he still held Keoh's urn, tucked carefully under his arm.

"What the fucking hell was that for?"

"Allie Tei, you drunken ass. I told you to help her! And she almost died because you were so fucking drunk you forgot about her."

Ishmael grimaced. He turned his face away and spat, but it wouldn't have been enough to clear all the blood from his mouth. "Fine, I guess I deserved that, then. She alright?"

"She took care of herself," Tashué grunted. "She shouldn't have needed to, though."

"I'm sorry."

"Tell her yourself. General Wolfe is protecting her now."

Ishmael spat again, wiping his mouth with the back of his hand. "I must still be drunk. It's been a while since anyone sucker punched me like that. You hit hard for an old man."

"Fuck you."

"At least buy me a drink first."

Tashué almost laughed. Ishmael was so ridiculous. Were it not for the fact that he'd seen the deep well of darkness in the man himself, he would have thought that Ishmael didn't take anything seriously. But he took *everything* seriously, and the charm and the jokes and the endless snacks were just his way to protect himself from his own anger.

Tashué's gaze drifted down to Keoh's urn, still tucked and safe under Ishmael's arm. He took a deep breath and headed into the *Pint Under*. It was dark inside, but warm with the fire crackling in the hearth. The familiar smell of stew made him sick. He was eating it when Lizanne washed up on the back and he was eating it when the Officers from Drystone came for their fight and he didn't think he would ever eat it again.

Pallwyth greeted him with a smile. It faded when the little man's gaze swept over them both. "Will you be skipping the pint this morning then, and heading straight for the whisky?"

"Yes please, Pallwyth," Tashué grunted, fishing in his pocket for some coins. He laid a silver on the bar. Powell Iwan's silver. "The whole bottle, please."

Pallwyth's eyebrows shot up and he looked between Tashué and the silver crown a few times, as if he was waiting for Tashué to tell him that it was a joke. "I don't have any of the good ones, sir," he said softly, stepping back to look at the array of bottles he kept under the bar. "None of the single malts worth a whole silver, just the blended whiskies."

"It's fine, Pallwyth. Anything will do."

Pallwyth cast an eye at the urn. Perhaps he'd seen enough to know all the weight such a small thing could possess. He reached under the bar and plucked up an unopened bottle. Tashué took it and headed out again.

Tashué cracked the seal and took the first long pull. How long had it been since Stella left? He wasn't completely sure. He'd been drinking almost steadily since. Waiting for Powell Iwan to break Jason out of the Rift so that Tashué would know at least Jason was safe, and would know the price he would have to pay.

He passed the bottle to Ishmael as they made their way down the street, toward the water. He could hear the roar of the current, the sound of it rushing over his whole body and making him feel cold and small. There were fewer people than there had been that day. There was nothing exceptional here to draw the crowds, to keep them in groups, blood clots in a wound. That's what he thought of them, back then, blood clots in a wound. How terribly apt.

Ishmael handed the bottle back as they left the street, their feet sinking into the loose, damp shale of the bank. Water soaked into his boots, brutally cold, but he took another pull from the whisky and walked on.

He traded the bottle for the urn. Holding it in his hands again he felt the terrible weight of it, crushing his chest, clawing at his throat. He thought he would wait for this moment, until Jason was out. Jason should be here to see his mother's ashes laid to rest. But having that urn in his kitchen was driving him mad. He couldn't wait any longer.

The Brightwash was swollen with autumn rain. The spot where Lizanne lay was submerged now, but he waded in anyway. The chill of the water made him catch his breath, made his heart beat faster. It was so cold that his feet ached, but he kept walking, the shifting rock of the riverbank and the resistance of the water as it tugged on his legs slowing him. How long ago was it, that Lizanne washed up? It seemed like so long now, but surely it was only a few weeks. His whole life had been stretched out by this child. Everything he remembered was *before* and *after*, with that one cold moment like a mile marker on a long road.

"I don't know what to say," he blurted, glancing back over his shoulder. Ishmael was still there, not as deep but close enough that he could pass the whisky bottle back. "If she had a proper funeral, a

Sister of the North Star would say something good about her, and about how the Keeper of the Keys took her and the North Star blessed her. But I don't… I don't know what to say."

Ishmael took another pull from the whisky, handing it forward. Tashué shifted his grip on the urn so he held it in one hand, taking the bottle and taking a long drink. The heat of the whisky wasn't enough to keep him warm when he was up to knees in the frigid water, but it had to be this spot. It had to be where Lizanne lay on the bank, mother and daughter in the same place, if only for a fleeting moment.

"At a Qasani funeral, the body is laid in a shroud for three days, and the women of the family are in the room with it the entire time. They weep, and the louder the better, because the sound of their weeping will guide Ishka's messengers to the room, so that they can come take the soul away to heaven. A sign of a person's value in the world is how many women will come and weep for them. And then, after three days, an Im-Aqi—that's like a priest—comes and tells the women, 'this life belonged not to us, but to the gods, and the wisdom of the gods is absolute.' The women stop weeping because no one can argue with the wisdom of the gods. The Im-Aqi takes the body out to the burial ground, where everyone else is waiting. People take turns sharing their favourite story. There's a Qasani blessing that means, 'I hope your funeral lasts a moon,' because you were so well loved that people won't stop talking. And then the body is buried and people feast, because there's not a single life event that the Qasani won't feast for."

Tashué nodded, feeling the tears threatening again. He cleared his throat, fighting for a deep breath. "Why only women? In the room, I mean. With the body."

"Women are the guardians of the soul," Ishmael said. "The Goddess Ishka was the one who put souls into humans, and she asked women to tend to them while they were on earth. That's why women carry the child, to hold it in their bodies while they receive their souls from Ishka. So the women guard the body and the soul until Ishka reclaims it."

Tashué took another pull from the bottle—it was half empty

now—and passed it back to Ishmael. The lid was on the urn precariously and it was an easy thing to pull it off. The wind coming down the river lifted some of the ashes and set them swirling through the air, but at least they were headed the right direction. Toward the sea.

"I'm sorry, Keoh. I'm sorry I didn't know how to love you. I'm sorry I didn't know how to save you. I'm going to try to save your son. And all the rest of your children. But now you can rest with Lizanne so maybe that's something."

He bent down, pushing the open urn under the surface of the river. Water swirled in and then out, pulling the ashes away.

"This life belonged not to us," Ishmael murmured, "but to the gods, and the wisdom of the gods is absolute."

The cloud of ash billowed away in the current. Tashué lifted the urn again, pouring the water out, then submerged it again to make sure every last speck was taken by the river. Out to sea. He never thought to ask her why she wanted to go out to sea, but then she had loved travelling. Maybe she just wanted the sea to spread her across the whole world.

He retreated, back up the bank, water sluicing from his pants and his boots as he trekked back toward the cobbles. The whisky had him now though and he felt too light, too much like he was going to float away without the river to hold on to his feet. He sank down on the edge of the cobblestone road, taking another pull from the bottle and resting the empty urn beside him. Ishmael sat with him, silent as they both kicked off their boots and peeled away their sodden wool socks. Another few pulls emptied the bottle and Ishmael stood it beside them. What a pair they must look like, bare feet in the shale, an empty urn and an empty bottle flanking them, with the bitter autumn wind bringing winter down from the north.

"Is all that shit true?" Ishmael asked. "The things you said to Rainer?"

"Fucking hell, you're useless when you're drinking, aren't you?" Tashué ran a hand over his face. "I told General Wolfe all of this already."

"I told you, I wasn't working," Ishmael muttered, reaching into his pocket and pulling out a handful of dates. He offered some to Tashué, but Tashué waved them off. "What are you going to do next?"

"I'm going to find a way to fucking prove it," Tashué muttered. He stood, but all the whisky seemed to hit him in the face like a punch, making his knees weak. He sank back down, closing his eyes as the world tilted and spun.

"Easy there, Captain. Don't start puking, or I'll fucking join you and all that whisky will be wasted."

Tashué sucked in a deep breath. "It's all so fucked. How did I not know any of this? I worked for the Authority for nineteen fucking years, and I didn't know. I have to fix it…" He ran both his hands over his face, trying to scrub away the slow, foggy feeling in his brain. Shit, they'd finished that bottle too damned fast. "If I can find proof, maybe I can fix it. I can make it fucking stop. Energy units, for fuck's sake."

"Tashué Blackwood."

Tashué turned, looking over his shoulder. A half-dozen Patrollers were standing behind him, clustered in close. A few of the younger ones had the white faces and trembling hands of youths fearful of their first action, but the older ones had grim and unrelenting faces.

"Shit," Ishmael breathed. "Tashué, don't fight it. No matter what they do, don't fight them, or they'll kill you. Just do what they tell you. Look at me, you bastard! Don't fight it!"

"Put your hands behind your head, Mr. Blackwood. You're under arrest for uttering threats against the Chief Administrator of the National Tainted Registration Authority."

ABOUT THE AUTHOR

Krystle Matar has been writing for a long time, but things got serious when Tashué Blackwood walked into her life, an amber-eyed whirlwind.

When she isn't arguing with him or any of his friends, she parents and farms. She has a lot of children and even more animals and one very excellent husband.

She is currently working on lots of stories set in the Dominion. She expects to exist in this universe for a while.

Look for *Legacy of Brick & Bone* in 2022.

Check out krystlematar.com for publishing news, and high resolution images of the maps. You can also join the newsletter mailing list, which will have deleted scenes, extra stories, publishing news, and more!